The Night Land
and Other
Perilous
Romances

The Night Land and Other Perilous Romances

Being The Fourth Volume of
The Collected Fiction of William Hope Hodgson

Edited by Jeremy Lassen

Night Shade Books · New York

Night Shade books may be purchased in bulk at special discounts for sales promotion, corporate gifts, fund-raising, or educational purposes. Special editions can also be created to specifications. For details, contact the Special Sales Department, Night Shade Books, 307 West 36th Street, 11th Floor, New York, NY 10018 or info@skyhorsepublishing.com.

Night Shade Books® is a registered trademark of Skyhorse Publishing, Inc. ®, a Delaware corporation.

Visit our website at www.nightshadebooks.com.

10 9 8 7 6 5 4 3 2

Library of Congress Cataloging-in-Publication Data is available on file.

ISBN: 978-1-59780-959-7
Hardcover ISBN: 978-1-89238-942-8

Cover and interior artwork © 2005 by Jason Van Hollander
Interior layout and design by Jeremy Lassen
Introduction © 2005 by Jeremy Lassen
A Note on the Texts © 2005 by Jeremy Lassen

Printed in China

This series is dedicated to the readers, editors, publishers and scholars who have worked tirelessly since William Hope Hodgson's death to ensure that his work would not be lost or forgotten. Without their efforts, these volumes would not be possible.

In particular, the editor would like to thank S. T. Joshi, Mike Ashley, Jack Adrian and George Locke for their generous support.

Contents

Perilous Romances

A Masterpiece of Sorts

"W H. Hodgson's The Night Land would have made it in eminence from the unforgettable somber splendor of the images it presents, if it were not disfigured by a sentimental and irrelevant erotic interest and fry a foolish and flat archaism of style." — C. S. Lewis

"The supreme master of imaginative horror in science fiction was William Hope Hodgson and his tour de force was the apocalyptic novel The Night Land." — Sam Moskowitz

"An achievement without equal . . . a masterpiece of sorts." — Brian Stableford

*T*HE NIGHT LAND IS William Hope Hodgson's towering achievement. Awe inspiringly massive, convoluted and purposefully archaic, it is his most ambitious and influential work . . . a "tour de force." Numerous writers have taken up the gauntlet thrown down by Hodgson, and engage in similar thematic endeavors, many of which far surpass Hodgson's flawed masterpiece.

The Night Land was published in 1912 by Eveleigh Nash. This was Hodgson's first book from Eveleigh Nash, and was not particularly successful, from a commercial standpoint. It is telling that while Hodgson had four more books issued by this publisher, they were all collections, and two of them collected popular serial characters.

Critics like Lewis single out the sentiment of *The Night Land* as the source of its failure. Others suggest it is the falsely archaic style, which is even more overwrought and distracting than that the affected style of *The Boats of the "Glen Carrig"*. Still others point to its ponderous length. Despite all these flaws, and perhaps because of them, the novel does succeed. The unnatural tone, the epic length, and Hodgson's sentimentality all work together in a surprising way.

Some Hodgson scholars (notably Sam Gafford in his essay "Writing Backwards: The Novels of William Hope Hodgson") have suggested that *The Night Land* was the first novel written by Hodgson—that his novels were written in the opposite order in which they were published. This idea is an intriguing one, and Gafford cites certain letters written by Hodgson in 1905 which support this idea. Regardless of the order of composition, what is clear is that subse-

quent to the publication of *The Night Land*, increasingly commercial short fiction made up the bulk of Hodgson's output.

The subtitle of *The Night Land*—"A Love Tale"—provides the thematic glue that binds this fourth volume of his collected fiction together—Hodgson's most un-commercial "romance" is presented here with his overtly romantic "woman's" fiction. If C. S. Lewis had a problem with the "sentimental and irrelevant erotic interest" in *The Night Land*, he would be horrified by the stories contained in this volume, or at the very least, consigned them to the bins of crass commercial fiction from which they sprang.

Nash's Magazine, *The Grand Magazine*, *Red Magazine*, and *Blue Magazine* all provided outlets for Hodgson's romantic work, with "The Captain of the Onion Boat" being published prior to *The Night Land*, in 1910. In addition to its presence in Hodgson's collection *Men of Deep Waters*, "The Captain of the Onion Boat" was published in the U.S. in pamphlet form in 1911.

"The Smugglers" and "The Wailing Gully" are a bit more plot driven then the others in this volume, but they are, at their heart, tales of romance. *Grand Magazine* provided the commercial outlet for these stories in March and September of 1911, respectively (again, prior to *The Night Land* publication).

"The Girl with the Grey Eyes" and "Kind, Kind and Gentle is She" were published in *Red Magazine* in January and April of 1913, while "Timely Escape" wasn't published until after Hodgson's death in *Blue Magazine* in 1922.

The romantic fiction in this volume (along with other sentimental stories such as "The Valley of Lost Children" and "The Sea Horses," presented in Volume Five), as well as Hodgson's relationship to his wife, all provide insight into a man who, despite the cosmic alienation for which he is most remembered, had a profoundly sentimental side which often manifested itself in his fiction. This duality then becomes the defining contradiction of his novel, *The Night Land . . .* "a masterpiece of sorts . . ."

Jeremy Lassen
San Francisco

The Night Land

A Love Tale

The Dreams that are only Dreams

"This to be Love, that your spirit to live in a natural holiness with the Beloved, and your bodies to be a sweet and natural delight that shall be never lost of a lovely mystery. . . . And shame to be unborn, and all things to go wholesome and proper, out of an utter greatness of understanding; and the Man to be an Hero and a Child before the Woman; and the Woman to be an Holy Light of the Spirit and an Utter Companion and in the same time a glad Possession unto the Man. . . . And this doth be Human Love. . . ."

". . . for this to be the especial glory of Love, that it doth make unto all Sweetness and Greatness, and doth be a fire burning all Littleness; so that did all in this world to have met The Beloved, then did Wantonness be dead, and there to grow Gladness and Charity, dancing in the years."

Table of Contents

I

Mirdath the Beautiful

"And I cannot touch her face
And I cannot touch her hair,
And I kneel to empty shadows--
Just memories of her grace;
And her voice sings in the winds
And in the sobs of dawn
And among the flowers at night
And from the brooks at sunrise
And from the sea at sunset,
And I answer with vain callings
. ."

IT WAS THE JOY of the Sunset that brought us to speech. I was gone a long way from my house, walking lonely-wise, and stopping often that I view the piling upward of the Battlements of Evening, and to feel the dear and strange gathering of the Dusk come over all the world about me.

The last time that I paused, I was truly lost in a solemn joy of the Glory of the Coming Night; and maybe I laughed a little in my throat, standing there alone in the midst of the Dusk upon the World. And, lo! my content was answered out of the trees that bounded the country road upon my right; and it was so as that some one had said: "And thou also!" in glad understanding, that I laughed again a little in my throat; as though I had only a half-believing that any true human did answer my laugh; but rather some sweet Delusion or Spirit that was tuned to my mood.

But she spoke and called me by my name; and when I had gone to the side of the road, that I should see her somewhat, and discover whether I knew her, I saw that she was surely that lady, who for her beauty was known through all of that sweet County of Kent as Lady Mirdath the Beautiful; and a near neighbour to me; for the Estates of her Guardian abounded upon mine.

Yet, until that time, I had never met her; for I had been so oft and long abroad; and so much given to my Studies and my Exercises when at home, that I had no further Knowledge of her than Rumour gave to me odd time; and for the rest, I was well content; for as I have given hint, my books held me, and likewise my Exercises; for I was always

5

an athlete, and never met the man so quick or so strong as I did be; save in some fiction of a tale or in the mouth of a boaster.

Now, I stood instantly with my hat in my hand; and answered her gentle bantering so well as I might, the while that I peered intent and wondering at her through the gloom; for truly Rumour had told no tale to equal the beauty of this strange maid; who now stood jesting with so sweet a spirit, and claiming kinship of Cousinhood with me, as was truth, now that I did wake to think.

And, truly, she made no ado; but named me frank by my lad's name, and gave laughter and right to me to name her Mirdath, and nothing less or more—at that time. And she bid me then to come up through the hedge, and make use of a gap that was her own especial secret, as she confessed, when she took odd leave with her maid to some country frolic, drest as village maids; but not to deceive many, as I dare believe.

And I came up through the gap in the hedge and stood beside her; and tall she had seemed to me, when I looked up at her; and tall she was, in truth; but indeed I was a great head taller. And she invited me then to walk with her to the house, that I meet her Guardian and give word to my sorrow that I had so long neglected to make call upon them; and truly her eyes to shine with mischief and delight, as she named me so for my amissness.

But, indeed, she grew sober in a moment, and she set up her finger to me to hush, as that she heard somewhat in the wood that lay all the way upon our right. And, indeed, something I heard too; for there was surely a rustling of the leaves, and anon a dead twig crackt with a sound clear and sharp in the stillness.

And immediately there came three men running out of the wood at me; and I called to them sharply to keep off or beware of harm; and I put the maid to my back with my left hand, and had my oak staff ready for my use.

But the three men gave out no word of reply; but ran in at me; and I saw somewhat of the gleam of knives; and at that, I moved very glad and brisk to the attack; and behind me there went shrill and sweet, the call of a silver whistle; for the Maid was whistling for her dogs; and maybe the call was also a signal to the men-servants of her house.

Yet, truly, there was no use in help that was yet to come; for the need did be then and instant; and I nowise loath to use my strength before my sweet cousin. And I stepped forward, briskly, as I have told; and the end of my staff I drove into the body of the left-ward man, so that he dropped like a dead man. And I hit very sharply at the head

of another, and surely crackt it for him; for he made instantly upon the earth; but the third man I met with my fist, and neither had he any great need of a second blow; but went instant to join his companions, and the fight thus to have ended before it was even proper begun, and I laughing a little with a proper pride, to know the bewilderment that I perceived in the way that the Lady Mirdath, my cousin, stood and regarded me through the dusk of the hushed even.

But, indeed, there was no time left to us, before there came bounding up, three great boar-hounds, that had been loosed to her whistle; and she had some ado to keep the brutes off me; and I then to beat them off the men upon the earth, lest they maul them as they lay. And directly, there was a noise of men shouting, and the light of lanthorns in the night, and the footmen of the house to come running with lanthorns and cudgels; and knew not whether to deal with me, or not, in the first moment, even as the dogs; but when they saw the men upon the ground, and learned my name and saw me proper, they kept well their distance and had no lack of respect; but, indeed, my sweet cousin to have the most of any; only that she showed no intent to keep distance of me; but to have a new and deeper feeling of kinship than she at first had shown.

And the men-servants asked what should be done with the footpads; seeing that they were now recovering. But, indeed, I left the matter, along with some silver, to the servants; and very sound justice they dealt out to the men; for I heard their cries a good while after we had gone away.

Now, when we were come up to the Hall, my cousin must take me in to her Guardian, Sir Alfred Jarles, an old man and venerable that I knew a little in passing and because our estates abounded. And she praised me to my face, yet quaintly-wise; and the old man, her Guardian thanked me most honourably and with a nice courtesy; so that I was a welcome house-friend from that time onward.

And I stayed all that evening, and dined, and afterward went out again into the home-grounds with the Lady Mirdath; and she more friendly to me than ever any woman had been; and seemed to me as that she had known me always. And, truly, I had the same feeling in my heart towards her; for it was, somehow, as though we knew each the way and turn of the other, and had a constant delight to find this thing and that thing to be in common; but no surprise; save that so pleasant a truth had so natural a discovery.

And one thing there was that I perceived held the Lady Mirdath all that dear fore-night; and this was, indeed, the way that I had my

pleasure so easy with the three foot-pads. And she asked me plainly whether I was not truly very strong; and when I laughed with young and natural pride, she caught my arm suddenly to discover for herself how strong I might be. And, surely, she loosed it even the more sudden, and with a little gasping of astonishment, because it was so great and hard. And afterward, she walked by me very silent, and seeming thoughtful; but she went never any great way off from me.

And, truly, if the Lady Mirdath had a strange pleasure in my strength, I had likewise a constant wonder and marvel in her beauty, that had shown but the more lovely in the candle-light at dinner.

But there were further delights to me in the days that came; for I had happiness in the way that she had pleasure of the Mystery of the Evening, and the Glamour of Night, and the Joy of Dawn, and all suchlike.

And one evening, that I ever remember, as we wandered in the park-lands, she began to say—half unthinking—that it was truly an elves-night. And she stopped herself immediately; as though she thought I should have no understanding; but, indeed, I was upon mine own familiar ground of inward delight; and I replied in a quiet and usual voice, that the Towers of Sleep would grow that night, and I felt in my bones that it was a night to find the Giant's Tomb, or the Tree with the Great Painted Head, or— And surely I stopped very sudden; for she gripped me in that moment, and her hand shook as she held me; but when I would ask her what ailed, she bid me, very breathless, to say on, to say on. And, with a half understanding, I told her that I had but meant to speak of the Moon Garden, that was an olden and happy fancy of mine.

And, in verity, when I said that, the Lady Mirdath cried out something in a strange low voice, and brought me to a halt, that she might face me. And she questioned me very earnest; and I answered just so earnest as she; for I was grown suddenly to an excitement, in that I perceived she knew also. And, in verity, she told me that she had knowledge; but had thought that she was alone in the world with her knowledge of that strange land of her dreams; and now to find that I also had travelled in those dear, strange dream lands. And truly the marvel of it—the marvel of it! As she to say time and oft. And again, as we walked, she gave out word that there was little wonder she had been urged to call to me that night, as she saw me pause upon the road; though, indeed, she had learned of our cousin-ship before, having seen me go by on my horse pretty oft, and inquired concerning me; and mayhap daintily irked that I had so little heed of Lady Mirdath the

Beautiful. But, indeed, I had thought of other matters; yet had been human enough, had I but met her proper before I see her.

Now you must not think that I was not utter stirred by the wonder of this thing, that we had both a dreamful knowledge of the same matters, of which each had thought none other knew. Yet, when I questioned more, there was much that had been in my fancies that was foreign to her, and likewise much that had been familiar to her, that was of no meaning to me. But though there was this, that brought a little regret to us, there would be, time and again, some new thing that one told, that the other knew and could finish the telling of, to the gladness and amazement of both.

And so shall you picture us wandering and having constant speech, so that, hour by hour, we grew gladly aged in dear knowledge and sweet friendship of the other.

And truly, how the time passed, I know not; but there came presently a hullabaloo, and the shouts of men's voices and the baying of dogs, and the gleam of lanthorns, so that I knew not what to think; until, very sudden, and with a sweet and strange little laughter, the Lady Mirdath to perceive that we had missed the hours utter in our converse; so that her Guardian (made uneasy because of the three foot-pads) had ordered a search. And we all that time a-wander together in happy forgetfulness.

And we turned homeward, then, and came towards the lights; but indeed, the dogs found us before we were come there; and they had grown to know me now, and leaped about me, barking very friendly; and so in a minute the men had discovered us, and were gone back to tell Sir Jarles that all was well.

And this was the way of our meeting and the growing of our acquaintance, and the beginning of my great love for Mirdath the Beautiful.

Now, from that time onward, evening by evening would I go a-wander along the quiet and country road that led from my estate to the estate of Sir Jarles. And always I went inward by the hedge-gap; and oft I should find the Lady Mirdath walking in that part of the woods; but always with her great boar-hounds about her; for I had begged that she do this thing for her sweet safety; and she to seem wishful to pleasure me; but truly to be just so oft utter perverse in diverse matters; and to strive to plague me, as though she would discover how much I would endure and how far she might go to anger me.

And, truly, well I remember how that one night, coming to the hedge-gap, I saw two country-maids come thence out from the woods

of Sir Jarles' ; but they were naught to me, and I would have gone upward through the gap, as ever; only that, as they passed me, they curtseyed somewhat over-graceful for rough wenches. And I had a sudden thought, and came up to them to see them more anigh; and truly I thought the taller was surely the Lady Mirdath. But, indeed, I could not be sure; for when I asked who she did be, she only to simper and to curtsey again; and so was I very natural all in doubt; but yet sufficient in wonder (having some knowledge of the Lady Mirdath) to follow the wenches, the which I did.

And they then, very speedy and sedate, as though I were some rack-rape that they did well to be feared of alone at night; and so came at last to the village green, where a great dance was a-foot, with torches, and a wandering fiddler to set the tune; and ale in plenty.

And the two to join the dance, and danced very hearty; but had only each the other for a partner, and had a good care to avoid the torches. And by this, I was pretty sure that they were truly the Lady Mirdath and her maid; and so I took chance when they had danced somewhat my way, to step over to them, and ask boldly for a dance. But, indeed, the tall one answered, simpering, that she was promised; and immediately gave her hand to a great hulking farmer-lout, and went round the green with him; and well punished she was for her waywardness; for she had all her skill to save her pretty feet from his loutish stampings; and very glad she was to meet the end of the dance.

And I knew now for certainty that it was Mirdath the Beautiful, despite her plan of disguise, and the darkness and the wench's dress and the foot-gear that marred her step so great. And I walked across to her, and named her, whispering, by name; and gave her plain word to be done of this unwisdom, and I would take her home. But she to turn from me, and she stamped her foot, and went again to the lout; and when she had suffered another dance with him, she bid him be her escort a part of the way; the which he was nothing loath of.

And another lad, that was mate to him, went likewise; and in a moment, so soon as they were gone away from the light of the torches, the rough hind-lads made to set their arms about the waists of the two wenches, not wetting who they had for companions. And the Lady Mirdath was no longer able to endure, and cried out in her sudden fear and disgust, and struck the rough hind that embraced her, so hard that he loosed her a moment, swearing great oaths. And directly he came back to her again, and had her in a moment, to kiss her; and she, loathing him to the very death, beat him madly in the face with her hands; but to no end, only that I was close upon them.

And, in that moment, she screamed my name aloud; and I caught the poor lout and hit him once, but not to harm him overmuch; yet to give him a long memory of me; and afterward I threw him into the side of the road. But the second hind, having heard my name, loosed from the tiring-maid, and ran for his life; and, indeed, my strength was known all about that part.

And I caught Mirdath the Beautiful by her shoulders, and shook her very soundly, in my anger. And afterward, I sent the maid onward; and she, having no word from her Mistress to stay, went forward a little; and in this fashion we came at last to the hedge-gap, with the Lady Mirdath very hushed; but yet walking anigh to me, as that she had some secret pleasure of my nearness. And I led her through the gap, and so homeward to the Hall; and there bid her good-night at a side door that she held the key of. And, truly, she bid me good-night in an utter quiet voice; and was almost as that she had no haste to be gone from me that night.

Yet, when I met her on the morrow, she was full of a constant impudence to me; so that, having her alone to myself, when the dusk was come, I asked her why she would never be done of her way-wardness; because that I ached to have companionship of her; and, instead, she denied my need. And, at that, she was at once very gentle; and full of a sweet and winsome understanding; and surely knew that I wished to be rested; for she brought out her harp, and played me dear olden melodies of our childhood-days all that evening; and so had my love for her the more intent and glad. And she saw me that night to the hedge-gap, having her three great boar-hounds with her, to company her home again. But, indeed, I followed her afterwards, very silent, until I saw her safe into the Hall; for I would not have her alone in the night; though she believed that I was then far away on the country road. And as she walked with her dogs, one or another would run back to me, to nose against me friendly-wise; but I sent them off again very quiet; and she had no knowledge of aught; for she to go singing a love-song quietly all the way home. But whether she loved me, I could not tell; though she had a nice affection for me.

Now, on the following evening, I went somewhat early to the gap; and lo! who should be standing in the gap, talking to the Lady Mirdath; but a very clever-drest man, that had a look of the Court about him; and he, when I approached, made no way for me through the gap; but stood firm, and eyed me very insolent; so that I put out my hand, and lifted him from my way.

And lo! the Lady Mirdath turned a bitterness of speech upon me

that gave me an utter pain and astonishment; so that I was assured in a moment that she had no true love for me, or she had never striven so to put me to shame before the stranger, and named me uncouth and brutal to a smaller man. And, indeed, you shall perceive how I was in my heart in that moment.

And I saw that there was some seeming of justice in what the Lady Mirdath said; but yet might the man have shown a better spirit; and moreover Mirdath the Beautiful had no true call to shame me, her true friend and cousin, before this stranger. Yet did I not stop to argue; but bowed very low to the Lady Mirdath; and afterward I bowed a little to the man and made apology; for, indeed, he was neither great nor strong-made; and I had been better man to have shown courtesy to him; at least in the first.

And so, having done justice to my own respect, I turned and went on, and left them to their happiness.

Now, I walked then, maybe twenty good miles, before I came to my own home; for there was no rest in me all that night, or ever, because that I was grown deadly in love of Mirdath the Beautiful; and all my spirit and heart and body of me pained with the dreadful loss that I was come so sudden upon.

And for a great week I had my walks in another direction; but in the end of that week, I must take my walk along the olden way, that I might chance to have but a sight of My Lady. And, truly, I had all sight that ever man did need to put him in dread pain and jealousy; for, truly, as I came in view of the gap, there was the Lady Mirdath walking just without the borders of the great wood; and beside her there walked the clever-drest man of the Court, and she suffered his arm around her, so that I knew they were lovers; for the Lady Mirdath had no brothers nor any youthful men kin.

Yet, when Mirdath saw me upon the road, she shamed in a moment to be so caught; for she put her lover's arm from about her, and bowed to me, a little changed of colour in the face; and I bowed very low—being but a young man myself—; and so passed on, with my heart very dead in me. And as I went, I saw that her lover came again to her, and had his arm once more about her; and so, maybe, they looked after me, as I went very stiff and desperate; but, indeed, I looked not back on them, as you may think.

And for a great month then, I went not near to the gap; for my love raged in me, and I was hurt in my pride; and, truly, neither had a true justice been dealt to me by the Lady Mirdath.

Yet in that month, my love was a leaven in me, and made slowly

a sweetness and a tenderness and an understanding that were not in me before; and truly Love and Pain do shape the Character of Man.

And in the end of that time, I saw a little way into Life, with an understanding heart, and began presently to take my walks again past the gap; but truly Mirdath the Beautiful was never to my sight; though one evening I thought she might be not a great way off; for one of her great boar-hounds came out of the wood, and down into the road to nose against me, very friendly, as a dog oft doth with me.

Yet, though I waited a good time after the dog had left me, I had no sight of Mirdath, and so passed on again, with my heart heavy in me; but without bitterness, because of the understanding that was begun to grow in my heart.

Now, there passed two weary and lonely weeks, in which I grew sick to have knowledge of the beautiful maid. And, truly, in the end of that time, I made a sudden resolving that I would go in through the gap, and come to the home-grounds about the Hall, and so maybe have some sight of her.

And this resolving I had one evening; and I went out immediately, and came to the gap, and went in through the gap, and so by a long walking to the gardens about the Hall. And, truly, when I was come there, I saw a good light of lanthorns and torches, and a great company of people dancing; and all drest in quaint dress; so that I knew they had a festival for some cause. And there came suddenly a horrid dread into my heart that this might be the marriage-dance of the Lady Mirdath; but, indeed, this was foolishness; for I had surely heard of the marriage, if there had been any. And, truly, in a moment, I remembered that she was come one-and-twenty years of age on that day, and to the end of her ward-ship; and this surely to be festival in honour of the same.

And a very bright and pretty matter it was to watch, save that I was so heavy in the heart with loneliness and longing; for the company was great and gay, and the lights plentiful and set all about from the trees; and in leaf-made arbours about the great lawn. And a great table spread with eating matters and silver and crystal, and great lamps of bronze and silver went all a-down one end of the lawn; and the dance constant upon the other part.

And surely, the Lady Mirdath to step out of the dance, very lovely drest; yet seeming, to mine eyes, a little pale in the looming of the lights. And she to wander to a seat to rest; and, indeed, in a moment, there to be a dozen youths of the great families of the country-side, in attendance about her, making talk and laughter, and each eager for her favour; and she very lovely in the midst of them, but yet, as I did

think, lacking of somewhat, and a little pale-seeming, as I have told; and her glance to go odd-wise beyond the groupt men about her; so that I understood in a moment that her lover was not there, and she to be a-lack in the heart for him. Yet, why he was not there, I could not suppose, save that he might have been called back to the Court.

And, surely, as I watched the other young men about her, I burned with a fierce and miserable jealousy of them; so that I could near have stept forth and plucked her out from among them, and had her to walk with me in the woods, as in the olden days, when she also had seemed near to love. But, truly, what use to this? For it was not they who held her heart, as I saw plain; for I watched her, with an eager and lonesome heart, and knew that it was one small man of the Court that was lover to her, as I have told.

And I went away again then, and came not near to the gap for three great months, because that I could not bear the pain of my loss; but in the end of that time, my very pain to urge me to go, and to be worse than the pain of not going; so that I found myself one evening in the gap, peering, very eager and shaken, across the sward that lay between the gap and the woods; for this same place to be as an holy ground to me; for there was it that first I saw Mirdath the Beautiful, and surely lost my heart to her in that one night.

And a great time I stayed there in the gap, waiting and watching hopelessly. And lo! sudden there came something against me, touching my thigh very soft; and when I looked down, it was one of the boar-hounds, so that my heart leaped, near frightened; for truly My Lady was come somewhere nigh, as I did think.

And, as I waited, very hushed and watchful; yet with an utter beating heart; surely I heard a faint and low singing among the trees, so utter sad. And lo! it was Mirdath singing a broken love song, and a-wander there in the dark alone, save for her great dogs.

And I harked, with strange pain in me, that she did be so in pain; and I ached to bring her ease; yet moved not, but was very still there in the gap; save that my being was all in turmoil.

And presently, as I harked, there came a slim white figure out from among the trees; and the figure cried out something, and came to a quick pause, as I could see in the half-dark. And lo! in that moment, there came a sudden and unreasoned hope into me; and I came up out of the gap, and was come to Mirdath in a moment, calling very low and passionate and eager: "Mirdath! Mirdath! Mirdath!"

And this way I came to her; and her great dog that was with me, to bound beside me, in thought, mayhap, that it was some game. And

when I came to the Lady Mirdath, I held out my hands to her, not knowing what I did; but only the telling of my heart that needed her so utter, and craved to ease her of her pain. And lo! she put out her arms to me, and came into mine arms with a little run. And there she bode, weeping strangely; but yet with rest upon her; even as rest was come sudden and wondrous upon me.

And sudden, she moved in mine arms, and slipt her hands to me, very dear, and held her lips up to me, like some sweet child, that I kiss her; but, indeed, she was also a true woman, and in honest and dear love of me.

And this to be the way of our betrothal; and simple and wordless it was; yet sufficient, only that there is no sufficiency in Love.

Now, presently, she loosed herself out of mine arms, and we walked homeward through the woods, very quiet, and holding hands, as children do. And I then in a while to ask her about the man of the Court; and she laughed very sweet into the silence of the wood; but gave me no answer, save that I wait until we were come to the Hall.

And when we were come there, she took me into the great hall, and made a very dainty and impudent bow, mocking me. And so made me known to another lady, who sat there, upon her task of embroidering, which she did very demure, and as that she had also a dainty Mischief lurking in her.

And truly, the Lady Mirdath never to be done of naughty laughter, that made her dearly breathless with delight, and to sway a little, and set the trembling of pretty sounds in her throat; and surely she must pull down two great pistols from an arm-rack, that I fight a duel to the death with the lady of the embroidering, who held her face down over her work, and shook likewise with the wickedness of her laughter that she could not hide.

And in the end, the Lady of the Embroidering looked up sudden into my face; and I then to see somewhat of the mischief in a moment; for she had the face of the man of the Court suit, that had been lover to Mirdath.

And the Lady Mirdath then to explain to me how that Mistress Alison (which was her name) was a dear and bosom friend, and she it was that had been drest in the Court suit to play a prank for a wager with a certain young man who would be lover to her, an he might. And I then to come along, and so speedy to offence that truly I never saw her face plain, because that I was so utter jealous. And so the Lady Mirdath had been more justly in anger than I supposed, because that I had put hands upon her friend, as I have told.

And this to be all of it, save that they had planned to punish me, and had met every evening at the gap, to play at lovers, perchance I should pass, so that I should have greater cause for my jealousy, and truly they to have a good revenge upon me; for I had suffered very great a long while because of it.

Yet, as you do mind, when I came upon them, the Lady Mirdath had a half-regret, that was very natural, because even then she was in love of me, as I of her; and because of this, she drew away, as you shall remember, being—as she confessed—suddenly and strangely troubled and to want me; but afterwards as much set again to my punishment, because that I bowed so cold and went away. And indeed well I might.

Yet, truly, all was safe ended now, and I utter thankful and with a mad delight in the heart; so that I caught up Mirdath, and we danced very slow and stately around the great hall, the while that Mistress Alison whistled us a tune with her mouth, which she could very clever, as many another thing, I wot.

And each day and all day after this Gladness, Mirdath and I could never be apart; but must go a-wander always together, here and there, in an unending joy of our togetherness.

And in a thousand things were we at one in delight; for we had both of us that nature which doth love the blue of eternity which gathers beyond the wings of the sunset; and the invisible sound of the starlight falling upon the world; and the quiet of grey evenings when the Towers of Sleep are builded unto the mystery of the Dusk; and the solemn green of strange pastures in the moonlight; and the speech of the sycamore unto the beech; and the slow way of the sea when it doth mood; and the soft rustling of the night clouds. And likewise had we eyes to see the Dancer of the Sunset, casting her mighty robes so strange; and ears to know that there shakes a silent thunder over the Face of Dawn; and much else that we knew and saw and understood together in our utter joy.

Now, there happened to us about this time a certain adventure that came near to cause the death of Mirdath the Beautiful; for one day as we wandered, as ever, like two children in our contentment, I made remark to Mirdath that there went only two of the great boar-hounds with us; and she then told me that the third was to the kennels, being sick.

Yet, scarce had she told me so much; ere she cried out something and pointed; and lo! I saw that the third hound came towards us, at a run, yet very strange-seeming in his going. And in a moment, Mirdath cried out that the hound was mad; and truly, I saw then that the brute slavered as he came running.

And in a moment he was upon us, and made never a sound; but leaped at me in one instant of time; all before I had any thought of such intent. But surely, My Beautiful One had a dreadful love for me, for she cast herself at the dog, to save me, calling to the other hounds. And she was bitten in a moment by the brute, as she strove to hold him off from me. But I to have him instant by the neck and the body, and brake him, so that he died at once; and I cast him to the earth, and gave help to Mirdath, that I draw the poison from the wounds.

And this I did so well as I might, despite that she would have me stop. And afterwards, I took her into mine arms, and ran very fierce all the long and weary way to the Hall, and with hot skewers I burned the wounds; so that when the doctor came, he to say I have saved her by my care, if indeed she to be saved. But, truly, she had saved me in any wise, as you shall think; so that I could never be done of honour to her.

And she very pale; but yet to laugh at my fears, and to say that she soon to have her health, and the wounds healed very speedy; but, indeed, it was a long and bitter time before they were proper healed, and she so well as ever. Yet, in time, so it was; and an utter weight off my heart.

And when Mirdath was grown full strong again, we set our wedding day. And well do I mind how she stood there in her bridal dress, on that day, so slender and lovely as may Love have stood in the Dawn of Life; and the beauty of her eyes that had such sober sweetness in them, despite the dear mischief of her nature; and the way of her little feet, and the loveliness of her hair; and the dainty rogue-grace of her movements; and her mouth an enticement, as that a child and a woman smiled out of the one face. And this to be no more than but an hint of the loveliness of My Beautiful One.

And so we were married.

* * * *

Mirdath, My Beautiful One, lay dying, and I had no power to hold Death backward from such dread intent. In another room, I heard the little wail of the child; and the wail of the child waked my wife back into this life, so that her hands fluttered white and desperately needful upon the coverlid.

I kneeled beside My Beautiful One, and reached out and took her hands very gentle into mine; but still they fluttered so needful; and she looked at me, dumbly; but her eyes beseeching.

Then I went out of the room, and called gently to the Nurse; and the Nurse brought in the child, wrapped very softly in a long, white robe. And I saw the eyes of My Beautiful One grow clearer with a strange, lovely light; and I beckoned to the Nurse to bring the babe near.

My wife moved her hands very weakly upon the coverlid, and I knew that she craved to touch her child; and I signed to the Nurse, and took my child in mine arms; and the Nurse went out from the room, and so we three were alone together.

Then I sat very gentle upon the bed; and I held the babe near to My Beautiful One, so that the wee cheek of the babe touched the white cheek of my dying wife; but the weight of the child I kept off from her.

And presently, I knew that Mirdath, My Wife, strove dumbly to reach for the hands of the babe; and I turned the child more towards her, and slipped the hands of the child into the weak hands of My Beautiful One. And I held the babe above my wife, with an utter care; so that the eyes of my dying One, looked into the young eyes of the child. And presently, in but a few moments of time; though it had been someways an eternity, My Beautiful One closed her eyes and lay very quiet. And I took away the child to the Nurse, who stood beyond the door. And I closed the door, and came back to Mine Own, that we have those last instants alone together.

And the hands of my wife lay very still and white; but presently they began to move softly and weakly, searching for somewhat; and I put out my great hands to her, and took her hands with an utter care; and so a little time passed.

Then her eyes opened, quiet and grey, and a little dazed seeming; and she rolled her head on the pillow and saw me; and the pain of forgetfulness went out of her eyes, and she looked at me with a look that grew in strength, unto a sweetness of tenderness and full understanding.

And I bent a little to her; and her eyes told me to take her into mine arms for those last minutes. Then I went very gentle upon the bed, and lifted her with an utter and tender care, so that she lay suddenly strangely restful against my breast; for Love gave me skill to hold her, and Love gave My Beautiful One a sweetness of ease in that little time that was left to us.

And so we twain were together; and Love seemed that it had made a truce with Death in the air about us, that we be undisturbed; for there came a drowse of rest even upon my tense heart, that had known nothing but a dreadful pain through the weary hours.

And I whispered my love silently to My Beautiful One, and her eyes answered; and the strangely beautiful and terrible moments passed by into the hush of eternity.

And suddenly, Mirdath My Beautiful One, spoke,—whispering something. And I stooped gently to hark; and Mine Own spoke again; and lo! it was to call me by the olden Love Name that had been mine through all the utter lovely months of our togetherness.

And I began again to tell her of my love, that should pass beyond death; and lo! in that one moment of time, the light went out of her eyes; and My Beautiful One lay dead in mine arms . . . My Beautiful One. . . .

II

The Last Redoubt

SINCE MIRDATH, MY BEAUTIFUL One, died and left me lonely in this world, I have suffered an anguish, and an utter and dreadful pain of longing, such as truly no words shall ever tell; for, in truth, I that had all the world through her sweet love and companionship, and knew all the joy and gladness of Life, have known such lonesome misery as doth stun me to think upon.

Yet am I to my pen again; for of late a wondrous hope has grown in me, in that I have, at night in my sleep, waked into the future of this world, and seen strange things and utter marvels, and known once more the gladness of life; for I have learned the promise of the future, and have visited in my dreams those places where in the womb of Time, she and I shall come together, and part, and again come together—breaking asunder most drearly in pain, and again reuniting after strange ages, in a glad and mighty wonder.

And this is the utter strange story of that which I have seen, and which, truly, I must set out, if the task be not too great; so that, in the setting out thereof, I may gain a little ease of the heart; and likewise, mayhap, give ease of hope to some other poor human, that doth suffer, even as I have suffered so dreadful with longing for Mine Own that is dead.

And some shall read and say that this thing was not, and some shall dispute with them; but to them all I say naught, save "Read!" And having read that which I set down, then shall one and all have looked towards Eternity with me—unto its very portals. And so to my telling:

To me, in this last time of my visions, of which I would tell, it was not as if I dreamed; but, as it were, that I waked there into the dark, in the future of this world. And the sun had died; and for me thus newly waked into that Future, to look back upon this, our Present Age, was to look back into dreams that my soul knew to be of reality;

20

but which to those newly-seeing eyes of mine, appeared but as a far vision, strangely hallowed with peacefulness and light.

Always, it seemed to me when I awaked into the Future, into the Everlasting Night that lapped this world, that I saw near to me, and girdling me all about, a blurred greyness. And presently this, the greyness, would clear and fade from about me, even as a dusky cloud, and I would look out upon a world of darkness, lit here and there with strange sights. And with my waking into that Future, I waked not to ignorance; but to a full knowledge of those things which lit the Night Land; even as a man wakes from sleep each morning, and knows immediately he wakes, the names and knowledge of the Time which has bred him, and in which he lives. And the same while, a knowledge I had, as it were sub-conscious, of this Present—this early life, which now I live so utterly alone.

In my earliest knowledge of that place, I was a youth, seventeen years grown, and my memory tells me that when first I waked, or came, as it might be said, to myself, in that Future, I stood in one of the embrasures of the Last Redoubt—that great Pyramid of grey metal which held the last millions of this world from the Powers of the Slayers.

And so full am I of the knowledge of that Place, that scarce can I believe that none here know; and because I have such difficulty, it may be that I speak over familiarly of those things of which I know; and heed not to explain much that it is needful that I should explain to those who must read here, in this our present day. For there, as I stood and looked out, I was less the man of years of this age, than the youth of that, with the natural knowledge of that life which I had gathered by living all my seventeen years of life there; though, until that my first vision, I (of this Age) knew not of that other and Future Existence; yet woke to it so naturally as may a man wake here in his bed to the shining of the morning sun, and know it by name, and the meaning of aught else. And yet, as I stood there in the vast embrasure, I had also a knowledge, or memory, of this present life of ours, deep down within me; but touched with a halo of dreams, and yet with a conscious longing for One, known even there in a half memory as Mirdath.

As I have said, in my earliest memory, I mind that I stood in an embrasure, high up in the side of the Pyramid, and looked outwards through a queer spy-glass to the North-West. Aye, full of youth and with an adventurous and yet half-fearful heart.

And in my brain was, as I have told, the knowledge that had come

to me in all the years of my life in the Redoubt; and yet until that moment, this Man of this Present Time had no knowledge of that future existence; and now I stood and had suddenly the knowledge of a life already spent in that strange land, and deeper within me the misty knowings of this our present Age, and, maybe, also of some others.

To the North-West I looked through the queer spy-glass, and saw a landscape that I had looked upon and pored upon through all the years of that life, so that I knew how to name this thing and that thing, and give the very distances of each and every one from the "Centre-Point" of the Pyramid, which was that which had neither length nor breadth, and was made of polished metal in the Room of Mathematics, where I went daily to my studies.

To the North-West I looked, and in the wide field of my glass, saw plain the bright glare of the fire from the Red Pit, shine upwards against the underside of the vast chin of the North-West Watcher—The Watching Thing of the North-West. . . . "That which hath Watched from the Beginning, and until the opening of the Gateway of Eternity" came into my thoughts, as I looked through the glass . . . the words of Æsworpth, the Ancient Poet (though incredibly future to this our time). And suddenly they seemed at fault; for I looked deep down into my being, and saw, as dreams are seen, the sunlight and splendour of this our Present Age. And I was amazed.

And here I must make it clear to all that, even as I waked from this Age, suddenly into that life, so must I—that youth there in the embrasure—have awakened then to the knowledge of this far-back life of ours—seeming to him a vision of the very beginnings of eternity, in the dawn of the world. Oh! I do but dread I make it not sufficient clear that I and he were both I—the same soul. He of that far date seeing vaguely the life that was (that I do now live in this present Age); and I of this time beholding the life that I yet shall live. How utterly strange!

And yet, I do not know that I speak holy truth to say that I, in that future time, had no knowledge of this life and Age, before that awakening; for I woke to find that I was one who stood apart from the other youths, in that I had a dim knowledge—visionary, as it were, of the past, which confounded, whilst yet it angered, those who were the men of learning of that age; though of this matter, more anon. But this I do know, that from that time, onwards, my knowledge and assuredness of the Past was tenfold; for this my memory of that life told me.

And so to further my telling. Yet before I pass onwards, one other thing is there of which I shall speak—In the moment in which I

waked out of that youthfulness, into the assured awareness of this our Age, in that moment the hunger of this my love flew to me across the ages; so that what had been but a memory-dream, grew to the pain of Reality, and I knew suddenly that I lacked; and from that time onwards, I went, listening, as even now my life is spent.

And so it was that I (fresh-born in that future time) hungered strangely for My Beautiful One with all the strength of that new life, knowing that she had been mine, and might live again, even as I. And so, as I have said, I hungered, and found that I listened.

And now, to go back from my digression, it was, as I have said, I had amazement at perceiving, in memory, the unknowable sunshine and splendour of this age breaking so clear through my hitherto most vague and hazy visions; so that the ignorance of Æsworpth was shouted to me by the things which now I knew.

And from that time, onward, for a little space, I was stunned with all that I knew and guessed and felt; and all of a long while the hunger grew for that one I had lost in the early days—she who had sung to me in those faery days of light, that had been in verity. And the especial thoughts of that age looked back with a keen, regretful wonder into the gulf of forgetfulness.

But, presently, I turned from the haze and pain of my dream-memories, once more to the inconceivable mystery of the Night Land, which I viewed through the great embrasure. For on none did it ever come with weariness to look out upon all the hideous mysteries; so that old and young watched, from early years to death, the black monstrosity of the Night Land, which this our last refuge of humanity held at bay.

To the right of the Red Pit there lay a long, sinuous glare, which I knew as the Vale of Red Fire, and beyond that for many dreary miles the blackness of the Night Land; across which came the coldness of the light from the Plain of Blue Fire.

And then, on the very borders of the Unknown Lands, there lay a range of low volcanoes, which lit up, far away in the outer darkness, the Black Hills, where shone the Seven Lights, which neither twinkled nor moved nor faltered through Eternity; and of which even the great spy-glass could make no understanding; nor had any adventurer from the Pyramid ever come back to tell us aught of them. And here let me say, that down in the Great Library of the Redoubt, were the histories of all those, with their discoveries, who had ventured out into the monstrousness of the Night Land, risking not the life only, but the spirit of life.

And surely it is all so strange and wonderful to set out, that I could

24 WILLIAM HOPE HODGSON

almost despair with the contemplation of that which I must achieve;
for there is so much to tell, and so few words given to man by which
he may make clear that which lies beyond the sight and the present
and general knowings of Peoples.

How shall you ever know, as I know in verity, of the greatness
and reality and terror of the thing that I would tell plain to all; for we,
with our puny span of recorded life must have great histories to tell,
but the few bare details we know concerning years that are but a few
thousands in all; and I must set out to you in the short pages of this my
life there, a sufficiency of the life that had been, and the life that was,
both within and without that mighty Pyramid, to make clear to those
who may read, the truth of that which I would tell; and the histories
of that great Redoubt dealt not with odd thousands of years; but with
very millions; aye, away back into what they of that Age conceived to
be the early days of the earth, when the sun, maybe, still gloomed dully
in the night sky of the world. But of all that went before, nothing,
save as myths, and matters to be taken most cautiously, and believed
not by men of sanity and proved wisdom.

And I, . . . how shall I make all this clear to you who may read?
The thing cannot be; and yet I must tell my history; for to be silent
before so much wonder would be to suffer of too full a heart; and I
must even ease my spirit by this my struggle to tell to all how it was
with me, and how it will be. Aye, even to the memories which were
the possession of that far future youth, who was indeed I, of his
childhood's days, when his nurse of that Age swung him, and crooned
impossible lullabies of this mythical sun which, according to those
future fairy-tales, had once passed across the blackness that now lay
above the Pyramid.

Such is the monstrous futureness of this which I have seen through
the body of that far-off youth.

And so back to my telling. To my right, which was to the North,
there stood, very far away, the House of Silence, upon a low hill. And
in that House were many lights, and no sound. And so had it been
through an uncountable Eternity of Years. Always those steady lights,
and no whisper of sound—not even such as our distance-microphones
could have discovered. And the danger of this House was accounted
the greatest danger of all those Lands.

And round by the House of Silence, wound the Road Where The
Silent Ones Walk. And concerning this Road, which passed out of
the Unknown Lands, nigh by the Place of the Ab-humans, where was
always the green, luminous mist, nothing was known; save that it was

held that, of all the works about the Mighty Pyramid, it was, alone, the one that was bred, long ages past, of healthy human toil and labour. And on this point alone, had a thousand books, and more, been writ; and all contrary, and so to no end, as is ever the way in such matters.

And as it was with the Road Where The Silent Ones Walk, so it was with all those other monstrous things . . . whole libraries had there been made upon this and upon that; and many a thousand million mouldered into the forgotten dust of the earlier world.

I mind me now that presently I stepped upon the central travelling-roadway which spanned the one thousandth plateau of the Great Redoubt. And this lay six miles and thirty fathoms above the Plain of the Night Land, and was somewhat of a great mile or more across. And so, in a few minutes, I was at the South-Eastern wall, and looking out through The Great Embrasure towards the Three Silver-fire Holes, that shone before the Thing That Nods, away down, far in the South-East. Southward of this, but nearer, there rose the vast bulk of the South-East Watcher—The Watching Thing of the South-East. And to the right and to the left of the squat monster burned the Torches; maybe half-a-mile upon each side; yet sufficient light they threw to show the lumbered-forward head of the never-sleeping Brute.

To the East, as I stood there in the quietness of the Sleeping-Time on the One Thousandth Plateau, I heard a far, dreadful sound, down in the lightless East; and, presently, again—a strange, dreadful laughter, deep as a low thunder among the mountains. And because this sound came odd whiles from the Unknown Lands beyond the Valley of The Hounds, we had named that far and never-seen Place "The Country Whence Comes The Great Laughter." And though I had heard the sound, many and oft a time, yet did I never hear it without a most strange thrilling of my heart, and a sense of my littleness, and of the utter terror which had beset the last millions of the world.

Yet, because I had heard the Laughter oft, I paid not over-long attention to my thoughts upon it; and when, in a little it died away into that Eastern Darkness, I turned my spy-glass upon the Giants' Pit, which lay to the South of the Giants' Kilns. And these same Kilns were tended by the giants, and the light of the Kilns was red and fitful, and threw wavering shadows and lights across the mouth of the pit; so that I saw giants crawling up out of the pit; but not properly seen, by reason of the dance of the shadows. And so, because ever there was so much to behold, I looked away, presently, to that which was plainer to be examined.

To the back of the Giants' Pit was a great, black Headland, that

stood vast, between the Valley of The Hounds (where lived the monstrous Night Hounds) and the Giants. And the light of the Kilns struck the brow of this black Headland; so that, constantly, I saw things peer over the edge, coming forward a little into the light of the Kilns, and drawing back swiftly into the shadows.

And thus it had been ever, through the uncounted ages; so that the Headland was known as The Headland From Which Strange Things Peer; and thus was it marked in our maps and charts of that grim world.

And so I could go on ever; but that I fear to weary; and yet, whether I do weary, or not, I must tell of this country that I see, even now as I set my thoughts down, so plainly that my memory wanders in a hushed and secret fashion along its starkness, and amid its strange and dread habitants, so that it is but by an effort I realise me that my body is not there in this very moment that I write. And so to further tellings:

Before me ran the Road Where The Silent Ones Walk; and I searched it, as many a time in my earlier youth had I, with the spy-glass; for my heart was always stirred mightily by the sight of those Silent Ones.

And, presently, alone in all the miles of that night-grey road, I saw one in the field of my glass—a quiet, cloaked figure, moving along, shrouded, and looking neither to right nor left. And thus was it with these beings ever. It was told about in the Redoubt that they would harm no human, if but the human did keep a fair distance from them; but that it were wise never to come close upon one. And this I can well believe.

And so, searching the road with my gaze, I passed beyond this Silent One, and past the place where the road, sweeping vastly to the South-East, was lit a space, strangely, by the light from the Silver-fire Holes. And thus at last to where it swayed to the South of the Dark Palace, and thence Southward still, until it passed round to the Westward, beyond the mountain bulk of the Watching Thing in the South—the hugest monster in all the visible Night Lands. My spy-glass showed it to me with clearness—a living hill of watchfulness, known to us as The Watcher Of The South. It brooded there, squat and tremendous, hunched over the pale radiance of the Glowing Dome.

Much, I know, had been writ concerning this Odd, Vast Watcher; for it had grown out of the blackness of the South Unknown Lands a million years gone; and the steady growing nearness of it had been noted and set out at length by the men they called Monstruwacans; so that it was possible to search in our libraries, and learn of the very coming of this Beast in the olden-time.

And, while I mind me, there were even then, and always, men named Monstruwacans, whose duty it was to take heed of the great Forces, and to watch the Monsters and the Beasts that beset the great Pyramid, and measure and record, and have so full a knowledge of these same that, did one but sway an head in the darkness, the same matter was set down with particularness in the Records.

And, so to tell more about the South Watcher. A million years gone, as I have told, came it out from the blackness of the South, and grew steadily nearer through twenty thousand years; but so slow that in no one year could a man perceive that it had moved.

Yet it had movement, and had come thus far upon its road to the Redoubt, when the Glowing Dome rose out of the ground before it—growing slowly. And this had stayed the way of the Monster; so that through an eternity it had looked towards the Pyramid across the pale glare of the Dome, and seeming to have no power to advance nearer.

And because of this, much had been writ to prove that there were other forces than evil at work in the Night Lands, about the Last Redoubt. And this I have always thought to be wisely said; and, indeed, there to be no doubt to the matter, for there were many things in the time of which I have knowledge, which seemed to make clear that, even as the Forces of Darkness were loose upon the End of Man; so were there other Forces out to do battle with the Terror; though in ways most strange and unthought of by the human mind. And of this I shall have more to tell anon.

And here, before I go further with my telling, let me set out some of that knowledge which yet remains so clear within my mind and heart. Of the coming of these monstrosities and evil Forces, no man could say much with verity; for the evil of it began before the Histories of the Great Redoubt were shaped; aye, even before the sun had lost all power to light; though, it must not be a thing of certainty, that even at this far time the invisible, black heavens held no warmth for this world; but of this I have no room to tell; and must pass on to that of which I have a more certain knowledge.

The evil must surely have begun in the Days of the Darkening (which I might liken to a story which was believed doubtfully, much as we of this day believe the story of the Creation). A dim record there was of olden sciences (that are yet far off in our future) which, disturbing the unmeasurable Outward Powers, had allowed to pass the Barrier of Life some of those Monsters and Ab-human creatures, which are so wondrously cushioned from us at this normal present. And thus there had materialized, and in other cases developed, gro-

tesque and horrible Creatures, which now beset the humans of this world. And where there was no power to take on material form, there had been allowed to certain dreadful Forces to have power to affect the life of the human spirit. And this growing very dreadful, and the world full of lawlessness and degeneracy, there had banded together the sound millions, and built the Last Redoubt; there in the twilight of the world—so it seems to us, and yet to them (bred at last to the peace of usage) as it were the Beginning; and this I can make no clearer; and none hath right to expect it; for my task is very great, and beyond the power of human skill.

And when the humans had built the great Pyramid, it had one thousand three hundred and twenty floors; and the thickness of each floor was according to the strength of its need. And the whole height of this pyramid exceeded seven miles, by near a mile, and above it was a tower from which the Watchmen looked (these being called the Monstruwacans). But where the Redoubt was built, I know not; save that I believe in a mighty valley, of which I may tell more in due time.

And when the Pyramid was built, the last millions, who were the Builders thereof, went within, and made themselves a great house and city of this Last Redoubt. And thus began the Second History of this world. And how shall I set it all down in these little pages! For my task, even as I see it, is too great for the power of a single life and a single pen. Yet, to it!

And, later, through hundreds and thousands of years, there grew up in the Outer Lands, beyond those which lay under the guard of the Redoubt, mighty and lost races of terrible creatures, half men and half beast, and evil and dreadful; and these made war upon the Redoubt; but were beaten off from that grim, metal mountain, with a vast slaughter. Yet, must there have been many such attacks, until the electric circle was put about the Pyramid, and lit from the Earth-Current. And the lowest half-mile of the Pyramid was sealed; and so at last there was a peace, and the beginnings of that Eternity of quiet watching for the day when the Earth-Current shall become exhausted.

And, at whiles, through the forgotten centuries, had the Creatures been glutted time and again upon such odd bands of daring ones as had adventured forth to explore through the mystery of the Night Lands; for of those who went, scarce any did ever return; for there were eyes in all that dark; and Powers and Forces abroad which had all knowledge; or so we must fain believe.

And then, so it would seem, as that Eternal Night lengthened itself upon the world, the power of terror grew and strengthened. And

fresh and greater monsters developed and bred out of all space and Outward Dimensions, attracted, even as it might be Infernal sharks, by that lonely and mighty hill of humanity, facing its end—so near to the Eternal, and yet so far deferred in the minds and to the senses of those humans. And thus hath it been ever.

And all this but by the way, and vague and ill told, and set out in despair to make a little clear the beginnings of that State which is so strange to our conceptions, and yet which had become a Condition of Naturalness to Humanity in that stupendous future.

Thus had the giants come, fathered of bestial humans and mothered of monsters. And many and diverse were the creatures which had some human semblance; and intelligence, mechanical and cunning; so that certain of these lesser Brutes had machinery and underground ways, having need to secure to themselves warmth and air, even as healthy humans; only that they were incredibly inured to hardship, as they might be wolves set in comparison with tender children. And surely, do I make this thing clear?

And now to continue my telling concerning the Night Land. The Watcher of the South was, as I have set to make known, a monster differing from those other Watching Things, of which I have spoken, and of which there were in all four. One to the North-West, and one to the South-East, and of these I have told; and the other twain lay brooding, one to the South-West, and the other to the North-East; and thus the four watchers kept ward through the darkness, upon the Pyramid, and moved not, neither gave they out any sound. Yet did we know them to be mountains of living watchfulness and hideous and steadfast intelligence.

And so, in a while, having listened to the sorrowful sound which came ever to us over the Grey Dunes, from the Country of Wailing, which lay to the South, midway between the Redoubt and the Watcher of the South, I passed upon one of the moving roadways over to the South-Western side of the Pyramid, and looked from a narrow embrasure thence far down into the Deep Valley, which was four miles deep, and in which was the Pit of the Red Smoke.

And the mouth of this Pit was one full mile across, and the smoke of the Pit filled the Valley at times, so that it seemed but as a glowing red circle amid dull thunderous clouds of redness. Yet the red smoke rose never much above the Valley; so that there was clear sight across to the country beyond. And there, along the further edge of that great depth, were the Towers, each, maybe, a mile high, grey and quiet; but with a shimmer upon them.

Beyond these, South and West of them, was the enormous bulk of the South-West Watcher, and from the ground rose what we named the Eye Beam—a single ray of grey light, which came up out of the ground, and lit the right eye of the monster. And because of this light, that eye had been mightily examined through unknown thousands of years; and some held that the eye looked through the light steadfastly at the Pyramid; but others set out that the light blinded it, and was the work of those Other Powers which were abroad to do combat with the Evil Forces. But however this may be, as I stood there in the embrasure, and looked at the thing through the spy-glass, it seemed to my soul that the Brute looked straightly at me, unwinking and steadfast, and fully of a knowledge that I spied upon it. And this is how I felt.

To the North of this, in the direction of the West, I saw The Place Where The Silent Ones Kill; and this was so named, because there, maybe ten thousand years gone, certain humans adventuring from the Pyramid, came off the Road Where The Silent Ones Walk, and into that place, and were immediately destroyed. And this was told by one who escaped; though he died also very quickly; for his heart was frozen. And this I cannot explain; but so it was set out in the Records.

Far away beyond The Place Where The Silent Ones Kill, in the very mouth of the Western Night was the Place of the Ab-humans, where was lost the Road Where The Silent Ones Walk, in a dull green, luminous mist. And of this place nothing was known; though much it held the thoughts and attentions of our thinkers and imaginers; for some said that there was a Place Of Safety, differing from the Redoubt (as we of this day suppose Heaven to differ from the Earth), and that the Road led thence; but was barred by the Ab-humans. And this I can only set down here; but with no thought to justify or uphold it.

Later, I travelled over to the North-Eastern wall of the Redoubt, and looked thence with my spy-glass at the Watcher of the North-East—the Crowned Watcher it was called, in that within the air above its vast head there hung always a blue, luminous ring, which shed a strange light downwards over the monster—showing a vast, wrinkled brow (upon which an whole library had been writ); but putting to the shadow all the lower face; all save the ear, which came out from the back of the head, and belled towards the Redoubt, and had been said by some observers in the past to have been seen to quiver; but how that might be, I knew not; for no man of our days had seen such a thing.

And beyond the Watching Thing was The Place Where The Silent Ones Are Never, close by the great road; which was bounded upon the far side by The Giant's Sea; and upon the far side of that, was a Road

which was always named The Road By The Quiet City; for it passed along that place where burned forever the constant and never-moving lights of a strange city; but no glass had ever shown life there; neither had any light ever ceased to burn.

And beyond that again was the Black Mist. And here, let me say, that the Valley of The Hounds ended towards the Lights of the Quiet City.

And so have I set out something of that land, and of those creatures and circumstances which beset us about, waiting until the Day of Doom, when our Earth-Current should cease, and leave us helpless to the Watchers and the Abundant Terror.

And there I stood, and looked forth composedly, as may one who has been born to know of such matters, and reared in the knowledge of them. And, anon, I would look upward, and see the grey, metalled mountain going up measureless into the gloom of the everlasting night; and from my feet the sheer downward sweep of the grim, metal walls, six full miles, and more, to the plain below.

And one thing (aye! and I fear me, many) have I missed to set out with particularness:

There was, as you do know, all around the base of the Pyramid, which was five and one-quarter miles every way, a great circle of light, which was set up by the Earth-Current, and burned within a transparent tube; or had that appearance. And it bounded the Pyramid for a clear mile upon every side, and burned for ever; and none of the monsters had power ever to pass across, because of what we did call The Air Clog that it did make, as an invisible Wall of Safety. And it did give out also a more subtile vibration, that did affect the weak Brain-Elements of the monsters and the Lower Men-Brutes. And some did hold that there went from it a further vibration of a greater subtileness that gave a protecting against the Evil Forces. And some quality it had truly thiswise; for the Evil Powers had no ability to cause harm to any within. Yet were there some dangers against which it might not avail; but these had no cunning to bring harm to any within the Great Redoubt who had wisdom to meddle with no dreadfulness. And so were those last millions guarded until the Earth-Current should be used to its end. And this circle is that which I have called the Electric Circle; though with failure to explain. But there it was called only, The Circle.

And thus have I, with great effort, made a little clear that grim land of night, where, presently, my listening heard one calling across the dark. And how that this grew upon me, I will set out forthwith.

III

The Quiet Calling

NOW, OFT HAD I heard tell, not only in that great city which occupied the thousandth floor, but in others of the one thousand, three hundred and twenty cities of the Pyramid, that there was somewhere out in the desolation of the Night Lands a second Place of Refuge, where had gathered, in another part of this dead world, some last millions of the human race, to fight unto the end.

And this story I heard everywhere in my travels through the cities of the Great Redoubt, which travels began when I came upon my seventeenth year, and continued for three years and two hundred and twenty-five days, being even then but one day in each city, as was the custom in the training of every child.

And truly it was a great journey, and in it I met with many, whom to know was to love; but whom never could I see again; for life has not space enough; and each must to his duty to the security and well-being of the Redoubt. Yet, for all that I have set down, we travelled much, always; but there were so many millions, and so few years.

And, as I have said, everywhere I went there was the same story of this other Place of Refuge; and in such of the Libraries of those cities as I had time to search, there were great numbers of works upon the existence of this other Refuge; and some, far back in the years, made assertion with confidence that such a Place was in verity; and, indeed, no doubt did there seem in those by-gone ages; but now these very Records were read only by Scholars, who doubted, even whilst they read. And so is it ever.

But of the reality of this Refuge, I had never a sound doubt, from the day of my hearing concerning it from our Master Monstruwacan, who with all his assistants occupied the Tower of Observation in the apex of the Pyramid. And here let me tell that he and I had always an affinity and close friendship one for the other; though he was full

grown, and I but a youth; yet so it was; and thus, when I had come to an age of twenty-one years of life, he opened to me a post within the Tower of Observation; and this was a most wondrous good fortune to me; for in all the vast Redoubt, to be appointed to the Tower of Observation was the most desired; for thereby, even as in these days doth Astronomy, was the natural curiosity of Man eased somewhat, even while thwarted.

Now, let me tell here also, lest it be thought that I was unduly favoured because of my friendship with the Master Monstruwacan, that there was a sound justification for his choice, in that to me had been given that strange gift of hearing, which we called Night-Hearing; though this was but a fanciful name, and meant little. Yet the peculiar gift was rare, and in all the millions of the Pyramid, there was none with the gift to a great degree, saving only myself.

And I, because of this gift, could hear the "invisible vibrations" of the æther; so that, without harking to the calling of our recording instruments, I could take the messages which came continually through the eternal darkness; aye, even better than they. And now, it may be the better understood, how much was to be counted that I had grown to listen for a voice that had not rung in mine ears for an eternity, and yet which sang sweet and clear in my memory-dreams; so that it seemed to me that Mirdath the Beautiful slept within my soul, and whispered to me out of all the ages.

And then, one day, at the fifteenth hour, when began the Sleep-Time, I had been pondering this love of mine that lived with me still; and marvelling that my memory-dreams held the voice of a love that had been in so remote an age. And pondering and dreaming thus, as a young man may, I could fancy this æon-lost One were whispering beauty into my ears, in verity; so clear had my memory grown, and so much had I pondered.

And lo! as I stood there, harking and communing with my thoughts, I thrilled suddenly, as if I had been smitten; for out of all the everlasting night a whisper was thrilling and thrilling upon my more subtile hearing.

Through four long years had I listened, since that awakening in the embrasure, when but a youth of seventeen; and now out of the world-darkness and all the eternal years of that lost life, which now I live in this Present Age of ours, was the whisper come; for I knew it upon that instant; and yet, because I was so taught to wisdom, I answered by no name; but sent the Master-Word through the night— sending it with my brain-elements, as I could, and as all may, much or little, as may be, if they be not clods. And, moreover, I knew that she

who called quietly would have the power to hear without instruments, if indeed it were she; and if it were but one of the false callings of the Evil Forces, or more cunning monsters, or as was sometimes thought concerning these callings, the House of Silence, meddling with our souls, then would they have no power to say the Master-Word; for this had been proven through all the Everlasting.

And lo! as I stood, trembling and striving not to be tense, which destroys the receptivity, there came thrilling round and round my spiritual essence the throb of the Master-Word, beating steadily in the night, as doth that marvellous sound. And then, with all that was sweet in my spirit, I called with my brain elements: "Mirdath! Mirdath! Mirdath!" And at that instant the Master Monstruwacan entered that part of the Tower of Observation, where I stood; and, seeing my face, stood very quiet; for though he had not the power of Night-Hearing, he was wise and thoughtful, and took much account of my gift; moreover, he had but come from the Receiving Instrument, and thought vaguely to have caught the throb of the Master-Word, though too faint to come proper through the Instrument, so that he searched for me, in that I, who had the Hearing, might listen for it, I being, as I have said, gifted in that wise.

And to him I told something of my story and my thoughts and my memories, and of that awakening; and thus up to this present happening, and he hearkened with sympathy and a troubled and wondering heart; for in that age a man might talk sanely upon that which, in this age of ours would be accounted foolishness and maybe the breathings of insanity; for there, by the refinement of arts of mentality and the results of strange experiments and the accomplishment of learning, men were abled to conceive of matters now closed to our conceptions, even as we of this day may haply give a calm ear to talk, that in the days of our fathers would have been surely set to the count of lunacy. And this is very clear.

And all the while that I told my story, I listened with my spirit; but save for a sense of faint, happy laughter that wrapped about me, I heard naught. And nothing more all that day.

Here let me put down that, because of my memories and half memories, I would time and again dispute with our learned men; they being in doubt as to the verity of that olden story of the Days of Light, and the existence of the Sun; though something of all this was set out, as of truth, in our oldest records; but I, remembering, told them many tales that seemed fairy-like to them, and entranced their hearts, even whilst I angered their brains, which refused to take

seriously and as verity that which their hearts accepted gladly, even as we receive the wonder of poetry into our souls. But the Master Monstruwacan would listen to aught I had to tell; aye! though I spoke through hours; and so it would be, odd times, that having talked long, drawing my stories from my Memory-Dreams, I would come back again into the present of that Future; and lo! all the Monstruwacans would have left their instruments and observations and recording, and be gathered about me; and the Master so sunken in interest that he not to have discovered them; neither had I noticed, being so full of the things which had been.

But when the Master came back to knowledge of that present, he would rouse and chide, and they, all those lesser ones, would fly swiftly and guiltily to their various works; and yet, so I have thought since, each with a muddled and bewildered and thoughtful air upon him; and hungry they were for more, and ever wondering and setting questions about.

And so it was also with those others—those learned ones who were not of the Tower of Observation, and who disbelieved even whilst they hungered. Listen would they, though I talked from the first hour, which was the "dawn," to the fifteenth hour, which was the beginning of the "night"; for the Sleep-Time was set thus, after other usage and experiment. And, odd whiles, I found that there were among them, men of extraordinary learning who upheld my tellings as tales of verity; and so there was a faction; but, later, there grew more to believe; and whether they believed, or not, all were ready to listen; so that I might have spent my days in talk; only that I had my work to do.

But the Master Monstruwacan believed from the beginning, and was wise always to understand; so that I loved him for this, as for many another dear quality.

And so, as may be conceived, among all those millions I was singled out to be known; for the stories that I told went downward through a thousand cities; and, presently, in the lowest tier of the Underground Fields, an hundred miles deep in the earth below the Redoubt, I found that the very ploughboys knew something concerning my tellings; and gathered about me one time and another when the Master Monstruwacan and I had gone down, regarding some matter that dealt with the Earth-Current and our Instruments.

And of the Underground Fields (though in that age we called them no more than "The Fields") I should set down a little; for they were the mightiest work of this world; so that even the Last Redoubt was but a small thing beside them. An hundred miles deep lay the lowest of the Underground Fields, and was an hundred miles from side to

side, every way; and above it there were three hundred and six fields, each one less in area than that beneath; and in this wise they tapered, until the topmost field which lay direct beneath the lowermost floor of the Great Redoubt, was but four miles every way.

And thus it will be seen that these fields, lying one beneath the other, formed a mighty and incredible Pyramid of Country Lands in the deep earth, an hundred miles from the base unto the topmost field.

And the whole was sheathed-in at the sides with the grey metal of which the Redoubt was builded; and each field was pillared, and floored beneath the soil, with this same compound of wonder; and so was it secure, and the monsters could not dig into that mighty garden from without.

And all of that Underground Land was lit, where needed, by the Earth-Current, and that same life-stream fructified the soil, and gave life and blood to the plants and to the trees, and to every bush and natural thing.

And the making of those Fields had taken maybe a million years, and the "dump" thereof had been cast into the "Crack," whence came the Earth-Current, and which had bottom beyond all soundings. And this Underground Country had its own winds and air-currents; so that, to my memory, it was in no ways connected to the monstrous air-shafts of the Pyramid; but in this I may be mistaken; for it has not been given to me to know all that is to be known concerning that vast Redoubt; nor by any one man could so much knowledge be achieved.

Yet that there were wise and justly promoted winds in that Underground Country, I do know; for healthful and sweet they were, and in the corn-fields there was the sweet rustle of grain, and the glad, silken laughter of poppies, all beneath a warm and happy light. And here, did the millions walk and take excursion, and go orderly or not, even as in these days.

And all this have I seen, and the talk of a thousand lovers in the gardens of that place, comes back to me; and with it all the memory of my dear one; and of a faint calling that would seem to whisper about me at times; but so faint and attenuated, that even I, who had the Night-Hearing, could not catch its import; and so went, listening ever the more intently. And oft times calling.

Now there was a Law in the Pyramid, tried and healthful, which held that no male should have freedom to adventure into the Night Land, before the age of twenty-two; and no female ever. Yet that, after such age, if a youth desired greatly to make the adventure, he should receive three lectures upon the dangers of which we had knowledge,

and a strict account of the mutilatings and horrid deeds done to those who had so adventured. And if, after this had passed over him, he still desired, and if he were accounted healthful and sane; then should he be allowed to make the adventure; and it was accounted honour to the youth who should add to the knowledge of the Pyramid.

But to all such as went forth into the danger of the Night Land, there was set beneath the skin of the inner side of the left forearm, a small capsule, and when the wound had healed, then might the youth make the adventure.

And the wherefore of this, was that the spirit of the youth might be saved, if he were entrapped; for then, upon the honour of his soul, must he bite forth the capsule, and immediately his spirit would have safety in death. And by this shall you know somewhat the grim and horrid danger of the Dark Land.

And this I have set down because later I was to make huge adventure into those Lands; and even at this time, some thought of the same had come to me; for always I went listening for that quiet calling; and twice I sent the Master-Word throbbing solemnly through the everlasting night; yet this I did no more, without certainty; for the Word must not be used lightly. But often would I say with my brain-elements "Mirdath! Mirdath!"—sending the name out into the darkness; and sometimes would I seem to hear the faint thrilling of the æther around me; as though one answered; but weakly, as it were with a weakened spirit, or by instrument that lacked of its earth-force.

And thus, for a great while there was no certainty; but only a strange anxiousness and no clear answer.

Then, one day as I stood by the instruments in the Tower of Observation, at the thirteenth hour there came the thrilling of beaten æther all about me, as it were that all the void was disturbed. And I made the Sign for Silence; so that the men moved not in all the Tower; but bowed over their breathing-bells, that all disturbance might cease.

And again came the gentle thrilling, and broke out into a clear, low calling in my brain; and the calling was my name—the old-earth name of this day, and not the name of that age. And the name smote me, with a frightenedness of fresh awakening memories. And, immediately, I sent the Master-Word into the night; and all the æther was full of movement. And a silence came; and later a beat afar off in the void of night, which only I in all that great Redoubt could hear, until the heavier vibrations were come. And in a moment there was all about me the throbbing of the Master-Word, beating in the night a sure answer. Yet, before this I knew that Mirdath had called; but now had surety.

And immediately, I said "Mirdath," making use of the instruments; and there came a swift and beautiful answer; for out of the dark there stole an old love-name, that she only had ever used to me.

And, presently, I minded me of the men, and signed to them that they should continue; for the Records must not be broken; and now I had the communication full established.

And by me stood the Master Monstruwacan, quietly as any young Monstruwacan, waiting with slips to make any notes that were needful; and keeping a strict eye upon those others; but not unkindly. And so, for a space of wonder, I had speech with that girl out in the darkness of the world, who had knowledge of my name, and of the old-earth love-name, and named herself Mirdath.

And much I questioned her, and presently to my sorrow; for it seemed that her name was not truly Mirdath; but Naani; neither had she known my name; but that in the library of that place where she abode, there had been a story of one named by my name, and called by that sweet love-name which she had sent out somewhat ruthless into the night; and the girl's name had been Mirdath; and when first she, Naani had called, there had come back to her a cry of Mirdath, Mirdath; and this had minded her so strangely of that olden story which had stayed in her memory; that she had answered as the maid in that book might have answered.

And thus did it seem that the utter Romance of my Memory-love had vanished, and I stood strangely troubled for sorrow of a love of olden times. Yet, even then I marvelled that any book should have story so much like to mine; not heeding that the history of all love is writ with one pen.

Yet, even then in that hour of my strange, and quaintly foolish pain, there came a thing that set me thrilling; though more afterwards, when I came to think afresh upon it. For the girl who spoke to me through the night made some wonder that my voice were not deeper; yet in quiet fashion, and as one who says a thing, scarce wotting what they say. But even to me then, there came a sudden hope; for in the olden days of this Present Age my voice had been very deep. And I said to her that maybe the man in the book was said to have had a deep tone of speech; but she, seeming puzzled, said nay; and at that I questioned her the more; but only to the trouble of her memory and understanding.

And strange must it seem that we two should talk on so trivial a matter, when there was so much else that we had need to exchange thought upon; for were a man in this present day to have speech with

those who may live within that red planet of Mars within the sky, scarce could the wonder of it exceed the wonder of a human voice coming through that night unto the Great Redoubt, out of all that lost darkness. For, indeed, this must have been the breaking of, maybe, a million years of silence.

And already, as I came to know later, was the news passing downward from City to City through all the vast Pyramid; so that the Hour-Slips were full of the news; and every City eager and excited, and waiting. And I better known in that one moment, than in all my life before. For that previous calling, had been but vaguely put about; and then set to the count of a nature, blown upon over-easily by spirit-winds of the half-memory of dreams. Though it is indeed true, as I have set down before this, that my tales concerning the early days of the world, when the sun was visible, and full of light, had gone down through all the cities, and had much comment and setting forth in the Hour-Slips, and were a cause for speech and argument.

Now concerning the voice of this girl coming to us through the darkness of the world, I will set out that which she had to tell; and this, indeed, but verified the tellings of our most ancient Records, which had so long been treated over lightly: There was, it would seem, somewhere out in the lonesome dark of the Outer Lands, but at what distance none could ever discover, a second Redoubt; that was a three-sided Pyramid, and moderate small; being no more than a mile in height, and scarce three quarters of a mile along the bases.

When this Redoubt was first builded, it had been upon the far shore of a sea, where now was no sea; and it had been raised by those wandering humans who had grown weary of wandering, and weary of the danger of night attacks by the tribes of half-human monsters which began to inhabit the earth even so early as the days when the half-gloom was upon the world. And he that had made the plan upon which it was builded, was one who had seen the Great Redoubt, having lived there in the beginning, but escaped because of a correction set upon him for his spirit of irresponsibility, which had made him to cause disturbance among the orderly ones in the lowest city of the Great Redoubt.

Yet, in time, he too had come to be tamed by the weight of fear of the ever-growing hordes of monsters, and the Forces that were abroad. And so he, being a master-spirit, planned and builded the smaller Redoubt, being aided thereto by four millions, who also were weary of the harass of the monsters; but until then had been wanderers, because of the restlessness of their blood.

And they had chosen that place, because there they had discovered a sign of the Earth-Current in a great valley which led to the shore; for without the Earth-Current no Refuge could have existence. And whilst many builded and guarded, and cared for the Great Camp in which all lived, others worked within a great shaft; and in ten years had made this to a distance of many miles, and therewith they tapt the Earth-Current; but not a great stream; yet a sufficiency, as was believed.

And, presently, after many years, they had builded the Pyramid, and taken up their refuge there, and made them instruments, and ordained Monstruwacans; so that they had speech daily with the Great Pyramid; and thus for many long ages.

And the Earth-Current then to begin to fail; and though they laboured through many thousands of years, they came to no better resource. And so it was they ceased to have communication with the Great Redoubt; for the current had a lack of power to work the instruments; and the recording instruments ceased to be sensible of our messages.

And thereafter came a million years, maybe, of silence; with ever the birthing and marrying and dying of those lonesome humans. And they grew less; and some put this to the lack of the Earth-Current, which dwindled slowly through the centuries of that Eternity.

And once in a thousand years, maybe, one among them would be Sensitive, and abled to hear beyond ordinary; and to these, at times, there would seem to come the thrilling of the æther; so that such an one would go listening; and sometimes seem to catch half messages; and so awaken a great interest in all the Pyramid; and there would be turning up of old Records, and many words and writings, and attempts to send the Master-Word through the night; in which, doubtless sometimes they succeeded; for there was set down in the Records of the Great Redoubt certain occasions on which there had come the call of the Master-Word, which had been arranged and made holy between the two Redoubts in the early days of that second life of this world.

Yet, now for an hundred thousand years, there had been none Sensitive; and in that time the people of the Pyramid had become no more than ten thousand; and the Earth-Current was weak and powerless to put the joy of life into them; so that they went listlessly; but deemed it not strange, because of so many æons of usage.

And then, to the wonder of all, the Earth-Current had put forth a new power; so that young people ceased to be old over-soon; and there was happiness and a certain joy in the living; and a strange birthing of children, such as had not been through half a million years.

And then came a new thing. Naani, the daughter of the Master Monstruwacan of that Redoubt had shown to all that she was Sensitive; for she had perceived odd vibrations afloat in the night; and concerning these she told her father; and presently, because their blood moved afresh in their bodies, they had heart to discover the plans of the ancient instruments; for the instruments had long rusted, and been forgotten.

And so they builded them a new instrument to send forth a message; for they had no memory at that time that the brain-elements had power to do thus; though, mayhap, their brain-elements were weakened, through so many ages of starvation of the Earth-Current, and could not have obeyed, even had their masters known all that we of the Great Redoubt knew.

And when the instrument was finished, to Naani was given the right to call first across the dark to discover whether indeed, after that million years of silence, they were yet companied upon this earth, or whether they were in truth lonely—the last poor thousands of the Humans.

And a great and painful excitement came upon the people of the lesser pyramid; for the loneliness of the world pressed upon them; and it was to them as though we in this age called to a star across the abyss of space.

And because of the excitement and pain of the moment, Naani called only vaguely with the instrument into the dark; and lo! in a moment, as it seemed, there came all about her in the night the solemn throb of the Master-Word, beating in the night. And Naani cried out that she was answered, and, as may be thought, many of the people wept, and some prayed, and some were silent; but others beseeched her that she call again and quickly to have further speech with those of their kind.

And Naani spoke the Master-Word into the night, and directly there came a calling all about her: "Mirdath! Mirdath!" and the strange wonder of it made her silent a moment; but when she would have made reply, the instrument had ceased to work, and she could have no further speech at that time.

This, as may be thought, occasioned much distress; and constant work they had between the instrument and the Earth-Current, to discover the reason for this failing; but could not for a great while. And in that time, oft did Naani hear the call of "Mirdath" thrilling about her; and twice there came the solemn beat of the Master-Word in the night. Yet never had she the power to answer. And all that while, as I

learned in time, was she stirred with a quaint ache at heart by the voice that called "Mirdath!" as it might be the Spirit of Love, searching for its mate; for this is how she put it.

And thus it chanced, that the constant thrilling of this name about her, woke her to memory of a book she had read in early years, and but half understood; for it was ancient, and writ in an olden fashion, and it set out the love of a man and a maid, and the maid's name was Mirdath. And so, because she was full of this great awakening of those ages of silence, and the calling of that name, she found the book again, and read it many times, and grew to a sound love of the beauty of that tale.

And, presently, when the instrument was made right, she called into the night the name of that man within the book; and so it came about that I had hoped too much; yet even now was I strangely unsure whether to cease from hoping.

And one other thing there is which I would make clear. Many and oft a time had I heard a thrilling of sweet, faint laughter about me, and the stirring of the æther by words too gentle to come clearly; and these I make no doubt came from Naani, using her brain-elements unwittingly and in ignorance; but very eager to answer my callings; and having no knowledge that, far off across the blackness of the world, they thrilled about me, constantly.

And after Naani had made clear all that I have set out concerning the Lesser Refuge, she told further how that food was not plentiful with them; though, until the reawakening of the Earth-Current, they had gone unknowing of this, being of small appetite, and caring little for aught; but now wakened, and newly hungry, they savoured a lack of taste in all that they ate; and this we could well conceive, from our reasonings and theory; but happily not from our knowledge.

And we said unto them, that the soil had lost its life, and the crops therefrom were not vital; and a great while it would take for the earth within their pyramid to receive back the life-elements. And we told them certain ways by which they might bring a more speedy life to the soil; and this they were eager to do, being freshly alive after so long a time of half-life.

And now, you must know that in all the great Redoubt the story went downwards swiftly, and was published in all the Hour-Sheets, with many comments; and the libraries were full of those who would look up the olden Records, which for so long had been forgotten, or taken, as we of this day would say, with a pinch of salt.

And all the time I was pestered with questions; so that, had I not

been determined, I should scarce have been allowed to sleep; moreover, so much was writ about me, and my power to hear, and divers stories concerning tales of love, that I had been like to have grown mazed to take note of it all; yet some note I did take, and much I found pleasant; but some displeasing.

And, for the rest, I was not spoiled, as the saying goes; for I had my work to do; moreover, I was always busied Listening, and having speech through the darkness. Though if any saw me so, they would question; and because of this, I kept much to the Tower of Observation, where was the Master Monstruwacan, and a greater discipline.

And then began a fresh matter; though but an old enough trick; for I speak now of the days that followed that re-opening of the talk between the Pyramids. Oft would speech come to us out of the night; and there would be tales of the sore need of the Lesser Redoubt, and callings for help. Yet, when I sent the Master-Word abroad, there would be no answering. And so I feared that the Monsters and Forces of Evil knew.

Yet, at times, the Master-Word would answer to us, beating steadily in the night; and when we questioned afresh, we knew that they in the Lesser Redoubt had caught the beat of the Master-Word, and so made reply; though it had not been they who had made the previous talk, which we had sought to test by the Word. And then they would make contradiction of all that had been spoken so cunningly; so that we knew the Monsters and Forces had sought to tempt some from the safety of the Redoubt. Yet, was this no new thing, as I have made to hint; saving that it grew now to a greater persistence, and there was a loathsome cunning in the using of this new knowledge to the making of wicked and false messages by those evil things of the Night Land. And it told to us, as I have made remark, how that those Monsters and Forces had a full awareness of the speech between the Pyramids; yet could they have no power to say the Master-Word; so had we some test left, and a way to sure knowledge of what made talk in the night.

And all that I have told should bring to those of this Age something of the yet unbegotten terror of that; and a quiet and sound thankfulness to God, that we suffer not as humanity shall yet suffer.

But, for all this, let it not be thought that they of that Age accounted it as suffering; but as no more than the usual of human existence. And by this may we know that we can meet all circumstances, and use ourselves to them and live through them wisely, if we be but prudent and consider means of invention.

And through all the Night Land there was an extraordinary awak-

ening among the Monsters and Forces; so that the instruments made constant note of greater powers at work out there in the darkness; and the Monstruwacans were busied recording, and keeping a very strict watch. And so was there at all that time a sense of difference and awakening, and of wonders about, and to come.

And from The Country Whence Comes The Great Laughter, the Laughter sounded constant . . . as it were an uncomfortable and heart-shaking voice-thunder rolling thence over the Lands, out from the unknown East. And the Pit of the Red Smoke filled all the Deep Valley with redness, so that the smoke rose above the edge, and hid the bases of the Towers upon the far side.

And the Giants could be seen plentiful around the Kilns to the East; and from the Kilns great belches of fire; though the meaning of it, as of all else, we could not say; but only the cause.

And from the Mountain Of The Voice, which rose to the South-East of the South-East Watcher, and of which I have made no telling hitherto, in this faulty setting-out, I heard for the first time in that life, the calling of the Voice. And though the Records made mention of it; yet not often was it heard. And the calling was shrill, and very peculiar and distressful and horrible; as though a giant-woman, hungering strangely, shouted unknown words across the night. And this was how it seemed to me; and many thought this to describe the sound.

And, by all this, may you perceive how that Land was awakened.

And other tricks there were to entice us into the Night Land; and once a call came thrilling in the æther, and told to us that certain humans had escaped from the Lesser Redoubt, and drew nigh to us; but were faint for food, and craved succour. Yet, when we sent the Master-Word into the night, the creatures without could make no reply; which was a very happy thing for our souls; for we had been all mightily exercised in our hearts by this one message; and now had proof that it was but a trap.

And constantly, and at all hours, I would have speech with Naani of the Lesser Redoubt; for I had taught her how she might send her thoughts through the night, with her brain-elements; but not to over-use this power; for it exhausts the body and the powers of the mind, if it be abused by exceeding usage.

Yet, despite that I had taught her the use of her brain-elements, she sent her message always without strength, save when she had use of the instrument; and this I set to the cause that she had not the health force needful; but, apart from this, she had the Night-Hearing very keen; though less than mine.

And so, with many times of speech, and constant tellings of our doings and thoughts, we drew near in the spirit to one another; and had always a feeling in our hearts that we had been given previous acquaintance.

And this, as may be thought, thrilled my heart very strangely.

IV
The Hushing of the Voice

("Dearest, thine own feet tread the world at night--
Treading, as moon-flakes step across a dark--
Kissing the very dew to holier light . . .
Thy Voice a song past mountains, which to hark
Frightens my soul with an utter lost delight.")

NOW, ONE NIGHT, TOWARDS the end of the sixteenth hour, as I made ready to sleep, there came all about me the thrilling of the æther, as happened oft in those days; but the thrilling had a strange power in it; and in my soul the voice of Naani sounded plain, all within and about me.

Yet, though I knew it to be the voice of Naani, I answered not immediately; save to send the sure question of the Master-Word into the night. And, directly, I heard the answer, the Master-Word beating steadily in the night; and I questioned Naani why she had speech with me by the Instrument at that time, when all were sleeping, and the watch set among the Monstruwacans; for they in the little Pyramid had their sleep-time to commence at the eleventh hour; so that by this it was five hours advanced towards the time of waking; and Naani should have slept; nor have been abroad to the Tower of Observation, apart from her father. For I supposed that she spoke by the Instrument, her voice sounding very clear in my brain. Yet, to this question, she made no answer in kind; but gave a certain thing into my spirit, which set me trembling; for she said certain words, that began:

"Dearest, thine own feet tread the world at night——"

And it well may be that she set me to tremble; for as the words grew about me, there wakened a memory-dream how that I had made these same words to Mirdath the Beautiful in the long-gone Eternity of this our Age, when she had died and left me alone in all the world. And I was weak a little with the tumult and force of my emotion; but in a moment I called eagerly with my brain-elements to Naani to give some explaining of this thing that she had spoken to the utter troubling of my heart.

Yet, once more she made no direct answer; but spoke the words again to me across all the dark of the world. And it came to me

suddenly, that it was not Naani that spoke; but Mirdath the Beautiful, from out of all the everlasting night. And I called: "Mirdath! Mirdath," with my brain-elements, into the night; and lo! the far, faint voice spoke again to my spirit through all the darkness of eternity, saying again those words. Yet, though the voice was the voice of Mirdath the Beautiful, it was also the voice of Naani; and I knew in all my heart that this thing was in verity; and that it had been given to me to be birthed once more into this world in the living-time of that Only One, with whom my spirit and essence hath mated in all ages through the everlasting. And I called with my brain-elements and all my strength to Naani; but there came no answer; neither sign of hearing, though through hours I called.

And thus at last I came to an utter exhaustion; but neither could be quiet, nor sleep. Yet, presently, I slept.

And when I waked, my first memory was of the wondrous thing which had befallen in the sleep-time; for none in all this world could have known those words; save it had been the spirit of Mirdath, my Beautiful One, looking from above my shoulder in that utter-lost time, as I made those words to her, out of an aching and a broken heart. And the voice had been the voice of Mirdath; and the voice of Mirdath had been the voice of Naani. And what shall any say to this, save that which I had in my heart.

And immediately I called to Naani, once, and again twice; and in a little moment there came all about me the throbbing of the Master-Word, beating solemnly in the night; and I sent the Master-Word to give assurance, and immediately the voice of Naani, a little weak as was it always when she had not the Instrument, but sent the message with her brain-elements.

And I answered her, and questioned her eagerly concerning her sayings of the past time of sleep; but she disclaimed, and made clear to me that she had no knowledge of having spoken; but had slept through all that time of which I made to tell; and, indeed, had dreamed a very strange dream.

And for a little while I was confused, and meditated, not knowing what to think; but came suddenly again to a knowledge that Naani's far voice was thrilling the æther all about; and that she would tell to me her dream; which had set strong upon her mind.

And she told the dream to me, and in the dream she had seen a tall, dark man, built very big, and dressed in unfamiliar clothing. And the man had been in a little room, and very sorrowful, and lonesome; and in her dream she had gone nigh to him.

And presently the man made to write, that he might ease him by giving expression to his sorrow; and Naani had been able to read the words that he wrote; though to her waking spirit the language in which they were writ was strange and unknown. Yet she could not remember what he had writ, save but one short line, and this she had mind of in that he had writ the word Mirdath above. And she spoke of the strangeness of this thing, that she should dream of this name; but supposed that I had fixed it upon her, by my first callings.

And then did I, with something of a tremble in my spirit, ask Naani to tell me what she remembered of the writing of that big, sorrowful stranger. And, in a little moment, her far voice said these words all about me:

"Dearest, thine own feet tread the world at night——"

But no more had she memory of. Yet it was a sufficiency; and I, maybe with a mad, strange triumph in my soul, said unto her with my brain-elements that which remained of those words. And my spirit felt them strike upon the spirit of Naani, and awake her memory, as with the violence of a blow. And for a little while she stumbled, dumb before so much newness and certainty. And her spirit then to waken, and she near wept with the fright and the sudden, new wonder of this thing.

And immediately, all about me there came her voice thrilling, and the voice was the voice of Mirdath, and the voice of Naani; and I heard the tears of her spirit make pure and wonderful the bewildered and growing gladness of her far voice. And she asked me, as one who had suddenly opened the Gates of Memory, whether she might be truly Mirdath. And I, utter weak and shaken strangely because of this splendour of fulfilment, could make no instant answer. And she asked again, but using mine old love-name, and with a sureness in her far voice. And still I was so strangely dumb, and the blood to thud peculiar in mine ears; and this to pass; and speech to come swift.

And this way to be that meeting of our spirits, across all the everlasting night.

And you shall have for a memory-picture, how that Naani stood there in the world in that far eternity, and, with her spirit having speech with mine, looked back through the part-opened gates of her memory, into the past of this our life and Age. Yet more than this she saw, and more than was given to me in that Age; for she had memory now and sight of other instances, and of other comings together, which had some confusion and but half-meanings to me. Yet of this our present Age and life, we spoke as of some yesterday; but very hallowed.

Now, as may be conceived, the wonder of this surety which had

come into my life stirred me fiercely to its completion; for all my heart and spirit cried out to be with that one who was Mirdath, and now spoke with the voice of Naani.

Yet, how should this be won; for none among all the learned men of that Mighty Pyramid knew the position of the Lesser Redoubt; neither could the Records and Histories of the World give us that knowledge; only that there was a general thought among the Students and the Monstruwacans that it lay between the North-West and the North-East. But no man had any surety; neither could any conceive of the distance from us of that Refuge.

And counting all this, there was yet the incredible danger and peril of the Night Land, and the hunger and desolation of the Outer Lands, which were sometimes named the Unknown Lands.

And I spoke much with Naani concerning this matter of their position; yet neither she nor her father, the Master Monstruwacan of that Refuge, had any knowing either of our position; only that the Builder of the Lesser Redoubt had come out of the Southward World in the Beginning, as they had knowledge of by the Records.

Also, the father of Naani set that ancient Compass to bear; for, as he made explanation to us through the Instrument, so great a power of the Earth-Current must be ours that, perchance it was our force which did affect the pointer from steadfastness. For, indeed, the needle did swing in an arc, as we heard, that held between the North and the South; within the Westward arc; but this it had done ever with them, and so was a very helpless guide; save that, maybe, as we had thought, the force of the Earth-Current that was with us, had in truth some power to pull the needle towards us. And if this were so of verity, we made a reckoning that set the Lesser Redoubt to the North; and they did likewise, and put us to the South; yet was it all built upon the sand of guess-work; and nothing to adventure the life and soul upon.

Now we, of curiosity; though a million times had it been done in the past ages, set the compass before us, having it from the Great Museum. But, as ever in that age, it did spin if we but stirred the needle, and would stop nowheres with surety; for the flow of the Earth-Current from the "Crack" beneath the Pyramid had a power to affect it away from the North, and to set it wandering. And this may seem very strange to this present Age; yet to that, it was most true to the seeming nature of things; and harder to believe that ever it did once point steadfastly, to prove a guide of sureness, and unfailing.

For, be it known, we knew the positions of the Land by tradition, coming from that ancient time when, in the Half-Gloom they had build-

ed the Pyramid; they having known the use of that ancient compass, and with sight of the Sun had named the Positions; though we of that far future day had forgotten the very beginnings of those Names of Direction; and used them but because our fathers did a million years and more. And likewise we did the same with the names of the day and the night and the weeks and the months and the years; though of the visible markings of these there was nothing but only and always the everlasting night; yet the same seeming very natural to that people.

Now, Naani, having heed to my constant questions, craved with an utter keen hunger that I might come to her; but yet forbade it, in that it were better to live and commune in the spirit, than to risk my soul, and mayhaps die, in the foolishness of trying to find her in all the darkness of the dead world. Yet, no heed had I taken of her commands, had I but known of a surety the direction in which she might be discovered; and gained some knowledge of the space between, for this might be named by thousands of miles, or but by hundreds; though a great distance it was surely.

Yet, one other thing there was, that has point in this place; for when I sent my speech out into the night, using my brain-elements, I came to know that, whether I had a knowledge of the North, or no knowledge at the moment, yet did I turn oft with a sure instinction to that Direction. And of this, the Master Monstruwacan took very great note, and had me to experiment many a time and way, and so enclosed about with screens, or with bandages across mine eyes, that I could not, save by that inward Knowing, have any knowledge to point me the way. Yet would I turn Northwards very frequent, by a certain feeling; and seemed unable of speech, if I were turned otherwise by force.

But when we asked Naani whether she had an unusualness in this matter, she could discover none; and we could but take note curiously of that which affected my habits; and which truly I set to the attracting of her spirit; for I had mind that she did be somewheres out that way in the darkness of the world; but yet was this no more than to suppose, as you perceive.

And the Master Monstruwacan wrote a study of this matter of the Northwardness of my turning; and it was set out in the Hour-Slips of the Tower of Observation; and so it came to be copied by the Hour-Slips of the great cities, and made much comment, and much calling up to me through the home instruments; so that with this, and the speech that went about concerning my powers to hear, I was much in talk, and diversely pleased and oft angered by overmuch attention and importunity.

And now, whilst I pondered this matter in all my spirit and being, how that I should some way come to Naani, there befell a very terrible thing. And in this wise must I tell it: .

It was at the seventeenth hour, when all the millions of the Mighty Pyramid slept, that I was with the Master Monstruwacan in the Tower of Observation taking my due turn. And sudden, I heard the thrilling of the æther all about me, and the voice of Naani in my soul, speaking. And I sent the Master-Word into the darkness of the world, and presently, I heard the solemn answer beating steadfastly in the night; and immediately I called to Naani with my brain-elements, to know what thing troubled her in her sleep.

And her voice came into my spirit, weak and far and faint, and so that scarce I could make to hear the words. Yet, in a while I gathered that all the peoples of the Lesser Redoubt were in very deadly trouble; for that the Earth-Current had failed suddenly and mightily; and they had called her from her sleep, that she might listen whether we answered their callings by the Instrument; but, indeed, no calling had come to us.

And they who had been of late so joyful, were now grown old with sorrow in but an hour or two; for they feared that the fresh coming of the Earth-Current had been but the final flicker and outburst before the end. And, even in this short while of our speech, did it seem to me that the voice of Naani grew further off from me; and I felt like to have broken my heart with the trouble of this thing.

And through all that remained of that sleep-time, did I converse with Naani, as might two lovers who shall presently part for ever. And when the cities awoke, the news went throughout them, and all our millions were in sorrow and trouble.

And thus was it for, maybe, a little month; and in that time had the voice of Naani grown so weak and far-off that even I that had the Night-Hearing, could scarce make real its meaning. And every word was to me a treasure and a touch upon my soul; and my grief and trouble before this certain parting drove me that I could not eat, neither have rest; and this did the Master Monstruwacan take upon him to chide and correct; for that, if any were to help, how should it be done if I that had the Night-Hearing, and heard even now that the recording Instruments were dumb, came to ill-health.

And because of this, and such wisdom as was mine, I made to eat and order my life that I might have my full powers. Yet was this beyond all my strength; for, presently, I knew that the people of the Lesser Pyramid were threatened by the monsters that beset them; and

later I had knowledge from faint, far words whispered in my brain, that there had been a fight with an outside Force that had harmed many in their minds; so that in madness they had opened the gate and had run from the Lesser Pyramid, out into the darkness of the Lands about them; and there had their physical bodies fallen to the monsters of those Lands; but of their souls who may know?

And this, we set assuredly to the failure of the Earth-Current, which had robbed them of all force and power; so that, in those few weeks all life and joy of living had left them; and neither hunger nor thirst had they, much, nor any great desire to live; but yet a new and mighty fear of death. And this doth seem very strange.

And, as may be thought, all this made the Peoples of the Great Redoubt think newly of the Earth-Current that issued from the "Crack" beneath the Pyramid; and of their latter end; so that much was writ in the Hour-Slips concerning this matter; yet in the main to assure us that we ourselves might each be free from a disturbed heart; though some went foolishly to the other event, and spoke of a speedy danger to us, likewise; as is ever the way. But the truth of our own case lay, maybe, somewhere between.

And all the Hour-Slips were full also of imaginings of the terror of those poor humans out in the darkness of the world, facing that end which must come upon all, even upon our mighty Pyramid; though, as most would believe, so far away in some future eternity, that we have no cause to trouble.

And there were sad poems writ to the peoples of that Lesser Redoubt, and foolish plans set about to rescue them; but none to put them to effect; and no way by which so great a thing might be done; and doth but show how loosely people will speak out of an over-security. Yet to me, there had come a certain knowledge that I must make the adventure, though I achieved naught save mine own end. Yet, it were better to cease quickly, than that I should feel, as now I did feel.

That same night, in the Eighteenth Hour, there was a great disturbance in the æther about the Mighty Pyramid; and I was awakened suddenly by the Master Monstruwacan; that I might use my gift of the Night-Hearing to hearken for the throbbing of the Master-Word, which they had thought to come vaguely through the Instruments; but no one of the Monstruwacans was sensitive enough of soul to account truly whether this was so.

And lo! as I sat up in the bed, there came the sound of the Master-Word, beating in the night about the Pyramid. And immediately there was a crying in the æther all about me: "We are coming! We are coming!"

And mine inwards leaped and sickened me a moment, so shaken was I with a sudden belief; for the message seemed some ways to come to me from very near to the Great Redoubt; as that they who sent it were nigh to hand.

And, forthwith, I called the Master-Word into the night; but no answer did there come for a while, and then a faint thrilling of the æther about me, and the weak pulse of the Master-Word in the night, sent by a far voice, strangely distant. And I knew that the voice was the voice of Naani; and I put a question through all the darkness of the dead world, whether she were within the Lesser Redoubt, and safe thus far.

And presently, there came a faint disturbance about me, and a small voice in my soul, speaking weakly and out of an infinite distance; and I knew that far away through the night Naani spoke feebly, with her brain-elements; and that she abode within the Lesser Pyramid; but that she too had heard that strange pulse of the Master-Word in the night, and that message: "We are coming! We are coming!" And vastly had this thing disturbed her, waking her within her sleep; so that she knew not what to think; save that we were devising some method to come to them.

But this I removed from doubt, saying that she must not build on vain hoping; for I would not have her doubly tortured by the vanity of such believing. And, thereafter, having said such things as I might, though few they were, to comfort her, I bade her, gently, to sleep; and turned therewith to the Master Monstruwacan, who waited in quiet patience; and had no knowledge of that which I had heard and sent; for his hearing was but the normal; though his brain and heart were such as made me to love him.

And I told the Master Monstruwacan many things as I put my clothing about me; how that there had indeed been the calling of the Master-Word; but not by any of that Lesser Redoubt; but that, to my belief, it had come from nigh about the Great Pyramid. Moreover, it was sent by no instrument; as I wotted that he did guess; but, as it seemed to me, by the brain-elements of many, calling in unison.

And all this did I set out to the Master Monstruwacan; and with something uncertain of fear and trouble in my heart; yet with a blind expectation; as, indeed, who would not. Though, no longer was I shaken by that first thought of Her nearness.

And I said to the Master Monstruwacan that we should go to the Tower of Observation, and search the Night Lands with the great spy-glass.

And we did this, and lo! presently, we saw a great number of men pass over the Electric Circle that went about the Pyramid; yet they came not to us; but went outwards towards the blackness and the strange fires and hideous mysteries of the Night Land. And we ceased from spying, and looked swiftly at one another, and knew in our hearts that some had left the Mighty Pyramid in the Sleep-Time.

Then the Master Monstruwacan sent word to the Master Watchman that his wardership had been outraged, and that people left the great Pyramid in the Sleep-Time; for this was against the Law; and none ever went out into the Night Land, save the Full Watch were posted to the Great Door; and at a due time, when all were wakeful; for the Opening Of The Door was made known to all the Millions of the Great Redoubt; so that all might be aware; and know that no foolishness was done without their wotting.

Moreover, ere any had power to leave the Pyramid, they must pass The Examination, and Be Prepared; and some of this have I set out already. And so stern was the framing of the Law, that there were yet the metal pegs upon the inner side of the Great Gate, where had been stretched the skin of one who disobeyed; and was flayed and his hide set there to be a warning in the Early Days. Yet the tradition was remembered; for, as I might say it, we lived very close about the place; and Memory had no room whereby she might escape.

Now the Master Watchman, when he heard that which the Master Monstruwacan had to tell, went hastily with some of the Central Watch from the Watch-Dome, to the Great Gate; and he found the men of the Sleep-Time Watch, with the Warder of the Gate, all bound, and stopt in the mouth, so that none could make outcry.

And he freed them, and learned that nigh five hundred young men, from the Upper Cities, by the bigness of their chests, had come upon them suddenly, and bound them, and escaped into the night through the Eye-Gate in the top of the Great Gate.

And the Master Watchman was angry, and demanded why that none had called by the instruments of the Watch House; but lo! some had made to call thus, and found them unable to wake the recorders which lay in the central Watch-Dome; for there had been tampering.

Now, after this, they made certain new rules and Laws concerning the order of Watching, and made tests of the lesser instruments of the inward Pyramid, nightly, upon the coming of the Sleep-Time, which was, even in that strange age, by tradition called the Night, as I have given hint; though hitherto, until the way of my story was known, I have used a word for the sleep hours that was yet not of that time;

but somewhat an invention to make this history free from the confu-
sion of "night" and "day," when, in truth, it was always night without
upon the world. Yet, after this, shall I keep to mine use the luxury of
the true names of that time; and yet, how strange is it that the truth
should be of so little to our thinking.

And so to go forward with my telling; for, though all this care were
now taken, it had no force until afterward; and at this moment were
those poor foolish youths out in all the danger of the Night Land,
and no way by which they might be succoured, or called back; save
that Fear or Wisdom should come to them quickly, that they cease
from so wild an attempt. For it was to make rescue of those in that
other, unknown Pyramid, out in all the darkness of the World's Night
that was their intent, as we had speedy knowledge from those boon
friends that had been in the secret of their plot, which had seemed
to them great and heroic; and was so, in verity, but that neither they
who went, nor they who stayed, had a true awaredness of the danger
they had dealing with, being all naught but raw and crude youths; yet,
doubtless, with the makings of many fine and great men among them.

And because some had thus abetted that which they knew to be
against the Law, which was framed to the well-being and safety of all,
there were certain floggings, which might the better help their mem-
ories in the future as to the properness of their actions and wisdom.

Moreover, they who returned, if any, would be flogged, as seemed
proper, after due examination. And though the news of their beat-
ings might help all others to hesitation, ere they did foolishly, in like
fashion, yet was the principle of the flogging not on this base, which
would be both improper and unjust; but only that the one in question
be corrected to the best advantage for his own well-being; for it is not
meet that any principle of correction should shape to the making of
human signposts of pain for the benefit of others; for in verity, this
were to make one pay the cost of many's learning; and each should owe
to pay only so much as shall suffice for the teaching of his own body
and spirit. And if others profit thereby, this is but accident, however
helpful. And this is wisdom, and denoteth now that a sound Principle
shall prevent Practice from becoming monstrous.

Yet, now I must hasten that I set down how it fared with those five
hundred youths that had made so sad an adventure of their lives and
unprepared souls; and were beyond our aid to help them, who might
not so much as make any calling to them, to bid them to return; for
to do this would have been to tell to all the Monsters of the Land that
humans were abroad from the Mighty Pyramid.

And this would have been to cause the monsters to search the youths out to their destruction, and maybe even to awaken the Forces to work them some dread Spiritual harm, which was the chief Fear.

Now, presently, through all the cities of the Great Redoubt, the news had gone how that five hundred foolish Youths had adventured out into the despair of the Night Land; and the whole Pyramid waked to life, and the Peoples of the South came to the Northern sides, for the Great Gate lay in the North-West side; and the Youths had made from there, not straightly outwards, but towards the North; and so were to be seen from the North-East embrasures, and from those within the North-West wall.

And thus, in a while were they watched by all the mighty multitudes of the Great Pyramid, through millions of spy-glasses; for each human had a spying-glass, as may be thought; and some were an hundred years old, and some, maybe ten thousand, and handed down through many generations; and some but newly made, and very strange. But all those people had some instrument by which they might spy out upon the wonder of the Night Land; for so had it been ever through all the eternity of darkness, and a great diversion and wonder of life was it to behold the monsters about their work; and to know that they plotted always to our destruction; yet were ever foiled.

And never did all that great and terrible Land grow stale upon the soul of any, from birth until death; and by this you shall know the constant wonder of it, and that sense of enemies in the night about us, which ever filled the heart and spirit of all Beholders; so that never were the embrasures utterly empty.

Yet, many beheld not the Land from the embrasures; but sat about the View-Tables, which were set properly in certain places throughout the cities, and so beheld the Night Land, without undue cranings, or poising of spy-glasses, though less plain-seen. And these same tables were some form of that which we of this age name Camera Obscura; but made very great, and with inventions, and low to the floor, so that ten thousand people might sit about them in the raised galleries, and have comfortable sight. Yet this attracted not the young people, save they were lovers; and then, in truth, were they comfortable seats for quietness and gentle whisperings.

Yet now, as may be supposed, with all the Peoples of the Mighty Pyramid grown eager to look towards one part of the Night Land, the embrasures hid in the crowds; and such as could gain no view therethrough, thronged about the View-Tables. And so was it in all the hours of leisure; so that women had scarce patience to attend

their children; but must hasten to watch again, that lonesome band of foolish youths making so blind and unshaped a trial to come upon that unknown Lesser Redoubt, somewhere out in all the night of the world.

And in this wise passed three days and nights; yet both in the sleep-time and the time of waking did great multitudes cease not to watch; so that many went hungry for sleep, as in truth did I. And sometimes we saw those Youths with plainness; but other times they were lost to our sight in the utter shadows of the Night Land. Yet, by the telling of our instruments, and the sense of my hearing, there was no awaredness among the Monsters, and the Forces of Evil, that any were abroad from the Pyramid; so that a little hope came into our hearts that yet there might be no tragedy.

And times, would they cease from their way, and sit about in circles among the shadows and the grey moss-bushes, which grew hardly here or there about. And we knew that they had food with them to eat; for this could we see with plainness, as some odd, grim flare of light from the infernal fires struck upon one or another strangely, and passed, and left them in the darkness.

And who of you shall conceive what was in the hearts of the fathers, and the mothers that bore the youths, and who never ceased away from the Northward embrasures; but spied out in terror and in tears, and maybe oft with so good glasses as did show them the very features and look upon the face of son and son.

And the kin of the watchers brought to them food, and tended them, so that they had no need to cease from their watching; and beds were made in the embrasures, rough and resourceful, that they might sleep quickly a little; yet be ever ready, if those cruel Monsters without made discovery of those their children.

Thrice in those three days of journeying to the Northward, did the Youths sleep, and we perceived that some kept a watch, and so knew that there was a kind of order and leadership among them; also, they had each his weapon upon his hip, and this gave to us a further plea to hope.

And concerning this same carrying of weapons, I can but set out here that no healthful male or female in all the Mighty Pyramid but possessed such a weapon, and was trained to it from childhood; so that a ripe and extraordinary skill in the use thereof was common to most. Yet some breaking of Rule had there been, that the Youths had each achieved to be armed; for the weapons were stored in every tenth house of the cities, in the care of the charging-masters.

And here I must make known that these weapons did not shoot;

but had a disk of grey metal, sharp and wonderful, that spun in the end of a rod of grey metal, and were someways charged by the Earth-Current, so that were any but stricken thereby, they were cut in twain so easy as aught. And the weapons were contrived to the repelling of any Army of Monsters that might make to win entrance to the Redoubt. And to the eye they had somewhat the look of strange battle-axes, and might be lengthened by the pulling out of the handles.

Now, the Youths made, as I have told, to the Northward; but had first to keep a long way to the North-East, that they might come clear of the Vale of Red Fire. And this wise they journeyed, and kept the Vale about seven miles to the North-West of them, and so were presently beyond the Watcher of the North-East, and going with a greater freedom, and having less care to hide.

And this way, it may be, certain of the giants, wandering, perceived them, and went swiftly to make attack and destroy them. But some order went about among the youths, and they made a long line, with a certain space between each, because of the terror of their weapon, and immediately, it seemed, the Giants were upon them, a score and seven they were, and seeming to be haired like to mighty crabs, as I saw with the Great Spy-Glass, when the great flares of far and mighty fires threw their fierce light across the Dark Lands.

And there was a very great and horrid fight; for the Youths broke into circles about each of the Giants, and many of those young men were torn in pieces; but they smote the Monsters from behind and upon every side, and we of the Mighty Pyramid could behold at times the grey, strange gleam of their weapons; and the æther was stirred about me by the passing of those that died; yet, by reason of the great miles, their screams came not to us, neither heard we the roars of the Monsters; but into our hearts, even from that great distance and safety, there stole the terror of those awesome Brutes; and in the Great Spy-Glass I could behold the great joints and limbs and e'en, I thought, the foul sweat of them; and their size and brutishness was like to that of odd and monstrous animals of the olden world; yet part human. And it must be borne to mind that the Fathers and the Mothers of those Youths beheld all this dread fight from the embrasures, and their other kin likewise watched, and a very drear sight was it to their hearts and their human, natural feelings, and like to breed old age, ere its due.

Then, in a time, the fight ceased; for of those seven and twenty Giant Brutes there remained none; only that there cumbered the ground seven and twenty lumbering hillocks, dreadful and grim. For the lesser dead we could not see proper.

And we that were within the Pyramid saw the Youths sorted together by their leaders, all in the dim twilight of that place; and with the Great Spy-Glass I made a rough count, and found that there lived of them, three hundred; and by this shall you know the power of those few monstrous things, which had slain full two hundred, though each youth was armed with so wondrous a weapon. And I set the word through the Pyramid, that all might have some knowledge of the number that had died; for it was better to know, than to be in doubt. And no spy-glass had the power of The Great Spy-Glass.

After this fight, the youths spent a time having a care to their bodies and wounds; and some were made separate from the others, and of these I counted upon fifty; and whilst the others made to continue their march towards the Road Where The Silent Ones Walk, these were constrained by one who was the Leader, to return to the Pyramid. And in a little, I saw that they came towards us, wearily and with many a halt, as that they suffered great wounds and harm of the fight.

But those others (maybe two hundred and fifty Youths) went onwards into the Night Land; and though we sorrowed at this thing; yet was there come a huge pride into our hearts that those raw ones, who yesterday were but children, had so held themselves in the battle, and done a great deed that day. And I wot that whilst their mothers wept, easeless, their fathers' hearts swelled within them, and held somewhat of their Pain away from them for a time.

And all this while, those wounded Youths came slowly, and rested, and came on again, the better helping the worse; and a great excitement and trouble there was in all the Mighty Pyramid, to learn which were they that came, and they that went, and who lay out there quietly among the slain. But none might say anything with surety; for, even with that great spy-glass in the Tower of Observation, they were not overplain; save when some light from the fires of the Land flared high, and lit them. For they stood not up into the glare of the fires, as had the Giants. And though I saw them with clearness, yet I knew them not; for there was so mighty a multitude in that Vast Redoubt, that none might ever know the half even of their rulers.

And about this time, there came a fresh matter of trouble to our minds; for one of the Monstruwacans made report that the instruments were recording an influence abroad in the night; so that we had knowledge that one of the Evil Forces was Out. And to me there came an awaredness that a strange unquiet stole over the Land; yet I knew it not with mine ears; but my spirit heard, and it was as though trouble and an expectation of horror did swarm about me.

And once, listening, I heard the Master-Word beating strangely low, and I knew the æther to thrill about me, and a faint stirring was there in my soul, as of a faint voice, speaking; and I knew that Naani called to me some message across the night of the world; yet weak and coming without clear meaning; so that I was tormented and could but send comfort to her, with my brain-elements. And presently I knew that she ceased to speak.

And, later, I heard that there was a new matter forward in the Redoubt; for ten thousand men had assembled to attend the Room of Preparation for the Short Preparation; and by this we knew that those poor Youths who stumbled towards us through the dark, were presently to have help.

And through all that Sleep-Time, there went forward the Spiritual and the Physical Preparation of the ten thousand; and upon the morrow they slept, whilst an hundred thousand made ready their arms.

And in this space of time the two hundred and fifty Youths that went towards the Road Where The Silent Ones Walk, had come very nigh thereto; having gone very warily and with some slowness, because, as may be, of the lesson of the Giants.

And to us in the Pyramid, the instruments made known constantly that Influence which was abroad, and which all those of the Tower of Observation thought to proceed from the House of Silence. Yet, nothing could we see with the Great Spy-Glass, and so could come to no sure knowing; but only to fear and wonder.

And, presently, the Youths were upon the Great Road, and turned to the Northward. And beyond them, a great way, stood the House of Silence, upon a low hill at a certain distance to the right of the Road.

By now, they that were wounded had come to within, maybe, fifteen miles of the Great Redoubt; and the news went through all the Cities, that the ten thousand men that were Prepared, made to arm themselves. And I went down by the Tower Lift, and saw them come down by thousands from the Room of Preparation; and none might go nigh to them, or cause them to speak; for they were made Ready, and were, as it might be, holy.

And all the millions of the Mighty Pyramid stood in their cities about certain of the Main Lifts, and watched those thousands go downwards, all in their armour of grey metal, and each one armed with the Diskos, which was that same very terrible weapon, which all had training to.

And I doubt not but that the Young Men of the Pyramid looked, with longing in their hearts, that they might have been among those

that went forth to succour. Yet, the older men had graver thoughts in their hearts; for the blood ran more soberly in them, and they had knowledge and memory of the Peril. And by this, I would make clear that I speak less of the peril of the body, which is common to every state of life; but of the peril of the spirit.

And it may be thought by those of this age, that it was most strange that they of that, having all the knowledge of eternity to aid them, had no weapon by which to shoot, and kill at a distance.

But, indeed, this had not been so in the past; as our Histories did show; for some wondrous weapons there had been, that might slay without sound or flash at a full score miles and more; and some we had whole within the Great Museum; and of others but the parts in decay; for they had been foolish things, and reckless to use; for we of that Great Pyramid, wanted not to kill a few of the Monsters that lay at a great distance; but only those which came nigh, to harm us.

And concerning those same weapons that killed silently at a great distance, we had now little knowledge, save that they did waste the Earth-Current; and no practice had we concerning their workings; for it was, maybe, an hundred thousand years gone that they had been used, and found to be of no great worth in a close attack, and harmful otherwise to the peace, in that they angered, unneedful, the Forces of that land, slaying wantonly those monsters which did no more than beset the Mighty Redoubt at a great distance.

For, as may be seen by a little thought, we did very gladly keep a reasonable quietness, and refrained from aught that should wake that Land; for we were born to the custom of that strange life, and lived and died in peace, for the most part; and were very content to have security, and to be neutral in all things that did not overbear us; but, as it were, always armed, and ready.

But concerning the great and Evil Forces that were abroad in the Night Land, these we had no power to harm; nor could we hope for more than that we had security from them, which indeed we had; but the hugeness of their power was about us, and we dared not to wake it; save through such extremity as had come to pass by this folly of the Youths; though, even now, we had no thought to attack aught; but only to succour those wounded ones.

And concerning this simplicity of weapons, which excites some-what even my wonder in this our present age, it may be that the powers of chemistry were someways quaintly limited by conditions in that age; and there to be always a need to spare the Earth-Current; and hence, by this cause and by that, we were brought, by the extreme, nigh to the

simplicity of the early world; yet with a strange and mighty difference, as all may know who have read.

Now, presently, the Word was sent to every City throughout the Great Redoubt—as was the Law—that the Great Gate should be opened; and each city sent its Master, to form the Full Watch, as was the Law. And each went clad in grey armour, and carrying the Diskos. And the Full Watch numbered, two thousand; for there were also the Watchmen.

Then the lights in the Great Causeway were made dim; so that the opening of the Gate should cast no great glare from within into the Night Land, to tell the Watcher of the North-West, and all the Monsters, that certain humans went out from the Mighty Pyramid. But whether the vast and hidden Forces of Evil had knowledge, we knew not; and they who went must but chance it, remembering that they were Prepared, and had the Capsule.

And the ten thousand that were Prepared, went out through the Great Gateway, into the night; and the Full Watch stood back from them, and spoke no word, but saluted silently with the Diskos; and they that went, raised each the Diskos a little, and passed out into the dark.

Then the Great Gate was shut; and we made to wait and to watch, with trouble and expectation within our hearts. And at the embrasures many did comfort the women of those men.

And I went back, upwards by miles, until I came to the Tower of Observation; and I looked out from there into the Night Land, and saw that the ten thousand halted at the Circle, and made arrangement of themselves, and sent some before and upon either hand, and so went forward into the Night Land.

And after that, I went to the Great Spy-Glass, and turned it towards the two hundred and fifty Youths that were far off, upon the Road Where The Silent Ones Walk; yet for awhile I could not perceive them, for all the Road seemed empty. But afterward I saw them, and they were clambering back into the Road, having gone aside, as I thought, because of the passing of one of those Silent Ones, that I saw now at a distance to the Southward of them.

There passed then, some three hours; and in that time I varied my watching between those far-off Youths, and the Ten-thousand that went forward to succour the wounded, that were now, maybe, scarce nine miles distant from the Mighty Pyramid, and the Ten-thousand came very close to them. And, in truth, in a little while, they spied one the other, and I gathered, in spirit, something of the rejoicing of those youths; yet weak and troubled were they, because of their wounds, and their knowledge of failure, and their disobedience of the Law.

And, presently, they were surrounded by the Ten-thousand, and carried upon slings; and all that body swung round towards the Pyramid, and came back at a great pace.

And, in the same time, I heard the sound that made them so swift to hasten; for there smote up through the night the Baying of the Hounds; and we knew that they were discovered. And I swept the Great Spy-Glass over the Land, towards the Valley Of The Hounds, that I might discover them quickly; and I saw them come lumbering, at a strange gallop, and great as horses, and it might be only ten miles to the East.

And I looked once upon the Watcher of the North-East, and I saw and marvelled that the great bell-ear quivered constantly; and I knew that it had knowledge, and gave signal to all the Land. Then did one of the Monstruwacans report that a new and terrible Influence was abroad in the Land; and by the instrument, we had knowledge that it approached; and some of the Monstruwacans called foolishly with weak voices to the Ten-thousand to haste; forgetting, and desiring only their safety from that which came near.

Then, looking with the Great Spy-Glass, I saw that there moved across the Land, from the direction of the Plain of Blue Fire, a mighty Hump, seeming of Black Mist, and came with prodigious swiftness. And I called to the Master Monstruwacan, that he come and look through one of the eye-pieces that were about the Great Spy-Glass; and he came quickly, and when he had looked a while, he called to the Monstruwacan that had made report. And the Monstruwacan answered, and replied that the Influence drew nearer, by the reading of the instrument; yet of the thing itself the man had no sight.

And I ceased not to look, and in a little while, the Humped thing passed downwards into the Vale of Red Fire, which lay across the Land that way. But I watched steadfastly, and presently I saw the black Hump climb up from the Vale of Red Fire upon this side, and come through the night, so that in scarce a minute it had come half way across that part of the Night Land.

And my heart stood quiet with fear, and the utter terror of this Monster, which I knew to be surely one of the Great Forces of Evil of that Land, and had power, without doubt, to destroy the spirit. And the Master Monstruwacan leapt towards the Home-Call, and sent the great Sound down to the Ten-thousand, that they might attend, and immediately, he signalled to them to Beware. Yet, already I perceived that they knew of this Utter Danger that was upon them; for I saw them slay the Youths quickly, that their spirits might not be lost; for

they were Unprepared. But the men, being Prepared, had the Capsule, and would die swiftly in the last moment.

I looked again towards the Hump, and saw that it came like a Hill of Blackness in the Land, and was almost anigh. Then there happened a wonder; for in that moment when all had else gone quickly, that they might save their souls, out of the earth there rose a little Light, like to the crescent of the young moon of this early day. And the crescent rose up into an arch of bright and cold fire, glowing but little; and it spanned above the Ten-thousand and the dead; and the Hump stood still, and went backwards and was presently lost.

And the men came swiftly towards the Mighty Pyramid. Yet, ere they were come to safety, the Baying of the Hounds sounded close upon them, and they faced to the danger; yet, as I could know, without despair, because that they yet lived after so enormous a peril.

And the Hounds were very nigh, as now I beheld with the Great Spy-Glass; and I counted five score, running with mighty heads low, and in a pack. And lo! as the Hounds came at them, the Ten-thousand drew apart, and had a space between the men, that they might have full use of that terrible Diskos; and they fought with the handles at length, and I saw the disks spin and glisten and send out fire.

Then was there a very great battle; for the Light that arched above them, and held away The Power from their souls, made not to protect them from this danger of the lesser monsters. And at an hundred thousand embrasures within the Mighty Pyramid, the women cried and sobbed, and looked again. And in the lower cities it was told, after, that the Peoples could hear the crash and splinter of the armour, as the Hounds ran to and fro, slaying; aye, even the sound of the armour between their teeth.

Yet, the Ten-thousand ceased not to smite with the Diskos; and they hewed the Hounds in pieces; but of the men that went forth, there were a thousand and seven hundred slain by the Hounds, ere the men won to victory.

Then came that wearied band of heroes back to the home shelter of the Vast Redoubt; and they bore their dead with them, and the Youths that they slew. And they were received with great honour, and with exceeding grief, and in a great silence; for the thing admitted not of words, until a time had passed. And in the cities of the Pyramid there was mourning; for there had been no sorrow like unto this through, mayhap, an hundred thousand years.

And they bore the Youths to their Mothers and to their Fathers; and the Father of each made thanks to the men that they had saved the

soul of his son; but the women were silent. Yet, neither to the Father nor to the Mother, was ever made known the name of the slayers; for this might not be; as all shall see with a little thought.

And some did remember that, in verity, all was due to the un-wisdom of those Youths, who had heeded not the Law and their life-teachings. Yet had they paid to the uttermost, and passed outwards; and the account of their Deeds was closed.

And all this while did great numbers spy toward the Road Where The Silent Ones Walk, that they might watch that band of Youths afar in the Night Land, who went forward amid those horrid dangers. Yet, when the dead Youths had been brought in, many had ceased to look out for a time and had turned to questioning, and some had made inspection that they might know which had come back, and which lay out there where the Giants had slain them, or went forward to more dreadful matters.

But who of those that were abroad, were slain, or still went onward, we had but indifferent knowledge; though the men of the Ten-thousand knew somewhat, having had speech with the wounded Youths, ere they slew them. And, as may be thought, these men were sorely questioned by the Mothers and the Fathers of those Youths that were not accounted of; yet I doubt that few had much knowledge wherewith to console them.

Now there was presently, in the Garden of Silence, which was the lowermost of all the Underground Fields, the Ending of those seventeen hundred heroes, and of the Youths that they saved and slew. And the Garden was a great country, and an hundred miles every way, and the roof thereof was three great miles above, and shaped to a mighty dome; as it had been that the Builders and Makers thereof did remember in their spirits the visible sky of this our present age.

And the making of that Country was all set out in a single History of seven thousand and seventy Volumes. And there were likewise seven thousand and seventy years spent to the making of that Country; so that there had unremembered generations lived and laboured and died, and seen not the end of their labour. And Love had shaped it and hallowed it; so that of all the wonders of the world, there has been none that shall ever come anigh to that Country of Silence—an hundred miles every way of Silence to the Dead.

And there were in that roof seven moons set in a mighty circle, and lit by the Earth-Current; and the circle was sixty miles across, so that all that Country of Quiet was visible; yet to no great glare, but a sweet and holy light; so that I did always feel in my heart that a man might weep there, and be unashamed.

And in the midst of that silent Country, there was a great hill, and upon the hill a vast Dome. And the Dome was full of a Light that might be seen in all that Country, which was the Garden of Silence. And beneath the Dome was the "Crack," and within it the glory of the Earth-Current, from which all had life and light and safety. And in the Dome, at the North, there was a gateway; and a narrow road went upward to the gateway; and the Road was named The Last Road; and the Gateway was named by no name, but known to all as The Gateway.

And there were in that mighty Country, long roadways, and hidden methods to help travel; and constant temples of rest along the miles; and groves; and the charm of water, falling. And everywhere the Statues of Memory, and the Tablets of Memory; and the whole of that Great Underground Country full of an echo of Eternity and of Memory and Love and Greatness; so that to walk alone in that Land was to grow back to the wonder and mystery of Childhood; and presently to go upwards again to the Cities of the Mighty Pyramid, purified and sweetened of soul and mind.

And in my boyhood, I have wandered oft a week of days in that Country of Silence, and had my food with me, and slept quietly amid the memories; and gone on again, wrapped about with the quiet of the Everlasting. And the man-soul within would be drawn mightily to those places where the Great Ones of the past Eternity of the World had their Memory named; but there was that within me which ever drew me, in the ending, to the Hills of the Babes; those little hills where might be heard amid the lonesomeness of an utter quiet, a strange and wondrous echo, as of a little child calling over the hills. But how this was I know not, save by the sweet cunning of some dead Maker in the forgotten years.

And here, mayhaps by reason of this Voice of Pathos, were to be found the countless Tokens of Memory to all the babes of the Mighty Pyramid, through a thousand ages. And, odd whiles, would I come upon some Mother, sitting there lonely, or mayhaps companied by others. And by this little telling shall you know somewhat of the quietness and the wonder and the holiness of that great Country hallowed to all Memory and to Eternity and to our Dead.

And it was here, into the Country of Silence, that they brought down the Dead to their Burial. And there came down into the Country of Silence, maybe an Hundred Million, out of the Cities of the Pyramid, to be present, and to do Honour.

Now they that had charge of the Dead, did lay them upon the road which ran up unto The Gateway, even that same road which was named

The Last Road. And the Road moved upwards slowly with the Dead; and the Dead went inward through The Gateway; first the poor Youths, and afterward they that had given up life that they might save them.

And as the Dead went upwards, there was a very great Silence over all the miles of the Country of Silence. But in a little while there came from afar off, a sound as of a wind wailing; and it came onwards out of the distance, and passed over the Hills of the Babes, which were a great way off. And so came anigh to the place where I stood. Even as the blowing of a sorrowful wind did it come; and I knew that all the great multitudes did sing quietly; and the singing passed onwards, and left behind it an utter silence; even as the wind doth rustle the corn, and pass onwards, and all fall to a greater seeming quietness than before. And the Dead passed inward through The Gateway, into the great light and silence of the Dome; and came out no more.

And again from beyond the far Hills of the Babes there was that sound of the millions singing; and there rose up out of the earth beneath, the voices of the underground organs; and the noise of the sorrow passed over me, and went again into the distance, and left all hushed.

And lo! as there passed inward to the silence of the Dome the last of those dead Heroes, there came again the sound from beyond the Hills of the Babes; and as it came more nigh, I knew that it was the Song of Honour, loud and triumphant, and sung by countless multitudes. And the Voices of the Organs rose up into thunder from the deep earth. And there was a great Honour done to the glory of the Dead. And afterwards, once more a silence.

Then did the Peoples of the Cities arrange themselves so that from every city whence had come a Hero, were the People of that City gathered together. And when they were so gathered, they set up Tokens of Memory to the Dead of their City. But afterwards did charge Artists to the making of sculpture great and beautiful to that same end; and now did but place Tablets against that time.

And afterwards the People did wander over that Country of Silence, and made visit and honour to their Ancestors, if such were deserving.

And presently, the mighty lifts did raise them all to the Cities of the Pyramid; and thereafter there was something more of usualness; save that ever the embrasures were full of those that watched the Youths afar upon the Great Road. And in this place I to remember how that our spy-glasses had surely some power of the Earth-Current to make greater the impulse of the light upon the eye. And they were like no

spy-glass that ever you did see; but oddly shaped and to touch both the forehead and the eyes; and gave wonderful sight of the Land. But the Great Spy-Glass to be beyond all this; for it had the Eyes of it upon every side of The Mighty Pyramid, and did be truly an Huge Machine.

And to me, as I went about my duties, or peered forth through the Great Spy-Glass at the Youths upon the Road Where The Silent Ones Walk, there came at times a far faint thrilling of the æther; so that sometimes I was aware that there was the beating of the Master-Word in the night; but so strange and weak, that the Instruments had no wotting of it. And when this came, then would I call back through all the everlasting night to Naani, who was indeed Mirdath; and I would send the Master-Word with my brain-elements; and afterwards such comfort as I might.

Yet hard and bitter was the truth of my helplessness and weakness, and the utter terror and might of the Evil Forces and Monsters of the Night Land. So that I was like to have brake my heart with pondering.

And the silence would come again; and anon the weak thrilling of the æther; but no more the far voice speaking in my soul.

V
Into the Night Land

ΠOW, AFTER THAT DESTRUCTION which had come upon the Ten-thousand, and the fresh assurance that was upon us of the terror of the Night Land, it may be known that there could be no more thought to succour. Though, in truth, those Youths that went now upon the Road Where The Silent Ones Walk were far beyond our aid.

Yet might it be thought that we should have signalled to them, calling by the Home-Call, which was that great Voice which went forth from the Machine above the sealed base of the Mighty Pyramid. But this we might not do; for then we gave signal to the Monsters of that Land, that some were even now abroad from the Pyramid; yet we could no more than hope that the Evil Forces had no wotting of them; for, in verity, none might ever know the knowledge or the Ignorance which those Powers did possess.

Yet, it must be kept to the mind that we knew even then there was an Influence abroad in the Land, strange and quiet; so that the Instruments did not more than make record of it. And as I have surely set down ere now, we had belief that it did come from that House of Silence, afar in the Night Land, upon that low hill to the North of the Great Road. And many among the Monstruwacans feared that it was directed upon the Youths; but of this there could be no surety; and we could but wait and watch.

Now, about this time those poor Youths did draw nigh to that part of the Road Where The Silent Ones Walk, where it turned more swiftly to the North; and they to be now at no mighty distance from that grim and horrid House.

And presently we knew that the Influence had a greater Power in the Land; and I had an assuredness that it came from the House; yet no certain proof was this. But I set out my feelings to the Master Monstruwacan; and he had trust in them and in my power; moreover,

he also had belief within himself that some secret Power came out from the House of Silence.

And some talk there was at times that we send the Home-Call into the night, to give warning to the Youths of our knowledge and our fear; and to entreat them to make a safe endeavour to return swiftly. Yet was this an error; and refused by the Master Monstruwacan; for it was not meet that we put the souls of those Youths in peril, until such time as we had certainty that they should be lost if we did not bestir ourselves. For, indeed, this Home-Call was as a mighty Voice, calling over the world, and did have so exceeding a noise, that it had immediately told all that Land how that some were yet abroad from the Great Redoubt. And here will I set down how that the Home-Call had no use in those ages; but had been a Call in the olden time when yet the great flying-ships went abroad over the world.

And there passed now a day and a night; and in all that time there ceased not great multitudes to peer forth into the Night Land at the Youths. For it was known concerning the Influence, and all felt that the Youths did draw nigh very speedy to their fate; and much talk there was; and many things said, and much foolish speech, and kind intent; but no courage to go forth to make further attempt to rescue; which, in truth, calls not for great astonishment, as I have surely writ or oft thought.

And in this place let me set down that the Land was, as it might be said, waked, and unquiet, and a sense of things passing in the night, and of horrid watchfulness; and there were, at this time and at that, low roars that went across the Land. And if I have not told the same before this time, it must be set to count against me and my telling; for, indeed, I should have writ it down before this place. Yet is the difficulty of my task great; and all must bear with me, and entreat for me that I have courage, so that I may come at last to strength and wisdom to tell all that I did see.

Now, in the space of this day and night, it was known that the Youths had not slept, neither had they eaten, save once, as they who had the watch through the Great Spy-Glass did affirm. But they to hasten alway at a woeful speed towards the North, along that Great Dismal Road, so that presently they must cease, or slay themselves with their endeavour.

And all this did give surety to our fears that they were under a spell from that horrid House afar in the Land; and we had an assurance that this thing was. For, presently, there came a Monstruwacan to the Master Monstruwacan to report that there had come sudden a mighty

Influence into the Land; and in the same moment, as it might be, I spied through the Great Spy-Glass, and did see those Youths break swiftly from the Road Where The Silent Ones Walk, and begin to run very swift that they might come quickly to the House of Silence.

Then did the Master Monstruwacan hesitate not; but did send the Home-Call across the world, aye, even to those poor doomed ones that hastened, unknowing, to the terror which did compel them. And immediately upon the sound, the Master did send a message to the natural eye, in set language, and made warning that they suffered themselves to be drawn to their destruction by a Force that came from within the House of Silence.

And he besought them to put forth the strength of their spirits, and do battle for their souls; and if they could in no wise compass a victory over that which drew them onwards, to slay themselves quickly, ere they went into that House to the horror of utter destruction.

And in all the Pyramid was there a great silence; for the bellowing of the Home-Call bred a quietness, because of that which it did portend; and it was swiftly known by the millions that the Master Monstruwacan did plead for the souls of the Youths; and there went forth, unknowingly, a counter-force from the Mighty Pyramid, by reason of the prayers and soul-wishings of the countless millions.

And the counter-force was plain to my inward hearing, and beat all the æther of the world into a surge of supplication; so that it stunned my spirit with the great power of it. And it seemed to me, as it were, that there was a vast spiritual-noise in all the night; and I spied tremblingly through the Great Spy-Glass, and lo! the Youths did cease from their swift running, and were come together in a crowd, and had a seeming to be confused; as might some who have waked suddenly from sleep, to find that they walked in their sleep, and had come to a strange place.

Then came there a great roar from all the millions that spied from the embrasures—from nigh five hundred thousand embrasures they did look, and I count not the great View-Tables. And the shouting rose up like to the roaring of a mighty wind of triumph, yet was it over-early to sound for victory. For the counter-force which came from the intensity of so many wills blent to one intent, was brake, and the Evil Force which came forth out of the House did draw the Youths again; so that they heeded not their salvation; but turned once again to their running.

And the Mighty Pyramid was full of a shaken silence, and immediately of lamentation and sorrow and horror at this thing. But in that

moment there did happen a fresh wonder; for there grew suddenly before those poor Youths, billows of mist—as it had been of pure white fire, shining very chill; yet giving no light upon them.

And the mist of cold fire stayed their way, so that we had knowledge that there fought for the souls of them, one of those sweet Powers of Goodness, which we had belief did strive to ward our spirits at all times from those Forces of Evil and Destruction. And all the millions saw the thing; but some with a great clearness, and many doubtful; yet were all advanced more in spiritual sight and hearing than the normal Peoples of this Age.

But of them all, none had the Night-Hearing, to know a soul having speech in the æther half across the world. Yet, as I have said, some there had been aforetime who were thus given the Hearing, even as was I.

And there came a Monstruwacan to the Master Monstruwacan to make report that the Influence had ceased to work upon the Instruments; and by this thing we knew that in verity the Force which proceeded out from the House of Silence was cut off from us, and from those Youths; and we had assurance that there fought a very mighty Power for the salvation of the souls of the Youths.

And all the Peoples were silent, save for an underbreath of wonder and talk; for all were utter stirred with hope and fear, perceiving that the Youths had some chance given unto them to return.

And whilst the Youths yet wavered in their minds, as I perceived with the Great Spy-Glass, and the knowledge of my soul, and of my natural wit, lo! the Master Monstruwacan sent once more the great Voice of the Home-Call abroad into the Land; and immediately besought those Youths for the sake of their souls and the love which their Mothers had for them, to come swiftly Homewards, whilst they had yet this great Power to shield them, and allow them sweet sanity.

And I thought that some did look towards the Pyramid, as that they answered to the mighty Voice of the Home-Call, and did read the message which the Master Monstruwacan made to them. But in a moment they faced about, seeming to have a good obedience to one who did always lead; and of whom I had inquired, and found to be one named Aschoff, who was a great athlete of the Nine-Hundredth-City. And this same Aschoff, out of the boldness and bravery of his heart, did make, unwitting, to destroy the souls of them all; for he went forward and leapt into the billows of the bright shining fire that made a Barrier in the way of their Destruction.

And immediately the fire ceased from its shining, and gave way

and sank and grew to a nothingness; and Aschoff of the Nine-Hun-dredth-City began again to run towards the House of Silence; and all they that were with him, did follow faithfully, and ceased not to run.

And they came presently to the low Hill whereon was that horrid House; and they went up swiftly—and they were two hundred and fifty, and wholesome of heart, and innocent; save for a natural way-wardness of spirit.

And they came to the great open doorway that "hath been open since the Beginning," and through which the cold steadfast light and the inscrutable silence of Evil "hath made for ever a silence that may be felt in all the Land." And the great, uncased windows gave out the silence and the light—aye, the utter silence of an unholy desolation.

And Aschoff ran in through the great doorway of silence, and they that followed. And they nevermore came out or were seen by any human.

And it must be known that the Mothers and the Fathers of those Youths looked out into the Night Land, and saw that thing which came to pass.

And all the people were silent; but some said presently that the Youths would come forth again; yet the people knew in their hearts that the young men had gone in to Destruction; for, in truth, there was that in the night which spoke horror to the souls of all, and a sudden utter quiet in all the Land.

But unto me (that had the Night-Hearing) there came a great Fear of that which might be whispered into my spirit, out of the Quietness of the night—of the agony of those young men. Yet there came no sound, to the hearing of the soul; neither then nor in all the years that were to come; for, in verity, had those Youths passed into a Silence of which the heart cannot think.

And here will I tell how that the strange Quiet which did fill all the Land, seeming to brood within the night, was horrid beyond all the roarings which had passed over the darkness in the time that went before; so that it had given my spirit some rest and assurance to hear but the far-echoing, low thunder of the Great Laughter, or the whining which was used at times to sound in the night from the South-East, where were the Silver-fire Holes that opened before the Thing that Nods. Or the Baying of the Hounds, or the Roaring of the Giants, or any of those dreadful sounds that did often pass through the night. For they could not have offended me as did that time of silence; and so shall you judge how dreadful was that quiet, which did hold so much of horror.

And surely it will be known that none had thinkings now, even in idle speech, that any should have power to succour the Peoples of the Lesser Redoubt. Neither, as I have said, had any the knowledge of the place where it did stand.

And so was it made plain that those Peoples must suffer and come unhelped and alone to their end; which was a sad and dreadful thought to any. Yet had those within the Great Pyramid come already to much sorrow and calamity because that some had made attempt in this matter. And there had been for gain, only failure, and the sorrow of Mothers, and the loneliness of Wives, and of kin. And now this dread horror upon us, which concerned those lost Youths.

Now, as may be conceived, this sure knowledge that we might give no succour to the People of the Lesser Redoubt, weighed heavy upon my heart; for I had, maybe with foolishness, held vague hopes and wonders concerning our power to make expedition secretly into the Night, to discover that Lesser Pyramid, and rescue those poor thousands; and above all, as may be thought, had I the thought of that sweet moment in which I should step forward out of the night and all mystery and terror, and put forth mine arms to Naani, saying: "I am That One." And knowing, in my soul, that she that had been mine in that bygone Eternity, should surely know me upon the instant; and call out swiftly, and come swiftly; and be again unto me in that age, even as she had been in this.

And to think upon it, and to know that this thing should never be; but that, even in that moment of thought, she that had been mine in these olden days of sweetness, might be even then suffering horror in the Power of some foul Monster, was like a kind of madness; so that nearly I could seize the Diskos, and run forth unprepared into the evil and terror of the Night Land, that I should make one attempt to come to that Place where she abode, or else to cast off my life in the attempt.

And oft did I call to Naani; and always I sent the Master-Word beating through the night, that she might have assurance that it was indeed I that did speak unto her spirit, and no foul thing or Monster, spelling evil and lies unto her.

And oft did I make to instruct her that never should she be tempted forth from the shelter of that Redoubt in which she did live, by any message out of the night; but always to await the Master-Word; and, moreover, to have a sure knowledge that none that was her Friend would ever seek to entice her into the night.

And this way and that way would I speak with Naani, sending my words silently with my brain-elements; yet was it doleful and weariful

and dreadful always to have speech into the dark, and never to hear the answering beat of the Master-Word, and the sweet, faint voice whispering within my soul. Yet, once and again, would I have knowledge that the æther did thrill about me, weakly; and to mine inward hearing it would seem that the Master-Word did beat faintly in the night; and thereafter would my heart have a little comfort, in that I had assurance, of a kind, that the love-maid of my memory-dreams did still live.

And constant, I put forth my soul to hark; so that my health failed me, with the effort of my harking; and I would chide my being, that I had not a wiser control; and so make a fight to do sanely.

Yet, day by day, did my heart grow more weary and restless; for, indeed, it did seem that life was but a very little matter, against so great a loss as my heart did feel to suffer.

And oft, at this time and that, did there come a Voice speaking plainly out of the night, and did purport to be the voice of Naani; but ever I did say the Master-Word unto the Voice, and the Voice had no power by which it could make the one answer. Yet I jeered not at the Voice, to show contempt of its failing to bewit me; but let the matter bide; and the Voice would be silent a time; and again would make a calling unto me; but never did I make speech with it (for therein lies the danger to the soul), but always did speak the Master-Word to its silencing; and thereafter would shut the thing from my memory, and think only upon sweet and holy matters, as it might be Truth and Courage, but more often of Naani, which was both sweet and holy to my spirit and heart and being.

And so it was as I have set down, there were Monsters without in the Night that did torment me; having, it may be, intent to lure me unto destruction; or indeed it doth chance that they had no hope but to plague me with malice.

And, as may be thought, all this considering of my trouble, and the giving of my strength unto Naani through the night of the world, that she might have comfort and help, did work upon me; so that I grew thin, plainly to the eye of those that loved me.

And the Master Monstruwacan, he that did love me, as I were his son, chid me gently, and had wise speech with me; so that I but loved him the more, yet without having gain of health; for my heart destroyed me, as it doth if love be held back and made always to weep.

And it may be thought strange that my Mother and my Father did not talk also with me; but I had neither Mother nor Father those many years; and this thing I should have set down early; so that none should waste thought pondering to no end. But the blame is to my telling.

Now, concerning my love-trouble, there did happen a certain thing which gave me to decide; for one night I waked from a sore troubled sleep, and it did seem that Naani did call my name, mine olden love name, and in a voice of utter anguish and with beseeching. And I sat up in the bed, and sent the Master-Word into the Night, with my brain-elements; and presently all about me there was the solemn beat of the Master-Word, answering; but weak, and gone faint, that scarce I might hear it.

And I called again with my brain-elements unto Naani, that was Mirdath; and spoke to give her assurance, and to haste to tell unto me that which was so wrong and pitiful with her. And who shall be amazed that I was shaken with the eagerness of my spirit, in that it was so long since Naani had spoken clear within my soul; and now behold, her voice.

Yet, though I did call many a time unto the everlasting night, there came no more the voice of Naani, speaking strangely within my spirit; but only at times a weak thrilling of the æther about me.

And, at the last I grew maddened with the sorrow of this thing, and the sense and knowledge of harm about the maid; and I stood upright upon my feet, and I raised my hands, and gave word and honour unto Naani through all the blackness of the night, that I would no more abide within the Mighty Pyramid to my safety, whilst she, that had been mine Own through Eternity, came to horror and destruction by the Beasts and Evil Powers of that Dark World. And I gave the word with my brain-elements, and bade her to be of heart; for that until I died I would seek her. But out of the Darkness there came naught but the silence.

Then I clothed me swiftly, and went up quickly to the Tower of Observation, that I might speak instant with the Master Monstruwacan; for my heart burned in me to intention, and to be doing speedily that which I had set upon myself to do.

And I came to the Master Monstruwacan, and told all to him; and how that I did mean no more to suffer in quiet and to no end; but to make adventure into the Night Land, that I find Naani, or perchance find a swift peace from this my long troubling.

Now, when the Master Monstruwacan heard that which I had to say, it sat heavily upon him, and he besought me long and many times that I refrain from this thing; for that none might achieve so great a task; but that I should be lost in my Youth before many days were gone by. Yet to all his speech I said naught, save that this thing was laid upon me, and even as I had promised, so should I make to act.

And in the ending, the Master Monstruwacan perceived that I was set to this thing, and not to be moved; and he did put it to me how that I had grown to leanness, with so much troubling, and that I should have wisdom to wait awhile, that I put on my full strength.

But even as I was, so would I go; and this I told to him, gently; and showed how that the thing was meet and helpful to the safety of my soul; for that my strength was still in me; yet was I sweeter in spirit because that I stood lean and pure, and much poor dross and littleness had been burned from me; so that fear was not in me. And all do I lay to the count of my love, which doth purify and make sweet and fearless the human heart.

And because I was even as I have said, so was I the less in trouble of the Forces of Evil; for long and sore had been my Preparation of Spirit; and I wot that none had ever gone forth into the Darkness, so long withholden from that which doth weaken and taint the spirit.

And here let me set down how that the Three Days of Preparation, which were Proper to those that willed to go forth into the Night Land, had for their chief aim the cleansing of the spirit; so that the Powers of Evil did have a less ableness to harm.

But also it was, as I have said, that none should go forth in ignorance of the full dreadfulness of all that held the Night; for it was at the Preparation that there was made known certain horrors that were not told unto the young; and of horrid mutilations, and of abasements of the soul, that did shake the heart with fear, if but they were whispered into the hearing. And these things were not set down in any book that might be lightly come by; but were warded and safe locked by the Master of The Preparation, in the Room of Preparation.

And, indeed, when I did hear that which presently I was to hear, I had wonder in my heart that ever any went out into the Night Land; or that ever the Room of Preparation should have other than Students that meant not to go forth, but only to achieve some knowledge of that which hath been done, and mayhaps shall be once again.

Yet, in verity, is this but the way of the human heart; and hath always been, and will be so in all the years, for ever. For to adventure is the lust of Youth; and to leave Safety is the natural waywardness of the spirit; and who shall reprove or regret; for it were sorrowful that this Spirit of Man should cease. Yet must it not be thought that I do uphold fightings to the death or to mutilation, between man and man; but rather do sorrow upon this thought.

Now, when the morrow came, if thus I shall speak of that which was outwardly even as the night, though changing alway within the

Mighty Pyramid, I went unto the Room of Preparation; and the Door was closed upon me; and I underwent the Full Preparation; that I might have full power and aid to come to success through all the terror of the Night Land.

And three days and three nights did I abide within the Room of Preparation; and upon the fourth day was mine armour brought unto me; and the Master of the Preparation stood away from me, silent and with sorrow upon his face; but touching me not, neither coming anigh to aid me; nor having any speech with me; for none might crowd upon me, or cause me to answer.

And, presently, was I clad with the grey armour; and below the armour a close-knit suit of special shaping and texture, to have the shape of the armour, and that I might not die by the cold of the Night Land. And I placed upon me a scrip of food and drink, that might keep the life within me for a great time, by reason of its preparation; and this lay ready to me, with the armour, and was stitched about with the Mark of Honour; so that I knew loving women thus to speed me.

And when all was done and made ready, I took up the Diskos, and bowed in silence to the Master of the Preparation; and he went towards the door, and opened it; and signalled that the People stand back; so that I might go forth untouched. And the People stood back; for many had crowded to the door of the Room of Preparation, so that I knew how that my story must be to the heart of all, in all the Cities of the Great Redoubt; for to come unbidden anigh that Door was against the Lesser Law, and that any erred in this matter, betokened much.

And I went out through the Door; and there was a mighty lane of people unto the Great Lift. And about the Great Lift, as I went downwards, did the countless millions stand; and all in a great silence; but having dear sympathy in their souls; yet loyal unto my safety, in that none in all the Mighty Pyramid did make speech unto me, or call out aught. And as I went downward through the miles, lo! all the æther of the world seemed to be surged with the silent prayers and speedings of those quiet multitudes.

And I came at last unto the Great Gate; and behold the dear Master Monstruwacan did stand in full armour, and with the Diskos, to do me honour, with the Full Watch, as I went forth. And I looked at him, quietly, and he looked unto me, and I bent my head to show respect; and he made silent salute with the Diskos; and afterwards I went onwards towards the Great Gateway.

And they made dim the lights in the Great Causeway, that there should no glare go forth into the Land, when the Gate was opened;

and behold, they opened not the lesser gate within the greater, for me; but did honour my journey, in that they swung wide the Great Gate itself, through which a monstrous army might pass. And there was an utter silence all about the Gate; and in the hushed light the two thousand that made the Full Watch, held up each the Diskos, silently, to make salute; and humbly, I held up the Diskos reversed, and went forward into the Dark.

VI

The Way That I Did Go

NOW I WENT FORWARD for a space, and took heed not to
look backwards; but to be strong of heart and spirit; for that which
did lie before me had need of all my manhood and courage of soul,
that I come to the succour of that Maid afar in the darkness of the
World, or meet my death proper, as it might need to be.

And thus did I go forward steadfastly, and conscious in all my
being of the emotions of that parting from my mighty Home, and
of the tenderness and wiseness that did underlie so much curbed rule
and guidance.

And my heart was warm towards the Master Monstruwacan for
that great honour, that he should come downward in armour to make
one with the Full Watch, that he might uphold me to a lofty spirit at
the moment of my going.

And all that time as I went forward, was the æther of the night
about me, in tumult with the thoughts and blind wishings of the great
millions I had but now left to my back.

And, presently, as I steadied somewhat upon my emotions, I
was conscious of the exceeding coldness of the night air, and of the
different taste of it upon my lungs and in the mouth; and it had, as it
were, a wondrous keen sharping upon my palate, and did fill the lips
more in the breathing; so that it may be supposed it had more body
within it than that air which did fill the plateau of the Thousandth
City where was my home; for the air of every City was of difference,
and the greater between one that was afar up and another nigh to the
earth, as may be thought; so that many Peoples did migrate unto that
level which gave them best healthfulness; but under rule, and with a
guidance of quantities. And not all that were lacking of health; for
some are ever contrary.

And here let me set down that, within the deeps of the Fields, there

was air utter varied and wonderful, that might charm one here and likewise sorrow another that were happier elsewhere; so that all might have suiting, did they but wander, and have Reason to companion them.

And thus did I go forward, full of new thoughts and olden memories, and fresh-breaking wonders; neither forgetting something of doubts and fears more than a little. And again was it most cunning strange to be out there in the Night Land—though not yet afar—where often had my fancies and imaginings led me; yet until that time never had I touched foot, in all that life, upon the outward earth. And this must be a wondrous quaint seeming thought to those of this present day.

And so came I, at last, nigh to the Circle that did go about the Redoubt; and presently I was come to it; and something astonished was I that it had no great bigness; for I had looked for this by reasoning; having always a mind to picture things as they might be truly, and hence coming sometimes to the wonder of a great truth; but odd whiles to errors that others had not made. And now, lo! I did find it but a small, clear tube that had not two inches of thickness; yet sent out a very bright and strong light, so that it seemed greater to the eye, did one but behold from a distance.

And this is but a little thing to set to the telling; yet may it give something of the newness of all; and, moreover, shall you have memory with me in this place, how that oft had I seen Things and Beast-Monsters peer over that same little tube of light, their faces coming forward out of the night.

And this had I seen as child and man; for as children, we did use to keep oft a watch by hours upon an holiday-time, through the great glasses of the embrasures. And we did always hope each to be that one that should first discover a monster looking inwards upon the Mighty Pyramid, across the shining of the Circle. And these to come oft; yet presently to slink away into the night; having, in verity, no liking for that light.

And pride had we taken of ourselves to perceive those monsters which had most of ugliness and horror to commend them; for, thereby did we stand to have won the game of watching, until such time as a more fearsome Brute be discovered. And so went the play; yet with ever, it doth seem to me now, something of a half-known shudder to the heart, and a child's rejoicing unknowingly in that safety which had power to make light the seeming of such matters.

And this, also, is but a small matter; yet doth it bear upon the inwardness of my feelings; for the memories of all my youth and of

the many Beasts that I had seen to peer across the Light, did come upwards in my mind in that moment; so that I did give back a little, unthinking of what I did; but having upon me the sudden imagining of that which might come out of the Dark, beyond.

And I to stand a little moment, and presently had grown free in my heart to have courage of farewell; and so did turn me at last to the viewing of that wondrous Home of the Last Millions of this World. And the sight was an astonishment and an uplifting, that indeed there was so mighty a thing in all the earth.

And well might be that there were Monsters and Forces gathered together about that Hill of Life, out of all the Darkness of the World; for the thing was as a Mighty Mountain that went up measureless into the night; and spread out upon the earth to the right and to the left of me, so that it did seem to hold all the world with its might.

And in the nearer slope were there three hundred thousand great embrasures, as well I did know; there being in all the four sides of the Redoubt, twelve hundred thousand embrasures, as was set out in the books of the schools, and upon the cover of Atlas-books as they still quaintly to be called, and many another place, as might be supposed.

And half a mile upward was the lowest tier of those great window-places, and above that, countless other tiers. And a great light came out from them into the darkness; so that I looked up into the night many miles, and yet did see them in shining rows; and did make separate each embrasure from its fellow for a great way. But there grew yet more, above in the mighty distance, so that they were lost in the upward space of the night, and did seem to me presently but as a constant, glimmering fire, that did shape a shining Peak into the blackness of the heavens, dwindling into the utmost height. And thus was that Everlasting Monument.

Then did it come to me that those little things, which I did see to cluster against the embrasures, were in truth the countless millions of the Mighty Redoubt; and this I could make out with some plainness in those lower embrasures, which were the more near to me than they above; for the Peoples were set against the light within, yet were as small things like unto insects, in that distance, and within so Huge a Bulk.

And I knew that they looked out upon me, and did watch through their spy-glasses. And I sent my gaze upwards again along that great Slope of grey metal, aye! upward again to where it strode glimmering into the Blackness, and so at last to the little star that did crown that Wonder of the World in the eternal night. And, for a little, I did stare towards that far light; for it came from within that Tower of Obser-

vation, where so lately I had spended my life; and I had knowledge within my heart that the dear Master Monstruwacan did bend the Great Spy-Glass upon me, through which so oft had I spied. And I raised the Diskos unto him, in salutation and farewell, though I saw him not at all through that vast space.

And my heart was very full; yet my soul but the stronger for it. And then, behold, I was aware of a murmur in the night, coming to me, dim and from afar off; and I saw the little shapes of the Peoples in the lower embrasures, in constant movement; and I knew upon the instant that the Multitudes did take that salute unto themselves, and cried out and waved to me their farewells, or to come back—as may be.

And, indeed, I was but a lonesome person looking up at that great mountain of metal and Life. And I knew that I had danger to realise my plight; and I stayed no more; but did raise the Diskos, reversed, as was but meet from one young man unto all the Millions.

And I looked swiftly upward through those eight great miles of night, unto that Final Light which did shine in the black heavens; so that my friend should know that I thought of him that was beyond my sight, in that last moment. And it may be that the invisible millions that were far up in the night, in the Upper Cities, did take that also to be a meaning of farewell to themselves; for there came down out of the monstrous height, a far, faint murmur of sound, as of a vague wind up in the night.

Then did I lower the Diskos, and turn me about. And I breasted strangely against the Air Clog, and stept forward across the Circle, into the lonesomeness of the Night Land. And I looked no more behind; for that which was my Home did weaken my heart somewhat, to behold; so that I made determination that I look not again to my back, for a great while.

Yet, about me as I went, there was constant surging in the æther of the world; and it did tell unto me how that those, my people and kin, had continual mind of me, both in prayer and wishings, and in a perpetual watching. And the same gave to me a feeling as of being something companied; yet, in a time, it came to me that this disturbance of the æther should tell to some Evil Force how that I was there abroad in the Land. But how to stop this thing, who should have power? For, of truth, had I been among them to make a full explaining of the danger, they had been yet powerless to cease; for but to have such great multitudes a-think upon one matter, was to set a disturbance about, as should be most clear to all.

Now, at the beginning, I did walk outwards into the Night Land,

somewhat blindly, and without sure direction; being intent only to put a good space to my back, that I might cure somewhat the ache which did weaken my heart at the first.

But, in awhile, I ceased somewhat from my overswiftness, and did put thought to my going. And I came quickly to reason that I should try a new way through the Land; for it might be that there was an over-watchfulness in that part which had been trod by the Youths.

And I began therewith to set this thought to the practice; and went not direct towards the North; but to the North and West; and so in the end to mean to circle around to the back of the North-West Watcher, and thence to the North of the Plain Of Blue Fire; and afterwards, as might be, have a true and straight way to the North; and by this planning come a long way clear of that House of Silence, which did put more fear upon me than all else that was horrid in the Land.

Yet, as all will see, this made to me a greater journey; though, in verity, it were better to go slowly and win to success, than to make a greater haste towards Destruction; which was, indeed, surely to be mine end, did I not go warily.

Now it may be thought upon with wonder, that I did go so assuredly to the North; but I went thiswise, part by an inward Knowing, and part come upon by much latter studying, within the Pyramid, of olden books; and by reasoning upon all things that I did observe, that had seemings of verity in them.

And because of this constant searching upon one matter, I had come, but a while back, upon a little book of metal, very strange and ancient, that had lain forgot in a hid place in the Great Library through ten hundred thousand years, maybe, or less or more, for all that I had knowing.

And much that was writ in the book was common knowledge, and set mostly to the count of fairy-tales and suchlike, even as we of this our age take not over-surely any belief in Myths of olden times. Yet had I always much liking for such matters, perceiving behind that outer shell which did win always so much unbelief, the kernel of ancient truths and happenings.

And thus was it, concerning this little book which I had made discovery of; for it told again, that which oft I had heard (even as we in this age, read of the Deluge) how that once, in a time monstrous far back from that, but utter future to this age of ours, the world did brake upwards in a vast earth-quaking, that did rend the world for a thousand miles.

And there came a mighty chasm, so deep that none might see the bottom thereof; and there rushed therein an ocean, and the earth did

burst afresh with a sound that did shake all the cities of the world; and a great mist lay upon the earth for many days, and there was a mighty rain.

And, indeed, this was just so set in certain Histories of the Ancient World. Also, there was made reference to it, within some olden Records. Yet nowise to be taken with a serious mind, to the seeming of the peoples of the Mighty Pyramid; but only as a quaint study for the Students, and to be set out in little tales that did entertain the nurseries; or, as it might be, wise men and the general.

Yet, there was this, about that small and peculiar book, that it did speak of many of these things, as it were that it did quote from the pens of those that did have actual witness; and set all out with a strange gravity, that did cause one to consider it as meant to be indeed the tellings of Truth, and to seem thiswise to have great difference from all that I had read before concerning those matters.

And there was, further, a part in the ending of the book, that did seem to be writ of a time that came afterwards, maybe an hundred thousand, and maybe a million years; but who shall say.

And therein it did tell of an huge and mighty Valley that did come out of the West, towards the South-East, and made turning thence Northwards, and was a thousand miles both ways. And the sides thereof were an hundred miles deep, and the Sun did stand in the Western end, and made a red gloom for a thousand miles. And in the bottom there were great seas; and beasts strange and awesome, and very plentiful.

Now this, as may be seen, was as the talk of Romance; yet did I turn my wits to their natural end, and made thus plain of it. For, in truth, I to have something of belief, and it to seem to me that in a bygone Eternity, when the world was yet light, as in my heart I knew to have been indeed a thing of verity, there was a great and wondrous earthquake.

And the earthquake did burst the world up, along a certain great curve where it had weakness; and there fell into the yawning furnace of the world, one of the great oceans; and immediately made of itself steam, and so brake upwards again, and tore the earth mightily in its swift uprising.

And thereafter there was a mist and confusion and rain upon the world. And, indeed, all very seemly put; and not to be taken as a light tale.

Then, in that ending of the book, there was one that did write, having lived in a vast later age, when the Sun had come anigh to his dying, and the upward earth was grown quiet and cold and not good to

live upon. And in that time the Mighty Chasm had been calmed by the weight of an Eternity, so that it was now a most deep and wondrous Valley, that did hold Seas and great Hills and Mountains; and in it were great forests of kinds, and Lands that were good and healthful; and Places given over to Fire, and to Steamings, and Sulphur Clouds; so that they held Poisons that had ill for Man.

And Great Beasts were there down in that far depth, that none might see ever, save by a strong spy-glass. And such there were in the Early World, and had now been bred in the Ending by those inward forces of Nature which did make the Valley a place of Good Warmth; so that there was, as it were, once more the Primal World born to give new birth unto such olden Monsters, and to others, new and Peculiar to that Age and Circumstance.

And all this, indeed, did the book give also; but constrained and difficult to take clearly to the heart, and not like to the wise plain speech of the early tellings; so that I must even set it out here in mine own speech.

And it did seem to me, by my reading, that Man had come at one time to a great softness of Heart and Spirit through many ages of over-ease. But that the World did come to coldness and unfriendliness, by reason of the Sun's slow ceasing.

And there was presently, in naturalness, a Race upon the earth that were hardy, and made to fight for their lives; and did perceive that the Mighty Valley that cut the World in twain, was a place of Warmth and Life; and so did make to adventure their bodies down that wondrous Height; and were many Ages coming safe to the Bottom; but did find safe places in the downward way where they built them Houses, and made to live, and begot them children; and these grew up to that life of constant and great climbings, and of hard workings upon The Road, which was the One Intent of that People; so that the book did speak of them always as The Road Makers.

And thus did they make downwards through the long years and the ages; and many generations did live and die, and saw not the reaching of the Road down into that Great Vale that lay so monstrous deep in the World.

But in the end they did come there with the Road; and they were very Hardy; and they did fight with the Monsters and slay many; and they built them many Cities, through great years in the Mighty Valley, and did make the Road from City unto City along that Great Valley, even unto the Bight of the Valley. And they found here a constant darkness and Shadow; for that the Sun could not make a shining

around that Great Corner. Yet, even here they ceased not to make the
Road; but took it around, and a mighty way unto the North; passing
it among strange Fires and Pits that burned from out of the earth.

But there was presently, such a power and horror of Monsters
and Evil Things in that Valley of Shadow, that the Road Makers were
made to go Backwards into the Red Light which did fill the Westward
Valley, and came from that low Sun.

And they went back unto their Cities; and lived there mayhaps an
hundred thousand years; and grew wise and cunning in all matters;
and their Wise People did make dealings and had experiment with
those Forces which are Distasteful and Harmful unto Life; but they
did this in Ignorance; for all that they had much wisdom; thinking only
to Experiment, that they come to greater knowings. But they did open
a way for those Forces; and much harm and Pity did come thereby.
And then had all People to have Regret; yet too late.

Now, presently, when an hundred thousand years had gone, or
it may be a greater space; there came slowly the utter twilight of the
world, as the sun to die the more; so that presently it gave but an utter
gloomy light. And there grew upon many of the Peoples of the Cities
of the Valley, a strangeness and a wildness; so that strange things were
done, that had been shameful to all in the Light. And there were wan-
derings, and consortings with strange outward beings, and presently,
many Cities were attacked by monsters that did come from the West;
and there was a Pandemonium.

Then was an Age of Sorrows and Fightings, and Hardenings of
the Spirit and of the Heart, for all that were of good Fibre; and this
did breed a Determined Generation; and there grew up into the World
a Leader; and he took all the sound Millions; and did make a mighty
Battle upon all Foulness and upon all that did harm and trouble them;
and they drave their Enemies down the Valley, and up the Valley, and
did utterly scatter and put them to flight.

Then did that Man call all his Peoples together; and did make it
plain how that the Darkness grew upon the World, and that the Foul
and dreadful Powers abroad, were like to be more Horrid when a
greater Gloom came.

And he put to them that they Build a Mighty Refuge; and the
Peoples did acclaim; and lo! there was built, presently, a Great House.
But the Great House was not Proper; and that Man did take all the
Peoples to Wander; and they came to the Bight; and there was built
at last that Great and Mighty Pyramid.

Now this is the sense and telling of that book; and but late had

I read it; and talked somewhat of it with my dear friend, the Master Monstruwacan; but not overmuch; for I had taken so sudden a mind to GO, that all else had dropped from about me. Yet, to us it did seem clear that there was no life in all the invisible upper world; and that, surely, that Great Road whereon the Silent Ones did walk, must be that same Road which the hardy Peoples of that age did make.

And it did seem wise to the Master Monstruwacan, and unto me, that if any should find the Lesser Redoubt, they must surely do so somewhere within the mighty Valley; but whether The Road that led into the West, where was the Place of the Ab-humans, should bring me to it, I had no knowing; nor whether it might lie on the Northward way. And I, maybe, to wander a thousand miles wrong; if, in truth, I were not into some dreadful trouble before.

And, indeed, no reason of value was there to give me hope that the Lesser Pyramid lay either to the West, or where the Road went Northward, beyond the House of Silence. Yet I did so feel it to be somewhere to the North, that I had made a determination to search that way for a great distance, the first; and if I could not come upon aught, then I should have sober thought that it did lie Westward. But in the Valley someways, I had feeling of assurance that it must be; for it was plain that the telling of the book was sound in its bottom sense; as might be seen; for how should any live in the utter bleak and deadly chill of the silent upper world that lay an hundred miles up in the night, hid and lost for ever.

And strange is it to think of those wondrous and mighty cliffs that girt us about, and yet were fast held from us in the dark; so that I had not known of them, save for the telling of that book; though, in truth, it had been always supposed that we lived in a great deep of the world; but, indeed, it was rather held in belief that we abode in the bed of some ancient sea, that did surely slope gradual away from us, and not go up abrupt and savage.

And here let me make so clear as I may that the general peoples had no clear thought upon any such matters; though there was something of it taught in the schools; yet rather this and that, of diverse conclusions, as it might be thinkings of the Teachers, after much study, and some ponderings. For one man, having a lack of imagining, would scoff, and another, maybe, to take it very staidly; but some would build Fancy upon the tellings of the Records, and make foolish and fantastic that which had groundings in Truth; and thus is it ever. But to the most Peoples of the Pyramid, there was no deep conviction nor thought of any great hid World afar in the darkness. For they gave attention and

belief only to that which lay to their view; nor could a great lot come to imagine that there had been ever any other Condition.

And to them, it did seem right and meet that there should be strange things, and fires from the earth, and an ever-abiding night, and monsters, and matters hid and tangled much in mystery.

And very content were the most of them; though some had in them the yeast of imaginings, or the pimples of fancy upon them, and to these there seemed many possibilities; though the first to read out to sanity; and the second, to expect and have speech towards much that was foolish or to no purpose.

And of these vague believings of the peoples, have I made hint before, and need not have much trouble to it now. Save that, with the children, as is ever the way, those olden tales had much believing; and the simplicity of the Wise did mate with the beliefs of the Young; and between them did lie the Truth.

And so did I make speed towards the North, having a strong surety in my heart and mind that there were but two ways to my search; for without of the Valley, afar up in the dead lonesomeness of the hidden world, was a cold that was shapen ready to Death, and a lacking, as I must believe, of the sweet, needful air that yet did lie in plenty in that deep place of the earth. So that, surely, the mighty Valley somewheres to hold that other Redoubt.

Yet, as I have said, I went not direct to my journey; but otherwise, for those sound reasons which I did set down a time back.

VII

The Night Land

NOW, AS I WENT towards the North and West, I steered me warily for a great while, that I come safe of that Great Watcher of the North-West. And as I made forward, I put thought to all matters which must concern me; so far as I had imagining to see. And first I did consider the speed that I should keep; and found presently that I did well to be moderate; for that I had before me a great and mighty journey; and indeed, who might speak knowingly of the end thereof?

And another matter, I did arrange; for I would make the times of my goings forward, and the times of mine eatings and sleepings all to a wise and regular fashion; that, thereby, I might go a great way, with the less harm to my body; so that I should be strong when the need did come for my strength. And I made in the end that I should eat and drink, at every sixth hour, and at the eighteenth hour sleep me until the twenty-fourth.

And by this means did I eat thrice in that time, and have six hours of sleep. And this seemed very good to me, and I did strive always to manage thus in all my great journeying in the Night Land. Yet, as may be supposed, there were times oft and many when I must watch without ceasing, and leave my slumber unto the future; for the Land was full of grim and dreadful Perils.

And, as doth be human, I brake my rule straightway in the beginning; for I ceased not to walk for one-and-twenty hours, hiding and creeping, as the need did be in those places that were like to show me unto the Watcher; and when I did think upon food, it did sicken me; so that I would eat by and by, as I made it within my thoughts.

But when one-and-twenty hours had gone, I grew very weary and something faint; and was forced that I look about for some place where I might have rest. And, in a little while, I did see, away off, a small fire-hole, the like of which I had passed odd times even so early. And

I made to come nigh to that part; for there would be warmth from the chill of the Night Land, and mayhaps a place dry and convenient to my slumber.

And when I came anigh, I saw that it was a cheerful place, as it might be said, amid so much gloom; for the hole was but a few paces wide, and full of a dull, glowing fire, that did bubble somewhat, and throw off a small sulphur-smoke. And I sat me down, at no great way, and did place the Diskos on the rock to my hand.

And I moved not, awhile; but was aweary, so that I had not the courage to eat, neither to drink; but must turn me and look back to the Mighty Pyramid; and, in truth, though I had come a very good space, yet was I so anigh to it, that I was both cheered and put out of heart; for it did seem close upon me, by reason of its greatness, so that I, who had journeyed a hard and weariful way, was shaken with the greatness of the task that was upon me.

Yet was this but one side of my heart; for it was good to feel the nearness of my Mighty Home; and I knew that there did countless millions make watch upon me, as I sat; yet did I make no sign; for it is not meet to make a constant farewell; but to GO. Yet was it very strange to be thus near, and to show such behaviour as were proper to one afar from all humanity. But so it was that I ordered my ways; for it did seem proper to me; yet was I happy to know that the dear Master Monstruwacan must, time and oft, have spied upon me through the Great Spy-Glass; and mayhaps did watch me in that moment.

And it grew in me that I did act weakly to hold off from mine Vittles, and showed foolishness before my kind friend afar; and I did ope my scrip, and take therefrom three tablets, the which I chewed and did eat; for this was a strong food, treated that it had but small bulk. Yet were they not filling to the belly; and I made that I would drink well, that I might feel that something was therein.

And to this end, I shook from a strong and especial tube, a dust; and I caught the dust within a little cup; and the air did make an action upon that dust, as it were of chemistry; and the dust did boil and make a fizzing in the cup, and rose up and filled it with a liquid that was of simple water; yet very strange to see come that way; but ordinary after a time.

And in this way, as might be seen, had I such food and drink in but a little scrip, that might keep life within me for a great time. Yet was it a way of discomfort, and lacking to the mouth and to the belly; but a sufficient thing unto the need of the body, and good matter for a thankful heart, in that dark and hungry Land.

Now, when I had eaten, I did go over in their order, those things which I did carry; for there was, beside the Diskos and that scrip of food, a pouch that did contain matters various. And these, I did look into; and afterward did take out a small compass that I had been give by the Master Monstruwacan, so that I might find of its workings without the Great Redoubt; and, he had said unto me, that it might be that I should pass far off into the Night Land, and lose the Mighty Pyramid amid so great a Country and so plentiful a Darkness. Then, perchance, if that ancient principle did still lurk within the machine, though turned no more to the North, but unto the Pyramid, then should it guide my feet Homeward out of the Everlasting Night, and thus have once more that ancient use which, as I do know, is common unto this age.

And this was a very cunning thing to have with me, if but it held service to the Earth-Current, and a rare thing, which the Master Monstruwacan did make with his own hands and much skill and pains, from an olden one that had place within the Great Museum, and concerning which I have told somewhat, before this place.

And I set the thing upon the ground; but it had no certain way with it; but did spin and waver constantly; and this I made to consider, and remembered that I was yet above that part where, afar in the earth did spread the greatness of the Underground Fields; and I was, haply, but a little way off from the "Crack"; though a mighty way above.

And it pleasured me to wonder whether the dear Master Monstruwacan did behold how that I made test with the compass; for the light was good from the fire-hole; and the Great Spy-Glass had a great strength. Yet, had I no certainty; for, as I did know, from much watchings, there was no surety in the searching of the Land, by the Glass; for there was oft plainness where you did think surely none should see, and anon a dullness where might be thought that the sight went gaily. And this may be plain to all; for the wavering of the lights from the strange fires was not to be accounted to rule; but made a light here, and a darkness there, and then did change about, oddly. Moreover, there were smokes and mists that did come upwards from the earth, in this place and in that; and had somewhiles a greatness; but oft were small, and did lurk low, and had no power but to confuse the sight.

And, presently, I did put by the compass in my pouch, and made to compose myself unto sleep. But here would I now set down how that, in the end, after I had gone many days' journeyings outward from the Mighty Pyramid, I did indeed find it to draw the Northward part of the needle unto it; and this was a comfort and a pleasure to my

spirit; moreover, if ever I did get back, as I did think, it would be a matter for great interest unto the Master Monstruwacan; yet, in verity, were there other matters that should hold him more; for he was right human, as all should know.

And, moreover, concerning this same compass, I did find a fresh thing; for, after a yet greater time, as I shall set out in a due place, if I do but remember, which doubt is ever my fear to fret me, I came a mighty way from the Redoubt, and, lo! fearing that I might indeed lose that, My Great Home, in the Darkness of the World, I did pull out that strange wonder of the needle, that I might have comfort by its homeward pointing. And I did discover a new power in the night; for the machine did point no more directwards unto the Great Redoubt; but was a point unto the Westwards; so that I had knowledge that some Great Power afar in the Darkness of the World did sway upon it; and I had a childlike wonder that this might be, in truth, that same Power of the North, of which the books, and my Memory-Dreams did tell. And, indeed, no doubt should there be upon this matter; yet who might not have doubt in that time, that they should perceive after an eternity, that ancient Northward Force swaying that small servant unto an olden obedience. And it was, as it were, a revealing unto me, how that to know within the brain is one matter; but to have knowledge within the heart is another; for I had always known concerning this Northward Force; but yet had not known with the true meaning of Knowledge.

And yet one other matter there was to cause doubt, at that moment of this new knowing; for it came to me that maybe the power of that Lesser Redoubt did begin to act upon the machine, even as the Earth-Current of the Great Pyramid did hold yet a strong drawing upon the needle; and were this so, then did I not surely begin to stand anigh unto my Journey's end; for that less power of the Lesser Redoubt could have no impudence to pull, save that I had come to a closeness with it.

Yet, in truth, as I do now have knowledge, it was the North that drew; and I do seem to make a great telling about this little matter; but how else shall I show to you mine inward mind, and the lack of knowledge and likewise the peculiar knowings that did go to the making of that time, and the Peoples thereof, which is but to say the same thing twice over.

And now, as I did say, I made to compose myself for sleep; and to this end, I took a cloak-matter which did cross my shoulder and hip, and wrapt it about me, and lay down there in the darkness of the Night, by that strange fire-hole.

And I lay the Diskos beside me, within the cloak; for it was, indeed, my companion and friend in bitter need; so that I had pleasure to feel the strange thing anigh to me. And as I did lie there, in those moments that do drowse the Soul, as it were that they do proceed as breath out of the mouth of Sleep, I had a half-knowing that the æther did surge about me; and I doubt not but that there had watched my every doing, many of the Millions, and had been humanly stirred, at my commending of my spirit unto sleep; and thus did shake the æther of the world about me, with their unity of sympathy.

And, mayhaps, I had some little knowing of this thing, as I did pass, drowsy, into slumber; and it is surely like that I slept the better for it. Moreover, I was wondrous tired and worn, and thus did sleep very strong and heavy; yet I mind me that my last dim thinkings were upon that sweet maid I did go to find. And in slumber did I have speech with her in dreams, and a strange happiness about me, and all seeming to be touched by fairy-light, and freed from the sorrow of life.

And it was from a sweet and lovely sleeping, such as this, that I was waked suddenly by a great and mighty sound; and I came instant to a possessing of my senses; and I knew that the mighty Voice of the Home-Call did go howling across the Night. And, swift and silent, I slid the cloak from about me, and took the haft of that wondrous Diskos into mine hand.

And I did look towards the Pyramid, quickly, for a message; for I had a sure knowledge that there had a great Need arisen, and that some Terror came towards me out of the Dark; else they had never waked all the Night Land to a knowing that an human was abroad out of the Mighty Refuge.

And even as I did peer towards the Great Redoubt, I could not abide to keep my gaze entire that way; but did take a large and fearful look all about me; yet could make to see nothing; and so did stare, eager and anxious, afar into the upper blackness of the Night, where did shine that Final Light of the Tower of Observation; and the same while crouched, and holding the Diskos, and making to glance across my shoulders, and to watch for the message, and all in the same moment.

And then, afar upwards in the prodigious height, I did see the great, and bright and quick darting flashes of a strange green fire, and did know that they spelled to me in the Set-Speech a swift warning that a grey monster, that was a Great Grey Man, had made scent of me in the dark, and was even in that moment of time, crawling towards me through the low moss-bushes that lay off beyond the fire-hole to my back. And the message was sharp; and bade me to leap into the

bushes unto my left; and to hide there; so that I might chance to take the thing to an advantage.

And, as may be thought, they had scarce flashed the tale unto me; but I was gone in among the shadows of a clump of the moss-bush that did grow anigh; and I sweat with a strange terror, and a cold and excited shaking of the heart; yet was my spirit set strong to conquer.

And lo! as I did crouch there, hidden, I saw something come very quiet out of the bushes that did grow beyond the fire-hole; and it was great, and crept, and was noways coloured but by greyness in all its parts. And the glare from the fire-hole did seem to trouble it; so that it looked, laying its head to the ground, and spying along the earth, in a strange and Brutish fashion; that it might oversee the glare of the fire-hole. Yet, I doubt that it saw beyond the fire with plainness; for, in a moment, it crept swift in among the bushes again, and came out towards the edge of the fire-hole in another place; and this it did thrice unto my left, and thrice unto my right; and every time did lay its head to the earth, and spy along; and did hunch its shoulders, and thrust forward the jaw horridly and turn the neck, as a very nasty beast might go, wanton.

Now, as you may think, this manner of the Beast-Man did shake my courage mightily; for I did think each time that it did go inward among the moss-bushes, that it had made discovery of me, and would make to take me in the back, from out of the dark of the bushes; and this was an uncomfortable thing to consider, as others might think also, had any been there in the bush with me. And then, in truth, did that same swift sense of mine Hearing, prove helpful to my saving; for, behold, the thing did go back into the moss-bushes, after that last coming out; and did seem to make as it had made a failing to discover me, and had no further intent, save to return unto the Night; and I had this thought truly in mine heart, and for maybe a minute; and then, lo! within my soul a voice did speak plain, and did warn me that the thing did make a great compass among the moss-bushes about the fire-hole, having made discovery of me; and it did go warily to take me in the back, from the other side.

Now, when I heard this voice speak within my spirit, I had knowledge that the dear Master Monstruwacan made watch from the Tower of Observation, and did send the speech with his brain-elements, having in mind that I had the Night-Hearing. And I trusted the speech; for in the same moment of time there did beat all about me in the Night the solemn throb of the Master-Word, as that it had been added with speed, to give instant assurance. And I leapt quick from that clump

of the moss-bush, unto another, and crouched, and made a watch all about me; and kept the ears of my spirit open, knowing that the Master Monstruwacan did also watch all, for me.

And, suddenly, I saw a little moving of a bush that grew to the back of those bushes in which I had been hid; and there came out of the bush that moved, a great grey hand, and moved the moss of the clump where I had been, as it were that something peered out of the moving bush. And there followed the great grey head of the Grey Man, and the head went into the clump of the moss-bush where I had been.

And I knew that I must strike now; and I leapt, and smote with the Diskos; and the thing fell upon its side, and the great grey legs came out of the hither bushes, and twitched and drew upwards; but the head remained in the bush where I had been hid. And I stood away from the thing whilst it died; and in mine hand the Diskos did spin and send forth fire; as it were that it did live, and did know that it had slain a great and horrid monster.

And presently the Grey Man was dead; and I went away from those bushes, unto the far side of the fire-hole. And I stood with the Diskos held high and spinning and sending out fire, that they within the Mighty Pyramid might know that I had slain the Beast-Man; for it might be that it lay too much in the shadow for them to look upon.

But the Master Monstruwacan spoke not again to me; for, indeed, it was not meet to do so, except it might save me from a sure danger; for, as you may know from my past tellings, there were Powers of the Night Land that did hearken unto such matters; and it was like enough that there had been overmuch done, even thus, for my further safety. Yet the thing could not be helped.

And now that I was a little calmed, and eased from my fear, I could know that all that the æther of the night was disturbed by the gladness of the millions within the Great Redoubt; so that it was plain how great a multitude had given note unto the fight; and their hearts to beat in sweet sympathy and natural fear; so that I did feel companied and befriended; though, as it may be thought, something shaken yet about the heart.

Now, in a little time, I did gather unto me my wits and had myself to order; and I looked to see how the hours did go, and I found that I had surely slumbered through ten hours. And I reproached myself; for, indeed, I had slept oversound by reason of my having lacked a regular way and time, as I had with a proper wisdom made to be my rule. And I resolved that I would obey the wit of my Reason in all the future time, and make to eat and rest in due season, as you will wot that I did before intend.

Then, with a self-reproachful heart, I went around the small fire-hole, and caught up my cloak and other matters. And I turned me towards the Mighty Pyramid, and did look once upwards along all the great slope, where it did go measureless into the far blackness of the Everlasting Night; and I made no salutation; for I had so resolved, as you will know; moreover, I desired not to call forth any unneedful disturbance of the æther of the world, which indeed must be, did I make to stir the emotions of the Millions.

And I turned me then away, and went off into the night, going swift and cautious, and bearing the Diskos cunningly and almost, as it were, with a love for that strange and wondrous weapon that had so befriended me, and slain the foul Grey Man with one stroke. And I had feeling that it did know me, and had a comradeship for me; and I doubt none will understand this; save, it might be, they of the olden days that did carry one strong sword always. Yet was the Diskos more than the sword; for it did in truth seem to live with the fire and the flame of the Earth-Current that did beat within it.

And it was well acknowledged within the Great Redoubt, that none might touch the Diskos of another; for that the thing went crustily, as it might be said, in the hands of a stranger; and if any made foolish-ness of this knowledge, and did persist much to such an handling, or making to use, the same would presently act clumsy with the weapon, and come to an hurt; and this was a sure thing, and had been known maybe an hundred thousand years; or perchance a greater time.

And by this it doth seem wise to believe that there did grow al-ways an affinity between the nature of the man—which doth, as ever, include the woman—and the Diskos that he did use in his Practice; and because of this known thing, and that the place would elsewise be lumbered with olden weapons of those that did die, it was a Law and Usage that there was placed with the Dead, the Diskos of the Dead, there upon The Last Road in the Country Of Silence, and was thus made to give back unto the Earth-Current, the power that did lie in it.

And this doth seem to a careless thinker, as it were that I told once again those olden customs of the Ancient Folk; but this is otherwise, and had a sound reason to it; yet, if you do so believe, I doubt not but that a right human sentiment was something at the bottom, which is proper; for it is meet that Love should mate with Wisdom to mother Comfort in our sorrows; and it is a warm thing to do aught for our dead; and none may say nay to this.

Now, as I did go onwards into the Night Land, looking ever to this shadow and to that, it may be conceived how my heart would stir

with swift fear, at this and that; and that my body would oft quiver to leap aside; and as swift discover that naught assailed.

And so did I go forward, and always with imaginings and wonders concerning what manner of uncouth Being or Brute might come out of the darknesses all about. Yet, in all that time, there was a certain proudness of the heart, that I did come safe out of the power of the Grey Man, and did surely slay him. But, truly, it were well that the praise be considered, and not overmuch given unto me; for I had died as I slept, but that they of the Great Redoubt, had made a watch over me, and waked me unto my saving.

Now, presently, as I walked, I grew something faint, and had knowledge that I did foolishly; for, indeed, I should have eat after my fight; yet may I be forgiven for this forgetting, in that I had been much shaked and put about.

And I sat me down in a little clear place among the bushes, and did eat three of the tablets, and did once more shake forth the dust that did turn in the air to a natural water by a proper and natural chemistry of these matters. And after I had eat, I sat a little while, and did think, and did look upwards at the great slope of the Pyramid in the night; and all the time did I listen with mine ears and with my spirit; and kept the Diskos across my knees, and looked this way and that, very frequent; but nothing came anigh.

And so I rose presently, and went onwards, and walked for six hours towards the North and the West. And I made much to the West, for a little, that I might come clear of the North-West Watcher. Yet, after a space, I made to do foolishly; for I changed my mind about, and kept something more towards the North, so that I should have a surer sight of that Monster.

And this was, in truth, a rash and naughty thing to consider; for if I were but seen, then should that grim Brute make a signal unto the Evil Powers, and I be met swiftly with destruction. But surely the heart is a strange and wayward thing, and given to quick fears, and immediately unto great and uncountable rashnesses. And so I did go forward unwisely to the Northward of a safe and proper going; and it may be that an influence was upon me, and drew me thatwards; but who shall say.

Now, a great time I walked, and made a halt upon every sixth hour, and did eat and drink, and look a little unto the monstrous towering of the Great Redoubt; and afterwards make strong mine heart, and go forward again. And always I did go warily, and chiefly among the low moss-bush; but sometimes out upon stony ground, and oft across

places where sulphur did puff somewhat from the ground in a low smoke, very strong in the nostrils and not liked inwardly.

And as I made onwards, I looked always to my right and to my left, and anon to the rear; yet made a constant observation of the Mighty Watcher, that I did begin to draw nigh unto. And oft did I stoop to crawl, and my hands did bleed somewhat; but after I was troubled so, I put on the great gloves that made complete the grey armour, and so was shod proper to such journeying.

And, presently, when eighteen hours did have passed since that my sudden awakening to the peril of the Grey Man, I did search about for a place to slumber; for I would keep wisely unto my ruling, and go not over long lacking of sleep; and by this planning I should be the less like to sleep oversound, and so should set my spirit to listen whilst I did sleep; and by so much as my spirit should serve me with faith, should I have safety. And this thing is plain, and wants not more to the saying thereof.

And I came presently unto a sudden place where the land did go downwards brokenly, as that it had been burst a great while gone by the inward fires; and I looked downwards over the edge of that place, and went round about it, and did see presently a ledge upon the far side, that was difficult to come upon; yet a place of some little safety to any that might go down to it; for it was awkward to see, and did any monster seek to come at me, I should have chance of warning; and might go downwards a greater way in time to my salvation.

And by this determination, I abode; and came down to that place with labour; but was cheerful of heart that I had found so sure a shelter. And I eat my three tablets, and drank the water that I did get from the powder. And so made to compose my body to sleep. Yet, at this time, a thought did come to me, and I made calculation afresh; and laughed somewhat at that my poor counting; for, indeed, I had thought to eat but thrice in the twenty and four hours; yet by my arranging, I was made, indeed, to eat four times, as you shall see immediately by a little thought. And this thing came more strong upon my spirit than any might think; for I did eat overmuch for the lasting of the food; though, in verity, it was but little to my belly; as you must all think, and have sympathy for my discomfort.

And I considered a little, and had determined that I should afterwards in my journeying, eat but two of the tablets to my meal; and this was a wise thought, and like much wisdom, a discomposing thing. But so it was, and I set it down that you may know the arranging of my ways at that time.

Now, in all this while of meditation, I had been setting my cloak about me, and was fast set to my sleeping; for I had walked a weary way. And I lay me down upon my left side, with my back to the rock, which did overhang me something above; so that I was contented to feel hid from things that might pass by in the Night. And I had the cloak about me, and the Diskos close against my breast, within the cloak, and my head upon my pouch and upon my scrip.

And as I lay thus a moment easeful, I could see that so mighty was the uprising of the Great Pyramid that it was not hid from me even thus, but did stand upward into the night, and did shine, and was plain to be seen above the further edge of that deep place where I did lie.

And I fell upon sleep, looking upward at that Final Light, where, as might be, the Master Monstruwacan did bend the Great Spy-Glass upon my lonesomeness, as I lay there upon the ledge.

And this was a thought of sweet comfort upon which to slumber; the which I did; but my spirit lay wakeful within my breast, and did listen through the night; and harked for all evil matters and things that did make to come anigh. But also my spirit did whisper unto Naani as I went into sleep; and so passed I into dreams.

Now, it may be thought that I did act with a strange valiance, in that I composed my body so properly to slumber, and with but a little trouble of the heart concerning the coming of monsters. And in truth this hath seemed somewhat so to me, thinking since that time; but I do but set the thing that is truth; and make not to labour to an illusion of truth; and so must tell much that doth seem improper to the Reality. Yet must all bear with me, and have understanding of the hardness of setting forth with true seeming the honesty of Truth, which, in verity, is better served oft times by timely and cunning lies. And so shall you understand this matter so well as I.

And presently my spirit waked me there in the half dark of the Night Land; and I looked swift about me, and upwards, and saw nothing to fear. Then did I peer at my dial; and made to discover that I had slept full over six quiet hours; and by this I knew the reason of mine awaking; for it was so great impressed upon me by mine inward sense and being. And this you shall understand, someways, who have thought, ere sleep, to wake to a certain time of the morning; and by understanding shall you believe and give me all your kind harking and human sympathy.

And I made to have a smartness of going, which is ever hard to the newly waked; and I eat two tablets, the while my belly did cry out for an wholesome and proper filling; but I drank some of the water, and so did ease somewhat of my hunger.

Then did I wind my cloak to its shape, and put upon me my gear, which was the scrip and the pouch, and the Diskos to my hip; and I clomb out from that place of rest. Yet, before I did come rightly up into the open, I peered about, and made some surety that no evil Brute was anigh. And then I gat me out, and stood upon my feet, and looked for a little upwards at the mighty slope of the Great Redoubt, which did seem yet very nigh unto me, by reason of it being so monstrous in bigness.

And I wondered whether in that moment the Master Monstruwacan did look down upon me, with the Great Spy-Glass. And afterwards I turned away swiftly, and went on into the Night Land; for it did always make me shaken with lonesomeness to look upon my Great Home. And so I did go forward with a strong and uncaring stride; but grew presently to quietness, and to have back the proper caution of my going. Yet had I not gone all foolishly; for I had taken the Diskos from my hip, ere this; so that I possessed it handily.

Now there is one matter which shall seem but a small and natural occurring unto you; yet was strong upon me in that time; and this thing was that I did begin now to see the Night Land from the new outlooking of my distance from the Mighty Pyramid. And it was as that a man of this day did go from the earth to travel among the stars, and lo! should he not find them to shift upon his vision; so that the Great Bear and this and that shaping of the star clusterings, should make a new order, as he did wander onwards; and so should he find that there was naught that was truly fixed, as he did before then think; but all to alter according unto the place whence the looking! And this thing shall be plain unto you, though no thought be put to the matter; for it is of an evident verity that doth need not argument to expound. And so shall you have memory of me, there a-wander among those strange shapings and wonders of that grim Land, the which I had never but supposed to seem but as my memory did retain them, from the lookings of all my life within the Great Redoubt. And so it was; and ever there did this thing and that open out to a new view, and the Night Land take to itself a constant new aspect to mine eyes which had never until that time had but the one fixed vision of the same.

And you shall understand with me how that when, about the fourteenth hour of that day's travel, I did draw very nigh unto the monstrous Watcher of the North-West, it did seem so utter strange from this fresh aspect that I had been like to think that I did see a new Monster. For, in truth, when I did come at last to creep to within a mile of it, among the low moss-bushes, I was confounded that the mighty chin did come forward towards the Great Redoubt, even as

the upward part of a vast cliff, which the sea doth make hollow about the bottom; for it did hang out into the air above the glare of the fire from the Red Pit, as it had been a thing of Rock, all scored and be-weathered, and dull red and seeming burned and blasted by reason of the bloody shine that beat upward from the deep of the Red Pit.

And by the way in which I do tell upon it, you shall know that I did surely view it something from the side at this immediate time; for, in truth, it was then that I did draw the nearer; and, moreover, I was the more astonished at this viewing, than I had been to the front; for it was so utter strange, and shapen so different from the Brute that did hang in my memory.

And a great time I did lie there upon my belly; and shaken by a fear of the Beast; yet emboldened, as you may conceive, by having come to the side; and being hopeful in my heart that I was very secure within so great a shadow and the thick sheltering of the moss-bushes.

And surely it was that I did creep more nigh, the while that I did look; for presently I had a very plain seeing of the Great Monster; and did know where I had gotten to, and thereby did acknowledge unto myself that this was an utter foolishness; and like, for all that any might say, to lead unto destruction. Yet, as all must know, there was the first fear, and the ceasing of this fear, as I did wot that I was so little a thing to heed out there in the shadows. And presently a gaining of courage, and the prick of my Being that did crave to see clear this exceeding Wonder. And so was I come close, more or less, having gone far upon my hands and knees; yet sometimes to pause; but afterwards on again.

Now by this nearness, I was the more truly able to perceive how that the Bulk of the Watcher did rise up into the Night, like a Hill; and the colour was mostly black, save and indeed where it did face to the red shine of the Pit; and concerning this I have done telling.

And so did I lie there, and stare a great while, parting a small hole in the moss-bushes that I might spy through the same. And the thing was squat there, and might have root within the earth, so it did seem to mine imaginings, as I did stare with a dumb wonder. And there were monstrous warts upon the thing, and indents and a mighty ruggedness and lumpings; as it were that it did be pimpled with great boulders that were inbred within that monstrous hide. And where the shine from the Pit of Red Fire did strike upon these, they did stand out into the darkness away from the skin, as you of this Age shall see mountains of the moon catch a bright fire from the Sun, and show plain upon the night of the moon.

Now, as I have set down, I did lie there and look a great while; and it came presently to me that there was unease within the Mighty Pyramid, among the Millions; for I did feel the æther of the world to be disturbed by their distress; and so had a knowing that they had a cunning wareness concerning the place where I did hide among the moss-bushes.

And the thrilling in the night did bring a wisdom into my head; for, in verity, as I have said, this was a foolish matter that I was upon. And I gat a thought that the Watcher might have an awareness of the trouble of the Multitudes; and, indeed, for all that I did know, it had a full knowledge of all my wandering; though concerning this, I did think otherwise truly in my heart; as is a most human and proper way to make comfortable the spirit, where Doubt can have no ease from Reason.

And I made that I would go backwards to a good distance from the Watcher, and go forward again upon my journeying, if but that I come safe from so unwise an adventuring. And as I did begin to return, it was to me as that all my senses were newly awake; for I had a sudden knowing that I was within the atmosphere, should I not call it, of the Monster.

And I gat an abrupt and horrid shaking of the spirit; for I did feel in verity that my soul had come too anigh; and that the Beast had a sure knowledge concerning me; yet did make to my destruction with no haste; but after that way and fashion that did seem proper unto it.

And this feeling you shall understand the better, maybe, when I do tell that it was to me as that the air all about me was full of a quiet and steadfast life and keen intelligence that I did believe to come forth from the Watcher on every side; so that I did feel as one already within the gaze of some Great and Evil Power.

Yet, though I had a great terror upon me, I made no foolish haste; but commanded my soul to courage, and put a guard upon my way of going, and so made a very quiet journey for maybe two full miles; and afterwards did allow myself something more of haste; for I was now grown easier in my spirit; and felt apart from the spirit of the Great Watcher.

And after a longer while, I did leave that hill of watchfulness to my rear; and was gone onward into the night; yet, as may be known, with a vague unease and trouble to my heart, and a swift and frequent turning to learn surely that no Evil Thing came after me. For, as you may know, I could nowise have forgetting, concerning that great quiet Life which did seem to be living in all the air around that Mighty Bulk. For it had been all about me in the night, as I have told, and I to

feel that I had been surely discovered! And thus shall you know how shaken was my spirit, in verity.

Now, presently, at the eighteenth hour of that day's travel, I ceased from my journeying, that I might eat and drink; and I did sit a little while, and looked back upon the strange and monstrous thing which I had come beyond. And the great humped back and vast shoulders of the Watching-Thing rose up into the night, black and cumbrous against the red shine of the Pit. And thus, as you shall think, had that Brute looked always unto the Mighty Pyramid, through Eternity, and did cease not from watching, and was steadfast and silent and alone; and none did understand.

And after I had eat, and drunk some of the water, I went onward for a full matter of six hours more; being minded to have no sleep until I had put a great way between me and the Watcher. And in this part of my journey did I come to The Place Where The Silent Ones Kill, as it was named in the Maps. And I observed a very wondrous caution, and went away from it a little, unto the North, where I did see at a distance the shinings of fire-holes; the which did promise me warmth through my slumber.

And here you must know that the Place Where The Silent Ones Kill was an utter bare place, where all did seem of rock, and no bush did seem to grow thereon; so that a man might not come to any hiding; though, in truth, there might be some hole here or there; yet was none shown in any map within the Pyramid; neither did there seem to be any such to me, as I did creep there among the moss-bushes to the Northward of the Place, and look constant and fearful towards it; so that I should see quickly whether any Silent One did move across all the grey quiet of that rocky plain.

And concerning this same Place Where The Silent Ones Kill, it were well to make an explanation how that there was always a little and far-spreaded light over all that lonesomeness; and the light was something grey-seeming; as it were that a lichen might grow upon the rocks, and send out a little uncomfortable glowing, even as certain matters do in these times, if you do but know the place and the time to seek them. Yet was the light exceeding weak, and very cold and dismal, and did seem truly to show naught with a sureness; so that it did appear to the eye, if one did look fixedly, that there were shadows that did move here or there, as it were of silent beings; and none might know, in truth, whether this shaping of the greyness was to the clouding of the Reason, or that the eye did see of Reality. Yet, if one did look with the Great Spy-Glass, then might there be some surety and plainness;

and likewise was it so, if one did have come sufficient anigh to that uncomfortable Place, even as I then did be.

And so you shall conceive how that I did slide very quiet from bush unto bush; for I had alway in all my life had a very dread fear of this place; and oft did I peer out into the dim grey light of the lonesome plain unto my left; and would think sometimes to perceive the shapes of the Silent Ones stood vague and watchful; yet, on the instant, to see nothing.

And thus I did go onward, and came presently to a part where the grey plain did stretch out a bareness into the Night Land to my front; so that my way ended, unless I did make a long passing round about.

And I sat there among the moss-bushes, and did consider, and lookt out cunningly through a spy-hole of the bush in which I did sit. And I perceived that the part of the plain which did jut bareness into the Land before me had no greatness of size; but might be passed swiftly in but a little running. And this thing should save me a wearisome going round; so that I made to consider it with a serious mind; and all the time did I search the bare greyness before me, and saw presently that it was surely empty.

And I made to adventure myself across, running very swift until I had come to the far side. And lo! as I did go to rise up out of the bush, mine eyes were opened, as it were, and I saw that there was something amid the constant greyness; and I fell quickly into the bush; and did sweat very chill; but yet did haste to look.

And I saw now that there were, in truth, matters that did show vague upon that part of the plain that was before me. And I did peer very constant and anxious, and, behold, I saw that there was facing me, a great line of quiet and lofty figures, shrouded unto their feet; and they moved not, neither made they any sound; but stood there amid the greyness, and did seem to make an unending watch upon me; so that my heart went unto weakness, and I did feel that there was no power of the moss-bushes to hide me; for, in verity, they that stood so silent were certain of the Silent Ones; and I was very nigh to the Place of Destruction.

Now, I moved not for a time; but was made stiff by the greatness of my fear. Yet I was presently aware that the Silent Ones came not towards me; but stood quiet; as that they did mind not to slay me, if but I did keep from that Place.

And there grew therefrom a little courage into mine heart, and I obeyed my spirit, and took an hold of my strength and went slowly backward in the bushes. And presently I was come a long way off. Yet troubled and disturbed, and very strict to my going.

And I made a great circling about that place where the plain of
the Silent Ones did come outward; and so did gain to the North-West;
and was thence something the happier in my heart; and went easily,
and oft upon my feet; yet making a strong watching to every side.

And so I came at the last to a time when I had walked through
four-and-twenty weariful hours; and was eager that I should come to
a safe place for my sleep; yet did lack a happy belief of safety, in that
I had come twice anigh to so grim trouble; and unsure I was that I
did not be secretly pursued in the night. And this you shall believe to
be a very desperate feeling; and a plight to make the heart sick, and to
long with a great longing for the safety of that mine Home. Yet had
I put myself to the task; and truly I did never cease to the sorrowful
remembering of that utter despair that had sounded to me plain in the
last calling of mine own love, out of all the mystery of the night. And
but to think upon this was to grow strong in the spirit; yet to have a
fresh anxiousness that I did the more surely keep my life within me,
and so come to that maid's salvation.

Now, as you shall mind, I had spied the shine of certain fire-holes
somewhat to the Northward, and had thought to make thereabouts
a place for my sleep; for, in truth, there was a bitterness of cold in
all the air of night that did surround me; and I was warmed nigh to a
slow happiness, by thinking upon a fire to lie beside; and small wonder,
as you shall say.

And I made presently a strong walking unto that place where did
glow in the night the shine of the fire-holes, as I did well judge them
to be; and so was like to have come over-swiftly upon my death, as you
shall presently see; for, as I came anigh to the first, I perceived that
the light came upward out of a great hollow among the moss-bushes,
and that the fire-hole burned somewhere in the deep of the hollow;
so that I did but look upon the shine thereof.

Yet very eager was I to come to that warmth; and I made more
of haste than care, as I did hint; and so came very swift to the top of
the hollow; yet was still hidden by the kindness of the moss-bushes.

And as I made to thrust forward out of the bushes, that I might
look and go downward into the hollow, there rose up to me the sound
of a very large voice, and deep and husky. And the voice was a dreadful
voice that did speak as that it said ordinary things, and in a fashion so
monstrous as that it were that a house did speak, and, in verity, this
is a strange thing to say; yet shall it have the truth of my feelings and
terror in that moment.

And I drew back swiftly from discovering myself; and was then all

feared to move, or to make to go more backward, lest that I should give knowledge that I was come anigh. And likewise did I shiver lest that I was even then perceived. And so shall you have something of the utter fear that did shake me. And I abode there, very quiet, and moved not for a very great space; but did sweat and shake; for there was a monstrous horridness in the voice that did speak.

And as I crouched there within the moss-bushes, there came again the large voice, and it was answered by a second voice; and thereupon there arose, as it did seem, the speech of Men that must have the bigness of elephants, and that did have no kindness in all their thoughts; but were utter monstrous. And the speech was slow, and it rose up out of the hollow, brutish and hoarse and mighty. And I would that I could make you to hear it, and that you could but borrow mine ears for a little moment, and forthwith be shaken with that utter horror and an afraidness, even as was I.

Now, presently, there was a very long quiet, and I ceased at last a little from mine over-fear; and later I did calm somewhat; so that I made to shift my position, which was grown very uneasy.

And there was still no sound from the hollow. Wherefore, having a little boldness and much curiousness, and these despite my great fearfulness, I put forth mine hand, very cautious, and did move the moss-bush a little from my face. And I went forward upon the earth, and did lie upon my belly; and was by this so close upon the edge of that place, that I was abled to look downwards.

And you shall know that I peered down into that great hollow, and did see a very strange and horrid sight; for, in truth, there was a large fire-hole in the centre of that place, and all about the sides there were great holes into the slopes of the hollow, and there were great men laid in the holes, so that I might see a great head that did show out to my sight here, from one of those holes, and would seem to be that of a monstrous man heavy with sleep. And there I would see but the buttocks of another, as that he did curl himself inward to his brutish slumbering. And so was it all about; and to my memory there were maybe a score of these holes; yet had I not time to the counting, as you shall see. For, after that I had made but a glance, as it were, at these sleeping and utter monstrous men, I perceived that there sat beyond the fire-hole, three great men, and they were each greater than elephants, and covered a large part with a stiff and horrid hair, that did be of a reddish seeming. And there were upon them great segs and warts, as that their skin had been hides that had never known covering. And there was between them the body of a mighty hound,

so big as an horse, that they did skin; and I judged that this beast was one of those fearsome brutes which we did call the Night Hounds.

Yet, as I should set down, they did nothing in that time in which I lookt at them; but did sit each with a sharp and monstrous bloody stone in his fist, and did look to the ground, as that they heeded not the earth or the food that they did prepare; but did listen to some outward sound. And you shall know that this brought to me a very swift and sudden terror; for I perceived now the why of their long silence; for, in verity, they had an unease upon them, being subtly aware that one was anigh, even as are the brute beasts in this manner and kind, as all do know.

And I made to draw back, and win unto safety, if indeed this thing were to be done. And as I moved me, it may be that I shook a little earth into the hollow; for there was, indeed, a little sifting of dry dust below me, as I did wot, being very keen to hear, by reason of my fright. And immediately did those three monstrous men look upward, and did seem to me to stare into mine eyes, as I did lie there hid amid the moss-bushes. And I was so put in fear that I did clumsily, and sent another siftering of dust downward, as I did strive to go backward swift and quiet from the edge. And all the time I did look through the bushes very fixedly into the eyes of the giants; and lo, their eyes did shine red and green, like to the eyes of animals. And there rose up a roar from them that did nigh slay my soul with the horridness of the noise. And at that roaring, all the giants that did lie in the holes did awake, and began to come outward into the hollow.

Now, I was surely lost, and given over to destruction; for they had possessed me immediately; but that in that moment, as I went backward, the earth gave behind me, and I fell into a hole among the moss-bushes to my back, and I made first to come out very hurried, and all choked with a dust of sand and ash; but in a moment I was sane to know that I had come to a sudden hiding-place; and I lay very still and strove neither to cough nor to breathe. And well for me, I came to so close a hiding; for there were all about me the sounds of monstrous footsteps, running, that seemed to shake the ground; though maybe this to be an imagining bred of my fear.

And shoutings of great voices there were; and the thudding of huge feet all about; and the noises of the bushes rustling; but presently the search drew away to the Southward. And I perceived that there had surely fought for me some power of good fortune. And I came up out of the hole, very cautious, and shaken and a moment weak with the beating of my heart; yet with a lovely thankfulness for my salvation.

And I gat me about, and went swift through the moss-bushes to the North and West for three hours, and ceased not to run upon my hands and knees. And by that time was I come a great way, and did have a surety in my heart of present safety.

And I ceased to run, and lay quiet; for, in truth, I did near swoon away with the hardness of my travel. And indeed as you shall know, I had slept not for seven-and-twenty hours, and had scarce ceased to labour in all that time. Moreover, I had eat not, neither drunk, for nine hours; and so shall you conceive that I was truly a-weary.

And, presently I did slumber there as I lay, and all abroad to any monstrous thing that should come along. Yet did I wake unharmed, and found by my dial there had gone by a full ten hours, the while that I did lie there and sleep unwotting. And I was sore perished with the cold of the Night; for I had not the warmth of my cloak about me, and my belly was very empty.

And I stood me up, and did peer about for any dread matter; but all seemed proper, and I began to stamp my feet against the earth, as that I would drive it from me, and this I do say as a whimsy, and I swung mine arms, as often you shall do in the cold days; and so I was presently something warmed. And I dismantled my cloak, and wrapped it about me, and did feel that the Diskos was safe to my hip.

Then did I sit me down, and did glow a little with relish, in that I should now eat four of the tablets; for, indeed, these were my proper due, by reason of my shiftless fasting ere I came so wotless to my slumbering. And the memory of that eating doth live with me now, so that I could near to smile; for the eagerness of mine inwards was proper and human; yet were even four tablets but a little matter to so great an emptyness; and I drank a double portion of the water, that I might make less the void. And this thing was seemly; for, indeed, there were two portions due unto me.

And when I had eat and drunk, I did fold the cloak once more to shape across my shoulder, as I did carry it; and afterwards I took the Diskos into my hand, and went forward again to the North and West.

Yet, as you shall know, I did pause a little in the beginning, and peer to every side for any close danger; and then did look more abroad of that place; but could nowhere see any matter to have me to immediate fear. And afterwards, I looked a little while at the monstrous humped back of the Watcher of the North-West; and it did grow to me how steadfast that thing did look toward the Mighty Pyramid; and this set me to new hatred and horror of the Monster, as you shall conceive and believe.

And presently, I looked beyond the Watcher, unto the vast Mountain of the Great Redoubt; and I was still seeming close upon it; yet, in truth, gone a long and weariful distance. But this you shall understand was by the greatness and utter height and bulk of that shining Mountain of Life.

And strange and wonderful it was to me to think that even in that one moment, it might be that the dear Master Monstruwacan did look upon my face, through the Great Spy-Glass. And I should not seem utter far to him, by reason of the power of the big Glass. But to me, as I did look upward through the Night, unto that far and utmost light in the upper blackness of the everlasting gloom, it did seem doubly to me that I was afar off and lost forever from mine Home. And this thinking did breed in me such a great and lonesome feeling, and a weakness of the heart and spirit, that forthwith I took my courage close unto me, and did turn away quickly; and went onward to the North and West, as I have told.

Now I walked for twelve hours, and in that time, did eat and drink twice; and made onward again very steadfast, and happy that all did go so quiet with me; so that it was as if I had at last come to a part of the Land that was given over to quietness, and lacking of monsters. Yet, in truth was I come to a worse place than any, maybe; for as I went forward, striding very strong, and making a good speed, I did hear presently a little noise upward in the night, and someways unto my left, that had seeming as that it were a strange low sound that did come down to me out of an hidden doorway above; for, indeed, though the sound did come from very nigh, as it did seem no more than a score feet above my head, yet was it a noise that did come out of a great and mighty distance, and out of a Foreign Place. And I did know the Sound; though never, as you may suppose, could I have heard it in all my life. Yet had I read in one of the Records, and again in a second and a third, how that certain of all they that had adventured from the Pyramid into the Night Land to seek for knowledge, had chanced to hear a queer and improper noise above them in the Night; and the noise had been strange, and did come from but a little way upward in the darkness; yet was also from a great and monstrous distance; and did seem to moan and hum quietly, and to have a different sounding from all noises of earth. And in the Records it was set forth that these were those same Doorways In The Night, which were told of in an ancient and half-doubted Tale of the World, that was much in favour of the children of the Pyramid, and not disdained by certain of our wiser men, and had been thus through all the latter ages.

And I did seem to know the sound upon the moment; for my heart grew swift to understand. And it was a very dread uncomfortable sound; and you shall know how it did seem, if you will conceive of a strange noise that doth happen far away in the Country, and the same noise to seem to come to you through an opened door near by. And this is but a poor way to put it; yet how shall I make the thing more known to you? So that I must even trust unto your wit and true sympathy that you shall conceive of the fullness of my meaning.

Now, in all the Histories of those that had adventured into the Night Land, there were but three sure Records that did concern this Sound; and each did tell of a Great Horror; and of them that did hear the Sound there had died the most part, out in the Night Land. And the Records did make always that they had come upon Destruction, and not simply unto Death; but were destroyed by a strange and Invisible Evil Power from the Night.

And of those that came alive unto the Pyramid, they had all one strange tale to tell, how that there were secret and horrid Doorways In The Night. Yet how this thing could be plain to them, who may know truly; save it be that the eyes of their spirits did behold that which was hid to the eyes of the flesh.

And there was afterwards writ a proper and careful treatise, and did set out that there did be ruptures of the Æther, the which did constitute doorways, as those more fanciful ones did name them; and through these shatterings, which might be likened unto openings— there being no better word to their naming—there did come into this Particular Condition Of Life, those Monstrous Forces Of Evil, that did dominate the Night, and which many did hold surely to have been given this improper entrance through the foolish and unwise wisdom of those olden men of learning, that did meddle overfar with matters that did reach in the end beyond their understanding. And this thing have I told before, and it doth seem proper unto my belief; for it is always thus, and I have that same taint within me, as must all that have the zest of life.

Now, by this that I have set down swiftly, to make a little clear the sure horridness of this Sound, you shall know, even with me, the great horror that did come immediately upon my Spirit; and I did know that my Search was surely like to have an end in that moment; and I bared mine arm, for my teeth, where the Capsule did lie below the skin; and so was ready to an instant Death, if that Destruction did come upon me. And in the same moment, I did fall silent, inward among the moss-bushes, and did begin to creep very quiet toward the right;

for, as you will mind, I had heard the Sound over beyond my left. And all that time, as I did creep, there was a great sickness upon me, and it did seem that my mouth had weakened unto water; so that I could scarce hold my teeth tightly from unseemly clitterings.

And I crept always very silent, and did often stare quick and painful over my shoulder, upwards, and this way and that; but did never see anything; neither could I hear now the Sound.

And I went thiswise for a great hour, and was like to faint through the effort of my care and the soreness of my going. But upon the end of that long while, I grew something easier in the Spirit, and did perceive that I was saved from the Destruction that I had come so dreadful anigh. And this thing, it may be, was because that I did chance to hear it, whilst yet it was beyond, and before I did come right unto it, to pass below. Yet may I be wrong in this thought, and do but make a guessing. But, as I shall here explain; after that time, I kept mine ears newly keen unto hearing; and did chide my Spirit, for that it had not taken account of that Sound a great while earlier. Yet, as I did presently conceive, the spirit had no power to hear that thing; which was very strange; but truly so.

Now, because that I went with a very wary hearing, I heard the Sound once a far way off before me, and I hid upon the moment, and went backward, and after a while, did judge myself to have come unto safety; and so it was, in verity; for I heard no more that time. And so did I come presently unto the eighteenth hour, and did eat and drink, and made me a place of slumber in a little hollow of a rock that stood upward out of the moss-bushes. And I slept for six hours, and afterwards waked, and was come to no harm.

And after I had eat and drunk again, I did look outward over the Night Land, and with particularness to that part that I did travel in, as it might be called, the yesterday. And I did observe it to be a very bleak and desolate Country, and not given over to fire, or other warmth, nor to sulphur-vapours; but to be very quiet, and with but a little light in all its breadth. And I could conceive that it was no place for anything of life to desire; but rather to avoid; and that Country did seem to be yet all about me; for I was by no means come clear from it at that time; though, Northward, there was a glimmer, as of fire-holes; and beyond those, the strange shining of the Plain of Blue Fire.

And, after that I had thought awhile, I did believe that I should meet no Monster of Natural Life in all that Country of Desolation, until I did draw nigh, once more unto fire. And I conceived that this Sound from out of the invisible Doorways might yet trouble me; but

whether the quietness of that part was because all of natural life did fear the Sound, or because that there was neither fire nor warmth, I do not say, having no knowing in this matter; but may yet believe that it was to be laid to both causes; and this doth seem of common reason, as you shall agree.

And when I had looked a while unto the Mighty Pyramid, which was now truly a great way off; for I had walked so many weary hours; I turned me once more to my journeying. And here let me observe that I had gone very far; yet not so distant, as might be thought; for, oft, I did go less than one mile in an hour or maybe two hours, having to be of great caution, and oft to hide, and to go upon my belly, or to crawl, all as might be. And, further, as you may have perceived, I made not a straight forwardness; but did strike this way and that way, being very intent to escape the Monsters and Evil Forces that were all about.

Now, because that I believed that I travelled in a Place where was surely to be discovered those strange Doorways within the Night, I made an especial care of my going; and did stop oft that I might listen, and watch, and keep a very strict ward in all the Night about me. Yet, as you shall see, this served not to prevent me from going forward into the fearfulness of that which did haunt all the void; for, sudden, as I went carefully, I heard a faint humming noise come downward from the night a little unto my rear; and the humming noise did grow more plain, as that a door were opened slowly above, and did let out that Sound ever more loud. And surely, after I did hear that, I could not doubt that a door were opened upward there; for the noise did grow in such wise as you shall hear a distant sound come through, when a door truly is oped; for, if the noise had been made just in that place, it had seemed to come from there; but this Sound, though it did come through there, was as that it did come outward from some far lost and foreign Eternity. And this I do struggle always to make plain; and you shall not blame me that I think overmuch upon it; for, in truth there was an horror so wondrous and drear about it, that I can forget not; but do strive always that others should know with me that peculiar woe and terror that did haunt the night.

Now, as you will see, I had in truth gone past the place where the Doorway in the Night did open; yet had come to no harm; but rather it did seem that it opened by chance, unwotting that I was anigh; or it may be that my quiet passing did disturb an Evil Power, so that it did even come to listen, or to make search. And all this doth pass through my brain, as I do write, and it doth seem to me that my thoughts are but the thoughts of a little child, before so great a mystery; and that

I touch not even the edge and fringe of the truth with my thinkings, and so do cease upon them; and will but go forward so plain as I may with my telling. Now, as you may truly believe, when I heard that Sound, and did understand that I had, in verity, come past beneath that Place, I did surely sicken to an utter weakness of body and heart, though it was but for a moment; and then was I swift hid within the close shelter of the low and thick moss-bushes.

And I shook in all my being, and crept, shaking, upon my hands and knees, and did near totter to my face thrice, so weak gone was I in that moment of terror; and I did have a wickedness of forgetting in that time; for I bared not mine arm, to have the Capsule to a readiness for my death, if that did need to be; and this was an abominable foolishness, and I do shake now when I think upon it; for Death is but a little matter by the side of Destruction; though, in truth, dreadful enough for all. Yet, as it did chance, no harm came to me, and I gat away, as that some wondrous power did cast a viewless cloak about me, that I might be utter hid; and oft have I wondered whether this was truly so; but have no knowing.

And, presently, I ceased from fleeing, and had some calmness, and did eat and drink; and so came to the comfort of a firm spirit, the which had been sore troubled, above all understanded causes, by that horrid sounding upward in the Night. And after that I had eat and drunk, I did rest a little; but afterward, went onward to the Northward, going towards that place where the fire-holes did glimmer, the same being by this time no great way off.

Then, as I did come anigh, I thought to hear once again the Sound in the night, and I stopt very swift, and hid into the moss-bushes, and did listen; but did hear naught; and so was hopeful that fancy did play upon me. Yet, because of this matter, I went upon my hands and knees for a good way; and so came at last nigh unto the shine of one of those fire-holes, the which I did see for so long.

Now, as you shall suppose, I went very cautious through the bushes, unto that red-shining fire; being careful, both that I did attract not any Evil Force that might listen in the Night, and because that there might be some Monster nigh to the fire-hole. But, presently, when I was come so that I could peer through the bushes, I did see a little fire-hole set in a small hollow, and there did no thing seem to lurk anigh; and the sight of that warmth did cheer me; for it was long since I did have the comfort of such a matter.

And when I had lain hid awhile, that I might watch all about, I saw the place to be safe and quiet; and I went out from the moss-bushes,

and sat down a space from the fire, which did fill the pit in which it did lift and bubble. And the noise that it sent out was strange and slow, and it did seem to gruntle gently unto itself in that lonesome hollow, as that it had made a long and quiet grumbling there, through Eternity. And oft was it still, and made no sound; and again would give an odd bubbling in the quietness, and send off, as it did seem, a little smoke of sulphur, and afterward fall once more upon a quiet.

And so I did sit there very hushed and restful, and the loneliness did lie all about me, and the red shine of the fire-hole did glow soft in the hollow; and I was glad to be quiet, for my heart was weary.

And there was to my back a little rock that did jut upward so high as a man; and the rock was warm and pleasant to lean upon, and moreover did seem to guard me from behind. And there I eat and drunk, and kept very still; and so was presently rested. And this I did need, as you have perceived; for I was gone sudden weary of the heart, as I did say; and this might be because that I did never cease to have Destruction over me to companion my way; though as you will mind, I had been no more than twelve hours afoot, since my last sleeping. Yet I doubt not you do understand.

And presently my heart grew strong again within me, and I had a warmth in my Spirit; and I got up from the earth, and stretched out mine arms; and I saw that my gear was safe upon me, and afterward did grip the Diskos, as it were newly.

Then I went away from the fire-hole, and climbed the far slope of the hollow, and went Northward. And there were before me many of the fire-holes; for I did perceive them to shine in the Night for a great way; as it did seem that they were a path of red shinings that led me onward to the North-West of the light of the Plain of Blue Fire.

Now, I had a believing that I had come out of the Country where did lurk those horrid Doorways in the Night; and I went not with so utter a weight upon my heart; and did feel that naught should come now upon the back of my neck, which had been an odd and trouble-some fancy whilst that I did creep through that Country of Gloom. Yet, as you shall know, I went with no foolish confidence; but with a great caution, and mine hearing keen to hark, and a care to my steps, and did ever watch around me as I journeyed.

And because that I went forward in this proper and sedate manner, I had great cause for a thankful heart, as you may perceive; for I had come after a long way to another of those hollows where did burn one of the fire-holes; and I made a pause upon the edge of the hollow in which it did lie, and looked downward, keeping guarded within the

moss-bushes, where they grew anigh to the top thereof. But there was no living thing there to be seen, and I went downward, so that I should warm my body at the fire. And lo! as I stood upon this side of the fire-hole, and turned myself about, I looked presently more keenly to the other side; for the yellowness of the earth did seem a little strange in one place. But I could see with no plainness, because that there arose a glare from the fire against mine eyes; and I went round, that I should look the better; yet with no fear or thought of Evil in my heart. And, truly! when I was come upon that far side of the fire-hole, lo! there was spread out in the yellow sand of that place, a Curious Thing; and I went more nigh, and stooped to look upon it; and behold it moved, and the sand all about did move for a great space; so that I gave back very swift, and swung upward with the Diskos.

And, strangely, I heard the sand to stir at my back, and I looked round very quick, and the sand rose upward in parts, and sifted back, and there came to my sight odd things that did move and curl about.

And immediately, before I knew which way to go, I knew that the sand did shift under my feet, and did work and heave, so that I was tottered, and was shaken also in the heart; for I knew not what to think in that instant. Then did I perceive that I was all surrounded, and I ran swift upon the heaving sand, unto the edge of the fire-hole, and I turned there, and looked quickly; for I did not know what this new Terror should be.

And I saw that a Yellow Thing did hump upward from out of the sand, as it had been a low hillock that did live, and the sand shed downward from it, and it did gather to itself strange and horrid arms from the sand all about it. And it stretched two of the arms unto me; but I smote with the Diskos, and I smote thrice; and afterward they did wriggle upon the sand. But this was not the end, as I did hope; for the Yellow Thing arose, and ran at me, as it might be that you should see a spider run. And I did leap backward, this way and that; but the monster had a great swiftness; so that I did seem surely lost.

Then made I a strong and instant resolve; for I perceived that I had no hope to slay this thing; save that I should come at it in the body. And I put everything to the chance, and made not to escape any more; but ran straight in among the legs; and there were great hairs like to spines upon the legs, and these had pricked me to the death, but that the armour saved me.

Now, I had done this thing with a wondrous quickness; so that I was under the mighty arching of the legs before the Yellow Thing did wot of my intent. And the body was bristled with the great hairs, and

poison did seem to come from them, and to ooze from them strangely in great and shining drops. And the Monster heaved itself up to one side, that it might bring certain of the legs inward to grasp me; yet in that moment did I smite utter fierce with the Diskos—thrusting. And the Diskos did spin, and hum, and roar, and sent out a wondrous blaze of flame, as that it had been a devouring Death; and it sundered the body of the Yellow Thing, and did seem as that it screamed to rage amid the entrails thereof; so wondrous was the fury and energy of that trusted Weapon.

And I was covered with the muck of the thing; and the claws upon the legs seized me, so that the grey armour did bend and crack to the might thereof, and I grew sick unto death with the pain within; but smote with the shining Diskos, using my left hand weakly; for my right was gript dreadful fast to my body. And lo! I was sudden free, and a great blow did knock me far across the hollow, so that I was like to have fallen into the fire-hole; but fell instead upon the edge, and came backward unto safety.

And I turned me about, and the Yellow Thing did throw the sand all ways, as it did die; but had lost power to come upon me. And for my part, I lay weak upon the earth, and was no more able to fight; nor could I do more than breathe for a great while; but yet came presently to health, and made to examine my hurts.

Then I saw there was no great wound anywhere upon me; but only an utter bruising; and I found upon my right leg that there was a sharp and hairy claw clipt about it; but the armour had saved me from harm of the horrid thing; so that I did but kick it free with my left foot, and thence into the fire-hole.

Now, by this time, that Monstrous Creature was dead; but I held off from it, and went upon the other side of the fire; for I was yet surely in horror of it. And I sat for a time, and did think upon all matters that did concern me; and I saw that I should have not comfort of heart, until I was washed clean from the taint of the Monster.

And I gat me up wearily to go forth into the Night again, that I should make a search for a hot spring, of which I had come past many. And I had oft found them to be nigh unto the fire-holes; so that I was trustful that I should see one ere long. And lo! there was a little hollow just beyond, and scarce a hundred paces off; and in the hollow, there did shine three small fire-holes, and there was a steaming puddle, as did seem, beyond the third of the holes.

Now, before I adventured downward into this place, I went all about the topmost edge, and made a search of the moss-bushes

about; but found naught that should scare me. And afterward, I went all across the hollow; but did find no monstrous thing hid anywheres. Yet, there was that in the place that discouraged me, and did keep me from stripping mine armour, so that I should bathe in the hot puddle; for I stept upon a small serpent, and the same did lap about my leg; but could do me no hurt, for the armour, which was a very blessed protection. And I freed myself from it with the handle of the Diskos.

And because that I could not go naked to my cleansing, I tried first the hotness of the water, which was not over great, and afterward did take off the scrip and the pouch, and the cloak, and laid them with the Diskos upon the edge of the warm puddle.

Then I stept into the water, and was immediately gone downward a great way; for, truly it was no puddle as I had supposed; but a deep well, as you might call it, of hot and sulphury water. And this doth show how a man may act foolishly, even when he doth believe that he hath a great caution; and surely it is borne in upon me afresh that none should trust over freely unto unproven matters, the which shall you heartily agree with; but yet do as foolishly, according to your lights and characters. And so shall you laugh not over hardly upon me.

Now I had gone over the head, and, surely I do not know what deepness was there. Yet, as you shall think, I stayed not to consider upon this matter; but made to climb out, and much shaken with my splutterings and the smartings of mine eyes; for, truly, the water was strong with sulphur matters. Yet, very cleansing was it, as I did presently see; for there was no more any taint or horridness upon mine armour, or the flesh of my face or hands. And I took the Diskos, and washed it clean, also; and then the cloak, and afterward the scrip and the pouch, and the bands of the same.

And after I had done this, I was minded to dry myself by the little fire-holes; but when I was come there, lo! maybe a score small serpents were about those places; and I was strongly pleased that I should keep away. Yet that I must warm and dry me in that desolate and bitter Night Land, you shall agree. And to this end, I put the scrip and the pouch upon me, and afterwards took the Diskos readily into my hand, and ran quietly unto the hollow where I did fight with the Yellow Thing. And the cloak I bore in my left hand.

Now, when I was gat there, I was truly glad to think that there were no serpents in that place; and because that I had slain the Monster of the Place, how should it be that any harm might come unto me; for truly, was it not like that a Creature of such Might should keep all that Hollow unto itself, and slay any that did come therein, and thereby

preserve that place from all other horror; though, surely, until it did die and cease to Be, there had been no call for any greater abomination.

Now, all this did go through my brain, as I did sit to dry mine armour and my body and my gear, upon that side of the fire-hole which was away from the slain Monster. And I made presently to think that this would be a sure and proper refuge wherein to sleep; for, truly, it must have gotten a place where none other Creature should be like to come to work me harm. And it must be that you do all see with me in this matter, and commend me that I thought with properness.

And so did I resolve that I put my disgust within my pocket, as we do say, and stay safe and quiet within that Hollow. And this thing I did surely, and did eat and drink; and presently I went over to the dead Monster, and made very sure that it was truly slain; which indeed it was. And after that I had seen to this matter, I returned unto the fire-hole, and made a comfortable place in the sand, for my rest; for I was well dry by this.

And I wrapped the cloak about me, and took the Diskos to my breast, for a sure Companion, as it had truly proved in my need. And I could think almost that it did nestle unto me, as that it knew and loved me; but this thing can be no more than a fancy; and I do but set it down as such, and that it doth show my feeling and mind at that time.

Then, ere I did compose myself to slumber, I looked about me, upward to the edges of the Hollow, and I perceived that I was lost to the sight of the Mighty Pyramid; for I was come so far off that it looked not down from so wondrous a height, as you shall perceive; and moreover, the Hollow was something deep.

And afterward, as I lay my head back upon the scrip and the pouch, which were to me my pillow, I went to think a little upon Naani, as alway I did in my constant journeying; yet, presently, I strove sometimes that I put her from my mind, that I should sleep; for a bitter sorrow and anxiousness was oft upon me when that I did think upon her; and this you may know; for truly I knew not what terror was come to her, afar in the silence of the Night. And did I think overmuch, I should feel that I could have no calmness needful to sleep; but to need to walk for ever until I died, which could not be long; and so should I make a foolishness of mine anxious journeying to do her true service and to save her from Destruction, if such did truly threaten.

And I was soon gone over to sleep, and waked not for seven hours, being much wearied by the fight and the soreness of my body, the which did put me into a great pain as I did rise upward from my slumber. But this was presently something less, and I eat two of the

tablets and drank some of the water, and afterward did put my gear upon me, and went forward into the Night, having the Diskos in my hand. And my heart was glad that I had come safe through the time of my sleep.

Now I walked six hours, and did stop a little to eat and drink, and went on again. And it was in this second Third of the day that I saw afar to my right, two strange and wondrous men, and they did shine, as they had been made of a pale mist. And they came anigh, going very swift, and did seem as that they were maybe forty feet high, yet having no thickness; and I hid downward into the moss-bushes. And they past me, so quiet as a cloud of this day might go, and did appear to be, if I did guess, but an hundred fathoms off; yet was this no sure thing; for their position had no more surety than shall a rainbow have in this age. And so they were gone onward into the Night, and did seem to come out of the North. And they did appear not to wot of me; and whether they were harmful, I know not, for they harmed not me.

And I lay there in the moss-bushes, until they were well gone away; and I had belief that they must be those same mist-men that were told of in certain of the olden Records; but were never seen anigh to the Pyramid; though I had thought, odd times, to see men, as of mist, through the Great Spy-Glass, when I was within the Tower of Observation. But they were always a mighty way off; and some would say it was but a bright vapour that did move; yet would others be in doubt, and so is it ever in such matters.

And here let me take chance to say how that it is a hard thing to speak of such happenings to men of this age, and to make the truth proper unto them; and because of this, oft am I tempted to say no word upon many things that I did see; yet must I tell my tale, or suffer from the weight of it within me. And so shall you hark to me and give me your sympathy and human understanding.

And concerning these mist-men, I have wondered oft whether they were the visible shape of some of those many Forces that were abroad in the Night Land; for they did truly seem to me as that a thing of Strange Life were half shown to my human eyes; yet I do not know, and am but telling of my natural thoughts and ponderings.

Now, as I did say, those mist-men were never seen nigh unto the Pyramid, and were, as I did hint, always so far off that they were half given over to the fables of the olden days, in the beliefs of the Peoples of the Mighty Redoubt; and set about with an halo of unrealness, for none within the Great Pyramid had ever beheld them with surety.

And because that now I saw them anigh to me, it was borne in

afresh upon my spirit how greatly I had wandered away, and how that I stood afar in the lonesomeness of that Land of Night; as it had been that a man of this Age did wander amid the stars, and perceive a great comet to go by him very close; for then he should know in his heart how that he was far off in the Void. And this I do say to you, that you may know somewhat of the emotions of my heart in that moment.

Yet, presently I shook free of my melancholy and lonesomeness and rose up out of the moss-bushes, and went onward. And, as ever, I thought much upon the Maid that I did search for; yet strove to think quietly concerning her state; else should I have turned to running, and wrecked my body before that I had gone any great way.

And that day, I passed seven large fire-holes, and two that were small; and always I came softly unto them; for there were oft living things about the warmth. And at the sixth fire-hole, I did see that which I did think to be a great man, that did sit to the fire, with monstrous knees drawn upward unto his chin. And the nose was great and bent downward; and the eyes very large, and did shine with the light from the fire-hole, and moved, watching, always this way and that, so that the white parts did show, now this side and now that. But it was not properly a man.

And I went away very quiet from that place, and looked oft backward, until that I was sure of safety; for it was a very horrid Monster, and had that place to be for a Lair, as I did judge from the smell thereof.

And when the eighteenth hour was come, I looked about for a safe place to my sleep; and I kept away now from the fire-holes; for I did always find the more life there. Yet, when I came to my rest, I was lacking of warmth, by reason of this care; and could scarce sleep at all, because that I was so cold. Yet managed something of slumber after a while; but woke very stiff, and was glad to beat my hands and bestir myself that I should come to some warmth of life.

And after that I had eat and drunk, I put my gear upon me, and took the Diskos in my hand, and went forward again upon my journey. And here I should tell that I was come soon unto the North-West border of the Plain of Blue Fire. And presently, I was but a little way off from it, and did go direct to the North; so that the Plain was always upon my right.

Now this Plain was a strange and fearsome place, as you shall see; for it was as that a blue void did rise upward from the earth in all the country of that Plain. For, surely, the Plain did not lumber with flame; but was hid with a strange and inburning light, as of a shining atmosphere of a cold blue colour. And it did throw no sure light upon

the Night Land, as had seemed proper; but was a very dreadful, cold shining, as of a luminous and blue void. And the moss-bushes grew nigh to the edge of the plain, and did show to me black and strange against that horrid gloom of light.

And you shall know that I could not see into the plain; for it was as that the cold blue light was a void that swallowed all within it; and gave no power to the eye that aught should be perceived. And it stood between me and the Mighty Pyramid, and I could nowise see across. And I know not whether I do make all this matter clear unto you; for surely it is no easy task.

And presently I had gone very quiet upon my hands and knees through the moss-bushes; and I came near upon the edge of the Plain, and hid there in a clump of the moss-bush, and peered forth and harked. And I heard constant voices that did call to one another across the Plain; as it were that strange peoples of Spirits did wander within that blue Shining, and did make a calling one to the other, and were all hid and held apart. And surely I could see naught, and did judge, as I have writ, that they likewise went blindly. And truly is this a strange matter to set out; and easy to think on with doubt. Yet as I did see, so have I told; for, in verity, there were surely hidden Peoples of Spirits scattered and lost afar upon that improper Plain.

And you shall judge that I kept safe hid; for whether this might have any natural explaining, or whether it was a matter that did go utter beyond knowledge of man, I did not know; for surely in that strange Land, it did like to be an Horrid Danger in any case; and whether of some Monstrous Creatures, or of the Evil Forces of the Land, I did wisely to be away.

And for two days I did make a safe coasting of the Plain of Blue Fire; and did keep well off, maybe two great miles, among the moss-bushes. And I made a very good speed through the darkness. And at the eighteenth hour of each journey, I made a place for my slumber; and the first I did manage under a thick bush; but the second was high upon the ledge of a rock that grew upward in the night amid the bushes. And, save that I was bitter cold there did no harm come to me. And in all that time of journeying, I had no sight of the Mighty Pyramid; for the blind shining of the Plain of Blue Fire was ever between.

Now there had been certain little matters in my journey beside the Plain of Blue Fire, which I have not set down; for they were of no account, and do but repeat much that I have told before. And, indeed, there was naught in that part of my journey, save that I did pass nineteen great fire-holes, and four small; and did observe no life

beside any, save about one of the great holes that there was no hollow around, and here I did happen to see some strange and ugly creatures so big as my head, that did have a look of the scorpion of this Age; but proportioned more squat and thick. Yet, though they were naught to remark upon in that Land, they had been but woeful bedmates to any man; as you may think.

And you shall know how it gave a rest to my spirit, that I did go so long with no trouble of the Monsters of the Night, or the Evil Forces thereof. And I grew bolder to my journeying, and made ever a greater speed of going; and it was like that I took presently a less heed for my safety, which was a wrong and foolish state. Yet there came no harm unto me, in all that part of my travel.

Then, it was in the sixteenth hour of the third day of my journey beside the Plain, that I did come out beyond the end of it, and had fresh sight of the Mighty Pyramid, afar in the night upon my Right. And I stopt there in a bare place among the moss-bushes, and did in a weak moment hold up the Diskos, so that I make a salute unto the Pyramid, Mine Home; for truly was I so utter glad to behold it once more.

And in a little while was I aware that there was a disturbance of the æther of the world all about me; so that it did seem that there had been one at the Great Spy-Glass to watch for my coming into their sight from behind the shining of the Plain of Blue Fire.

And it was like that news had gone downward through the Cities of the Great Redoubt; so that they did print the word of it in the Hour-Slips; and by this there would be many great Millions thinking upon me, and a rushing unto the Embrasures, that they might spy out at me. Yet I doubt that any glass might perceive me surely at so great a space, save the power of the Great Spy-Glass in the Tower of Observation. But the Emotion of the Millions to reach to me.

And you shall know that it did seem homely and sweet unto me to hear all about me the shaking of the æther of the world, and to be ware that so many did think humanly upon me, and had prayers unto my safety.

And it was a strange thing to stand so utter far off in the Night, and to look back to that Everlasting Hill of Light, that was grown something small by the distance, and to have surety that I was lookt upon through the Great Spy-Glass, maybe by the kindly eye of my dear friend the Master Monstruwacan, and so keenly that he could, it might be, make almost to guess the look within mine eyes, as I did gaze backward unto that Mine Home.

Yet, though this dear and homely sympathy was a sweet and com-

panionable thing to my heart, it came swift to my thought that I was in a sore danger, if that they ceased not quickly to think so onely upon me; for surely was I not come over-near unto that dreadful House of Silence; and well might so much Emotion of the Millions tell unto the Horrid Power that dwelt within, how that I was even anigh. And so shall you see the mixt feelings that came upon me everyway.

Yet, as it did chance, the æther was quieted in a little; for it did need unity of the Millions (being that they were untrained to their spiritual powers) to stir the æther. And so was I more easy of mind, and went forward again upon my way.

Now, as it did chance, at the eighteenth hour, I was come to a place where I heard a noise of water; and I went to my left, that I might come upon it; and there boiled a hot fountain that went up out of the rock of that place. And the water rose upward in a column, and was, maybe, so thick as my body; and it fell unto the North, for the water came not up straightly; but did shoot out from the earth unto that way. And I saw the thing plain; for there were many fire-holes all about, as you shall have wotted from my telling; and so was there a certain and constant light in that part of the Land.

And I followed the water that ran from the fountain, and tried it with mine hand; but found it to burn; and so did go further beside it; for presently it should be no hotter than I did need. And it went onward, winding among the moss-bushes, and sent up a constant steam, that hung about it; and the steam made a red cloud about the way that it did go; for the lights from the fire-holes made a shining upon it; and so was it a wondrous pretty sight.

Now, presently, I tried the stream again, and found it to be nicely warm; and I sat upon a little rock, and took off my foot-gear, that I might bathe my feet, which were gone something tender; moreover, I did ache to have the sweetness of water about me. And I made that I should bathe my feet, and afterwards find a place among the moss-bushes, and so eat and drink, and have my slumber.

Then, as I did sit there beside that warm stream, with my feet dabbled therein, I heard sudden, afar off, the voice of a mighty Night-Hound, baying in the night. And the sound came from the North-West of the Plain of Blue Fire. And there was afterward a quiet; and you shall see me sitting there upon the rock by the side of that smoking river, and the steam all about me, and my feet within the lovely warmth of the water; and I very still and frozen with a sudden fear; for, it did seem to me, in an instant, that the NightHound might surely be upon the track of my goings.

And after that there had passed a little time, the while that I did listen very keen, lo! there burst out in the night, as it did seem scarce a mile off, the monstrous deep baying of the giant Hound. And I knew surely that the Brute did track me, and a sick and utter horror did fall upon me; so that I could scarce get my foot-gear upon me, once more. Yet, in truth, I was not long to the matter, and was to my feet, and did hold the Diskos ready; and very desperate I was to the heart; for it is ever a fearsome thing to be put in chase, and the worse an hundred times when there is a sure knowledge that a deathly Monster doth be the pursuer.

Now, I did stand there but a moment it did seem, to make an anxious considering how that I might best assure me some chance to live through this swift coming Danger. And then did I think upon the stream, to use it, and I leapt quick therein, and did run very strong down the middle part, which was nowheres so much as thigh-deep, and oft not above mine ankles. And as I did run, there came again the bellow of that dire Brute, following, and was now, as mine ears did say, scarce the half of a mile to my rear.

And I did run but the stronger, for the dread of the sound; and so, maybe, for a little minute; and after that time, I stopt from mine heavy running, and went very wary, that I made no loud splashing; for by now the Monster-Brute should be something anigh to that place where I did enter the stream. And I looked round, with a constant looking; but did see no surely visible thing; though my fear did shape me an Hound from every shadow of the moss-bushes about me.

Then, in a moment, I did hear the Great Beast; for it bayed but a little way up the stream, as that it had overshot the place where the scent did end. And immediately, I sank swiftly into the water, which was there so deep as my knee, and turned upon my belly. And the water surged over my shoulders; for I kept my head above. And so I did look eager and fearful through the steam into the shadows and the half-darkness, towards where I did think to see the Night-Hound.

And in a moment I saw it coming; and it was a little vague, by reason of the smoke of the river; yet did seem black and monstrous in the gloom, and great as a mighty horse. And it went past me at a vast and lumbersome gallop; but I did not see it in that moment; for I dived my head down unto the rock of the river bottom, and held downward, until that I was like to burst for sore longing of breath.

Then I put upward my head, and took swift and deep breathings, and lookt about me, very cautious and fearful, as you can know. And I heard the Night-Hound casting round among the moss-bushes, and it

did send up a wild and awesome baying; and I heard the bushes brake and smash beneath it, as it did run to and hither. And afterward there was a quiet; yet I moved not; but stayed there, very low in the water, and did have a thankful heart that it was warm and easy to persist in; for I had surely died of a frozen heart, if that it had been cold; for, by this time, you do know even with me, how bitter was the chill of the Land.

Now, I had been awhile lain thus upon my belly, and heard no sound from the monstrous Hound. Yet, I ceased not to be full of an horrid unease, concerning the Great Beast; for I did better to know what it did, than to have no knowing. And, sudden, I heard the sound of it, running very swiftly and coming nigh; and it passed me, and did go up the stream; and there was surely a quick stupor upon me; for I ducked not my head under the water; but stayed very still; which as it did chance, was maybe not such an utter foolishness; for my head did seem in that half-gloom to be, mayhap, no more than a little rock in the water, and I made no move to tell of life; yet should the Hound have smelled me; and that it failed in this matter, doth be a puzzle to me.

And as the great Night-Hound past me, it tore the earth and the bushes, with the exceeding strength that it put forth to run, and clods of the earth and stones of bigness were cast this way and that by the feet of the Hound, running. And so shall you have a little knowledge of the strength of that Beast.

And the Hound ran on into the distance, and presently, I heard it baying in the Night. Then I rose, and went onward, down the warm stream, and made a strong walking, yet keeping alway to the water; and oft did stop a little that I should listen; and always I heard the Night-Hound a great way off in the night, baying, and seeming that it did surely run to and fro, searching.

Now, I journeyed thus for twelve hours, and the baying of the Hound making search, did never cease. And I kept always to the water, as I did say, that I should leave no scent unto the Hound. And by that twelve weary hours had gone, I found that I was come anigh unto the House of Silence. And this put me in great trouble; as you may perceive; for surely had mine whole effort been to the end that I should avoid that House, by a great way. Yet had the Hound driven me thus a-near.

Now I saw that the small river did go onward, and did make a breach across the Road Where The Silent Ones Walk; and I determined in my heart that I should leave the water, which was now grown nigh to a bitter cold, in that it was so long upon the face of the Land. Yet

chiefly did I mind to leave the water, that I should come no more anigh unto that House of Silence; for the water did go that way. And I stood awhile, and did listen for the baying of the Hound; but could hear it no more; and did have a surety within me that it was indeed gone from searching for me.

Then I came out of the water, and went forward, stooping and creeping, among the moss-bushes, going outward to the Westward of North, so that I should go away so quickly as I might from the nearness of the House. Yet, lo! I was gone upon my hands and knees no more than an hundred fathoms, when I did find the moss-bushes to cease to the Westward, for a great way, and there to be a great bareness of rock, which, in truth, was much shown thereabout. And I dared not to go outward upon that naked Land; for then I had not been hid by the moss-bushes; but had stood plain there for all things of the Night to behold; and moreover, though I could nowise have a sure knowledge concerning this matter, yet did I hope within me that I should make a sure hiding from the Power of the House of Silence, did I but go very low among the bushes. But, indeed, it was like enough that naught could give me hiding; yet should I lose no chance unto my safety.

And because of this, I went backward among the bushes, and ceased to escape out unto the Westward. And I found presently, that the moss-bushes made but a narrow growth in that path, and grew only for a while by the side of the Great Road; so that I was surely fain to keep nigh to the Road, that I have the covering of the bushes.

And, in a while, I found the Road Where The Silent Ones Walk, to bend inward at the North of the House of Silence; so that it came right horridly close unto the House; for here the hill on which the House did stand, was very abrupt and fell steeply unto the Road. And so was that Dreadful House stood up there above me in the Silence, as that it did seem to brood there upon the Land. And this side did seem truly as the other; and equal lone and dreadful.

And the House was monstrous and huge, and full of quiet lights; and it was truly as that there had been no Sound ever in that House through Eternity; but yet was it as that the heart did think each moment to see quiet and shrouded figures within, and yet never were they seen; and this I do but set down that I bring all home unto your hearts also, as that you crouched there with me in those low moss-bushes, there beside the Great Road, and did look upward unto that Monstrous House of Everlasting Silence, and did feel the utterness of silence to hang about it in the night; and to know in your spirits the quiet threat that lived silent there within.

And so shall you have mind of me, hid there among the bushes, and sodden and cold; and yet, as you will perceive, so held in my spirit by an utter terror and loathing and solemn wonder and awe of that Mighty House of Quietness loomed above me in the Night, that I wotted not of the misery of my body, because that my spirit was put so greatly in dread and terror for the life of my Being.

And also you shall have before you, how that I knew in all my body and soul, that I stood anigh to that Place where but a little while gone there had passed inward so dreadful to an everlasting Silence and Horrid Mystery those poor Youths.

And after that you have minded you of this, you shall consider how that the memory of all my life held dread thoughts of the monstrousness of that House; and now was I anigh unto it. And it did seem to my soul that the very Night about it, held an anguish of quiet terror. And always my mind did come back to the sheer matter that I was so anigh. And this thing I do say unto you once and again; for truly, as you do see, it hath imprinted itself deep into my spirit. Yet shall I now cease from saying further in this manner; for, surely, you shall never know all that was in mine heart; and if I cease not, I do but be like to weary you.

And so did I hide and creep, and oft pause to a time of shaking quiet; and afterward gather something of new courage, and go onward; and peer upward at that monstrous House, stood above me in the night. Yet, as it did come about, I came presently clear of that horrid place; for the Road came round again unto the North, and I began that I made a better way through the moss-bushes; but never that I grew to much speed; for I had oft to go about, that I should miss a naked part here, and another there; for truly there was an abundance and bareness of rock, so that the bushes grew not so thick as I could wish.

And in the space of five hours was I clear of that House; and did have a greater ease about my heart; but yet was not free to come to food nor to slumber, the both of which I did sorely need; for I had slept neither eat for a weariful time, as you do know. But first I must go further off from the House, and afterwards come to some firehole, that I should dry myself and get warmth again into my body, which was bitter cold.

And now that I had come unto the Northward of the House of Silence, there came to me a great Wonder, which bred in me a mighty Hope and Gladness. For as I did go among the bushes, there broke sudden all around me in the æther, the low and solemn beat of the Master-Word. And the throb of the Word was utter weak; so that one

moment I did say unto myself that I heard, and in a moment that I did not; yet had I no proper doubt in my heart.

And I reasoned with myself, and with a great shaking of excitement and expectation upon me, that the Master-Word came not from the Great Pyramid, which should have power to send it as a Great Force across the everlasting Night; whilst that this that throbbed about me was faint and scarce to be known even unto the keenness of the Night-Hearing, which was mine.

And, immediately, as I crouched low there, and thrilled with the hope that was bred in me, lo! there seemed to come the far faint voice of Naani, calling with a little voice within my spirit. And I thought the cry to have an utterness of supplication within it; so that I grew desperate to up and go to running; yet did curb such foolishness, and stayed very hushed, to listen.

But I heard no more; yet was shaken continually with the Joy and Hope which this calling did breed in me, for truly did it seem now that I was right that I did determine to go unto the North; for sure was I now that the Lesser Redoubt lay that way in the Night. And it did seem plain unto me, that the House of Silence had put a barrier between; and had power to withhold so weak a calling. And now had I come beyond the Barrier. And I did perceive in my heart how that Naani had called oft, maybe in the sadness of Despair; yet had the weak crying of her brain-elements been held from me by the horrid power of the House; and surely, as I did think, it was well named; for it did make a silence.

And so shall you stay with me in your hearts, and take to yourselves something of the new Gladness that held all my being; for it did seem truly that my bitter task and adventuring should not in the end be offered to Uselessness; and that I did truly draw unto that far place in the Everlasting Night, where mine own Maid did cry for me, that I should succour her.

And ever as I went, did I hark; but there was no more the low beating of the Master-Word in the Night; not at that time.

And presently, I spied outward to the West, as it did seem a good mile off in the night, the shining of a fire-hole; and I began to plan that I should come unto that place, and have warmth and dryness, and food and slumber. And, in verity, so set was I to the need of these matters that if there did be a Monstrous Thing nigh to the fire—as was so oft the case—then would I give battle unto it; for neither my Joy nor my labours did serve to put warmth into my body; and I must surely come anigh to fire, or die.

Then, as I kneeled upward among the moss-bushes, and made to lay a true course unto the fire-hole, I perceived that there came a Being along the Road unto my right; and I went low into the bushes, and moved not; for truly I had seen that there drew nigh one of the Silent Ones.

And I made a little place that should let me to see; and I spied out, with an utter caution; and lo! the Being came on very quiet, and with no hurry. And in a time, it went by me on the road, and did take no heed to me; yet did I feel that it had knowledge that I stoopt there among the moss-bushes. And it made no sound as it went; and was a Dreadful thing; yet, it did seem unto my heart, as that it had no trouble of Wanton Malice to work needless Destruction to any. And this, I crave strangely that you to understand; for it was so to me that I had a quiet and great respect for that thing; and did feel no hatred; yet was very dreadly in fear of it. And it was Huge in size, and was shrouded unto its feet, and seemed, maybe ten feet high. Yet, presently, it was gone onward down the Road, and I was no more troubled by it.

Then did I make no waste of time; but set off unto the fire-hole; and kept so much to shelter as I might; but was oft made to run over baked places, ere that I should come to more of the bushes.

And I came presently nigh unto the fire-hole, and made a pause, and crept unto it, with a great care. And I found it to be in the bottom of a deep hollow of the rock of that part. And the rock was clear looking of all living matters, the which did make me to be glad. And I went round about the top of the hollow, carrying the Diskos very handily; but there was nowhere any living thing; and I feared not to go downward into the deep hollow, and so unto the fire-hole, which lay in the bottom, as you have perceived.

And when I was come there, I made a close search of the rock, and found it was very sweet and warm; and there were no serpents, neither any stinging creatures; so that a certain comfort came upon my spirit.

Then stript I off mine armour and gear, and afterward all my garments, so that I stood naked there in the hollow. Yet was that place almost so warm as some mild oven, and I had no fear to suffer from the cold of the Night Land; but was uneasy lest that any monstrous thing should be anigh to come to take me so unawares.

Now I wrung the garments, and spread them upon the rock near unto the fire-hole, where it was hot; and I did rub my body very brisk with my hands, so that I glowed into health and had no fear of a stiffness.

And afterward, I did look to my food and drink, and to the matters

in the pouch; but there had no harm come to any, by reason of the tightness of the scrip and the pouch, that had kept off the water. And I eat and drank, there as I stood waiting for the garments to come to dryness; and I walked about a little, as I eat; for I was restless to be into mine armour swiftly. And now I did turn this garment upward of the dry side, and now that; but did find them to steam, so that I turned them many times before they were proper.

Yet, in truth, they dried in but a little while, and I gat me into them very swift, and into the armour; and I felt the strength and courage of my spirit to come back into me, which had gone outward somewhat when I did stand there so naked. And this feeling you shall all have understanding of; and know that you would have felt that way, likewise, had you but stood there in that Land in so unhappy a plight.

And when I had come into mine armour, I put my gear upon me, and took the Diskos into my hand, and did climb out of the hollow; for I would find a more secure place to my slumber, and did not dare to sleep in that place; for it was beyond seven and thirty hours since that I did have sleep; though as I do see by my count, I have made it to seem but as five and thirty; yet was a part consumed in diverse matters that I have not set down. And you shall mind how bitter had been my labour and weariness in all that time; and I did know of a surety that sleep must come heavily upon me; so that I was sorely in need that I should search out a safe place; for I should not be lightly waked, until that I had slept away the tiredness of my heart, and the weariful achings from my body. And, indeed, I should mind you how that I was not yet come perfect from the bruising which I had gotten from the fight with the Yellow Thing.

And presently, when I had searched but a little while, I did find that a rock stood upward from a great clumping of the moss-bushes unto my left; and I went over to the rock, and made a search about it. And I found that there was a hole into the bottom part of the rock, and I thrust the Diskos into the hole, and made the blade to spin a little, so that it sent out a light; but there was no thing in the hole, and it did seem a dry and safe place for my sleep.

Then I turned me about, and went into the hole with my feet that way; and I found that it was so deep into the rock as the length of two men, and just so wide as I could lie in it without having it to pinch me. And there I made my bed in the hole, and went swift unto my sleep, and scarce had but a moment even to think upon Naani; and by this thing shall you know how utter was my weariness.

Now I waked of a sudden, and was very clear and refreshed. And

I crept to the mouth of the hole, and lookt out; but there was all a quietness round about, and nothing to threaten.

And I found that I had slept ten hours; so that I made a haste to eat and drink, that I should go forward swiftly upon my journey. And at that time, as in the time when I did eat, naked, in the hollow, by the fire-hole, I eat four of the tablets; and this you shall understand to be rightly due unto me, in that I had gone so long fasting in that my great journeying to come safe from the Hound, and to come past the House of Silence. And this shall seem but a little thing to you; yet was it a wondrous important matter unto me, that had gone so long with an empty belly, and was never satisfied. And neither should any be, that had eat so little as I did eat, and made to fill their belly always with a drink of water. Yet, I doubt not but that it did keep my soul sweet and wholesome and no useful thing to the Powers of Evil of the Land.

And when I had made an end of so great a gorging, and had ceased to be drunken with water, I gat my gear upon me, and took the Diskos into mine hand, and so went forth once more towards the North.

And presently, I was nigh unto the Road again; for it did curve something Westward a space beyond. And I was sore tempted to go upon the Road; for the ground was rough and the moss-bushes did catch my feet. Yet did I stay among the bushes, though the Road was true and smooth, by compare. And by this telling, you will perceive that I walked once more upright, and had given over to crawl between the bushes. And, in truth, this was so; for the Land did seem very quiet in all that part; and I had less of fear, now that I stood beyond the horrid unease of the House of Silence.

Now, after that I had journeyed twelve hours, I saw that I was come upon the commencement of a great and mighty slope, as that the world did slope downward always towards the North. And I went on again, after that I had eat and drunk, as I did likewise before this at the sixth hour of that day's journey.

And presently, I perceived the Road to cease; and surely this did confound me; as that a man of this age had come to a part where the world did end; for you shall know that the Road was that which had seemed to go on for ever; and you shall mind the way of my life up till that time, and so shall you the better conceive of my bewilderment, and as it were a feeling of great strangeness unto one that was overprest, as you would believe, with strange matters.

Yet, truly, was this all as the little book of metal had told unto me; and so should I have been something prepared; yet are we ever thus needing eye-proof; and perhaps it is more proper that it be so.

Yet, you shall perceive me adrift somewhat as to direction; for I had steered before this time so that I should come to the North of the House of Silence; and afterward had shaped my way by the Road. But now was I adrift, as it might be set down, in the wilderness.

And so did I stand and consider, and presently did look unto the far Pyramid, which was now a great way off in the night, and had seemed but small by that which I knew it to be. And lo! as I did look, I perceived that I could but see the high upper-point of the light of the Great Pyramid, where did shine the Last Light; and I was confounded afresh; yet in a moment I saw that the greatness of the slope did account for this. But here I should tell to you that the slope was nowise steep; but did seem as that it should never cease. And mayhaps this is clear unto you.

And I perceived surely that the time was come when I should make an utter parting from the Great Redoubt; and the thought came very heavy upon me. And in the same time I knew that the æther was stirred by the emotions of the Millions; so that I had knowledge they watched me with the Great Spy-Glass, and did send word down unto the Hour-Slips; and by this did the Millions know, and have a great thinking upon me in that moment.

And you shall perceive how utter lost and lonesome I did feel. And it was at that time that I did test the compass, to comfort me, as I did tell before this, and feared I must sure forget, when I did come to the proper place; yet have I minded me, as I did desire.

And I saw now that the Night Land that I did wot of, was hid from me by the slope. And I turned and looked down the slope; and surely all before me was utter wildness of a dark desolation; for it did seem to go nowhither but into an everlasting night. And there was no fire down there, neither light of any kind; but only Darkness and, as I did feel, Eternity. And downward into that Blackness did the great slope seem to go for ever.

Now, as I did stand there, looking downward into the Dark, and often backward unto the shining of the Final Light, and put to a horrid desolateness, behold! there came the low beating of the Master-Word in the Night. And it did appear as that it had been sent to give me courage and strength in that moment; and did seem unto my fancy that surely it did come upward unto me from out of the mighty blackness into which the Great Slope ran. Yet could this have been but a belief; for the æther doth have no regard unto direction to show you whence the spiritual sound doth come; and this did my knowledge and Reason know full well.

And I made that I would send back the Master-Word, sending it with my brain-elements, and so give news unto Naani how that I did struggle to come unto her. Yet did I have caution in time; for in verity, had I sent the Master-Word, then had the Evil Forces of the Land wotted that I was out; and mayhaps had come swift unto my Destruction; and so did I contain my spirit and desire, and made to do wisely.

Yet was I put in courage by the low beat of the Master-Word; and did listen very keen, that some message should follow; but there came none, neither did the weak throb of the Word come about me again, at that time. And because that I was now grown more to my natural state, and did feel that I should indeed find the Maid, I looked once more unto the Great Pyramid, long and eager and with a solemn heart; yet with no sign or salutation, as I was before determined. And afterward, I turned and went downward into the dark.

VIII
Down the Mighty Slope

NOW I WENT DOWNWARD very quiet and slow into that Dark ness; and did make but a cautious way; for now you shall know me truly wrapped about with such a night as did seem to press upon my very soul, and such as you shall never have seen nor felt; so that I did seem lost even from my self, and did appear as that I went presently in unreal fashion, and did pass onward for ever and for ever through everlasting night; so that odd whiles I did make to walk with random, as that I stept no more upon this earth; but did go offwards into the Void. Yet was this foolishness of the mind set straight and proper each time that it did come about; for lo! I did kick against an upjutting rock here, and fall upon a great and unseen boulder there, and so was shaken very quickly to a sound knowledge that I trode the hard and actual earth; and had no true dealings with unreal matters.

And ever I did go downward; and by this only did I have a guide to my way. Yet, as you shall think, through reason of the utter dark I made scarce a mile in an hour or even two full hours; and so grew bitter by reason of mine unableness to go forward with a proper and free stride.

But I did think me presently upon a thing that I should do to light my path; and to this end, I did make the Diskos to spin, odd whiles, and did look down the mighty slope, the little way that the strange glis-tening of the Diskos did show, and so fixed my path into mine inward remembering, and would go forward afresh, until that I was shaken once more by the darkness, and would fain to look once again upon the blessedness of light, and make me some knowledge of my way.

And, truly, the light from the Diskos did seem astonishing great, and this to be because there was so monstrous a darkness all about me there forever. And thereafter would I go onward again, until the pain of my stumblings did bid me surely to have that sweet shining once more unto my path.

And so shall you perceive my going; and sore and miserable was it unto the heart; and like to shake the courage of the spirit; yet, in verity, I had come through much, and did have intent to give way to no foolishness of thought.

And you shall well believe that I did make the light not more oft than I did surely need; for it was no properness of wisdom to use the power of the Diskos, save for mine extremity.

Now, presently, when I had done thiswise through six long and bitter hours, and it being now beyond the twentieth hour since I did last slumber, I sat me down there upon the Mighty Slope, in the everlasting Dark, and did eat two of the tablets, and made the water, and could but feel and hearken whether I did this thing right and that.

And when I had eat and drunk, I unfolded my cloak, and wrapt it around me, and placed the scrip and the pouch under my head; and the Diskos I took to company me; and so fell swiftly upon sleep; yet did think earnestly but vaguely upon Naani, as I came unto slumber.

And I slept all but six hours, and did waken very sudden there in the utter dark; and I got me to mine elbow, and did listen very keen; for I had waked immediately, as that something had touched me or come nigh unto me; and I gript the Diskos, and listened; but there did not even a little sound come to me out of all that night.

And presently I had more assuredness that naught did make harm about me; and I sat me up in the dark, and reached for my scrip, and did eat and drink, there in that utter night; and fumbled somewhat, as you shall think. Yet I was done in a while, and got my gear upon me, and the Diskos into my hand, and so to my feet and forward.

Now all that day, I did have a strange unease of the spirit, so that I stopt oft to listen, as that my soul told of something nigh unto me that did follow very quiet. Yet did mine ears perceive nothing; and so I alway to go downward again into the night that held the slope.

And here should I tell how that in the early part of the seventh hour, after I had eat and drunk, and went forward as ever, upon my journey down the Mighty Slope, I did have a very sore tumble against a sharp rock; for I put my foot sudden into a small hole, and this did make me to pitch. And I was utter shaked by the fall and lay very quiet for a time; for the rock had surely ript my body, but for the armour.

And after that I was something renewed of strength and spirit, I made that I should go no more upon my feet, but upon my hands and knees; and thus should I feel the way that I went, and have a less need of the Diskos, which had not overmuch use to light my way, in that I shone it not often, and did guess more than I did perceive, as you may think.

And so I crept all that day, which was a bitter way of travel; yet had I done many a sore mile thus through the Night Land. And when that I had gone downward for eighteen hours, and eat and drunk thrice, I ceased from my labour, and did feel about in the darkness, that I come to a level place for my rest; and so did find presently, a place not so bad, and did push and cast away such small boulders as had been like to irk me.

Then did I eat and drink, and afterward composed me to my sleep, and had many a thought of Naani, as I did drift unto slumber; yet also had I memories of the strange half-fear that had been with me all that day, as though something went constantly near me in the Dark. And because of this, twice did I rise unto mine elbow, and listen; but heard no sound to trouble me, and afterward did trust that I did but fancy; and so came at last unto slumber, that yet was not over-restful, for truly I did listen even as I slept.

And when I had been asleep scarce six hours, I waked again very sudden, as I had done before, and had belief that something did be anigh unto me; and I gript the Diskos, and did hearken; yet was there no sound that mine ears did wot of; neither aught that had power to be surely known of the spirit.

And all that day was as the day before; save that about the eighth hour I came near to fall into some monstrous pit in the Great Slope; but did only fall with my breast upon the edge, and so drew back, and presently did crawl all around it in the dark, and come safe unto the lower side; yet shaken and put more in trouble of spirit than before, and fearful how I should go; for I knew not whether I had come among such things, or whether I had but few to sorrow me.

And so you shall perceive that I went over-cautious for a great while in all that utter dark; but did think at last upon a plan to go with more surety and speed. But to this I did need a cord, and surely I had no cord upon me; and if a boy be no boy that hath none such about him, shall not the same be said of any man! And this I did think, as I searched me; for the sayings of that day had many that were like to this.

Yet in the end I did compass my plan; for I did buckle the scrip and the pouch together, and took one of the straps from the pouch; and this strap was long and thin, and well suited unto my purpose. Then I fixt a stone into the end of the strap, and buckled it there, and after that, I cast the stone before me, as I went upon my hands and knees; and I did hold to the hither end of the strap, and so was abled to have something of knowledge whether there lay any great deepness immediately before me, and thiswise to strive that I fall not down some monstrous cliff in the night.

And so did I go, casting the stone continually to my front, down the slope; and this you shall think to be a cumbersome fashion of travel; yet was I in better case than in all the time since I had begun to go downward of the Mighty Slope in the everlasting darkness.

And at the eighteenth hour I did sleep; and was waked strangely before the sixth hour, even as I had waked before. And this did put always upon me a new wonder and unease. Yet did no harm seem to come unto me, and I did strive that I have no needful trouble of mind. But that something was always nigh unto me in the dark, I do truly believe; yet have I no knowing that it was evil; for it harmed not me.

And three days more I journeyed thus, and did never cease to creep downward weariful upon my hands and knees; and the Diskos I had to my hip, and so shall you know how I carried it. And by this, as you do know, I had been on the Great Slope six days of utter Dark; and did have no wotting but that I went unto some dire and dreadful place; for, surely, I had gone for ever downward a monstrous way.

And here, before I tell further, I must set down how that the cold was much gone from out of the air upon the slope; and the air was grown, as it did seem, very heavy unto my chest. And concerning this matter I should say something. For, if I do mind me, I have said not overmuch concerning the air of the Night Land and the Mighty Pyramid; for truly I have been so set to tell my story of all that I did truly see and adventure upon. Yet, though I have said but little, you will surely have perceived that the air of that far and chill time was not as the air of this; but was thin and keen within the Night Land, and lay not, as I do think, to a great height above the land, but only nigh to the earth.

And as you do know through my tellings, there was a wondrous difference between the air within the Mighty Pyramid, and that which lay without around the base; for upward beyond that, I did understand that there was no outward air that any should breathe; and so was all the Pyramid sealed in certain wise in all the upper Cities for ever; and whether it was sealed utterly from the outward air at the base, I do not surely remember, if, in truth that I did ever bother my head to such matters.

Yet, if I be set proper in memory and understanding, we did draw air from the Underground Fields; but whether they gat any change or newness of air from the Night Land, I have no knowledge; and do lament that I have no sure knowing. Yet, as you shall believe, I could surely write an hundred books upon that Wonder of the Future, and be still lacking in the half of all that there is to be told; and so do I try

to have courage to this my task, and to have no over-trouble, because that I do tell but a little of a Great Tale.

And here in this place will I set down how that the Peoples of the Pyramid were greater to the chest, methinks, than we of this age; but yet do I have no oversurety in the matter; for well it may be that the Reason of this age doth blind within me somewhat the Knowledge that I have concerning that; for, in verity, is it not but a natural thing to believe those Peoples to be great of the chest, so that they should make a proper dealing with the thin air of that place and that time? And yet, as I do strive to make plain unto you, because that this thing should be, by the making of my Reason, I do the more distrust that Reason shall make foolish my Knowledge; for even a fool should suppose that which I have told; and the truth may be even otherwise.

Yet that the Peoples of the Upper Cities had great chests, I do well know; for this was a common knowledge; even as we of this age do acknowledge the Peoples of Africa to be of blackness, or those of Patagonia to be of great stature. And by this one thing should any know a man of the Upper Cities, from a man of the Lower Cities. And because that there grew this difference among the Peoples, there had been once, as any could learn from the Histories, a plan whereby the Peoples should be moved upward and downward through the great height of the Mighty Pyramid, from this city unto that. Yet had it met with great disfavour; and was put out of force; and this is easy to be seen as the natural way of the human heart.

And here it doth occur unto me that it was like enough to be a plan for health, beside of training of the mind, that each youth and maid was put to travel through all the cities of the Mighty Pyramid; the which did take three years and two hundred and twenty-five days, as I have told before this. For by this plan, were they made to breathe the air of every height, and this, mayhaps, unto the good of their developing. And they also to discover that air which was best to their need.

And concerning the air of the Night Land, you shall know that there was in all that Land no flying thing, because that the air was grown very thin; yet, as the Records did show, there had once been monstrous flying-brutes, that went over the Land in mighty bounds; but this was in a long gone age; and we could but suppose that the Records gave truth.

And here you shall know that, when the Monstruwacans did learn that I would journey through the Night Land, in search of Naani, there had been some foolish and well-intended talk among them that I take a small flying-ship, that was in the Great Museum beside the models of

the Great Ships. For, truly, this machine was yet sound to go; for it was made of the grey metal of the Mighty Pyramid, that did seem to have no power to cease. Yet, in verity, I had no skill to manage this, neither had it flown, through an hundred thousand years; so that none did know the mastership of that art, which did be learned but by a constant practice, and oft made uneasy by fallings that did wreck the machine, as I did know from the Book of Flying. And, moreover, as I have told, the air of the Night Land was grown over-weak to uphold such a thing; which, I doubt not, had made the Peoples of the Pyramid to cease from flyings, quite so much as that they did fear the Forces of Evil in the night.

And if that there had been air and skill sufficient unto this purpose of flying, yet had I been wicked with foolishness that I should work to be hung upward in the night, for all the Evil of the Night Land to behold. And though I had gone up some great way, yet the machine had surely made a great noise in the quietness of the eternal night, as you shall suppose.

Now indeed am I gone weary that I should need to tell so much concerning the air of that Time and Place; for surely I do seem to make this my story as that I did make a lecturing upon matters of chemistry; and so do I cast about, that I may not bother to tell more upon this matter. Yet, in truth, a little more of my thinkings and observings had I better set down here, and so be done with it. But you shall have patience with me, and know that had this, my story, been no more than an idle tale, I had been free to make no labour with such matters.

Now there doth a wonder come to me why that the Road Makers, who were of that far-off Age which was before the Age of the Mighty Pyramid, did not fly downward from the upper world into the deep of the monstrous valley; but did instead build a road.

Yet it may be that the air of the upper world had grown thin a great age, so that they had truly forgot that once man did have power to fly. But even if that they did have proper machines to this purpose, surely it were a wondrous and fearful thing to fly downward an hundred great miles; for they surely to have a dread that they never to rise again through so huge a deep.

And, moreover, the downward world that was the bottom of the Great Valley, was full of monsters, as was told in the little metal book. And the monsters were very strange and unknown; and foreign to the whole world, that had never come unto the deep of the Valley. And the Valley had come, as you shall mind, when the earth did split; and this thing was, in truth, like to be thought that same Ending of the World, which all Nations have been taught to believe shall come. For

in verity, when the world did split and burst, and the oceans rushed downward into the earth, and there was fire, and storms, and a mighty chaos, surely it was proper to think that the End had come. Yet was it, in truth, but the beginning of hope of a new Eternity of Life; so that out of the End came the Beginning, and Life out of Death, and Good out of that which did seem a dire matter. And so is it always.

Yet doth this go past my first wonder, which did concern the wherefore that they made not to descend in Things of Flight. Yet, maybe, shall my reasons stand to show why this was not.

And again, mayhap it did chance that some were wild adventurers, and did leap over the edge of the upper world, having to ease their flight certain contrivings, like to parachutes. And these you shall picture, as that you watched them to leap; and so shall you see them go downward into the gloom; and you shall see them for maybe ten miles, and maybe for twenty miles; and afterward shall they be lost utterly in that Great Deep, and seen no more of any man for ever.

But when the Nations became Road-Makers, and came downward slowly to the monstrous Deep of the Mighty Valley that did split the World, then were they come there by millions, and with power sufficient to fight against the Beasts; and afterward to grow back again to an ancient Civilizing; and so to the building of the great airships that were yet shown in the Great Museum of the Pyramid. And here shall I cease from these my thinkings on this matter; for indeed, who shall say what did be truly a Reason for those peoples and what was their Need? And so do I come to no surety by my wonderings.

Yet, as you do know, all things do seem verily to go in a circle; for, behold, in time, they of the Mighty Pyramid, were likewise held off from the glory of the airships; and so were gone backward a great way, according as we do look upon this matter. And so hath this been the way always, as you shall know who have studied and thought, and seen the true ways and goings of Life.

And now will I go forward in my telling; and here will set down a sure thing that I did perceive, both by mine ears and by my fingers; for, as I did make clear to you but a while gone, there had come a change into the air as I did go downward of the Mighty Slope; and truly I was come to a great and new Deepness, even beyond that of the wondrous depth where did stand the Last Redoubt. So that I was afar down and in a monstrous night. And the air here was of a great thickness and abundancy, even as it might be the air of this our Age; or maybe more or maybe less; for who may compare two matters with a sure guessing, that do have an eternity to keep them asunder.

And because that the air was grown very strong and apparent, it shall be, mayhaps, that it was by reason of this thing that the water, when I did make it, did fizz upward in a moment very loud and plentiful, and did boil overward to the earth from out of the cup, and wet upon my hand. And surely this thought did come very keen to my Reason, as I did fumble, each time of mine eating, there in the everlasting night and lonesomeness of the Great Slope.

And so shall you have knowledge now of this and that thing which did come upon my thought, and of the little and the big wonders, and all shall help something to give unto you the ache of newness and bewilderment that was constant companion unto me.

Now by this time, as I have said, I was gone downward ever for six great days; and I did seem as that I should presently come to the middle of the world; for of going downward there was no end.

And then, when it did be that I was near ready to believe this, I perceived far off in the deep of the night a little shining that was yet weak and unsure. And I do not know whether I can truly give unto you the great astonishment and pain of hope that did come upon me; so that I grew sick in all my being but to behold once again the blessedness of light, and to have help unto my belief that I went not downward to an utter desolation.

And I stood upward from my knees, and did look very earnest, and surely it did seem that a light was there afar downward in the night; and again it did seem that I must be plagued by my hopes and by my fancy, and that there was nowhere any light. And then again I did see it very clear, and not to be mistaken, and I had a shaking to come upon me, and I gat me to a run, and made a great and mad speed down the dark slope. And lo! I was not gone any way, but I went headlong, and near brake myself; and could but hold my teeth together very fierce and quiet until that the pain was something gone from me.

And afterward, I gat me again to mine hands and knees, and went slowly, as before; and so for a great hour or more, and did look oft; and alway the light became more plain to my sight; but ever to come and go, oddly-wise. Yet did I go six hours, before that I was come anywise near to it. And by this shall you know how great a space off it had been. And lo! when that I did seem surely anigh unto it, truly was it still far away in the night; and I came not indeed near to it until that I was gone onward again for three hours more. And all that time did I yet go downward into the night; but the Slope now did not be so utter dark.

Now, presently, I made a pause, and stood upward to my feet, so

that I should the better perceive the light. And lo! as I did look toward it, I heard a faraway sound in the dark, as that something did set up a strange and monstrous piping in the night. And immediately, I went to mine hands and knees among the stones of the Slope, and kept myself low in the darkness, so that I should be the less plain to be seen, did any Monster approach.

But there came nothing to trouble me, and I went downward of the Slope for yet another hour; and all the time that I did go, the sound of the piping grew more in the great eternity of the night upon the Slope.

And by this time was I come truly near unto the light; but yet did not behold it plainly; for it did burn beyond certain monstrous rocks that stood between. And I went to the left for, maybe, the half of a big mile; and all the while that I did go, the piping made a mightier whistling in the Night; and it did seem presently as that the earth sent forth the sound and revelry of wild roarings. And I went the more silent; and later did kneel among three rocks, and peered forth for a while upon the place before me.

And now, being come nigh unto the light—though yet it was not unhid from behind the great barriers of the uprising rocks, I perceived that I crouched within the mouth of a mighty gorge; and the left side was a great way off, and I saw it plain at whiles when the light did rise; but the light was to the right, and it was so wondrous great that it did make clear to me that a mountain was to that side of the gorge, and went upward into the everlasting night, as it did seem for ever.

And afar down the gorge, I did see the shinings of strange fires, faint and a great way off. And so was I come at last to the bottom of the Mighty Slope. Yet the gorge also to go downward, but not so great.

And presently I did go forward again; and so did open the point of the rocks, as the sailors do say. And I saw now that there gushed forth a great blue flame from the earth; and the mighty rocks stood about it, as that they were olden giants groupt there to some strange service.

And concerning this flame I was not overmuch astonished in my Reason; for it had seemed to me as I drew anigh, that the fire and the sound should be made by the roaring and whistling of a burning gas that did issue forth among the rocks. Yet, truly, though it did be a natural matter, it was yet a wondrous sight, and set amazement on my senses; for the flame did dance, and sway whitherward monstrously, and sometimes did seem that it dropt so low as an hundred feet, and afterward went upward with a vast roaring unto the utter height, and did stand mighty and blazing, maybe a full thousand feet, so that the far side of the gorge was lit, and surely it was seven great miles off or

more; but yet did show plain and wondrous. And the light did show me the flank of the mountain, that made the right hand side of the Gorge, to go up measureless into the night.

And so shall you perceive that I stayed awhile among the rocks that were in the mouth of the gorge, that I should gaze upon this thing; but afterward I lookt this way and that way, so that I should have a knowing of the place where I was come.

And it was a wild and stark and empty place, as you must perceive. And the far side did be great miles off, as I did say; and everywhere there was abundance of rock and lonesomeness. And before me there went the great and dim length of the gorge, and there were lights here and lights there, in a great distance, and oft—as it did seem—the quiet dancing of lights in diverse places; but yet were these gone on the instant. And ever there was a strong and vacant silence upon that place.

And presently, after that I had looked once more unto the mighty dancing flame, and perceived nowhere any life around it, I went onward down the quiet gorge. And for a great way as I journeyed was my path lit by the dancing of the blue flame; and oft should I seem to be going but dimly among the rocks, and my shadow faint and long; and lo! the flame would leap, and all the gorge come to a wondrous brightness, and my figure to shorten, and the shadows to be black and strong. And so shall you perceive how I went.

And oft did I turn me about to behold the dancing of the Great Light; for it was solemn to my spirit, even amid so much of Greatness and Eternity, to think upon that Flame, and to conceive that it had an utter age danced there at the foot of the Mighty Slope, unseen, through lonesome Eternities. And this I do tell unto you; that thereby may you have some knowledge of the strangeness and the bitter loneliness of that place; which, in verity, did seem the expressing of all the lonesomeness of my wanderings.

And all the time as I did go downward of the great Gorge, there sounded the blast of the roaring, that was presently afar to my back; and the mountain sides did catch it here and in that place, and sent it offwards with strange and improper echoings, as of a chill piping, or oddwise as hushed whisperings of monstrous creatures; so that I did oft stoop to hide a little among the boulders; for truly I knew not but that some unnatural thing called from the darkness of the mountain side.

And for six hours I walked onward thus, and sometimes did hide, having a sudden fear, as I have told.

And presently, in a great while, the roaring was sunk to a far and

monstrous piping; but in the end to no more than a far and uncertain whistling, that yet did catch strange echoes in the night. And in the end there was only a quietness. And yet, as you do perceive, there had been always a silence in that Gorge, as I have told, and this to the despite of the whistling. And I do hope that you have understanding with me in this matter; for it was truly as I have told, and there is no contrariness of telling in this matter.

Now in all this time that I had walked in the great Gorge, I had past four of the far lights that I did see from the bottom of the Slope; and the two first and the fourth were blue, but the third was green; and all did dance and quake, and sent fitful shinings into the belly of the Gorge. And there came also from them whistlings, and from the second one a low and strange moaning noise; and I doubted not the gas did come oddly and with trouble. And I past these things with no great thought; for truly they were no matters for notice, after that which I had beheld.

Now, as you shall mind, it was surely in the early Third of the seventh day of my journey down the Mighty Slope that I saw the first shining of the monstrous gas fountain; and from that time until now had there past maybe sixteen hours. And, as you do wot, I had eat not in all my travel since that I had seen the light; so that I was gone to a proper lack inward; and moreover, it was full nineteen hours or more since that I had slept; and all that while had I laboured.

And I ceased me from wandering, and lookt about that I should come to a safe and proper place for my slumber; and this I saw very quick; for there was dry stone and rock everywhere, and no failing of holes and diverse places to my purpose; so that I was soon in a little cave between two mighty boulders.

And here I eat four of the tablets; for truly so many were my due, and I had not been violent had I eat more. And afterward, I made some of the water, and it did fizz up in a moment; so that I perceived that but a good pinch made a great cup-full. And this I set to the count of the strong and heavy air, as I have told, which I did think to have a greater power of chemistry.

And presently I slept, having my gear about me as ever, and the Diskos to my breast. And as I went into slumber, I thought sweetly upon Naani, as I had done, indeed, an hundred times since I was come to the hopefulness of the lights of the Gorge.

Now, whilst I slept, I dreamed that the Master-Word did presently beat all about me in the night. Yet, as I do mind, I waked not; and because that I continued to sleep, I have no sure knowing whether

this was truly a dream, or an Happening. And I minded me upon it, when I waked; but this was after that I had slept seven hours; and I could have no sureness anywise of the matter; but only that I was come safe through my sleep; though heavy within my head and limbs, as that the air did call me unto a further slumbering, as is like enough.

And after that I had eat and drunk, I put my gear about me, and the Diskos to my hip, for I needed both my hands to the task of journeying amid the great boulders. And I set forth again down the half-light of the mighty Gorge, and through eighteen hours I made a strong going, save when I did pause at the sixth and the twelfth hours to mine eating.

And by the eighteenth hour was come, I was very ready to my food and slumber; and presently I was asleep in a place of the rocks. And that day had I past three and twenty of the dancing gas fires; and five been like a white fire; but the others blue and green. And all did dance and made a strange and uncertain light within the great Gorge; yet was it a peaceful thing unto my spirit that there was truly light, as you shall understand.

And I slept six hours, and waked, and did want more sleep, as you shall think. But I eat and drunk and put my gear upon me, and went on downward of the Gorge.

And at the sixth hour, after that I had eat and drunk, I came to a part where the big gas fires did cease to dance, and there was a certain darkness upon that place. Yet was it not a proper dark; for there came the glimmer of a flame here and the glimmer of a flame there, as that little flames came upward between the stones, and did vanish, and come upward in another part. And so did light and die out constant and forever amid the stones and the boulders of that lonesome Gorge; and made a low-spread light, so that it did seem unto me that strange shudders of light beat upward through the dark of that place.

And I went onward, and a heavy fume did seem to hang in the air, and horrid gases to come upward from the earth in odd puffings; and anon a light would leap upward beyond the next stone, and afterward vanish, and there would be an hundred thousand such upon every hand, running to and fore; and afterward for a moment an utter dark, and again the little flames everywhere; so that it did seem I went one moment amid the heart of a strange country of fire, and immediately through a country of utter night. And this was to me strange and a peculiar matter. Yet, as I do think, the gases did bother me the more; for they did seem as that they were like to hurt mine health utterly; for, in verity, oft did I seem as that I should choke and breathe no more,

by reason of the poison that came upward from among the stones and the boulders.

And all that time, as they came or went, did the little flames make small phlocks of sound in the Gorge as they did flash or die; and the sounds did seem, to my likening, as stones cast into an utter silent pool; for they but made apparent the everlasting quiet of the Gorge.

And afterward, I came beyond this place, and you shall see me going very lonesome among the rocks of the Gorge, beyond. And by this, it was come nigh unto the eighteenth hour; and I did find a place proper to my slumber, and did eat and drink, and was quickly gone over unto sleep.

And here, I should tell how that I had not an over-fear of Evil Powers whilst I was in the great Gorge; for truly it did seem as that nothing that ever did live came anigh to that wild and silent place of stone and rock; but that I journeyed through it alone, and was surely the first that did go that way for maybe a million years. And this feeling that was upon me, I do hope you to perceive and take unto yourselves, and thus have an understanding of my heart at that time.

And as you shall know, I went always unto slumber with sweet and with troubled thoughts of the Maid. Yet, for a great while, I had been put so mightily to the labour of my way that my heart did suffer less at this time than should be thought; and truly it doth show me how I was drawn unto that One with all my being, that I did surely think so oft and sweetly upon her amid so many perils and matters of horror. And this doth seem something strange to say, when that you do consider that I was adventured unto these same perils and horrors but only for the sake of the Maid.

And in six hours did I wake, as I did strive alway to set myself to do; yet was I very heavy and slow for a little, until that I was more properly come to wakefulness. And surely, as I did think before, this was like to be put upon me by the weighty air of the place; but yet it might be that the gas which did float in the Gorge was upon my lungs. And also, as you have perceived, if but you have attended my way, the air was grown warm, and oft were the rocks pleasant to the seat, and all of these matters did contrive to make me slumbrous.

Now, presently, the gas fires did cease utterly in the Gorge, and I lookt downward, along that great place, and saw only a greyness, but above the greyness there was, as it did seem, something of a vague and ruddy shining in the night. And this did wake me to wonder what new thing lay before; so that I grew more eager among the boulders.

And, later, when I had eat at the sixth and the twelfth hours, and

gone on awhile, I came to a place where the Gorge made a quick turning unto my left, and at the end of the turning was a red and glowing light that was very great and wonderful; so that I was utter keen to come to that place, that I should discover what made the shining. And the place where I was come then, was very dark, because that I was nigh under the mighty wall of the mountain of the right side of the Gorge. Yet above, as it did seem to me, there was a far red upward glowing in the night.

Then did I go forward very fast, and presently, in a good while, I discovered that I drew near to a second great turning, that went to the right. And about the seventeenth hour, I came nigh unto the second great turning. And here did I put caution upon me, and crept for a while among the dark rocks of that place, that I should come to a sight of that which made the monstrous red shining.

And presently, I was beyond the corner of the mountain, and did look downward into a mighty Country of Seas, and the burning of great volcanoes. And the volcanoes did seem as that they burned in the Seas. And the country was full of a great ruddy light from the volcanoes. And so shall you perceive me there among the rocks that did all stand upward strange and bold and silent in the red and monstrous glare of the light. And I, as it did seem, the one thing of life in all that desolation and eternity of rock and stone, there in the end part of the great Gorge.

And I peered forth into the wonder of the light, and was full of thrillings and fancies that I was surely come to the place where the Lesser Redoubt had been builded. And immediately I knew that this was not so, for surer had not Naani told how that they were in a land of darkness. And if this did be so, truly, how wondrous and dread a way had I yet to go, if that this Country of Seas and mighty volcanoes stood between.

Surely, it did seem to me then as that I must wander searching unto the world's end. And so shall you be company unto me there with my trouble and my thoughts, and the immediate wonder and strange glory of that mighty Country.

IX

The Dark Pyramid

NOW IN TWO HOURS more I was come clear down out of the Gorge, and stood in that Country; and for all that I did feel fresh troubled and bewildered, yet was I rejoiceful, as you may believe, in the surprising light and splendour of that sudden Land.

And before that I had come down out of the great Gorge, I had stood high within the mouth thereof, and lookt well out over the mighty Country. And I had counted seven and twenty great volcanoes, and this doth not take heed of two monstrous ranges of fire-hills that burned afar off, something unto my right. Neither doth it take account of an hundred thousand lesser places of fire.

And truly it did seem a very land of fire and water. For there was a small fire-hill stood within a sea, as it did seem no more than a little mile from that place where I did stand. And maybe a score to the back of it, spread all about. And here shall I do proper to tell concerning the seas. For there were of these, that I did count at that time, three that were small, and a mighty sea that went onward for ever into the red light of the fire-hills, so that it was gone utterly out of my sight, and did show no ending.

And there rose up out of the seas, islands; and on the islands, volcanoes. But in other parts the fire-hills did come upward straightly from the sea. And over the near sea, as it did seem, there lay a plenti-tude of steam, as that the sea did boil at whiles and in diverse places.

And there did seem to me, as it were within the red atmosphere of that place, as that there were a muttering thunder, low and constant, shaking the air, now from that distance and now from this, and this did I judge to be the voices of the fire-hills, speaking with the fire that lived in them.

And you shall conceive how utter new was all this unto me; for there was in that Country a constant Voice of the Energy of Life, so

that the World-Noise of this our Age was even there again, and with a keen and undoubted apparentness; and the more so, some ways, than now.

And here shall I set down more closely the things that were ready to my gaze.

And first, that it did much attract me, there was a huge and blackened mountain unto the left of the mouth of the Gorge, and the mountain did go upward into the night, maybe fifteen and maybe twenty miles. And there was a mighty peaked volcano that grew out from the side of the mountain so high up as five miles, as I did guess that height; and this was upon the far side. And above this there was a second, maybe nine or ten great miles up in the blackness of the night that hung afar upward. And, as that this were not great wonder enough, there did burn and glow two other mighty fire-hills, at an utter height, upon the left crest of that black mountain; and these were upward so monstrous a way, as that they did seem to make strange and smouldering suns within the night. And truly, as you shall perceive, this was a wondrous thing.

And below these upward fire-hills there rose up from the earth vast mountains of ash and burned stuff, that had been cast forth by these perched volcanoes, and had poured downward unto the earth throughout Eternity, and so to build grey and sombre monuments unto the dreadful glory of Time.

And to my right there was always sea and sea and the red blazing of the fire-hills; but unto my left, there were mighty forests, and there rose upward here and in that place, as that they were beyond the great woods, monstrous fire-hills. And so do you take from me something of that first impressing upon my brain and sense.

And after that I had come down out of the mouth of the great Gorge, as I did tell a little while gone, I came upon a pause; for, surely, which way was the way proper unto my search. And I lookt about for a great while, and afterward did climb back into the Gorge, and called myself foolish, that I had not thought to map my way ere I came down.

And when I was come up into the Gorge again, lo! I saw that there was but one way that I should go; for truly, as I have said, there was only the seas unto my right; but unto the left, where the shores did meet the seas, there seemed, so far as mine eyes did tell to me, a clear way for a space. And mayhap, when I had come so far, I should even find a further way to go forward. And so did I descend again unto the Country of the Seas, as I did ever call that red-shining country of water and fire.

And by, that I was come again from the height of the Gorge, it was four and twenty hours since that I did last sleep; so that I was fain that I should put into some nook, and come to slumber, as you shall well believe.

And I found me a neat and proper place, where three great trees grew about a little basin of rock that was very dry and warm. And here, after that I had eat three of the tablets, and drunk some of the water—the while that my belly did yearn, as ever, for proper eat-ing-stuff—I made my bed in the little basin of the rock, and lay me down, and did begin to think awhile upon Naani; but was gone over to sleep before that I was aware.

And lo! I was suddenly awake, and did find that I swam in a hot water; and a mercy, I did think, was it that I was not drowned as I did sleep. And I gat me to my feet, and the basin was full of water, hot and steaming, and pungent to the taste, as well I did know. And I perceived now that the water poured in from a smoothed slit upon the far side, and did come with a strange gurgling and bubbling, so that I conceived some deep well to boil, and thus to drive upward this water into the basin; and glad was I that it did not boil as it came forth.

And surely, now that I was upon the dry land, and did consider, I did quickly suppose that the water had poured forth at seasons into the basin for an eternity of time, and afterward did go back by fissures in the bottom of the basin; and this to happen, as I soon did find, a little beyond the length of every hour; and, indeed the basin to empty slow as I did watch.

Now, being much wetted, I stript off mine armour, having before this dipt out mine effects from the hot pool, and so did come down to the naked flesh, and I found a place where the rock was hot, and here I did spread my garments. And whilst that they came to dryness, I gat me into the hot pool, and had a very pleasant bathing, and did have no great fear of any dangerous thing; for, as it did seem, I had surely left all such behind, within the Night Lands. Yet did I have the Diskos upon the pool edge to my hand; for I had no proper assurance in this matter. Yet, as it did prove, there were many monstrous beasts in that Country; but never did I feel the nearness and horrid power of any Evil Force; for these, as I do conceive, were congregate and gathered about the Mighty Pyramid, being attracted thereto by the great spiritual essence of so wondrous a multitude of humans gotten so close in one spot, even as sharks do come after the ship that hath bullocks within. Yet, how that the Evil Powers were given entrance unto this State of our Life, I have no sure knowing; yet have I put

forward certain thoughts on this matter in an earlier place; and more than such thinkings is surely vanity; for there is no certainty in my Reasoning concerning the thing.

Now, presently was my clothing dry; yet before this, I had come out from that bath, which truly was nigh all gone backward into the earth. And I dressed me again, and got my armour upon me, and afterward was I in a more lightsome state of the mind; and yet very ready to come again unto my sleep. And this I did, and had six hours more beside the pool; and once was wakened somewhat by the gruntling and bubbling noise of the water, that was made as the pool did fill time and again.

And when the six hours were gone, I waked very well fitted in my senses and feelings to go forward again through that red-lighted Country; and this I did, after that I had eat and drunk.

Now all that day I went forward at a great pace; and the nameless woods were unto my left, and the shores of the seas unto my right. And oft did I find that the trees grew even into the water, so that oft did I go forward among the trees, and a very wonderful thing was this to me, that never had known before in all my life, until I was come into that Country, how that a glad and wild mystery doth live among forest trees. For there was no such strange wildness among the groves of the Underground Fields; though a solemn beauty in plenty. And the scent of the woods was sweet unto my spirit, as you shall wot.

Now all the time that I did go, there was the shore unto my right; but alway to my left, and around me oft-times as I did say, the great forests. And as I did go, lo! there was life in all those darksome woods, and living eyes did peer out odd whiles upon me, and afterward go backward into the dark; so that I wotted not whether to fear, or to have no heed of trouble. Yet naught did come anigh to me, to make any hurt.

And thrice in that day did I come to little fire-hills that burnt redly, and sent out fire and noise, so that I heard their trouble each time through the forest, before that I was come to them. And about each was there a deadness and desolation, where the fire had killed the big trees; yet, as I did observe, the quick life of little plants did grow more nigh, as that they were born and lived between the times of the fire-bursts. And this I do take it that you perceive.

And in that one day I past thirty and seven boiling springs; but whether they boiled truly, I do have no knowledge; only that they sent out a great steam oft-times; and some did make a strong roaring noise; so that to hear them afar off in the forests was to think odd times that some wild beast roared strangely.

Now, when the eighteenth hour was come, I sat me down, as I had done upon the sixth and the twelfth hours, and eat two of the tablets, and drank some of the water, which here did fizz very rich and quick.

And afterward I lay down to my slumber, for I was greatly wearied. And I had chosen a place against a great rock, which was so that no creature might come upon me from behind. And I came easy upon sleep; but yet I did fix it upon me that I slumber only with the body; for I did know, by the shining of the eyes in the darksome woods, that strange creatures abode in the mighty forests.

And ere I was gone over to sleep, I thought upon Naani, as I had done much all that day, as though her spirit did hover near unto mine, and did strive pitiful to speak with me. And this I set out to you, that you shall know how it did seem unto me in my thoughts and fancyings. And as I lay there, I put a blessing upon her, and a determination into my heart that I make a more desperate speed of my going, if that might be; so that I come the sooner to that strange, and unknown place in the dead world where did stand the lesser Refuge. And I was then asleep in a moment.

And lo! sudden I was awake. And lovely was the brightness of that Country, that did show me in a moment my danger, and did not keep me suspend in fearful Doubt, as did the grey darkness and strange shadows and lights of the Night Land. For I saw, on the instant that I got me to mine elbow, how that certain things did crouch within the borders of the trees, no more than a score paces off. And I perceived in a moment that my spirit had been given knowledge, and had wakened me. And I stared, the while that I did grip the Diskos; and I saw that there were six squat men that were humpt at the neck and shoulder; and they did crouch all there in a row, and were something hid by the shadows; and I perceived that they watched me; and the eyes of the men did shine like the eyes of beasts; and so shall you know somewhat of the strange terror that came upon me. Yet had I the Diskos and mine armour; and though my heart did shake a little, yet was my spirit assured to conquer.

Now I gat me to my feet, and had the Diskos ready within my hand; and behold! I could not see the Humped Men, for they were gone from that place; yet never did I see them go, though I had kept my gaze very steadfast upon that part where they did hide. And, as you shall understand, I was near ready to believe that there had been nothing there within the border of the wood; yet truly I knew that the men with the humps had been there, as I had seen.

Now, I looked presently, and found that I had slept five hours; and

I eat two of the tablets, as I did stand there, watchful; and afterward drank some of the water; and so was ready to go forward again; for I was grown very anxious to be gone from that place; and did have no knowledge but that those strangely humpt Men were but a little way off, among the trees, and might come upon me in a moment; or, further, that they did go to call an army of other humped men to my destruction.

And after that I was ready, and had my gear secure upon me, I set off at a great stride, and did hold the Diskos very handy, and lookt this way and lookt that way, and all the while made onward with speed; for, truly, I was grown so lean and hard that it did seem to me that I had power to out-pace those men or aught else of their kind.

And all that day, through thirty great hours did I go forward, at that stride, and did always watch; and at every sixth hour, I eat two of the tablets and drank a little of the water, and went onward again.

And so did I hope that I was lost from those Humped Men. Yet, though I did hope, my faith was not this wise; for twice and thrice did it come to me that there went things through the woods to my left all that day, and did keep always to a level with my speed; yet were always hid. And, as you shall believe, this did be a very shaking thing to my heart, and did make my hope of but little account.

Now, because that I had no faith to company my hope, I was not easy to have slumber, until that I was come to a place proper and safe. And so, as I have told, I went onward through thirty great hours; and, in truth, in all that while I did find nowhere that did seem to fit my need.

And lo! about the end of the thirtieth hour, I perceived that there was water ahead, besides the water of the sea that was ever to my right. And I thought, maybe, that the sea did go inward at that part of the land; but it was otherwise; for when I was gotten to that place, I found that a river came into the sea, and did come out of all the country that lay unto my left.

And in the mouth of this river, there was a small island; and surely I did look across to the island, and think it a refuge from the Humped Men that did surely play dog upon my going. Yet, truly, this was but an idle thought, and my need was that I should come to some way to cross over the river, that I go forward beside the great sea, which did stretch onward, as it did seem for ever, before me upon the far side.

And I knew not how to go across; for I had no power to swim, and had I swum, there were surely monsters in that great and warm-flowing river, as you shall believe.

And I went upward of the river-bank, that I might come to some

place where the river did narrow; and surely I had been like to walk a mighty distance to this purpose, but that I came soon to a second river that did enter the first, not a mile above the shore of the sea; so that, as you do perceive, there was the sea to one side of me, and this second river unto the other, and the first river before me; and thus was I sorely perplexed, as any had been truly that was in a like trouble.

Yet, as it did chance, the need to go forward, and the danger of the Humped Men, put wit into me, so that I lookt about for a tree that was fallen. And there were many, yet great, so that I was much wearied and something strained of the spirit, before that I gat two little trees unto the water.

Now, when this was done, I made me a rough pole of a young tree-plant; and afterward, I lashed the two trees together with my belts and straps, and so had somewhat of a raft.

And you shall picture that, all the time as I did go about this business, I was very heedful lest the Humped Men should come upon me, ere that I was gone free upon the water. And this constant heeding did double the labour of my work, as you shall perceive; yet, in the end, it was done, and I ready to adventure over the river.

And so I did push off with the pole, and I pusht and paddled maybe the half of an hour, for, indeed it was all a clumsy contriving, and mayhap I the more so in my labours. Yet, presently, I was come so far over, that I drew nigh to the island; and it did seem a wise and proper thing that I should have my slumber there, and afterward go onward to the farther shore. And this I did; and after that I had eat and drunk, as ever, I lay down to sleep.

And by this time it was three and thirty hours since last I did slumber; so that I was bitterly awearied.

And I had a great and restful sleep; for, truly, the island did seem a very safe place; and, in verity, I came to no harm, though I was as a dead man for nine great hours; and so shall you perceive my weariness.

And when I was come proper awake, I eat two of the tablets, and drank some of the water; and afterward made an end of my voyage, and then did take back my belts and straps from binding the trees, and so forward again upon my way, and no more fearful of the Humped Men; for, surely, I did think I had left them all upon the far shore of the river; though afterward I minded me that they might grow likewise upon the two sides; but yet was I only discovered by those upon the one, as you do know.

And all that day I went very swift, and past many strange matters and did coast upon wonders oft. And at the sixth and the twelfth hours

did I eat and drink, as ever; and between the eighth and the fourteenth hours did I come past two mighty fire-hills, that made all the Country to tremble with their noise. And four times did monstrous creatures pass by me; but I was swift hid, and came to no harm.

And oft as I did go, were my thoughts upon the dear Maid that I journeyed to save from destruction. Yet, as you must see, always were my thinkings brought sharply unto my going; so that scarce was I ever set off to ponder upon Naani, but that there came some danger or wonder to give me heed to my way. And because of this, as you have learned, I was more put to plan free of the instant trouble and peril of my way, through all that mighty journey, than to have quiet chance for thoughts of love unto mine Own. Yet, truly, was not my journey one whole thought of love unto Naani? And, that peril made oft dumb my brain, was but the truer song unto my Maid.

And at times I was among trees; but oft did go past unnumbered boiling springs and small fire-hills; and oft was the air full of the noise of the little fire-hills, and the roar of the boiling springs; but there came no harm unto me.

And a thousand times did I perceive things that had life; and I made a very cautious way; though with a great speed and cleverness of going that made my heart glad.

And oft did I come to parts where a great life held the trees, and green stuff did flourish exceedingly, and the air rich and full and wondrous sweet; so that I was fain to think how that in some far-off time, it might be that our children's children should come down unto this Country, when the Upper Valley of the Night Land was grown to an utter chill and lacking of air; and here build them a new Refuge, if, indeed any should come clear of the Evil Forces and the Monsters that did live about the Mighty Pyramid in the Night Land. Yet, how should they come clear of those things; so that this is, as you do perceive, no more than a thought that did rise vaguely in me. And yet, again, who shall say what may be?

And onward I did pass, and I do mind me how that I saw the lower fires of that Country to burn very fierce; and this I set to the richness of the air; but yet with no surety of knowledge; and do but tell the same that you shall see the oddments of thought that went oft across my brain, and so have so much knowledge as I, concerning this and that.

Now, a little before the eighteenth hour was come, I came out from among the trees, and the sea was downward of a great cliff unto my right, for I had gone upward for a long and weary hour. And I did

see now a thing that made me to be cautious, and yet that did hold my heart to go swiftly to perceive the thing; for it was very strange.

And I went forward quickly, yet with a wise care; and so was come presently more nigh. And I perceived that the thing was, in part, a high rock, very tall and pointed and maybe an hundred feet high; but afterward I did find it to be more. And there was a monstrous great thing upon the top of the rock, that did seem very strange; and I stopt and lookt, and afterward went forward again; and so for a time, until that I was but a little way off. And now I saw that there did seem to be a mighty long rock laid across the topmost part of the upstanding rock, and yet had a very strange and shapely appearance; and did seem upon the underpart to be as that I had lookt before upon it. And upon the upper part, there grew trees and green things, even as these did grow upon odd ledges of the upstanding rock. Yet, for the most, the rock was very stark, as that a blast had blown upon it, and made it bare.

Now, when I had lookt for a while, I bethought me that this should be a safe and proper place for my slumber, if that I had power to come safe to the top. And when I had thought this thing, I began at once to climb up the rock; and I found that the rock was very high; so that in a while I was come a great way off the earth, and yet was not come to the top of the rock. And because that I was aweiried, I lookt about for a safe place to mine hand, and lo! there was a shelf of the rock very nigh, that went inward a little to the side.

And I gat me to this ledge, and did eat and drink, and presently I slept, and scarce had thought of Naani in the moment of my slumbering; for a great weariness was upon me, the which I do think to have come by reason that I was not yet proper rested from the task of the day that was gone before that one.

Now I waked very sudden, maybe seven hours after; and I had knowledge within me that my spirit did wot of some nigh danger. And I gat upward from the rock, very quiet, and had the Diskos ready in my hand. And I lookt swift about me in the moment that I did wake; yet did see nothing; for there was naught on the ledge with me.

And I crept to the edge, and lookt downward, and lo! I did see that there came up the rock two Humped Men; and they did climb very swift and silent; and I perceived that they smelled me, and came to destroy me. And I made ready the Diskos to do battle, and ceased not to look downward. And I saw how that the Humped Men did seem to be humpt by reason of their being so monstrous thick and mighty of the neck and the shoulder, as that they had been human bulls. And I saw that they were very strong, and by the speed of their climbing, I

knew they were swift; and so did I make steady my attention and my heart to the saving of my life; for truly I did know that I should be dead in a little, or they.

Now I stept back a space from the edge of the rock, and had the Diskos very ready; for it was needful that I should kill one of those brute men speedy, that I have no danger that one take me in the back, whilst that I fight with the other.

Then, in a moment it did seem, there came upward of the rock edge, the great and brutish face of the man. And in that moment that I slew him, I did note curiously how that he had large teeth upon each side of the mouth; and was aware that he had come so quiet as a great cat. And in the backward parts of my brain, I bethought that even thus, maybe, was primal man, so that a strange and secondary questioning and wondering did live in that part of me; and I did learn from these scarce conscious reasonings that I was of belief the thing was truly a man; but very crude and dangerous. And surely it is strange that I had all this thought in that little moment; but in verity so it was; though I doubt not but I bettered it with after thoughts, when a while had gone.

Now the first man died ere his great haired breast was come upward over the rock; and he sank back, and sagged and fell dully, and I heard him bodge downward from rock to rock, very lumbersome; and so in a moment was silence.

Then did I look this way and that way of the ledge; for the second Humpt Man was not yet upon me; and I feared that the pause did mean a cunning mischief and strategy. And when a little time had past, and all the while I was ready with the Diskos, and naught did come upward to harm me, I stept very soft to the edge of the rock-ledge, and lookt downward; but there was nowhere any thing to see.

Now, for a little moment, I did think that the brutish man had run off, being feared by the death that I did deal unto the first; yet I put this from me at once; for I did wot that such a creature did not be like to fear in such wise; but was rather set to some horrid cunning of attack, as I did fear, and was somewhere below me among the holes of the great rock.

Then I did think sudden that he might be gone upward, so that he should come down upon my back, and I lookt upward of the mighty rock; but did see naught; and afterward I stoopt forward a great way beyond the edge, so that I should perceive whether the man did hide beneath. And, behold! he was there below me, and crouched under the rock-shelf, ready to his spring. And in that moment, he made unto me with so mighty a leap as any tiger should give. And he came half over

the edge, and gript the Diskos by the handle, in an instant.

And surely I had lost that trusted weapon, or been pulled over and cast into the depth, but that the Diskos did spin, and the Earth-Current did make live the handle—as was intended—save where the "grip" was set. And lo! the man gave loose the handle very swift, for it had burned and shaken the creature sore. And I staggered back, with the effort I had made to withhold the Diskos; and the brutish man came upward again over the rock edge, and leapt at me. Yet he gat me not; for I sprang unto my right, and made a blow with the Diskos, even as I did leap. And the blow came something short; but yet harmed the Humpt Man with a gash upon the belly, very sore and horrid among the great brown hairs of the man. And immediately he sprang after me; but I smote full at the face; so that he leaped back from the strange roar and blaze of the Diskos, and yet was harmed; for he gat not right free of the blow; but did be cut very sore on the mighty and haired arm.

Now, seeing that he was something feared of the weapon, I ran in upon him, and smote again at the face; yet was the man gone out of my reach before that the blow did reach; for, truly, he was quick as a panther. And immediately, he did leap unto the ending of the ledge, where it did join upon the Rock; and he caught the living Rock between his two hands. And truly the Rock must have been splitten there; for he tore out a monstrous lump, so great near as my body; and did run upon me with the rock above the head of him.

Now, I perceived I should be smashed in a moment, if that I did not slay the man very quick. For so mighty was he, that he did leap this way and that way after me, as though the great rock did cumber him no more than it had been but a light matter.

And you shall perceive that I leapt this way and that way, to avoid the man; and twice did strike him; but yet was feared to brake the Diskos upon the rock, which the man did use as a shield each time that I did make a blow. And all the while, I did act to escape when that the man should cast the rock, as I did conceive at the first to be his intent. Yet, truly, it was as that he had no wotting that a rock may be thrown; for he strave only to come at me with the rock, that he should crush me, as with a monstrous club. And, in verity, what should a man do against so horrid an attack.

And time and oft did I leap now to the right and now to the left, and again in a moment, I did cut the Humpt Man; but the blow was something turned off by the great rock in the hands of the man; yet so strange and mighty was the power of the Diskos, that it shore away a small portion of the rock, and did come to no hurt in itself.

And, surely I had presently failed in wind and limb, because of the leapings and chargings that I did make; and because of the weight of the armour, that was not overmuch, yet to be considered; but that I fainted not, was by reason of the wondrous hardness and leanness that I was grown to, with so constant a journeying and strait living; for the tablets did keep the strength in a man, though, truly, they eased not the yearnings of the belly.

And lo! even the brutish man did grow weary, and the hot breath and body-stink to come from him; and surely who shall wonder, for always he did rush to and fro upon me, with the monstrous rock to crush me. And sudden, I leapt unto the right of the man, thinking within me that I did perceive a chance that I should cut him upon that side; but, truly, he was less aweary than I did know; for he came very sharp upon me, and had me between him and the wall of the Rock; and surely I had no room to make escape, and had died in a moment, but that I made a sudden sham toward the left with the Diskos, as that I should leap that way. And in the same instant, I did go to the right with a strong bounding; and immediately did come in upon the Humpt Man from that side; and I put my fortune of life to the stroke, and stood anigh to the man, and I smote him across the middle part, before that he did wot of my intent. And the blow slew the man very surely, and did nigh cut the mighty creature in twain. And surely he fell, half leaping even as he died, so that the monstrous rock that was in the hands of the brutish man, did crash down almost upon my feet, and I leapt very high that I should escape the thundering of the rock; for in verity, I was near slain in that last moment of the life of the Humpt Man. But yet I lived and came free of death, and did have a relief of happiness about my heart, as you shall believe.

Yet, truly, I was much shaken; and a little weakness took me, so that I was fain to go down upon the rock-shelf, that I have back my strength.

And presently, I was grown steady again, and I took my gear, and did haste down the Rock, and so was come presently to the earth again. And I saw the first of the Humpt Men that I did slay, lying very quiet a little off from the bottom of the Rock; so that I went round upon the other side to avoid the man; for it was no pleasure to mine eyes or to my heart. And, truly, it did trouble me always to make a death.

And when I was come round upon the other, which was the seaward, side of the Rock, I perceived that I was yet shaken; and I remembered that it were wise to eat and drink and rest a little, before that I did go further upon my way.

Now, as I did sit there at the bottom of the Rock, I looked upward at the strange crown thereof; and until that time, I had been taken up with the fight and with gazings this way and that to see whether there came others of the Humped Men to work me an harm.

But now that I was given some ease of the mind and of the body, I saw plainly that I knew the thing that lay upward upon the Rock; for the shape had been something strange and half-known to me even before that moment, as that I had a vague knowledge concerning it; but yet with no surety. And now, truly, I did know in a little instant that the thing was one of the olden flying-ships, the which, as you shall mind, there were certain in the Great Museum of the Mighty Pyramid.

And surely, I was ready to wonder why that I had not seen the thing plain before that moment; yet was this like to be because that there was a shadow upon the other side of the great Rock; but upon this side there was a little fire-hill a way off to the cliff edge, and this did throw a warm light that made a glimmer upon the dull metal of the ship's bottom, which was uncovered to my sight, and was surely of that same deathless grey metal that made the Great Redoubt.

And yet, as you shall believe, even as I said this thing to my mind, that the strange matter upon the top of the Rock was truly one of the olden air-ships, I did feel that I should be proper to doubt; for it was a very wondrous thing to perceive a thing common to man, in that utter strange Country, and after that I was gone so far off from the Mighty Pyramid. Yet, in verity, I did know in my heart that it was indeed that which I did perceive it to be; and I did stand and walk to and fore and look upward constant; for I was very keen that I look well upon it.

And truly, as I did look from this place and from that place, it was scarce a thing for wonder that I had not wotted it to be an air vessel; for there were great trees and abundance of earth and living matters upon the topmost side of the ship; so that none could easy perceive it to be aught save a great and desolate rock that did lie upon the other rock. Yet, truly, it was as I have told; and presently I did make to climb upward of the great Rock, that I should come to the air vessel to enter it. But yet was this not proper; for I had surely no duty save to go forward forever, until that I found the Maid; but yet did I spend a little while to this searching of the ship; and I do but set down that which I did, and with a serious spirit. And truly, as it doth here occur to me, I do be ever seeming a serious young man, as you maybe shall have grown to think; but yet was I to a dread and serious business, and the strain did be too great upon me and the trouble too much prest upon my heart to give me much of laughter, as you do surely

perceive, and so you to give me your ear and your understanding. For, indeed, before that I did lose Mirdath my Beautiful One, I was not over-grave; but so young and joyous as any.

Now it took me a great time to go upward of the Rock; for it was so monstrous steep and high. Yet, presently was I come nigh under the bottom of the ship; and here I did perceive that she had been sore battered in that far-off age when she did come upon the Rock; for, surely, as I did perceive, the peak of the Rock was through the bottom of the ship, so that the metal was burst this way and that, and very plain to be seen in some parts; but in other places the earth and growing matters did make a hiding.

And after that I had climbed this way and that way, I perceived that I must come to the topmost part by the plants that did hang over, and grow downward. And after that I had pulled upon them, to know that they were strong to hold me, I went upon them, and was soon to the top of the ship. Yet, truly, I might so well have been upon the earth; for the ship was covered above by the earth and dust of a monstrous age of years; so that I was like to need much time to dig downward unto the ship; and because of this, I considered a little while, and afterward made no more to search her; but did go downward again, that I should come once more to my journey. Yet, as you shall think, it was with a queer thrilling of the heart, and with strange thoughts upon the end of those that did come, maybe, to a bitter and lonesome dying in that ship of the air, in that far-off time when she did fly.

And surely, it did seem to me as I went downward of the great Rock, how that the flying-ship had been there for an hundred thousand years; and that mayhaps the sea did live all about the Rock in that Age; and truly this was no improper thing to think, for it was like that the sea had been monstrous high and great in those days; so that the Rock was but a little island in the midst of the sea; and now was the sea gone small from a great sea to lesser seas, and this through an eternity of years. And always, as it doth seem to me, had the ship lain upon the Rock, and lookt quiet and silent over the change and wonder and the lonesomeness of all that Country of Fire and water, for ever.

But how the air-ship did come upon the rock, how shall I know; save, maybe, it doth seem as that she might have flown low over the sea in that olden age, and come hard upon the Rock, because, maybe, there was one to the helm that did steer unwittingly. And again, it shall well be otherwise, and I do but set down mine odd thoughts; and such as they be, they have no especial use, save that they do show to you the different workings of my mind at that time, as I did go

downward. And so to set you the more in possession of all that I did have knowledge of.

And presently, I was come again to the earth, and did go forward with a great speed, so that I should waste no more of that day. Yet, oft did I think upon that ship hid there upon the mighty Rock, under the wondrous quiet ashes of eternity.

And I went eighteen hours walking, and in all that time I did see no more of the Humped Men; yet three times was I put in a sudden danger, for there went past me thrice, between the fourteenth and the seventeenth hours, great flying monsters, that were winged very ugly, and did go, as I thought, in a great bounding, rather than that they did fly proper as doth a bird. Yet I suffered no hurt from these; for I was swift to hide between the great boulders that were very plenty in that part; but no trees. For I was gone now past the forests of trees; there being none since that I had gone through a very shallow river, that I came to about the thirteenth hour. And this had I waded, and sounded my path with the staff of the Diskos; but I had kept mine armour upon me, lest there be things, even in water so shallow, that might bite and work harm upon me. But I gat through pretty quick, and had no hurt done me.

Now I had eat, as ever, at the sixth and the twelfth hours; and by that the eighteenth hour was come, I was nigh again unto a forest, that came down to the shore that went alway upon my right; and I to be very sore and wearied, as you shall know; for I had fought very desperate after my waking, and afterward climbed the great Rock, and then again to journey; so that it was, by this, nigh to one and twenty hours since that I did sleep.

And surely, I lookt this way and that way, constant, and did see no place proper to my slumber. But afterward, I considered I did be a fool, to lack such; for truly the trees were plentiful, and I could climb a great one, and strap my body safe, and so have a sure bed for my rest. And I did this thing, and went upward into a great tree, and did tie my body to the tree, with my belts; yet I eat and drank before that I went up the tree.

Now when I was fast upward in the tree, and had made a bed upon a monstrous branch, and had the Diskos ready upon my hip, so that it should not fall but be nigh to my hand, I lay a little while thinking upon Naani; and I went not over to sleep immediately, which was strange; yet mayhaps because that my bed was so uncertain.

And I considered very gravely how that it was a monstrous long while since that I did hear the Master-Word from the dear Maid; and

truly I was come a dreadful way from mine home, which was the Mighty Pyramid; for I had gone onward for ever through five and twenty great days of travel, and was not yet come to any place that did appear like to be that place where the Maid did abide.

And it did seem that I might even wander onward in that great Country of Fire and Water for a time beyond all that I had before gone; and this thought did put a great weight of trouble and weariness upon my heart; for the Maid had been in sore need of me, and I did feel sudden to be all adrift in the wilderness. But before this time, it had seemed as that I surely went aright. And mayhaps your sympathy shall tell you just how I to feel in the heart.

And after that I had lain there very awkward, and thought upon all matters, I minded me that I would try the compass again upon the morrow; but had no great hopes of the machine; yet did be willing to try aught to see where I had gotten to. And truly, as it did come to my mind, if that the compass did point a little as I did wot it was used to point in the Lesser Redoubt, then, in verity, I was surely come something more anigh to that unknown place of the world than I did dare to believe. And this to be plain to you.

Then a little time did pass in which I did wake and sleep, and wake and sleep, a little; but with no surety of sleep; but as that I was very tired of the heart, and did but lie too wearied to come properly to sleep.

And odd whiles I did lie with mine eyes half to open, and did look very dreamful upward among the dark branches of the tree, as they did show black and pretty against the redness of the shining that came from the sea; for there was stood a great and bright-burning fire-hill in that part of the sea that lay off the shore from me. And above the glaring of the fire-hill, there was the deep night that did brood for ever above in a monstrous black gloom of eternity, and did make the red smoke of the volcano to show deep and mighty and thunderous-seeming, afar up in the great dark. And the red and shining smoke did but show the utter hugeness of the night, that had been upon the world through the great ages.

And, in verity, as I did lie there so dreamful, it did come to me afresh how wondrous strange was mine adventure; and how that I did lie warm and alive in a Country of red light and smoking seas. And, truly, as I did remember and consider, there was a great and lost world above me, upward through the dark . . . maybe an hundred and fifty great miles up in the grim night.

And this thing did strike me very solemn, as I did lie; and I do trust that you conceive how that there was, in truth, afar above in the

eternal and unknown night, the stupendous desolation of the dead world, and the eternal snow and starless dark. And, as I do think, a cold so bitter that it held death to all living that should come anigh to it. Yet, bethink you, if one had lived in that far height of the dead world, and come upon the edge of that mighty valley in which all life that was left of earth, did abide, they should have been like to look downward vaguely into so monstrous a deep that they had seen naught, mayhaps, save a dull and utter strange glowing far downward in the great night, in this place and in that.

And surely, as you shall have seen, I have set the Great Deep of the Valley to be, maybe, an hundred and fifty miles of night; for, as you do mind, it was conceived that the Valley of the Night Land was an hundred miles deep, and mayhap to be more; and I had come from that Place downward of the Mighty Slope, and of the Gorge, a very great way. Yet, in verity, I do believe in my heart this measuring was utter wrong; for I think the deep to have been monstrous, beyond these miles that I do give; yet have I no proving of this belief, and do set it down for no more than it is.

Now, presently, I had ceased from these vague thinkings and half dreamings, and was gone truly to sleep. Yet, nowise did I sleep very strong; but did seem to come anigh to wakefulness, this time and that. And, as it did chance, this was mayhaps a very good thing for my life; for I did presently come awake more surely, and did turn on the great branch; for there was a noise in the air, that was not the noise of the great fire-hill.

And the noise did grow, very heavy and lumbersome. And, in a moment, there came seven Humped Men, running among the trees, as that some monstrous thing did pursue. And immediately they were beneath the tree in which I did lie; so that a great fear came upon me, and I loosed the belt from the branch, that I should be free to fight.

And, directly upon this, I saw that the men did leap upward into the tree, beneath me; but not as that they did wot of me or make to come at me; but as that they did pay a great heed to some creature or happening that was far off among the trees. And surely, the noise did seem to come from that part, and did grow loud and mighty, and the Humped Men did all crouch very silent, and did make no noise or motion one to the other; but were quiet upon the lower branches.

And, as I did look now more to my ease, I perceived that they had each a great stone, and bloody, that did seem as that it were split to a certain sharpness, even as a stone doth break very natural. And they carried the stone under this arm or under that arm, so that they had their hands free to all matters.

And, alway the noise did come the more anigh, and I saw that a Humped Man did come running from among the trees, and did run beneath that place where the seven Humped Men did be on the branches. But they made no sign to the man, to save him; yet truly it was very plain that some monster pursued the man.

And immediately I saw how this thing was; for the Humped Man upon the ground, did not run so fast as might be; and I conceived that he did act to make some creature to come after him, to pass under the men within the tree. And surely this thing did prove to be; for there came very quick, a great and ugly thing, that had an ugly way of putting down the feet, and did have seven feet to each side, which was very strange; and the back was as that it were horny, and the belly of the thing did seem to brush heavy upon the earth, and it grunted, as it went, and shook the earth with the weight of it; so that a monstrous noise came from it, upon so hasty a journey. And I did wot that it was not such a thing as did properly pursue after matters of food; but did rather eat of that which did need little haste, but a monstrous strength, to gain. And that it did so make after the man, was in truth because that it had been wounded and made fierce; for, indeed, there came blood from the creature from great wounds upon the back; but how these were made, I could not know in that instant.

And it did go under the tree in which I was hid; and in that moment when it past under the tree, the seven Humped Men did leap out of the branches, and did catch to the brute by the great horns of the spine; and I saw that the wounds were in the joints of the spine, as was plain when the back did work, with the going of the creature. And the seven Humped Men took the sharp stones from under their arms, and did strike very brutal in the wounds that were in the joints of the spine; and the creature roared and cried, and went onward into the trees at a great speed; and in all the time that it ran, the Humped Men ceased not to strike with the stones.

And sudden, when it was gone a distance off, it did roll very swift over upon the back, first to the right, as that it would go that way; so that the Humped Men did leap off upon the other side. And immediately the creature rolled to that side; and there ran clear of the brute only four of the Humped Men; so that I knew that three were slain. And afterwards, they that lived, ran beyond the beast, and gat up into a second tree, and the one that was chased, did entice the creature to follow, and so did tease it once more to pass beneath the other men; and they very swiftly again to the back of the creature; and so from my sight, striking with the great stones, and the beast bellowing very

loud and piteous. And how many of the Humped Men there were to
the beginning of that strange hunting, I know not; but surely there
were few that lived to the end.

And surely there were such things as this thing in the beginning
of the world, and again was it thus in the end; and I did ponder this
a little while, as I did sit upon the great branch, and hearken unto the
sound of the hunting, that was now gone a great way off, and was
presently beyond my hearing.

And afterward, I gat me to the earth, and did look this way and that
way, to see that no beast was anigh, neither any of the Humped Men;
and afterward, I eat two of the tablets and drank some of the water.

And when I had gat this far to a readiness for my going, I minded
me that I should try the compass again, as I did intend. And surely
the machine did point between the North and the South, upon the
Westward arc, even as Naani had told unto me; yet, as it did seem, with
somewhat more of a Southward pointing than she had made me to
think. And because of this telling of the compass, a great ease came
upon my spirit; for, surely, was not this but a sure sign that I did go
direct unto that hidden place of the world where the Lesser Refuge
did abide; but yet was not come over-close, so that the pull of the
Mighty Earth-Current of the Great Redoubt was something stronger
than in the place where was the Little Pyramid.

And all this did I think very swift to myself, and had a glad uplift-
ing of the heart, as you do perceive; so that I went forward upon my
journey, with a great stride, and did scarce fear any strange thing that
all the Country did hold, in that moment.

And I went all that day at a strong pace, and did be oft tempted
to send the Master-Word unto Naani; yet did keep from so foolish an
acting, the which, mayhaps, had brought straightway upon me an Evil
Power, and had given me to Destruction when that I was near come
to the succour of the Maid. And it was this quick and constant fear of
the Evil Forces of the Night Land, that did keep me ever from calling
unto Naani, lest that they should discover me, and follow after; and
this, I doubt not, you to know by now so well as I.

Now, by the sixth hour, I was come into a part of the Country
where there were an exceeding abundance of steam fountains and
sprayings and great upboilings of water in basins of rock; and the
air did be full of the sounds and the roarings of the boilings and the
spoutings, and of a hot mist and spray; so that, truly, I had scarce the
power to see to my front, nor to any side.

And here, presently, I made a pause, and did eat and drink, and

afterward went forward again; and I did keep the shore of the sea always to my right, and so did go proper to my way; yet with no great ease; for the sea also did steam very strong in that part, and because of this great fog of steam, I was surely much laboured to make a great speed, lest unseeing I go headlong into an hole of the boiling water.

And in the ninth hour, I did go clear of the hot boilings, and was come again free of the mist and the steam, and might look with mine eyes to my going. And, surely, as I did perceive, I was come to the end of the great sea that had been ever to my right; for it did go against the feet of great and monstrous mountains, that went upward for ever into the night, and did seem as that they were the hither wall of that strange Country of Fire and Water. And so was I stood there very much taken upon doubt; for how should I go farther.

And after that I had been there a while, in a bewilderment of doubt and of wit, I went to the left, along the feet of the mountains; and truly this but of common sense; for how might I go any other way, save I go back again!

And at the twelfth hour I eat two of the tablets, and drank some of the water, and went forward once more. And lo! at the fifteenth hour, I was come to a place between the mountains, even an upward gorge, very dark and gloomy, and without light for a great way.

And, in verity, I did not want to go up the gorge, in that it was so dreary a place and narrow and horrid and drear-seeming, after the light and wideness of the Country in which I did yet stand.

And presently, I did go past the mouth of the gorge, that I should learn whether there went another way out of that Country. And this-wise, for a great hour more, along the feet of the mountains, and did presently come to a monstrous black river, that was, maybe, a mile wide. And it to be very shallow, and seeming as that the water scarce to cover the mud of the bottom. And here and there a great steam did come from it, and spirtings and moundings-up of the mud in many places, and monstrous babblings and puffings-up of strange smoke, as that a great heat went beneath it in this place and in that.

And surely it went backward into the country for a mighty way, so far as my sight did go; and I did think it to be no river, but truly a further sea. And there was no way across; for there were no trees anigh, to make me a raft, neither might I wade across; for it might be shallow here and deep there, and the mud be in all places. And, moreover, I had been like to be caught in one of those upburstings of mud, even did I have a raft to go upon. And because of all these things, I gat me back again to the Gorge, and presently I did go upward into the darkness.

Now, I went upward very steady, save that I did stumble oft, and did go through six great hours. And truly it did seem that I went in an utter dark, because that I had been awhile in so constant a light.

And, by that I had been six hours in the Gorge, I was gone right away from the Country of the Seas, and did be as that I was back into some place that was like to the dreadness of the Night Land. For there were in this place and in that place of the Gorge, red fire-holes, even as in the Night Land. Yet not many until that I was come a great way up of the Gorge. And there did be life of horrid things about the fires, as soon I did wot; so that I made to keep off from them. Yet, as you shall perceive, I must come oft pretty near, because that the Gorge was nowheres scarce an hundred good paces across, and did oft come very narrow, so that I did come oft anigh to the fire-holes, whether that I did heed to or not.

And all that time, and ever, did the Gorge go very sharp upward, so that it was a very weary thing to make great trial of speed, as you shall know. But yet I went so fast as I could do; for I was grown sudden very excited about the heart, and to feel as that I did surely draw anigh to that strange and hid place of the world, where was the Lesser Refuge.

And when I had gone upward through six great hours, as I did say, I took caution for a place proper to slumber; for I was surely very wearied.

And I saw a place presently, afar upward of the dark side of the Gorge, upon the right, where a ledge of the Rock did show in the glaring from one of the fire-holes that made a gloomy light in that place. And I climbed unto this ledge, and did find it to be secure, and awkward to come upon. And presently, after that I had eat and drunk, I did compose myself unto sleep, the which came very speedy upon me, whilst yet I did believe I thought only upon the sweetness of the Maid. And truly it had been something over three and twenty hours, since last I did sleep; so that I was greatly awearied.

And in six hours I waked and did eat, and did climb downward again to the Gorge, and so unto mine upward journey.

Now, as you do perceive, when that I was come properly a great way up the Gorge, and had come among the fire-holes, there was no more an utter darkness, for the dull red glare of the pits beat upward upon the black sides of the rock-mountains, that did make the sides of the Gorge; so that oft I did see both sides very plain in the lower parts; yet of the height of the Gorge, who might know aught; for the black sides did go upward for ever into the everlasting night.

And because of the light from the fire-pits, I did see, time and oft

about the fires, horrid monsters, both that were snakes, and others like to scorpions so great as my head; but no more than these for a long while. And afterward I perceived that surely other matters did move among the rocks of the Gorge; so that I did keep the Diskos very ready in mine hand; yet had truly no use for it all that day.

Now I eat and drank at the sixth and the twelfth hours, and went onward at a very strong speed. And at the sixteenth hour, I did seem as that I knew the æther to be stirred about me, and the beat of the Master-Word very faint upon mine inward ear. And immediately, a wondrous great and lovely thrilling did wake all my being; for surely, I said, this was the spirit of my love, calling unto me with her brain-elements. And, indeed, this was a very proper and sensible thinking; for had the Master-Word been sent from the Mighty Pyramid, I had been like to hear it very plain, by reason of the force of the Earth-Current which was with them and to their command. But, as you do know, the Earth-Current was nigh gone from the Peoples of the Lesser Refuge; so that they were over-weak to make any proper calling. And this I have spoken of before this place.

Yet, in a little while, as I did stand very hushed, that I should hark the better, I was come to doubt whether that I did truly hear the Master-Word. And one moment I did say that it had surely beat in the night about me; and immediately would I be just so unsure; and so in a while I gat once more to my journey, and had doubt in my heart; yet, as you shall conceive, more of hope. And because of this thing, I went onward for thirty great hours from the time that I did wake; for my heart was excited within me.

And when that I had gone so long forward as this, I did see how that I did foolishly; and I lookt about for a place for my slumber; and I found a small cave that was clean and empty, as I did discover by the shining of the Diskos which I made to spin a little time. And the cave was in the cliff of the mountain that made the right side of the Gorge, and was nigh twenty good feet from the bottom of the Gorge, and hard to approach.

And when I was come secure into the cave, and sure that it was proper to my purpose, I eat four of the tablets, as was just and nice to my belly, and did afterward drink some of the water, and so to my slumber; and all the while, very sweet and strong in my thoughts upon Naani; so that surely I was a little time before that I had myself rightly unto sleep.

And I slept six hours, and did wake, for I had set my spirit hard unto such wakening; yet was I still greatly yearning for sleep. But this

did go somewhat, when that I had fought a little with my need. And afterward, I eat two of the tablets, and drank some of the water, and did gat my gear upon me, and was presently down unto the Gorge; and so again to my journey.

Now in all that day I did go with a very stern speed; for it did seem as that my soul did know for surety that I was truly come something nigh unto that hid place in the night where I should find mine Olden Love again. And the sweet hope that was bred of the calling that had seemed truly to sound about my spirit, was in all my being, and more sure on that day, than before that I had slept.

And I went thirty hours in all, even as before, ere that I did come again to sleep, and I eat and drank at every sixth hour, so that my strength should abide within me. And by that I was come to the ending of the thirty hours, I was sorely awearied, and gat me upward of the monstrous cliff that did make the left side of the Gorge, having perceived in a place a great ledge of the rock, that did seem very proper for my purpose of slumber.

And when I was come upward upon the ledge of the rock, I saw that there did seem something, like to a mighty spider, that did stay half without of a hole in the back part of the ledge. And I smote the thing gently with the Diskos, so that it was very quickly dead; and afterward I searched well about; but did gladly perceive that there abode there no other horrid creature.

And I eat two of the tablets, and drank some of the water; and did afterward make me ready for slumber, as ever. But now I did put the cloak well about me; for truly there was grown a chill into the air of the Gorge; and here also will I tell how that it did seem unto me that the air was gone something from that great thickness and strength which had been with me in the past days of my journeying.

Now I was gone so tired, that I fell upon sleep in a moment, yet with a dear thought and anxious, concerning Naani; but was so starved of the body for slumber, that even mine anxiousness kept me not awake. And I was then so fast with sleep that I knew naught for eight hours of very sound slumber. And then did I awake, and very thankful of the heart that no evil beast or creeping thing had come upon me whilst that I was so utter lost in sleep.

And now, truly, was I something fresh and ready; and I ate and drank, and had my gear once more upon me, and so down into the Gorge. And afterward, I went upon my journey for eighteen hours, and did pause but a little while at the sixth and the twelfth hours that I should eat and drink.

And when the eighteenth hour was nigh come, I perceived that the nature of the Gorge was grown very horrid and dank. And in verity, I did feel as that afar upward in the night the black mountains that did make the sides of the Gorge had come together, and did make a monstrous roof unseen in the utter height.

And this thing I do tell, only as of my belief; for I have no very sure proof. Yet, truly, my reason doth say likewise; for there did oft drip water upon me out of the darkness, even though I walked in the middle way of the Gorge; and how should this thing be, save that there went an overreaching of the sides, that should let the mildew down upon me.

And in this place, and for more than eleven great hours, there were fire-holes and fire-pits only in this part and in that, and each a great way off from another. And they burned very dull, and did seem to throw a fume of sulphur into all the air, as that there was no freedom above for the stink to pass away. And in every place were the rocks of the Gorge very thick and slippery with strange growths; so that it was a sorrow to walk upon them. And all that time was there an heavy wetness and slowness in the air; and a smell, beside the stink of the fire-pits, as that I did go forward through a place where dead things did be.

And for a great time there was a horrid darkness, as it had been that the air was grown thick with the fumings of the fire-pits, as I do believe; and beside this thing there was, as I have said, but a dull fire here and another there; so that it was like that there should be a heavy dark. And because that it was so utter black, and because that there were growths upon the rocks in the bottom of the Gorge, I did go but slowly, and with pain of stumblings; and always with the stink of that place to trouble me half unto a sickness.

And sudden, as I did go past one of the fire-pits, I saw that the fire made a dull shining upon some monstrous thing that did move before me, upon the far side of the fire. And I came in one moment unto a swift silence, and hid among the rocks of the bottom of the Gorge. And I lookt very cautious at the thing that moved beyond the fire, and surely I had seen no thing so monstrous since that I had come free of the Night Land; for it was as that some huge Creature, like to the hull of a great ship did move down out of the dark of the upper way of the Gorge. And it went by the fire-hole, and onward into the dark of the lower way of the Gorge; and I had perceived somewhat of it, as it did go past the fire, and, surely, it was black and beslimed, and utter great in height and in length, and it went always without

noise, so that I had not known it to be there, but that I saw it plain with mine eyes. And, truly, if I do say that it was somewhat as that I had seen a monstrous slug-thing, surely I should use wise and proper words to make known to you this horrid brute.

And I stayed very quiet a time, and afterward I went upward again of the Gorge, and did use a new caution to my way, and saw that the Diskos was free upon my hip; for even thus I did carry the weapon, being that I must use both hands to my way, and to save me in my stumblings and slidings over the slippery rocks.

And once it did seem to me that some great thing moved in the darkness, and I went downward among the rocks, and stirred not my body for a great while; and sure am I that there went some living monster past me, that did stink as a loathsome grave. And afterward, I went on again.

And three hours did I go thus, and came at last to a place where a fire-hole did shine more ruddy; and I did look well about me, that I should perceive that part of the Gorge the better. And as I stood there, very quiet, away off from the fire, so that it did show no great light upon my person, I did note how utter still was that place; and this to take me anew, as though it had come fresh upon me. And here, there would be the drip of water, and again in that place, and again elsewhere; and all very solemn and very dismal. And the silence to be constant.

And presently, as I lookt, now to this way and again to that, I saw that there was a monstrous slug-thing laid upward against the black side of the Gorge, as that it had stood up on end; and the one end of the monster went upward beyond the light from the fire-pit; but the other part did come down and trail into the Gorge, as a long hillock, very ugly and black and beslimed.

And I near sweat with a disgust and horror of the thing; but afterward I had more courage, and spied well upon the brute. And surely, it moved not at all, any more than the side of the cliff of the Gorge; and I conceived that it stood not upward upon any feet; but clung to the rock, even as you shall see a slug to go. And for a great space I was very quiet and moved not, neither did I make to hide, but stood there very stupid.

Yet, in a time, I had more of courage which brought strength unto my heart, and I began again to go upon my way, but with an utter caution, and I then to creep for a weary time upon my hands and knees among the dank and weariful rocks and boulders that lay in the bottom of the Gorge. And thrice between four hours was I passed by hidden and monstrous things in the horrid dark places of the Gorge;

yet with no noise, save, as it might be, the odd rattle of a rock in this place and that; but with an utter and dreadful stinking. And I to be quiet as they went, as you shall think.

And each time now that I did go by the fire-pits and fire-holes that lay odd-ways in the Gorge, I did pause and search about me with mine eyes, very cautious, and oft now did I perceive how that the monstrous slug creatures did lie in this place and in that against the cliffs of the Gorge. And I did go then utter still, from this space to that space among the rocks, and oft upon the flat of my belly, and with a constant heed that I make not mine armour to knock against the boulders.

And always as I did go, there was a monstrous stench, and the choking of sulphurous smoke very oft. And here and there, as mine heart doth believe, there were utter great caverns within the mountains to the right and to the left; and of this thing I have some small proof; for once I did go by a place where a fire did burn, as it should be a fire-hole, afar inward of the mountain side upon my right; so that I saw in a moment that I looked in the darkness through the mouth of a mighty cave-place; and I went past very quick and silent, for I knew not whether any horrid thing should come forth out of that place to slay me.

And, truly, as I did think, if there did be one such place, there were like to be many; and mayhaps the slugs came forth from those caverns, where, as I did conceive there was naught save an eternal dripping of waters and the foul growth of things in all parts. Yet is this last but a thought, as I do say; and you shall wisely take it for no more than that.

Now, I came clear of the darkness and the slime and the stinking in about twelve hours after the time that I did think the mountains to be a roof unto the Gorge; and the air was now free and did seem as that some life and health did abound in it; and the fires did be more plentiful, and burned very bright and clean, and threw all their fumings upward, so that there was no more any bitter pain of sulphur within my throat.

And surely, it was with a thankful heart that I went onward, and with a good speed; for there was much of light all about me, in that there burned an hundred fire-pits here and in that place; so that I saw clear before me and behind, and conceived that the slugs did abide only in the closed part of the Gorge. And oft I did take the air very full into my lungs, for the sweetness of it, after the horrid stenchings that I had abode all those hours.

And presently, when I was come free of the roofed part of the

Gorge, maybe some three good hours, I lookt for a place proper to slumber; for it was surely something over three and thirty hours since that I did last come upon sleep; and I was utter worn and lost of strength with so much of creeping and harking for monsters, as you shall believe; moreover, about that time I had gone bitter long whiles between slumberings through more than an hundred hours, as you shall have perceived from my tellings.

Now, presently, I saw a small cave that went inward of the side of the Gorge. And I lookt into the cave, and found it to be sweet and clean, and very dry. And there was a small fire-pit off from the mouth of the cave that did throw a good light for my purpose; so that I saw there was no creeping thing or horror in the place; and I went in, and made to prepare for my slumber.

But truly, when I was come to look upon myself, I was utter soiled and did seem as that I stank with the slime and disgust of the dark part of the Gorge, where I had gone upon my hands, and upon my belly. And because of this, I was set that I should not eat or come to sleep, without I washed me.

And I went out from the cave, and there was a spring near to the fire-pit, as was oft in that part of the Gorge. And the spring was hot and did fill a hollow of the rock, very quiet and with a fuming of sulphur, as I did bend above it. And I washed mine hands and face and mine armour and gear, in the hot spring, and did dry me with my pocket-cloth; and so was sweetened and put to happiness of mind.

And I went back into the cave, and did sit in the mouth of the cave, with the Diskos to mine hand; and I eat four of the tablets, for I was gone a mortal long while without, and afterward I drank some of the water. And as I did eat and drink, I lookt out upon the lightness of the Gorge before me, and with a cheerful and composed heart.

And I saw presently that there came certain creatures out from their holes, even as it might be that they were part rats; but very strange looking, and not properly such. And some did lie about the fire-hole, and some did hunt about in the rocks; and one came presently, and had a snake by the neck. And it stood upon the snake, and did eat it, even while that the snake did lash about upon the rock. And the snake did lash until that it was nigh all eat; and a very strange thing this was to see, and something troublesome to the pity. Yet was I glad to perceive that there were enemies to the serpents of that place.

And when the rat creature did make an end of the snake, it made across to the spring, and did drink the hot water a while; and afterward back unto the fire, and there laid down anigh to the edge, and seeming

very sweetly comforted of the belly, which, in truth, was much otherwise with me. And, after that, I saw many creatures that went about the fire, and did have warmth from the fire and drink from the spring; and surely I did ponder that the Peoples of this our Age should say, if they had stood with me, that Providence had made nigh together the warmth and the drink that were needful unto life (for it was grown to a bitter chill now in the Gorge). But rather did this thing seem to me otherwise, that these creatures did be but of their circumstance, and if that it had been another way, then had they grown of their wits to meet it to their means of life. Yet, as some would say, the arguments do but meet, and be the same thing. And neither way do I care in this place; but do no more than to show unto you the working of my brain, in this way and that, as I made my journey.

Now, presently, when I was done eating, and come very ready to fall upon sleep, I went out from the cave and gat me certain boulders, the which I did carry into the cave. And when I was come back for the last time, I put them very secure in the entrance-way, that no small stinging creature come at me as I slept. And after that, I made ready, and went to my sleep, having sweet thoughts and slumbrous, of the Maid.

Now I slept very quiet that time, and was not over troubled with the chill of the Gorge, which was but little in that place, both by reason of the fire-pit and because that the cave did help to keep my warmth to me. And I had a deep slumber for eight hours, and waked then pretty tired, but strong to go upon my way. And after that I had sat a little while, I came full to wakefulness and afterward did eat two of the tablets and drink some of the water, the which I did, sitting in the mouth-part of the cave, after that I had cast free the boulders.

And afterward, I gat my gear upon me, and I went again upon my journey. And the Gorge did continue very light and cheerful, with the shining of the fires; and oft there did be a little steam that did hiss from this part or that of the bottom of the Gorge and did blow very quaint and noisy in the quiet of that place. And oft there did be hot pools, and everywhere the great boulders in the bottom way, and to the right and to the left the black and mighty sides of the Gorge that did go upward for ever into the everlasting night.

And so I did go, and had eat and drunk at the sixth hour, and gone onward again. And, lo! at the eighth hour, I did thrill sudden with a wondrous great thrilling; for, in verity, it did seem to me that the Master-Word did beat softly about me, out of all the night of the world. And all my heart did throb with great glowings of joy; yet was the beat of the Word unsure, so that I knew not truly whether my

spirit had indeed heard aught, for there was immediately a silence, as ever, about mine inward being. Yet, as you shall believe, there was a new hope and strength of courage in all my body and soul.

And I went forward very swift, and all renewed, as it were; and my strength and hope did make naught of any terror that should lie to bar my way, neither did I have further heed of the boulders that lay always upon my path, but did go over them with quick leapings, and a wondrous and thrilling eagerness of the heart within me.

And, sudden, in the end of the tenth hour, I perceived that the mighty walls of blackness that made the sides of the Gorge did be no more there, and that I was come truly upon the end of the Gorge. And I near trembled with hope and astonishment; for when I was gone a little way on, I had ceased to go upward any more, and was come clear out from the mouth of the Gorge, and did peer forth across a mighty country of night.

And it did seem to me as that I was come to a second Land of Strange matters, even as the Night Land where did lie the wonder of the Mighty Pyramid. And surely, I did think within my heart that I was come at last to that far and hidden place of the world where did be the Lesser Redoubt. But yet was there no place in all that night where did tower the shining lights of the Lesser Pyramid, the which I did hope vainly to perceive. And because that I saw them not, a great heaviness came upon my spirits for a time; but afterward the heaviness did go; for I put Reason to help my courage, and did plan this cause and that to show why that I was not come to sight of the shining embrasures of the Lesser Redoubt. But yet was there left an ache of doubting, as you shall well conceive.

Now this Land was very new and strange, and had a great light in this part, and a wondrous grim darkness in that. And I did pause a great while to determine how that I should go properly. And presently I bethought me of the compass, and did draw it forth, and set it upon the earth, that I should see how it did act. And truly it did go almost as Naani had told to me; so that I was very sure in all my being that I was in verity come anigh to the hidden Refuge. But yet did the compass give me no proper guiding to my way; so that I was no more wise to this end than before, only that I had the comfort of that which it did seem to assure.

And, in a little while, I went forward into the Land, and did hope that I should come presently to some matter to help my choice. And I went first toward a certain great glowing of fire that lay before me, and did seem joined to another great glare that went afar to my left.

And I found the ground of that Land to be very fair for my feet, and to have in this place and that certain bushes, even as it did seem to me, of the kind that we named moss-bushes in the Night Land, as you do know. And I made a very good speed, and went thus until I had gone for maybe six long hours. And by that time, I was come anigh to the glowing of light; and did keep now a strong caution to my going; for truly, as I did know from the tellings of the Maid, there were very horrid and dreadful Powers in that Land, and I did well to remember that I was come again to parts where might be the destruction of the spirit.

Now I made a pause, and lookt toward the glowing light; and it seemed to me that for a monstrous way unto the right and unto the left, there did be surely a great, hid valley in the earth before me. For the shining did seem as that it came up from out of a valley, as that there burned a deep light in such a place; but yet was I all unsure, and had no proper knowing whether indeed there did be any valley there, but only a strange and luminous shining that did come upward from the earth.

And I made no great haste now to go unto that place; but went down sudden into the bushes, and lay upon my belly, and had a new great fear upon my spirit. And presently, I parted the bushes a little, and made a place for spying.

And I looked a great time unto the place of the light, and now to this part and now to that. And sudden, I saw, as it did seem, a monstrous head within the glowing; for the glowing did seem at whiles as that it swept to and fore, as should a shining smoke that went obedient to a quiet wind: and so to hide and again to uncover. And in a moment I lost the great face, and was all unsure that ever I had seen aught.

And lo! in a little minute, I did see it again; but whether it did be the shape of some utter monster of eternity—even as the Watchers about the Mighty Pyramid—or whether it did be no more than a carven mountain of rock, shaped unto the dire picturing of a Monster, I did have no knowing. But I made that I should get hence very quick, and I did turn me about in the bushes, and went upon my hands and knees; and so came at last a great way off.

Now, presently, I came again upon my feet, and did take a new look around that Land. And I had the mouth of the Gorge to my back, and this I perceived by the shining of the fire-pits that made the place shown to me.

And to the left of the Gorge was an utter blackness, as I did conceive of black and monstrous mountains, through which the Gorge

did come. And to the right side of the Gorge there were many low volcanoes, that went always along the feet of the great mountains that made the right wall of the Gorge. And I saw the feet of these dark mountains, because that the light from the little volcanoes made a glare upon the lower slopes.

And so shall you have some knowing of that part of this second Land of Night.

And a good way off, was the shining that I had journeyed unto, and the shining went into a distant light through a part of the Land that lay afar to my left, for it stretched a great and strange way toward me, out of the leftward gloom, and came unto my front, and so away into an utter distance. Yet, though it was so great, you shall not think that it made any huge light in the Land; but was rather as that it had a shining made unto other ends; for it made not a great lightness in the Land.

And you do now perceive something roughly how the Land did seem to my back part and unto my left, and somewhat before my face. And because that I did think to have no profit to my search, if that I went to the left, I made attention unto the Right. And here there was much of darkness; yet oft the shining of fire-holes in this place and that amid the darkness. And, as I did look, it grew very plain upon me how great was the spread and drear wideness of that Country of Night; and how that I did be an utter lonesome person in all that dark. And so shall you be with me in sympathy of the utter greatness of my task, and know of the fear that did breed, odd whiles, that I should search until I die, and never find. And you to give me good human understanding.

Now I made no more to delay, but went unto the right, and did keep the chain of the little volcanoes something level to my course; though a great way off. And I went thus with a strange growing of hope, and an excitement, for ten hours, and had eat not then for more than twenty hours, and surely not since the sixth hour of that day and this because that I was so utter shaken from my calmness of going.

And at the tenth hour, I went utter weak, and did seem surely as that I must swoon. And lo! I bethought me how that I was gone so long without aught for my belly. And surely, when I was quiet a time, I eat four of the tablets, and in a good while did feel all renewed, and would rest no more, after that I had drunk some of the water, but went onward; for, in verity, my spirit did be as that it had slain me, if that I had lain down at that time. And this because hope was so fierce in me; for I to feel indeed that I was come near to the Maid.

And I went ten hours more, until that I did truly totter upon my feet, with utter and dreadful weariness; for I had gone now through someways of forty great hours, and had been foolish in mine eating and drinking, as you have perceived; but yet was this to be forgiven; for I was as that I should come any little minute upon the wonder of the Lesser Pyramid, shining afar in the night. Yet, truly, there was nowhere anything that might be likened unto it.

And I lay down there, just as I did be, and with no proper heed to my safety. And I was gone asleep in one moment, as it did seem; and waked not for twelve hours; and then did come suddenly unto knowledge; and thankful was I in the heart that no monster had come upon me in that dead-time of slumbering. And I eat four of the tablets, as was surely due unto me, and drank some of the water, and so gat forward again into the night.

And truly I was mortal stiff and did ache for a great while, and this did be in part because that I had wrapped not the cloak about me, ere I slept; for the Land was bitter cold and did make the blood very chill.

Now when I had gone onward through six hours, I ate and drank; for I did mind now to be wise and keep my strength good within me. And I went onward again at a very great speed, and full of an excitement. And surely, I did be glad at last that the tablets were so easy gone in the mouth, and unfilling to the belly; for I had been without power and patience to eat proper victual.

And at the tenth hour, I saw that there rose a red-shining out of the Land before me, as that it came upward from a mighty pit. And I made slow my way, and so, when I was gone on for two great hours more, I saw that monstrous figures went about, against the red glare of the shining. And I gat me down into the bushes which were very plentiful in that part.

And I stayed there for a certain while, and made a watch upon the red-shining and the figures; and, truly, it did seem to me that there were horrid giants in that Land, even as in the Night Land. And afterward, I crept away, and went outward from the little volcanoes, into that part of the Land that was dark, save, as you do mind, for the glare of fire-holes in this part and that.

And I went now with an utter care; for the giants had put a new caution into my heart, and I did surely mean that I should live to rescue mine own Maid, and have joy through all my life. And thereafter, I went with the Diskos in my hand, and at each hour that was the sixth, I eat two of the tablets, and drank some of the water, and so did keep my strength very good within me.

Now, presently, I was come to a place where the Land did go downward a great slope, and there was a difference in the earth that went beneath my feet, and no great plenty of the bushes; but only one in this place and one in that, and nowhere any fire-hole.

And I gat me down and did feel the earth with my hands, and lo! I did find presently smooth stones, and afterward olden shells. And immediately, a great delight took me; for Naani had told how that the Lesser Pyramid stood something nigh to the shore of an ancient sea, that was long dried up in the years of eternity. And surely it might be that I was come down into the dry bottom of that same olden sea, and should presently have sight of the Little Pyramid.

And because that hope was put so fresh into me, I went forward through, maybe, thirty hours, across the olden sea-bed; but in all that time I had no sight of the lights of the Lesser Redoubt. And a great trouble began to take me; for, indeed, Naani had not told me how great was the sea; and it might be that I should wander a weariful age across it, before that I come to the far side.

And it did come to me, presently, how that I should be wise to see that my way was very straight, so that I waste not my strength in useless wanderings. And I had a great care now to observe that the red-shining did be always upon my right, to my rear; and by this reasonable cunning did I make to steer very nicely through the great gloom of that place.

Now, as I did go across the bed of the great sea, I heard strange sounds, now in this part of the darkness, and now in that; and oft did there be a noise, as if things did run this way and that way in the bed of the sea. And once, afar off in the night, there did be a strange and horrid screaming; so that I did know truly that the monsters of that Land were out, and did go about in the dark.

And, as you shall perceive and understand, I was all unknowing of the lore of that Land; so that I knew not what to think of this strange sound or that, neither knew I what they might portend, but only that, as I did say, there were Monsters abroad. And I could do no more than have my way forward with an utter care always, and be very ready with the Diskos, or to hide, each as maybe according to the need.

And, surely, I went one-and-forty hours that day, and eat and drank after every sixth hour. And before this, in the seven-and-thirtieth hour, I heard a great roaring and bellowing in the night, coming nigh unto me; and afterward the thudding of monstrous feet, as that a giant ran past me in the darkness, and did make a chase of some creature. And the thudding of the feet and the roaring went far off into the night;

and there did seem presently to come back to me from a great way, a little screaming; but of this thing I had no surety; and I abode very hushed in a clump of bush, until quietness was come again all about; for there had been an utter frightening sound in the horrid voice and in the thudding of the great feet.

Now, in the one-and-fortieth hour of that day, I came upon the farther shore of the olden sea. But lo! there was nowhere any light to tell me aught of the Lesser Refuge. And truly, a great doubt and bewilderment took me; for, indeed, I could not perceive how it might be that I saw not the lights of the embrasures of the Lesser Pyramid. And a great despair took me; so that I sat down there upon the shore of the olden sea, and had no heed of anything for a while.

But afterward, I ate and drunk, and went into a clump of bush, and wrapt the cloak about me, and so went fast unto sleep, with the Diskos handy to my breast. And, in verity, the pain of the despair and the bewilderment of mine heart did make rather for sleep, than to keep me wakeful; for, indeed, I was half stunned of the brain and of my courage; and did seem now the farther off from the ending of my search than ever I had been.

And I slept six hours, and waked then, sudden. And I leaned up upon mine elbow in the bush, and harked very quiet, perchance some noise had shaken my sleep from me. But, indeed, there was nothing, only that I was wakeful, and did mind me of my trouble of failure. Yet now, I did invent this thing and that thing to make natural account that I was not come to the Lesser Redoubt; and so had hope again within me; yet much also of doubt and bewilderment.

And I eat two of the tablets, and drank some of the water, and again to my journey. And I made that I should keep along the shore of the sea, the which I did through twelve hours, and was then still so much in doubt as ever.

And I ceased from my journeying, and lookt about me over the Land, and lo! I did note how that a weak and strange shining was in the air of the Land, at a great way; as it had been that a far spreaded and faint glowing made a little glare into all the night unto my left and before me.

Now I ate and drank, and made to steady my spirit; for I did fear lest I should feel utter lost in all the night of the world, and to know not where to make any more my search, and so to grow desperate in despair. And this thing you will understand.

And afterward, I did make across that Land, unto the place where it did seem that the dull shining was something bright. And I went

thus through eighteen hours, and did make pause at each sixth hour, and ate and drank very resolute; though, in verity, it did seem as that even so small a matter as the tablets did be like to choke me. And by this is it plain to me how great an anguish was come upon my spirit, lest that I was all astray, and should have no joy to succour mine Own.

And thrice in the time that I did go, there did be a running of feet amid the darkness; and odd whiles strange and horrid cryings in the night; so that I put a force upon my despair, and hid me; for, indeed, I had no right to lose care of my life, if there did be any chance yet that I find the Maid.

And lo! in the eighteenth hour, which was truly the thirtieth of that day, I found the shining in the night to be grown very plain, and an utter stinking of sulphur; and truly I did be aware that the Land went upward.

And I made upward through seven hours, and the light did grow more plain, and was of a dull redness, very sombre and heavy. And in the end of six more hours, I ceased to go upward, and did know of a strange low sound, that did be like to no other sound that ever I did hear; and was like to a dull roar that did never have ceased through eternity.

And I went forward unto the light, and the Land to be now as that I went over an upland plain. And I did go thus through five hours, and the low roar did grow ever upon mine ears. And truly! even as I did shape my thoughts to take a caution for my body, I went upward again a little, and came out upon the edge of a mighty cliff, and the low and constant roar did moan upward against me with an everlasting muttering. And I lookt downward a monstrous way, and surely there was spread out a mighty sea, as it did seem, of dull fire, as that a red-hot mud did lap very deep and quiet below me in all that night.

And I lookt outward across the strange sea, and the far side was hid from me; for, surely, there were dull and solemn clouds that came off the sea, and hid the distance from me. And the clouds to glow a little redly; and so to rise, and presently to blacken into the night. And I lookt to the right and to the left, and it was plain that the black cliffs did stretch out both ways, and did go downward ever into that monstrous sea of slow fire. And there were great headlands that went out into the fire, as into a sea; and the fire did lap very quiet about these, and where the fire lapt about them, there did shine and spirt out green flames and vapours at diverse times.

And, indeed, as I did perceive, I was come to an upward sea of fire, as it were the deep inwards of a low and utter monstrous volcano,

that was flat of the top and utter big across. And, in verity, I did look downward into the fires of the inward earth, and a very wondrous sight was it, to stand there alone upon the cliffs of that everlasting sea. And a great heat came upward from the dull and grim fire of that gloomy sea, and a reek of sulphur; so that I was like to be choked, and did go backward from the edge of the cliff.

And surely, I was come to the end of that Dark Land upon that side, and had nowhere perceived the Lesser Pyramid in all the night of my travel. And a new despair came upon me; for, indeed, it seemed I was come all astray in the night of the World, and did nowise have any knowing whether I stood near to the Country of the Lesser Redoubt, or whether that I was gone half across the World unto a strange place.

And, then, as the despair troubled my spirit and dulled the beating of my heart, a sudden thought did light up a fresh hope within me; for, indeed, as you do know, I was come upward of a great height, and did surely have a huge view over all that Land; and mayhaps the Lesser Pyramid did lie somewhere in a valley, if, in verity, it did be anywheres at all in that Country. And I turned me from the cliffs, and lookt backward over all the night of the Land; but there was nowhere in all that Country the shining of the Lights of the Lesser Pyramid.

And lo! of a sudden I did know that there was something in the night. And I stared, with a very keen and anxious look. And behold, there was the black shape of a great pyramid afar off in the night, that did show against the shining of the distant light; for it did stand between me and the far-off fires. But until I was come to that place, whence I did look, I had not stood to have it plain against the shining upon the other side of that Land.

And how I did feel in that moment, I have no words to set out unto you. But surely was my heart gracious with thankfulness, and I ready to leap with joy and hope, and all my body thrilled with an excitement that would not have me to be silent; so that, suddenly, I began to shout foolishly across the night. But I came soon to wisdom and silence, as you shall think.

X

The Maid of the Olden Days

NOW, AS YOU SHALL perceive, all mine utter despair was turned in a moment into an huge gladness and a great hope; so that it did seem to me that I should be with my dear One in but a little while. Yet was this an over-hope and expectation, and was not like to have a swift satisfying; for, truly, I was made aware of naught, save that I did perceive the shape of a great pyramid, going upward into the night.

And I knew that the Pyramid did surely stand upon an hill in the midst of that dark Country, for only so might it show so great and high. And I set me to run swift downward into the Land, so that I should make a strong going unto the Pyramid.

And I ran for a few little minutes, and lo! I fell headlong, and did truly feel as that I had brake my neck with the hardness and pain of my fall. And I had no power to go forward any more for a great while; but did just be there where I did fall, and very helpless and moaning a little; so that any creature had been able to slay me, if that it had come upon me in that time.

Yet, presently, I was able to sit upon the earth, and did hold my neck with my hands, and afterward the pain went away; so that I gat once more to my feet. But now I went forward very wisely, and had, moreover, an anxiousness in my heart; for, indeed, how did it be that the Pyramid was so utter dark, if that it did be the Lesser Refuge, in truth. And immediately there did rise in me a fear that it should be some House of Evil in the dark of that Land, or some wicked Force working a Pretence and a bewilderment upon my sight. Yet, truly, the thing was plain now against the far-off fires of the Land; and I did have little thought but that it should be, in verity, the Lesser Refuge.

Now in the first moment that I did perceive the dark Pyramid, I had been without wit, save to run very quick and blind unto the place; for you to remember how long I had made so great a search. And af-

terward, I had been minded to call unto Naani with my brain-elements, sending the Master-Word, and my speech after to tell how that I was come unto her. But now I did heed to have caution, and to discover what this darkness should truly mean.

And so did I go downward again into the night of that Land, at the first with a carefulness; but presently with a fierce eagerness and expecting of the heart, the which had been dulled a little time with the horrid shaking and pain of my fall.

Now I had climbed unto the upper plain of the great volcano in, maybe, thirteen hours; but I went downward of that great Hill in ten, and had made a greater speed, but that I was sore shaken and unsure, by reason of my fall.

And in the end of the tenth hour, I perceived that I was come again to the great Plain of the Land; and I had no more any proper sight of the Refuge, because that it was upward afar in the darkness of the night. Yet was I abled now to see that there went a bulk between me and the far shinings, and did know that this great thing was surely the hill on which the Pyramid did stand.

And I went four hours across the Land, and did pass in this place and that, fire-holes that made a little red-shining in the night; and because of the fires in those far parts and a-near, there was not an utter dark.

And when I was gone four hours towards the Pyramid, I could no more see the distant shinings, for the bulk of the hill-bottom stood up between, and made all a blackness that way. And by this thing, I did guess that I was come nigh unto the hill; but yet was a great hour more before that I came to it. And in that five hours, since I was come down from the great Volcano, there had past me thrice and again, the sounds of things running in the night, and once there did be a sound as of a giant roaring afar, and a strange and horrid screaming.

Now I began to go up the hill. And, at the first, an utter excitement took me in the heart; so that I could have shouted the name of the Maid aloud in the night, with vain hopings that she should hear me and make an answer. But this state went from me very swift, as I did go upward, and there came a caution again about me, and a coldness of fear, as that my spirit did wot of something that my heart did not perceive.

And, presently, I was come upward almost to the top of the hill, the which took me nigh three hours. And surely, when I was come that I could see the grimness of the Pyramid, going upward very desolate and silent into the night, lo! an utter shaking fear did take me; for the

sweet cunning of my spirit did know that there abode no human in all
that great and dark bulk; but that there did await me there, monstrous
and horrid things that should bring destruction upon my soul. And I
went downward of the hill, very quiet in the darkness; and so in the
end, away from that place.

And I was four great hours before that I was come clear away
from the hill, and I did feel that there was not any safety for my spirit
in all that Land. And surely I went a little blindly, in the first, and did
go with no heed unto my way.

And presently, I was upon the shore of the olden sea, and had no
knowing how that I was come there; for, surely, I did think it to be a
great way off. But now I do think that the dry bed of the sea did curve
around unto that place, or that there did be two, or more, olden seas
in that Country of Night.

Now, presently, I sat me down, very weak and bewildered; for it
was as that my heart did lie dead within me. And, in verity, you shall
perceive how this thing was, for I did know by the tellings of my spirit
that there abode evil things in the dark Pyramid upon the hill; and I
doubted not but that destruction had come upon the Peoples of the
Lesser Pyramid, and that evil creatures and Powers did now abide in
that place. And if this thing did be truly so, I was come over-late to the
saving of the Maid; and with this thought I was very glad that some
evil thing should come that I should fight with it and die quickly; for
there was naught then in all the world to make me glad to have life.

And so shall you know the utter desolation that was in my heart;
and, truly, I can perceive both the wiseness and the unwisdom of
my reasonings; for, indeed, I did have no sure knowing that the dark
Pyramid did be truly the Lesser Refuge. But yet, in verity, my spirit
did know with a certain sureness, and there was no doubt concerning
this thing, in all my being.

And, after that I had sat there awhile, I did mind me suddenly that
I should send the Master-Word through the night; for, indeed, how
else might I ever know whether Naani did yet live; though, in truth,
I had little, save desperate hope in this matter; but yet did remember
how that I had seemed odd times of my journey to hear the beat of
the Master-Word with my spirit, out of all the dark of the world.
And, in verity, if Naani answered not to the Word, but there came
instead an Evil Power to destroy me, I should but cease me of mine
utter heart-ache.

And I stood me upon my feet, and looked outward about me
into the blackness of that Land. And I sent the Master-Word with

my brain-elements; and immediately I called Naani, thrice, sending the call with my brain-elements.

And lo! in a moment, as it did seem, there broke around me out of all the mystery of night, low and solemn, the Master-Word, beating in the night. And immediately there did sound within my brain a far, small voice, very lone and faint, as that it had come from the end of the world. And the voice was the voice of Naani and the voice of Mirdath, and did call me by mine olden love-name.

Then, indeed, I did near to choke with the utter affright of joy that did take me in the heart, and also I was shaken with a mighty excitement, and my despair was gone, as that I had never known it. For, in verity, Naani did live and did call unto me with her brain-elements; and surely I had not heard the voice of mine Own for an utter age of grim labour and dread.

And the voice was, as I did say, as that it came from one that did be in a far place of the earth. And, in verity, whilst I stood dazed with a great joy that the Maid did live, I knew within me, concerning the fear that she was utter far off; and what peril might come anigh to her, before that I should stand to her side, to do battle for her life and well-being and mine own joy.

And lo! in the same moment, and before that I made further speech unto Naani, I did wot that someone did be a little way off from me, in the bushes, where a fire-hole did burn anigh to me; and it was as that my spirit knew this thing, and told of it unto my brain. And I made no answer unto the Maid, across all the dark of the world; but went very swift into a great bush that was nigh to the fire-hole, upon this side.

And I lookt through, into the open space that did be about the fire-hole. And there was a little figure that did kneel, sobbing, upon the earth, beside the fire-hole; and truly it was a slim maid, and she did seem as that she harked very desperate, even whilst yet she did sob. And surely, mine own soul did Know, all in one white moment of life. And she there, unknowing, and harking unto a cry of the spirit, that she did think to come through all the desolation of the night—even from the Mighty Pyramid. For oft, as I did perceive, had she cried unto me in all that lonesome month, and known no answer; neither that I was making a desperate way unto her; for, indeed, her weakness was great, so that she had no power to throw the Word strongly afar, neither to make plain her spiritual cryings through any mighty space of the æther.

And lo! I drew in my breath, and set my teeth a moment, to steady my lips; and I said: "MIRDATH," out of the bush where I did be, and

using natural human speech. And the Maid ceased from her weeping, and lookt this way and that, with an utter new fear, and with a frightened hope that did shine with her tears in the light from the fire-hole. And I divided the bush before me, and went through the bush, so that I came out before her, and did be there in my grey armour; and I did pause then, and was all adrift in myself; for my heart said that I should take this Maid into mine arms again; for that I was come again to be with Mirdath after an utter lost Eternity. But yet was I all paused; for truly she was Naani and she was Mirdath, and she did be a stranger in mine eyes, and very dainty and pretty and shaken with woe and sore trouble and grief.

And in that same moment of my coming unto her out of the bush, she screamed and fell back from me, and strove weakly to gain unto the hither bushes; for, truly, she knew not what was come upon her in that first little moment. And immediately she saw that it did be an human man, and no monster to slay her, and in that instant I said the Master-Word unto her, aloud, that she should have knowledge of peace and help. And I told my name, and said I am That One. And she knew this thing, even as my lips made the sounds. And she cried out something in an utter broke voice, and ran unto me, and thrust her two small hands into my charge and keeping, and fell thence into a great sobbing and shaking, so that I was all in trouble to ease her; but did keep a silence and held fast her hands, for I had not on mine armoured gloves.

And she leaned against me, very weak, and seeming wondrous like to a child. And lo! in a while she ceased to sob, and did but catch her breath this time and that, but said no word. And I bethought me that she did suffer of hunger, for I perceived that she had been long wandering and alone, and was come unto the end of hope, when that I did come.

And the Maid stood there yet silent, for she might not yet command her mouth to speak. And she trembled as she stood. And I opened my left hand, and lookt at the hand within my palm, and surely it was utter thin and wasted. And I made no more pause, but lifted mine Own and set her easy upon the earth, with an hump of smooth rock unto her back. And I stript off my cloak very quick, and put it about her, for she was scarce covered with her clothes that had been all torn among the bushes; so that part she shook with an utter chill, and part because of weakness, for she was nigh to be starved unto her death, and destroyed with her grief and lonesomeness.

And I took from my back the scrip and the pouch, and I gat a tablet

from the scrip, and brake it into my cup, and with the water I made a little broth very swift upon an hot rock that was to the edge of the fire-hole. And I fed the broth unto the Maid, for truly her hands did shake so that she had spilt it all, if that I had done otherwise.

And she drank the broth, and was so weak that presently she did fall again to sobbing, yet very quiet; so that I strove not to be troubled in the heart; for, indeed, this thing was but reasonable, and not cause for me to have an anxiousness. But I put my hands under the cloak and took her hands into mine and held them strong and firm; and this did seem to bring something of peace and strength unto her; so that presently the trembling and the weeping went from her. And, indeed, the broth was surely helpful in this matter.

And presently, I knew that her hands did stir a little within mine, and I loosed somewhat of my grip; and immediately, she graspt my hands with a weak and gentle grasp; but lookt not yet at me; only did stay very quiet, as that she did gather her strength within her. And, indeed, I was content; save that an anxiousness of the heart did stir me this time and that, lest some monster should come upon us. And because of this trouble, I did hark about me, now and oft, and with a new and strange fearfulness of danger, because that now mine Own was given unto my charge; and surely my heart would break, if that there came any hurt unto her.

Now, of a sudden, the Maid did make as that she would rise, and I loosed free from her, to give help. And she gat me by the hand, and slipt sudden to her knees, and did kiss my hand, and did begin again to weep. And surely I was so utter abashed that I stood very stupid and let her do this thing. But in a moment I drew free from her; for this thing might not be. And I gat me to my knee likewise before her, and took her hands, and kist them once, newly humbled, as it were; and thus should she know all that was in my heart, and of mine understanding. And she did but sob the more; for she was so weak, and utter moved unto me, because that I had come to her through the night of the world. And this thing I knew, though no speech had yet past between us. And I gave up her hands, lest she need them for her tears; but she left them to lie in my palms, as she did kneel there; and she bowed her head a little over her weeping; but did show that she was mine, in verity, unto the very essence of her dear spirit.

And I took her into mine arms, very gently and without caress; but presently I stroked her hair, and called her Naani and Mirdath, and said many things unto her, that now I scarce do wot of, but she did know them in the after time. And she was very quiet in mine arms,

and seeming wondrous content; but yet did sob onward for a great time. And oft did I coax her and say vague things of comfort, as I have told. But truly she did ask no more comfort at that time than that she be sheltered where she did be. And truly she had been lonesome and in terror and in grief and dread, a great and horrid time.

Now, presently, she was grown quiet; and I made to put her comfortable in the cloak against the rock, that I should have freedom to make her more of the broth. But yet she did nestle unto me, with a little sweet wistfulness, that made warm my heart in a most wondrous fashion; for surely she was mine Own. And she to begin to say odd words to me. And so to have gentle obedience, and to rest quiet against the rock, the while that I did make the broth. Yet ever her gaze did follow me, as I knew; for I must look oft her way.

And I took the broth to her, and she drank it, using her own two hands; and I sat by, and eat three of the tablets and drank some of the water, for truly it was a foolish great time since last I had eat.

Now, in a while, the broth did make bright the eyes of the Maid, and she did begin to talk; and at whiles had pauses, because that she lacked of strength, and there was more to be told than an human may have the heart-strength and cunning to make plain. And twice she did come again to sobbing; for, truly, her father was dead and the Peoples of the Lesser Redoubt all slain and dispersed through the night of that Land.

And I learned that an Evil Force had made action upon the Peoples within the Lesser Redoubt; so that some, being utter weak by reason of the failing of the Earth-Current, had opened the Great Door, and gone forth into the night. And immediately there had come into the Lesser Pyramid, great and horrid monsters, and had made a great and brutish chase, and had slain many; but some had escaped forth into the night.

And with these had come Naani, after that her father, the Master Monstruwacan, had been slain by a shaggy man, very brutal and monstrous. And there had been three maids with Naani, when that she made escape into the night; but there had come certain creatures upon them, as they did sleep among the bushes, and had stolen two, and the other maid had run off, as did Naani, and they had neither met the other any more.

And this dreadful happening unto the Peoples of the Lesser Redoubt, had been a great while gone, as it to seem to her; but she had no means to tell me how long this time should be; for, in verity, how should she make a count. Yet had it been a dread long while unto her;

and I found presently, that she had been lost through all that time that I did make my journey unto her; for, indeed, this thing I discovered by asking concerning my callings unto her. And she had heard none that did come to her, in any time since she had escaped out of the Lost Refuge into this dreadful Land.

Yet, in verity, oft had she callen unto me, until that her heart did grow sick with the desolation of her lonesomeness and her utter forsakeness. And her callings had told unto the Evil things of the Land that she did be in this part and that; for there had come things and beasts in search for her; but having the gift of the hearing, she had known of their approach, most whiles, and had come free from them; yet oft-times with piteous and fearful runnings and hiding among the rocks and the bushes, so that she had grown afterward to make no calling unto me, save odd whiles, lest she bring the monsters upon her. And, indeed, as you do know, naught had come plain unto me, for she was so utter weak that she had no power of her brain-elements to send the Word afar or the tellings of her spirit.

And because that she was so sorely chased, she had come nigh to be naked, even as I found her; for the bushes and the rocks had torn her garments from her, and she had naught with which to make any proper mending of them. And for food she had eat the moss upon the rocks, and odd strange berries and growths, and had drunk of the waters of the hot springs; and oft had she been made utter sick, because of the sulphur, or somewhat, of the water and, maybe, the poison of odd plants. Yet, as I did think, it was like that the first did save her life from the second; but in this thing I do make only a guessing.

And in all that dreadful time, since that she had come to be quite alone, she had heard a score drear things; for there had been once the slaying of a young maid nigh unto her, by some Brute out in the darkness of the Land; and thrice and more had she heard the feet of people running this way and that, and the tread of giants pursuing. And by this telling I did understand those things which mine ears had told to me as I did go across that Land, and surely a new pity and sorrow and horror did come upward within me. And the Maid told me how that she came once upon certain of the Peoples of the Lesser Redoubt, as they did hide among the bushes; but they ran, with no heed to her callings that she did be human, even as they; and by this is it plain the sore and dreadful panic that was upon the hearts of such.

And the bitter chill of the Land had made her to strive alway to be nigh unto the fire-holes that were very plentiful; but even as this did be needful unto her, so was it a thing that drew the Monstrous

Brutes of that Land, even as I had found in the Night Land, and in
the Upward Gorge. And because of this, she was oft made to stay afar
off in the utter cold of the night.

Yet, in truth, odd whiles she did be so desperate, that she would
make the venture, and so mayhaps have a time of warmth; and be-
cause of this, she had been nigh slain in her sleep, twice and thrice.
Moreover, there were snakes about the fires, though not over-plentiful
in all parts, and there did be spider-crabs and monstrous scorpions.

And, indeed, even as she had lain by the fire-hole, very weak and
seeming near unto her death, even this time when my call had come
unto her to stir her unto life and bitter knowledge of despair, even
then was she all surround by creatures that were like to crabs, that did
squat all about her, and did but wait for her to die; so that she had
been feared to sleep, lest they destroy her in her slumber.

And by this thing, she had known that her death was surely nigh;
and lo! out of all the night of the world had come the beat of the Mas-
ter-Word, strong and powerful, beating as a low and spiritual thunder
out of all the dark of the night. Yet had she thought of me, only as
speaking from the far-off Mighty Pyramid; so that the cry had brought
naught of hope unto her, but only a newer and more known despair.
And, behold, in a little minute, there had come her name, spoken surely
with the tongue; and a name that was different from the name that
my spirit had said after the beat of the Word. And immediately, I had
come out of the bush, and she had fallen back in a sudden great fear
that a monster was stolen upon her; and then did see a young man in
grey armour, and did know in one instant that I was that olden one
of her memory dreams, and the one that had spoken unto her in the
spirit across half of the dead world, as it did seem. And now was I
come through all that unknown desolation and affright, to succour
her. And she was immediately safe; but yet all broken because of her
weakness and her utter joy and her sweet honour for me.

And this is the chief of that which she did tell unto me; and the
way that she had seen and did regard the marvel of this our coming
together. But, surely, no man was made ever to be worthy of the way
that she did look upon me, or of the words that she did say unto me
in her weakness and happiness.

Now, with the Maid having speech concerning the spider-crabs, I
lookt presently well around, and surely, in a minute, I saw that they were
not gone away; but did be a circle of silent and steadfast watching and
impudence and horror all about us. And surely this thing put an anger
and disgust upon me; so that I gat to my feet, and went unto the border

of the light, and I spurned this little monster and that, and did truly kick maybe a dozen, before that they were content to be gone. And by this thing shall you know of their calm and foolish assurance; but yet were they seemingly without courage; for they made not to attack me. Yet a true crab of this day been wishful to pinch me, had I put my toe forth unto it.

Now, I went back to the Maid, and she did laugh with a little, weak gleefulness; so that I perceived that she was like to be a very joyous maiden, if but I did have her in health. And I made her another cup of the broth, and she drank it very easy. And afterward, I made a very stern and playful order that she must sleep, and, indeed, she to need it sore, for she was gone again from her excitement, and her weakness upon her; yet very happy and content and without fear.

And I made a smooth place for her, and put the pouch and the scrip to be for a pillow, and I did lay her there very quiet and sweet in the cloak, and covered her feet; but, indeed, I saw first that they did be sore cut and without any gear to them; so that I perceived that Mine Own had worn out her foot-gear utter in her lonesome journeyings, and in running from Brutes that did come to find her. And so I to know more in the heart, somewhat of the true dreadfulness and fear that had companioned Mine Own. And I was minded then that I would wash and bind up her feet; but yet was she so utter worn, that I did prefer that she sleep so soon as she might, and afterward, when she was come wakeful again, then should I take a proper heed of her feet. And truly, they were very small and shapely.

And presently, she slept; and, surely, I doubt whether she had slumbered so peaceful and proper for a great month; for she never to have known when any evil thing should come upon her in her sleep. And this to be a very dreadful feeling, as you do know well; for you do know how I had been in this same matter.

Now, while Naani did sleep, I stript off mine armour, and took off mine under-suit, which was named the Armour-Suit, and a very warm and proper garment, and made thick that it should ease the chafe of the armour. And afterward, I put on the armour again; but the suit I folded, and laid beside the Maid; for, truly, she was nigh unclothed, by reason of the bushes and the rocks, that had rent her garments all-wise.

And I stood watch for the Maid, the while that she did slumber; and surely she went ten long hours. And I walked upon this side of the fire-hole and now upon that, and did oft cease, that I might hearken both with mine ears and with my spirit; for, truly, I was all wakened to a new care and delight, and did have a fresh and doubled fear of any Horrid Creature or Force of Evil. And this shall be very plain to you.

And in the end of ten long hours, the Maid wakened, and I ran to her all joyed that she was come again to knowledge and to be that I could talk with her.

And she sat upward and looked at me, and there was new light and movement in her, so that I knew her strength was come back into her. And for a little minute, she said naught unto me, the while that I did ask how she did be; and she lookt at me very keen, so that I wondered some wise in a daze, what was in her mind.

And she askt me, of a sudden, how long it did be since that I had slept. And having not thought to put away her asking, because that the question was over sudden, I said four-and-eighty hours, which should be three days and the half of a day of four hours and twenty; and this thing I knew, because that I kept alway a very careful counting of the hours, lest that I get all adrift, and know not how long I was taken to come to this place and that.

And, truly, even as I told this thing to the Maid, I was grown very quaint in the head; for, indeed, I was gone a wondrous while without slumber, and had done much and bitter work in that time; and before then had been much lacking of rest, as you do know.

And, sudden the Maid cried out something, and tost the cloak from her, and had me into her arms, and did heed not to have any foolish shame of her nakedness. And, in verity, I knew not how I was gone so strange; but do see now that I was nigh to swoon for lack of slumber and rest.

And she kept me very steady for a little, and afterward helped me to be laid upon the ground; and she put the scrip and the pouch under my head; and so I did lie very calm and restful, and did be the more so, because that I was grown so tired in the heart, the which did make my head to be very husht, as that all the world was grown very quiet in a moment.

And the Maid did mind then that she did lack to be properly covered, and she gat the cloak, and put it about her, and did afterward sit a little beside me, and did rub my hands. And presently, I was something more to myself, and she did grow more happy of her mind, and made to give me something for my stomach; for, indeed, I was grown those late hours to be foolish and to have no wiseness to proper eating.

And she did lift my head, the while that she did take the scrip from under, and kept me very sweetly upon her knee, and so until she had gat free a pack of the tablets, and the flask and the cup; for I had put all matters back into the scrip before Naani had gone unto sleep, and because of this, I had not been able to eat or drink aught, save by

wakening her, as you perceive; for, indeed I had put the scrip and the pouch under her head for a pillow, as I have told.

And she would not bide that I should do aught; but only did ask concerning the making of the water, and was wondrous amazed to see how the powder did fizz up and become water; and indeed, she had too much into the cup, for, truly, it rose up and ran to the ground. And when she had done thus, and ceased to marvel, she put three of the tablets into the water, and made me a broth, even as I had made a broth for her; but, indeed, I was in no need, and had done very well to eat the tablets and drink the water. Yet, truly, I was not wishful to lack the love of her way, as you may think.

Now while I did drink the broth, I did be very restful upon the earth, and mine head against mine own Maid; and I did mind me now that I tell her concerning the Armour-Suit that I did mean for her wear.

Yet I said not that I had stript it from me, for then she had been like to say nay, and to trouble that I was like to come to a chill, as is the way of a woman. But, indeed, I might so well have told her, for truly, she did know on the moment, and set to a little unto weeping; yet very gentle and sweet, and did kiss me as I lay there, and say such things as should make a young man the better to have heard, if but that his own dear Love doth say the same.

And she would nowise wear the garment; but yet in the end I prevailed by gentle reasonings and because that I was her master, as I was born to be; and moreover, her own sweet sense did show that I spoke for wisdom; for how should she come through all the bitter way before, if that she had not a strong and close-made garment; and as you do mind, her coverings did be in utter rags, as I have told; yet very sweet and clean, as I had known; so that I ween she had stript oft in the lonesome night, and washt her garments in this or that hot spring of the sulphur waters and other matters.

And, in verity, alway she was much given to washings, as I did soon perceive.

Now, presently, I did be very well again; but with a sore slumber that did press upon my head. Yet, ere I should sleep, I did mean that I bathe her feet and bind them with ointment and with my pocket-cloth; and truly her feet were very small and pretty.

And I sat me up, talking my head from her knee; and told her of mine intent. But, in verity, she did but throw her arms about my neck and give me one loving kiss, and laught so hearty that I did think to do this thing when indeed she was the better able to mind it, and I the better suited to have me to my rest. And, surely, this was very

true, and I made no ado, save to give her the ointment; but lay back, and did be quiet.

Now I did be upon my right side, and she went to my back, and took the cloak from about her, and spread it upon me, and afterward stoopt over very dainty, and kist me, and bade me to go very swift to my sleep, for that she did mean to make her toilet and to get into mine Armour-Suit.

And I made no foolishness in this matter; yet told her to ease the cloak a little about me, so that I should have room to take the Diskos from my hip; and this thing I did, and took the Diskos to my breast, as was my habit; and surely I saw that her eyes did look at me with a little shining, because that I had so strange and fierce a bed-mate.

And I made her to promise that she keep a very keen harking, the which was like that she should do, and to call me on the instant that she did perceive any unease in the night. And after that, I shut mine eyes, that I should not shame her, and put out mine arms, and kist her once and turned from her unto my slumber; and she away to my back that she might be modest to her needs.

And surely, I was asleep in but a little moment, and with a great love and delight in my heart and in all my being.

And, truly, I waked not for twelve great hours. And when that time was gone, lo! I came awake, and surely the Maid did sit beside me, so bonny, and so winsome and pretty that mine arms went unto her in a moment, and she into them, and gave me a loving and tender kiss; and afterward slipt away from me, very sensible and loving; and did stand up and turn about to be lookt at. For she did wear the Armour-Suit, and surely it was loose upon her; but yet very pleasing, being close-knit. And I to my seat, from lying, that I might see the Maid the better. And, in verity, I must kiss her again; for she did be with her hair all about her, that she look pretty unto me; and her little feet did be bare, and so that they made my heart new tender to look upon them; for truly she was utter lost of foot-gear. And I to my knee to her; and she, not to deny me, did come to be kist again.

Now when I found how great a time I had slept, I did scold Mine Own; but yet, as she did say, I must have long slumber if that I go so long wakeful, else should I lose my strength. And I askt how oft she had eat, and she told me but the once, and that six hours off.

And on this I did scold again; but surely she put a very pretty finger sudden upon my lips, so that I might do naught but laugh, and kiss that same finger.

And, after that, we did eat and drink, and made plans. And once I

did comfort the Maid; for, indeed, her sorrow did rise in her, because that her father was come unto his death, and the Peoples of the Lesser Redoubt all destroyed, and adrift in the night amid the monsters of that Land.

And, in verity, I was set that we go quickly out of that place, ere there came an horrid Destruction upon us; and, surely, there should scarce be any human, beside, in all that Land; for there must have come death upon the chief of those that did make escape.

And after we had eat and drunk, I did count the packs of the tablets, and was thankful in all my being that I had been careful and denied my belly; for I did perceive that there were left enough for our needs, if that we made a good speed, and did not fear to be empty. And of the water-powder, as it might be named, there were left two full flasks, and somewhat of that one that I had drunk from, all my journeying. And by this thing you shall perceive that we did not be like to die for the need of such matters.

And here, as it doth occur unto me, I do ponder how it did be that we had no thought to slay any small creature for our food; but, mayhap, we had no knowledge this way; for surely, they did not this thing to my knowing in the Mighty Pyramid. But yet, as I have said before this, I have not all knowledge of the doings of the Peoples. But, in verity, I never saw joint meat in all the time of that far Life that I do wot of. Yet, had we but slain somewhat for our hunger in that great wandering, we had been less empty in the belly.

Now, before that we should do aught beside, we must contrive that Naani have some gear for her feet; and to this intent, I did make a search into the pouch, and surely I found that there did be a change pair of inner shoes, that were made to go within mine own shoes of the grey metal.

And at this I was wondrous glad, and did make the Maid to sit upon a little rock, while that I made a fitting of the shoes. And, surely, they did be utter big and clumsy upon her little feet; so that I was in surprise to know how great is a man, beside a Maid. But in the end I had a cunning thought, for I cut off all the side of a strap, through-out the length of the strap, very thin and careful, and so had a lace to tie the boots around the tops, which were soft and easy for such a purpose. And after that, I stood away to look at the Maid, and neither she nor I were truly pleased; for, indeed, she was too pretty to be so hid and muffled. Yet were we glad otherwise; for now she might go without hurt to her feet.

And afterward, we packt our gear, and she did make a bundle of

her torn garments; for, truly, they might be proper somewise to our need. And so we to begin the way out of that Desolate Land.

And we went forward together across the Land, and the journey was no more a weariness, but of a close and sweet joy; yet did I have a new anxiousness, as you do perceive, lest that any monster come to harm Mine Own.

And we went twelve great hours in the bed of the olden sea, and did eat twice in that time. And surely the Maid did grow utter weak and weary; for she was not come proper unto her strength; yet did she make no odd saying to tell me of this thing. But indeed, I did know; and I stopt in the thirteenth hour, and took her into mine arms, even as I should carry a babe; and I went forward with her, and did hush her protesting with a kiss, and afterward she did but nestle unto me and shelter against my breast.

And I bade the Maid to sleep; but, indeed, she had no power to this end, for her body did ache very sore; but yet did she strive to give me an obedience in this thing. And in the eighteenth hour, when that I stopt to have food and drink, surely she did be awake, yet had she been utter silent; and I made to scold her; but she gat from mine arms, and did go upward upon her toes, and put her finger against my lips very naughtily. And afterward she did be impudent unto me, and did deny me to kiss her. But she went unto my back, and did open the scrip, and gat me to my food, even as a quiet and proper wife should go. As she did be so sedate that I knew she had mischief her heart of harmless kind.

But afterward this did pass sudden into weeping; for she had a quick and sore memory of her father and of the Destruction; and I took the Maid into mine arms, and did let her be there very gentle, and made not to kiss or to comfort her; but yet to give comfort.

And presently she ceased from weeping, and did slip her hand into mine, and I to keep it within, very soft and quiet; and afterward, she began to eat her tablets, yet always she did be very husht; so that I did be quiet also, and feel as that my love did be round her as a shield. And I knew that she had knowledge of this thing in her heart.

And oft I harked into the night of the Land; but there was nowhere any sound, or disturbing of the æther, to trouble me. And the Maid in mine arms did know when that I harked; for in verity, she had the Night-Hearing and the understanding spirit that doth be needful to such. And odd whiles did I look down to her through the gloom that did be about us; and presently I did perceive that she lookt up to me, out of mine arms.

And I kist her.

Now, in all that day, we had come nowhere upon any fire-hole in the bed of the olden sea; and truly I did ache to be nigh unto the warmth of such; for I did feel the cold of the Land, because that I was weary, and because that I had not the thickness of the Armour-Suit below mine armour to warm me.

And the cloak did be about the Maid; for I had feared that she should grow cold as I carried her. Yet, now she did know subtly that I was come to feel the utter chill of the Land; and she gat from mine arms, and put the cloak about me, and afterward came again into mine arms. And I let the cloak bide there, and drew it forward to be around her, also. Yet, truly, I was joyful that I did be cold, as you shall perceive. For it was sweet to the heart to bear somewhat of that dread chill for Mine Own; and she half troubled and likewise with understanding of my heart, because that I was less clothed than I had been.

Now, in a little while, the Maid did pack the scrip; and so we did make ready again to go forward, for I was grown anxious, as you may suppose, that we should come to some fire-hole, that we have a place for sleep that had warmth and light; for, truly, the cold of the Land did be drear and horrid.

And I stoopt to take the Maid into mine arms, that I should carry her; but she did say nay, that she did be well rested. And I not to gainsay her, for she did mean the thing, as I perceived, and I had no desire to force my way upon her, save when I saw truly that she did seem to go unwisely. And, indeed, when such did be the case I did strive with her, only with a nice reasonableness, as you shall know.

And the Maid walkt by my side, and wondrous silent; but yet very nigh to me, so that I knew she did be very full of love to me, and of that quaint and sweet humbleness that love doth breed odd whiles in a woman when she doth be with her man, if but that man be also her master.

And presently, I perceived that the cloak did be over mine own shoulders, and I took it and would have put it about the Maid; but truly she did not allow this; and when I did be stern with her, that she obey me in this matter, she did stand upon her toes, that she might kiss me, and pulled my head down, and surely she kist me and coaxed me that I wear the cloak, else should I give pain to her, in that I did surely be cold because she did wear the Armour-Suit.

Yet, I would not hark to this thing; so that the Maid did be truly in trouble. And first she made a threatening that she wear but her olden garments that did be only rags, if that I did persist. But this I saw to be

foolishness and scarce-meant, and did as much need to smile at her as that I did think to scold her; but I did be firm that she wear the cloak.

And lo! she went sudden into crying; and this had been beyond my thoughts. And truly, it set me all adrift; for I perceived that she did be greatly distrest concerning this matter, when I had conceived that she did but mean this thing for tenderness' sake. But mine heart helped me to understand, and I saw how she did be truly shamed, in her sweet womanhood, if that I helped her not in this matter; for she did feel that she was made to do hurt unto that one that was her Love. And this thing I do pray you to think upon, that you understand; for, indeed, until that I was made to think, I had not seen it thiswise, for her.

And in the end, I came to agreement with the Maid, that we wear the garment hour by hour, in turn; and she to wear it the first hour and I to wear it the second hour; and so to go forward.

And truly, this did be an happy arranging; but yet she stampt her foot a little, as I put the cloak about her. And thrice in the hour did she ask me concerning the time that was gone; and surely, when the hour was but up, she had the cloak off in a moment, and went to my back and cast it upon my shoulders, and after to my front, and made it fast upon my breast; and so eager and naughty was she to this, that I took her by the shoulders, and shook her, somewhat, even as she had made to stamp at me; yet mayhaps with more of laughter. And she to take no heed at all; but to button the cloak and be very sedate. Yet, in verity, I caught her up into mine arms, and kissed her, for a sweet and naughty Maid; and she very willing, now that she had gotten something of her way.

But yet in an hour, I did have the cloak about her, again; and so did straiten matters, as you shall conceive.

Now, when we had gone forward, through five great hours, I perceived that the Maid did be utter worn, but yet did make presence that she was unwearied. And because I saw how she did be, I did heed and be anxious only that we come to some rock, to be for our safe refuge, and mayhap there to find an hole or cave, that should be somewhat to keep our heat about us; for there was nowhere any fire-hole anigh in all those hours.

And presently, we came to a part where there did be rocks, and we went to and fro in the gloom, and came in the end to a place where the rocks did go upward into the night, as that it had been a small and ancient cliff.

And surely in a while I found a hole that did go inwards of the rock; and the hole did be above mine head; yet when I was come to

it, and had made the Diskos to spin therein, that I should have light to see whether there did be any creature or creeping thing in the hole, I was well pleased; for truly it did be sweet and dry.

Now the Maid had cried out a little to see the sudden shining that did come from within the hole, when I made the Diskos to spin, and because of the low roar of the weapon. But I answered her that there did be naught to have fear concerning; and so was she peaceful again, but yet a little trembling when that I came down to her; for, indeed, the Diskos did make always a strange sounding and a quaint and drear shining, as you do know; and she did be feared for me that some Evil Force had come upon me out of the cave; for she had neither knowledge nor conceiving that ever there did be so wondrous a weapon in all the world.

And I gave the Maid an help upward to the little cave, and came after, myself; and so we did be in a very nice and cosy place, that did not be easily gotten at by any monstrous thing. And surely I was utter glad for such a place, so that both should have safety that we might sleep in the same hours.

And, in truth, this was a needful plan; for if one had stayed wakeful to keep a watch for the other, then had our sleep taken us double hours; and this thing might not be, else should our food be done, and we to be twice so long as need be, ere ever we did come unto the refuge of the Mighty Pyramid; and I utter wearied and anxious of the heart and spirit that I bring Mine Own soon unto the safety and glory of my Mighty Home, and so free from the Destruction that did hang above our two souls for ever in that Land, and the peril that did be everywhere, save in the Last Redoubt.

Now when we were come into the hole of the rock, the Maid did slip the scrip and the pouch from my shoulders; and she gat out the tablets, and made some of the water, and did be very swift and natty, and all to the despite of the gloom that did be utter in that little cave.

And we eat each of us two of the tablets and drank some of the water; and I made jest with the Maid how that the tablets did be proper for strength, yet very lacking to fill the belly; though, indeed, I named it otherwise.

And she to agree, and did pat mine arm, and did tell me how that she should cook me a monstrous tasty and great meal when that we were come unto the Mighty Pyramid. And immediately afterward, she did make to laugh upon me, and to name me impudently for so much thought unto my feeding; and afterward again to silence, and to patting my hand.

Now, when that we had made an end of eating and drinking, I was very ready for sleep; for, truly, it was six and twenty great hours since that I did last slumber; but for the Maid it did be eight and thirty great hours; for, as you do mind, she had made no sleeping when that she did lie in mine arms for six hours of our journeying.

And I made how we should sleep; and put the cloak about the Maid; but surely she did refuse, very piteous, and seeming to have also somewhat of doubt and puzzlement. But in this thing I did be very stern and intending; for she did not be over-warm clad, as you do know, and moreover, she was but a little One, while I did be wondrous hardy.

And, in verity, I made her to obey, and gave her the scrip and the pouch for her pillow; and she, as it did seem to me, to sob to herself a little in the gloom of the night. But yet did I stay my heart a little stern to mine intent. And I wrapt the cloak about her, and set the scrip and the pouch very nice beneath her head; and afterward, I knelt over to kiss her, before that I came unto mine own slumber. Yet did she turn her mouth from me, and did put her hand above her face to ward me off, the which did grieve me; for truly, I did heed alway that I should never thrust my love upon her in her lonesomeness; but only let it be to her for a shield and for all comfort unto her heart.

And I turned my back, and went a pace away and lay down; for truly there did be no way else but to be near unto the Maid, for it was but a little cave. And I lay very husht, because that I was so sore in the heart. Yet, truly, I could not come unto my slumber, for I was so disturbed in my love; and I stayed very quiet maybe for a great hour; and did fight that I shake not mine armour to jinglings with the utter cold that did make me to tremble. But the Maid did sleep very sweet and calm, as I perceived by her breathings.

Yet, in verity, the Maid did be so much awake as I, and with some sweet and naughty intent of the heart, as my spirit did sudden perceive. And I lay very husht, and did wait to discover what this thing might be.

And I made my breathing to seem as the breathing of one that did sleep, even as that naughty Maid did make pretending. And surely, in a while I did know that she moved very quiet, and came unto me; and I made yet that I slept very sound and strong; though the cold did nigh to conquer all my quietness.

And in a moment I perceived the intent of the Maid; for I did feel the cloak spread over me with a wondrous gentleness; and afterward there did be a soft kiss put upon my hand; and the Maid back then to her pillow; yet, as I did hear, she brought it something more nigh to me; as that she did crave to be near unto me that was her own Love.

And I sat up, and I put forth my hands suddenly and took the Maid into mine arms; and she to nestle unto me so that I did be wordless, because that I loved her so utter.

And presently, I felt her to stir in mine arms; and I loost her somewhat; for I did be always very mindful that I impose not upon her dear liberty of maidenhood. Yet she made not to go from me, but only to gather the cloak about her; so that we did both be in the cloak. And she askt why this might not be; for surely it did be madness that one should starve and the other be very nice in warmth. And, indeed, this did be but wisdom; yet it might not come the first from me.

And I said to Mine Own that this thing should be; and she reached out, and brought the scrip and the pouch, and placed them for a pillow for my head, and told me that I should put my head thereon. And I askt her how this did be right; for she did need a pillow the more than I. But she bid me to bide, and to have obedience in my turn. And when I was so, she spread the cloak over me, and afterward crept under, and did lie down beside me, and did seem as that she was asleep in one moment.

Yet, though she did be so sedate and matter-of-the-fact, as we do say, while that she was wakeful, she did yet nestle unto me very sweet and childlike in her sleep. And surely I did want to kiss her; but yet did refrain from my love; for, truly, I did well that I treat her very gently, at such a time, as you do perceive. And, in verity, such a Maid doth make a reverence in the soul of a man.

Now, presently, I was gone over unto sleep; and in seven hours I waked; and in that time had the Maid slumbered through eight hours; yet did I intend that she be not disturbed, until that we were aready to the journey. And I slipt from under the cloak, and put it round her, very gentle. Yet it to be as she did miss me, even in her sleep; for it to seem to me that she put out her arms in the darkness, and she made a little moaning in her slumber. Yet, in a moment, she did be quiet, and afterward I put the cloak about her again.

And I went then to the opening of the little cave, and put forth my head, and lookt well about, and harked a long while; but there stirred nothing in the night thereabout; neither did my spirit wot of any matter for trouble unto us.

And presently, I gat out two of the tablets; for, as you do know, the Maid had given me the scrip and the pouch to be my pillow, so that I had power to come at these matters, without awaking her; but for her own part, as I did learn after, she had used her torn garments to be for a pillow; yet had made no explaining, as you do mind; and

surely this was one of her naughty whimsies; and mayhap she had been so full of a playful happiness—as doth take the heart betimes—that she had made a little mystery where there did be no mystery; and this but to release her joy, and so to say masterful things unto me, out of her impudence; and afterward had meant that she tell me; but yet was gone unto slumber, ere that she did mind her.

Yet, since that time, a new thought hath come unto me that she did mean in the first that she should come into mine arms to sleep, and thereby need no pillow. But afterward, it may hap that she saw with a sudden olden wisdom, all in one moment; and afterward did act lovingly, yet with understanding. And so did change from her intent; yet with no improperness of modesty; but only with a niceness of Sense, which she did make no talk of; but yet did have. And surely, how oft is a man thus wisely ordered, unknowing.

And to cease from these thinkings, and to go forward, I eat two of the tablets, and afterward made some of the water. And lo! the fizzing of the water waked the Maid; and I knew that she reached out very sudden to me; but afterward knew in a moment what did make the sound, and that I did be up and making ready for the journeying.

And she gat up in the darkness, and said my name, and came unto me, and kist my forehead in the dark; and immediately she ran her hands gently downward of my left arm, and when she came to the cup, she took it from me, and slapt my hand, very dainty. And afterward I knew that she took a sip from the cup, and then did turn that side to me, and so gave me to drink, and did scold me that I had not waked her to tend to my needs; for surely she did be Mine Own, to have her duties to me.

And after that I had drank, she took the cup, and did finish it; and she gat two of the tablets, as I did think, and came afterward and sat upon the rock to my side, and did nestle somewhat against mine armour, and took mine arm and set it about her; and so did make to eat.

But first she put her tablet unto my lips, in the dark, that I should kiss it; and surely this was an olden way of Mirdath My Beautiful One; so that I did be all shaken of the heart. And I kist the tablet; and immediately she nestled unto me, and did begin to eat.

And truly it was as that Eternity had been rolled backward; for I had discovered the soul of mine olden Love in this dainty Maid to my side. Yet, in looks had Mirdath been of an utter differing; but, in verity Naani was wondrous lovely. But, though I to be so stirred, I did be silent; for my heart was very full of memory.

And as the Maid eat, she slipt her fingers between mine, curling

them softly; and surely her fingers did be very little; and she stirred mine olden memories again in this thing. And surely I was dumb before my Memory.

And presently, she put up the second tablet, as I did think, that I should kiss it; and I kist it, as before. Yet, ere she did begin again to eat, I did wot suddenly that she hid some intent from me.

And I caught her hand very quick in the dark; and her fingers did close upon the tablet, very guilty; so that I perceived that I had guessed aright. And I opened her fingers; and I found that there did be but the half of a tablet within her hand. And surely she had taken but that one tablet, and had given me the one end to kiss, and afterward the other; so that I should suppose she did eat two proper and complete tablets.

And I perceived that she had done this thing secretly, being minded that if she eat always but one tablet, then should I never lack, even if that we did be over-long coming unto the Mighty Pyramid.

And I askt how oft already had she eat but one, for two. And she confessed in a very quiet voice that this did make the fifth time. And I was so angered, that I took her hand and whipt it thrice, so hard that she had screamed if that she had been any coward. And she said nothing to me, neither went away.

And she began again to eat the half of the tablet, and did eat it from the other hand, as I to be aware, because that her left hand did be hurt. And she wept not, but was very quiet by me; and presently I knew that she kist the whipt hand secretly in the dark.

And afterward, I put mine arm again about her; and she did be there in it, very sober and happy. And when she had made an end of the first tablet, I gave her the second, and she eat it very quiet and content.

And presently I talked with her, and showed her how that this thing did hurt my heart, even as she had been hurt that I did be cold garmented, the while that she did be warm. And I showed her the wickedness that she had done, that she did play so foolish with her life and strength; and well might she be weak and all a-lack.

Yet, did I think a little sweet impudence came into her, as I told her concerning her wickednesses. And I took her then into mine arms, and I showed her how that I knew all the unselfishness and wonder of her heart; and I kist her, and truly her lips did have a lovely glad humbleness as they came unto mine; so that it was as that I had not kist her truly until that moment. And I made her to promise that she never deceive me in such matter again. And indeed she promised; but yet with no ready tongue.

And afterward, we made proper for the journey; and when we had

gotten our gear together, I went downward of the rock, and gave the Maid help to come down. And when we did stand at last upon the bottom of the rock, I askt Naani how she did feel, and whether her feet did hurt. And she answered that she did be very well and had no soreness in her feet.

And we went forward then, and she close unto me; and odd whiles with low speech, but more oft with silence, because that we did need that we hark alway for any danger or horror; and also there did be so utter a silence upon that part of the Land, which did be the bottom of the olden sea.

And we eat and drank at the sixth and the twelfth hours; and in the fifteenth hour, we came upon a great slope of the earth; and lo! it did be the far side of the sea. And we went upward for a long hour; and so came to the upward part, and did be able once more to look over the greatness of that Land.

XI
The Homeward Way

NOW, TRULY, IT DID seem very light, after the horrid and lonesome gloom that did lie all-ways in the bottom of the olden sea; and I saw that I was come out upon a part of the Land that did be surely to the right of that place where I made entry into the sea-bed, on mine outward going. And there did be a great plenty of fire-holes, so that mine heart was warmed to see them; yet did I mind to be wary in coming unto them; for, as you do know, there did so oft be life of this kind and that about these fires.

And I lookt now down to the Maid, and she upward to me, and did come more anigh to me, and truly she did be most wondrous pretty and sweet; yet did seem very awearied and pale in the face; so that I made blame upon myself that I had overwalked her; for, in verity, I do think that I was so strong and hard as that I had been made from iron; and she but a dear and tender Maid. Yet did she refuse that I should so reproach myself; and did but stand anigh to me and look at me with eyes that were very beautiful. And so I put mine arms about her, and kist her; and afterward lookt again over the Land, that I should shape out our further journeying.

And from that place where I did stand, there spread out all before me the blue shining that I had seen from the mouth-part of the Upward Gorge; yet did it be a great way off. And, indeed, I should tell you in this place, that it was by the glimmering of this shine within the sky of the night that I had steered, as we did come across the olden sea-bed. And, truly, it was but a broad thing to go toward; but yet did serve me, in that it told me that I went toward the far side of the sea-bed, and made not to go all about in blind circles in the night.

And after that I had considered a while, I did know somewhat where the Gorge should be, and perceived that I should go unto my left; but not overmuch, for indeed I saw the red-shining of the giants'

hole that lay at a great space that way; and surely I must go so that I missed the place of the giants so much as I might, and in the same going, come not overnear unto the blue-shining that lay before me, across all the far part of that Country; for, in verity, I mistrusted the place where that shining did be.

Now when I had gained somewhat of knowledge where should be found the Mouth of the Upward Gorge, I put mine arm about the Maid, where she did stand so nigh to me, and very husht, the while that I had lookt about. And I pointed outward over the dark Land unto my left, and told her that the Gorge did be somewhere that way, a great distance off; yet utter out of my sight, and only to be known that it did be somewise there by the things that I did mind of, concerning my way after I came into the Land.

Now the Maid, having stood very quiet, had lookt all that time about her; and so had come to some knowing of the place where she did be in the Land, for she to know the land someways, as you shall think. And she askt me how I did mind to go; and truly I said, so straight as we might; but yet so that we come neither too nigh to the shining nor to the great red fire-pit of the Giants.

And the Maid bade me to look in the way that I did mind to go; and I lookt, but yet there was nothing save, as they did seem, certain fire-holes that had a green-shining about them. And she set out unto me then, how that there did go a tract of bad gas in that part of the Land, that should be utter poisonous unto any; and this had been well known in the Lesser Redoubt, by the reading of their instruments. And where the gas did go, there was there a green-shining about the fire-holes.

And she showed me how that the Place of the Gas went a great way unto the North-West, so that I learned now somewhat how the land did lie, as we do say in these days. And it was in all the North-West that the great blue-shining did burn. And I askt Naani how they named this, and she told me by no name, save but The Shine.

And Mine Own made very earnest to warn me, regarding The Shine; and urged that we go no more that-wards than should be needful to our lives—the which, indeed, was no wish of mine. And her reason to be that the Fixed Giants did be within the borders of The Shine, and all hid in the light thereof, save when the burning mist did roll this way or that. And I took a great heed of this thing, and did guess that these Fixed Giants were somewhat even as the Great Watchers that were about the Mighty Pyramid, as you do know. And immediately I minded me of that utter monstrous face that I did see

amid the bright smoke of The Shine, when that I came first into the Land; and surely this had been one of the Fixed Giants, that Naani told me were Forces of great and very horrid Evil.

And I askt Mine Own how far the Place of the Gas went across the Land; and she pointed and made further explaining. And, in verity, in the end, I saw not how I should come that way to the mouth of the Gorge, if that I would keep off-wards from The Shine. Yet, in a moment, Naani askt me how I did come across the Land, when that I searched for her. And, truly, as I showed her, I had walked then by a sweet chance, or guiding, alway upon the far side of the Place of the Gas, and so unto the Olden Sea bed; and was in this way come free of the gas, and all unknowing of it.

And at this telling, the Maid said that we go downward again into the bed of the Olden Sea, and walk some great hours below the shore, but in the way that should take us unto the South-West, and so until we were come beyond the Place of the Gas. And afterward up again into the Land, and then to have an utter caution that we escape the watching of the giants who did be ever about the Great Red Fire-Hole. And by this plan very speedy to the entering-part of the Upward Gorge.

And, truly, this did be very good and sound, and such as I should have planned in a moment; for, indeed, I am not over-slow in such matters; only the Maid did be very eager and quick; and it was very sweet to me that she should thus plan; for, in verity, I loved alway the sounding of her voice, and to hear her have speech and to plan and think, and so to show me the workings of her inward self and her dear qualities and human niceness. And to have part and lot alway with me in all things and thinkings.

And, we shaped to this plan that Naani made; but at that time, as you do mind, it was somewhat of seventeen hours since last we had slumber; and the Maid was sore wearied, as I did see. And I showed to her how that it did be wise that we have our rest very soon, and so forward again in new strength and ability.

And the Maid did soon agree with me; for indeed she was very weary; and we made it that we should venture unto one of the fire-holes that lay no great seeming away, a little upon our right, which was the Northward-way of that Land.

And we went toward the fire-hole; and, truly, it did be further off than we had thought; for it was a good hour before that we came anigh to it; and, indeed, it to prove a very great and red-glowing shine that went upward into the night, out of the hollow place where it did burn among rocks.

And when we were come near unto it, I made a sign to the Maid that she be utter husht; and I took the Diskos from mine hip, and went forward before her; and afterward to my knees and hands, and beckoned backward to Mine Own, that she do likewise.

And we came this way to the edge of the hollow-place where the fire-hole did burn; and so were able in the end to look downward. And truly it was a great fire that burned in the earth in that place; yet, as I perceived very swift, there did seem nowhere any monstrous thing about the fire, the which set some peace upon mine heart; but yet not overmuch; for it was come fresh upon me that we did well to stay afar off from the fires of the Land, in that it was about the fires that all living things did congregate.

And I lookt a great time, and the Maid crept unto mine elbow, and lookt with me; and afterward we harked, very keen, into the night; but there was nowhere any trouble of the air or of the æther of the Land. Yet I spoke quiet with the Maid, and showed unto her how that we did well to stay off-ward from the fires; but, truly, she was so utter cold and chill, that she did beg that we go down by the fire-hole, even should it be that we stay no more there than should put a warmth through the utter chill of our bodies.

And, in verity, I was so bitter cold that I was all weak to go beside the fire; yet, truly, I do think that the shiverings of the Maid was that which did force my heart, to go against the teachings of my head; so that in the end, we came down into the hollow, and very swift unto the fire.

Now, truly, it doth seem a strange thing to be so diverse-minded as this, when that, as you do know, I had been so long a-search for a fire-pit; and mayhaps you shall perceive the better how my heart and brain did be contrary, when that I tell to you, now, how that I have belief that my spirit did even then be subtly set to warn me. And, also, as all do know, it doth be easy to forget this warning and that of experience; by which saying, I do mean that, oft as I had come to know the dangers that did be alway about the fire-holes, yet when I did be far off from them, and Mine Own broken and a-shiver with the chill of the Land, the danger did seem but a small thing and afar off from my mind, and unreal; but the cold to be doubly real. Yet, when we did come even unto the fire-hole, then did come again all about my heart the truth of those dangers that had seemed, but a while gone, so little. And, indeed, I do hope you perceive me in this thing, and how that I strive alway to set unto you the utter truth, so that you shall go with me all the way, and lend me your nice understanding.

Now, when we were come down unto the fire-pit, I went this way and that among the rocks that did be in the bottom of the hollow, so that I should perceive whether there did be any living creature there hid, that should mayhap come out, unknown, to work us harm.

But, indeed, I discovered nothing of any greatness; yet I saw three snakes, and there were, beside, two scorpion-creatures, as I did name them, that neither went backward from me, nor came against me; but did bide where I saw them, each in an hole of the rock.

And because I had seen these things, I saw that we should not do wise to sleep nigh unto the fire-hole; for the creeping things did mortally like the heat, and should be like to come upon us in our slumber. And, indeed, this did but uphold my caution, that we should be well actioned, if that we chose some other part to our rest.

Yet, as you shall suppose, I said naught unto the Maid concerning the creeping and the poisonous things; for I did mean that she have rest and happiness the while that we did stay beside the fire-hole; and afterward, I should tell her, and so she be the more ready to see the properness that we go elsewhere to our sleep. But, as you to understand, if that she not to see wisely and be still intent to the fire-hole, I should have her to obey; for surely she was Mine Own, and I did love her and did mean alway to have her to safety.

Now, presently, the Maid was something warmed, and afterward, she slipt the scrip from my shoulder, and so had food and drink very swift to my need.

And we sat together, and eat and drank; and the Maid very sweet and quiet, as she did begin to eat her second tablet; and, truly, I had knowing that she did remember in all her body that I had whipt her. And, indeed, she did be utter mine.

And oft as we did eat and drink, I lookt this way and that, so that no creeping thing should come anigh to us; and presently, when we had made an end of our food, the Maid saw that I did look about, and she then very swift to catch some of mine unease, and to stare over her shoulder. And, indeed, in a little while she saw a snake go among the rocks; and she then to be very eager that we find some place that should be secure from creeping things. And we to begin then to look for such.

But in the end, we stayed in the hollow; for we found a little cave that did be in an upstanding rock of the hollow, and the upstanding rock was, mayhaps, an hundred good feet off from the fire; for the hollow was very great. And the cave did be a hole that was thrice my height up from the bottom rocks; and it was dry and sweet and with

no creeping thing within it, neither did there be any place to hide such therein.

And when we were gotten into the hole, surely it did be very sweet and cozy; for the shine of the fire-hole did shine therein; and surely we had felt it a very haven, but that there was ever the fear of the Land upon our hearts; and upon mine the more than upon the Maid; for, truly, Mine Own did seem to trust me utter; and to seem that she feared not any evil monster, but to have surety that I had power to succour her in all ways. And truly this trust had been very sweet unto my heart, if that I had lacked somewhat of my terror for the safe home-going of Mine Own.

And we slept that night as we had done before, and shared the cloak over us; for truly, the fire-hole made no great warmth unto us; yet was it less bitter in that part than in the darkness of the Land.

And by that we had come unto sleep, it was twenty good hours since last we had slumber; and truly we did be very wearied; but yet came unto our rest with our spirits set anxious to harken on danger the while that we did sleep.

And we slept seven hours, and did know suddenly of some matter that had need to waken us; and lo! in a moment I did wake, and the Maid in the same instant of time; and there was a great screaming and crying out in the night, that surely affrighted us both; yet did hurt our hearts the more; for it did be the utter cryings and terror of poor humans in the night of that Land. Yet might I do naught; but only wait that I learn more of the matter; for my duty was unto Mine Own, and I had no leave of rashness any more.

Yet, as you do suppose, I was all shaken to go downward of the rock, and afterward to climb out from the hollow, that I should give some help unto they that did need help; but yet might I not leave the Maid.

And immediately, there was a great roaring in one part of the night, and again another roaring in another part of the night; and lo! in a moment the roarings did be answered; and the roarings were the sounds of big and husky voices; so that it did seem that we harked to men so big as houses that did run and shout in the night.

And the Maid did begin to shake, and I put mine arm about her, and drew her backward into the hole so that she did be into the shadow; and she to tremble like one that was broken in courage; for, truly, she had heard those sounds oft in the night in all the long and dreadful month that she had wandered.

And, indeed, I was all shaken in my courage; for it did be the

shouting of giants that I heard; and you do know somewhat of the utter horror and terror that did be alway in the heart that did harken unto those monstrous voices, for you do know my tale.

And there came in a moment, a dreadful screaming out in the night, and the screaming did be the screaming of a young maid that doth be slain very brutal. And my heart sickened, because of Mine Own; but my spirit did swell with a strange and utter anger, as that it should burst my body. And the Maid to my side broke into an utter sobbing.

And the screaming of the maid afar off in the dark did end very sudden; but in a moment there did be other screamings in diverse places, and the hoarse shoutings of the great men and the thudding of mighty feet that ran this way and that, a-chase.

And the cryings of the humans came nearer, and the thuddings of the great feet. And, in verity, in a little minute, it did seem unto me that the sounds did be right upon the hollow; and I crept forward, and peered out. And I felt the night to be full of people running; and immediately there passed by the hollow a clustering of humans that ran ever, and screamed and gasped and wept, panting, as they ran. And the shining of the fire-hole made them plain seen and clear, and they did be both men and women, and were but in rags or utter naked, and all torn by the rocks and the bushes, and did seem, indeed, as that they had been wild things that did go by so swift and lost.

And mine heart troubled me with the pain and longing that it did know; so that I had gone in a moment after those people, but that I should leave Mine Own and put her to peril. And even while that I felt so utter in this thing, there came a great thudding of monstrous feet; and there ran four great men out of the night, and went past the hollow very quick. And three did be dull coloured and seeming much haired and brutish; but the other did be an horrid white, and livid-blotched; so that it did seem to my spirit that there went by, a thing that did be a very man-monster filled of unwholesome life. And surely they did be gone from out of the shine of the fire, in one moment, as we do say; and again into the night to their dreadful chasing.

And when the thudding of their feet had gone a long way off over the Land, I heard them bellowing, and afterward a far away screaming, that did have a death note in it; and I knew that those dreadful brute-men did be taking the life from some poor wild humans; and afterward there did be the silence again.

And, surely, it did come to me with a fierce impatience of sorrow, that those people did be without spirit of courage; else had they turned them upon the giants, and slain them with their hands, even

if that all had died to compass that slaying; for, truly, they should all die anywise by the giant-men; and they had died then with somewhat to comfort their hate

Yet, as I do know, the Peoples of the Lesser Redoubt had long been born of parents that were starved of the Earth-Current through an hundred-thousand years and more, and because of this thing, they did surely lack somewhat in all ways. Yet was Naani otherwise; but this not to prove aught, save the rule, as we do say.

Now, sudden, as I stooped very husht and troubled in the mouth of the little cave, I knew that Mine Own sobbed dryly in the back part of the cave. And I had gone to comfort her, but that in the same moment, I saw a naked maid run very swift over the edge of the hollow, and did look over her shoulder, as she ran. And she came to the bottom, and crept in under a ledge of rock that did be in that place; and she did seem utter worn, and gone of the spirit, and desperate. And I perceived in the same instant why that she did go stealthy and swift in that fashion, and to cower, as for her very life; for there came a squat, haired man, so broad as a bullock, who did come silent down into the hollow, looking this way and that, even as a wild beast doth peer, very sudden.

And the Squat Man had instant knowing of the place where the maid did be; and ran in upon her, with no sound.

And I paused not; but leaped all the great way unto the bottom of the hollow, which did be, mayhaps, twenty good feet and more; for mine anger was upon me, and I did mean that I save that one, though I did be powerless to give succour unto those others.

And I fell strong upon my feet, and had no harm of my limbs, for all that the leap did be so high. And in that moment, before that I had time to save the maid, the Squat Man ript her; and she cried out once with a very dreadful scream, and was suddenly dead in the hands of the Brute-Man.

And my heart made my blood to burn with wrath in mine eyes, so that I had scarce power in that instant to see the Squat Man, as I ran upon him. And the roar of the Diskos filled all the hollow, as I made it to spin, as that it did rage with an anger, and to be glut of the Man.

And the Man came round upon me; and thought, mayhaps, to deal with me, as it had dealt with that poor maid, but not all thatwise, as you must know. And I swung the Diskos, and it did seem to sing and to cry eager in my hands. And I smote at the Squat Man, even as it did leap silent upon me, as a tiger doth leap, making no sound. But I gat not home the blow; for the Man dropt sudden down upon the

hands, and the blow went overwards. And the Brute-Man caught me by the legs, to rip me; and I cut quick with the Diskos, and it did have but one monstrous talon left unto it. And immediately, it cast me with the other, half across the hollow, and I fell with mine armour clanging mightily, and the Diskos did ring like a bell.

And by the graciousness of all good things, I was harmed not by that monster throw; but was to my feet in one instant, and had not loosed the Diskos from my hand. And the Beast-Man did be upon me with two quick boundings; and I stood up to the Man, and it made no sound or cry as it came at me; and there did a great froth of brute anger and intent come from the mouth of it, and the teeth came down on each side of the mouth, very great and sharp. And I leaped and smote, so that my blow should come the more speedy, and the Diskos took away the head and the shoulder of the Squat Man; and the dead thing knockt me backward, with the spring that it had made; but it harmed me not greatly. Yet afterward I did know how sore and bruised I did be, in all my body and being. And I came back very swift against the Man; but it did be truly dead and greatly horrid.

And I went from the dead monster, and did go, all heart-shaken, unto the dead maid. And I took the torn body of the maid, very sorrowful, and cast it into the fire-hole.

And I turned me then that I should look unto the cave, that I should know that all did be well with Mine Own, and whether she did have seen the horror, or be gone into a swoon.

And lo! Mine Own did run toward me; and she had in her hand my belt-knife which I did give her, before that time, to be a weapon for her defence. And I perceived that she had come to be mine aid, if that I did need such. And she did be utter pale, yet very steadfast and not seeming to tremble.

And I made to take her from that place; but she went beyond me, and lookt at the monstrous bulk of the Squat Man; and was very silent. And she came back unto me; and still so silent. And she stood before me, and said no word; but my heart knew what she did be thinking; for I am not foolish, to have lacked to know what did be in her heart; though mine effort had not shown itself that way unto me, before that moment.

And I had no pretending of modesty, but received with gladness and a strangeness of humbleness the honour that her eyes did give to me; for, indeed, she did be so, that she might not give word to her joy of me and her glad respecting, the which is so wondrous good unto the heart of all men that do be loving of a dear and honest maid.

And she said nothing, neither then nor afterward; but I did be

honoured all my life after, when that I did anytime mind me of the way that Mine Own lookt upward at me in those moments.

And afterward she did need and allow herself to come unto mine arms, that I hold her from the trembling of heart which did come to her, after that there did be no need for courage; for surely we had both seen a very dreadful thing, and there was a great horror upon us.

And I climbed upward again to the little cave, and did help Naani; and when we were come there again, we did rest awhile. And presently we eat, each of us, two of the tablets and drank some of the water, and indeed we were both utter thirsty.

And in about an hour, after that we had harked very keen a time, we came downward again from the cave, and had our gear with us; and we came up out of the hollow, and set forward with a great caution unto the olden sea-bed. And we came there in two long hours; for we went very slow and with constant harkings; for the fear of the monstrous men was upon us. But there came no harm anigh, neither did we perceive any disturbance in the night of the Land.

And we went down an hour into the olden sea-bed, and did go now the more swift; for our fear was something eased from us, because that we had come away from that place where we had perceived so great and dread an hunting. But yet had we all care about us; for the giants surely to be everywhere in that Land; but yet, as I do think, they to roam more oft anigh to the fire-holes; for the humans did surely wander in such parts, that they have warmth of the fires.

And after we had gone downward an hour into the sea-bed, we turned somewhat unto the South-West, and went for twelve great hours, and did never be any huge space from the shore; for it did run that way, as you do know. And I made to steer by the shinings of the Land, and with advices from Mine Own.

And in the end of the twelfth hour, I did count our distance, making that we did walk somewhat of a certain speed; and by the tellings of the Maid, we did be surely come beyond the place of the Land where the Poison Gas did lie.

And by this, it did be something after seventeen hours since we did sleep; and surely we did be very ready to have rest; for we had gone forward strongly, and with anxiousness; and truly my hurts did be come upon me, so that my whole body did ache; for the quick fight had been bitter, and I had been thrown very hard and brutal; and, indeed, it was wondrous that I had not been all smashed, only that the armour did save me.

And this doth show truly how hard and strong I did be; and

Naani did speak upon this, and was oft a-wonder, and at that time did beg me that I make some rest to cure my hurts; for she had not conceived that a man did grow so strong and hardy; and, in verity, the men of the Lesser Redoubt did be soft-made and lacking of grimness, as I did perceive, both through my reason and from her tellings; for they did lack the strong life that doth breed where is the beat of the Earth-Current, as we to have in the Mighty Pyramid. And this thing I have said somewise before this time.

And because that we did be so wearied, I said unto Naani that we find a place for our slumber, and she very willing, as I have shown, and to counsel me likewise.

Yet did we search about in that gloom for a great hour more, and found no cave or hole to give us a safe refuge for our sleep.

And when that we could not find such, I told Naani that we should put the boulders together, somewhat, and so have them about us, that we be greatly hid; and, in truth, even as I began to tell her my plan, she did have the same words in her mouth, so that we caught our little fingers, there in the dark of that grim Land in the end of the world, even as she and I had done oft in the early years, before that eternity, when that she did be Mirdath the Beautiful. And we did both be silent, and after that we had wished very solemn and earnest, we said each a name; even as lad and maid shall do in this age; and so to laughter and kist one the other. And truly, the world doth seem not to alter in the heart, as you shall think. And this was what I did find.

And we set-to, and gathered together the boulders which did be very plentiful in that part. And she carry those that did be thin and flat, and I to roll those that did be great and round. And I made a place that did be long and narrow; and afterward, I set the flat stones round the sides, that there be no little hole by which any creeping thing should come inward to sting us in our sleep.

And afterward we gat inside; and surely it did be very cozy, as we do say; but yet not so secure as I did wish, only that I could not shift to plan aught better. And, indeed, it should keep off from us any small thing, and should be like to save us from any monstrous Brute treading upon us; but otherwise, it did be but a poor affair.

Now we eat two of the tablets, each, and drank some of the water, even as we had done in the sixth and the twelfth hours; and afterward we shared the cloak for our slumber; and we kist very sedate and loving, and charged our spirits that we wake if that any horrid thing should come anigh to us in our sleep; and afterward we did be gone very swift to slumbering, and suffered no harm.

And I waked seven hours after, and surely I did ache very bitter, as I did move my body; for the bruisings did be gotten hold of me.

And I slipt away from the Maid, very gentle; for I had mind that she sleep a while more, as I did mean that we make a great journey that day.

And after I had harked a while, and perceived that there was no evil thing anigh, I went outward of the stones. And I walked to and fore and moved mine arms, that I be eased somewhat of the stiffness and ache; but surely it did seem that many hours must go ere I should make any speed of travel; for I did be all clumsy and slow and nigh to groan with the pain of going and aught that I did.

And I minded me that I should do somewhat to ease this thing, lest that I cause us both to come to an harm by staying over-long in that Land.

And I went back into the stones, and gat an ointment from the pouch, that I did carry. And surely the Maid did yet sleep. And I went outward of the stones, again; and stript off the armour, and all my garments; and I rubbed my body with the ointment, and surely the pain did be so that I groaned at this time and that; but yet must I rub good and strong so that I die not of the cold of the Land; and beside I was greatly anxious to cure myself.

And sudden, as I did rub very strong and savage, and heeding so well as I might that I groan not, the Maid did speak close beside me. And, indeed, she could see me but dimly, and had waked sudden to hear my groaning, and I was not to her side. And immediately she had thought that some evil thing harmed me, and was come in an instant that she be with me.

And she cared not that I did be naked; but was utter in anger that I strove to do this thing alone, and with none to aid me, and all uncovered to the chill of the Land. And she ran back into the stones, and brought the cloak and put it about me; and was so angered that she stampt, and had no impudence, but rather as that she did be minded to have tears.

And she sent me back into the sheltering of the stones, and gathered mine armour, and brought these things after me. But the Diskos I took in my hand. And she took the pot of the ointment from me, and made me to lie, and she rubbed me very strong and tender, and kept me warm with the cloak; and surely she was a wise and lovely Maid, and utter Mine Own.

And in the end, she askt me how I was, and I said that I did be different; and she hurried me that I be clothed very quick; for she did be sore afraid that I should come to a chill.

And when I was gotten again into mine armour, she came to me, and showed me where I did lack wisdom, and spoke very straitly and gentle and serious; and afterward kist me, and gave me my tablets, and to sit beside me. And we eat and drank; and I with a new lovingness unto Mine Own; and she somewhat as that she did mother me; but when I put mine arm about her, she did be only a maid. And we did be thus, with but little talk and a great content.

And afterward, we gat our gear together, and went from that little refuge that we had made; and in a while we did go upward out of the olden sea-bed.

And when we were come again to the top of the shore, the which we did in two good hours, I lookt over the Land, a time, with Mine Own anigh to me. And I perceived that the Great Red Fire-Pit of the Giants did be no mighty way off unto the South and West; and surely in a little moment, we saw that there went monstrous figures against the shine of the mighty fire-pit; and we stoopt unto the earth; for it did seem that the light did be like to show us standing there, though truly we did be afar off, as you perceive. Yet, mayhaps, you do share with us the utter horror and distress that those horrid Men did cast about the heart, and so have a kindly understanding of our fear.

And over all the Land, in this place and that, there did be the small shining of little fire-holes and pits, that did be alway red, save in that part where the Poison Gas did lie, the which we had now come safe past.

And beyond the fire-holes, was the great Shine, that lay from the West unto the North of all that Land; and, in verity, we did need that we steer so that we come not anigh to it, neither unto the Great Red Fire-Pit of the Giants; neither unto the low volcanoes, which were beyond the Great Red Fire-Pit, as you do know, and someways unto the Mouth of the Upward Gorge.

And the way of our journey was between the West and the South-West of that Land; and to be made with cunning and wisdom, that we come clear of all unseemly danger unto Mine Own. And I askt her concerning this thing and that of the Land; and surely she told me so much of terror that I was half in a wonder that ever I did live in the end to come unto her.

And it was because of the things that she set out to me, that I perceived how we must come nowise anigh to the low volcanoes that were upon this side of the mouth of the Upward Gorge; for it had been known alway in the Lesser Redoubt that there went very horrid men in that part that did be called wolf-men; but whether there did

be any such thing in that age, she had no knowing; for she told me
the things that did be set down in the Records and the Histories; and
truly no man of the Lesser Redoubt had found heart in a thousand
great years to make a journeying through the Land, for the desire of
glad and dreadful adventuring, such as our young men did be oft set
to; though it was not all such that went.

And because there did be no adventuring for so monstrous a space
of years, there was no certain new knowledge of the Land of that
age. And this thing is plain to you, and needing not of many words,
which do so irk me.

And Naani set out to me how that The Shine was conceived to be
a land where Evil did live for ever, and whence came all those Forces
of Evil that did work upon the Lesser Refuge. And afterward, she did
quiet; so that presently I perceived that she did weep to herself, because
that her memory was all new-stirred by my questionings. And I took her
very gentle into mine arms, as we did be there kneeled upon the earth.

And after that time, I askt her no question, save as it did be needful
to our health and life; yet oft did she tell me this thing and that of her
knowledge, to be for mine help and guiding.

Now we went forward, going a space toward the North-West, so
that we come the more clear of the place where did be the Great Red
Fire-Pit of the Giants. And we journeyed with a care alway that we
show not ourselves over-plain unto the light that shone over the Land
from the great Pit; and oft we did creep a while over this stark place
and that; and went nimbly amid the bushes that grew oft in great parts.

And we made six hours this way; and did then have pause, that we
eat and drink; and truly it was nine hours since first I did wake; yet had
we made no pausing, because that we were so set to our journeying
to come clear of the place where did be the Giants.

And after that we had eat and drunk, we went onward again; and
made now unto the South-West; for we did heed that we go no more unto
the North-West, because that should bring us over-near to The Shine.

And in the fourteenth hour of that day's travel, we came to a part
where the Land dipt downward into a broad valley; and surely it did
be very dark down there, and did be seeming shallow, yet truly of a
great deepness; but we went that way, because that it did be a weary
long journey to go around the place where the valley did be.

And the Valley had a different darkness from the gloom that went
alway in the olden sea-bed; for the gloom of the sea-bed did be ever
of a greyness; but the gloom of this Valley had a greater dark within
it; yet did the air seem more clear.

And we went downward three hours into the Valley, and stopt then that we eat and drink; and truly I had not paused then; but that Mine Own did insist; for our methods did be like, else, to go all adrift, and we to be lacking of proper strength.

And this was wisdom of the Maid; but I to be a little irked-like and restless; and this mayhap because that my blood did itch me, because that it did be so full of the poison of my bruises.

And it was gone now of seventeen hours since last we did sleep; but yet did we be ready to go forward, that we come so quick as maybe out of the dark of that Valley; for there did seem nowheres any fire-hole to make a light; only that in this place and that, there did be a little blue shining, as that there burned a strange gas in this part or that.

Now, in two hours after the time that we did eat, we stopt, both of us, very sudden; for there did be some vague and curious sound in the night. And we went very swift to the earth, that we be hid, and harked. But did hear nothing.

And in a while, we to go onward again; yet there did be an unease upon our spirits; for our spirits did perceive something afar off in the night; but yet had we no surety in this matter.

And we went forward through a great hour more; and did pass in that time, two places where the blue-shining did be; and truly it seemed as that a low gas hung to the earth in this part and that, and made a slow burning, having neither noise nor spurtings; but slow, as that it did smoulder and be all to shine and luminous. And oft there did be a strong smelling of a bitter gas, very horrid in the throat.

And in the end of another hour, while that we were a space off from one of those gas-shinings, there went past us at a distance, as it did seem people, running in the night; as that they did be lost spirits; yet with a rustling very soft; so that they did be like to be barefoot.

And I thought mayhap that these did be some of the Peoples of the Lesser Pyramid; yet did they be only as that shadows went among the blue-shinings. And I pondered a moment, whether that I send my voice over the Valley, to question what they did be; but yet had caution, and harked through the utter silence of the night; for I had no surety of aught.

And, surely, in that moment that we harked very keen, there did be a sound afar off in the night of the Land; and it was as that we had heard the sound before; and, in verity, our spirits had perceived the sound, those two hours back; and now our bodies did wot, and perceived that we had known it subtly before that moment. And the sound was as that something went spinning in the night.

And a very great terror came upon the Maid; for she did know the sound; and the sound was that which did show that one of the great Evil Forces of the Land did approach; and the sound had been known alway in the Lesser Refuge to show this thing. And, indeed, mine own spirit had been half to know that a Power of Evil did come through the night; but yet was the assurance very terrible; for how should I protect Mine Own.

And the spinning came toward us, and was presently in the Valley; and it came swiftly across the dark of the Valley. And my heart was all broken within me, because that there had been happiness with us, but a little time gone; and now there did be our death anigh.

And Mine Own gave me the knife that I had given to her; meaning that I slay her, in the last moment; for she did heed even in that moment that she be not gashed horridly by the terror of the Diskos. And I took the knife. And I kist not Mine Own; but stood there, very shaken and desperate, and gript her fast unto me, scarce heeding the hardness of my gripe; and alway I lookt unto the way of the coming of the Sound. And presently did unbare my wrist where the Capsule did be.

And the sound of the thing Spinning came anigh, across the Valley; and my heart did dull and my spirit go black with my desperateness, because that this thing must be, and because that I could nowhere see hope that I should save Mine Own.

And, of a sudden, the Maid put up her arms, and pulled me downward, and kist me once on the lips; but I wot not whether I kist her; for I did burn with despair and was all adrift in my being. Yet was there a sharp comfort that mine own dying did be so nigh.

And the Maid stood gently against me; so that she did be convenient unto my hand. And afterward I remembered this thing; and do you pray that you be never to have such a matter on your hearts! But, indeed, there was a wonder in this thing, beside the horror; so that my memory doth be alway knowing of this wonder; and mayhap you do see with me, and love Mine Own also in your hearts.

And in the moment that the Maid stood thus, as I have told, I perceived sudden that there did be a little glowing in the night, and the glowing was pale and horrid. And there was no more any sound of the Spinning; only there did be, as it were, the trunk of a great tree, that did show in the glowing; and the trunk of the tree came toward us across the darkness.

And I turned the Maid from the Tree, and she did flutter a little in my hands, as I did know, scarce-knowing; for she perceived that she

did be going to die in that moment. And I had my body thus between the Evil Thing and the Maid. And lo! the Tree came no more anigh to us; but went backward, and the pale glowing did fade, and the Tree no more to be seen.

And I cried unto the Maid, very husky, that we did live; for that the Evil Power was gone off from us; but she answered not, and did be heavy against me. And I held her, and lookt alway about us, lest the Tree come in upon the other side.

And, as I lookt this way and that, I saw naught; and afterward, in a moment, I searched the night above, lest that the Thing come from above. And, behold, I saw that there abode over us a clear light, as it were a clear burning Circle, above us in the night. And my heart did leap with an holy joy and an utter great thankfulness; and I was no more in fear of the Tree; for, in verity, there fought for our souls one of those sweet Powers of Goodness, that did strive ever to stand between the Forces of Evil and the spirit of man; and this matter have I shown to you, before this time.

And concerning this holy Defense, I have thought that it should not, mayhap, to have had so strong a power to save us, if that we had shown an over-weakness and fear, but because that we did rather stand so well as we might to make battle of escape from so dire a Destruction.

And, surely, this doth seem but a sane thinking unto me; but yet without proof, and to be said to you, only as the shapings of my thoughts. And this the chief end of that happening, that the holy Circle did truly deliver us, and burned through twelve great hours above us; and by this, do I know that the Evil Power hovered anigh, to destroy us, all that while; for, indeed, it doth not be proper of reason to suppose that such an utter wondrous thing did be needlessly over us, save to be a Shield of Great and Lovely Force against a waiting Evil Thing. And surely you do see thiswise with me?

And, truly, so soon as my Spirit and Reason perceived that we did be no more to suffer from the Evil Thing, I remembered that I did know that Mine Own had swooned. And, in verity, you shall mind how that she did face her death so utter sweet and brave, and had given no cry, but made quietly to help me in that dreadful moment, and did stand brave and gentle to the stroke. And so fell into a swoon, as you have seen, because that she did suffer an hundred deaths as she did stand so brave, waiting to be slain, for the blow did be so long delayed, yet to come in any moment.

And I gat her to come-to unto her life again, and I set the lovely tale very swift to ease her, and surely with love and warmth, and kist

her with a great joy. And I showed how I did honour her for her good courage.

And she to weep a little, with the ease come so sudden upon her; and afterward to kiss me upon the lips an hundred times, and to need that she be very safe in mine arms, because that I had meant that I do so dread an office to her. And surely I do wonder whether you perceive all that did be then in her heart.

And the holy light that did be over us, she did watch with a sweetness of awe; and rest did come more great upon her in the heart, as she did learn how sure was the seeming of that Lovely Power to deliver us.

And, presently, we made forward again in the Valley. And did go steadfast, and newly-loving each to the other, and so through twelve great and body-weary hours; but our hearts could never be done singing within us, nor our hands to cease from the hands of the other, because that we did so crave each unto the beloved.

And in the ninth hour, a monstrous way off in the dark of the Valley, there did seem as that there went a far and dreadful screaming in the night. And it did be as that our spirits perceived the sound of something Spinning in the night; yet faint and a great way off; but yet had we no surety that we did truly hear the sound of the Spinning; only we did be so shaken in the heart, for truly there was some horror done unto humans, downward in the mighty darkness of the Valley. And to think upon the sound of the Spinning, was to be in a shaking trouble of the spirit; and to bless the quiet and holy light that went above us in all that time; and to ache only that it should stay to be to our protecting. And surely it did be plain that there were the signs of great Forces in that Land.

And three hours after that time when we did hear the far-off screaming, we were come up over the edge of the Valley, and did be once more unto such light as did be general in the Land; and truly it did seem a wondrous lightness, after so utter a dark.

And we did be all exhaust, and Mine Own drew her feet so weary that it was as that she must go no more, until we did rest; for indeed it was three and thirty hours since last that we had slept; and a bitter trouble and work there had been in that space, as you do know.

Now we had eat some of the tablets a few hours back, as we did walk, and had drunk some of the water; but had made no rest; for we did crave only that we come free of that Valley. And now it was needful that we rest, if but a little time.

And I minded that we find some place where I should have a hot pool, that I be able to bathe Naani's feet. And, surely, we came in a

while to a hollow-place, and there did be two dull-burning fire-holes in this place, and a hot-bubbling spring, the which did seem to be a rare thing in that Land; so that we were the more fortunate to perceive it.

And I made Mine Own to sit, with her feet in the hot-spring; for it was not over-hot, and did seem pretty natural to my taste, as I did prove in the first. And also I did search about the hollow, lest there be any harmful creature near-by; and this you will have truly supposed, because you do know the methods of my journeying. But yet did I not have so much care as did be proper; for I was so dull in the mind, by reason of my weariness; but, indeed, there came naught to work us any harm; and so we came to no suffering, through mine aches and dullness.

And I sat beside the Maid, and made her to eat a tablet, and saw that the cloak did be nice about her, and her head to rest against my knee, and I laid the palm of my hand to be as a pillow, because of the armour, to ease the hardness.

And I eat with the Maid, and we both drank after; and so there came back somewhat of our strength. Then I took the Maid's little feet, and rubbed a portion of the ointment from the pot all about them, very gentle and constant; and so did they be new-rested and eased; and she presently fit again to the journey; for I was strong set that we go quickly hence out of that Land, and stay no more there to sleep, lest we come unto Destruction.

And when we had rested an hour, I put the shoes again upon the Maid, and made them secure; and so gat my gear about me, and made to the journey.

And lo! as we did leave the hollow, I lookt upward unto the Holy Light; and behold it was gone from us, and by this thing I supposed that we had come free of instant danger; but yet did there be to me a seeming of nakedness and unprotection, as you must perceive.

And because that the Light was vanished, I was the more set that we come speedy out of the Land. And we went forward at a strong speed, and had the Great Red Fire-Pit of the Giants to our rear unto the left, and a mighty way off in the night; but yet I did wish it the further. And before us, was a small ridging up of the dark Land, as I did judge, because that our view of the lights and the shinings was bounded; and to our left at a great way the low volcanoes, and somewhat to our right, across all that part of the Land went the cold and horrid glare of the Shine.

Now, in a little while, I felt that the ground did be sloped upward before us a little, and by this thing I saw that I had known aright, for

that there did be a ridge that hid the Land somewise over unto the part where I lookt to find the mouth of the Upward Gorge. And we went up this slope at a strong pace, because that I was so eager that I find where we did be in nearness unto the mouth of the Upward Gorge.

And surely, I was something forgetful, in mine eagerness, and came somewhat ahead of Mine Own, who did make to hide from me that she did begin to lag, because that her new strength was near gone from her.

And sudden there did be a very dreadful cry, to my back; and I came round in one instant, so quick as a light doth flash; for it was the voice of Mine Own, and all my being did suddenly burn with fear that kindled through me in a moment of thought.

And lo! Mine Own did struggle terribly with a yellow thing which I perceived to be a man with four arms; and the Man had two arms about the Maid, and with two did make to choke her unto death; for she cried out no more.

And I came unto the Man with a quick leaping, and stopt not to pluck the Diskos from my hip; and surely I did be very strong, and mine anger and rage to make me monstrous; for I caught the two upper arms of the Man, and brought them backward in an instant, so fierce and savage, and so wrencht upon them, that I brake them in the shoulders of the Man.

And the Man roared and shriekt, even as a wild and dreadful Beast should cry out, and came round upon me with the two lower arms. And surely it was a mighty and brutish thing, and so broad and bulkt as an ox, and the lower arms were huge and greatly haired, and the fingers of the hands did have the nails grown into horrid talons, as that they should grip very bitter.

And it caught me by the thighs, to rip me upward, as I did fear; but yet this did not be the intent of the Man; for in a moment it caught me round the body; and on the instant, I gat the Man by the great throat, and the throat did be haired, and so great as the neck of a bull. And I strove with mine armoured hands that I choke the Man, and surely I made it to suffer great trouble; yet, I could not harm it in the life.

And so I did be an horrid minute, and fought with the Beast, with no more than the strength of my body; and it was as that an human went with his hands to slay a monster so strong as an horse. And the breath of the Man-Beast came at me, and did sicken me; and I held the face off from me; for I had died with horror, if that it had come more anigh; and surely the mouth of the Man was small and shaped so that I knew that it did never eat of aught that it did slay; but to drink

as a vampire; and in truth, I did mean that I chop the Man to pieces, if that I have chance to the Diskos.

And I did sway this way and that, as we did struggle; and surely it was as that the Man had never made to use the lower arms, save to hold unto prey, the while that it did use the upper arms to strangle, as I do think. For all that weary minute of the fight, the Man made not to loose from me, that it should tear my hands from their grip to the throat; but made vain waggings with the arms that I brake, as that it would use these to the attack; but surely they had no more power to do hurt.

And sudden, it put forth an utter power about my body, so that mine armour did be like to crack; and truly I had died in a moment; but for the strongness of the armour. And the man hugged me thus for an horrid time, the while that I did hold off from me the brutish face, and gript very savage into the haired throat.

And lo! the creature did work slow in the brain, and in the end loost from me, abrupt, and went back with a leap, so that my hands did be ript from the throat of the Beast. And in one instant it did be back unto me, and gave me no moment to free the Diskos. But I made anew to fight, and shaped as I had learned in the Exercises of mine Upbringing; for truly I had been alway deep in practice of such matters. And I slipt from the great hands of the Man, as it did try to take me by the head; and I hit the Man with mine armoured fist, and put a great power and skill to the blow. And I went instant to the side with a swift stepping, and evaded the Man, and I smote the Man again, and took him very savage in the neck; but all the while grown very cold and brutal and cruel; for I was set to the slaying. And the Man-Beast came round on me; and lo! I slipt the gripe of the great hands, and my body and my legs and mine arms did work together unto that last blow; so that I did hit so hard as a great hammer. And I gat the Beast in the throat, and the Beast went backward to the earth, even as it did think to hold me.

And lo! in a moment, I was free, and I pluckt forth the Diskos from my hip. And the Yellow Beast-Man grunted upon the ground; and it rose up again to come at me; and it stood and did grunt, and did seem as that it was gone mazed; for it did make other sounds, and an horrid screeching, so that truly, by the way of it, I conceived that it cried out unknown and half-shapen words at me. And in a moment, it came again at me; but I cut the head from the Beast-Man, that was in verity an horrid monster, and the Man died, and was quiet upon the earth.

And truly, in that moment, the distress of mine efforts and mine

utter tiredness and the ache of the bruises took me; so that I do surely think I rockt as I stood; but yet was my head strong to think and my heart set in anxiousness; for I wotted not how great an hurt had been done upon Mine Own.

And I ran to her, and came to where she did be upon the ground; and surely she was all huddled, and had her hands very piteous to her throat, that did be so pretty. And it did shake me in that moment that she was truly slain; for she was gone so utter still and as that she did be broken unto death.

And I took her hands from her throat, and surely it did be a little torn; yet not to be much, or so that it should loose her of her dear life. And I strove that I steady the trembling of my hands; and I gat free of mine armoured gloves; and made that I feel whether her throat did be deadly hurt; and, in verity, it seemed not so; only that my hands did so shake, because that I was so frightened for Mine Own, and because that I was but new come from the battle; and because of this, I had not power of touch to assure me.

I made then that I quieten my breath, which did yet come very full and laboured; and I put mine ear above the heart of the Maid, and lo! her heart did beat, and the horridness of my fear went from me in a moment.

And I had the scrip from my back very speedy, and some of the water to fizz, and I dashed the water upon her face and upon her throat; and surely there did be a little quivering and an answering of her body.

And I strove with her for a while more; and she came unto her life again; and in the first, she was all a-lack, as you may think; and immediately she began that she remembered, and she then to shake.

And I told her how that the Four-Armed Man was surely dead and could harm her no more; and she then to weep, because that she had been put to such shock and horror, and held by so brutish a thing. But I took her into mine arms, and so she did come presently to an ease; and I perceived in all my being that she was as a little ship that doth lie in harbour; for she did cling and nestle unto me; and did be safe with me in all her heart and body and belief. And surely she was Mine Own, and I to have glory in that knowing.

And presently, I put her from mine arms, to lie; yet so that she might not perceive the body of the Yellow Beast-Man. And I made clean the Diskos, from her sight, and afterward I put on the scrip; and I took the Maid to mine arms again, and had the Diskos in my hand beside her.

And she made protest that she should truly walk; for that I was

all a-weary, and she come to her strength again. And, indeed, I carried her a certain way, and did then put her down to her feet; and truly her knees did so tremble that she had not stood, let be to walk! And I caught her up again; and I kist her, and I told her that I did be surely her Master, in verity, and she mine own Baby-Slave. And truly you shall not laugh upon me; for I was so human as any; and a man doth talk this way with his maid.

And she did be quiet and sweet and to obey wisely; for she was gone very weak. And thiswise we did go; and I to say loving words, in the first; but afterward I did heed more of my going, now that she was something eased and at rest within mine arms. And I did peer everywhere about, lest that some other evil thing come outward of the bushes, to have at us ere I did ware. And, truly, the bushes grew here and there in that place, very plentiful, in great clumpings.

And presently I was come to the top part of the ridge; and lo! a great gladness took me, and some amazement; for there did be the lights that did be in the mouth of the Upward Gorge, and they did show me that I was come anigh to that place. Yet had I feared that we were surely a dozen great miles off; and now I to learn that we did be scarce of two or maybe three, as I did judge.

And I told this thing to the Maid; and she rejoiced in mine arms, with a deep and quiet thankfulness. And I set forward then at so good a pace as I might; and I was come into the mouth-part of the Upward Gorge in about an hour; and surely I did be very weary, for it was beyond six and thirty hours that we had gone since last we did sleep; and there had been sore labour and terror to our share in that time, as I have told.

And I turned in the mouth of the Gorge, and told Mine Own, very gentle, that we did take our last look upon that Land. And she askt that I put her down to her feet; and I put her down. And therewith we stood in that place, and mine arm about her; and so did I support the Maid, the while that she lookt silent over the dark of the Land.

And presently she askt me in a very husht voice, whether that I knew where the Lesser Pyramid did be in all that Darkness; for she was all adrift of her bearings, and was as a stranger, because that she had never lookt upon the Land from that place, before then. And I showed her where I thought the Pyramid to stand hid in the everlasting night; and she nodded, very quiet, as that she did think thatwise, also.

And so a time did pass, and I knew that Naani said good-bye forever unto all that she had known of the world in all her life; and she did be whispering a goodbye in her soul unto her Dead.

And I was very husht, and deeply sorrowful for the Maid, and did understand; for in verity, there should no other human look upon that Land of terror through all the quiet of eternity; and the Maid did lose all her young life into that blackness, and the Father that was her Father; and the grave of her Mother; and the friends of all her years. And there went death in the Land, even then, after those that did live.

And Mine Own shook a little within mine arm; so that I knew she strove that she be brave, to weep not; but afterward, she made not to cease from her tears; and truly I was there, to be her understanding; and she did be sweet and natural ever with me; for she was Mine Own, and did be hourly the more so.

And presently, I moved a little, to sign that we go downward of the Gorge; and she stayed me one moment, that she look once more over all that Land; and afterward, she submitted, and turned with me, and did break into very bitter sobbing as she did go stumbling beside me; for the sorrow of memory did fill her; and she was truly a very lonesome Maid in that moment, and had come through much dreadfulness.

And in a minute, I stoopt and lifted her; and she wept in mine arms against mine armour; and I very silent and tender with her; and carried her downward of the Gorge for a great hour more. And presently she was grown calm, and I knew that she slept in mine arms.

And in thiswise we made farewell of that dark Land, and left it unto Eternity.

XII

Downward of the Gorge

NOW I CARRIED THE Maid an hour downward of the Gorge, as I did say; and I was then grown so weary that I near fell, as I walked, and stumbled everywhile, because that I had lost somewhat of guiding in my feet, the which did show mine utter alackness.

And I saw that I must come very swift to a place for slumber, or that I did be like to fall headlong with the Maid; for I nigh slept as I walkt.

And I began that I give attention to the sides of the Gorge; and surely I had gone that hour all in a dream; for I was fresh-waked, as it were, in that I did give my will to perceive aught; and when I did come to have power to attend, I knew that I had gone, even as a sleep-walker; for the Gorge did seem a fresh matter unto me, and as that I had come awake sudden to find myself a-walk in that strange and narrow place.

And presently, I saw somewhat where I did be; for I minded the memory of mine outward journey; and truly I have a good power to know and remember a way that I have gone. And I saw that there was a great and ruddy fire-hole anigh to me; and I was all sure that I had perceived certain caves in the wall of the Gorge, near to that fire, as I past it on mine upward way; and I had been given a mighty longing of heart at that time, that it be given to me that I should bring safe Mine Own out of the peril that beset her, and have her unto just such a place for her slumber, on the way of our journey backward.

And surely I tell you this thing as a child in pleasure; for, truly, it was a wondrous happy matter that my desiring should be like to have a true ending; as, indeed, it did seem was truly to be, if that my memory had set me aright.

And I went onward somewhat; and lo! I to be right, for the little caves did be there, a little past the great fire-hole; and there were seven of them in the left side of the great cliff of the Gorge; and one did be as that it were very cozy and a place of sure safety, if that we could win unto it.

And truly, as I did conceive, we had come safe from the Evil Forces of that Land; but yet did I mind that there was no surety in this thing; and neither did I know but that some Monster should come downward of the Gorge, out of that Land; and so work our deaths, as we did sleep; if that we have no sure place for our slumber. And, indeed, I had wished that we were come a greater way downward of the Gorge, but this might not be; for I was all adrift with weariness. And truly, if that we gat upward to the top-most cave, there did be few Monsters that should have power to come at us, ere we be warned of their coming. And afterward they should be like to come upward against the Diskos; and this should be indeed a thing difficult, as you shall conceive.

Now it did be needful that I wake the Maid, and I kist her, as she did be in mine arms; and surely that dear One did kiss back again in her sleep, and was yet asleep. And truly I did love her with all my being; and I kist her again, and shook her very gentle, and so had her to wakefulness, and told how we did be come to a place fit for our slumber.

And she to look about, very sleepy, as I set her to her feet; and then to upbraid herself that she did over to slumber, the while that I did labour with her carrying. And, in verity, I kist her again, as she did stand making to steady herself, and looking so pretty with the sleep that did lie yet in her eyes. And she to kiss me very dear and all mine; and even then scarce proper come to wakefulness; and did say with something of a little dear abandon, that she did love me utter and forever.

And afterward, I climbed to the topmost of the caves, and told Mine Own the while that she walk up and down a little; so that she come to a full awakedness; and this I was careful to, because that she should have a need of all her powers that she come safe upward unto the cave.

And when I was come to the cave, lo! it did be so sweet and dry, as did make glad my heart. And there did be a warmth in the cave, as that there went a fire somewhere through the rocks anigh. And the light from the fire-hole did make a reflection inward, and so this did seem a place safe, and fit to our slumbering.

And I came downward unto Naani, calling that the cave was very proper for our use; and presently I gave her mine aid to the climbing, and so we came in the end safe into the cave; and truly we did feel very safe and happy.

Yet, before we did sleep, I set free the scrip and the pouch, and took the straps and went downward again into the Gorge; and I gat a

good boulder, so heavy as I might carry, and strapt it to my back, and came upward again to the cave, and the Maid very grave and anxious, lest that I slip to my hurt. And when I was come to the cave again, I set the boulder in the mouth of the cave, and did balance it so light upon the edge, that a touch should send it rolling downward.

And by this devising, I conceived that any Beast or Monstrous thing that should climb upward whilst that we slept, should be like to set the rock adrift, and mayhaps the rock to work an harm to such, but the chief end to be that I should be swiftly waked by the noise.

And then I did turn that we go to our slumber; and lo! the Maid had spread the cloak upon the rock, that we should sleep upon it; for truly there did be no need that we have it now to our covering, because that the cave did be so warm as I have told before.

And surely, there did be no cause either that I should have the cloak for a bed; for how should I perceive any softness from the cloak, through all the sternness of mine armour; but yet did I see that the Maid had made a couch that should be for the two of us, and did be so sweet and natural, and to lie by me; but yet to preserve her sweet modesty, and to do the thing with no thought, save that it was natural to our hearts; and that she did long alway to be anigh to me; but yet, mayhaps, scarce full conscious that her heart did prompt her in this thing.

And, in verity, I loved her very dear.

And surely, Naani showed me the where that I should lie upon my side; and when I had obeyed, she kneeled, and kist me on the lips, very sober and loving; and she lay down then upon the cloak beside me; and truly we had both gone to sleep in one little minute, as I do think.

Now I did be waked twelve great hours after, by the fizzing of the water; and lo! when I lookt, the Maid was not beside me; but did make ready our simple eating and drinking. And she laughed at me, very sweet and tender, because that she loved me so, and did be so glad to have me awake to her; and she came over to me, and kist me, very bright and loving upon the lips.

And after that she had kist me, she kneeled beside me, and lookt at me, very dear and tender; so that I knew in a moment that she had waked a while gone, and watched me, somewise motherlike, as I did sleep. But how I knew this thing, I am not sure, save that my spirit did know, or that her thoughts did have tongues unto mine.

And truly I needed that I be so loved, and all of you to say like with me; and I put up mine arms to her, as I did yet lie; and she not to deny me, but came into mine arms, and did snuggle there so sweet and happy and gladly, and with so true a delight, that it did be plain

how she did love in all her body and spirit to be anigh to me, as I to her. Yet, truly, as you do mind, the armour did be upon me; so that I feared to take her very strong in mine arms, lest I hurt the dear Maid; and surely the armour did be a stern matter for her to nestle unto; but yet, mayhaps, did the sternness something please her womanheart, and yet, again, mayhaps to lack.

And presently, she made that she would go from me, and I loosed mine arms from her very ready, because that I did heed alway that she have full sweet liberty of her dear Maidenhood; and I to be watchful sufficient unto this end, yet always honest and wholesome and not over-pondering even in this my care; and this proper intending you shall ever perceive, if that your hearts do strive to hearken unto my heart, which doth speak alway before you.

And the Maid went from me, over to where she had put the cup of the water, and the tablets; and I to make to rise, that I look that the boulder did be safe untouched in the mouth of the cave. But she called unto me that I lie backward; for that she did mean gently to spoil me that once; and that I have no heed to the boulder or whether there did be any Monster or Beast anigh in the Gorge; for that the boulder did be safe as I did balance it; and nowheres any Creature to sight in the Gorge; for she had lookt oft, since waking, to this end.

And truly I obeyed, and lay back, and did like that I should be spoilt, as we do say. And Naani brought the cup of the water, and the tablets over to me; for she gat them from the scrip before I had it to my pillow, in that while when I had gone downward for the boulder. And surely, even when she brought the cup, she would not have me to rise; but took my head upon her knees, and kist me once very dainty on the lips, and I very happy to be so loved, and wishful no otherwise.

And she took a tablet and kist it and gave it to me; and afterward touched another to my lips, and had that to be for her own. And so we eat and were very glad and happy, someways as children are happy, and our hearts all at ease.

And presently, we eat each our second tablet, in the same wise as the first. And truly I did be kist more than once. And afterward, we drank each of the water.

And when we had made an end, Naani told me that I move to stand; and surely I wondered; and I stood up, and lo! I near cried out with the pains of my bruisings; for I was all gone stiff in my sleep, and as that I did be more sore than ever; and this to be because I had fought again, as you do know, and surely had been hurt more by the Four-Armed Man than I had known.

And I perceived then that Naani had supposed that I should be thus pained, and had given dear thought to the matter; and truly she had the pot of the ointment, ready, if that I did be very bad, that she rub me.

And she gave me aid with mine armour, and afterward eased me with my garments; and surely I did be utter bruised in the body, by reason of the violence of the Yellow Beast-Man. And the Maid had somewhat so tender and sweet in her eyes as she looked upon the bruisings, that I did be very happy and to glow with contentment.

And she had me to lie, and made me in comfort with the cloak, so loving and grave, so that I was as a child that doth be cared of by his mother. And she did rub me very skilful and gentle for a great hour, until I was all refreshed. And in verity she was a lovely wise maid.

And as the Maid ministered unto me, I lay alway very restful, and harked to the low sound of the muttering of the fire-hole that did be in the bottom of the Gorge; and alway I did feel as an happy child that doth be clothed in love and guided in wisdom.

And presently, when that the Maid had ended her dear care, she put by the ointment, and gave me her hands very dainty, that she mean to aid me to rise; and surely when I was come again to my feet, I was all eased, and to have movement with no great pain; and truly this made me wondrous pleased and to feel new couraged; for I had been troubled that I should be so helpless, in that I did be the Protector of Mine Own.

And when I had tried my limbs, and found them to be in command and ready, I lookt about for my garments. And lo, the Maid brought me my spare body-vest, from the Pouch, and had it upon her arm, to give to me. But surely she denied me a moment, of the vest, and stood before me, and had an admiring and wonder, very sweet and honest, because that my arms did be so great and hard with muscles.

And, indeed, I did be very strong, as you have perceived; for I did be alway in affection of the Exercises that were taught in the Upbringing of all the Peoples of the Mighty Pyramid; and by this explaining, you shall understand that I was like to be strong; but indeed, I owed the straightness and shaping of my body to the Mother that bore me. And afterward, in all my life, had I taken pride of my body to be of health and to have strength; and surely this is a matter very fit for pride; and to be told bravely and with honesty.

And the admiring of the Maid was very sweet to me; and, in verity, I did be to deceive, if that I said otherwise. And in a moment, she dropt my body-vest, and put out her hands to me that I take her into mine arms.

And I took the Maid into mine arms with a great gladness and with somewhat of humbleness that I was nowise good enough to hold her, for my heart was young, and I loved her very dear and youthful. And she did lie there very quiet and happy, a little; and surely I did find presently that she kist the great muscling of my breast, very sweet and sly, where her face did be press against it. And lo, in a moment, she came free of mine arms, and gave me an aid with my garments, and afterward with mine armour.

And when that this was done, she stood off from me; and she lookt at me, half shy and half of sweetness and naughtiness. And she came then in a moment, and put her hands upward to my shoulders, and so stood her eyelids something down over her eyes; and did steal a little look up, this time and that. And lo! in a sudden moment, before I did wot, she was to her knees before me, and did weep; and I down very swift to kneel with her.

And I askt not why she wept; for I perceived that she did have joy and glad happiness and sweet trouble of her man; and that she did be a true woman, and one part of the woman did worship, so that she did be strangely humble and nigh to be shy; and another did love, and need that she be anigh to me; and a third to have a calm wisdom. And all did now be a-tremble, together in her heart; and I knew that I did be truly an hero to her, though but usual to all others. And my heart was wondrous proud and wondrous humble, so that I was in the same moment upraised and to feel dreadly unworthy. But I made no pretending to discredit myself to her, but only did resolve that I win alway her dear respect; and I did be natural and truthful of my manner and without foolish denial of her sweet worship, for she was utter Mine Own, and it did be a pitiful thing if that I seem otherwise than an hero unto her.

But of you I ask kind understanding, and to call me not a thing of conceit because that I did understand; for truly I knew my faults, even so well as you, that do know all of my going. And you to look backward upon the love-days, and to mind how that your maid did ever to make you great in manhood with her dear belief and uplooking; and so shall you conceive of all my feelings; for we do be all so human in this matter, and to meet on a dear natural ground, as you will say.

And, truly, in a little time, Mine Own did be steadied, and wiped her pretty eyes, and nestled to me a while, very husht and to need that she be close. And I to have her gentle against mine armour, and to be in my heart as that I did be her father and her lover in the one man, and surely to be silent and joyful that I lived.

And presently I slipt her shoes from her little feet, with my right hand, the while that she did rest within my left arm; and I condemned myself that I had thought not more swift to this end; but indeed I had thought upon it while that Naani rubbed me, and had intention thiswise; but afterward forgat, as you shall understand, that have been with me alway. And truly Mine Own did be hurt that I say aught to my blame; and I to cease, but yet to feel reproached by my heart.

And when I had lookt to the Maid's feet, I tied on her shoes again; and we gat together our gear. And afterward we came down from the cave, with a great care, because that it did be so high up in the cliff of the Gorge.

And afterward, we made downward of the Gorge, and had a good care to our going, and so much of speed as we could make, that we come something off from the Dark Land of the Lesser Redoubt, so quick as we might.

And in six hours we had gone very well, and we stopt then that we eat and drink; and afterward, I lookt again to the feet of the Maid. And I bathed them in a great rock basin of warm water that did be anigh to the place of our eating; and afterward I put the ointment about them very thorough and gentle and for a good while; and so she had some ease and comfort.

And afterward, we made onward again; but now we did go pretty easy; for I had considered the notings of mine outward journey, and so did perceive that we should be but six or seven hours off that part of the Gorge, where did be the Slugs.

And I was minded that we rest and sleep, ere that we make through that dire and dreadful place; for that we should be twelve great hours, and more, to go through, and to have no rest or pause, until that we did be safe outward again, as you shall think. And so did we need to be strong and well rested, and this to be wise also for the feet of the Maid.

Now surely the Maid did be in delight of the fires of that part of the Gorge where we were come, and she had beside a rest of the soul, in that she had feeling that there did be no Evil Force to trouble us to our destruction; and I bothered her not yet awhile with tellings of the horrid place that we should to journey through in a while, as you do know.

And so we did go, and alway with a good caution, lest that some Beast or Creature should come upon us; and alway with the fire-holes before and behind, and in the air of the Gorge the little whistlings of steam that did spirt out in this place and that; and a good warmth in many parts, by reason of the fires; and odd whiles a smelling of sul-

phur; but not greatly, nor to our trouble. And alway the low muttering of the fire-holes and pits, and the red lights, and the dancing of the shadows when that we did go by a fire-pit where the fire did frisk and burn lively. And upon either side, the grim walls of the Gorge going up measureless into the night.

And so we were gone presently, pretty comfortable, for six good hours, since last that we eat; and we made halt, and eat and drank; and I showed the Maid how that we should make a short journey that day, and sleep, and so be ready to the horrid journey through the dark part of the Gorge, where the Slugs did be.

And we made search then, that we have a safe place to our slumber; and surely I perceived where we did be; for we came upon that same cave where I did sleep after that I was come free of the Slugs; and that we were come no farther, doth show how easy did be our present going, and this you do know. And there did be the spring where I washed, and the fire-hole anigh, and truly they were not like to be gone away, as you shall say! Yet did we exclaim, very natural; for the Maid did be so deep in interest of the matters of my coming, and to be at once that no other place should serve for our rest and slumber.

And, indeed, this was a natural thing, and the place so good as any, save that I did wish it had been upward unto a high place of the Gorge, as you shall understand. But yet might we block the mouth-part of the cave with boulders, somewise as I did before, and so to have a defence against any thing that should make to enter upon our sleep; or at the least to be waked by the falling of the boulders.

Now Mine Own went inward of the little cave, which did be very light from the fire-pit that was to the front; but before that she did go, I made a swift search of the place, that there should be no creeping thing; and truly it was sweet and free. And the Maid did be strangely taken that she should come to the veritable place where once I did lie on mine outward way; and truly I do understand, and so shall many that do have these feelings about matters.

And afterward, we went unto the hot spring that was in the hollow of the rock, anigh to the fire-pit. And I saw that there did be no snakes, neither any of the rat-things anigh; and so I had the Maid to sit very comfortable on the side of the pool, and I freed her shoes, and bathed her feet, and afterward rubbed them very steady with the ointment; and so for a good time, and alway to keep a looking out upon the Gorge.

And presently, when that I had taken a loving care of her pretty feet, I tied the shoes again upon the Maid, and so back to the cave;

and the two of us to carry boulders, according to our strength. And when we had a sufficient, we builded a rough and clumsy wall, after that we were gone into the cave; and the wall rose nigh to fill the mouth of the cave, and made us to be somewise in darkness, but yet to feel in safety. And I had a good heed to make the chinks of the wall very close in the bottom, so that no small creeping thing should come through unto us whilst that we slept.

And afterward, Naani set the scrip and the pouch to be for my pillow; but had the bundle of her torn garments to be for her own purpose.

And I perceived that she had the water-powder and a pack of the tablets to her hand for our waking, that she might prepare our food, and mayhap to wake a little before me, so that she have all ready to greet me from my sleep. But, indeed, I said naught to show that I knew; for I saw that this thing did give her a dear pleasure, and truly it was very sweet to have her to these gentle duties, that did be to her so sure and quiet a delight.

And Mine Own bade me that I lie; and she put the Diskos upon the outward side of me, to mine hand; and with a dainty and fearful touch; for the weapon did be very dreadful unto her thoughts; but yet a comforting thing to abide for our defence. And afterward, she covered me with the cloak, and kist me very sedate upon the lips; and then to her own side, and to come very nice and happy under the cloak, and so to her rest.

And presently she did sleep, as I perceived by her breathings; and surely it did seem to my spirit that she had an utter and dear content in this arranging of our slumber, so that she did be all at peace in all her being, because that she did be nigh unto me, that did be her Own Love.

But, indeed, I could not sleep for a time; and surely, in a while, Mine Own did nestle unto me in her sleep, so sweet and dear as a child, and likewise as that it did be her right to be so anigh unto me; and I to be that I should put mine arms about her, but indeed I moved not, neither did I kiss her, as I did wish; for truly I should be very manly with mine own maid that did be so trustful and utter mine in her sleep.

And presently I was over unto slumber also, and stirred not for eight good hours, and did wake then to the hissing of the water, so that I knew Mine Own was awake before me, as she had planned, and was making ready that we eat.

And when she saw me move in the half-light, she gave out a little word of joy, that I did be again to knowledge of her; and she came over, and put her arms about my neck, and kist me very loving, thrice upon the lips. And, in verity, it came to me in that moment that I had

been kist a while gone in my dreams, but scarce to know it; yet I perceived now that Mine Own had taken a naughty advantaging of my slumber, that she kiss me to her own pleasure; yet did the Maid say no word of her naughtiness; and I to be likewise; but to resolve that I waken, mayhaps, on the next time, and so catch her in her sweet and secret delight of me.

And, truly, this doth sound quaint; but to be true.

And I rose, and took down the half of the wall that did be across the mouth of the cave, and afterward lookt out; but there was no sight of any horrid thing in the Gorge, save that one of the rat-things did slumber, very gorged-seeming, upon the side of the little fire hole.

And afterwards, we eat and drank; and the Maid then to rub me, as before; for I was greatly stiff on my waking, as you shall think; but she came not into mine arms presently, as I did hope; but only kist my shoulders, when that she had finished, and so bid me to dress.

Yet, after that I was drest, and had mine armour full upon me, she must come unto me, and she slipt her two small hands into the one of mine, and so stood by me, very silent. And sudden she put up her lips very quiet and passionate, that I should kiss her; and she kist me once, as it did be as that her spirit kist mine, and all her being came unto me; and she gave me but that one kiss, and afterward slipt her hands very gentle from mine, and made to the gathering of our gear.

But truly, I that loved her so great, knew that a tumult of love did be hid in her heart. And, indeed, she looked once at me in such wise, that I grew near to a true humbleness of heart because of the honour and love that did be in her eyes.

And surely, it is a very little thing to die for such an One as Mine Own did be. And by this saying, shall you perceive my heart in that moment, and that I did pant, as it were, that I do some deed of love to show my love. And truly this is but a natural desiring and human, and the cause proper to the uplifting of manhood. And surely you shall all mind you of such feelings in the past love-days, that I do pray should be never past.

And when we had our gear together, I left it in the cave, and took Mine Own over unto the hot pool that was anigh to the fire-pit; and she to exclaim upon the rat-thing that did be yet a-slumber upon the side of the fire-pit; and I to say that the thing did be no cause for fear, but rather, indeed, a good friend, in that it was a devourer of snakes, as you shall mind.

And while that we talked, I bathed the little feet of Naani; and surely, as I dried them upon my pocket-cloth, I was taken that I should

kiss them; and surely I kist them, and they did be very shapely and dainty, and all eased of travel by the care that I did take to this end.

And afterward I rubbed them with the ointment for a good while, and so had them again into the shoes, and the Maid very quiet, after that I had kist her feet that did be so dainty, but yet with a sweet naughtiness in her way, as my heart perceived, though she did nothing, neither said anything, to this end; and was truly very obedient, and orderly to all my wishes.

And we went back then to the cave, and the Maid put the pot of the ointment back into the pouch, and she buckled the pouch and the scrip upon me; and the Diskos I had upon my hip; for I went nowise anywhere, without it, as you shall suppose. And she had the little bundle of her clothing for her burden, and truly, I was ready that she should carry so much; for we did be to act wisely, and she well able to carry so small a thing, and I better to have my hands alway free to the Diskos and to the needs of the way.

And we went downward of the Gorge at a strong speed, for there did be somewise of fifteen hours good journey, ere that we come out upon the far side of that place where the Monsters did be, and this did be three hours to the upward beginning of that place, and twelve hours journey then, in the least, that we should take to go through again into the light of the Gorge below. And this I did reckon from my notings of mine upward journey, as you do know.

And I made all clear to the Maid, of the thing that did be before us, and made not to hide the danger and horror, but yet to make not overmuch of the same. And she to walk close beside me, very sweet and trustful, and to say that she feared naught, so that I should be there to have care of her; but only that she did fear harm for me; and yet to have confidence that I should slay all hurtful things that should be like to trouble us. And, truly, I did kiss her for her dear belief and love.

Now, in the middle part of the third hour, the air of the Gorge did begin that it was heavy, and to have a seeming of fumes that stang something upon the throat, odd whiles. And there were presently less of the fire-holes, and soon, as we did go the more downward, the beginnings of a great gloom, and to have smoke therein that made us to feel husky.

And in the end of the fourth hour, we were come truly far downward within the gloom; and to be as that we groped in a fog of distaste; and to know not how we went with any surety; for oft there did be an utter darkness about us; and awhile the shine of a dull-glowing fire-pit upon our sight, that did show us the gloom and dread of that place.

And we went alway very husht, and the Maid to my back; but I did halt now and this time, and make to know how she did be; and surely she whispered very brave to me through the dimness, and once did slip her hand into mine, and I to take off mine armoured glove for a little moment, that I hold her hand, and give her nice assurance. But, in verity, there was terror in mine heart, that did be a terror far beyond the trouble of mine upward way; and surely I was shaken newly with every danger, lest that I should lose Mine Own, or she to come to any hurt. And, indeed, you shall perceive how I did be; for so should you be in a like case, and, in truth, it doth be an utter anxiousness and suffering.

Now when we had been two hours in the dark part of the Gorge, I smelled of the dread and horrid stink that you do wot of. And surely a great fear came upon me; for I perceived that we did come among the Monsters, or that one came anigh to us.

And I whispered unto the Maid that she halt; and we stood very husht a while, and surely the stink did grow, and to be very dreadful in the nostrils, so that I felt Mine Own Maid to shake somewhat with the fear and disgust that this thing did make in us. And presently the stinking did ease somewhat from about us; but whether there had gone past us a monster Slug, I have no sure knowing; for there did be no fire-pit anigh to that place; so that there was a great darkness all about.

And surely there was a great slowness and wetness of the air, and dismal drippings that made desolation in the silence; and the feel of strange growths upon the boulders, as you do know; and oft an horrid slime and dankness; and the stink to be everywhere, so that we knew a constant disgust and fear. And alway the fumings of sulphur, that did seem, in verity, to beat down upon us, utter heavy and sore upon our lungs.

And so went we onward amid the smell that did be as of dead things; and oft did we make pause and hark, and had a great care as we did go by the dull fire-holes and fire-pits, that we should make no showing of ourselves in the light.

And sudden, as we did go by a great pit that burned very deep and red, I reached back and caught Mine Own by the arm, and I set her gaze unto the right side of the Gorge, which was beyond the fire. And the Maid went very still, as she did see the thing that was there; for in verity it was utter monstrous, and did shine very wet-looking in the light of the fire. And truly it moved a little with the head, this way and that, stretching through the dark and the shadows, as you shall see a slug to move, and with no speed or sound, and nowise seeming

heedful of aught. But yet did I fear that it smelled us, if this might be; and this, as you shall think, to be a very natural fear.

And alway, as I do mind, it seemed to go blindly somewise, or to have that slow and strange moving that doth make one to think of a blindness; but whether it did be truly blind, how shall I say; only that it was an utter Monstrous Brute, so great as the black hull of a ship, and very dreadful unto our hearts.

And we moved not for a while, save that I pulled Mine Own down into the hiding of the boulders of that part; and she to put her hand very anxious unto me; yet not to be comforted, as I did half to think, but to persuade me, lest that I go to some adventuring that should set me in a surer danger. And this I perceived in a little moment, and loved her for her care.

But, indeed, I had no mind to aught, save that we come clear of that place; and I watched the Monster, through places between the boulders; and surely, in a little while, it swayed the great head very slow and quiet unto the cliff that did make that side of the Gorge; and the Brute set unto the Cliff, and began that it went upward with a strange moving of muscles that did go wavewise under the wet and horrid-gleaming hide.

And so, in a little time, it was gone quiet against the cliff, and the head-part did be upward in the darkness above, so that it did be from our sight. But the monster body did be plain for a great way, and was seeming clung to the cliff, and to come downward out of the dark, as that it did be a great black ridge of soft and dreadful life upon the face of the cliff; and the tail was something less bulked, and to taper, and did trail outward into the Gorge upon the boulders.

And surely the thing did seem as that it slept, but that odd whiles the tail did lift a little off the boulders, and curl somewise, and afterward come down again upon the boulders, mayhap in this place and mayhap in that place, as we did watch, all hid.

And it was as that our sense and our Spirits did assure us that the thing had no wotting of us; but surely our fears did nigh to equal the comfort of this sweet reason, and to make us think otherwise

Yet, in a time, I made that we go forward together through the spaces that did be among the boulders. And I went creeping, and the Maid to follow likewise.

And oft I did pause, and made a watching upon the monster; but truly it moved not, save as I have told; and I kept a great heed upon the Maid, that she follow alway close unto my feet.

And in the end we came safe from that place where the monster did be clung unto the great cliff in the night.

And we went then for two great hours without adventure, save that once the Maid touched me that we pause; for that something went by us where we did be in an utter dark place of the Gorge, and no fire-hole anigh.

And I knew that the thing did be near, even as the Maid toucht me. And caught I the Maid in the dark, and thrust her under the side of a boulder; and I crouched then before her, with mine armour, that I should protect her from any Brutish thing. And the Diskos in my hand, and afterward an horrid time of waiting.

And the stink of that part of the Gorge grew very dreadful, so that it did be as that we should not breathe, with the horror of the stink. And there went past us some horrid and utter Monster, that made neither sound nor anything, save that there seemed a strange noise that might be the breathing of a great thing; but yet did be all uncertain, in that the sides of the Gorge cast the sound this way and that, in an horrid whispering of echoes; so that we did not know whether the sound be made nigh to us, or afar upward in the eternity of the night, where I did suppose the mountains to be joined over the Gorge in a monstrous roof in that part.

And presently, the strange noisings died in the upward height, and all about us; and the utter disgust of the stink went from us; so that we knew that the Monster had gone past us, and did make downward through the dark Gorge; and mayhap then to some lone and dreadful cavern of the world, as I did think.

And, indeed, as I do mind, I had a sudden wonder at that time, and other whiles, as it did chance, whether this way did be truly the olden way that the Peoples of the Lesser Refuge did travel in the Olden Days. And surely, as I did suppose, they had come some other way, or the Gorge to be different and less dreadful in the far-off years. And this thing you shall agree with me to be a reasonable thinking.

And after that the Monster had gone a good while we went onward again, and with a great caution; and dreading alway lest that we come upon that Monster, in the darkness; but yet did we know by smell, and by all our consciousness, whether that we came nigh unto one of the monster Slugs.

Then, in the end of the fifth hour in the dark part of the Gorge, we came by the mouth of that great cavern, upon our left; and you to remember the same.

And I made pause in the darkness, and had the Maid very gentle by the arm, that she should look with me. And I whispered how that I past this place, to my right, upon mine upward way; and how that I

did think there to be a-plenty of monster caverns within the mountains that made the sides of the Gorge, and that, mayhap, the Slug-Creatures had there an home in such places, or came up, it might be, from some utter strange deepness and mystery of the great world.

And the Maid did bide very close unto me, and silent, whilst that I whispered; for the terror of the place did be on her, yet not to make her lacking of courage, but yet to put a monstrous awe upon her and a great and natural fear; and I likewise, as you do know.

And we stayed there, where we did be, a little moment, and looked downward into the bowels of the monster cavern; and the shine of the fire-hole beat over the cavern in the near part; but there did be an utter mystery and deathly dark beyond the shining of the pit that did be within, as you shall remember.

And, in verity, as we stayed but to glance, I perceived that there lay humped things about the fire, and some to be black-seeming, and some to have a seeming of whiteness, but with no sureness in the colour to mine eyes.

And there came a moving in one of the humpt things, so that it did be as that an hill did wake unto an horrid life. And immediately I knew that the humps did be some utter monsters, mayhaps even the great Slugs, a-slumber about the fire-pit that did burn in that strange deeply cavern. And I saw that I did ill for our lives, that I should pause even for a little moment to such staring.

And immediately I whispered to Mine Own that we go with all our speed; for, indeed, I knew not whether that our nearness had waked that Monster, or whether that it had but waked by chance. And truly, I was utter eager that we be gone from that place, so swift as we might.

And we went on then through all of the sixth hour that we did be in the Slug part of the Gorge, as I named it unto myself. And in all that hour, there did nothing harmful come anigh; only, as I did know presently, there came an unease upon our spirits, but yet to be very little at that time, and we to be scarce knowing of it.

And alway, as we went, there did be darkness for the most, and odd-whiles a vague murmuring of the night far above, as it did seem; and presently the dull glare of a fire-pit to shine out far off below us in the Gorge, and to seem very dim and unreal unto us, by reason of the smokes and the fumes that made a haze and a distaste in the Gorge.

And presently, the murmuring of the night to grow somewhat, and, afterward, the sound of the muttering of the fire-pit to come unto us; and the murmuring to die unto our ears that did be hearing now only the dull muttering, and so we to know that the murmuring

of the night did be truly the far-off muttering of the fire-holes, and our eyes to guide our hearing, and our reason to explain and knit the sounds; and so we to pass by the fire-hole with a great quiet and caution and ever with watchfulness, as you shall suppose. And afterward again into the dark; and presently again the murmuring, to tell that we came unto another of the fire-pits, that was yet afar off in the Gorge, and made dim echoes in the night.

And alway we went very watchful, and in grim fear; but with steadfastness and good intention to win forth out of that desolation and horror, and having alway so great a speed as the darkness and the dangers and the trouble of the way did allow.

And in this place I will make explanation why that I speak somewhiles of fire-pits and otherwhiles of fire-holes; for the holes did be those fires that burned nigh to the brim of the holes; but the pits were those places where the fire was deeply in the earth. And this thing I give for your enlightenment, even on a small matter; so that you shall have a clear knowledge to abide with me all the way; and you to agree of this for wisdom, and I to be pleased that you so agree.

And here also, I should tell that there did not come a muttering from all of the fire-holes and the fire-pits; but mayhap from this one, and mayhap not from that one, according to the way of the fire therein. And this shall be plain unto you.

And so shall you see us go, and the smoke and the bitterness of the sulphur to be all about us; and oddwhiles the murmuring of a far-off pit, and oft the utter silence; and to pass this time a lonesome fire-hole; and afterward the utter dark, or the half-gloom, all as might chance, according to the nearness of the fires. And upward in the everlasting night, the grim mountains to make a roof over us, as I did suppose.

And all this while did the unease, of which I have told, make upon us; so that, presently, Mine Own whispered unto me the thing that already my spirit did half to perceive, that there came after us through the night some harmful thing, that did be surely no great way off, as I did feel within me, and the Maid to have a likeways belief.

And, truly I thought at once upon that Brute that did wake downward in the mighty Cavern, where did be the great inward fire-hole, as I have told; but whether this did be true knowledge that we did be chased in the dark by that thing, or whether there came after us some other Monster, I could have no sureness; but only that we did be chased, and of this I had assuredness.

And I set the Maid before me, that I have myself ready to the danger that followed; and we made forward again then, so quick as

we were abled; and she went very wisely; for she had good wit and had noted the ways of my leading.

And we went thus until the end of the seventh hour. And surely, in that time, we heard the murmuring in the night which told of a fire-hole somewise before us; and soon to have the red glare plain to our eyes, and the noise of the murmuring to die away into the nearer mutter of the fire; and so presently to be anigh; and we to make forward with a good speed, because that we feared utterly the thing that made quiet chase of us through the night.

And oft I did look backward, and smelt the air, that I know whether it did be a monster Slug-beast that chased us; but there did be no worseness of the smell, to tell me aught.

And alway, I did be fretted in the heart, that we could make no greater speed; but, indeed, as you shall perceive, our going did be but a slow thing in the dark places, and even thus we had many a sore tumbling and bruising.

And by this, we were come almost unto the fire-hole; and immediately, I saw that I knew the place, for there went upward beside the fire, a great jaggedness of rock, that I had seen upon mine upward way.

And surely, I caught the Maid in an instant, and bent her, and she quick to obey with her body. And we were both immediately hid downward among the boulders. And this I did, because I minded how that there did be many of the Monsters nigh to this same fire-hole, as I did go upon mine upward way.

And we went forward then with an utter care; but yet to keep onward, because that there did be somewhat in chase of us. And, in verity, when that we were come opposite unto the fire-hole, I saw that there did be seven of the monster Slugs against the far side of the Gorge, and did be all set upon their bellies against the cliff, and their horrid heads to be hid in the upward dark, and their tails to lie very great and soft-seeming in the bottom of the gorge, upon the boulders.

And, lo! the Maid toucht me, and she drew me to look upon the near cliff of the Gorge. And truly there did be three of the Brutish Things laid upward there, and a fourth did be humped somewhat upon a great ledge that did be upward of the Gorge, and just to be plain to our eyes.

And surely, it was as that we did be all surround by such Monsters, and to make the heart sink, and fear to lie upon our hopefulness. But, indeed, the Maid showed a good spirit, and I to have fierce determining that we come free of that Gorge, and afterward, in time, unto our Mighty Home.

And we made forward again, and did go creeping among the rocks and the boulders; and so came presently past that place, and had not waked the Monsters, if that indeed they did truly sleep.

And I made halt a moment upon the far border of the light from the fire-hole, and I lookt backward up the Gorge, perchance that I should see the thing that followed us. But, indeed, there came nothing out of the dark of the upward Gorge, so that I knew that there did be some safe space to our backs, which did be truly a comforting thing.

And here I should tell how that there was no great stinking in that place where did be so many of the Slug-beasts, and this to puzzle me; and in the end to make me think that some of those horrid things did stench more great than others; but yet I to have no certainty in this matter, as you do perceive. And, truly, this thing troubled me; for I had been comforted that my nose should tell me when that the thing that made chase of us should draw nigh in the darkness; and now, in verity, I knew not what to have for assurance; for the awaredness of the spirit was but a vague thing, and no more in such a matter, than a feeling as of an inward warning.

And we went onward then for a great hour, and with an horrid unease upon us; and thrice we did go by fire-pits in the darkness; and alway I made pause upon the far side of the light, that I should look backward; but did have no sight of aught; yet did my spirit or my fears warn me with new fear, and a greater sense of nearness; and the Maid to confess also to this thing.

Now, we saw not any of the Slugs for a long while, neither had there been any about the three fire-holes; and the air of the Gorge was grown something sweet and free somewhat of the stench of dead-seeming things; but yet to be very bitter with fumings and smoke and sulphur stinks.

And lo! in the middle of the tenth hour, as we did go, painful and with anxiousness in a very dark place of the Gorge, there came unto us again the smell that told to us that one of the Monsters did be anigh. And surely we had both a great fear, in that we had belief that it did be a sign that the thing that made chase, did draw near upon us. But yet did I to use my Reason also, and to know that the stink might be from some Monster that we were come nigh to in the darkness of that place; and I whispered this unto the Maid, and she to say, very husht, that it might be so; but to have no belief; and I to be likewise, as you do see.

And we pusht forward at a new speed, and had many bitter falls, so that we did be all bruised; but not to know it at that time, because

that our fear did be so keen. And oft we made a little pause and harkt; but there did be only the dismal drip of water from on high; and presently the murmur of the night, that told that we drew near unto a new fire-pit.

And surely this was a great easement to our spirits, in that we should have light to perceive our danger, and mayhap to win free. But to be in that utter dark, was a thing to break the courage, and to breed belief that we did be utter helpless, and all wrapt in horror and despair.

And the stink grew ever, as we made forward; so that I knew not whether there did be great Monsters beside the fire-pit that was to our front, as I have told, or whether it made plain the advancing of the Pursuer. And we only to be able to make our best speed, and to be weary with hope that we rush not blind into death; and alway to be chilled in the back with the belief that the thing that made chase did be very close in that utter dark, and to gain upon us.

And we knew not whether to make our belief to be the tellings of the spirit or the utterings of our fears; and so shall you perceive our plight; and we but to be able to make forward. And, in verity, the dreadfulness of that time doth shake me now to think upon, and you also, if that you have gotten my tellings to your hearts, so that your human sympathy doth be with me.

And there came presently to our ears the far mutter of the fire-pit, so that very soon the murmuring was lost to us in the night, and only the slow mutter to be plain. And the dull looming of the fire shone afar off, through the night and the smoke and fumings; and we to a great speed, and to pant with fear; but yet with a freshness of hope again to sweeten us.

And we came nigh to the fire-pit, and lo! the smell did be grown very drear and foul; but there did be no Slug-Beast near the fire. And by this, we perceived that we did be truly in an utter danger, in that the Pursuer did be upon us, and the stinking to tell this to be truth, and our spirits to have warned us very strong and proper.

And I stopt near to the fire-pit, which did be great, and very red-glowing; and I lookt upward of the Gorge, into the night of the Gorge that we did come from; but the Monster was not yet upon us to work our death. And I lookt to the sides of the Gorge, and the Maid to have the same thought that did be mine, that we climb the mountains that made the sides of the Gorge.

And I lookt very keen first to this side, and then did run overward, that I look more close upon the other; and afterward back again; for it did seem that we should have a greater ease upon the side that we did be.

And I askt the Maid whether that she did be prepared; and she to be very white and wearied, and all besmirched with the dankness and growths upon the boulders and the hidden pools of the Gorge and the dripping of the waters; but yet did she be sound in her courage, and to show that she had all belief and abiding in me, and her judgement likewise to be with mine, in that her own Reason did approve.

And I took the bundle of her torn clothing from her, for it did be at her girdle, and like to trouble her movings; but she to refuse, very determined, in that I did be already over-burdened. And I to be firm in my deciding, and to make her to yield the bundle, the which I hookt unto the "hold" of the Diskos, where it did be to mine hip.

And the Maid to be there, a little figure, and white in the face, and strangely angered, and her anger mixt with hidden acknowledgement that I did be her master, and half to be minded that she move not from where she did stand, and part to be reasonable and fearful of the hidden Beast; and in part also to thrill in her womanhood unto the man that did be so masterful unto her. And all to pass in a little moment, and we to be to the Gorge side, and busied very eager to the climb.

And the Maid to be first, as I did heed, and I to follow, and have constant looking to the task and to her safety, and alway to be bitter anxious for our speed to be good, and to be anxious the more then, lest that Mine Own should slip; for there did be an horrid wetness upon the sides of the Gorge, as you shall have guessed, and horrid growths that blotched the great rocks mightily, and made an utter slipperiness, if that they did be trod upon; and we to have to come so clear of all such matters, as we might, and yet to be speedy for our lives, and likewise to lack no care and thought to the setting of our hands and of our feet in places fitted to the lifting of our weight.

And truly you shall see that we went very desperate, and I to give word to the Maid that she look not downward, the which I was urgent upon, lest that she come giddy in the heart. But I, as you shall think, could scarce to keep from fearful peerings below, so that I learn speedy whether the Pursuer did come yet into the light of the fire-hole, beneath.

And presently, the Maid did gasp very weak and troubled with the soreness of the climb; and I came higher, and set mine arm about her, as we did be there upon the face of the cliff; and she stopt very still a little while, and an ease did come to her, and an assurance of safety. And surely, I kist her there where we did be in that upward place, and her lips did tremble unto mine; and her courage and strength to come back into her, so that in a minute she did make once more to the climbing.

And we came presently to a place where a great ledge did be, that jutted out from the mighty cliff, and was surely a huge way above the Gorge bottom. And the ledge sloped, and there were on the ledge, great stones and boulders that did make lodgement there through eternity.

And I lookt very careful to our way, and saw that we did be in the path of a mighty rock that was over-nigh unto the edge of the shelf-place, and did put fear upon me, in that it seemed that it should come down with great thundering upon us, if that we but shook the place where it did be.

And I caught the Maid very swift and gentle, and shaped our path unto one side of that great rock, and did presently lose my fear, when that we did come safe from under it.

And in a minute after, we were come upward upon the ledge, and a very safe place it did seem, and surely as that no monster should be abled to come upward upon us. And this I did try to make for comfort unto ourselves; but that we both to know how that the great Slugs could lie up against the sides of the Gorge, and surely it did be like that they should be able to come upward clear of the Gorge, and so to the place where we made to have safety. And I had no thought to deny this thing, when that it was clear to my brain; but set rather that we should have some way to fight the Monster, if that we did be discovered.

And I thought in a moment upon the stones that did be about; and the Maid in the same moment cried out that we should push the big rock down upon the Slug that we believed to have chase of us, and indeed, the rock to be a great weapon, if we could but stir it, as you shall think.

And alway, as we talked, very hushed, we lookt downward into the deepness of the Gorge, unto the upward end of the fire-light; but there came no thing yet unto our knowledge, only that the stinking did rise up to us through that great distance.

And the fire-pit to seem now a very small burning, and to give no great light up to us; and we neither to be abled to see very clear of the Gorge bottom, in that the haze of the fumes and the smoke was in the air of the Gorge, and made uncertainty; and we to be nowise proper free of the smoke. even where we did be.

And we watched, very set with anxiousness and fearful expecting of the monster; and did be both yet lost of breath, and the Maid that she made her words something broken for a little while.

And lo! in a moment, Naani cried out very low and sharp that the thing did come; and I to see a moving of somewhat, in the same instant, in the Gorge that lay upon the upward side of the fire-pit.

And immediately I saw the great and monster head of the Beast come forward into the shine from the pit; and the head did be of a blotched white, and to have the eyes upon great stalks that came from the forward part of the head; and the stalks to be set downward, so that the eyes lookt upon the bottom parts of the Gorge. And surely this doth be very horrid-seeming to the mind of this age, but yet to have a less strangeness unto the two of us that had seen many horrid sights, as you do know.

And as the Monster came forward the more into the light, I saw that the great and utter mighty bulk did be all of that same whiteness, that did be so set over with blotchings and a seeming of unhealth. But, truly the colour was proper to a creature that did abide in so great a darkness, as you shall say; yet had those Slugs that we did see, been black and shining, for the most, as I have told; and this to be as I saw, and I not to heed here that I try unto explainings in this place; else should I be never eased of my task, as you do see.

And the Monster Slug came onward, and as it did go, it set the stalks of the eyes in among the boulders, as that it did search; swayed now this way and now that way, from side to side of the Gorge, and alway it pushed the stalks of the eyes inward among the boulders; and so to go forward, searching. And truly it was very dreadful to see the thing make search for us, and to go so steadfast to so dread a purpose.

And, indeed, I saw it not so plain as might be, because of the haze of the fumes and the smoke that did lie in the air of the Gorge, as I have told, and made something vague the sight at this time and that; but yet we did both see a strange thing; for when that the great white body did be come half into the light, the Slug-Beast set out a big tongue among the boulders, after that it did peer thereunder; and the tongue did be very long, and white, and something thin-seeming; and the Monster lapped inward in a moment a great snake from among the boulders, and the tongue did hold upon the snake, as that there did be surely teeth or roughness upon the tongue; but yet the distance to be too great for any surety of the sight, as you do know; and moreover, there did be the uncertainty of the haze within the air.

And the Slug took the snake inward, all as it did lash and wriggle, and swallowed it in a moment; and, in verity, that snake did be a big and horrid creature, else had it been not so plain to our sight; but it did be as a worm unto the monster, and gone instant.

And immediately, the Slug-Beast went again to searching, and the head to sway from this side unto that side of the Gorge; and by the wideness and ease of this swaying shall you perceive the utter greatness of the Beast.

And alway, as it did come downward of the Gorge, it thrust the stalks of the eyes inward among the boulders, looking all ways; and oft the breath did come from it, as a cloud; and the stink to rise up unto us, very plain and an abomination.

And again, we saw the Beast set the tongue in among the boulders of the Gorge bottom; and it lickt forth a snake that did seem so thick as a man in the body; and the snake to thrash in the great white tongue, and to be immediately drawn inward, and gone utter.

And surely, as the thought did stir in me, there did be a great Mercy over us, in that we did not die by such a serpent in some dark and horrid place of the Gorge. But yet, as it is like to be, mayhap the snakes did be only anigh to the fire-holes; yet doth it be anywise a wondrous thing that we had come so free of them alway; and truly to learn, was to be given a new terror.

Now the Monster was come fully into the shining of the fire-pit, and was upon this side; and the fire to make a shining against the side of the Slug, so that odd whiles I did perceive very plain the huge wrinklings and musclings of the skin, as the Beast made onward. And alway it did search, thrusting in the eye-stalks among the boulders.

And sudden, it made pause, and did begin that it brought all the mighty body together, and humpt itself, and brought the head-part round unto the bottom of the cliff that made this side of the Gorge. And it gathered itself, and afterward did lengthen upward against the cliff, and begin to climb. And lo! I saw that the Beast did scent of us, and made to come upward to destroy us.

And as the mighty hill of the body did come into length against the great cliff-side, the Beast set the eye-stalks into this cave and that, as it did go, and into all crannies; and so lengthened upward very straight and monstrous and dreadful unto us, and did be as a white and mildewed hill, that had an horrid life. And the stink to come up, so that we did be like to lose our breath with the dreadfulness of it, as you shall think.

And surely, for a moment, I lookt unto the rocks upon the ledge, and this way and that way, and upward unto the everlasting darkness that did be above us, and again unto the great rock that did seem to quiver upon the edge, as I have told. And I was grown utter desperate in a moment; for, truly, it did seem in that instant that there did be no power in the world that should slay so utter mighty a Monster.

And immediately, even as I did despair, I had run very swift unto the great rock, and the Maid with me, both very strained and shaken with the horror of the thing that did make upward unto us so sure and intent.

And I set my strength unto the rock, and heaved; but indeed the rock gave not from the place where it did be; so that I had a dreadful despair; for I saw that it did be more secure than had seemed. And the Maid lent her strength unto mine, and we heaved together, with sore pantings, and little cries to guide our endeavours and because we could not be contained in that moment.

And surely it seemed that the great rock moved, and lo! as we strove together to the task, there came a vast and sudden grinding, and the rock to cease from our shoulders, and to be gone from us, or scarce we did wot of the happening. And the rock went over, and rushed downward upon the Monster, and with mighty crashings, as it did grind and crush the face of the cliff-side with a quick and constant thundering. And I caught the Maid, as she did stagger upon that dire upward edge because that she had set her strength so utter to the endeavour, and the rock to be gone so sudden, as you do see, and she to be like to follow after. And she clung unto me, and I to hold her very safe as I lookt down upon the falling of the Rock. And behold! the Great Rock smote the Monster in the humpt part of the back, below of the head, and did enter into the Monster, even as a bullet doth strike, and was gone instant from my sight into the Vitals.

And there came a mighty sound of anguish from the Monster; and the Monster did loosen from the cliff, and to crumple, as it did seem, and sink backward. And a great steam of dread breathing to go upward from the Beast, and a reek; and it made again the strange and horrid noise of pain, and the Gorge to be yet full of the echoes of the Rock thundering, and with the noise of the rock there was now mingled the horrid sounding of the death-crying of the Beast. And the Gorge to be filled with dull and dreadful echoings, as that an hundred Monsters died in this place and that of the darkness in the Gorge, and all to be bred of the noise of that mildewed hill a-dying.

And the echoes ceased not for a while, even after that the Monster did be utter quiet; for truly they came presently from far upward and downward of the Gorge, out of all the eternity of the night, and to be as that they came backward very faint out of lonesome miles, and out of the strange deepness of unknown caverns of the world. And so in the end to silence; and the far bottom of the Gorge to be filled with a white and horrid hill, very dreadful, and that did yet quiver to show the slowness of Death. And alway a dreadful reek and stinking to fill all the air, even unto the height, as of the grave.

And I stood upward in that far, high place, and held the Maid very strong and tender; and she to have covered her ears from that

dreadful crying; and to be yet shaken with the greatness and horror of the dying of the Monster, and the nearness that she did come unto falling, as you have seen.

And presently she came less to tremble, and did weep very easeful, even as a babe doth weep; and I, mayhap, to be not over-steady, as you shall think; but yet to have a great gladness set in my heart, and a triumph, and an utter grace of thankfulness.

And I held Mine Own, very tender and sure, as I did say; and she very soon to be eased of her trouble, and the shock to be something gone from her. And she lookt up at me, and slipt her arms upward about my neck, and pulled me downward unto her, that she might kiss me.

And we to talk then, of the going down; and surely this did seem a great and dangerous task; for, truly, we had come upward pretty easy in the excess of our fear; but how we might go down, with our blood cool, I did be all in doubt.

Yet, before that we did aught else, I led the Maid upward on to the safe part of the ledge; and we sat there, very quiet and weary, and she did be leaned against me. And we eat, each of us, two of the tablets, and I to scold and coax Mine Own to this end, and she to obey and to be better afterward, because that she had eat. And we drank some of the water, and did rest a time longer.

And presently, our courage and strength was come back into us; and we packt the scrip again, and the Maid set it fast to my back; and we went then to the edge of the shelf, and lookt downward, this way and that; and surely, there did be no way to go, save the way we came; only that we might shape our downward climbing to bring us a little below that place where the dead Monster did be.

And I saw by mine own heart and by the paleness of the Maid, that we should do well that we consider the thing no more; but make to the task.

And I went immediately over the edge of the shelf, upon my belly, and I bade Naani to follow. And we began then that we go downward; and, in verity, we went downward for, mayhap, a great hour; and I gave help alway unto Mine Own, as I could; and she to come after me very brave, and made that she hold back her fear, and come downward of that cliff, that did be oft like to a mighty wall. And surely, even as we came down, I marvelled how we did ever go upward, even though fear did aid us; but, indeed, I do think it doth be easier to climb safely, than to come backward; for this is how I have found.

And we made rest thrice upon ledges of the cliff. And afterward

came downward again; and alway very slow and with exceeding heed where our hands and our feet did go, that we slip not suddenly to our death.

And once, as I did see, the Maid was lost of all her strength, and did be going to fall, because that she did be all gone into a sudden weakness of the head in an instant. And she did be silent, even in that moment, the which doth be marvellous unto me, and to give me a strong pride of her, as you shall understand, if that ever you have loved. And surely, I came upward, in a moment, that little space that was between, and had mine arm about Mine Own very swift, and held her hard and fierce against the cliff; and this I did that she should feel how that she could never fall; and immediately, her strength and her dear courage came back into her; and I kist her, there against the mighty cliff; and afterward she did have power again to come downward safe.

And presently we were come to the Gorge bottom, and maybe an hundred paces down the Gorge from that place where did be the dead Monster, all sunk into an ugly and horrid heap, so great as a small hill.

And a dreadful stinking did hang in all that part of the Gorge, by reason of the Slug; and signs of disgust, as you shall think; and the great and mildewed body of the thing yet to settle and twitch, as I did look, as it did come properly unto death in all that mighty bulk. And everywhere, the skin of the Beast did be set into great wrinklings, and horrid blotchings to be upon the improper whiteness thereof; and truly I did be in haste that I turn the Maid away from that thing, and that we haste downward of the Gorge.

And we went then for two good hours, and alway I did hearten the Maid, and she to go very husht and trustful by me; but truly I did be in an anguish of heart, because that I was newly aware that there did be such great and dreadful serpents in that part of the Gorge, as you do also know. And I was not over-feared for myself, but for the Maid that did have no armour to protect her dear body. And because that I was so set with this trouble, I took the Maid presently into mine arms, that I carry her, and so to have her clear of aught that should lie among the boulders.

And, in verity, Mine Own did show an anger very surprising and determined; for I said not why I should carry her—fearing to give her a greater unease—but only that she did be weary, and I very strong and willing.

And, indeed, I could not bring her to reason, without I told her, which was not mine intent; for she did refuse me to carry her; and said that truly I had need of no added burden unto my labours.

And when she saw that I would not be moved by her reasonings, she made to win upon me by her loving ways; but, indeed, I only kist her; and went forward with her in mine arms. And she half naughty, that I did be so heedless of her wishings, and somewise hurt also; and so to be silent in mine arms; yet mayhap to be something stirred in her nature, that I did be steadfast to mine intention, despite that her will did be contrary.

And this I do believe to be truth, because that, afterward, I do think that she lay there in mine arms, only as a woman that doth be in the hands of her Master that hath all her love.

And in thiswise we went forward.

And in the end of the two hours that we did go, there was come the end of the dark part of the Gorge; and we to be outward of that mighty roof of the mountains, as I do think it to have been; and the air to be free of the stink of the Monsters, and the fire-holes to be very plenty, and their smokings to go upward very proper; so that we had no more the bitterness of their fumings in our throats.

And there did be a pretty good light, to go by the contrast of the past hours; and I set Mine Own again to her feet, and made that she keep to my rearward, so that if there did be any serpents to our path, they should come first under my feet, and thiswise to work no harm to me, because of mine armour, neither to Naani, Mine Own Maid.

Now by this time, it was somewhat of nineteen great hours since we did sleep; for we had been a long while making that we come safe from the Slug; and, indeed, we had come downward with a less speed than I did go through upon mine upward way, as you shall mind; and this to be that Mine Own did not have the hard strength that was in my body to the enduring of great labour and stress; and this surely all to be plain unto you that have been with me in all my journey. And, moreover, there must be kept to mind the three hours that we had gone, ere we were come proper into the dark part of the Gorge; and so all to be remembered unto you; and also you to mind that we did be wakeful a time, ere that we set forward upon that day's journeying.

And we did go almost in joyous-wise, because that we were come safe out of that dreadful place; and surely, odd whiles I did feel the hands of Mine Own Naughty One to be hookt very pretty and sly into the backward part of my belt, as that she did make a pretending that she drive me before her; and surely this doth be a strange thing to tell upon; for there did be no knowledge of the olden horse in all the eternity of that dark world; but yet, maybe, some dear olden memory-dream did set her hands unconscious to this pretty work.

And, in verity, once I turned very sudden, and had her swift into mine arms, as she did pretend to drive me; and she to laugh with a sweet and joyous gurgle against mine armour; and I to heed that I hurt her not, because I did be like an iron man that should put arms about a tender maid.

And we lookt alway now for a place that should be proper to our rest and to our sleep; and when it did be close upon the end of the twentieth hour of that journey, the Maid showed me a cave that was, mayhap, fifty good feet upward in the right side of the Gorge.

And I lookt about, and saw that there did be two fire-holes anigh, and a warm spring to make a basin of water, that did lie between the fires; and all very well set to our need, as I did perceive; for, indeed, we did be utter besmirched with the filth of the Slug part of the Gorge, and to need that we be nice and fitly washed, before that we have any comfort of our selves.

And I bade Naani to wait a little minute; and I lookt well up the Gorge and well down the Gorge; and lo! there did be no thing to set me in unease; and I told Mine Own that she keep a sharp and stead-fast watching, and not to heed me; and this I said, because I knew she did be like otherwise to look at me and be over-anxious, as I go upward to the cave; and, indeed, she to be better anyway in watch of the Gorge, and to cry out to me, if that anything came anigh, whilst that I went upward.

And I made upward to the cave; and was come there pretty quick; and truly it did be good for our purpose, and fresh-seeming and dry, and to have no holes that I could see for the hiding of creeping things.

And I called down gently to the Maid that the cave did be proper; and she to show her gladness, and to be looking upward at me, instead of the way of the Gorge, as I set her; and truly she did be a dear and human little Maid, and utter Mine; so that I did find a new joy in each small lack of wisdom, and this just so much as that she had done a wondrous proper thing. And truly, you shall say, there was some properness to her heart, in that she could abide not but to watch me.

And I went quickly down to Mine Own; for there was alway an unease upon me, save when I did be nigh to her, in chance of trouble.

And when I was come down to her, the Maid did be seeming a little in thought; and afterward showed me how that she did be all in a pitiful disgust of the dirt and slime and the drippings of the Gorge, that did be on her, and had made her garment utter wet and bemired, so that she did feel that her very body was a repulse unto her.

And I saw how it did be with Naani; and I went to the warm pool,

and felt that it did be not over-hot, and afterward found the deepness, by the handle of the Diskos, and this to be scarce of three feet, and the water very clear to show me the bottom, so that it was surely a nice and proper place to be for such a purpose as I did think. And I set some of the water to my mouth, using my hand; and truly there did seem no hurtful chemical in the water; and therefore was I eased that the Maid should have the desire that I did see to be in her mind.

And I saw that I should be helpful to Mine Own, if that I make the arranging of things to be in mine own hands. And I went back unto the Maid, and told her that the pool was very nice to be for a bath-place; and that she to haste to wash herself, whilst the Gorge did be free of any Creature or Monster.

Now I saw that Naani was troubled, and feared that I did be going to leave her, and yet did be paused a little in her words, to show me all that she did wish.

And surely, I stoopt and kist her, as she did look so wistful in her little puzzlement; and immediately I removed her trouble very natural, and told that I should stand guard anigh to her, the while that she bathed. And, truly she did be at ease on the moment, and mayhap something surprised to know wherefore she had been something a-lack to ask me. But, in truth, it did be very natural.

And I told her to be so quick as she might, which was a needless thing to say, yet to start her; and she to go quietly to obey me; but first to take the cloak out of the hold upon my shoulders, and to unfold it, and so to the pool. And I to stand with my back thatwards, and to lean, ready, upon the Diskos.

And presently she did be in the water, as I knew; and I to be her man, very sure and gentle to her and sedate. And truly, as you shall think, I did love that I be to stand guard to her in her dear maidenhood; and she, after that she was cheered and warmed by the delight of the water, to sing very low and happy to herself, where she did be to my back.

And, sudden, the singing to cease, and the Maid screamed; and I to have no thought of improper modesty but turned instant to the Maid. And in a moment, I saw what did trouble her; for there came a serpent out of the water; and the Maid to be all adrift with natural modesty, and with her fear of the serpent. And I was come into the pool in a moment, in mine armour, and did lift the Maid, naked and wet into mine arms, and had her instant from the water, and upon the side of the pool; and there I wrapt the cloak about her; and ran very quick and killed the serpent, as it did go offwards among the boulders.

And surely it did be so thick as mine arm, and to have come from some hole that did be hid in the bottom of the pool.

And I came back then to Mine Own, and took her into mine arms, and set the cloak well about her; and she to cry and to tremble with the shock and disturbance of the thing; but soon to be eased, and ready to laugh with me.

And so she was come proper to her happiness again, and I very gentle and joyous with her, for truly my heart had been sick that she had come so nigh to that horrid danger.

And I eased the scrip from me, and opened it, and made her to take two of the tablets, and she to refuse to eat, save I company her also; and indeed I did be very willing, for truly my belly was alway empty. And she to be very glad to eat, because she did be clean now, and to have no more disgust of herself. And afterward, we drank some of the water.

And soon we did be finished, and she to ask for her girdle that I did give her with the knife, as I have surely told. And she belted the cloak very graceful about her; and lookt very dear and pretty with her little bare feet; and her hair very lovely upon her shoulders, for she did wear alway in the Gorge the lining of my head-piece, and so had her hair dry and sweet.

And, in verity, I did mind now, how that she did look very beautiful in her bath, as I had gone to succour her from the snake; and I to be nicely wholesome in this remembering, because of my love, but yet to be knowing that I was sweetly stirred to new things; and did not know before that a maid lookt in the same moment so holy and so human. And afterward, in odd whiles, I remembered; but never to think overmuch, because that I did feel inwardly that I should be gently wise in such things; and you to understand my heart in this, if that ever you have loved.

And surely, the Maid brought me from my dreamings very sensible, in that she had me to stand; and she was gone about me very swift and natty with her pretty fingers, that she ease me of mine armour.

And afterward, she bade me to strip and wash, whilst that she keep watch for me of the Gorge. And she took the Diskos, and leaned upon it, very brave and proper; but yet, as I do think, with somewhat of roguishness within her, very deep hid, and scarce known unto herself.

And I warned her to be very wise with the great weapon; for it did fit only to fight in my hands, and did be like to cause harm to any that should meddle with it or make to use it, save me.

And Naani to nod that she did hear me, and to be half in fear of

the thing, and half to feel that it did be friendly to her; and so to stand guard for me; and truly to seem a very sweet and slender maid, despite the bigness of the cloak; and the great weapon to seem more great in her small hands; and to mind me how strong I did be. And surely you shall think me in conceit; but truly I did be glad to be so strong; and a proper thing for pride, if that there be no scorn for others therein. And you to agree with me in this thing, or to be lacking of sympathy and good human understanding.

Now I washt me, not by going down into the pool; for indeed I did not wot whether there be any more snakes hid there in some other hole. And the way I washt, was that I dipt my head-piece into the hot pool, and poured the water over me, and rubbed my body very strong with my hands; and there to be, surely, some certain chemical in the water that aided mine efforts; for the water went very smooth under my hands.

And when I was done, I washt my pocket-cloth very speedy in the pool, and wrung it, and did then wipe my body so dry as I should; and afterward I wrung the cloth again, and set it about my loins, and so to be as proper as I might.

And I did call to the Maid that I was proper, and she to come then and kiss me; and she gave back to me the Diskos, and set me that I stand anigh to the nearer fire-hole, and so to be that I should guard her, and in the same time be come free of the chill of the Gorge, which was not great in that place.

And surely I did mean that I help her; but she would have no help in her work that she did say to be her glad right; but bade me that I to mine own work to be her dear protector, as she did call me. And I to lift that Wilful One into mine arms, a moment, and to give her a very loving hug, and for that time to have no fear that I harm her, because that I was freed of the hardness of the armour about me, as you do know.

And surely she to feel very dear and pretty in mine arms, and she kist me the once with a little passion of love; and immediately to want to go from me; so that I freed her in a moment, as was ever my way. And she then to pause a small space off from me, and lookt at me with a light in her eyes, and half to put out her arms that she be taken again into mine; but so to cease, ere she yield to her heart; and turned from me immediately to the task of the washing.

And she took first my body-vest, and washt it very quick and clever in the pool, and afterward came over by me, and spread it upon the hot flat rock anigh to the fire-hole.

And she got then my change body-vest from the bundle of her torn garments, where she did put it to be washt on opportunity, even as now; and mayhap to like that it should lie in her bundle with her own garments, for so, as I do mind, the thought came to me very natural; but she to say naught to lead me thus; yet to be a very honest and dear Maid, and to have little secret ways of love, as I did perceive, that I did not be told of.

And she washt the second body-vest, and set it to dry by the first; and afterward did likewise with all my garments, and came then to the washing of her own.

And lo! as she spread it also to the drying, there came to mine heart that the Maid did have only this one rough and thick garment, that did be the armour-suit, as I have told. And surely it did be dreadful that she have the hardness of that strong knitted and fibrous garment to be next to her dear body, and I to be in comfort with the softness of my body-vest.

And I was all angered in a moment, that she had gone thiswise, while that I had been gentled, as it might be. And I bade Naani take the second vest to her own use when it did be dry. And she to look upward from where she did turn the garments upon the hot rock; and to mean in the first to deny me. But indeed she was quick to see that I did be truly in anger; and mine anger to come because that I was hurt that this did be, and because that I was shamed that she had gone so rough-clad, the while that I had no thought to the matter. And moreover because that she had known her lack, and did not tell me of the thing.

But yet I did have a great tenderness in the backward part of mine anger, because that I perceived all the unselfishness and delight of her love that did be about this little matter, as you shall see, if you have gone alway with me.

But mine anger yet to be something hard, because I did see that I have need to watch the Maid, that she put not her dear body to pain, that I might come unknowing to some little pleasuring or ease, as did be now as I have shown. And truly it did be sweetly done in love; but to be somewise lacking of judgement; and so shall you know somewhat of the way that I did be angered, and to have understanding with me; but if you have not, you shall think it to be naught, and that the Maid did need only that she be kist, and to be shaken a little in playfulness, and warned to heed that I did be earnest; and mayhap you to be somewise right, and not to guess far off from the inward deepness of my heart. But yet it doth be verity that I was truly angered, and fit

to shake Mine Own, and in the same moment to be utter tender unto her. And surely this doth be all a contradiction, and the human heart to be a wayward thing, whether it doth be of a man or of a woman.

And Naani, as I do think, to have loved the chafe of that rough garment for love's sake, and to go very humble and loving, as I lookt at her; but in verity to be never gone from the sweet naughtiness that did be alway in her heart, and to plan even in that moment some new and secret service unto me, that should be for her quiet joy, and to be hid from me, until that my wit should come upon it to uncover it. And in verity a young man doth want that he whip his maid and kiss her, and all in the one moment. And, indeed, he to have delight in both.

And she obeyed me that time, as alway when I did be earnest, without more word. And surely that Naughty One did know how I loved her.

And the Maid washt then her torn garments that did be in the bundle, and had gotten soiled by the slime of the dark part of the Gorge. And she put these to dry, and afterward washed mine armour and the scrip and the pouch and the cloak-hold, and all such matters of our gear; and so to be presently done.

And she was heedful then that she turned the garments upon the hot rock; and afterward did attend to my bruisings. And when she did rest, I lookt to her pretty feet, and rubbed them very gentle and constant with the ointment; and surely they did be pretty well; but I to like that I should tend them, and to have joy to feel their littleness within my palms, and surely she did know how it did be with me; for presently she took her feet inward under the cloak; and I, maybe, to look something woeful; for she put one out presently, when that I did the least expect, and slipt it very cosy into my hand; and surely I kist her naughty toes; and she then to be very sedate.

Now, presently, when Naani found the garments to be proper dry, she gave those to me that were mine, and bid me to turn my back and be drest very speedy. And lo! in a little time, when I was nigh done, she came over and stood before me, and was drest again in the armour-suit, and to look very slender and dainty. And she lookt at me, so that I put out my hands, that I kiss her; but she went from me, very proper, and brought mine armour, and gave me help with it, and alway very grave and quiet; but yet to have naughtiness underneath, as I did believe.

And when I was full armed, she took my hand, and set mine arm about her waist, and she leaned her head against my breast, and put up her lips to be kist, as that she did be a child maiden; yet when I kist her, she did be a woman, and to kiss me very dear and loving, and to

look at me then from under her eye-lids; and sudden to make a dainty growling, and to pretend that she did be a fierce thing that should be like to eat me; and I to be utter feared, as you shall think, and to be scarce able that I kiss Mine Own Pretty Fierce One, because that I did laugh so hearty, and to be so taken with a surprise that the Maid did show this new playfulness; and in the same moment to be stirred and waked anew that she did be so lovely and graceful in mine arms, and to make her naughty growling so pretty that I did be eager that she make it again; but she to do this playing only as her mood did stir her.

And she made then that she would go from me, and I to loose her, as ever; and she bade me that I guard her the while that she washt the outward part of the cloak; for the inward did be clean, and the cloak proof to water; but the outward part to be something needful of washing.

And surely, when this was made clean, it dried very quick, because that the water went not into it; and whilst that it dried, I gave Mine Own an aid upward unto the cave, and afterward I passed up the gear, and the cloak when it did be dry; and so came upward also myself, and brought with me a boulder, that I balanced very light in the mouth of the cave, so that it should fall, if that anything toucht it; and this plan you do know of; for I used it before, as I have told.

And truly we did be utter wearied, and the time to be something beyond three and twenty hours, since last we had slumber. And the Maid had the scrip and the pouch set to be for my pillow, and the bundle of her torn garment to be for her own. And she to have me to my pillow, and to tuck the cloak about me, and the Diskos to my hand; and afterward to kiss me very sedate upon the lips, and then to come in under the cloak, with a quiet and lovely happiness, as I did know; and to be gone to slumber very content and sweet.

And I waked eight good hours after, with the fizzing of the water in mine ears; and lo! Mine Own did be waked and to make ready our breakfast; and I came upward upon mine elbow, to see whether that the boulder did be unmoved; and indeed it was not touched.

And Mine Own saw that I was come awake; and she ran to me, very dear and glad, and kist my lips very eager and loving. And surely, as she kist me, I did feel that she had taken again a naughty advantaging of my slumber, and had kist me as I did sleep; but truly I said no word of my thoughts; for I did mind that I should wake sudden one time, and so to catch her in this, and to call her then Mine Own, and that she did be a rogue; and all as you shall know, that have loved.

And I scolded the Maid a little, in that she had not waked me;

but I said not that I would attend to the duties that she did heed to; for I knew that she had joy of these things, in that she did love to do aught that should be done unto me. And when I scolded her, she to make but a little mouth at me, as we do say, and to put her tablets to my lips, that I kiss them, and she to kiss mine; and so to our breakfast.

And when we were done, we gat together our gear, and went downward from the cave, and began again to journey. And we went eighteen hours that day, and eat and drunk at every sixth hour, as ever.

And in the fourteenth hour, I perceived that I did be like to over-travel the Maid, though I made alway to have a less speed than did be natural unto me. And surely then, I took her up into mine arms; and she to refuse, and to be troubled that I should so carry her; for she did think that I was like to be wearied by the task.

And I to take no heed to her protestings; but to laugh gently with her, and to carry her, even as a babe in mine arms; and she to love that she be in mine arms, if but she be able to have assuredness that I come not to weariness through her. And truly it did be a dear love task, and to be set unto the needing of mine especial heart.

And I carried Mine Own then for four hours; and in the eigh-teenth hour we were come to that part of the Gorge where did be the ledge where I killed the spider, ere I slept, as you shall mayhap to mind. And here I aided the Maid to climb, and we had the same ledge that night to be our refuge; and did sleep very happy and unharmed, and alway with our spirits set to warn us, if that harm did make to come nigh to us.

And we went then through three days of eighteen hours' journey each; and alway I did carry Mine Own, from the twelfth unto the eighteenth hour of each journeying; and this to be very dear unto me, and to give me a new rejoicing that I did be strong and easy to carry Mine Own; and she to lie in mine arms very content, when that she perceived how that I did be so glad to go thiswise and that I had no weariness by the carrying.

And thus I did rest her feet, and wore not her dear and slender body overmuch with the vigour of my going; and was abled to make a very good speed.

And Mine Own, this time and that, to make sayings of impudence unto me, and to hide her naughty lips, when that I should kiss them; and to have quaint nestlings unto me, and odd whiles to kiss me very dainty when that I did be going thoughtful of the way. And surely never did there be so dear a maid as Mine Own; so that I did go many

a mile, and to be scarce that I knew that I was gone any way, because of the stirrings of my heart and the content of my spirit.

And oft as we did go, there were great scorpions in the path, and odd whiles they to have no heed to go from my way; but to be so great as my head, and very fat and lazy; so that surely I kickt a good number, from my path, even as you shall kick a ball with the foot; and three I burst in this way. And truly it did be well that I had on me mine armour, else had they been like to sting me very quick unto death; for they were so great.

And likewise, in this place and that, there were snakes; but none to come anigh to me; and I to choose alway the open goings; for I did think there to be many hid snakes and lesser monsters in the dark places between the great boulders. And alway, when the Maid did walk, I to go before, that I see clear her way; and this thing to be but a matter of wiseness, as you shall think.

And odd whiles, as I did carry Mine Own, she to talk a little with me of her memory-dreams of the olden days; and mayhap you to think it strange that we said not overmuch on this wise; but the way of our journey to have been so utter bitter, as you have seen; and we to be more of that far age, than we did be of this present age; and this present life to seem but a dream of Memory; and we to be set then with the realness of that life. And this telling, indeed, to be a plain thing to your understanding. Yet did we have a greater talk to these ends, when that we were come free of the Gorge; but yet, oft there to be an odd saying and a sweet memory, like to an olden and forgot fragrance of dreams, to pass between Mine Own and me. And do you to set your sympathy of understanding with me in this thing, and to know how holy these things did be, and far off, and to hold memory, as a mist that doth shine with golden lights, that did make an holy pain upon the eyes of the spirit, even as a quiet dawn of this day doth set a pleasure of vague pain upon the heart.

And once, as I did carry the Maid, I saw that she wept a little, very husht unto herself; and I to say naught; for I saw that it did be a natural sorrow for her father, and for the dead Peoples of the Lesser Redoubt; that did be left for ever unto the desolation of Eternity. And so, because I did be wise to leave her be, she to be eased presently, and to wipe her eyes, quiet and secret, and mayhap to think that I did not perceive; and then to nestle unto me; and so to be the more Mine Own.

And about the middle part of the second day, we came past the cave where I did sleep on the upward journey; and I to tell Naani, and she to look upward to the cave, and to wish that she might come a moment

into it; only that it did be twenty good feet upward, and I to desire that she run no risk of her dear life, when that there did be no need.

And so to go onward; and odd whiles to see strange things a-lurk among the boulders; but none to come anigh to us; yet did I keep the Diskos very ready in my hand, as you shall think; and had mine eyes alway to look upon every side, and mine ears to be wary; and to use my spirit alway to mine aid.

And surely, as we did come lower in the Gorge, the Maid was all a-wondered at the warmness that did grow, and something disturbed in the first, by the new thickness, as it did seem, of the air. And she to waste some of the water, because that it did fizz up so quick, even as I, until that she was come used to this newness. And all this to be very plain unto you.

And in the end of every journey, we slept eight good hours in a safe place; and so to go onward again; and the Maid to grow very eager as I did tell her this thing and that of the Country that we did come downward unto.

And she askt me questions, time and oft, and much I told her, and she to think upon it with a growing wonder and desire, even as a gladsome child that hath never seen the sea, and doth be told that it shall presently be there. And this to be but to shadow the way that Naani did be; for truly she did be a very live and eager maid, in all things.

And we to be still within the Gorge, and to go constant by the fire-holes and the fire-pits, and to see the flames leap upward in this place and that, so that the mighty walls of the Gorge would show very plain in an instant; and immediately to come the shadows again, and afterward the leaping of the flames. And so did it be forever. And oft the muttering of the fire-pits; and oft the utter quiet and the shadows.

And this time and that there did be a snake to go by us, and the scuttling of the monster scorpions; and mayhap a moving in the shadows of the great boulders, that did tell me there went maybe some peculiar monster in that place; so that I did be very wary, and to have the Diskos alway ready.

And when the fourth day was come, I showed the Maid, in the sixth hour, the ledge that did be my first sleeping place, when that I was entered into the Gorge.

Now presently, in the eleventh hour, after that we had gone five hours in a gloom, there did show afar off a shining; and I caught the Maid, and I pointed; and she also to perceive that it did be surely the shining of the light of that great Country that I did tell upon.

And immediately we did begin to run downward, and with sore stumblings in this place and that; but not to halt us; for we did be so mad as two children for the gladsome light.

And we came down presently in the twelfth hour of that journey into the warm light and wonder of the Country of the Seas.

XIII

Homeward by the Shore

NOW WE CAME PRESENTLY out of that sad and dreary place that did go inward of the great mountains, and which I have named the Upward Gorge; and we to halt soon between the feet of the mountains, beyond the mouth-part of the Gorge.

And Naani alway to look every way about her, and to breathe very quick, and her eyes to be gone bright with wonder and the seeing of new things, and the coming of freedom from so great a dread.

And she turned, now, and did look upward into the dark of the Gorge, and to spy upon the great mouth thereof, and to be feared then, and must run a greater way downward into the lightness of the Country of the Seas; and to come once more to pause, and to look backward, and with an awe and a relieved soul; and so again to the wonder of the spreaded Country and the great Sea; and did near to laugh and cry in the same moment, with the amazement and gladness and great astonishment that did be upon her. And she to turn constant this way and that, and to be never ceased of looking, and of deep breathings of the wide air; for never in that life had she been in a broad place of light, as you shall have perceived.

And we to feel, both, that there did be no more need to talk husht, as we did alway in the gloom and narrow dark of the gorge. And surely she to shout, as a child that doth try an echo; and her voice to go very pretty into the distance, and to be lost afar off in that Country.

And lo! in a moment, an echo to come out of the dark mountains to our backs; so that we lookt round very sudden; but whether the echo did be truly an echo, or some strangeness, or some unnatural call to come downward out of the gloom and horror of the Gorge, we did be all unsure; and indeed must run downward a while more, until that we did be all breathed, and to halt presently where we did feel to be utter free of the Gorge and of the strangeness that did

seem to our minds, in that moment, to lie upward in the darkness of the great mountains.

And surely we did look about for a flat rock to be for our use, and we came presently to a place nice to our purpose, that did be yet upward over the Land; and we climbed up on to the rock and sat thereon to have our food and drink.

And as we eat and drank, we did sit very close and happy; but yet to have a wise looking about anigh to us, so that we be caught by no danger of the Humpt Men, or by any other danger that might be.

And alway, the Maid did question, and did stare afar over the Country; and to have a shining wonder and joy of the sea, and to be stirred in all her being, so that she was pained with vague and sudden memories, that did be as strange dreams, and all mixt with pleasure and pain. And, indeed, she sudden to weeping, and to need that she be in mine arms, until that she know herself once again; and so to her dear natural joy and way.

And oft did Mine Own speak upon the clear wonder of the air, as it did seem to her; and to me it did seem likewise, that had lived my life also in a Dark Land, as you do know.

And she to break sudden from her rapture, and to set back her speech an Eternity with vague words, and memories so olden and englamoured that they did be as moonlight that once hath shone. And in a moment she to be forward again into that far future time and speech, and all her being to be close unto me, and oft in a solemn silence of the heart.

And the greatness of the sea to call unto her with an olden voice, and to half waken her; and I with her to be thus half-wakened, yet had I been not thus as I did come mine outward way; but truly I did stir to the stirring of the Maid, and all mine olden thoughts that did be my memory-dreams, to come afresh upon my spirit.

And so we two to sit there all shaken with dreamings that did concern happenings of the olden world that did lie upward in that dreadful night which made a mighty and deeply roof over that Country. And surely I am dumb, in that I have no speech to make known to you all the troublings and stirrings of our spirits that we did know in that moment.

And far off, by miles, beyond the feet of the mountain, where went the shore of the sea, upon our left, there was a great mist and steam; and this to be that mist and steam that I did come through on mine outward way; and Naani to ask concerning it, and I to tell her so much as I knew, and how that we must indeed come presently through it, upon our journey.

And she to be in wonder of the volcanoes that did burn in the sea, and in this place and that of the wide Country; and the height and grandness to exalt her, and in the same time to give her a strange humbleness of her mind; so that presently I did take her into mine arms, for I must kiss her, because that she did be so utter a sweet maiden, and lovely with interest and naturalness. And truly she to kiss me in turn; and to make her questionings between her kissings; and this to be because she didyearn for a greater knowing of the Country; but also, as I do half to think, because she did be sweetly impudent unto me; and this to be of her joy.

And presently, she to kiss me thrice very passionate and warm upon the mouth; and immediately to take my shoulders, with her small hands, that did seem so pretty upon my broadness and upon the metal of the armour. And she to strive thus that she shake me to a speedier answering; and she, all that while, to be full of a dear naughtiness, and to need that she be kist very hard.

And I to answer her; but after mine own fashion which did be a word between each kiss that I gave to her. And she very quick and naughty to put her hand between our lips; and I then to kiss the palm, that did be in my way, and did be very small and pretty. And she, when I had no thought, to open her fingers very quick, and kiss me through between the fingers, and immediately to shut the fingers, so that I did be stopt from the same.

And afterward, I made her to stand upon the rock, and I set free her hair over her shoulders; and I took then the boots from her, so that her little feet did show bare and pretty. And she, at the first, half to refuse me; but afterward to stand very dear and obedient that I should have my way with her; and to be a little shy, and the more pretty because of her sweet blushings.

And surely, when that I had her to my likings, I stept back a little pace, and lookt at her. And she to look again at me, very quaint and naughty; and then to turn her about, very grave; and to make pretend that she did be a dummy figure. And, surely, when she did be come right round, and to face me again, and had a very sedate look, she stretched out her pretty foot, all in a moment, and put her pink toes sudden upon my lips; and I to be so in surprise, that I had not wit to do aught, ere she had them back swift from me. And she then to make one glad spring into mine arms, and to want that she be hugged, and to be loved very great. And I to laugh, all tender; for I loved her so utter, as you do know; and I to tell her, as you sure likewise to have told your maid, that I wanted a pocket sufficient, that I might have her therein alway anigh to my heart; and this thing I to say to her, as

a man that doth love, shall say it; and you to know the way of it so well as I. And she to laugh very mischievous, and to tell me that she should truly tickle me, if that I carried her thatwise; aye and to pinch me, too. And I to have no answer, save that I shake her, very gentle, but indeed she to kiss me very naughty on the mouth, in the midst of my shaking; and truly, what shall a man do with such an one.

And she then to want to be more sedate and to be set down upon the rock; and she to make me to turn around, so that she should come at the pouch, which did be upon my back.

And she gat thence the comb that was a fitment, and did comb her pretty hair, and I to sit and talk with her, and to jest, with a heart that did be so light as it had not been for a great while; for though I did dread the Humpt Men and the monstrous animals of the Country of Seas, I had not any abiding horror of aught that I had seen in that Country; for there seemed a naturalness in all things, so that I did have no loathing; neither any fear of an Evil Force.

And presently, when that the Maid had combed her hair, she to bind it upon her head; but I to ask that she leave it upon her shoulders, because that it did be so pretty; and she to smile at me, and to be happy to my pleasuring.

Now we did be truly sedate, and to set our gear together; and I to put the boots upon the Maid; and afterward we to begin again to journey downward into the Country of the Seas.

And we went at a good pace; but not to bring us to any great weariness; for it was mine intent that we rest for our slumber upon this side of the place where did be the steam of the boilings, that was anigh to the shore of the sea, as you shall mind.

And we at this time to be passing along the feet of the mountains, unto the place of the steam; and to go thiswise for six good hours, and still to be a great hour off that part; for we went not so fierce as did be the speed of mine outward way, which was utter strong, as you do mind, that have gone with me in all my journey.

And so, when we had walkt six hours, we did be gone something beyond the eighteenth hour of that day's journeying; and to be very ready to our slumber.

Now, presently we found a tall rock, very hard to climb, that had a flat top so great as may be twice my length everyways; and this to be very good to our purpose. And when we were come safe to the top, we to eat and drink, and presently to sleep, and to have the cloak under us, as did be the will of the Maid; for the Country did be utter warm and nice, so that we had no occasion for covering.

And surely, we waked, both of us when that we had slept seven good hours; and we sat upward, and lookt newly each at the other; and to be as that we did each see the other anew in that good light, and to have a fresh joy each in the look of the other. And she to come into mine arms, and to kiss and to need that she be kist; and truly, we both to have our need; but yet to be something the more hungry of the other, for the having.

And Mine Own then to make our breakfast; and the water to fizz very strong and surprising; and we to eat and drink, and to be utter happy each with the other, and to talk on this thing and that, and the Maid to look about, as we eat; and she to look afar off at the wonders and the newness of the Country to her knowledge; but I to look near, lest there be any danger that might be anigh.

And in a while, Mine Own to draw my gaze to the Mountains that the Gorge came through. And, in verity, now that I did look in ease, I to see with her how that they did be truly monstrous, even as a monstrous wall that did go upward for ever until that they were gone out of the light of that Country, into the dark night of the deathly Upper World, that did be lost an eternity. And I to mind that I had some vague thoughts thiswise, on the outward way; but now I to have ease, and the Maid to speak with, and so to perceive odd matters the more. And I to tell you this little thing, so that you shall perceive the way that restfulness did be upon me, by compare with the Outward Going.

And, truly, we had no great speed with our talk and with our eating; but in the end did make somewhat to hurry, because that we did be conscious that we leaned to slackness. And indeed, we came down then pretty speedy from the rock where we did sleep; and had forward to our way at a good pace.

And when we had gone a while, we to begin to hear the far hissing of the steam and the noise of the upward burstings of waters that did boil; and the sound to be very strange; but I to have heard it before, as you do know; so that it to trouble me the less than the Maid. And I to assure her; and she to come nigh to me, and thiswise we to enter presently into the steam.

And we went then for more than three hours; and I had the Maid to my back, that I should be the first; and this I did, that she have no danger to walk into a boiling pool in the mazingness of the steam, which was everywhere. And I to be something guided in my path by the shore of the sea which did be unto our left alway; only that we could see neither the sea nor otherwise, except that we go so close that we near into the water.

And, truly, the sea to seem to boil in parts, and there to be hot pools in all places; so that who should say with ease whether we did go by one of the great hot pools or by the true sea. And this, our constant puzzle, shall be likewise to you; and you to perceive how that we did go utter wary.

And about us from every part there did come the strange burstings and shriekings and whistlings of the boil of the waters breaking upward from the deep world. And odd whiles the sounds to be as of great monsters; and the earth to shake under us; and other-whiles there to be a hush and only the steam about us, and somewhere in the distance and uncertainness a low piping of some steam cranny, very strange and lonesome-sounding.

And when it did be somewheres nigh upon the fourth hour, we came out of the thick steam; and the pipings and the roarings to be to our rearward; and soon the steam to be gone thin, as but a mist, and the noises to be very far-seeming; and presently we to be come clear out into the air of that Country.

And the Maid now to perceive the trees, which did be in great forests unto our right hand, while that the shore of the sea did go alway upon our left. And she to be utter in wonder of the trees; and to need that she pluck branches, and smell of them and look at each leaf; and so to be all stirred; for never in that life did she to have seen such a matter as those great trees did be; but yet to be all stirred by vague memories that did seem no more than dreams. And you to think but a moment, and to perceive how the thing did be with her; and you to have been likewise stirred, if that you did be so strangely waked in a corner part of the heart; though but a little matter to wake you.

Now when the sixth hour did be full come, we made a halt in a wise place, and had there our tablets and the water; and afterward, the Maid bid me that I take her unto a warm pool that did be near by, and to ask that I turn from her, but yet to be anigh for her Protector, as I did be ever.

And so she to wash and to make herself happy with a sweet cleanness that did be proper to her; and afterward, when she did be done, she to act watch whilst I to mine; and to help me in all matters, that she was able; and truly, I to be happy indeed that she did so have delight to attend upon me and to treat me mother-wise; yet truly with her maid-heart not all hid, as you have perceived, this time and that.

And surely thus did we go alway in these matters; and oft that I have not space to have told; and oft that you shall remember, if that I do be too full of other happenings to give heed to tell upon.

And afterward we to our journeying again; and to talk upon this thing and that thing; and I to be watchful as we talked, and to tell the Maid that she keep her eyes wary, but yet not to be of unease.

And when we did go thiswise for seven good hours, we were come nigh opposed to the bright-burning fire-hill that did be offward in the sea, and had made me a warm light in that time when I did sleep in the tree, as you do remember. And truly, as I shall here mind you, we did be past seven hours coming to this place, from the part where the steam did be; yet had I gone that space upon the outward way at a speed that was greater; but truly I might not set so great a pace to the Maid, save, mayhap, odd whiles; and this thing I beg that you have alway in your mind, and so to understand why that we did be oft long upon this part of the journey and that, by compare with mine outward going.

And, in verity, I had set off our hour for food, because that I saw we did come nigh to the place where the tree did be; and I to know that the Maid should like to eat and drink anigh to that place, and to know that I did sleep there.

And surely I took her to the tree, and when that I told her, she to beg me that I indulge her and that we go upward to that branch where I did sleep, and there to eat our tablets.

And I to be willing, and to enter into her wishing; for, indeed, there was no danger in the climb, and I to go alway below her, so that I could be surety for her safeness. And we came up to the great branch; and she to make how we should sit, and I to have to show just where I did lie, and she to look very close, and to see that my weight had surely marked the hardness of the armour upon the bark; and she then to be upon that branch alone, as she did eat and drink; and to look outward at the light from the fire-hill, and to be very husht, and to think, and I not to disturb her with speech.

And when she did be done, she gat from the branch, and kist the place where I did lie; and lo! in a moment a thought came into her, and she drew her knife, and cut out a piece of the bark, and put it into her breast to be for a keepsake; and so to seem somewise contented.

And truly, I told her about the great beast, when we were come down again to the earth; and she to cry out and to show me that there did be yet the mark where the belly of the monstrous beast did brush upon the earth, as it ran, and moreover the broken places of the foot-marks; and she by this to see how great a beast it did be; but yet did it be a little thing beside the Slug; only that it did be a thing of horn and hardness of skin, as you have perceived.

And truly, I do mind how that the observings of the Maid did bring very keen to me how that there had past but seventeen days since that I did go onward from this place; and this to seem very strange and scarce credible unto me; for I had thought it, somewise, as a great time; and truly this to be because it was so marked by stress of the mind and great happenings; and you to agree in this thing. But yet, also, we shall truly mind that those times that I have called days, did hold oft the hours of two days, and mayhap three, as you do remember.

Now we went onward then to our journeying; and I to make to carry the Maid, as ever, after that she had walked twelve hours, though she did walk thirteen hours this time as you have seen. And she to say that she go now upon her own feet through the next six hours, and so to ease me from the labour that did be needful to carry her.

But I to know how that she did be like to be all gone of her strength thiswise, in but a day or two, and we to make the better speed, if that I keep to my way, and to have her to walk twelve hours of every journey, and afterward to come into mine arms; for, truly, she did be bred less hardy than I, as you shall think from all that I have told concerning the Peoples of the Lesser Pyramid; and moreover she was yet something weakened, as I did think, by the dreadful month of her lonesomeness and escapings, before that I was come to succour her.

And truly, as I did carry her, the Maid did make remark of her wonderment concerning me, in that I did be so hard of my body and set in the determination of my mind. And, in verity, I did be exceeding strong and of great hardness of body; and mayhap my will did be somewhat this way also, else do I think I had never borne to come unto Mine Own through so much desolation. And I to smile very happy upon her; for I did love that I was so strong, and very truly in delight that Mine Own Maid did take gladness in this thing. And you to mind how you did be also in the love-days; and so to have nice understanding of my naturalness and human pride.

And surely the Maid did nestle unto me, as she did talk; even, somewise, as a Child shall come nigh to the Mother, but yet also as a Maid doth love to be nigh unto her Man, if that she doth truly love. And I to lift her more nigh to my lips; but she to refuse to kiss me, and to be a Sweet Impertinence that did lie in mine arms; yet when I did make to lower her again to the way that had her easy to carry, she to slip her pretty face very snug under my chin, and to kiss me there, after her own fashion; and afterward to be willing that she be as usual into mine arms.

Now, as I set the Maid again comfortable, it seemed to me that

she was something tender; and sudden it came to me that mayhap the armour to be very hard and painful unto her; and I to ask this thing of her, in a moment; and she to see that I would not be put off; and so to tell me. And, truly, I was utter angered with myself; and somewise also with her, in that she did not waken mine unthinkingness to this thing.

And I set her instant to the earth, and made her to bare her shoulders to me; and truly they did be much bruised where that she had lain so oft in mine arms, against the hardness of mine armour.

And I to be so angered that I near shook her, and she to see how I did be, and that she did be nigh to be shaken, because that I was grown so angry that she should let herself come to this foolish hurt, that yet I did know was very dear unto her secret heart. And, in truth, she put up her lips to me, very sudden, and with a strange naughtiness, that she have her own way with me to tempt me from mine anger, that yet she did half to like. And, in verity, I near slapt her then upon her pretty shoulders, but that she ceased from her tempting of me; and instead she turned her shoulders to me, even as a child, that I button her garment for her.

And surely, when I had buttoned her garment, she came round unto me, and closed her hand, so that it did be a little fist, even as I did love her to do, because that it was so small beside my great hand.

And she slipt her shut hand into mine; and surely I let it stay within, very quiet, and made not to close upon it, as I did wont. And the Maid did move her hand around in mine, that she make me to take notice upon her, and to grasp her little fist. Yet I did be very stern, for I was truly angered; and neither did I put her hand from mine, nor made to hold it; but only to let it bide; yet, truly, I to be something stirred in the heart-part by her pretty ways.

And in a little while, she took her hand from out of mine, and did have daring to be cold unto me. And mine anger then to be quaintly renewed, and to think that she did well need to be whipt. And she made a naughty and foolish impudence upon that which I said to her; so that presently I did say that she did need such as should make her to heed her manners; but yet, as you shall conceive, I to know inwardly all that time how that even this true naughtiness did not stir me to proper anger; but more that it made me masterful and to lack not that I make her to know truly that I did be her Master; and in the same time to be strangely touched in a very deep and secret place of my heart. And truly love doth have strange actings upon the heart.

And the Maid to ask me in a very saucy fashion that did be intentioned to anger me, what I did mean that she to need. And truly I

said that she did go the way to earn that she be flogged like any boy, and I to mean actual all that I did say, which doth something amaze me now; but, as I do know, I yet to be constant stirred inwardly by her beloved quaintness that did be alway so dainty, even when that she did mean her naughtiness to be truly to anger me.

And lo! when I told the Maid this thing, that she did well go to earn a sharp reproof, she turned in a quick instant, and came close to me, all tender and small and to need to be nigh to me. And she slipt both her closed hands into the one of mine, and truly they did be little fists. And because I could be no more stern with Mine Own, I put mine arm about her, and she did nestle to me, so that all my being did want to be a shield about her.

And she to hark very quiet and humble to my counsellings; and in the end did be so strangely husht that I lookt down to where her pretty face did be hid against mine armour, as she did love to do, when that I did be those odd whiles a little stern with her. And I held her face away from mine armour; and surely she did be smiling, very quiet and naughty; so that I perceived that she did be good only for that time, and did be like to show again this wrongful and impudent spirit. Yet I not then to be in trouble of the future; but to hope only that I do wisely, if that she show again this waywardness. And, truly, I to perceive now that I did be very young; but, anywise, as you do know, I to act alway from the natural telling of my heart.

And I shook Naani a little, for this naughty spirit which did not be gone from her. For I perceived that my manhood had but stirred the woman in her to that strange quick humbleness that had seemed to be a quenching of her wayward unwisdom; and truly it had not been stilled, but only sunken for a little moment in the uprising of her dear nature, which had responded unto me.

And the Maid to look at me from under her lids, as I did shake her with gentleness; and I to know that Mine Own did be a wondrous maiden, full of all life and spirit, and to be held wisely and to be loosed wisely, all as did be for the best to bring out the uttermost of her goodness which did be in all her being, and to be very lovely; and to make me feel as that I did be a giant that held a white flower very tender; but I to feel also that I did be her Master. And this mayhap you to understand, if that you look into your hearts.

And by all my telling, you to know that I did be very dainty with Mine Own Maid that did be all of daintiness; but yet I to be masterful, as did be my nature, and a very proper way it did be with the Maid, so that she did be alway reasonable in the main; and this to come out

of her love, which did have pleasure to know that I did be Master unto her, all in the same while that she did fight to show that I did be otherwise. And truly, and in part by this same showing, you shall perceive that her naughtiness to come likewise from her love, and the way that my nature did work upon her.

Now I to shake the Maid very gentle, as I have said, and with much that did be of play, but in the same wise there to be also somewhat of tender reproof. And surely, that naughty maid to spring very light upon her toes, and had kist me sudden and dainty upon the mouth, before that I did wot.

And I to put mine arm about her, and to give her a little hug; and immediately then to matters that did be practical; for I was eager to have come across that stony part of the journey, that did be before us, as you do know, before that we look for a place for our slumber. And this eagerness of haste to be, because of the great bird things which I had seen to go bounding over that waste, when that I was upon mine outward way.

And, surely, after that I had thought a little moment, I bid the Maid that she dress in her torn garments, so that these should be over the top of the armour-suit, and thiswise to make a soft thickness upon the top of the armour-suit, that should act for a cushion between mine armour and her dear body.

But indeed, the Maid would nowise to do this thing; and I not to make her, because that my heart perceived how it did be with her. And her reasons to be someways mixt, as doth be proper in all humans, and the more so when that it doth be a maid that hath reasons, as you to know, if that you have ever held such dear perverseness in your arms.

And she, as I could know, to be strangely in love that her gentle body be bruised by the hardness of mine armour; and if this might not be, she to be not wishful that she wear her torn clothing upon her neat suit and so to seem careless and to lack to be dainty in mine eyes; for, indeed, she did be alway to wash herself and to make tidiness; and she to have a way now that she did set the armour-suit upon her, that had it to seem different, and she to have set a little sprig from the trees upon her breast, and in her girdle, and so to seem the more of a maid; and surely a man doth know and love these things; but not alway to have full knowing how that they be done. And, indeed, you to be likewise with me in this thing. And we all to think we know, but somewise to be just a-lack when that it doth come to the proof.

And, in verity, the Maid to find a way that she be eased of the hardness of the armour; and I to have come to the same thing in the

same moment; but truly I do think she had been able to think upon it a long while, if that she had been so desired.

And truly, this was but that I fold the cloak very thick across mine arms and breast, and to take her then into the little nest that did be prepared.

And, surely, now that the Maid might no more have her secret wish that she lie close against mine armour, she to be helpful, and to have the cloak folded so in a very quick while; and so to be into mine arms again; and we to be once more upon the journey, and she to nestle to me, as that she did hunger to be nigh to me; and she to talk with me, odd whiles, and odd whiles to be silent.

And once, I to think that she wept a little; and to know that she did be like to think upon her father and her own Peoples; but she to have her face turned to me, so that I could but guess upon this thing; and she very soon to be husht again of this sorrow, and to lie content in mine arms.

And once, when that I had carried her for three hours, she to ask me that I kiss her; and truly I did kiss her, very gentle and with reverence, because that my heart did understand the holiness that did be in her heart in that moment.

And, surely, as I kist her, she to kiss me very tender; and I to know that some olden memory did be like to stir in her. And in a moment, she to take her lips from mine, where she had let them to nestle very light, and did whisper mine olden love-name; and I then to look at her, and her eyes to shine as the olden stars that did shine in the olden summers.

And I to be too shaken even that I kiss her. But she to put her arms about my neck, and to look steadfast into mine eyes. And immediately, after that she had lookt awhile, and I to have ceased from walking, she to put her hands upon each side of my face, within the metal of mine head-gear, where the guards did come down at the sides; and she to kiss me very sober upon the lips; but yet to mean utter by that kiss. And I not to return the kiss; for I saw that it did not be her need.

Now, in the beginning of the fourth hour, as I did go with the Maid, I to see afar off one of the half-bird monsters, that I did see before upon this place where there did be naught save great stones and boulders for a great way that did be many miles.

And truly, I to hide very swift with the Maid, where two great boulders did come together; and surely the bird-creature to go past at no great way, and to go with a great bounding, that did be half of flight and half of leaping, as that it did be too weighty in the body to make to fly proper.

And, indeed, I to have a sudden memory how that there did be a picture in some book that I did read in the Mighty Pyramid, where it did show such a bird-thing as this; and to make remark in the book that these things had been seen no more in the Night Land for a score thousand of years, or more; and to be extinct, as we do say.

But, indeed, now I do think that they did be come downward to that warm Country, a great while gone, and so to have new life and to breed through a great age, and this way to have set a pattern unto the Humans. And, in verity, it might be that in some age that did be far after that time, the Humans to find some way to journey from the Pyramid, and to build a new Refuge in that deep Country; and mayhap the Humans thiswise to have a new space of life, after that all the Night Land did be dead and lost in the bitter frost of Eternity. But this, indeed, to be no more than an odd thought; for how might any great multitude pass the Monsters; and I to ask that you take it for nothing of fact, but only as of my suppositions; and thiswise to come back again to happenings.

Now, when the bird-thing did be gone a long way off, I to go forward again with Mine Own, and to have a new care, and to look very swift and frequent everyway.

And, truly, it did be as that the creatures did inhabit that part of the Country; for in an hour after that, I to see a good score. And, I to free the Diskos from my hip, and to have it ready in mine arms beside the Maid; and so to journey.

And many times I to have to hide with Mine Own, and to crouch low among the rocks and the boulders; and this way to escape free of all for a great while.

Yet, when that the fifth hour did be nigh gone, I heard a noise sudden to my back, as we did go over a clear space. And, in verity, there did be one of the monsters that came upward over certain rocks that were to my rearward; and surely it to have been stayed hid there, or resting, and to have heard us or to have smelled us; but anywise then to have knowledge of us, and to come with low and brutish heavy boundings, very lumbersome, after us.

And I lookt every way in a moment; but there was nowhere any shelter anigh. And the Maid to leap sudden from mine arms, that I be free with the Diskos; and I to look swift to her, and to see that she have her knife ready in her hand, that she might chance to aid me. But surely I might not fight in ease of mind, if that Mine Own did be needless in danger; and I caught her very quick by the waist, and set her upon the ground between my feet. And she to make half to refuse;

but I to have no time for explaining, and to be sharp that I have her safe; so that I gave her a little shake that did sudden to make her feel the strength in me; and she then to be instant quiet in my hands, and to let me that I set her upon her face, and to cast the thick cloak above her; and in a moment to be stood over her, and to set down the visor of mine head-gear, lest that the bird-monster strike me in the face.

And surely, the bird-thing did be scarce an hundred good paces off; and to make two lumbering and monstrous bounds, and to come at me.

Yet, truly, it made sudden a pause, because that the Diskos did roar and send out fire, as I made it to spin; but in an mstant the great thing to come in at me upon the left side, and to strike me very hard with the bill, that did be so long as mine arm, and had surely gone through my body, if that I had been naked. And the bill of the monster rang upon mine armour; and it smote me twice thiswise, so that I staggered very sick and shaken. But in a moment, as it made to draw off, that it should come the more hard upon me, I swung the Diskos very sure and quick, and I smote the Bird-thing above the place where the great seeming-leathern wing did join upon the right side, as it should be the shoulder of the Bird-monster. And, in verity, the monster gave out a mighty squarking, and went backward this way and that, and beat all about upon the stones, and did strike with the great bill at the place where it did be hurt. And I heeded that I end it swiftly; and I ran in upon it, and the creature to strike at me with the great bill, very savage. But I jumpt speedy to this side, and again to that, and so in a moment to have chance to come in surely. And truly I split the skull of the Bird-thing, so that it died very quick and was gone from pain.

And the Bird-creature lay all spread upon the stones and the rock of that place; and surely it did be as that it were leathern, and made somewise as a bat doth be of this age, in that it did have no feathers.

And, truly, it lookt mighty, where it did be spread; and indeed the body to be full so big as the body of a young horse; and the bill to be very deadly and sharp and cumbrous, as you to have guessed. And I to be all and utter thankful that it did be there, dead, in the stead of mine own body. And the thing yet to twitch and stir a little, as the life did go from it.

And surely I was back then very speedy to the Maid, and she to be kneeled upward to watch me. And I took her into mine arms, and lookt well about; and made then forward again.

And about the middle part of the sixth hour of crossing that rocky land, I saw that we did draw near unto the shallow river, that you shall mind I came over, after that I had done with the olden flying ship.

And in all that time, since the Bird-monster to come after us, I had seen but two more, and they a great way off, so that I guessed that I was come beyond that part where they did go very frequent.

And I to wade over the river, and to carry Mine Own upon one arm, the while that I did sound my way with the staff of the Diskos; and truly I came across very easy, save that I did have to go around somewhat, where that the river did seem to have a deep place.

And when that we had crost the river, it did be full one and twenty hours since that we slumbered, as you shall know, if that you but count a little; for you do mind that we spent a certain time within the tree, as I have told; and this not to have been proper counted into the time of our journeying.

And surely, the Maid to have been very quiet, since that I did show my strength a little to her, when that I made her to lie, that she be safe from the bill of the Bird-monster. But she not to be anywise in anger upon me; but only, as I do think, that the woman in her did be something fresh waked unto me; and she to be very content that she be quiet in mine arms.

Now the place that we were come to, was much spread with boulders; but yet to have the beginnings again of the forests, as you to remember; for I to have made some small remark of the land in this part, upon mine outward way. And we lookt about for a fire-hole, that I should dry my lower garments; and truly, we had not past many in a great while; but we to be in fortune, that we came soon upon a little fire-hill that did be no more than so high as a man, and to have the rock all hot about; so that this did be a good place to our purpose.

And I kist the Maid, and set her down out of mine arms; and when that I had lookt well about, and seen that there did be naught to our sight to give us to fear, the Maid to help me with mine armour; and afterward with my garments, and to ease me all ways that she could think of with helpfulness.

And she set the garments of my lower parts to dry, and whilst that they did be drying, she to make ready the water and the tablets, and to have me to sit beside her, in my body-vest and gear, and we to eat and drink very comfortable in the warm hollow that was something anigh to the small fire-hill.

Now, truly, I did be very hungry that time, and indeed to be alway so, for the tablets did be very unfilling to the belly, as you do well know from my tellings. And when that I did be finished, I saw that the Maid lookt at me somewise oddways, and sudden she to come into laughter, and askt me whether that I did be very empty; and in the same moment

there to be a wondrous dear look within her eyes; so that I perceived that there went a mother-note under her impudence.

And she to yearn, as I could know, that she have some way to feed me; but truly there did be no way, for we thought not to make to slay aught for our purpose, and we did be feared that we eat any root or plant, lest that we be ill. And this to seem strange to my spirit of this our age, but to be natural unto that; so that I do think I did be so long bred from the primal obtaining of food, that I did be all lost to that which should seem natural unto the peoples of this early age of the world; though we truly to think that the world doth even now be old; and this to have seemed a true thing unto every age that ever did live.

Now, beside that we did lack somewise to think serious that we slay something to eat, in that the tablets did actually suffice to our strength, I to believe that there did be some other reason that I do forget, and mayhap never to have thought plain upon; but which to be set within me as an instinct, as we do say; and this to mean, if that I try to set it in other words, that the tablets did keep the body and the spirit in such condition that the Forces of Evil did have the less power to act upon us.

Yet, have I no remembering that I was taught in the preparation that I eat naught, save the tablets; and this mayhap never to have been set upon me; but to have been as a thing that doth never need to have been told; even as you shall not tell a grown man in this Age that he shall refrain from dung, and eat only wholesome matter.

And truly, I to hope that I have made this thing somewise clear unto you; for, indeed, it doth be something hard to set out; for every Age hath the subtleties peculiar to that Age; and these to be hard to the understanding of other Ages, but yet to seem plain and utter natural, even without thought, unto the Peoples of the Age.

And surely all this to be plain to you, and to be over-plain; for, in verity, I tell to you, and over-tell, until that I should be weary; and mayhap you to be the more so. And, indeed, I not to blame you; but only to hope that your understanding, which doth mean also in general your hearts, doth be with me all along my way. And, indeed, this my tale to be not easy told.

And, in verity, I to be back now unto the Maid a-laugh upon me, and in the same moment deeply loving and a-lack that she could not feed me, and I to laugh with her, and to have understanding with her, as you to know; and, indeed, I to have an heart that doth be made someways natural unto understanding; so that even though I be dead when you read this, my tale, you to feel that we be friends, and to know

that could I meet with you in pitiful trouble, I to have understanding and love to you, if that you be not utter brutish; and even-so, I to be sorrowful that you should be brutish, and to have understanding, in that I to know that by developement you to become wise unto sweetness and charity, and in love with all dear things, and kind pity of the rest. And thiswise you to be in human sympathy with me, because that you do feel that I be honest with you, and somewise even now to your elbow, as you read. And this to be writ now, and you mayhap not to be born a great while yet; but in the end to read and to have understanding with me, and to know how I did love Mine Own. And so we to go forward again, the closer, in that we do be the more knit in dear human sympathy.

And surely the Maid kist me very nice on the lips, and did promise again how that she should make me a great meal when that we did come to our Mighty Home; and, indeed, as she to say, she to join with me, and we both to be naughty gluttons for that once. And, surely, I laughed gently at the Maid, because that she should be so dainty a glutton; but for my part, I to feel that I could eat an horse, as we do say in this Age.

And by that we had eat and drunk and talked awhile, and lookt oft about, so that we know that no brutish thing came near, to our hurt, the Maid to tell me that my garments did be dry; and she then to give me aid that I dress very quick; and afterward she to help me with mine armour, the which she did wipe after that we had eat and drunk; and she to have had joy that she do this thing, and all things for me; and to have used a part of her torn garments to this end.

And so, truly, I to be clothed and armed very speedy, and to feel eased and the more sure in my mind; for in verity, I was alway in unease, when that I did not be ready that I be able to meet any horrid Brute that should be like to come upon us.

Now, when that I did be into mine armour again, the Maid to set the scrip and the pouch upon me, and all the while I scarce to be loosed of the Diskos, as ever. And we then to our way, which did be that we find a place proper to our slumber.

And when that we did be gone all-ways, and no cave proper to our sight, we found a great tree, that did be set off alone, and had a plenty of branches; but none that did be near to the bottom-part.

And surely, I gave the Maid a lift, and held her up so far as mine arms did go, so that she might stand upon the palms of my hands, and be steady against the trunk of the tree; and she thiswise to have a hold upon a branch, and so to go upward.

And, truly, when that she was safe, I loosed one of the straps from the pouch and the scrip, and I cast this up to the Maid, and she set it strong about the branch. And when I had caught the downward end, I went upward very easy; and afterward took loose the strap; and this way we did be something safe, as you shall see.

And we climbed upward then, and so came to a part of the tree where the branches did be very thick together; and we made here a place for our slumber, and the Maid set the cloak over the branches that did be so close, and afterward we lay down; but first I set the strap about her waist, and thence to a branch, and she to refuse sleep until that I be likewise; so that we did be both very safe from any fall.

And she kist me, and we then to our slumber, and very weary; for it did be two and twenty hours, by this, since that we had sleep.

Now we had eight hours in which we slept utter; and we both to awake, as it did seem in the same moment; but truly, I to think that Mine Own did be wakeful before that time; for, indeed, as she put her arms very dainty about my neck, that she kiss me, I did have a quick and sudden knowledge that I had been kist oft in my sleep, and this to have been but a little while gone. And surely, it did seem to me that Mine Own did have a sweet and contented Mischief inward of her eyes; but yet she to be very sedate outward, and to kiss me loving and dear, and then we to our breakfast, upon the cloak.

And afterward, I climbed to the topmost branches of the tree, and lookt well over the Country all about; but there was no brutish thing to my sight in any place, neither near nor far.

And I came down then to the Maid, and told her how that there was quietness of life all about. And we had our gear together, and went downward to the earth, and I to help Mine Own, and this way she to be safe.

Now, as we went forward upon our journeying, I perceived that the Maid had a wayward air; and truly, I thought that she did have her heart all set toward naughtiness and mischief; and in the same moment that I was in this belief, I did know in mine understanding that this did spring from the workings of my nature upon the nature of Mine Own Maiden.

And Naani to walk, in the first, beside me, and to have no word for me, because that she did be so filled with the stirrings of her naughtiness, that did be in the same moment very sweet unto me, and yet to waken all that did be masterful within me. And she to be that she did know, and to delight, in her secret heart that she waken that which did be masterful in me; but yet in the same moment to be

strong determined that she be not mastered by me. And surely this to seem contrarywise in the words; but to be clear to the heart, if indeed you have ever been loved by a dear maid of an high spirit.

And above all this, the Maid did be filled with a love for me, that did beat and dance in all her being; and this in truth to overweigh all; but yet from this same thing her dainty naughtiness to be born, because, as I did say, my manhood to stir all her nature up-wise in sweet trouble that did be half of rebellion, and half that she did ache that she be close unto me in mine arms.

And, in verity, you to be with me in all these things, if that you have had the love-days beside a dear and dainty maid, of an high and pure and natural spirit; so that if you be old these days, even but the light merriment of a passing maiden to bring a pain of wonderings and golden memories upon your heart.

And presently, I saw that Mine Own put a little space between us, as the naughtiness did work in her, as my heart to know; and she to be offward from me a little. And she still to have no speech with me; but in a little to begin that she sing in a low voice; and to have her pretty body very upright and lithesome, and to go forward with a wondrous dainty swing, so that my heart told me that she did all be stirred with small thrillings of defiance unto me, and with thrillings of love; and she to have the triumph of her Maidenhood and of her Womanhood, as it were both to contend in her and to thrill upon her tongue, and to show out the lilting and pretty warfare of her spirit that did go dancing and dearly naughty in her breast.

And surely I went, very lifted in my heart, and astir; for it did be wondrous to me that this lovely Maid did be so utter mine. And to see but the way that she set her feet to the earth, and the way that she did lift them sure and dainty; and the way that her body did be poised, and the way of her head; and the way of her naughtiness and the sweetness and the love that did be wrapt in with all, did make me want that I have her in mine arms.

But yet, I not to do this, because that in the same time that she did so stir me to love and admirings, she to set somewhat else in me at variance, so that I did half to feel stern with her, for I perceived that she had that naughtiness then within her, that she did be like to have a real intent of impertinence unto me, so that she should be naughtily outrageous, and to have no heed to my advisings, neither unto my desires, unless that I set my hand upon her, to make her to obey.

And truly, you that have had dear maids, shall follow mine explainings; but unto others, I know not whether they shall understand,

until they too have been possessed of One that shall set all their heart adrift, even as this One that did be Mine Own.

And sudden, I to know that Naani did change from her low singing unto an olden air that had surely not been heard in all that eternity. And in verity, for a little while, I not to know why that it did so shake all my heart; nor what it did be; nor whether that I had truly heard it before, or only to think so.

And, surely, it did be as that the silence of the olden moonlit world did steal all about me; and sudden, I to know that the Maid did sing an olden love-song of the olden world, and to go halting a little as she sang, because that the words did steal something odd-wise through the far veils of her memory, even as a song doth come backward out of dreams.

And I to feel all my blood to seem to tremble in my veins, and my throat to be troubled, as with vague sobs that did be the ghosts of forgotten tears. And the dim sorrow that had come so swift and strange upon me, to be likewise steeped in golden mists of the love that I once did love; and the glamour to be come all fresh upon me, and I to know in that moment how much we do forget, even when that we do believe that we have all memory and all sorrow within our hearts.

And I lookt unto the Maid, something dimly, because of the way that I did be; and I perceived in a moment that Mine Own did weep as she walked; but the less with pain than with the strange anguish of Memory, that doth have in it Tenderness and Sorrow and Love and all that Hath Been and all that Did Never Be, and all to make a Vale unto the Spirit, where doth be both a dim greyness and a warm and everlasting light, and an utter speechlessness, and the low and far music of forgotten songs, that do come downward over the shadowy mountains that do be builded of Years and Forgetfulness, and yet made to be seen with the light of that our Memory, which doth cast so many husht shadows.

And surely, as I did say, the Maid did weep as she went; but not to be cast down; but rather that she held her head upwise, as that she did walk in a glory. And the song to come oft-broke, and oddly, and to set her voice to little human quiverings, as her memory did shake her sweet spirit unto tears afresh; and she to walk with her pretty head upheld and as that she did go in a Triumph; and the tears to come down strangely upon her face, and all her soul to be there, pure and wondrous, and in the same time both troubled and glad.

And this thing to be very dear and amazing; and she to be as that she not to know then that she sang; but as that she did be lost in her

thoughts, as we do say; and this to have come sudden upon her, out of all her upliftedness of spirit, that had been like to make her very open unto all subtile and subtle powers of thought and inward stirrings, as you shall think.

And again the song to come full-remembered, and fresh, as that this Eternity did be but the yesterday of that moment. And Mine Own to be all in a sweet madness with those half-dreamed memories, and the wonder and pain of all that no man hath ever said, and that shall be never said; and of the utter lost years, and all that hath been lost, and all forgotten greatness and splendour, and the dreadfulness of parting, and the loveliness of beautiful things that do be hid in the abyss of the years.

And it did be sudden to my quickened fancy, that there did be low echoes all about us, of the voices of dear beautiful ones that have died; for so did memory set a strange and lovely mystery about my spirit in that moment, that I did be all shaken so much as Mine Own. And I to be as that I drew my breath anigh to tears, and did be there with Naani amid the quiet spareness of the trees and the rock of that part of the land; but yet did be to see half dimly that I stood within a light, even as the light that doth be the wonder of olden sunsets; and I to be, in the same time, both that man and this man that now doth write; and to have beside my spirit but one maid, that I did lack to know whether I say to her Naani or Mirdath; for though the two that have been Mine Own did be different-seeming to the eye, there to be but the spirit of one maid beside me in that moment.

And surely, I did be there, all shaken unto the seeing of visions, as it did seem; so that the Land about me to have grown half as that it did lack that it be real unto my sight, because that I lookt inward unto Lands that did be of Memory. And lo! in a moment this to go; and I to be in that Country of the Seas, and to look newly unto Naani, and she to go as I have told; and there to be the lonesome trees and the rocks in all parts for a great way about.

And sudden, as I lookt at Mine Own, she to come round unto me, and she held out her arms, and did gaze at me with such a love, as that she were transfigured, and to need strangely that she be in mine arms; and surely, I to an holy need that I have her unto me, because that, after all, there did be no wonder so great as that wonder, that when all did be said I did have Mine Own, after that all Eternity had nigh past.

And, in verity, we ran each to the other, and did be silent, because that there was no speech of words by which we could say aught of all that did be in our hearts. And truly you to be with me in understanding;

for you too, mayhap, to have suffered thiswise of dumbness; even if that it hath not been so great. But yet to make you to know.

And presently, we grew quiet in the spirit; and Mine Own to come back again to her joyousness, and to go beside by me, as we made forward.

And presently, Naani to begin that she look at me with dear impudences again, that did be very sweet unto me; but yet to be like to lead unto defyings.

And truly, by these things shall you know the spirit of Mine Own Maid; and there to be none to me that ever did be like her. But, indeed, you to think thatwise of the maid that you did love; and all the world to be thinking each these thoughts of one dear maiden that doth be the one maid in all the round world.

And this to be the lovely niceness of the human heart; and I not to have any grumble thereat; but yet, surely, you shall say that this Maid that did be Mine Own, did be very dear and lovely. And, in verity, I to show my human heart in this thing; for you likewise to want that I think your Maid to have been just so dear, and the more so. And indeed we ever to be going these ways; and to have good comradeship of understanding, because that we have all loved and suffered joy and had utter belief in a dear One.

And surely a defyingness to come presently into the way that the Maid did go, and she to walk a little offward from me; and truly I lookt at her, both with love and yet with somewhat that did be to reprove her gently, and all in the same moment that she to make my heart stirred with her sweet naughtiness.

And she to look sudden at me; and to be that she half to intend to run to kiss me; but also that she be minded in the same moment that she set herself up impertinently against me. And, in verity, she made me to harden my nature a little, as manhood doth make a man to do; and this because of the rebellion that I knew to be in her; and she likewise to know. But she hid her eyes, when that I shook my head, half with play and half with earnest; and was then impudent unto me; and gone from that in a moment to her pretty singing, and her naughty walking apart. But she no more to sing an olden love-song.

Now, in a while, we past a basin of rock, in a place among the trees; and there was a warm spring bubbling in the rock, and the basin to be full of water, very warm and with some smelling of chemistry.

And the Maid told me that she would wash, and I to think it a good place for that end. And when I had tasted the water, I found that it did seem smooth and proper for our intent, as that there did be averity of an alkali in it.

And truly we washed, and after that I was done, the Maid bid me that I turn my back; and I to do this, and she to mock me very naughty whilst that I could not see her, and to seem very quiet; for indeed, I heard no splashings of water, though I stood off from her a long while, and she alway to say naughty things unto me, as that she did mind truly to have me angered; for, indeed, she did have a plain intent that she mock at me, and to ease not her wit.

And surely, after that I had stood a great while, I askt the Maid when that she did be like to be done; but she to say that she was nowise ended of her toilets. And I knew very sudden that she made foolishness upon me also in this matter; and I turned upon her, and lo! she did be sitting upon a little rock, very sedate, even as when she had bid me turn from her; and to have made no more forward, but only to have been there at ease, that she keep me turned away to please her naughty mood, and all the while have a double liberty to have impudence upon me.

And, in verity, I did be a little angered; but scarce that I did know it; for I did love her very great, and was stirred inwardly with her dearness and that she did look just that-wise that I knew not whether I to need to kiss her, or to shake her; and truly, how should I know; for my heart did ache that I have her to mine arms; but my brain to say that she did go over-far in the joke; and truly you to see that I did not be unreasonable, neither to be lacking of grace; for indeed I do think that I was swayed all-ways, because that I saw all the dear way that her pretty nature did work; and to conceive of her mood and to understand and be stirred; but yet to shape a little in my manhood unto hardening, and in my judgement unto sternness.

Yet, truly, I scolded Mine Own with no more than a little jesting, and did be nice and gentle with her, because she did be so dear, and I to know just-wise her mood and the cause and working of it.

And I told her that I did love her, and that she hasten now and let us again to the journey. But, indeed, she only to make a face at me, so that I did be near like to shake her unto sedateness. And she then to be both merry, and a rogue, as we do say, and to stop her ears and again to sing very gleeful; and all so that she might not hear aught that I said. And surely she lookt a very dainty Rebellious One.

And I went then straightway to her, and took her hands from her ears; and I kist her pretty ears very gentle that I not to deafen her. And I kist her lips as she did sing; and afterward shook her, that she be not such a sweet Torment. But this to have no success that way; for she only to put out her toes to be kist; for her foot-gear was off

from her feet. And, indeed, I laughed, even as I made to frown; and truly I kist her pretty toes, and tried then to coax her to go forward something speedy with her hair, and to be ready to the journey. But she only to sing, and to refuse to be sedate.

And, in verity, in the end, I caught her up in mine arms, and had her bundle in my hand, and so went off with her very sudden, with her hair all loose upon me in a lovely and soft shining, and her feet bare as they did be.

And this action I made, because that I was grown truly a little stern with Mine Own; for, indeed, she did half to need that she be whipt unto properness, as you shall think, that have seen how she did be thiswise only because that her nature did be stirred strangely, and her Womanhood and her Maidenhood to be all unto war, and in part to make a rebellion against me that she did know glad to be her true Master; but yet she to be thus, even though she did be so glad.

And this to act so that she did be in the same moment both sweet and wise and yet to show a dainty foo}ishness and a true naughtiness that did make me to feel somewhat of a real anger; but yet did have me to know that all my being did be stirred by her; so that I did think with one thought that she did be very foolish, and with another that she did be lovely wayward.

Now, when that I took the Maid up so quick, and made off with her, she to give a little gasp and to submit to me with a quick humbleness; but immediately, she to regain her courage, and to be outraged of me. But, indeed, I took no heed, only that I was like to shake her; and did know also that her hair did be wondrous pretty upon mine armour. And she soon to lie very quiet and easy in mine arms, and to be demure.

And I to have a half knowledge of somewhat amiss; but yet to have no sureness, neither to think much upon this vague feeling.

And when that I had gone a good mile, she to put up her lips to be kist; and I to kiss her very loving, for she was so dear. And she then to say, very ordinary like, that I should do wisely now if that I went back for her foot-gear, which truly I had lacked thought to notice, when that I did pick up the Maid.

And I saw that she had known this thing all that while, and had made that mile of carrying all a waste and a foolishness, because of the naughty rebellion which did be in her. And lo! I set her instant to the ground; and she gave out a little cry as she saw that I did be gone somewise hard and stern with her.

And indeed I pulled a small branch from a tree that did be near,

to be for a switch as you shall whip a boy with; and I held her with my left hand, and in verity I laid the switch thrice very sharp across her pretty shoulders, that she know all that she did need to know. And she seeming to be ceased in a moment from her perverseness, and did nestle very quick unto me, that had whipt her; and did need that she be wondrous nigh unto me. And, truly, how shall even a young man flog such an one.

And the Maid to be very husht against mine armour, and to resist that I look into her face that did be prest so anigh me. But presently, I used a little and gentle force, and so to look into her face something sudden. And truly, that One did be smiling very naughty and dainty to herself; so that I perceived that I had not truly whipt her enough; but yet I could harden my heart no more at that time; for, in verity, there doth be a strange half-pain in the bosom, if that you have to flog a maid that doth be utter thine, and this to the despite that there hath been—as then—no properness of anger to have for an after self-reproach.

And surely, I to have done this thing only of a stern intent and steadfastness, that I steady Mine Own Maid unto wisdom; but yet to have been helpt by a little anger, because of the thing that she had done. Yet, alway, my love did be so strong, that mine anger never to have aught of bitterness, as you shall have seen, and to understand.

And we went back then for the foot-gear of the Maid; and she to be very husht in mine arms; but yet, as I perceived, not to be quiet, of an humble little heart, but only of the chance that her nature did be stirred that way for the while.

And truly, when we were gone back, the foot-gear did be there to the side of the pool, and the Maid gat shod very speedy, and would have no aid; and afterward did up her hair very tight upon her head, to have it utter from my sight; and this to be for a perverseness; for she knew that I did love to see it pretty upon her shoulders, or if that she must do it, that she do it up very loose and nice; and truly you to know how I mean; only that I have no skill of such matters; but yet a good taste to admirings, if that the thing be aright.

And I to say nothing, as I looked at her; and she presently to make a quick glance unto me, to see why I did say naught. And I shook my head, smiling at her waywardness; but she to look away from me, and to seem to be set to fresh naughtiness.

Now we went forward then upon our journey; and alway the Maid to walk onward from me; but yet to have no other impudence, neither to sing.

And I to go kindly with her; but yet to think that she did lack somewhat to know that I did be truly her Master; and I to wonder a little whether she did know proper that my gentleness with her did be not of weakness, but born of understanding and love, and the more proof that I did be fit to possess and to guide her.

And truly this was the thought of a young man, yet lacking not of Reason in the bottom part, though mayhap to be something clumsy-seeming unto the mind of a maid; and to be very human to my years; and you to have been likewise, if that you have tried all-ways with a dear One, and she to be yet over-wilful, so that you to wonder whether she did truly know how you did understand.

And surely a maid doth know much that doth be in the heart of a man, if that she be true woman in her own secret heart. And oft she doth know more of her mar. than her man doth wot of himself, and to go her own diverse ways that she search out and bring forth and waken all that is the inward being of the man that she doth love.

Yet, when that she have stirred you in the deeps that you scarce to know, she to be all fearful, and in the same moment to have no fear; and to be in rebellion, and in the same moment to be most strange humble. And all to be born of love, and nature in action upon nature.

And more than this how shall I have learning of the heart to tell you; for, in verity, there doth be much in these few lines, if that you know to read. And surely you to know, or to learn; but if neither, then have you gone short of joy and the true inwardness of life.

Now this way I did be, as I have told; and the Maid to be quietly naughty in perverseness, as also I have set out; yet to have a strict mind to her duties, and to go now wondrous sedate upon the journey; yet alway apart. And likewise, when that the sixth hour did come, and we to our halt, as ever, she to be very speedy and nice that the water and the tablets be ready for me; but yet to have no word; neither to eat by me, but again a little apart, and not to share the water, but to make a brewing to herself, when that I had done.

And likewise, the Maid held not up her tablets to be kist, as alway; but eat them, quiet and meditative, and with little nibblings, as that she did ponder upon other matters, or mayhap to be not hungry.

And these things I saw, as we eat and drank in a silence; and I to look at the Maid, somewise sad in the heart, and something stirred; and I to say to myself wisely, yet as a young man, that she did not yet be taught sufficient that I was her master. And this you to perceive.

And she never to seem to look at me; but to be quiet and demure, and to have her eyelids something down upon her eyes.

Now, presently, as I thought upon the matter, I saw that I do well that I take no heed of Mine Own; but to let her to come to a natural end of this naughtiness, that did be, in the same time, both pretty and a little foolish; so that in half I condemned it and in half I was stirred; and alway I loved the Maid very dear, and had a good understanding; and there to be also an interest in my heart at this new side that she did be showing. And also, she to stir me odd whiles unto masterfulness; and so you to know pretty well how it did be with me in the matter.

Now, surely, I found this plan, that I attend not to the Maid, to have something of success; for I knew presently that she did look upward at me, slyly, from under her pretty eyelashes; and after, to be demure in a moment; and this to go forward for a while; yet I to show no heed.

And in a while, I saw that she gave attention to her garments, in the way of nattiness; and afterward, she took down her hair, and made it up then very loose and pretty upon her head; so that she did be very lovely, and to tempt mine eyes that they look alway at her. But, indeed, I did make as that I had no heed that the Maid did shape her hair different upon her head.

And she very soon then to speak, and to have the lesser gear together, and to make that she attract me. But truly, I was very nice with her; yet to keep her now a little off from me in the spirit; and so to teach her that-wise, that she was somewhat of a dear naughty maid; but also, as I do think, I was this way, because that in part I would tease her, in great love of her prettiness and her makings up to me; and so maybe even that I make her to be the more defying of me. And this to be as that I also lacked somewhat of reason; for I did strangely that I think that she need to be whipt, and in the same time that I go to make her the more deserving of the same.

Yet, this to be the truth, as I know it; and surely to be the natural waywardness of love. But yet, there did be also in the backward part of my wisdom, an intent that I be wise and careful with Mine Own; and I surely to have no full realisings that I did be like to set her further unto perverseness than yet she did be.

Now, after that I had shown well that I lacked to heed the Maid, I found that I did be looking oft at her; and she to be so dear and pretty, and to be all husht, that truly I could not bear that I be longer silent to her advancements.

And I ceased then from pretending, and would have had her into mine arms; but she to be now in sweet dignity, and to keep me off with very sober graces. And because of this, I to feel someway that I did be someway in blame; and surely, now that I consider it, I can see

that I was something acted upon, even as had been the Maid; and so we two to be; and a most human pair, as you to say; and somewhat both a-lack; but indeed, we did be very wholesome, and in utter love each of the other; and mayhap both then to perceive something of the sweet foolishness within us that did be as yeast a-work in us; for I thought that Naani did smile a little to herself. But, surely, this clear-seeing, to be but for an odd time; and afterward we each again to earnestness in our way with the other; but alway, even when we did make to show indifference, we to be something troubled inwardly with sweet flashings of our bewildered natures.

Now, though I have shown you that I to know that I did be not utter free of this most strange and natural foolishness; yet you to perceive that I tell this only that I have utter truth of all things that did happen; for, in verity, because that I was something subtly touched this way at whiles, yet was this no full excusing of the Maid; though, in the same moment, you to perceive, that there did be only the half of me to think that she did need to be excused; for, in truth, mine understanding went alway, in the main, with the workings of her nature; and had a natural sympathy with her dear whimsies; but also, as you to know, I to be stirred constant in my manhood by her naughty defyings; and to be troubled in my Natural Sense, when that her whimsies made her to act that she be likely to come unto aught of harm.

And surely now you to see all the way of my heart, and to have understanding in things that do follow. And alway you shall mind that I did love her utter, and to crave alway that I be a shield unto her; though truly, there doth be, mayhap, somewhat in me that doth act to make me a little stern seeming in my love; but yet not oft so; as you do know, that have gone with me in all my tellings.

Now, we went then upon our journey; and the Maid to be somewhat before me, and offward to the side, upon my right; and to have no speech with me, but to make a good pace, and to be very dear and graceful as she went.

And now we did pass this thing of strangeness, and now that; and these I did point out to her, and made some telling concerning the same, having the memory of mine outward way, and how that I did see these things then, when that I was all in suffering of so lonesome a doubt.

And she to hark alway very intent, and to move her head nice and intelligent, to show that she heard me; and once I saw that she lookt sudden at me with a dear light in her eyes; but this to be done in a moment, and she to be again silent-seeming and in her new perversity of dignity.

And surely she did seem so utter sweet in this new way of naughtiness; but yet I did think, odd whiles, that I should like to shake her unto dear humbleness and her usual way.

And in the twelfth hour, we made halt again, and had our food and our drink; and the Maid to serve me very clever and quiet, as that I did be her Lord, and she an husht slave. And I saw that she made a constant and naughty mock upon me; and truly, as I did half think, she to need that she be in care that I not treat her sternly, as shall a slave-master, and to give her that which she did ask for so mute and impudent. But alway she did stir me mightily to have her to mine arms, and to love her very dear.

And presently, we did be again to our way; and to be yet silent; so that I scarce knew whether to have patience with Mine Own, or whether that I take her and speak seriously with her to cease this play, which did begin a little to dispirit me somewhat strangely.

And in the end I went over to her, as we did walk, and I put mine arm about her, and she to yield to me without word, and to hark very quiet to my speech of reasoning and gentle sayings, and to hide whether she did be stirred inwardly, or not; though, indeed, my spirit to know that her spirit did never be afar off from mine in all deep matters; but only this thing to be to the top, and to set somewhat between us that did be both a sweetness and a trouble.

And alway, as I talked with the Maid, I saw that she did make naughtily to act as that I did be a slave-master, and she but a chattel to me; for she to be husht before me, and neither to yield her slender body willing to mine arm, nor to resist me; but only to be still, as that she had no saying in this matter; and as that I was like to beat her at my pleasure, or to withhold my hand, all as might chance to be my desire. And this I perceived was the shaping of her actions, so that all her dumbness and her quiet obedience did be but a way to say this thing to me; and all to have come from her love of me and that she did be shaken in her nature by my manhood, and so to be but a new form of her naughtiness, that did have this change when that I whipt her.

And all this, you to perceive, that have gone with me.

And I saw that she would not cease from this perverseness, but made a dumb and naughty and hidden mock upon me, very dainty and constant, and scarce to be truly perceived, save by the inward sense. And truly, I grew something angered afresh, and to feel that she did need that she be shaken so stern that she come unto the reality that I did be her man and natural master; yet alway in love.

And surely I loosed her then, and went off a pace to her side; and

we again to go forward thiswise; yet she soon to have a greater distance between us, which she made very quiet and natural; but, indeed, I saw what she did.

Now, about the fourteenth hour of that journeying, I saw before us, in the far distance, the rock upon which did be the olden flying ship, that you shall remember.

And presently, as we came more nigh, I lookt oft to Mine Own; and I saw that she did be staring that way, and to be in wonder; but yet to say naught to me.

And soon, as we came very close, I did want that I tell her about the ship, and of mine adventuring there, and of the wonder of that olden ship, set there through Eternity.

But in the first, I hesitated, as you shall think, because of her way; but truly, my heart knew that her heart did be proper unto me; and, moreover, I should be small in my nature, if that I let any pettiness put a silence upon me; though, in verity, if that the Maid had not been inwardly loving to me, I had been that I had told her no word; and this to be very natural, whether it be of smallness or not.

And when that we were come beside the great uprising rock, I made halt, and the Maid to halt with me; and I showed her how that the thing upon the rock did be an olden flying ship from the Mighty Pyramid. And in the first, she askt no questions; but did be quiet and but to show with little noddings that she did be greatly interest.

And I to show to her how that this olden ship did be there mayhap an hundred thousand years; and to have been there, as it did seem to us (that were of that age) since the beginnings of the world; though, in verity, our two spirits did know that the beginnings of That Age, did be truly the ending of This, as you also to know.

And much I told Mine Own, and afterward concerning the two Humpt Men that did come after me; and she alway to be silent, until that I spoke of the fight; but then to come round upon me very swift, and with a dear light in her eyes; and had askt, before she did wot, whether they did hurt me.

And surely, this to have been the first thing of her olden sweet naturalness that she did say for a great while, and I to be so in delight, that I had her into mine arms, and kist her very loving, all in a moment, and she to submit with a nice gladness, and to nestle unto me, and all unwitting that she did be gone from her waywardness.

Yet, in verity, she did be a naughty Maid; for she minded in an instant that she did forget her pose unto me; and lo, her lips did be no more to search unto mine, but to be as that they did be kist only

of my will, and she to have no more live nestling unto me, but only to be quiet in mine arms. And I lookt into her face, and her lids to be down somewhat over her pretty eyes, and she did look very husht and demure; so that truly, I knew not whether to shake her or again to kiss her.

But in the end I loost her, and made then that we go forward; yet, indeed, she did rather stay awhile, to hark further concerning the olden ship and of mine adventurings; but she did then to mind that she obey as a slave shall obey; and truly, I did punish her, in that I told her no more; but went forward at a good pace, and had some natural wonder how that I deal with such a Maid, if that I spare to shake her.

And surely, I thought then again that I leave her be, and so to have her presently again to her old and natural way.

Now, in a while, I lifted the Maid into mine arms, that I carry her, as ever, through the last part of each journey, and so to have her never over-tired for the morrow. And she for a moment to resist; but instantly to give unto me, and to lie quiet in mine arms, as that she had no saying in aught that did be done, but must alway obey. And, indeed, you to see how dearly perverse she did be.

And I went on then through four hours from that time, and lookt oft upon every side, and walkt quietly; for truly we were come now into a part of the Country where I did feel that there might be near some of the Humpt Men.

But I saw nowhere anything to put me in dread.

And alway as we journeyed, there did seem a great stillness in all the Country near about; and afar off the low mutter of the Great Fire-Hills, in this place and that, and a drowse as of life and warmth about us, and everywhere the air very rich and plentiful.

And presently, when that we did be come down from that high place where did be set the rock and the olden ship, we came in among the trees that came very nigh to the shore for a great way; and oft as we did go, there were clumpings of small fire-hills that did cast fire and noise; and oft the roaring of monstrous springs a-boil; and then again the smell of the woods about us, and oft still in odd places the low near sound of a little fire-hill, that did burn, lonesome, in some clear space of the woods, in this place and that; and afterward we to be gone onward again into the dull low mutter that did be in all the air of that Country, and that did but make a seeming of silence, because that it did be so far and constant.

Now, about the eighteenth hour I to note that the noise of the Great Fire-Hills grew more loud; and I saw presently over the trees,

afar upward in the great night and gloom that did lie above, those two
mighty Fire-Hills that I did feel to make the earth tremble, in that part,
upon mine outward way. And surely I have told something of this
before; and you to remember, if that you but think a little moment.

Now, it may appear strange that I speak thiswise of seeing the
two Hills of fire; as that I had perceived them sudden. But, indeed, I
had been long abled to see them both, yet to have had no attention to
them, because that they did be a great way off, and because they did
be but two Hills of fire, in a Country that did be plentiful with such.

And, truly, I not to have said aught about them, only that our path
did take us now by their feet, and I to see them, as it were, newly; and
to have nice ease of heart to perceive how that they did be a wonder
unto the spirit and the brain for all time.

For it did be as that the earth had a constant shaking within miles
of them, and that a monstrous force of nature did be in that place.
But yet there to be no desolation around, as you should think; but in
all parts a wondrous growing of trees and great plants in abundance.

And the trees to grow upward upon the shoulders of the moun-
tain; and there to be no falling of hot rocks and ash, as you to think;
but all very sweet and wholesome, as that the mighty valley made a
chimney to the mountain, and mayhap to others, so that their waste,
if that they had such, did go free. But, indeed, you shall take no heed
of this explaining, save as an odd thinking that hath come to me, and
to be without foundation. And there to be no surety of the reason
to this; only that there did be no falling of ash in that part, as I do
know. Yet in other parts of that Country the Fire-Hills did make new
mountains of the matter that did come from them; but this not to be
alway so; and there to seem to my knowledge no cause to order why
this did not be constant; save that my guessings to be right, or naught
to be blown from some. But, indeed, I to be sure only of that which
did be plain to mine eyes. And mayhap there to be no mystery in the
thing; but a score of natural explainings, if that I did know, or had
patience to think long enough upon such.

Now when that the eighteenth hour did be proper come, we to
be anigh to the great Hills, and there to seem nowise any danger of
falling fire, so that I sought about for a place for our slumber.

And I found a cave in the side of a big rock; and the cave was dry
and comfortable, and had the mouth about a score feet above the earth.
And when that I had climbed and lookt well into the cave, I gave the
Maid an help, and had her safe into that place; and she then to prepare
the tablets and the water, the while that I brought up a boulder from

below, to set very light balanced in the mouth of the cave. And this I meant for a signal to fall, if that any creature should climb upward into the cave, while that we did sleep. And surely, you to know this plan; for I did it before, as you to have learned.

And the Maid sat near to me, and eat her tablets very quiet and with a demure naughtiness; but yet to be also in wonder, and to gaze outward at the Great Fire-Hills, and to be in awe, as I did know.

And I put my half-anger and my play from me, and told her of mine outward journeying, and how I did go by these same mighty Fire-Hills, that did seem as mighty torches to light me in my search, and to have held a new strangeness and wonder over my path.

And she still to be silent, but yet to look at me twice or thrice with a very dear and loving way; though she did hide her eyes in a moment, when that she saw that I perceived her.

And soon the Maid spread the cloak for our sleep; and while that she did this, I lookt well about for any creature that might be anigh; and I had an especial thought unto the Humpt Men; but, indeed, there was naught living, unto my sight, and nowhere did I see anything to put me in fear for our lives.

And truly I had a great viewing from that place; for we did be in an upward rock that stood in a high part, and the cave to be twenty good feet aloft, as I have told; so that all made to set us in a lofty place.

And the cave to look toward the two Mountains that did rise upward no more than twelve good miles off from us, as I do think; and the Country between to be somewise as a mighty park; for it was spread much about the feet of the Great Fire-Hills, and did be bare in this place and that, as that rock did make the earth naked there, or the falling of some later fire to have wrought thus. And between the bare parts, there went strange and romantic woods, seen mistily; and in parts the gleaming of waters, as that hot lakes did be half shown among the broken forests.

And presently the Land did go upward with a monstrous sweep, and was then in great terraces in the height, and trees to grow very plentiful upon the mountains, in sundry parts; and so those two Mighty Hills to go upward to meet the everlasting night; and presently to show strange uplands that did be seen very wondrous and queer in the light that did glow from the vast glowing of the fire that did be a crown upon the hills, that did seem in verity to be that they burned halfway between that known world, and the lost olden world, that was mayhap two hundred great miles above in the everlasting night and eternity of darkness.

And I lookt upward for awhile, and was much held by the mighty uplands that did be on high; yet did lie utter far below the burning crests of the Mountains, and showed vague and sombre and dreadful seeming, because that they did be so lost upward, and to have the mystery of the red shining and of the shadows upon them, and to seem to slope far under the great fires, but yet to be a place where no life should ever come, because that they did be so monstrous a way upward beyond the great shoulders of the Hills, the which did be themselves a huge way up. And truly, I should give you somewhat of the affecting of those grim and unknown Uplands, if that I said they did seem to my fancy to be a place where a sorrowful thing might wander lost forever. But why I to think this thing, how shall I say; and do tell it to you, only because that it doth seem to hold in the thought the grimness and utter desolation of those high and lonesome lands.

And by this, I was done looking, and turned me about, and so did find that Mine Own did stand silent, and waited that I come to my slumber. And surely, I lookt at her; but she did have her lids something downward, when that she saw me turn; and so in the end, I said naught, but went to my sleep, and had the Diskos very handy, as ever, beside me.

And I then to know that Mine Own did lie down beside me, to my back, as alway; and this to gladden me, as you shall think; for I perceived afresh how thin did be the crust of her naughtiness; and I to be alway stirred and touched in the heart by her loving naturalness, that did need alway that she be near to me, save when she did play this naughtiness upon me along the way.

And I saw that she had no mind to be perverse whilst that I did slumber; but must now be nigh unto me, and quietly loving; though nowise truly ceased from her naughty acting that I did be as an hard slave master, because that I had whipt her; yet she to have somewhat a truce with me, as my heart did know. But, indeed, she not to kiss me good-night upon the mouth, in her dear usual and sober fashion.

And surely I did lie awhile, and pondered upon the Maid and upon all her ways; and I perceived that she kist me not, only because that she did not be able to break utter from her perverseness, that did come from the stirring of her nature. And truly, I did love her, and was half minded that I turn about to her, and take her a moment into mine arms; but yet to abide from this, because that I was set that I wait awhile, and to bring her to me thiswise, mayhaps.

And presently, I knew that the Maid kist mine armour, very quiet and shy, because that she must kiss me; yet to be intent that I have no

knowledge of this pretty act. But, indeed, I did know in all my being, and did be newly tender unto her; yet to say naught, and to wait.

And thus I knew presently that her breathing did go easy, so that I perceived that she was all content and gone over unto slumber, somewise as a little child that doth be weary, and doth sleep without care, and with happy assurance.

And, in verity, did a man ever to have so sweet and gentle a maid, that did be in the same time so troublous and perverse.

And I to lie yet awhile, and to note the constant tremble and shake of the rock that did be under us; and this to be alway thus as I did lie, and to be the more plain, because that I did be quiet in thought. And this, as I conceived, did come from the earth-shaking that was made by the inward fire of the world, the which did make a vague trouble in all that part of the Land.

And then in a little, I was gone over into sleep, and waked not for seven good hours; and then to hear the fizzing of the water, very brisk and cheerful, and so to have mine eyes open in a moment, and to know by my time-keeper or dial, that was somewhat like to a watch of this age, that I had slumbered through seven good hours. But this to be learned after that I had lookt to see whether Mine Own did be well, and whether that the boulder did balance in the mouth-part of the cave.

And surely, there did be nothing in harm; for the boulder was there, as I did put it; and the Maid a little off from me, and did make ready the water and the tablets, that we eat before our journeying.

And I rose then, and in the same moment I did know that my mouth had been kist whilst that I slept; and the knowing to come to me vague, as that I had been kist in my dreams.

And I lookt over toward the Maid; but she to have her lids something down upon her eyes, and to seem very demure; so that I saw her naughtiness was come again upon her. Yet, truly, I could not bear that I not to have her into mine arms; for, indeed, her perverseness did seem as that she did the more tempt me unto her. And thus I came to her in a moment; but she neither to resist me, nor to give herself unto me; but only to be still in mine arms, and to do no more than submit very quiet.

And because of this, I loost her unkist, and was silent, and a little to be angered, even whilst that my heart perceived the way of the working of her heart. Yet truly I ached now that she come back to her dear natural fashion.

And I eat my tablets and drank some of the water; and the Maid to do likewise.

And afterward, I lookt well from the mouth of the cave; but did nowhere see aught to put me in trouble for our safety, though, truly, as presently I saw, there went an herd of strange creatures afar off in the Northwestward part, which did be that way of the Country, beyond the feet of the mountains, toward the In-Land.

Now, when that I was something assured of the safeness of the way, I gat the Diskos to my hip, and the Maid to have the scrip and the pouch ready to my back, and her bundle to her hand; and so all to be ready.

And I went downward from the cave, when that I was girt, and gave aid to Mine Own; and so to be soon upon the journey.

And surely, as we went onward, and I to look about me with different-seeing eyes from my looking on mine outward way, I to see how wondrous this part of the Land did be; and how that it did be truly like a great and wondrous park, that did be made of the skill and labour of godlike things; and truly this to show my feeling, as I lookt all-ways.

And all that part did be bred of the inward forces of the world, and did be burned clear in this place, and upheaved in that, and made to an hot lake in another part; and odd whiles there to go a great steam fountain, that did whistle a lonely song forever. And anon there to be a small wood, and again a wood; and oft the quietness of great and strange trees, that did stand alone. And here, and in that part, a little fire-hill, that did be surely no greater than an house, and we to pass seven of these in but three hours. And two to glow very steadfast, and to make no vigour of burning; but the five others did burn very strong, and sent out a smoke and ash, and made a small desolation all about them; and of these five, there did be one that cast stones oft and again, so that they went upward with a strange loud noise, and fell in this place and that, all about, so that we came downward more nigh to the shore, that we be a good way off.

And here, as I do mind, there was a strangeness, in that there did be many trees that had stones set in the branches; and this to be plainly the work of the little fire-hill; and I to think it but something new come, else surely there had been no trees within all that space that it did throw; but yet, mayhap, I am wrong in this; for all things did seem that they grew very easy in that Country; and indeed this to be for surprise to me, only that I saw it with mine own eyes, as we do say.

And alway as we did go, there were signs of inward life and forces; so that we but to stand quiet to feel that the earth did tremble gently in many parts.

And presently there sounded for a great while a low and dull

booming sound; and this we found to be from a place amid certain great rocks toward the mountains; for there came thence a mighty up-spouting of boiling water, that went so high as an hundred feet, and oft to be thrice so high, and belched a great steam; and there went up in the jet of the water, a great rock, that was so big as an house, and did dance and play in the might of the water, as that it had been no more than a thing very light and easy. And when that the water fell, as it did oft, the rock to go downward with the dull booming that we did hear.

And I minded how that I had heard the booming upon mine outward way; but had been then something more to the shore, so that it had been less plain to mine ears, as you shall suppose; neither had it been then to my sight, as now it did be to us because that we were come mayhap the half of a mile more toward the In-Land of the Country.

And truly, we lookt awhile at this huge great fountain and up-boiling, and came nearer unto it; but yet to be a large space off, because of the way that it did throw out a spattering of small stones odd whiles. And surely the thing did cough and roar in the deep earth, and anon to gruntle gently and to sob and gurgle; and lo! to come forth in a moment with a bellow, very hollow and strange, and the great rock to go spinning upward, and all a-shine in the light from the volcanoes, and was so round as a monstrous ball, and polished by the fret of the waters, so that I saw it had surely danced in the great jet through a weary time.

And anon the jet to cease and to go downward with a great soughing and thundering of waters, and the dancing rock to fall downward from that height which did show very huge, now that we did be come so near. And the rock surely to fall backward into some deep pit, whence came the waters, and as it fell, there was again the dull booming. But why the rock brake not, I could not perceive, save that it did alway fall into a boiling up of waters, and had no hurt from the rock of the place whence it was come.

And the Maid and I both to have stood a while, that we stare at this thing; for it did be more strange than I have made you to know; but now I did make to our journey again, and did think the Maid followed; but lo! in a moment, when that I lookt, she was to my back, and went toward the great boiling fountain. Then I stopt very swift, and called to her; but she did take no heed of me, and went onward very naughty, unto the danger of the great boil of the Jet, and the constant flying out of the stones, that you do know.

Now, even as I stood and lookt, the Maid drew nigh to the place

where the water did thunder; and the Jet in that moment to bellow, so that I knew it came upward again. And I ran then after the Maid, and she to see me, and began likewise to run from me toward the monstrous fountain; and surely I did think that I had done well if that I had whipt or beat her proper before this time; for truly it did be as that her naughtiness had gone nigh unto somewhat that did be near to a wayward madness, so that as I did perceive all her nature did surely work in her toward some deed that should be for regret; and this to come, because that she did be something pusht from her dear balance by her loving, and by the acting of my manhood upon her, so that her nature both to be in rebellion against me and to need me, and all in the same time. And this-way, she to be in an inward turmoil, and to be ready foolishly that she put in danger her beloved life, if only thereby she to make me something adrift, and in the same moment to have some ease of her perverseness. And, in verity, you to know all this, because that I have shown the working of her heart to you before this time.

Now, I caught the Maid among the great rocks, which did stand all about; and before her there did be a monstrous pit whence came the upbursting of the water; and the water to go upward before our faces in a mighty column, so that it did be as that a sea shot up on end, into a pillar of living water, and went upward forever, as it did seem in that moment. And how we should be saved, I knew not, for the water did be as that it overhung us, and should come down upon us and smother us in one moment, forever. And the roar was in our ears and shook all the air of that place with sound, as of an harsh and dreadful thunder; and there was a scalding of beaten water, as fine as an haze, all about us.

And I had the Maid in one instant into mine arms, and I ran very swift, with a fierce running, that I have her away speedy, and so made forlorn trial that I save her life. And lo! as I went from under that huge and dreadful overhang of the great waters, there came downward from the height a great stone that had been cast by the Jet, and it burst upon the rock to my back, and certain of the flinders did strike and ring upon mine armour, and made me to stagger as I ran. But I held the Maid crowded safe against my breast, and she did not be hurt; and truly I was yet able to run, and did save Mine Own, and brought her out from under that grim Spouting.

And I put the Maid down then to her feet; and she not to know how near that she had given us to death, neither of the way that the fragments did strike me; for she laughed very naughty and gleeful. But

truly I laughed not; for my heart had been nigh husht with terror for her; so that I did be yet sick in my spirit, and mayhap also something shaken by the blows that I gat from the broken stone.

And, in verity, I to have meant that I flog her, very sharp, if that there be no other way that I might bring her to reason; for, in surety, as you to see, she to be acting so wild as a child, and so unreasoning as only a Maid-in-love; and I to know that she did have to be brought back from this way of spirit, even though I have to hurt her pretty body, that I bring her again to her dear natural wiseness.

Yet, indeed, I could not whip her then, because that she did laugh so joyous, though with a naughty heart, and did look so wondrous dainty, so that even her defyings did but seem that which my heart desired. And you, mayhap, to have been something likewise in the love-days. Yet I pled and reasoned with her to be a wise maid; but, indeed, she only to make a gleeful mock of all that I did say.

Now I went forward again, for I was not harmed by the stone, only that I did be shaked, as you shall think. And the Maid to go offward from me, and to sing, and did oft dance naughtily as she went. But truly, I did be silent with her, for I was but human, and did lack that she come to mine arms, and love me, because that I had pluckt her safe from that place. And, indeed, this to be but a natural desiring; and you to have understanding with me, and to know that you also to have this lack and need, if that you to have done aught for love of your maid, and she to deny you a word of loving tenderness.

Yet, in verity, I to be even then able to perceive with mine inward senses, how that the Maid did have a wondrous up-pouring of love for me, but yet did be so perverse, and the more so, mayhap, because that her love did so urge her unto loving admittings that I did be her Man. And she, maybe, to have meant that she be the more humble presently, but yet to go naughtily awhile more, and not, indeed, to have had the power within her at that time, to have come unto me, and cast off her waywardness, and askt that she be in mine arms, as all my heart did desire.

And so, as I have told, I went silently, and mayhap with a little dullness, that did be part of anger and part of hurt and part of that same strange love-foolishness from which the Maid did suffer. And truly, this doth be very contrary-seeming, only that you have seen my heart; and all indeed the more human, that it doth be so contrariwise to the brain-reason; and all to be desired, else did a man be no better than an ant or a weariful machine.

And this to be truth and wholesomeness as you shall perceive, if that you look deep enough, and do modify Reason with heart-un-

derstanding; for, in verity, how shall that which we call Reason, bring any to the full and the great knowledge. And this doth be a power of holy things, and doth be a child that is born of Love and Reason, and in the one to hold the two, and to know all things is the gift of this power; so that no man may walk truly that hath only the first, neither any man do utter wise that hath only the second.

And surely, I to cease from these thoughts, and to my tellings; and you to your harkings and dear sympathy.

Now, when the sixth hour did be come, we made a halt and eat and drank, and afterward went onward again, and so came presently clear of the two monstrous fire-hills; and their great noise to be presently to our rear, and likewise that quiet country that did be round their feet, and did seem so utter husht and strange and doubly so, because of the upward noise of the mountains, and because of the slow and subtle earth-shaking that did be so constant, and because of all those things that I have told.

Now, when we had made halt, the Maid had done her hair very uncomely upon her head, and had lookt slyly to see whether I did note; but truly, I took no heed; so that in the end she had it again in a pretty fashion, and did sing naughtily and with an heart of mischief, as she did shape it loose and wondrous nice about her head.

And I still to have no word for her; neither to show that I did watch her with love and somewise a quaint pleasure of her perverseness, even whilst that I did strive by silence and an aloofness that I bring her to my side, as she did be in the first days; for truly I did ache that she be near unto me, and to cease from her waywardness that did put a distance of spirit between us, as you to perceive.

And so we did go forward again, as I have told, and the Maid did strive that she make me to give attention to her naughtiness, for she did walk alway offward from me, and did sing aloud, and truly they did be songs strange unto me, but yet to be of love, and much as the songs of this Age; for, truly, there doth be but one song upon all the earth, and she but to sing it in diverse ways.

And she did oft to make little glancing toward me, and did pout very pretty; and in a moment come something toward me, as that she did be humble, and would be forgiven; but all to be in a naughty mockery; so that, in verity, I lookt not at her, save odd whiles; but did go forward alway,and made as that I had no heed of her doings.

And surely this did presently to stir her to a new defying and to a pretty anger; for she did sing other songs of impudence, that she did fit very clever about me; and this way to have a constant impertinence.

And so we did go, and I never to speak with the Maid, but to wonder when that she cease, or how long it should be ere that I did run swift to her and have her into mine arms, that I shake her and kiss her, all as my heart did desire.

And when that the twelfth hour did be come, we made halt again and eat and drank; and the Maid to serve me very intent, and hand me the water, the while that she went down upon her knee, as a slave; but when I would have laughed gently at her mockings, and taken her into mine arms, she went from me very sudden and cold, and was afterward silent and did sit apart from me.

Now I also did be silent, and in the first because that I was a little pained, and also because that I did be new touched with the love-foolishness that did trouble Mine Own.

But afterward, I ceased from these feelings, and did be intent to another matter; for it did seem to my spirit that there was some danger anigh to us; and I had a thought of the Humpt Men, and lookt well about, and did beckon the Maid to come nigh, because that the trees did be plentiful thereabout, to hide any creature.

But Mine Own came not over to me, so that I loosed the Diskos from mine hip, and went that I be nigh to her. And she made that she saw me not; but did set the gear together, and had it presently a-ready for the journey, the while that I did look all-ways among the trees; but indeed I saw naught.

And when that I had the gear upon me, and the Maid her bundle, we went forward again; and I to be very wary, and bid the Maid keep close to my side; but indeed, she would not obey, and went offward among the trees, so that I was all an-haunted with dread for her, and ran and caught her, and talkt wisely with her; but indeed she did not hark to me; but did run off in the moment that I loost her.

And I caught her again, and I took one of the straps from around the Scrip and the Pouch, and set it about her pretty waist, and the end I held in my hand, and so had her to obey me in this thing which did be needful to her safety.

And the Maid to go with me very husht for two great hours, and I alway to look well about. And in the end of that time, the Maid did begin to sing impudently, and I did ask her that she be a quiet maid, lest that she bring danger upon us; but she to be the more impudent

And lo! as I did strive that I look all-ways, lest any harm did come upon us, and in the same moment to reason Mine Own from her pretty folly, she did grow very husht, so that I lookt round upon her in an instant. And truly, she had cut the strap with her belt-knife, and did

run away very swift among the trees. And surely my heart did slow a little in my breast, because that there did seem something a-move in the dark of the shadows, where the trees did grow thick, and the Maid did run that way in her foolishness and waywardness.

And I ran hard after the Maid, and did call her, not over-loud, lest I bring somewhat upon her; but she to have no heed, and to run very light and swift, so that I caught her not for the half of a minute, as it might be; for she was gone ahead, and I did be a little cumbered with mine armour.

And lo! when I caught her, I shook her, and pointed inward among the trees, for it did seem even then to me that something moved there; but she to struggle in my hand a moment, and afterward to be still, and to ask with an insolence and a defiance whether that I did mean to flog my chattel, the which she did call herself in her naughtiness.

And, in verity, ere I did know, she had twist from me, and did run with a true wickedness straight toward that place where somewhat had seemed to be a-move. And I ran then with all my strength, and with a fearful and an anxious heart. And because I put all my strength to the matter, I caught the Maid in a moment, ere she did be gone any way; and she again to fight to be gone from me. But I took her into mine arms, very strong, and I ran outward from that place where the trees made a darkness.

And surely, when I was come again to where the trees did be more spare, I saw that I was come nigh to that river which I crost on the raft, as you shall mind; and truly I did be glad, and to feel safe in a moment. Yet I was firm now to my purpose; for I set the Maid to the earth upon her feet, and kept my hold very sure upon her; for I did mean that I whip her, before that her love-foolishness bring her needless unto death.

And I took the belt from her pretty waist, for it did be but a light strap, and I whipt her very sharp over her shoulders with the belt. And, truly, she did make to nestle unto me in a moment, as that other time when that I whipt her; but I stayed her from this, and I set the belt thrice more across her shoulders, very sharp, so that she to learn wisdom at once, and I to be free for ever of this need to pain her, which did hurt me very strange.

And the Maid to stand very quiet, now that I did keep her from coming unto me; and her head did be something bent, so that I knew not whether I did mayhap have flogged her over-hard; for I did be something lacking in knowledge whether that a maid be very easy hurt.

And I stooped and lookt into her face; and lo! she did be smiling

naughtily, and kist me in a moment very saucy upon the mouth, ere I did be aware; and afterward, she laughed and made try to make a bitter mock upon me, and askt when that I should be pleased to cease from whipping my chattel; for that then she should run away immediately into the wood, and to trust the Humpt Men that they protect her from me.

And surely, I lookt at her very grave; for I perceived that she did not truly jest, but made to anger me, and did be half in a strange anger herself, and something adrift; for she had not been whipt enough, but only to stir her rebellion utterly. And I saw that if she be not set right then, ere she leave my hand, she to be like to have some new foolishness that should take her unto her death, even as she had come overnear already, as you to know. And this to be because that her nature did be stirred so that her natural wiseness was all overset, and she to be that she do aught of unwisdom that should come to her, because of her pretty love-foolishness, which did now be made the more strong, by reason of the half-rising of her anger.

And this way, as I have known, I perceived that, for her dear sake, I should not let my lovingness weaken me in that moment. And, in verity, I shifted my hand and loosed the fastenings of her garment, so that her pretty shoulders did be bared. And her face to change sudden, and she lookt up at me an instant, with a little gasp; so that I knew she did be all unbroken, as was mine intent; but she did not yet have learned deeply in her heart, all that I was minded that she to learn; for even in that moment, she made a sound that showed she did try to mock me; but truly, she did not know in that instant whether to mock or to weep; though she did try to suppose that she had yet an heart for mockery.

And I set the belt thrice across her pretty shoulders, where they did be bared; and surely the blows did be very stern and sharp. And lo! in one moment Mine Own broke into an utter weeping, so that I took her instant into mine arms, and did hold her strong and gentle against mine armour. And she to be as a child in mine arms, and did sob very strange and bitter, as that she did be all undone in the heart.

And presently she did be quiet in mine arms; though I to feel how she did yet tremble; and she did cling tight unto me, and her face to be against mine armour.

And afterward, when that she had ceased to tremble, I kist her, and surely her mouth did be very humble, and her lids to be downward, and she to be something pale. And she then to be awhile more in mine arms, very quiet; and so to come unto her dear self. And lo! presently,

she to want to kiss me of her own accord; and she put up her lips, very sweet and as a loving maid, that I kiss her. And surely I kist her, with an humble and a masterful love; and a strange pain to be about my heart, as you shall suppose; but yet my heart and my reason both to approve mine action; and the Maid to be but the more mine own, and to have come again to her dear natural wisdom.

Yet, as you shall know, there to be for a long while a strange and mixed pain, in my bosom, both dreadful and tender, because that I had been so stern with Mine Own Maid; so that even while that my heart and my reason did approve me, my heart to make somewhat of reproach. And this to have been someways of foolishness; but yet human of our Nature, and an wholesome trouble to the spirit, if that this troubling be not allowed to shape our actions to any harmful weakness.

Now, in a while, the Maid did come to composedness, and to be very gentle and sweetly natural. And she made presently that she would have me to loose her; and afterward, she turned her back to me, even as a dear child, that I fasten her garment again upon the shoulders. And she did be both shy and glad, and humble, and in dainty pride of submission, and utter Mine Own.

And surely, as I did this thing for her, I perceived that she lookt with a great shyness at the belt which did be yet in my hand. And when that I had made an end of fastening her garment, she did nestle unto me for a while, and afterward stood away and made shyly to show me that I put her belt again about her pretty waist. And I saw that she did be somewhat a-lack yet that she touch the belt, because that I had whipt her with it.

And truly you to perceive how her heart did be in this matter; but if you not to know, then how shall I to tell you; and do but bid you ask your own maid; though, in verity, she to be like that she but laugh at you, and leave you so wise as you be now; for the way of the heart of a maid doth be most hid to the maid, and she but to know the desire, and to lack the ending. But truly she doth know when that a man shall set the truth of her heart before her.

Now, when I had buckled the belt very nice again about Mine Own, we went backward a space, until that we found the bundle, which she had dropt, when that she ran off from me. And I saw also the portion of the strap, which she cut; and so all to be found.

And we went then at a good speed toward the river; for I was still minded regarding the seeming of movement which there had been among the trees; and very wishful that we have a raft made with haste,

so that we might come to the little island, where I did sleep before, upon the outward way, as you shall remember. And I thought to have our slumber again in that place, and to make that day's journeying something short, because that the island was near, and a good and safe place for our sleeping.

And I told the Maid concerning the island; and she to be in great delight and interest, because that it did be one of those halts of mine outward going, and did be all eager as a child, when that I said we should truly have need of a raft to come to the island.

And we came downward to the shore of the river, and, indeed, there did be those two same trees, that had been my raft, there upon the shore of that place. And I showed these to Mine Own, and truly she did nigh to weep upon them, because of her dear emotions and love, and did cut a small branch therefrom, with her belt-knife, and put the branch where she did put the piece of bark; and this to be for a remembrance and an after-delight and pondering.

Now we lookt well in all parts, that we find some other small tree that should be fallen; and the Maid did climb a rock that did be near, with a flat top, so that she might search out around.

And presently she cried out to me that there did be a tree to our purpose, and but an hundred paces away; and she to go with me to show me, and to aid, if need be; but, indeed I carried the tree very easy, and had it with the others; and afterward, we went about again for branches, and these I cut from live trees, using the Diskos with care and wiseness.

And with these branches to be for cross-pieces, and our belts and the straps for binders, I set the trees together into a raft, and made it pretty good for our need, and so that no monstrous thing in the river should have chance to snap upward between the trees at my dear One.

And when the raft was done, I gat it to the water, and the Maid did lend her strength; for the thing was heavy, as you shall think. And when this was done, I pushed a sharp branch downward into the shore, and I hookt a branch of the raft about this mooring, and so did be nigh ready for the voyage.

But first I did need a pole to push the raft, and did wonder now where the other did be gone, that I cut upon the outward way; for I had set the pole with the two trees, as I did mind, having some vague thought that mayhap I should live to come that way again.

And I had a little strange unease that the pole did be gone; but scarce to know that I did be troubled, yet to set me to a new haste. And I bid the Maid put the scrip and the pouch and her bundle secure

upon the raft; and in that time I lookt well about for a sapling tree that should do my purpose. And I saw that there grew an odd one a little to the side of the flat-topt rock that the Maid had lookt from; and whilst that I cut it, the Maid did come to watch, and made pretty chatter in the time that I trimmed the branches away.

And lo! whilst that I did be part divided in mine attention between her dear talk and my work and an haste that did be born of that little unease that was come upon me, my spirit to seem to be aware that there came a danger anigh to us; and the Maid to have this same knowing; for she ceased her speech, and lookt at me with somewhat of trouble. And lo! in that moment, as I balanced the pole in my hands, there came the noise of a sudden bounding to our backward part, where the trees did grow something anigh.

And I turned, instant, and lookt; and behold! there did be upon us an Humpt Man, very lumpish and mighty; and he stretched out his hands, and ran at me. And I had no time to the Diskos, which did be upon the earth to my feet; and I smote the Humpt Man with the point of the pole that did be in my hands, and the point took him very strong and horrid in the breast, and entered in, so that the Humpt Man gave out a strange howling, that did be half seeming of an animal and half of an human. And he clutched at the pole that did so hurt him, and I stoopt very swift for the Diskos, and had it in a moment. And the Humpt Man tore the pole out of his breast, and in the same instant I ript him from the head downward, so that he did be nigh in two halves; for I had no mercy in mine act, even though my heart did be something sorry.

Now, even as the man died, there did be a sound of running in the wood before me; and lo! I turned very speedy to the Maid, and she was there to my back, and had her belt-knife drawn in her hand; for she had it in her bosom, where she had put it when that I took her belt for the raft.

And I caught the Maid about the waist with my left arm, and was come with her to the top of the rock in two great houndings. And I set her there upon the rock, and turned again to the way I came and swung the Diskos free; for indeed, I had seen that there did come a number of the Humpt Men among the trees.

And there came running from the wood, mayhaps a great score of the Humpt Men; so that it did seem to me that we did be going to die; for how should one stand against so many, and they so quick and strong, as you shall mind.

Yet, in verity, I had no despair; but did be mixt in the heart with

a great fear for Mine Own, and a strange and exulting gladness that I should do that day some deed for Mine Own Maid; and truly this to be the pomp of love and the heart-cry of the barbarian, as you shall say. And this maybe; but truly I did be proper human, and to make no excuse because that I was natural; neither have I hid anywheres aught that I did think and feel.

And whether that you approve or not, if that you condemn me, you to condemn all Humanity, and to have vain words and vain regrettings; for these things that be named for faults, do but be the complement of our virtues, and if that you slay the first, you may chance to wither the last; for now I speak of things as they be now, and as they did be then; and nowise of lovely ideals that do live chief in the mind, and so much in mine as any; as you to know, if that you have gone with me all along my way.

And surely, I must cease from my thinkings, and go forward with my telling; for the Humpt Men did come forward at a wondrous quick run, and did swarm upward on to the rock, as that they did be panthers; and they made no outcry; but came silent to the killing; and I saw that they did be something smaller than he that I had but then slain. And, in verity, I did be all knit in that moment with speed and cleverness; for I split the heads of three, with but quick turns of my wrist, as I did wield the Diskos. And I kicked the face of another, in the same time, with my metal boot, so that he died; for there did be all my strength and all my skill working then for our salvation.

Now all this to have been done in but a few beats of the heart, as I might say; and these men to have been in the front of the attacking. Yet there did be no space to have breath; for there leaped three more of the Men upon the rock; and one smote me with a great piece of rock that he carried, so that mine armour did seem as that it crackt, and I to be driven backward upon the Maid; yet had slain one of the Humpt Men, even in that moment.

And surely, my dear One caught me in her arms, behind, and steadied me, so that I fell not; and I slew the Humpt Man with the rock, even in that moment whilst Mine Own held me, as he came again to strike me. And I then to be firm again upon my feet, and did spring at the third of the Humpt Men; and surely there was no room that he should be able to avoid me, even did that be his intent; and he came at me with a great leap. And I stood strong, looking clearly to my work; and I swung the Diskos with both my hands, and the blow took the Humpt Man in the middle part, and split him, whilst that he did be yet leaping. And in that instant there reached over the

edge of the rock, two of the Humpt Men, and gat me by the feet; so that I was pulled sudden to my back very hard and bitter; and this to be done, even whilst that the body of the Humpt Man did be yet in the air. And the body came forward over me, and did be utter dead already, and fell down upon the rock beyond me, and rolled horridly and went over the edge of the rock.

And I did be all shaken and something bemused by the hardness of my fall; and the hands of the two Humpt Men pluckt me sharp to the edge of the rock, the while that I did strike vaguely to wound them; but did only chip the rock, and fortunate that I harmed not the weapon.

And lo! in the moment that they had been like to have me downward to the earth into their midst, I to make a good stroke, for I cut the shoulder of one very dreadful, so that he loosed me; and immediately, I kicked very fierce with my freed foot, and surely I nigh crushed the hand of that other with my metal boot; and he likewise to cease from dragging upon me.

And immediately, I knew that Mine Own did be helping me that I get instant to my feet again; for I was yet something dazed.

And there came then a rush of the Humpt Men up the rock; and truly it did be a glad thing for our lives that they might come up only upon but one side; for the other sides did be utter steep and smooth worn; and this to have been unto our saving, as you shall think.

And I stood up to the rush of the Humpt Men, and did smite hard at them, with a quick circling of the Diskos, so that the great weapon did glow and roar. And they gave back from the blaze and the sound of the Diskos; and surely then I ran in upon them, whilst that they did be something bewildered; and I gat the foremost man full upon the head, so that he did be dead before he did know what thing happened. Yet, in verity, this did be a dread moment to me; for the Humpt Men leaped in at me upon every side in an instant of time; and I did be struck upon my head-piece and upon my back and breast with the stones that certain of them did carry, so that I rockt as I stood, and did near to swoon, and mine armour to be all dint and bent upon me, and I truly to seem that I had come to the time of my dying.

And lo! in that moment of time, there did come to my dazed sense a low and bitter cry of anguish from the Maid; and this to set all my life aglow in me. And, in verity, there went a strange greyness of fury before mine eyes, and I then to fight as I did never fight before; and I did smite as it did seem forever. And the greyness did ease from mine eyes, and the Maid did have her arms about me as I stood, and the dead Men to lie heapt upon the rock, and Mine Own to steady

me, for I did be near slain and the blood did go from me, and mine armour was all broke upon me by the smitings of the sharp stones.

And I lookt something slowly upon Mine Own; and she to know that I would ask whether that she did be harmed anywise; and she to be very brave with me, and to tell me that she did be well; and she to be all slain in the heart, because that I did be so hurt; but truly I had fought a good fight, and did lack only to know that she come to no harm.

Now my wits did come back into me very soon; but I did be utter weak, and scarce to stand; so that I did mind only that I get Mine Own safe unto the raft, and to put off then from the shore.

And I walkt slow to the edge of the rock, and lookt well about, that I learn whether the Humpt Men did be all gone away; and the Maid did steady me.

And lo! there came up in that instant the last of the Humpt Men, and they were five and did creep very stealthy, that they have me in surprise. And I loost from the Maid, for I saw that I must come upon them whilst that I had any strength left in my body; and they now to leap upward unto me, so that I gat the first upon the head, and he to go backward dead; but truly I did be more weak than I knew; for I swayed upon the edge of the rock, and sudden I went downward to the earth; and did be there upon my knees, and my back to the rock.

And, in verity, the Humpt Men did come in upon me very swift; yet did they give back from the Diskos, which I swung to and fro, so speedy as I might, for my weakness, which did be so utter that I could nowise come to my feet to stand.

And Mine Own came down swiftly from the rock, and ran past the Humpt Men, and I to make that I shout to her to go to the raft; but truly I had no voice in my body, and did be dumb and weak, and did know that I should be gone forever from Mine Own in a little moment, and she to have none to protect her, neither to know the way of our journey, save by reason.

And behold! Mine Own did shout to the Humpt Men, and I perceived that she made to draw them after her; for she ran to and fore and did shout continually. But, indeed, the Humpt Men had no heed of her; but did make alway to come at me; and surely, in that moment, one of the Humpt Men reached me, and smote me so shrewd that sure he nigh crackt his monstrous hand upon mine armour, and did drive me backward upon the rock, and to make me bleed afresh, so that I was all in a daze and near swooned away. And the Humpt Man caught at the Diskos; yet, in verity, he loost it on the instant, for it did

burn and shake him very sore; and immediately, he smote me again, and so made to end me.

And lo! in that moment, the Maid ran right in among the Humpt Men, and she struck the man that strove with me, and drove her belt-knife once and again through his arm, very savage and determined. And surely, the man turned upon her, and he caught her by her garments, and he ript her two garments utter from her, so that they came away and she did be free. And behold, mine utter despair for her did give me a new strength, so that I shouted to her that she run instant to the raft; and I cut the Humpt Man in twain, and did fall back then into a part swoon against the rock. And lo! the Maid ran out from the Humpt Men; but they neither to know whether that they follow her or that they come in upon me; and as they did pause, she to call to them, and to try that she tempt them from me toward the wood; for she had no thought of her life, but only that she free me and save me; and I too weak even to have power to command her to the raft; and she, truly, to have no heed to such command, even did I thus to call again. And there I did be, half-gone out from this life, and lookt at her with eyes that did scarce wot, save as in a dream.

And lo! the Humpt Men ceased sudden that they heed her; and the three that did be left came very sly unto me, and with slowness and cunning; for they wotted not whether I did be dead, or but a-wait for them. And the Maid perceived that they came not after her; and she let out a great cry that did be distant-seeming in my dulled ears, and came back, naked, and running very swift. And she ran by me as death should run, white and silent and her face set unto despair, and her eyes utter intent. And she struck her belt-knife into the shoulder of the near Humpt Man; and the Man howled and turned, and she did leap to the side, and the Humpt Man ran at her. But lo! she leaped again this way and that, and utter silent, and so quick as a light doth seem to dance all ways in a moment. And the two other Men did join with the first, that they catch her; and behold! she went about, and did run right away among the trees, and the three Men did come after her, running very lumbersome, yet with a great speed.

And the Maid had the knife in her hand, and I knew that she did mean to slay herself presently, when that she could run no more; and in that moment it seemed that my heart burst; for that I should never more see Mine Own Maid forever. And there came some power of movement into me, and I came forward from the rock and fell over upon my face. And I gat again to my knees, and began that I creep after the Maid, and I did shout in whispers, for my voice had no more

power to call. And the Maid went from my sight among the trees, as a far white figure, that did run very swift, and was presently lost utter to my sight; and the Humpt Men did go after; yet even in my weakness, I perceived that two did go something clumsy, as that they had been hurt in the fight; and they to be the rearward of the chasing; but he that the Maid did cut with the knife was to the fore, and did run very strong; and surely they were all gone inward of the trees with a dreadful speed, and were lost from me. And the world did become sudden an Emptyness and a great Horror, and there was no sound in all the Earth, as it did seem. And I knew that I was come to my feet, and did run toward the trees, and the Diskos did trail from mine arm by the hold-buckle; and the ground did be as that it moved and shifted under me, and I not to feel where I trod, but did only peer desperate and lost among the trees; and, as I to know now, I heard my voice calling strangely; and afterward there was a thundering in mine ears, and I came downward upon my face.

And I did know presently that I was alive, and there to be some dreadful terror at my heart; and surely I did remember and sickened and gat my head from the ground. And I lookt among the trees; but there did be nothing, and everywhere there did be a strange silence and a dimness of unreal seemings. And I knew that Mine Own was gone from me, and had surely died. And the earth did be all stained about me with my blood, and I did be utter glad; for I to need death.

And I swooned again and was lost to my pain; but did live presently to know.

And there was a little strength come into me, and I gat my head up somewhat from the ground, and did peer among the trees; and my head did be too heavy, and my face came against the earth once more. And because that I could not hold up my head, I rolled my head a little, until that my cheek did be to the ground, and I to look thiswise, so well as I might; but there did be nothing; and afterward, I rolled my head again to the other cheek, and so to stare very weak and desperate, and not abled to look proper to my front. And lo! there went something among the trees, and did show white in the gloom of the wood; and did come through the trees. And I not to believe in the first that I did truly see aught; and sudden I to know that I saw somewhat. And behold! my heart did bound in me, so that all my body did waken; for I knew that Mine Own Maid did run slow and staggering toward me, through the wood. And I did be now upon my knees and upon my hands, and did begin again to creep and to bleed; and did make little callings to Mine Own, that had no sounding.

And Mine Own drew nigh, and did rock and stagger, and did strike anon against the trunks of the trees, as that she did be gone near blind with her running. And in a moment she saw me, and that I did yet live and did come unto her; and she made a strange and loving crying unto me, with a great gladness and with an utter weakness.

And she came running, and was lost with faintness, and did sway this way and that, stumbling; and she went sudden to the earth, and did be still.

And I crept onward so speedy as I might, and the earth to seem alway as that it moved from my hands, and to slide; and this-seeming to be of my weakness; for my hands and my knees went everyway, and my head to be that it kept nodding forward very stupid to the earth.

And lo! as I came anigh unto the Maid, where she did lie so quiet, I saw that something moved in the wood, and was running. And truly it did be an Humpt Man, and came forward very silent and with a quick slyness, as that he did track the Maid secretly; for he lookt alway to the earth. And I perceived that he was that one of the Humpt Men which the Maid had cut with the knife; for the blood did show upon the shoulder and the breast; and this bleeding mayhap to have slowed the Man; so that Mine Own did be like to have supposed she had come utter free; yet he to have found her, by tracking, as I perceived.

And I strave to my feet, that I should come to the Maid, before the Humpt Man; and surely I gat upright, and went with a strange running, and did roll, and lo! I fell immediate, ere I was come to her. And the Humpt Man to run also; and surely it did be a dreadful race; for I went creeping and did be weak and as that I was of lead. And the Humpt Man came very swift and brutish; but I came the first to Mine Own Maid. And I rose up at the Humpt Man, upon my knees, and I swung the Diskos, and the great weapon did roar in my hands, as that it did know and did live. And the Humpt Man ran in upon me; but I smote him truly with the Diskos, and he ran past me, all blundering, and fell and died upon his face, a little way off.

And lo! my wounds had brake out into a great bleeding, and my head did roll upon my shoulders. And I lookt down dull, yet with an utter great love upon Mine Own; and there did be no proper wound upon her; but yet was she all bruised and knockt and marked with the trees, and where she did fall in her running. And she did be there, very still and dear, and I to have brake my heart with love for her, but that I did be so dulled, as I have told.

And I fought that I should be strong a little while more against my weakness; and I strove that I set mine ear gently upon her breast,

that I should listen for her heart. But my head did go downward something clumsy and heavy upon her; and I then to hearken, and surely she did live and her heart did beat; though, in verity, mine ears did have at first a thundering; but afterward a quietness in them, that made the sounding of her pulsing to seem an utter long way off; and very faint it did be. And surely, in that moment, even as I harked, I was gone over into a deadness, and had no more knowing; neither to have even a knowledge that I did be slipt from my senses. And, behold, the Maid did lie swooning; and I to be there in my broken armour, and my head upon the breast of Mine Own, and likewise to know naught; and about us the quietness of that Country, and the far noise of the great Fire-Hills that did sound through Eternity.

XIV
On the Island

NOW I CAME UNTO my senses, and did be in pain and a great forgetfulness and bewilderment. And I strove that I rise; but did be held by a strange force, that did be surely my weakness, as I to know afterward.

And I was upon my back; and a little sound did be near me, as that something did pant. And I turned my head, very slow, because that I did so lack of strength. And lo! I saw that the Maid did be anigh to me, and did be yet naked; and did pant, and pusht hard and desperate with a great pole, which did be surely that one which I had cut when that the Humpt Men came upon us. And therewith I remembered all, and perceived that I did be upon the raft, and the Maid to push the raft along with the pole.

And, at that, I made a little sound with my mouth; but the Maid not to hear me; for she did look backward, as I should think to the shore; and her face did be very set and anxious; and there to be a far noise of howling, that I knew to be the voices of the Humpt Men; and so to perceive that the Maid had come unto her senses, and had gat me somewise to the raft, whilst that I did yet be swoond. And thus to save me ere the Humpt Men had come. But, in verity, how she did this thing, I never to learn; neither she to know, but only that her love did give her a great and desperate strength that she save me, that did be her man.

And afterward, Mine Own Maid did tell me how that she had come into her senses, and did be there upon the earth, and somewhat did be upon her breast; and she saw that it was my head which did be heavy upon her, and I to be surely gone out from this life; for I was so still.

And she came from under me, and did ease me out upon the earth, and her heart nigh brake, because that I was so be-bled, and my blood to have stained all that did be near. But when she had gat me restful,

she saw that I did surely live; and a great hope to spring in her heart. And oft, as she had eased me, she had lookt about, and there did be naught to the sight, save the body of the Humpt Man anigh,and the others dead about and upon the flat-topped rock, as you to mind.

And she ran then very speedy to the raft, and brought water from the river in my headpiece, and she dasht the water upon me; but I to have no power to come unto my senses. And lo! in that moment, she to know by some subtile telling of the spirit, that there came some danger anigh; and she then to make that she save me, or that we die both of us together. And she strave with me, and did carry and draw me that weariful way unto the raft. And she gat me on to the raft; and she ran then for the pole that did be beside the rock; and whilst that she took the pole, she perceived her torn garments, that did be yet in the hands of the Humpt Man, even as she had slipt them to escape him. And she caught the garments very hasty from the hand of the Man, and ran then to the raft; and she pusht the raft out from the shore, and leaped aboard; and behold! as she made to use the pole, there came a sound out of the wood. And there ran from the wood the two Humpt Men that did yet live; and they to have trackt her, after that she did run from them; and they ran downward to the shore, very silent and intent upon her; but she to work with an utter despair, and to have the raft a good way out, ere they did be come. And surely, they either to have no power of swimming, or to know that there did be a Dread in the water; for they made not to come after; but did stand and stare very stupid, and afterward to howl; and this howling I did hear when that I was come unto myself upon the raft, as you do know. And by this telling, you to be so wise as I; for more I know not, save odd things that I did learn afterward, that did but set my love more holy unto Mine Own Maid; and these to have been but small matters of love-thoughts that we did have together; and scarce clear unto my remembering.

And lo! even as I harked unto the howling of the Humpt Men, the sound did grow more faint and far off; for the Maid worked very desperate with the pole. And I did feel that I would help her; but yet was so a-lack; and surely, even as I did mean to rise, I was gone again utter from my senses; and that dear naked One did pilot me safe and loving unto the safe harbouring of the little island, that you do mind; and had no thought unto herself; but only that she save me. And I to be there, scarce offward from my death, and to have no knowing of aught, and no more power to help or to be a shield unto Mine Own; but did be only an helpless man, that had surely died, save for the care of My Beloved.

Yet did I fight a good fight, and have alway a great joy in the remembering.

Now, I mind nothing very clear after this for a great time; but only of pain and weariness, and of half wakings and times when I did know naught, and others when that I did be awake, yet did have no realness, either in myself or in any land or place; and all to come back strange and vague; yet with a constant knowing that there went Love about me, and a great and gentle watchfulness; so that I was eased when that the black mists of my weakness did uprise about me to swamp me; and I was made to know hope, when that unknown despairs did live stealthy within me.

And lo! there came a time when I waked, and did be freed of uncertain burdenings and peculiar woes and that still haze through which great achings did come constant upon me. And surely, I was laid very nice upon somewhat that did be soft, and there went a sweet quietness about me, and an healthful drowse did grow in my bones.

And slowly I perceived that the Maid did kneel beside me, and did look upon me with so great a love and gladness that it did be as that I drank in health and a drowsy joy and peace. And surely, she stoopt and kist me with an utter gentle love, upon my mouth, and her tears to go sweet upon my face; and truly I kist her again, with an utter content.

And she took my head in the comfort of her arm, and gave me somewhat that I drink; and when I had drunk, she kist me once again, so light as that a pretty wind did blow husht upon my lips. And my head she made easy; and lo! I was gone over unto sleep, even as she tended me.

And thrice do I mind that this to happen; and at the third time, I knew that my strength was come something into me again; and I moved my hand a little, this way and that; and she to know that I did need her to hold my hand; and she to do this, and I to go into sleep again, even while that I lookt sleepy, yet with all my love, into her eyes.

And when I waked for the fourth time, I did whisper that I loved her; and surely she broke into a sudden weeping, and did hold my hand very dear against her breast.

And when I waked for the fifth time, I to know how things did be about me, and that I did lie naked in the cloak, and did be all bandaged about my body; and the bandages, as I did know afterward, did be from the torn garments of the Maid.

And I lookt at the Maid, and knew that she did be drest again, and did be in the garments that I did give to her, as you to mind; which did be that one, and the inner, that the Humpt Man tore from her, and which she had slipt, that she escape from the Man.

And afterward, I found that she had made a very cunning mend of the garments, whilst that she did sit so utter long beside me to tend me; for she had gotten threads from her torn garments, and had made needles from thorns that did grow on the little bushes of the island; and the thorns did brake oft, and she then to have another, and so to persist an hundred times. And this way she did be drest very nice and dainty.

And Mine Own Maid perceived how that I lookt with interest at her, and did mind, very natural, how that I last to have seen her; and she then to blush gently; and did kiss me, that she have her pretty face something from mine eyes. And truly, I to wish the more that I be strong, that I kneel in a glad reverence unto her; for this way did be my love, and ever so; and you likewise, that have truly loved.

Now I did begin that I grew very steady unto my strength, again, and Mine Own Maid did tend me alway, and she gave me a broth of tablets and the water at set times, by the telling of my timepiece. And oft she washt me and did change the bandages, and did wash and dry the bandages, that she use them over again; for we did be so lacking for such matters, as you to know.

And on the fifth day, I was come utter to ease; and did be wondrous happy, and Mine Own to make pretty talk unto me; but had me to be alway quiet, because that I did be yet so weak.

And on the sixth day, I to be let answer Mine Own, and to say how great I did love her, the which mine eyes had said alway, while that I did lie in silence. And I to be assured by the Maid that she did be in health, and recovered; but indeed, I saw that she was gone very thin, and that her eyes did be weary, even while that they had so great a love and a gladness to me.

And I made Mine Own to bring her tablets by me, as she did alway, and when that I had kist them, and she to have eat and drunk, I bade her to make me the broth ready; and when she had made the broth, I askt that the Diskos be set anigh to me. And afterward, I bid her to my side, and had her to lie by me; and I took her pretty head upon mine arm, and told her that she to lie thus and to sleep, and to have no fear that she weary me; for that I to be but the more rested to have her so, beside me.

And she in the first to trouble that she be too heavy for mine arm; but truly, I showed that my strength was something come back to me; for I prest her gentle unto me, and she then to nestle content, and to be gone into an utter sleep, and to have been in a sore need of the same.

And Mine Own did sleep for twelve great hours, and had scarce any life in all that time, save when once she did make a little and gentle

moaning, and did afterward set her pretty face more nigh to me in her sleep. And surely, I had neither weariness nor lonesomeness; but did lie with an utter content; and did look downward upon the Maid, where she did sleep in the hollow of mine arm; and truly she did be most wondrous lovely and dainty; and the goodness of her face did seem as that it made an holiness about my heart, so that my spirit was uplift in a quiet and constant glory of love.

And I drank a part of the broth at the third hour, and at the sixth hour, and at the ninth hour, when that I finished it; and my right arm did be free to this purpose and to the Diskos; and surely I did twice and thrice set my hand upon that great weapon, as to a true comrade; and, in verity, I could think the weapon did know and did love me. And this thinking to be because I did be so uplift, as I have told; yet truly, the Diskos did be a strange and wondrous thing, and did be alway thought to have an oneness with the man that did use it.

And in the twelfth hour, the Maid awoke sudden, and came upward out of mine arm, all in a sweet haste, that she know that I did be well; and she did be eased wondrous, when that she saw how I laughed with a quiet joy but to see her dear eyes, and her pretty trouble. Yet did she be in reproach to herself, when that she lookt to find how the hours had past. But, indeed, I did make a mocking sternness with her; and forbad that she even to say one little word more upon this matter; but to be glad that I did be so utter happy, and she likewise.

And truly, when I had said this, that impudent Maid did set her little fist against my nose, and to threaten me. And, in verity, I laught so hearty that the Maid did be in fear I should set my wounds again to bleed, and did reproach herself again; but, in truth, I came to no harm.

And when that I could speak, I askt the Maid whether that there had been brothers to her, because that she did play so natural. And this I askt, not thinking; and lo! in a moment I perceived my thoughtlessness; but said naught, save to take the hand of Mine Own, that she know utter that I did not be heartless. And she to nod very quiet, and afterward kist my hand, and slipt from me. And I knew that she was gone a little way off, lest she weep; and I did be in trouble for her and for mine a-lackness; but truly I could do naught, only that I called very gentle unto her.

And she to return soon, and did smile loving and cheerful upon me; but, indeed, I saw that she covered her weeping, whilst that she had made me new broth. Yet, before I would take the broth, I would have her to mine arms; and she to submit very glad and happy, but to keep her pretty weight from me, lest she hurt my woundings.

And afterward, we both to eat, and be happy in glad talk.

And presently, I did sleep; but would have her to be nigh to me, even though she did be wakeful; and so we to be utter content together.

Now, the seventh day, as it might be called, was a wondrous happy time; and when I waked, the Maid did be sleeping as a child to my side, and her face nestled against me. And she to waken in a moment; for thus had she drowsed and watched through all the hours whilst that I had slept.

And we then to eat and to drink together, after that Mine Own had made me easy with a gentle washing and care. And I now to be allowed that I have my tablets whole, and the water afterward, as when that I did be well; and this to please me, as you shall think; for I did ache that I be strong very speedy, that I have power to guard Mine Own Maid again, and to go forward with our journeying, that I have the Maid unto the safeness of the Mighty Pyramid; and surely, now that I had my tablets whole, I to feel that I did grow near unto fitness again; and moreover, they did satisfy my hunger the better than the broth.

And the Maid to give me my tablets oft, so that I eat a great many; and I did make her to count; and surely there did be sufficient, if that I get strong pretty quick. And so I made no refusing of the tablets; for I did need them, that I make blood again within me, else should I be lacking, when that there came any need anigh.

And we kist each the tablets of the other, and did drink from the same cup, and did be utter happy; and did be part like children, but also to be man and maid.

And presently, the Maid did shift my bandages, as alway, and washt me proper, and had me into comfort. But she did keep me alway very low-lying; and truly I scarce to mind; for I was not gotten enough of my strength, to give me to feel irked. And further, as you shall think, there did be that lovely One with me alway; and did make sweet quips unto me, and talkt and did laugh, and oft did come into singing; for she did be so sweetly joyed that I was in life and did mend so proper.

And afterward, she went off from me a little, to her toilet; but I to ask that she be so swift as might be, and she to promise very merry; and she came back in a little while, and her hair to be in a lovely cloud about her shoulders, and her pretty feet yet to be bared from her bath, which she had in a pool beyond some bushes; and she to say that I did be so impatient a man, that she to be forced that she do the half of her dressing with me; but truly, she came thiswise only because she to know how I did delight in her thus, and to watch the way that she set up her abundance of hair; and she to be hungry also that she be with

me, and to love me that I watch her, even while that there did be oft
a little and quaint stirring of shyness in her dear heart.

And I had her to come beside me, and to sit anigh to my hand; and
I made presently that I did scold her, because that she had no proper
care to her pretty feet; and I bid her to set her feet toward me, that
I look the more close at them. And she to be a pretty rogue, and did
think I to mean to kiss them—and truly not to think alway wrong—but
I then to have another planning; for I had pluckt a hair very sly from
her head, and she but to have said an Oh! to me, and to have thought
no more. But, indeed, when that she gave her feet to me, I held them
so strong as I might, and I bound her pretty toes together with the
hair; and surely she did be a captive unto me, and we to laugh, as that
we to be both children. And afterward she stole back her feet from
me; but, in verity, I knew that she had a wondrous heed that she brake
not the hair that bound her; but did sit beside me bound in that pretty
way; but yet to hide from me that she did not brake the hair.

And she then to do her hair upon her head, very lovely; and af-
terward, I put up my hands, and took it down again; and she then to
kiss me and to ask how that she should ever have it proper upon her
head, if that I did alway so tease her.

And she then to take her hair, and did set the abundance of it
upon both sides of my face, and then to kiss me, as I did look up at
her, from out of so much beauty.

And afterward she cut a lock of my hair, and a lock from her own
dear head; and she did plait the two locks together, so that our hair
did blend and be together; and afterward she hid it in her bosom. But
I did be then out of content, and would have done likewise, only that
it did so weary me to uphold my hands; and she to cut a second lock
from my head, and a second tress of her own most lovely hair; and she
made me to kiss the hair that did be from her, and she then to kiss the
hair that did be from me; and afterward, she did plait them together,
and gave them to me. And I set the hair, for that time, under the great
bandage that went over my heart; and truly, she did be then the one
that lackt content; for she to say that the second plaiting did be kist,
and the first to lack; but I to refuse to exchange; so that we made up
a quarrelling, and did presently have to be kist, unto forgiveness. And,
truly, have you not likewise known such glad foolishness, when that
you were in the love-days.

And she then to make me to be quiet, and to keep my hands down-
ward from her hair, because that the uplifting did prove overmuch to
me; and she took my great hands then, and did threaten how dreadful

she use me, if that I be not humble. And truly, I said that I did be an humble man; and she then to hold my hands with but one small one; and surely, her hand did be so small that she not able to hold me, save by the thumbs. And she then with her free hand to cover mine eyes, so that I might not see; and whilst that she did hold me thus so utter helpless, she to kiss me very dainty and impudent upon the mouth; and afterward she loost me, and did be demure.

And we did be then silent a space; and presently, I put forth my hand, that did be very great, yet to be gone white and to tremble, because that I did lack so utter of blood. And the Maid to know what I did mean, and she clenched her hands into two fists, and set them both into my one hand, and surely they did be little fists; and I then to be happy; for this did be a wondrous pleasure alway unto me; and she to have her lids a little downward upon her eyes, and to be quietly happy. And, truly, how I mind it all so plain.

And afterward, I did plague her very gentle that she to be all a-lack, if that she did try to use her hands to aught, because that they did be so small. And she in a moment to have her two arms very dear about my neck, and did kiss me with an utter love and tenderness upon the mouth, and afterward went from me, lest that she have me to overset myself.

And I did then to make her to sit by me, and I did tell her a tale how that a young man did once live in the olden days, and did meet with the One Maid Upon All The Earth. And how that they loved and did be married, and she to die, and of the utter and desperate madness of grief that nigh destroyed the man; and how that he sudden to wake into the future of the world, in a New Time, and did come to learn that His Own did also to live in that Time. And he then to make that he find her; and did truly come unto her. And how she did be different in her beauty; but yet to be utter lovely. And the man did hold an utter reverence to the Maid, that had been his wife in the olden dream-days, so that his reverence of love did live in him like a constant pain and anguish of sweetness and trouble, and of holy thoughts that did be bred of her lovely companionship, and of his memories

But, in truth, I gat not further in the tale than this; for Mine Own did have come sudden into weeping, and had gotten to her knees, and did hold my hand against her breast, and did put her hand gentle upon my lips. And, in a moment, she to whisper somewhat through her tears; and there to be dear Motherhood within her face; and a sudden shining of Memory in her eyes, that had been near dreadful, only that it did seem to be to her as that she were part dreaming. And

the strange and solemn pain did come also unto me through the part-open gateways of my Memory. And I to remember very clear and with an anguish in that moment. And I told Mine Own how that the babe had gone onward, after that the Beloved had died. And there did be then an utter quiet upon us.

And lo! sudden the Maid did bend unto me, and I to take her into mine arms, out of the vague dreamings of her Memory-dreams. But, ere she did be come outward entire from the haze of the Past, she to try to set somewhat into words concerning this memory-vision of the babe; but someways to be strangely dumb. And I did be silent likewise, because of all those things that did be between us forever and forever.

And presently, she kist me, and was herself again; and she went from me to attend unto our food.

Now, that did be truly a lovely day; for I to have gat sufficient of strength that I did be able to have interest, and talk with Mine Own Maid; and she now to be well rest, and to have ease in her dear heart concerning me.

And surely we oft to laugh, and did make jests utter glad and foolish. And indeed, I do mind how that I askt Mine Own an olden puzzle, that did come out of the vagueness of my Memory-dreams. And she to be like a person that doth hear a strange familiar thing; and lo! sudden she to say, as that she gat knowledge from beyond Eternity, that it did be when that he was a little hoarse. And you to know the jest, and to have troubled it oft at school; but, in verity, it did be a strange thing to have from our Memories out of all the deep of Time. And we, in truth, never in that Age to have seen or to have known that ever there did be an Horse, or to mind the likeness of one. And this to be but a little matter; yet of strange and peculiar interest, as you to agree. And, indeed, we did both to look one at the other, when that we had ended, and did wonder what an horse did be; yet in the same time did have a vague inward knowing.

And so we to look ever backward through dim Ages; and surely we gat presently from jests, unto solemnness; and the Maid to be nigh again unto tears. And, in truth, I then to bring our thoughts and our speech forward from the Abyss of the Years, and did cease from Memory-dreaming for that time; and so to have the Maid again in joy; yet mayhap something wistful odd whiles.

And presently, I to tell the Maid an hundred thousand things concerning the Mighty Pyramid, of which I had so oft said somewhat; but never to have gat so great a chance as this unto a plenty of time and so nice an oneness in the way that our minds did go.

And surely, the Maid did be eager in a moment, and did be husht; and again to ask constant concerning all matters.

And, in verity, there went a great while this way; and the Maid to have an utter wonder and excitement of all that I to tell; for truly, it did be as that a man of this age should come downward from a great star in the heavens, and to tell of wonders and new things; and you to understand how she did feel.

And of all things that did most have a happiness unto the Maid, I to perceive that the great Life and Humanness of the Millions to dwell within her imaginings as a cloud of warmth and quiet joy; for I did show this thing to her, so well as I was able; and, in truth, you shall tell me in honesty whether that I have made the same likewise clear-seen unto you?

And she, as you shall mind, did be a maid that had grown all her life in a Refuge that did be shaken with hauntings, because that it lackt the power of the Earth-Current to protect; and with a People that did be weak-conceived through great thousands of years; and where love did bloom something faded, even in youth; and youth to have lack of the life-blood of an utter joy, such as did be ours and likewise to many that did be of the Mighty Pyramid.

Though, truly, there did go millions then, as now, that did never to know love; though the name did be in their mouths, and they to have belief that the sweet kernel did be in their hearts; but, in verity, THIS to be love, that your life shall bound in you with abundance, and joy dwell round you, and your spirit to live in a natural holiness with the Beloved, and your bodies to be a sweet and natural delight that shall never be lost of a lovely mystery that doth hold a perfect peace each unto the need of the other; and all to be that there go round about you a wonder and a splendour all the days and the nights that you shall be—the Man with the Woman, the Woman with the Man. And Shame to be unborn, and all things to go natural and wholesome, out of an utter greatness of understanding; and the Man to be an Hero and a Child before the Woman; and the Woman to be an Holy Light of the Spirit and an utter Companion and in the same time a glad Possession unto the Man. And lo! if one to die, then the soul of the other shall fail; and that one never to have full life again, in that bitter parting. And this doth be the true Human Love; and all else that be not like to this with the Man and with the Woman, doth be but a borrowing of the name of Love for that quiet desiring, which is but an Endurance beside Love, which doth be between they that be not mated both in their souls and in their bodies. And this telling to take no heed to those

base joinings that be made for purposes of wealth or Desire or other piteous ends; for, in verity, these to have no more dealings with the thing that I do tell upon, than hath the merchanting of goods, or the need of a glutton. But the thing that I do have upon my heart doth be that dear and uplifting Power of Love, which I to set forth in this mine own story; for, in truth, I to have known love, and to need death when that I be parted from Mine Own.

Now, surely, Mine Own did come twice and thrice unto weeping, as I did tell of this thing and that, which did set her memory backward unto the ways of the Lesser Redoubt. And presently, I did cease from my tellings, because that she did so be gone into pain of her memories. But, indeed, she then to beg me that I go forward again; for, truly, she to need in the heart that she know, and to strive to be no more in grief for the telling.

And I then to say on, and did tell upon the Might and Wonder and great Olden Delight of the Underground Fields, that were below the Great Redoubt, as you do know. And I told how that they went downward an hundred strange miles, that did be dug of the labour of Millions and of the years of Eternity.

And I set out unto Mine Own concerning that there did be wondrous villages spread through that great and hidden Country that did be in the underground; and how that great millions of the Peoples did live there, and made a constant labour in those deep Lands and Countries, that did be truly so monstrous in all as an huge Continent.

And I showed Mine Own how that there did be wondrous processes that did be learned in the Ages; and how that water did be made in chemistry; and truly she to nod to this, because that she did mind upon the powder that we did use; but truly the powder to have to be made in the first, as you shall think; and we but to advantage ourselves of that which did result, and I to speak to her of the making of the powder, rather than of the way that it afterward to make chemistry with the air, unto water.

And I told the Maid how that there did be mighty underground pipes that went across the Night Land, and did be, mayhap, oft so much as twenty great miles deep in the world, and did come upward into the seas of the Land; and all to have been made secret and hid from the monsters of the Land, as I to know from much readings of the Histories.

And Mine Own then to tell me that they did lack to have any such great wonders below the Lesser Redoubt; but that there did be utter monstrous caverns, where that there had been alway a strange and uncouth

Country of Husbandry, and lit from the Earth-Current; and they also there to bury their Dead. And all had been a-lack through great thousands of years, as she did know of their Records, and had grown dim-lit and lonesome, and a Land of deepness to starve the spirit with an utter strangeness and discomfort, where that the men went quietly as ghosts, through many ages; and all a place in dire want of sound and laughter.

Yet this all to have been surely different a monstrous Age gone, when that the Earth-Current did be a power in the Lesser Redoubt, and the Humans to be in plenty, and of good and natural health and courage of life. And, truly, to mind upon that Place, doth alway to set a fresh wonder in me, that Mine Own did be so lovely and wholesome of spirit and wise and in knowledge and good force of her being. But so it did be with her; and she to have been surely alway That One that did be Mine Own.

And I then to tell Mine Own Maid concerning the Lowest Field, which did be the Country of Silence, and was the Place of Memory unto all the great Millions, where did linger and bide the ghosts of an hundred billion griefs and the drifted thoughts of sorrowful hearts; and there to live a great hallowedness and a mystery of silence and an holiness and a Greatness, as that it did be the Expressing of all that doth be Noble and Everlasting that ever did come out of the heart of Man and all the lost Dead of Eternity; so that the spirit of a man did seem to go on great wings, unto lovely and splendid resolvings, if that he but to walk lonely awhile in that Country, that surely did be never lonesome unto the spirit.

And lo! the Maid did be all husht, as I did speak, and did look downward unto me with her eyes very bright, and lovely with the thinkings and tears that did stir within her.

And sudden she to ask whether that I did make my resolve to my journey, whilst that I walkt in that place; and she to look very intent and beautiful upon me, as she did question. And, indeed, I saw that she to mean a lovely praise unto me, as you to perceive; and truly, I did feel a little strange, as that I did be both glad and shy in the same moment. And she then to ease me of any answer; for she gat upward upon her knees, and she put her two hands to the sides of my face, and bid me to look into her eyes and to know that she loved me with her soul and with all that did make her to be.

And afterward, she kist me very gentle upon the forehead, and did be then husht awhile, as that she to be in thought; yet oft she did look downward at me, and did have a beauty of love and honour within her eyes, so that they alway to shine, as she did look at me.

And presently, the Maid did sit again beside me, and slipt her two hands into the one of mine, as did be ever my desire, and she to love that she give me this delight, and likewise, she to have joy to herself in this lovingness.

And we then again to have talk; and I did tell Mine Own somewhat of the History of the Olden World! and she did have dim memories, as in dreams, of the days of light; yet scarce that she could believe it of truth. But she to have knowledge of the Olden Love Days within her spirit, and to mind that there did be alway, as it did be, a lovely and golden light upon the world; but she not to know truly whether this to be but the holy glamour-light that Memory doth set about a past loveliness; and to have no remembering of the Sun; but yet to be made ready by her memories unto believing. And I to know of certainty; but yet even I that do tell this My Tale, did but perceive the Days of the Light, as in a far and vague dream; and to remember it but in the chief by the glory of lost sunsets that had cast an holiness upon my heart, and of the hush of Dawns that had made ready my spirit in the Gone Ages to look quietly unto my death.

And surely you to go with me in all this thing, and to have felt within your own spirit that uplifted wonder that doth shake the soul with the lost Beginning and with the unknown End, when that you have lookt through the sorrow of the Sunset, and stood silent before the Quiet Voice that doth make promise in the Dawn.

But, in verity, we that had near lost our Memory of the surety of these great wonders, did have memory of Love; and this to be most beautiful unto my heart; for it but to show the more how that love doth live forever, and doth make an holiness in all places; and doth give Companionship and Satisfying; so that to have love, is to have all, and to have escaped this Wonder is to have missed to have Lived.

And I to find then that Mine Own did have no knowledge of the way that the World did be in that Future Age; and did lack to know that there abode mightily above us in the everlasting night, the dead starkness of the world, where did be—mayhap two hundred great miles above us—snow and the eternal desolation of a lost world, that did be once the lovely world of the olden days, which did be now given over unto Night and Silence.

And mayhap there did wander upward there Memory, and did go companioned by Grief. But, indeed, I to delight to think that Hope and Love did build houses of joy about the Dead; and there to be no true death; but only the dying of days. Yet, surely, this doth be sorrow enough unto the heart and the soul, if that they did be days when love

did make a mystery of light about the spirit, and the Beloved to have been anigh to make ever a sweet wonder unto the heart.

But I to cease from these thoughts; for we to face our life brave and wise, and to take both the sorrow and the joy unto our developing, and to hold up the face with courage when that Grief doth come anigh; and to see that we grow not to bitterness, but unto sweet wholesomeness. And there to be Joy again, and we then the better abled to have that delight into our hearts; for how shall Joy ever to come truly again to that heart which bitterness hath made a place for the abode of sorrow.

And truly, I to cease from these thinkings also; for my story to wait upon me, and these things that I do say do be plain unto you, and to have no need to the telling.

And so did I tell Mine Own Maid of the things that I did learn from the little metal book; and she to be in a constant wonder and delight and with an awe and newness upon her. And sudden, there did some olden memory stir within her; for she askt me, in one instant, whether that I did remember when that the Cities did move alway unto the Westward.

But truly I had no remembering of this thing, and did look at her awhile, with somewhat of a trouble upon me; for, that there should be aught lacking in my memory of those times that we did be together upon this world, was a fear unto me, and a vague sorrow alway, if that I did but to let my thought go that way; though, indeed, I did ever strive to wiseness, and did have knowledge that there doth be an heart-wearing and despair and needless trouble in vain regrets; but yet these to be natural unto the spirit, if that you to know love; and do be but the complement of the love-joy, and mayhap to have a use unto the sweetening of the spirit, if that they be not let to over-ride the reason.

And whilst that I did look unto Mine Own, that she help me to remember, she did strive with her Memory. But in the end, did fail to come unto aught of clearness, save that she did see, as in a far dream, yet very plain, a great metal roadway, set in two lines that went forever unto the setting Sun; and she then sudden to say that she did see in her memory the Sun, and she to have a strange and troubled amazement upon her. And there did be Cities upon the great road; and the houses did be strange-seeming, and did move forward eternally and at a constant speed; and behind them the Night did march forever; and they to have an even pace with the sun, that they live ever in the light, and so to escape the night which pursued forever, as she did tell, and a dread and terrible chill that did live in the night. And there did be cities far forward in the morning Sunshine, that did have gone before

at speed, and set the husbandry of the world, and to be finished and gone forward again ere that certain of the latter cities did come to that place to the reaping; and the night to come presently to that place; but this not to be for some part of a year after that the crops were taken. But how long this might be, she not to remember.

And all this the Maid did say to me, as out of a strange dream, and I to have set it down, and to have made it so clear to you as she to have told it; and surely it doth be plain then that she to speak of a time when that the day did be grown to a monstrous length, because that the world did turn but slow and weary.

And it to be a sureness, as you shall perceive, that but to stand still in that age of which Naani told, was to be left presently in an utter night and chill, that should last mayhap a great and weary year. And, in verity, it doth seem that all Humanity did travel forever in that strange age, when that to stay was to die unprepared in the bitter night, and to go forward, was to be forever in the sun. And truly, this doth be so strange seeming to me, as to you.

And much I questioned the Maid, and did have an hurt within my heart, and a pain of jealousy and sadness to grow in me; for surely she did speak of some life that she did live, when that I did be elsewhere, either in Life or Unknowing. And, in verity, what man then should have taught Mine Own to love him? And she then mayhap to have had no remembering of me.

And truly I questioned very desperate, and the more so because that I was yet weak, and lacking my strength to be composed. But she neither to remember me nor any other man of that time; and to have no memories, save these bare things that she to have spoken out so strange, and which did come sudden unto her out of all the deepness of the years and the lost sorrows and joys and wonders of that which doth make a World of Humans.

And surely my questionings brought a distress upon Mine Own, both because that she did be troubled by the way that my love did bring me to this strange anguish, and because that she also to have pain, and a sudden fear that there did be ever a time when she not to have known me, or to have permitted the arms of another.

And she did then strive that she be both wise and strong, and to give help unto me, and to take reason unto her own easing. And truly she to show how that she did be all unknowing of any love in that far backward time; but it to be possible in reason that she to have gone to another, in natural course, the while that her heart did yearn alway in vague trouble unto Her Own, that her spirit did mayhap never to have

forgotten. And, truly, this doth be the way of Life, and a bitter thing and a sorrow to Joyous Love to think upon; yet I here to be set to the tellings of Truth, and to have heed to all that reason doth show to be.

But Mine Own did also have us both to remember that there did be equal right to think that she had died Mine Own Maid in that life; for that it did be not out of reason to think that she had been void-hearted unto all men, because that she had known in her spirit that she did once to meet Her Own, and did be thereafter untuned unto all other men that ever did live. And this all to be in a mist, and we to go vainly. And of her will, she did think that no man did ever to have possessed her, save I; yet this to be mayhaps only the prompting of her love; and she then to kiss me, and to say that there did be no surety in aught, but only that we did have been together before, and have borne a love so great that it did live through Eternity; and we to be now together, and maybe all else to be but dreams.

And truly I did have a fierce hope that this be so; and the Maid likewise so to hope, yet to be less bitter with rebellion than I, though in pain upon the thought; for she did be so utter and dreadful glad and in happy thankfulness that we did be now come together again in the end; and did mean that she conquer all that should be like to set a greyness upon our joy, and to be steadfast unto this end.

And I afterward to be likewise in wisdom, when that I was come the more to strength, and to mind that I suffer vainly for that which did have no surety, as I have shown; and moreover I did have no power upon the past, either to learn aught or to mend aught; so that I did go the way of an Human, and did shake free from these broodings, and strove unto forgetfulness; which, in truth, doth be both a Terror and a Mercifulness, as doth chance. And I kist Mine Own Maid, with somewhat more of the years within my love; and she to kiss me very sober and dear; and to desire only for my happiness, and to be utter mine own.

Now, we then to eat and to drink, and the Maid to see me unto comfort in all things, and my bandages all right; and she then to make that she have on her footgear and her hair to be bound; but indeed I bid her that she to dare do this thing, when that she to know how I did delight that her little feet be bare to mine eyes, and her hair most lovely upon her shoulders; and she to be very happy that I so to have an utter pleasure in her dear beauties, and did sit beside me again, and set her feet very sly where they did be anigh to my hand; for she to know that she did be Mine Own, and I to be her Master, and she to have joy that she to have to render her beauty unto me; for she did

be that true complement unto me that the heart of a man doth ache for eternally.

And so, presently, did end that lovely day of quiet speech and togetherness; and the Maid did prepare me for my slumber, and she then to lie anigh to me, and her head to rest gentle beside me, so that her pretty face did be near unto my breast upon the right side; and she to give me at the first a loving and sober kiss that did be somewise to set a guard upon her tenderness, and afterward did sleep content and gentle, as that she did be in the same moment a child and a woman.

And I also to come unto slumbering; yet did know vaguely how that Mine Own did rise a little upon her elbow, this time and that, and look very loving into my face, that she have assurance of my comfort and well-being; and once I did waken, proper, and lookt at her, and she then to kiss me gentle upon mine eyelids, and bid me to sleep; and so did come herself unto her sweet slumber.

Now when that I did come to my proper wakening, I to hear the fizzing of the water, and to know that the Maid did be risen a good while, and had made her toilets, as I perceived in a moment, when that she came unto me; for her hair did be in a lovely cloud upon her shoulders, all combed and made ready against my waking; and she to have bathed, as I supposed, in some warm pool that did be among the bushes upon the island; and she now to slip her foot-gear, that her feet be bare unto me, as I did love, and to stand a moment, and her eyes to twinkle gently. And I lookt at her with love and honour in mine eyes, as you shall know, and she to have dancing of sweet pleasure in her heart, that I so to look upon her with holiness and with natural love, and surely the last doth be unnatural if that it do lack the first; but my love did burn upward out of my being, so that the flame of my spirit did light the fires of my heart, and my Reason to add coals unto that fire that hath lived for ever, and doth be as that it shall be never quenched.

And Mine Own in a moment did kneel beside me, and, truly, someways in her deep intenseness unto me; for our love did make all the world holy, and she to be both uplifted and as that she must give all the humbleness of her heart unto the greatness of my love; and this she to feel, and her deep and utter love, to make it as that she did be all a passion of humbleness unto me, so that in her soul I did rise in that moment upon the wings of my love, and to seem that I did be all the world and all time and all place and all that ever she did need unto her.

And she put out her arms to me, and her eyes did shine with those

tears that do never be shed; and lo! in a moment, she did be upon my heart, and we two to be husht together in content; for our need did be in the other. And truly, where there do be two together with love, there doth be neither lack nor need; but eternal fulfilment.

And in verity this to be my Hope for that which doth come Afterward—that all doth be leading unto so glad a joy as this, and that all pain and grief and all that doth make the shaping of Life, doth be but a process by which we be eternally perfected from living unto living, unto each Fulfilment that doth be but the doorway unto greater Fulfilment in the Beloved.

And, presently, Mine Own Maid did loose herself gentle from me, and washt me and tended me; and very husht and tender, and something down-ridded of her dear and lovely eyes.

And we then to eat and to drink together, and joy so great and quiet did be upon us, that it did be as that we had gone into an eternity of peace and an utter content. And surely, as the thought did stir in me, it did be of beauty that we did be both of us true unto the other, in that life, and I never to have kist a maid, until that I kist Mine Own, and she to have been likewise, and to have fended all men from her, because that they did be Strangers unto her inwardness, and so we two to be so utter together, both in that our spirits did be knit, being each the complement of the other, and because that we had no secret pains of remembered things, to set any apartness between our hearts.

And in verity, I to think back then upon my jealousies, that I have told, and to know that Mine Own did never to have given herself lightly to any, neither to have taken lightly; and her spirit to have been alway mine through all the Everlasting; and mayhap this to be how all Peoples shall come to be in the length of time, only that to us had come the great wonder that we did early meet; though this also to bring that utter pain, which doth seem to slay, when that once you have known the Beloved, and to be parted.

And so I to think, and did presently ponder with a great and strange pity upon they that did not yet have met the Beloved, and they mayhap not to have kept all for the Beloved; but to have been light with that which doth be the Treasure, because that Love had not come to show them that they did unknowingly squander the strange and holy glory which doth be the possession of they that shall come to the Beloved and say, All that is thine have I kept for thee. And the Beloved to know and to have peace in the remembering. But what doth be the peculiar sorrow of they that have gone over-lightly, when that they shall meet the Beloved; for then shall there be a constant and

inward regret, as a thorn in the heart, that they not to have observed alway that holy care of all which doth pertain unto love; and they nigh to moan in the spirit, if they had but known, if they had but known. Yet, in the end, of their pain, shall they grow unto all loveliness, if that now they have truly come upon Love, and to live with Love; for this to be the especial glory of love, that it doth make unto all Sweetness and Greatness, and doth be a fire burning all Littleness, so that did all in this world to have met The Beloved, then did Wantonness be dead, and there to grow Gladness and Charity, dancing in the years.

And there to be yet one thing upon which, mayhap, I not to have thought sufficient; for it doth be this, that they who did err, as I have shown, shall be the greater for their Pain; and let this be to cheer you, if that you have done foolishly, and thought not upon that day when the Beloved shall come; for Pain is but the voice of Development or Destruction; and truly you to suffer the first, if that Love doth work in you; but truly, the more that you have lacked, the greater shall be your pain; for the more change there doth need be in you.

And so would I have you now to think, and to know that the Beloved shall come, and so shall you live in glad care of all your being, that you be able to come unto the Beloved in that day, and to say with beauty and human joy in your heart, even as I have said; and thus shall you miss that bitter pain. But yet, truly, you to be like to heed not this, until that Love doth come upon you; and I therefore to cease from this vain setting of mine inward reasonings.

But truly, when that day be come, as I have told, you to know how that there went alway with me in this mine own story which I tell, the simplicity of Truth; and how that I did be minded only that you to know, and thereby that you have gentle wisdom that you lay not up pain for that day. Yet, if you do lack to go with me, you to need that developing which shall then come upon you.

And so shall you perceive how my thoughts did go to and fro, as I did eat with Mine Own; and so in the last I to find that I did think very serious; and I then to cast from me this pondering, and to have that utter joy which did be upon us, and to seem that it did fill all that strange Country of Seas.

And lo! after we did be done of eating and drinking, which did be but a little time, as you shall think, the Maid did ease me to an upward sitting, and had my back very nice to an olden stump which did be light, and she to push unto me.

And Mine Own did sit then beside me, so that mine arm did come most natural about her; and she there to be nestled all gleeful and con-

tent, so that my heart did be doubly tender unto her. And I took the abundance of her hair, and set it about my neck, and upon my breast, so that it did near to cover me in the upward part; and we both then to laugh as that we did be two children, because that Love did make us so utter young in the heart; and our hands to be hid under the beauty of the Maid's hair, and I to have her then that she explain just how great she did love me; and you that go with me, do know how that this doth be a delight that is never done, neither to be set only into words.

And all that day we did be wondrous happy, save once when we saw that there were Humpt Men upon the shore, about the Flat-Topt rock where did be the fight; but what they did there, we not to be able to see, only that presently they went away; and indeed seemed to have no thought unto us, neither any knowledge; and so did be gone again into the forests; and we saw no more of them, after that time. And afterward we to be lost utter in happiness.

Now, upon the tenth day, I did be so come into health that I to walk a little way to and fore upon the island; and Mine Own did go with me, and so I to pace a good while, and afterward to rest again.

And Mine Own then to bring mine armour to me, which she had scoured very nice; but truly, the Armour did be sore broke and bent, and did be jagged inward this place and that, with the monstrous strength of the Humpt Men, when that they did strike me with the great sharp stones.

And, in verity, how I should ever come again to wear this protection, I to be in doubt. Yet, truly it had been a wondrous suit of strength that had kept my life within me when that I had been so deadly beset; and I to know that it to be yet like to save both our lives, if that we could someway straighten it, and ease the broken jags from wounding me afresh.

And I thought a time, and the Maid with me; and afterward we gat that stump upon which I had leant, and had this to be for an anvil; and we found then smooth stones of different sizes, and these to be for hammers; and we wrought all that day, with restings, upon the armour; and surely, we beat it into a very good shape, from the inward, and the broken parts we beat smooth, so that they should not wound, and in the end to have mine armour fit to go upon me.

And I, by now, as you shall think, to be drest part in my garments; but not all; for there did be yet some of the bandages upon my body, so that for the main I did wear the cloak, that the bandages be easily come at. And all that day did be utter happy, whilst that we workt; for we to be together.

And on the morrow, as we do say, which was the eleventh wakening upon the island, the Maid and I to talk long and oft, whilst that we yet worked upon the armour; and we to ponder the best way that we continue to our journeying; for, indeed, I was not come to my strength; yet was I very earnest that we go forward early; but in the same time, I did fear, lest that we meet with aught of Danger, and I to be a-lack, because that I was yet weak.

And presently, the Maid and I both to think upon the same thing; for she to cry out concerning the raft, and I to have the same word in my mouth. And, in verity, this to be a great thought; for then should we be able alway to be free of the Humpt Men, and to have frequent rest when that we be weary, and to sleep with an ease in the mind; and, indeed, I to hope that the labour of oars should be something less than to go upon the feet.

And surely, we talkt upon this a good while, and afterward we left the armour, and went over to the raft, and so to learn whether we should have power to make it something more stable, and that we have some way that we should put a solid matter between our bodies and any monster that should chance to swim under us.

And we went then together over all the little island; for I did search for some bush that should have a long tendril in plenty, and supple, and so to suit for binding. But, truly, there did be no such bush in all the island; and this to put me in trouble, as you shall suppose; yet was there a sufficient plenty of small and upright trees, that did seem very good for any purpose of structure.

And when we had gone all about the island, and found naught that should bind, the Maid to say with a pretty jesting that we should cut her hair, and plait it to be for cords. And, surely, even as the words did come from her, they to set me upon the thing that should supply our need; for I stoopt sudden to the grass that did grow oft and plenty in this place and that, and was so tall as my thigh, and to my head in the middle of the clumpings where it did sprout. And lo! it was wondrous tough.

And the Maid to have likewise perceived the thought, almost at that moment; but I to have been the first this time, and so to tease her; for truly, we had grown that we did nigh alway to discover all things in the same instant, as you mayhap to have seen. But I did surely be first this time, and must kiss her, as we do kiss little ones, that they be eased in their dismays and disappointments; and she to see how I did mock her, and she to pretend to weep; and surely how could she even to pretend, when that she did not be able to keep her pretty mouth

from searching with laughter unto mine; but must be kissed full and plenty in our constant joyfulness.

And we cut then a good arm-load of the grasses, using the knife, and had those to our camp; for we did be homely now unto that place, as you shall think. And the Maid then to show me plaiting, and how that we could work in the grass piece by piece, so that we should plait unto any length that we to need.

And all that day we workt, and did be very happy together; but when that we came to the time of our slumber, the Maid had done twice and thrice so much as I; and surely she came over to me, and kist me very grave, that I should be not to fret, even as I did kiss her with gentle mocking concerning the thought about the grass; and so did she make level with me, by this impudence and quaint sweetness.

And on the next day, which did be the twelfth, I took the Diskos, and on that day I cut down six of the trees; and alway the Maid did bring her plaiting, that she be near me; and when I had cut the six trees, she had me to cease, lest that I risk to open any wound. And truly they to have healed very wonderful.

And afterward, we to plait all that day, and did also finish the armour; and did be content and utter happy.

And on the thirteenth day, I counted the tablets, and found that we yet to have sufficient, if that we came unto the Mighty Pyramid within any reasonable time. But I insist that I should eat no more now than did be my usual way; and though Mine Own did beg and to coax me, and even to try whether that a naughty and loving anger should do aught to shift me, I not to alter from my deciding, which was based upon my reason and upon my intention that Mine Own should never to go in hunger-danger, whilst that there did be life in my body. And when that the Maid did show this dear and pretty anger, I to take her into mine arms, and to tell her how I did reverence and love her, and that she did be all beauty unto me, and I but to love her the more, because that I did know the reason for her dear shaping of anger unto me.

And she then to kiss me, and yet to beg again that she have her way in this thing; but presently I did show her that my reasoning was sound in this matter; though I said not that my strongest thought did be unto her own needs. And she to have to agree with me in her brain, even whilst that her heart did ache to feed me. And truly, I to love her but the more, as you shall think.

And this way shall you ever to manage a dear and sensible woman that doth both love you and hath reason in her; for the wise man and he that hath an heart unto bigness, doth be never hasty to command.

But, indeed, I speak not now of the way that you shall go with a woman that hath the love-foolishness upon her; for this to be a different matter, as you do know; and a woman then to require a double wit and tenderness in the governing; but also to need to be commanded, mayhap with sternness; yet with the more love.

Now, when that we wakened on our fourteenth day upon the Island, we gat to work, so soon as we had washt and eat and drunk, and Mine Own to see how my scars did go.

And I cut seven more trees that day, which made thirteen in all; and afterward I trimmed the trees very nice. And when this was done, I cut twelve good sapling-trees, and two more very thin, that I did mean to be for paddling the raft upon the water. And Mine Own Maid did sit near me alway, and never to be ceased from her plaiting.

And whilst that the Maid did plait, and make gentle and happy talk with me, I presently to sit beside her, and had her belt-knife to my need; and therewith, when I had cut bark from a tree, I made a foot-long cross-piece of wood which I did fasten with pegs and some lashing unto the end of one of the paddle-shafts.

And I took then a piece of the bark, so big, mayhap, as would cover my thigh, and shaped broad one end and thence to a point; and when I had made holes in the piece of bark, I lasht the broad end to the crosspiece, and the end that did be narrowed, I lasht secure to the shaft, and likewise made holes down the length of the bark, and lasht it also thereby to the shaft, and thiswise I had a pretty good paddle, that did be about ten feet long in the clear shaft, and the head to be somewise two feet more, mayhap.

And when this was done, I shaped the handle so small as might come into the grasp of the Maid, and did jest her very loving and gentle that she give me so great a work, because that she have her hands so little. And truly, she presently to stop me of my mocking; for she put her pretty hands upon my mouth, and I then to have to mumble and to laugh, and so she to go forward again with the plaiting.

And when I had made the one paddle, I made also the other; but something more rough and heavy, and suited unto my strength; and so did be very well pleased; for they did be made more of my Reason than of memory; yet had I used somewhat of the kind upon the quiet lakes which did be in the Country of Silence.

And we then to join in the plaiting, and thus with happy talk and our times of eating, until that we did be come again to our slumber.

And on the fifteenth day, when that we had gotten up and washt and eat and drank, the Maid did look unto my bandages; and did

consider that I be healed very good, if but that I not to overstrain my body. And we then to dance, half in play and half in victory, but gentle; and afterward she to come with me that she give me aid that we get the trees unto the water.

And in six hours, we rolled the trees down to the shore, and did begin then that I lash the saplings across the trees, and thiswise to hold them secure into a raft. And the midmost tree I put something more forward than the next; and so, until that which did be the front was shaped somewise like to the bow of a ship. And the saplings to hold the trees thiswise, when that I had set the lashings about every sapling and every tree, where the saplings did go across.

And all that day I worked pretty constant and steady, until that Mine Own had me to cease awhile, lest that I bend overmuch, and so to put strain upon my scars. And I to be reasonable; but yet to go forward again with the work; only that I did rest now, this time and that; and so did all to prosper.

And on the morrow, which did be the sixteenth day upon the island, I made an end of lashing the saplings across the raft; and I set up also, two rests for the paddles, so that we might row if we stood upon the raft; and afterward, being ready, we gat together our gear, and set all upon the raft.

And I put the pole that the Maid had used, also upon the raft, and loosed the straps from that first raft, and had the straps for our requirement, as heretofore. And mine armour we made safe on the raft; but the Diskos I had to my hip, as ever; and so did we be ready to leave that little island of refuge, where we had been so near to sorrow, but yet had come utterly upon joy.

And surely, Mine Own did take me by the arm, and she to stand a little, and to look with me unto that bed of soft herbage where she had laid me, when that I did be so nigh unto death; and she then to kiss me very sweet and loving and gentle, and all a-tremble with the tears and love that did stir in her; and I to set mine arms about her in love; and so we to turn and to put off then in the Raft.

XV

Past the House of Silence

NOW IT WAS IN the tenth hour of that day, that we put off in the raft; and surely we found the paddles to go very easy and with somewhat of balance in the rests which I had set up, as you do mind; and the raft to go forward with not overmuch of labour; so that we stood, the Maid to the fore paddle and I did be to the hinder one, and we pusht very steady upon the paddles, and had the raft presently to a speed something less than we should walk over the rough way of the Land.

And about the twelfth hour we stopt and eat and drunk, and went on again with our easy labouring; and truly, when that we gat set to the movement, we scarce to wot that we did aught more than rock something fore and back upon our feet; and so the hours to pass, and we to have a constant gentle speech one with the other, and the Maid oft to look back unto me with love, and to set her lips that she tempt me; but yet to shake her head most dear, when that I would leave my paddle, that I go forward unto her.

And when that the eighteenth hour of that day was come, we to draw inward our paddles, and the Maid set the cloak very nice to be our bed, and afterward we eat and drank, and so presently to our slumber, and did have sleep, very sound and happy, all in a moment, as it to seem.

And eight good hours after, we did waken both of us, together; and lo! we scarce to mind where we did be for a little moment; but afterward to know and to perceive that we did be safe and naught to have come unto us in our sleep. And surely we laught each in the face of the other; for we did be so joyous to be wakened each unto the knowledge of the other. And after that we had kist, we washt somewhat in the water of the sea, and so to our food. And when we had eat and drunk, we made again to the paddling; and went forward thus along the coast very peaceful and content all that day.

Now, in all, that voyaging did talk four good days of four-and-twenty hours each, for we made no great haste or labour, but went easy, that I have time to gather my strength. And naught to happen in all that time, save that once we did see a great beast to come upward lumbersome out of the sea on to the shore, and there did eat and browse upon the herbage in that part; or so it did seem to us; though, truly, we did be over far off to have surety.

And this beast not to put us into any horror; but only to make us glad that we be afar off from it; and by this saying, I to mean that it did seem unto us a natural thing; and nowise to have an odour of aught monstrous to trouble our spirits. And this way did be all the creatures of that Country; and truly I do think the Early World did be somewise like to it; and this to seem to make true that olden saying that extreme things do meet, as doth be over-apparent; for thus doth it be somewise to our knowings, as you shall perceive by your Reasonings Upon Olden Days, and by the showings of this Mine Own Story; for that Deep World to have put forth natural creatures that did be even as might be those that did live in the Beginning; though I to make no point of this, but only that it doth occur to my thought; and all to seem that it did be bred of Circumstance and Condition; yet this to have no saying whether that there to be a spiritual-force something deeper than the Circumstance; for this to be outside of any surety; but not offensive unto my Reason.

But this thinking also neither to offend me, that although much—and mayhap all—doth be modified and shapen diverse ways by the Circumstance and the Condition, yet doth there be an inward force that doth be peculiar each unto each; though, mayhap, to be mixt and made monstrous or diverse by foul or foolish breeding—as you to have knowledge of in the bodies of those dread Monsters that did be both Man and Beast. Yet, also, I here to say that maybe all diverse breeding not to be monstrous; but this to be beside my point. For I to be now set to tell, as I have told, that it not to offend me to suppose that there to be this inward force peculiar to each shaping of all bodies that do hold that wondrous quality of Life. And if that you ask me that I give example to make clear my thought, I to say that it doth be reasonable to suppose that the Force or Spirit of the Human doth be peculiar to the Human, whether that it to be a Cause of Life, or the Result of that which hath been evolved out of a Condition. And whether it to be the one way or the other, you to know that where this Force or Spirit be found untainted, there is man; and I to be not opposed to think that Man doth be constant alway in matters of fundament, and

neither to have been ever truly different; though something modified in the body and surely, in the first, all undeveloped in the lovely things of the spirit, because that there to be no call to these. Yet, presently, they likewise to come, and to act upon the flesh with refinings; and likewise, mayhap, there to be some act of the flesh upon the spirit; and so to the state of this Age of this our day, and to that far Age of which I do tell. But development never to make the Human other than the Human; for the development to have limits peculiar to the Human. And surely, it doth appeal to me, that the development of Man doth lie between two points, that be not wondrous wide apart; and Man to have power that he arrive very speedy from one unto the other, and likewise that he go back so quick, or even the more hasty. Yet, even did it be ever proved that Man once to be a fish, I to have no cause to abate the first part of mine argument; but to have the more need of the thought, that I gain power to accept the Fact; for I still then to have no occasion that I think Man to have been truly a Fish, or aught truly different from a Man; but only that he did be once Modified physically to his need, and to be still possessed of the Man-Spirit, though all lackt of development. Yet, truly, I to be less offend in my Reason, if that it be shown that Man did be ever somewise in his present shape, though mayhap so brutish as the Humpt Men; but yet I do be ready to consider all matters, and do build no Walls about my Reason. Yet, neither I to have an over-ready acceptance of aught, but to need that my Reason shall approve.

And you to perceive, surely, that I here not to speak of that which may be Afterward, when that all This, our life, be done. For who shall say how much or how little we then to go forward unto loveliness; and I at this point to tell you that I do have a wondrous hope of beauteous things, and of sweet and mighty Uplifting and Furtherance unto that Glad World which we have beheld the shores of, when that we had stood in holiness with the Beloved.

And, in verity, I now once more to my story; and to be glad that I am done at this small setting forth of a matter which did need words, because that it did have root in this Mine Own Story, and to be grown of it and from it.

Now, there did be one other thing of note, beside the Sea Beast, whilst that we did be upon the Seas; and this did be the strangeness of a great Fire-Hill which did stand in the sea, and we to pass very nigh unto it. And surely the sea did boil about it, yet not in all places; and there did be a score great jets that did go upward a monstrous way, and did roar very plain to us across the sea between; and there

did come strange gruntings from the sea about the base of the Fire-Hill, and these I to conceive to be made by the upbursting of gases in this place and that; and surely, it all to make us to know of the great energy that did be wakeful in that deep Country; and we yet to stare backward upon that Hill of Fire and Force, for a great while after that we had come past.

Now, beyond this, there to be naught, except that we had a certain care as we did come to that place where the Great Sea did be broke to smaller seas; but all to be knit with passages of water, which let us through upon our way.

And surely, I did show Mine Own Maid those two places where I did sleep when first I was come into that Country; and she to be sweet in interest, and alway to have somewhat that she would learn of this and that.

And so, when that we did be four good days upon the water, as I have told, we to come to the land, upon a flat place of the shore, where the Country did slope upward unto the mouth of the First Gorge, of which you do mind. And this to be in the tenth hour of that day; and we likewise to have begun that voyage in the tenth hour, as you do remember; and surely it to have been a sweet and peaceful water-journey; and I to have been happy, if that all that did be yet before us, to hold so much of pleasantness and safe goings. But, indeed, there to be much danger yet to come, as you do know; and we to have our hearts set in courage, and to go forward to conquer; for surely, if that we to conquer, and to come safe into our Mighty Home, there to be then that we have all our lives together in loveliness; and this to be truly a worthy prize and a glory of the heart, to end and to repay our Stress.

And surely, the Maid and I did presently strand the raft, so well as we might, and did then to wonder whether any should evermore to behold it through all Eternity. And we lookt a little, each at the other; and the Maid then to cut free a small piece of the wood of the raft, to be for an after remembrance.

And so we to have our gear upon the shore; and the Maid then to give me aid that I get once more into mine armour; and so I presently to have the Scrip and the Pouch again to my back, and the Diskos in my hand, and all in readiness, and the Maid with her bundle (that was now grown small), and her belt about her body, that she have her knife unto her hand.

And surely, the Maid then to kneel and to kiss the raft; for memories did gather upon her; and she there to have one more breaking from all that did be the first part of her life; and you to give your

understanding, and so to have a quiet sympathy, and to perceive that her heart did be like that it should stir with a strange trouble of sorrowing in that moment.

And surely I stoopt then, very gentle and loving, and had Mine Own to her feet; and I led her from the raft, and she to need that she be near me; and so we to go forward, and to make upward unto the dark mouth of the Great Gorge.

And there to be some miles unto our right, that grim and utter huge Mountain, whereon afar upward in the monstrousness of the night did be perched those four fire-hills of which I have told. And below them, there to go upward the great hills of ash, that had been cast down throughout Eternity. And this thing had the Maid lookt upon for a great time, and did be never done of her wonder; neither I, nor any human that ever should have sight of so great a wonder.

And so we to have come presently upward into the high mouth of the Gorge, and did go onward then into the gloom, a little space, until that we were come to the place where the Gorge did bend sharp unto the left, into darkness.

And lo! we made pause here, and turned again unto the Country of Seas, that we have a last outward look over all that Deep and living Land, that did be hid so far downward in the everlasting night of the world.

And, in verity, it did be a solemn thing to know that we, mayhap, to be the last of the olden Humans that should ever to look upon that Country; and I to wonder, in that moment, whether that the Humpt Men should ever to develop, in some far eternity, unto the full sweetness of the spirit of Humanity which I did think to be inward of them. And this to be both an odd and a natural thought to have then, as I do see. But at that time, I only to think it, and not to wot or to trouble whether that it did be odd or otherwise. And I to think that Country did be somewise as the Olden Time renewed; but truly we to look upon early things with new eyes.

And we yet to look awhile, and to be husht, and to hark in those last moments unto the far mutter of the Great Fire-Mountains, and the Fire-Hills, and the noise of life which did go over that Land; and we even then to be but a few short pacings off from the silence of the Great Gorge, which should lead us presently toward the Eternal Strangeness which did be in the Night Land. And the Maid did hold mine arm very close, as we lookt our last into the red light of that Deep and Hid Country of the World, where, in verity, we had come so utter nigh to our Death.

And presently, I turned, and the Maid slipt her hand into mine, and the tears did go silent down her face, because of all that did be prest upon her heart; but yet not to be all of sorrow, for there to be both sorrow and happiness, and also there did be somewhat of vague emotion that she never more to look upon that dear island where she had nurst her man again unto life and well-being; and she to be in mind of all those places where she to know that in after-life her memory to wander; and she to have oft-told tales, mayhap, unto her children, of that Country that they never to see; but only to be for a wonder to them for ever.

And we past then round the Mighty Corner-place of the Gorge, and went forward, somewhat stumbling, into the gloom.

Now we went sixteen hours very steady, and with naught save the great darkness to trouble us; and we by this to have been twenty and six hours since last that we had sleep; and surely this did be a foolishness, because that I to need that I come into my full strength, ere we reach the Night Land; and it to be a folly that I should over-tire myself; and the Maid to have said so much.

And, indeed, then, we came to a safe place for our slumber, and whilst that we eat and drunk, we made count from my notings of the outward way; and so did decide that we go no more than sixteen hours' journey each day through the Gorge, and to sleep alway for eight good hours. And this we to do, both then, and until that we did be come out of the Great Gorge, which did take us in all, so much as five days thiswise.

And surely, when that we were come into the light places of the Gorge, we to be more cheered, as you shall suppose; yet oft did we be half smothered with the horrid gases that came upward in this part and that, as you do mind.

And my strength did grow constant, as we journeyed; yet would the Maid never suffer that I carry her; but went alway very light and clever, and was grown, in truth, set unto this constant wander.

And at this place and that, I to make pause that I show Mine Own those places where I did slumber, and she alway to need that she come unto the very part, and that she stand for a little moment where I did lie so lonesome, as I went outward unto that despairful searching. And alway she then to be utter tender with me, and to be something lacking of speech, because of the calling of her heart.

And surely, Mine Own did be alway now to ask me when that we should be come unto the Night Land; and to require how far it should be, and to be taken with a growing of excitement, very dear and nat-

ural; and, in verity, I to be almost so much so as she; and to wonder what she to think of the Mighty Redoubt, and of all that strange and monstrous Land. And, above all these, I to be shaken unto my very heart, that I have the Maid speedy unto safety; lest, after all, even though we to have come so far, there somewhat to happen of woe. And all this did make it a hard thing that we not to begin to race, and to exceed the hours that we did set; but truly we had wisdom in this matter, and slumbered alway after the sixteenth hour.

And we never to see aught of life in all that great and desolate Gorge; for there did be only the gas-burnings, and the boulders and the stark rocks, and oft the rank smellings of the gases. And alway an utter and everlasting quiet; save when some lonesome gas-fire did oddly to moan or to whistle, and the whistling to sound very dree across the great waste of the Gorge, and likewise the moaning to be but a thing to make the loneliness to be felt in the heart; and the Maid to feel thus with me.

And alway, as I did know, she to think in her heart that I did come through that place alone to make a searching for her into the unknown lands of the world; and surely, I did be but a natural man if that I was something happy in my heart that Mine Own so to ponder and to remember; for thereby did her love seem ever to grow. And likewise, a man doth be glad in his spirit and natural pride, that his Maid to know that he hath done wholesomely of his best for her need. And you but to think upon the love-days, and to hear the echoes of those dear proud thoughts that did so to swell in you; and doth not all to go so strangely with familiar pain in the old way?

Now it was upon the fifth day, in about the seventh hour, that I heard oddwhiles a sound in this place and that of the Gorge, as that the rocks made husht and strange sounds at us. And I to have the Maid instant very nigh to me, and the Diskos to my hand, and we then to go onward with a great caution.

And thrice we did pass places where gas-fires did burn and dance, and made oft a low moaning, and somewhiles a little whistling; and the other sounds yet to come oddly from the rocks, in this place and that, very strange and unthought of, yet to be something familiar.

And sudden, it did come to me that there to be a far-away noise in these sounds; though they to seem to come from this place and that almost to mine elbow, as you should say. And lo! I knew then that I harked unto little echoings, that did be caught by the near rocks, and to come from some far and mighty sound. And this should be surely the monstrous piping of the Great Gas Fountain, that you do well

mind. And, in verity, I told Mine Own in a moment; and she to be all eager with me, because that this did be both a wondrous thing, and to be also a landmark to show that we did be nigh to come out of the Gorge, and our journey to come the more near unto an ending.

And surely we lookt ahead very earnest; and there to be so many strange and leaping fires to our front, that we not to be very sure which did be the far and monstrous dance of the Great Gas Fountain; for truly it to be yet so distant that the near gas-fires did make more upon the eye up all of a weary length of the Gorge, than did the great dance of the far-off fire, that was now so small, by the distance.

And presently, when that we were gone onward something more, we to see that there went a lightening and a darkening afar along the Gorge, so that the background of the night was made to lose somewhat of the intensity of its darkness, as with constant shudders of light; and this to be surely the far away dance of the flame of the Great Gas Fountain. And we then to watch alway as we journeyed, and to see how that the vague shudderings of light did grow in the distance of the night, and did merge and become known presently in a strange uplifting and falling of a far away blue flame.

And the sound now to come more steady, and to grow in a long while into a monstrous piping, very great and wonderful, and having a constant change in the note.

And we to come past the last of the lesser fires, and to be in that part of the Gorge which did be fireless, save for the great upward dance of the Gas Fountain, which did now to be grown huge and plain-seen, and did make a quaking light over all the Gorge.

And so in the end, we to be come very nigh to the dance of the monstrous flame; and did be half stunned by the noise, which did be now an utter and furious roaring, as you shall remember; and the Maid and I did stand as but two lonesome strangers in the mouth-part of that deep and desolate Gorge, and did stare voiceless unto the great flaw; and mine arm did be about the Maid, and she to stand very nigh to me; and neither to speak; and surely, how should we anywise; for the noise did be so huge.

And after that we had stared a great while, we turned that we look each at the other; and we kist very sober, there in the light from the monster flame. And afterward, we did stare again at the Flame, and soon turned, and lookt all ways, and did marvel to see the great throw of the light go blue and spreading and strange unto great distances.

And a while we did be watching the way that the far-off side of the Gorge did come plain to sight, when that the Flame did leap; and,

truly, that did seem a far and lonesome Place, as that a lost and forgot world of desolate mountains did be there.

And lo! we now to look that we should see somewhat of the way that our journey to go; and surely naught to be clear shown save when the Flame did rise oddwhiles to a monstrous height; and this to be because of the huge rocks that did stand about the Flame. Yet something I was abled to show the Maid of the bottom part of the Mighty and Utter Monster Slope that did be the last way of our journey, ere we were come to the Night Land.

And we then to go onward for about a good mile, that we be not so deafened by the noise of the Gas Fountain; and it did be now beyond the seventeenth hour; so that we eat and drunk, and made our rest in a secure place among the great boulders.

And lo! when that we waked, we eat and drunk again, and did be something silent, as we to gaze at the Flame dancing monstrous, and lonesome and all set about with the stark and mighty Rocks, which did be like unto giants of silence that did watch forever.

And presently, we had our gear upon us, and we went forward toward the utter dark of the Mighty Slope; and we began that huge climb, that should last through days in an eternity of night.

And oft in the first hours did we turn about from our blind stumblings, and gaze downward out of the long height, unto the loom of the Flame, that did shudder far below in the night, and made a quaking light in that far darkness. And so did we leave it to dance forever through Eternity in that deep and lost place of the world; and we bent all our will and our strength unto the climb.

And this way went we stumbling for sixteen great hours; and by that time had come to a pace proper for that task, and to be something numbed, and seeming grown unreal, because of the affecting of the Darkness.

And lo! for eight days then did we go upward forever through that most dreadful night. And after the first day, we crept alway upon our hands and our knees, and I to go in the front, and had the Diskos ready upon my hip. And I took two of the straps from the pouch and the scrip, and so had a certain length; and I set them from the waistbelt of the Maid unto mine own belt, and so did know ever that she came close after me.

And we made journeys sixteen hours long, and did eat and drink at the sixth and the twelfth hours, and likewise we eat and drank ere we slept, and again upon our wakings; and our slumber-time to go alway somewheres about eight good hours; for thus did I be heedful that

we have all our strength for that dreadness of the journey, which did be yet before us, across the fear and horrid terror of the Night Land.

And oft, at this time and that, I was utter sickened and a-wearied of reaching forward and upward forever, and making blind fumblings that I find a way about great boulders and the rocks and holes that did be in our path in the dark; for it to seem that we went lost from all life and knowing, in a blackness that should be never slackened from about us.

And I, these times, to make a pause, and to call softly unto Mine Own that she creep up nigh unto me; and I then to take her into mine arms, out of the utter blackness of that night. And so to give and to have comfort.

And surely, Mine Own did whisper once unto me, that she did be stunned with love and wonder in the heart; for she to never cease to know that I did adventure through this great night, that I find her. And this thing did make me very warm in my heart, as you shall think; but yet I to stop her speech with a gentle kiss; and she then to know that she be dumb concerning her thought in this matter; yet she never to cease from remembering it, and did be the more stirred with the trouble of her lovely secret worship; for, in verity, she to have me to be for her hero; and this to make me in the same moment both something shamed and greatly proud.

And so we to be together, and after such pause, to go forward again, with a new courage.

And surely it did be a great comfort to me to think that, because we to go upward and not downward, we be not like to fall over any hid cliff in the night; for I to have now some little knowing of the Slope, from mine outward journey; yet to remember upon that monstrous pit that I then to escape, and so to go with care.

And, indeed, upon the second day, I had Mine Own to creep more nigh with me, and I then to have but one strap between us, and the other I set a stone into, and did cast the stone alway before us, as upon the outward way. And you to mind you of this, if you but to think a little minute.

And oft in those weary days in the Darkness, did I make gentle whisperings through the blackness, unto Mine Own, that I give cheer unto her; and she alway to answer, very sweet and loving; yet ever husht, as I did be; and in verity, it did be as that we could not set our voices loud upon that Mighty Slope, lest some enchantment come upon us, as it might be said. And, indeed, each time that I cast the stone, the noise of the stone to make a little trouble and dismalness

in mine ears; for all did be so quiet and desolate and lost in night, that it to make us to need to be likewise so quiet, and to desire that we might go upward so silent as shadows.

Now, surely, I must tell here how that the Maid to have alway at waking that same awareness that I did have upon the Outward Way, that somewhat did be nigh to us, and to seem to have been concerned with our waking; and I likewise to have also the same knowledge, as before. And oft as we did go, I to feel that somewhat did go near to us. And this to put something of a fear upon me, because that I was ever anxious for Mine Own; and I to have her to be alway the more nigh to me, and did set the strap from her to me, even when that she slept; so that she not to be touched, and I to lack to know. Yet she to have no fear concerning this thing; but to feel in her spirit that it did be a force that had no evil intent unto us; but more, neither she nor I to know; and I, in truth, to come in the end used to it; save that I did be, as I have told, anxious in all that did concern the life and well-being of My Beloved.

And so did we go onward through those eight days.

And it soon to be grown cold, so that we both to need the cloak over us in our slumbers; but in the journey-hours to need naught; for the upward-going did surely heat us very well.

And there also to be come presently a change and a seeming of thinness into the air; and the Maid to remark upon this, and likewise that the water-powder now to be that it not to fizz so plentiful.

And we went upward, as it did seem forever, and journeyed very husht and steadfast; and likewise did halt at set times, that we eat and drink; and did alway sit then very close and quiet and in love. And so alway to go never beyond sixteen hours' journey each day, and very weariful even so much; for it to be a sore and constant labour of climbing.

And I to learn the hour alway, by a little shining of the Diskos upon my time-dial, which I have told did be somewise as the watch of this our present Age. Yet, truly, I also to learn that I made somewhat of a constant number of forward-throws of the stone in an hour; and the Maid to be the first to discover this, as she did creep behind me and harked steadfast and quiet unto the clatter of the stone, each time that I cast it. And she sometimes to call low to me that it now to be this time or that time; and I to look at my Dial, as I have told, and oft to find that she did be curiously right.

Yet otherwhiles, we to have no thought to count; but made a constant husht talk one to the other; and did grow odd times, that it did

seem to us that we did be two spirits there in an Everlasting Darkness, that had quiet speech one to the other, and to be seeming gone from our bodies. And we then to need that we look each at the other, that we know truly that we yet to live and to be indeed with the Beloved. And I then alway to make the Diskos spin a little, yet something more than when I should see the hour; and, in verity, our faces then to show pale and strange seeming in that luminous glowing of the great weapon in the Darkness; and we to look very eager and an hungered of love, each at the other; and so to need that we be held loving by the Beloved, and so to have comfort and assuredness; and afterward to have peace to go onward again.

And it did be one such time as these, that Mine Own to give me a love name she had called me in those olden days of this Age; and which surely I had not heard since Mirdath died. And, in verity, you to have dear understanding with me, how that I then to be all troubled with vague troubles and ghostly love-aches in the heart; and likewise, I did be all set about in a moment by the olden enchantment and speechless glamour that did be so long hid and lost in the Spaces of Memory, where surely the spirit doth wander such oddwhiles, husht unto a dumb tearlessness and to know in the same moment both Agony and the voiceless Glory and lost Delight of the Hath-Been; so that it doth be as that you wandered in the spirit between the sorrowful pain of the Sunset, and the Promise of the Dawn which doth be builded upon the Need and Hope of the soul, and doth also to have an essence of pain within it; because that these do be knit with Longing which doth be the essential pang of Memory. And so, mayhap, you to have gone with me; for you to have also strange thoughts that do come out of the years, and do hurt the heart, even whilst that the heart doth hunger of that which doth so pain. Yet, truly, Mine Own did be now with me, as you do know so that I had joy all about my heart; yet did all the years of my lost delights and of my pain, be in the spaces of my memory, and Mine Own now to have stirred all; so that no words that did be ever shaped of man should help me to have ease in speech.

And Mine Own Maid to know how it did be with me; and she to have said the thing, scarce wotting, even as her spirit did set it through her lips; and she before then to have forgot so utter as I; and now she to be stirred likewise with me; so that, in verity, we to hold hands in the great Darkness upon the Slope, and to wait till the pain and strange trouble did go somewhat from our hearts; and we to have power again to know truly that we did be again together in sweet verity, after a mighty Eternity.

And thus did we go, and even in that strange Night to have an everlasting coming together; so that surely our two spirits to be nigh made one, somewise; and this to be that sweet and holy thing which I do name Love; and it to be my glory and Astonishment that Love hath come unto me. And with you that have love, I am as a Brother in holy delight; but with all that have not known Love, or to have missed Love, I am a Mourner, and my heart to pray that they to know this Wonder, ere they die; for else shall they die so green and bitter as they be born, and to have grown nowise unto Ripeness, which doth be Charity—the end of life and the Crown of Humanity.

And surely I to go forward again now with my telling. And you to know that on the eighth day upon the Slope, about the end of the ninth hour, there to be an upward seeming of light, afar before us in the Darkness, and did show as a dull and vague sheen above us in the night. And truly, I to know that we did be come at last a-near unto the Night Land.

And we went upward then very eager through the dark; and the dim shine did grow, ever; so that we soon to see it very plain, as a looming of light afar upward. And we ever to climb and to go onward. And lo! in the fourteenth hour of that day, we came up slowly out of the Night upon the Slope, and stood at the ending of that strange road Where The Silent Ones Walk.

And surely it did be as that I was come home, and to have set my feet again upon familiar Lands; and this to bring to you how far off I did seem to have gone; and now to be come again to a Known Place.

And we went upward upon the Road, until that we did truly have topt the Slope, and at last to look out over all the wonder and mystery of that Land. And I never to be rid of the utter gladness of knowing that I was come there again, after so strange a journey, and that Mine Own had I brought with me, out of all the unknown world. Yet, truly, I also never to have forgetting that this familiar Land of Strangeness did be the last test and the greatest dreadfulness of our journey; and anxiousness did hang upon me; for I now to have to take the preciousness of Mine Own among and beyond all that Danger of Horrid Forces and of Monstrous Things and Beast Men, and the like.

And truly, I did be like to trouble.

And, in verity, I did stare with a fierce eagerness unto the far-off place in the middle part of the Night Land, where did be the Mighty Pyramid; and surely it there to shine in the midst of the land, and did be mine Home, where never had I dared hope I should return. And I set mine arm very swift and eager about the Maid, and pointed, so

that she see quickly the wonder and safe Mightiness of that which did be our Refuge for all our life to come, if but that we to win unto it. And the Maid to look with a great and earnest soberness and a lovely gladness and utter soul and heart interest, unto that Place that bare me, and where I to have come from, and now to take her.

And long and long she lookt; and sudden came round unto me, and set her arms quick about my neck, and burst unto a strange and happy weeping. And I to hold her gentle to me, and let her cry very natural, until that she was something unpent.

And lo! when that she was eased, she to stand close beside me, and to look again unto the Mighty Pyramid; and afterward, as she to steady, she to ask an hundred questions, so utter eager and so to thrill with joy and excitement, as that she did be a glad child. And an hundred questions I answered, and showed her new things and Wonders uncounted.

And of all strangeness that she then to see, there did none so to shake her in the spirit with terror as did that dreadful and Horrid House, which did be the House of Silence. And it was as that her very being did know and be repulsed of some Horror that did concern and be in that House; so that she to want to hide in the bushes that did be anigh to the Road; and truly, I to think this wise, and to remember and to be ware suddenly that we did be indeed come now into the Power of Monstrosity which did be utter and forever abroad in that Land.

And surely, we went then in among the bushes that did grow clumpt upon the side of the Road, as you to remember; and afterward, I calmed this new fear that had come so quick upon Mine Own; and she then to peer forth with me from the bushes, and to have renewed sight over the Land.

And the House of Silence to stand upon that low hill of which you do know; and did not be a very great way off, somewise toward the right. Yet, as you shall have remembering, it did take me some long and bitter hours upon mine outward way, ere I did be come from under the shadow of it, as we do say, unto the top-part of the Mighty Slope.

But this to have been in the main, because of the utter care that I did need to bring me safe past the House; for I to have gone long and weary upon my hands and knees among the bushes, as you remember; and oft to pause, and to be so still as Death, lest that the Power of the House to have become aware of my passing. And truly, we to need again so utter a care, when that we make to go past, unto our Mighty Home; and this to be heavy upon my heart, and I to be in the same moment anxious that we have haste to the trial, and yet very willing, if it might be, that we not make it forever.

And, indeed, after that we had peered a good while from the bushes, I to consider that we do well to eat now, and afterward to have a safe place for our slumber, so that we go fresh to the horrid dangers and dreadfulness that did be before us upon our way.

And we then to look about, and soon to find a great boulder that did be set with the bushes. And we made our place for sleep against the boulder, and the bushes went all around, so that we did be complete hid.

And, in verity, we to be very cold, as we had been those two past days, whilst that we made toward the top of the Mighty Slope. And now we to have the full chill of the Night Land, and did be very glad to have the cloak, so that we eat and drank whilst that we sat together, and the cloak round us. And afterward, the Maid set the cloak about us for our sleep; and we then to kiss very sober, and I with anxiousness in the heart; but she with less, because she to have rest in me.

And so we lay down to our sleep, and the Diskos ready in my hand; and my spirit wakeful against any terror that should come anigh to us in our slumber; and the Maid I warned to be likewise wary.

And surely we slept and waked, and there had gone eight good hours, and naught was come anigh to us to harm us. And we eat and drank, and did hark oft, and lookt out from among the bushes; but there did be naught abroad to set dread upon our spirits; and so we did be more content, and well rest and a-ready for the further journeying.

Now I had the Maid to wear the cloak, because of the chill of the Land; but she in the first to refuse, save I also to have it in my turn; but truly, I did feel that it should smother me, and that I need all my freedom of my body, lest there come any thing sudden upon us; and all this I showed Mine Own, and also that we should have weary work, and to creep much, so that I should be warm by my labour of going, and she likewise, mayhap. And she then to consent, because she saw that I did be earnest and to burn with anxiousness; yet had me to promise that I take the cloak, if that the chill of the Land gat me anywise bitter.

Now we made a pause, when that we have our gear upon us, and we lookt well out over the Land; and surely alway our eyes did gaze in the ending upon that far Wonder of Light and Safeness, which did be the Mighty Pyramid; and I to be never ceased from telling Mine Own this thing and that thing concerning the Great Refuge; and she to be constant stunned unto silence and delight of wonder, and anon shaken unto a multitude of questionings, so that truly we did be as that we never to have done making known one unto the other.

Now, as you have knowledge, the House of Silence stood upon a low hill, and the Road did bend about the bottom of the hill; and this way did I come, when that I was on mine outward way.

Yet now there to be a new plan of journeying come into my mind; for, as you do remember, I did take somewise of eleven great days from the Pyramid unto the top-part of the Mighty Slope, because that I had gone diversely and round about to the North-West of the Plain of Blue Fire.

And surely, as now I lookt, it did seem that we should try a short passage, and thereby be come free out of all danger in but a space of four or five days, if only we to succeed. And I stood a good while very husht and anxious, and did consider this new way, and did presently point it out to the Maid, how that we saw the Mighty Redoubt straight to the back of the low hill where stood the House of Silence, and mayhap we might chance to find a safe going that way, and that I did ponder thatwise. For, indeed, as you do know, we must go nigh past the House, even did we return by the long journeying, and this to be because that the bushes did make a cover only near to the Road, and all to be a country of bare rock beyond the bushes on that side of the Road, which did be to the North and West.

Now, presently, I had formed my intention regarding our way, and told all to Mine Own, and how that we to have alway an utter caution; and the danger I made so plain to her as I did know it, and she then to beware in her heart the need there to be of care and wiseness forever, as we did go.

And we then to make forward into the Night Land, and to be gone from the top-part of that great deep, in which there to be hid strange lands, as you do know. And surely, it to be like that none should ever to go that way again for an eternity, or maybe forever.

And so went we forward, with a new caution.

And we came out from among the bushes upon the North-West of the Road, and crost unto the Eastward side; and here the bushes to grow very plentiful, so that I led on with a cheerfulness of hope within my heart. And alway I went so far to the South-East as the bushes would give us their cover, and this way I made that we should scarce to pass within a great mile of the dread and horrid House; though, in verity, this to be most dreadful close.

And we walked then for six hours, and went sometimes creeping, and oft stoopt, and ever with a great caution.

And in the sixth hour we made a rest, and eat and drank, and afterward went forward again.

And in the tenth hour were we come something nigh unto the House; for truly, we to be off from the Road Where The Silent Ones Walk, and so to go more straightly, and alway to save distance. And we kept so far outward from the House as we might; but could pass it not more than a great mile off, because that the bushes did have their margin near upon our left, as we went; and there to be barenness of rock beyond; and fire-holes in this part and that amid the starkness of the rocky spaces, that should be like to show us very plain, if that we came outward from the bushes.

And moreover, there went upward into the everlasting night one of those Towers of Silence, which did be in this part and that part of the land, and were thought to hold Strange Watchers. And the Tower stood great and monstrous afar off in the midst of the naked rocks, showing very grey and dim, save when the flare of some great fire did beat upward in the Land, and sent huge and monstrous lights upon it. And we to have need alway now to remember this Tower, and to keep the more so to the sheltered hiding of the bushes. Yet, in verity, we to have little thought of aught, save of the grim and threatening terror and monstrousness which did stand forever upon that low hill, and did be the House of Silence.

And in the eleventh hour, we did go creeping from bush unto bush, and did be as shadows that went in the mixt greyness and odd shinings of that Land. And the grim and dreadful House did be now unto our right, and did loom huge and utter silent above us in the night. And the lights of the House did shine steadfast and deathless with a noiseless shining, as that they shone out of the quiet of some drear and unnatural Eternity. And there did a seeming of Unholiness to brood in the air, and a sense of all and deathly Knowledge; so that, surely, our hiding did seem but a futile thing unto our spirits; for it was to us as that we did be watched quiet and alway by a Power, as we slipt gentle from bush unto bush.

And when the twelfth hour did be nigh, we to begin to draw clear of the House; and surely there to come somewhat of ease into my brain and heart; for it did be as that we should come clear of all harm.

And I turned to the Maid, that I whisper gentle and loving encouragement unto her. And lo! in that moment, Mine Own gave out a sudden low sobbing, and was gone still upon the earth. And, truly, my heart did seem to die in me; for I knew that there did be directed a Force out of the House of Silence, which did be aimed unto the Spirit of Mine Own Maid. And I caught the Maid instant into mine arms, and I set my body between her body and the dreadness of the

House; and surely, my spirit to perceive that there beat out at her a dreadful Force, which did have in it an utter Silence and a bleakness of Desolation. And lo! I saw in a moment that the Force had no power to slay me; but did surely make to slay the Maid. And I set my Spirit and my Will about her, for a shield, if this might be, and I had her to mine arms as that she did be mine own babe.

And I stood upright, for there did be no more use to hide; and I knew that I must walk forever until that I have Mine Own to the Shelter of the Mighty Refuge, or to walk until I die; for only with speed might I save her from the dread and horrid Malice of that Force.

And I set free the Diskos from my hip, and had it in mine arms beside the Maid, and I strode forward out of the bushes, and put forth my strength that I journey with an utter speed. And ever my Spirit did know of that monstrous Force which did be direct upon us, to the Destruction of Mine Own Maid.

And odd whiles, as I walkt, I called Mine Own by her olden love name, and by the new name of Naani; but never did she move or seem even that she lived; and surely my heart sickened within me with a mighty despair, so that a constant madness did begin to thrill in me and to make me something monstrous in strength, with my fierce agony and intentness to save. And one hope only had I, that I bring her yet living into the Shelter of the Mighty Refuge; and so, swift, to the care of the Doctors.

And lo! I did strive to be wise in my despair; for I made a quick halting soon, and I warmed a broth of the tablets and water upon a hot rock, and strove that I set some of the broth between the closed lips of Mine Own Maid; yet did it be useless, as I to have known before in my heart. And alway I kept my body and my Will and my Spirit and my Love between the Maid and the dreadfulness of the House. And I made some of the water, and dasht it upon the face of Mine Own, and I chafed her hands; but truly it to have no use; neither did I truly to think it should be like to.

And I wiped her face then, and harked to her dear heart; and surely it did beat, very slow and husht. And afterward, I wrapt her in the cloak.

And I forced myself then that I eat some of the tablets, and I drank a great lot of the water, for a fever did seem to burn in me, and moreover I to mean that I lack not for strength to my task.

And I set my gear upon me very speedy, and I lifted Mine Own Beloved, that did be now so husht, that once had been so merry and dearly naughty. And surely, I nigh choked as the thought uprase in me; but I set it back, and did but go the more furious. And surely no man

did ever go so fast and constant upon his feet, through an eternity; for I was come again to my strength, and there did be a madness of intention and despair upon me; and I went on forever.

And at each sixth hour when I stopt very brief to eat and to drink, I made to bring Mine Own to her senses; yet she never to come, and alway her heart to grow the more feeble; so that in the end I did utter fear to hark; and did but set food and drink into me, and onward again with an utter fierceness.

And why there came not any Sweet Power of Goodness to help me in my strait, I never to know; but did call desperate upon all Good things to aid me, as I went, to save Mine Own. But there naught to come; so that I had grown into cursings, but that I did not to lose my wisdom to any useless foolishness. And alway, as I went, I to see the Land blindly, and oft vague and grey as that I did look at naught real, and again with strange flashings of light, and the glare of fires; and anon to see the Land as it did be, and all odd whiles to have now to me the feel of a dread and monstrous dreaming.

And surely I sped forever through the dreadful hours, and went neither to the right nor to the left, neither did I strive to hide in the bushes nor to evade aught, for I knew that the Maid died slowly in mine arms, and there to be no more gain in life, save by speed, that I have her swift to the Mighty Pyramid to the care of the Doctors. And a great and despairing madness grew ever within me.

And thrice I to have a vague memory that there came creatures at me, from the dark of the Land; but surely I slew them with the Diskos, and have no remembering thereof, only that mine anger did boil in me, and I to know once that the Diskos did run blood in my hand.

And lo! there to come sudden unto my spirit the knowledge that the æther of the world did be stirred. And, indeed, I did be surely sighted by the great Millions of the Mighty Pyramid. And they to have seen me come forward into the sight of the spy-glasses, and that I did bring a maid in mine arms out of all the night of the world.

And truly, as I did after learn, the dear Master Monstruwacan had discovered me great hours before; for there had been a steadfast watch kept in the Tower of Observation for my returning, if that ever I should return; and the might of the Great Spy-Glass had shown me plain a good while gone, and that I did carry somewhat, that was surely the maid that I did go to find. Yet had the Master given an order that no word be set abroad to the Peoples, of this discovering, lest that the emotions of the Millions to tell overmuch unto the evil Powers of the Land. But now had the Millions also come unto knowledge;

for many had ceased not to watch through their spy-glasses, and the news to travel very speedy through the cities; and surely now there did be a constant spiritual noise in the night, to be heard only of the Spirit, yet to suffice to wake and to warn all that Land.

And truly, as I after to learn, the Master Monstruwacan did know by the instruments that there came a force out of the House of Silence, and this to trouble him greatly; so that he set the word through the Pyramid, by the Hour-Slips, that all the Peoples strive to contain their emotion, lest they bring an Harm and a Destruction upon me, by warning the Land with the greatness of their feelings.

Yet, in verity, this did be useless; for the Peoples did be very human, and could nowise check their gladness and great wonder and excitement; for it was to them so great a wonder almost as we should suffer if that a man in this Age should go beyond Death in search of his Beloved; and afterward to come backward unto the Living; and, surely, in such case, how mighty should be our amazement; and this to be somewise how they did be; yet with it also a sweet and natural gladness and strong welcoming, which doth be the true beat of the Human Heart unto the Wanderer.

And presently, and through all the time that I came forward across the Land, there did be mayhaps an hundred million that did never cease to watch me from the embrasures, from the View-Tables, and from all vantages. Yet, for a long while, only they which possessed strong spying-glasses did be abled to see me truly; for I was a great way off.

And millions did but stare vainly unto that part where I was said to be; and the Hour-Slips to come out four times in the hour, and to tell aught that did be known. And so shall you perceive that Humanity did but have grown the more Human.

And, in verity, I went forward with all my strength, and did drive heedless through the miles and the night, and scarce conscious of aught, because of the aching madness of despair that did grow ever within me; for I knew that Mine Own Maid died alway in mine arms, as I did carry her.

And later, a monstrous space of hours it to seem, I knew that I was come to that part of the Road, where it did bend somewhat unto the Vale Of Red Fire; and this did be something anigh to that wilderness where the Youths did fight with the giant-men.

And I came over the Road, and urged my body utter furious across the Land. And, surely, in that moment when I cross the Road, great numbers of the Millions did see me, that had not seen before. And there went a shaking in the æther of the World, because of the

sudden emotion of so mighty a Multitude; and lo! it did be as that in that moment the Land was at last waked; for there came from far away unto the Eastward, a faint and dreadful laughter, as that a monstrous Being laught unto Itself in some lost and dreadful country. And the Laughter passed over the Land, and did echo strangely, as it did seem, in this part and that part, and presently to go rolling round in the far and hid West Lands, and to be as that it wandered awhile amid the far mountains of the Outer Lands, and was presently lost from my hearing.

And my heart chilled a little maybe; but yet did I not care over-much; for I to lack all if that I lackt Death, if that I not to be given power to save Mine Own. Yet did I make a little pause, so that I gat the knife from the belt of the Maid, and did also to bare the Capsule; for if that there came a Destruction upon us, I to make instant sure that Mine Own Maid be safe unto death, and I then to go quickly with the Capsule.

And afterward I again upon my way.

And ever upon each sixth hour I did stop that I eat and drink, and did onward again, even as a machine; for I commanded myself to this duty of victual, that I lack not my strength unto the saving of the Maid. Yet, truly, I did seem to choke alway as I strove with the tablets.

And lo! ever as I went forward did the Land awake; and my spirit to know that Great Forces did be abroad, restless. And the Monsters to begin wild roamings, because that they also to know of the Unrest that did be come into the Land. And there to go presently odd roarings across the Land, from night unto night. And I to go forward the more desperate, and to step neither to the right nor to the left; but to make direct unto my Mighty Home.

And the Vale of Red Fire did be soon afar off unto my right, and the bulk of the Watcher of the North-East to be somewise unto my left, before me; and the great back to be toward me. And truly, I lookt at the Brute-Force, and it did be as that I drew nigh unto a Mountain of Watchfulness; and above it in the everlasting night did be the blue shining of the luminous ring, and the ring shed a light downward over the Monster-Force; and the shoulders did be huge and humpt, even as two small hills, and it lookt forever from me through eternity unto the Pyramid. And this to be plain, though I did be a great way off from it.

And sudden, as I went, there came Somewhat out of a bush unto my left, and rose up at me, very long and tall; and surely it did be some kind of a man, and came at me. And my fury and my despair came inward upon me in a moment, so that I troubled not to set down the Maid, but leaped at the thing, where it did be yet half hid in the dark.

And lo! it died in pieces, and the Diskos did roar to content my heart an instant. And I then onward again the more savage, so that my heart did be a dreadful thing within me.

And a great while I went then, and do have a vague remembering that this time and that there came things at me from out of the dark; but surely they to have died very speedy, that I not to remember more.

And the hours did pass in spaces of time that did be made of terror and numbness and an utter and evergrowing fury of despair. And I did be at last as that I did burn inward with a grim and dreadful energy, and to seem to grow the less tired, and to come over the Land with a stronger ease and somewhat as that I did desire things to come unto me, that I have something to ease my heart; for lo! Mine Own Maid did be dying in mine arms as I carried her; and I to be in a bleak and sickened dread, so that I lacked all courage now to listen unto her heart, as I have told; and went burning, and dry and hot in the eyes.

And ever there sounded the roarings across the Land; and there did be added presently lower and more horrid and dread noises. And later I heard a far thudding of the earth; and in a little there went past me a great Man, running so heavy that he did make a shaking as he past me; yet, in verity, by a sweet mercy, he saw me not, and was gone onward in a moment and lost utter into the night. And the æther of the world to be full of the trouble of the Peoples, as the Man past me; and afterward there to be a stirring of glad thankfulness. And truly, alway my spirit did know strangely as in a dream, that the Millions set their sympathy and pity and help about me, and did girt me about with Human love and with encouragement and with uplifted thoughts. Yet, in verity, did all be as water beside the fierce wine of my love and despair, which did urge me onward in a natural lacking of all dread, save for Mine Own. And truly this doth be the way of Love, and shall make fearless the heart of the weakest. And there to be prayers in the night, and all the æther to be surged with the spiritual trouble and callings and cryings of the Millions; so that, indeed, if that my spirit so to hear these things, it to be conceived that these do pass outward into the Everlasting, and to break upon the Shore of Eternity in an anguish, even as a visible foam of supplication.

And surely the unity of love of the Millions did make a natural Force about me; for, in verity, the Force that did come from the House to seem to be somewhat eased from the Maid; yet there to be no surety in this; for all did be desperation and turmoil in my heart, and I to have but one thought in my brain, that I bring Mine Own swift across the Land unto the Mighty Pyramid, and so unto the Doctors.

And lo! there stole presently from afar the deep and dreadful baying of the Hounds; so that I knew we did be surely dead, save that a miracle should happen. And I askt in my heart in a fierce and mad fashion why that they did not to rig one of the olden shooting weapons, that they shoot from the Pyramid, and so to give me some aid in mine extremity.

And behold, even as I did be so bitter, there went afar upward in the everlasting night, where did shine the Last Light, the sharp flashings of the Set Speech; and I did warm in my heart a little with hope; for the Master Monstruwacan did see that I was now all discovered, and there to be no more use for silence, and did speak straight and helpful unto me. And I made to read the Set Speech, but mine eyes had been mad and near blinded with lost hope. But in a moment I saw clear. And behold, the dear Master Monstruwacan bid me to keep good my courage, for that they did have made ready three of the olden weapons; and moreover, they to save me, even if that they have to turn loose the Earth-Current over the Land. And he commended me with Honour, and that I strive forward yet a little while; for that an Hundred Thousand Men did be Prepared, and did even then go downward in their armour by the Lifts.

And surely, as you shall think, my heart eased a little in me, and there burned somewhat of a hope in my spirit that I yet to bring Mine Own unto the Doctors, ere it be too late.

And the baying of the Hounds did grow nearer in the night; and there to grow ever the roarings over the Land; and a sense of Evil and monstrousness to be abroad in all the night.

And lo! I to have come by this so that the Watcher of the North-East did be backward upon my left; and I lookt keen and fearful now at the Monster-Force; and behold, the great bell-ear did quiver continually, so that I saw the Monster made somewhat known unto all the Land. And the Monster did look as ever, unto the Pyramid; and did be a great and silent Hill of Life that did lean toward the Pyramid; and the light from the Ring came downward upon the monstrous hide, which did be set in vast folds and wrinkles upon it. And the Monster to know of me; yet never to move, neither to show life, save that the ear did quiver so horridly.

And I knew that they made some great preparation in the Pyramid for our defence; for all the night did begin now to shake and to quiver with the mighty beat of the Earth-Current.

XVI
In the Country of Silence

\mathcal{A}ND LO! I DID be come something nigh unto the Mighty Pyramid; and my great Home went up vast into the everlasting night, as a very Mountain of sweet Life and Safety; and had surely amazed me afresh with the utter Bigness of it, only that despair and weariness did have too grim an hold upon my heart for me to care of aught, save to have Mine Own Maid within the safe wonder of the huge Refuge. And it did be still afar off from me.

And I to go forward across the Land with a strong going; and lo! as I past a hollow place where did burn a fire-hole, there came something out of the hollow. And the thing gat upward from crawling, and did be a great and haired Man. And the Man lookt at me, and afterward came unto me, and did put his hands forward, very eager, as he came. And I did see the hands plain in the light from the fire-hole, and the hands were monstrous, and did be armed brutish with horrid claws, so that the Man should have been able to rip aught, even as a wild beast.

And I put Mine Own very swift to the earth; and surely, I cared not for life or aught; for this thing did make to delay me, and I to be fierce with despair that aught should halt me. And lo! I leaped very furious and with cold anger at the giant; and I smote at the monstrous brute; but he unto the side in an instant of time, and so escaped the blow. And he flung forth his monstrous arm out of the half-dark of a shadow that did be cast by the dance of the fire-hole, and caught my head-piece and pluckt it from me so strong and brutish that he cast me nigh a dozen feet on to my back. Yet I was not harmed in the life, but only sore shaked and bruised; and I to be up in a moment, and came in upon the giant, and the Diskos did roar and blaze in my hands as I swung the weapon. And I gat the giant above the middle part, and the Diskos did glut itself, and went through the giant as that he did be naught, though so huge and monstrous and girt with strength. And

he to have surely turned his shoulders as he died; for the upper part of the giant-man went horrid to the earth, and the legs and the trunk stood plain in the light of the fire-hole, and the blood went upward as a fountain in the night.

And I made no pause, but leaped unto the Maid, and had her in a moment to mine arms, and onward again past that dead thing, that did only then to fall with an horrid sound. And surely the night did be full of an astonishment and upliftedness of the Millions, so that their spiritual cryings did go all about me, and did tell me that they had perceived this thing, and did cast their love and delight unto me, and a vast excitement to be upon them.

And lo! I scarce to have gone a great mile more, but there came two vague things out of a dark place, where certain rocks did upstand; and I smote them with the Diskos, and went onward; but what they did be, I never to know.

And surely, after that, I did seem to go smiting forever; for there to come, time and oft, strange things out from the bushes and the rocks, as that all the Land did be a-crawl with foul and monstrous life, and I to go smiting, as in a dream, and to speed forward ever with a more fierce despair; for surely the end of our lives did be come, and I not to be given power to save Mine Own Maid.

And all the Land did be full of grim and monstrous roarings, and odd-wise lower sounds, very deadly. And once I did hear the noise of giants running. And all the night to be Evil. And, in verity, how I did not be slain by some dread Force, I not to know, unless that I did be burned free of all weakness that an Evil Power should have chance to harm me through; for, indeed, I had been dealt a bitter training a monstrous time.

And lo! there to be again the deep and dreadful baying of the Night-Hounds unto the South-East, and to be nearer; and I to know now that no strength of mine should serve to protect Mine Own.

And lo! from the upwardness of the night, where did be the Last Light, there sudden to come downward a strange blue flash, that smote downward into the Land unto the South-East. And again the flash to come, and mayhap a score times after; and there to come down out of the height a peculiar crackling sound, that did be less than the thunder of this age, yet more loud than any other sound that you ever to hear. And lo! I knew that the Humans did begin to fight for me, that I bring Mine Own safe unto Home.

And behold! it did be as that all the wakefulness of the Land that had been, did be but as sleep, beside the wakefulness that now to come;

for surely the Night now to seem to rock with the roarings of the Monsters, and with the be-stirring of Great Forces. And ever there to go over the Land the yowling of that strange and dreadful Laughter, which did come from that hid Country in the night of the lost East.

And lo! there arose constant now the hoarse and dreadful bayings of the Hounds, and made known that a mighty pack did be out. And they to seem to be no more, maybe, than a good mile unto the South-East; and I to be all alone, save for the dying Maid that I held in mine arms. And I lookt vainly and with despair for the Hundred Thousand that did be Prepared, and had come downward, as you do know, unto mine aid. But truly, there did be naught to see anywheres, save the strange lights and shadows of the Land; and the movement of monstrous life in this place and that place. And the Hounds to come nearer with every moment of time; so that indeed, I knew that death did be very nigh.

And I ceased not from my stride; but went forward, and did begin to run; for the Pyramid was not a huge way off in the night; and the shine of the Circle about it, to be plain seen, save here and there, where it did be hid strangely. And I to have a despairing hope that I come yet with Mine Own into the safety of the Circle.

And the baying of the Hounds to come ever the more near; and surely it did be a doubly hideous bitter thing that I lose My Dear One, so nigh unto Home; and the great Mountain of my Home to go upward before me into the night, and to seem so near that surely I did be almost there; but yet, mayhap, two great miles off, even then. And, behold, I called out in vain despair and to no end, why that none come to give me aid in this extremity; for the Hounds did bay now but the half of a great mile, upon my left, and did surely have scent of me, by the way of their dreadful baying

And, truly, the Millions to have an anguish of sympathy for me; for the spiritual noise of their emotion did be plain unto my spirit; and they surely to have seen and to have interpreted the way that I did look about me and appear to call out in despair; for there came all about me in a moment the companioning of a great and sweet spiritual force, which did be bred of their quick going with me in their understanding and love; and they to have perceived how that I did be unto the end of hope; and the Hounds to be almost upon me.

And in this moment, there came afresh to my hearing the shaking beat of the Earth-Current; so that I knew the Humans to take desperate means to save. And there came to my view a vast pack of the Hounds unto my left, and they came running at a great pace, and their heads

did be low, and they to be so great as horses; and seen plain, and again in shadow, all in the same moment, as they did come.

And, in verity, I knew that we two to be dead indeed ere a minute be gone, if that the Humans not to haste. And I stood where I did be; for there was no more use to run; and I lookt from the Hounds unto the Mighty Pyramid, and again to the Hounds. And again I lookt with my hope gone, unto the Pyramid; for the Hounds did be scarce two hundred fathoms off from me; and there did be hundreds of the mighty beasts. And lo! even as I lookt that last time unto the Pyramid, there brake out a monstrous bursting flame, that did rush downward from the Sealed lower part of the Mighty Pyramid. And the flame smote downward upon the Land where the Hounds did run, and all the Night to be lost from my sight in the brightness and strangeness of that mighty flame; so that I saw no more the Pyramid, or aught; but only the shining and dreadful glory of that flame. And the Flame made a blast in the Night, and a hotness that did seem to wither me, even where I did be from it. And I perceived that the Humans had truly turned loose the Earth-Current upon the Hounds, that I be saved. And there went a constant great thundering over the Land, because that the Earth-Force did rend and split the air, and did tear up the earth. And the roaring of the Monsters did be husht and lost in that mighty sound; and I to see no place where the Hounds did be; but only flames and broken lands where the Earth-Force did strike; and great rocks did be hurled all whithers, with a vast noise; and truly it did be a mercy that I was not slain an hundred times, if this might be, by the failings and burstings of great rocks and boulders.

And lo! in a moment the Humans did cut off the Earth-Force, and had it again to their control. And there to seem now a great silence upon the Land, and an utter dark; save that flames and noise came from that part where the Current did strike. And I very speedy to come free of the dazedness that had me, and made again to my running; for, in truth, it to seem now that I should yet be let to win unto safety with Mine Own.

And mine eyes did grow presently unto their accustomed using; and I to look all ways about me, lest there come somewhat upon me even then to work our deaths. And for a good time there to be naught that I did see anywheres, neither there to be the wakeful sounds of the Land, save only the grim and horrid Laughter from afar in the dead East.

And oft as I did run, I to stare hungry hearted upward at the Mighty Pyramid; and surely it alway now to seem to be less bright than before.

And in the first, I to set this to the count that mine eyes did be yet dazed by the great Flame of the Earth-Force; but soon I to perceive that it did be otherwise; and that there did be truly a less brightness of the light that did shine throughout all the Mighty Redoubt. And this lack I conceived had owing to that great using of the force and power of the Earth-Current that had been loosed to save us. And I to have this new thing cold upon my heart; for, truly, if that the Force of the Current to be made over low, there to be a danger for all the Humans that did live, even for all the great Millions of the Mighty Refuge. And this, did be surely known by the Masters; and they to have no more power to aid me with the Current, until it flow strong again, lest that they destroy all the Peoples of the Earth. And all this to be plain to me in a moment, as I ran; and I to be but the more desperate to come unto instant safety with the Maid.

And surely, I to be yet in expecting of the Hundred Thousand to come unto me; but they not to come. And all about me the Land to begin again to give out the noises of the Monsters; and to send forth new and peculiar noises, as that there did be more awaked in the Land than did be ever heard by me before. And presently, I saw that there went living things, creeping, between me and the light of the Circle. And I to know that I yet to have to fight bitter, if that I would bring the Maid safe. And I swung the Diskos free, and ran on.

And sudden my Spirit to know that I did be warned of some new peril; and I to look upward into the night, that the Master Monstruwacan should mayhap to tell me the danger, by the Set Speech. But, in truth, there came not the quick flashings of the Set Speech; but only an upward stillness, and a dimness of the lights of the Mighty Pyramid. And afterward, I to learn that the dear Master Monstruwacan made to warn me of danger; but that all the instruments of the Tower of Observation to fail to work, and likewise all the machinery of the Pyramid to cease, even unto the moving of the great lifts, and the moan of the Air Pumps; and all to have been this way for nigh a great hour, until that the Earth-Current did flow again more full. And surely, this doth show that Death did nigh to come unto all the Millions, because of the great trial that did be made to save us.

But, truly, my spirit did be warned by the trouble of the Millions, and because the Master Monstruwacan called vaguely with his brain-elements; so that I went ever more warily, and did look all ways. And lo! sudden I to stare above me into the night; and there to be a pale circle, very quiet and steadfast that did go alway over the twain of us. And I saw that this did be surely one of those sweet Powers of Holiness,

that did stand between our souls and some dread Power that came anigh to work our Destruction. And I to have no over-fear; but did put my trust in the Force of Holiness, and went forward, running warily.

And surely, I came mayhap so nigh as to within four hundred paces of the Circle; and I to think that I yet to win Mine Own safe and undelayed within the guarding of the Circle. And the light of the Circle did burn dim; so that I had sudden fear whether that it be any more use for a Guard, until that the Earth-Current to come more free. And all this as I ran, swift and wary and utter anxious.

And lo! in that moment in a dim place there rose up three beast-men from the earth, and came at me, growling. And the first did be so close that I had no room to the Diskos; but beat in the head of the man with the haft-part. And I leaped unto the side then, and swung the Diskos, and did be utter mad, yet chill, with fury; so that the Maid did be no more than a babe in the crook of mine arm. And I came in sudden to meet the two beast-men as they ran at me; and I cut quick and light with the great Weapon, and did have that anger upon me which doth make the heart a place of cold and deadly intent; so that I had a wondrous and brutal judgement to the slaying. And, truly, I slew them as that they had been no more than mice; and I had no harm, neither so much as a touch from them. And, behold! in that moment there came a great Shout of wonder and of welcome from within the Circle. And I lookt swiftly, and began again to run; for there did be men in grey armour all within the Circle; yet came they not to mine aid.

And lo! in a moment I knew why that the Hundred Thousand did have held off from me in mine extremity; for, behold! there did be monstrous Black Mounds all along without of the Circle, and did rock and sway with a force of strange life that did set an horror into my soul as I ran; for truly they did be the visible signs of monstrous Forces of Evil. And did any Human have ventured outward beyond the Circle, then had that man been Destroyed in the Spirit, and lost utterly; so that none had dared to come; neither had it been of use if any had made themselves to be a sacrifice to aid me; for, truly, they to have been of no use, when dead, as you shall say.

And there came a constant shouting from the Hundred Thousand to me, that I haste, and indeed to haste. And truly I did haste with all my strength. And I lookt unto the dear Circle of Holiness that did be above us twain; and it to go steadfast over us; so that I saw we to be surely saved.

And lo! I to be no more than an hundred paces now from the glowing of the Circle. And behold! even in that instant, there must

come brutal things to destroy us; for there came an herd of squat and brutish men all about me in a moment from the shadows, where they had been hid. And they caught at me, and caught at the Maid to tear her from mine arm. And truly, it did be as that they surely to have success; for I could nowise in a moment free myself, and yet to guard the Maid and to use the Diskos. And lo! I kickt with my metal boots, and gave from them, and turned all ways in a moment, and wrenched free; and I leaped back; and the herd of horrid brutes after me.

And now I to have space for the Diskos, and a grimness in my heart; and I came round very sudden, and ran in among the men, smiting. And I hit very swift both from the right and the left, and to and fro with a constant quick circling. And the Diskos did spin and roar, and made a strange light upon the faces of the men, and they to have tusks like to the tusks of pigs. And surely I did rage through them, smiting. And they to strike me a thousand times with great stones, so that mine armour rang, and was all fresh burst, and I near to sicken under the blows and new wounds; but they not to harm the Maid, for I carried her above their squat and brutish reach.

And the brute-men to seem without end. But I made alway forward unto the glowing of the Circle; and the night to be full in that place of the fierce shoutings of the Hundred Thousand; and many—as I did learn—to have tried to come unto me, but that their comrades held them from so useless a dying.

And, in verity, I to be now scarce fifty paces from the glowing of the Circle; and did be nigh to fall; for I did be so utter dazed and wounded with the fight, and ill with a vast weariness and the despair and madness of my journey; and moreover, as you do know, I not to have slept, but to have carried the Maid forever through days and nights, and to have fought oft.

And lo! the Hundred Thousand stood just within the Circle, and they that were to the front did swing each man the Diskos; and they hurled each the Diskos in among the herd of the tuskt men that did make to slay me. And surely this to save me; for the herd did thin to my front; and I to gather my strength, and to charge with despair, and to smite and never be ceased of smiting; so that there did be dead creatures all about. And behold! I brake through the herd, with Mine Own, and did be upon the Circle. And lo! I stept over the Circle, that did scarce now to give out a Resistance; and a thousand hands did come forward to give me help; yet did none touch me, but gave back from me; for there did be that about me which held them off, as with a little awe; for I to be strange unto them.

And I stood there in a great silence, and the Diskos in my hand ran blood to the haft. And maybe I rockt as I stood; for many again did put out their hands, as to hold me, and again drew back, and were silent.

And I lookt unto them, and they lookt back at me; and I did gasp awhile, and was strangely dazed, and did try to tell them that I had need of the Doctors for the Life of Mine Own Maid, that did be dying in mine arms. And behold, in that moment, there did be a sound of giants running, out in the night. And some then to cry out different matters, to aid me, and to beware of the giants, and to bring the Doctors to attend me on the instant.

And other voices did call that the Holy Light was gone from above; and likewise the Black Mounds from the outer part of the Circle. And there did be a monstrous noise of roarings in the Land, and all to come bewildered unto my brain, which did surely fail now with the grim and utter stress which had been mine so long.

And there to be also a constant noise that came from near and from upward; and truly I to know, as in a dream, that it did be made of the shouting of the great Millions, that did make an eternal and vague roaring-sound upward in the night, that did come down from the upper heights, no more loud than a strange and continual murmuring out of the lofty miles.

And surely, I to find my voice in a little minute, and did ask a near man whether there be any Doctors with the men. And in that moment there came forward a Master of the Diskos, which doth be as a Commander of this age. And he made the Salute of Honour with the Diskos, and would have eased the Maid from me; but I to ask again, very slow, whether that there was a Doctor a-near. And he on the instant to give an order; and the great thousands to begin to shape, and did make a mighty lane unto the Great Gateway of the Mighty Pyramid.

And the Master of the Diskos made a sign to certain that did be near; and they stood about me, as I to know dully, lest I fall; but they not to touch me; for I did be as that I must not be laid hand upon; for I did near to choke with despair lest I to have come Home too late; and surely, also, the men to seem as that I did be strange unto them.

And there went orders swift and constant this way and that; and lo! in a little while, there came two big men of the Upward Cities, running; and they had a little man between them upon a sling. And the little man did be a Master of the Doctors; and he aided me gentle to lay Mine Own Maid upon the earth. And the Master of the Diskos

made a sign, and the men that did be near, turned each his back; and the Doctor to make examination for the life of Mine Own.

And there to come about that time a seeming of silence in the land. And truly the Hundred Thousand did be utter quiet; and a great quiet in the Mighty Pyramid; for, in truth, all to know, by this, that there to be a fear that the Maid I did bring out of the night, did be slain by the Evil Forces.

And sudden the little man that did be the Master Doctor, lookt up quiet and piteous at me; so that I knew in a moment that Mine Own Maid did be dead. And he to see that I knew; and he covered the face of Mine Own, and stood up very speedy; and he called softly to the men that did be to my back, and he signed to them that some to support me, and some to lift Mine Own Maid, and bear her unto the Great Gateway. And he lookt keen at me; and I to fight a little that I breathe; and afterward did make with my hands, that the men not to come near me, neither to touch Mine Own. And the Master Doctor to understand that I did be truly strong until I die, and did beckon the men from me, and from the Maid.

And I stoopt, in a little, and I lifted Mine Own Maid into mine arms for that last journeying.

And I came down the mighty lane of the Hundred Thousand, all in their grey armour. And they did make silent salute with the Diskos reversed, each man as I passed him, and did be utter silent. And I scarce to wot of aught, save that all the world did be quiet and emptied, and my task to have failed, and Mine Own to lie dead in mine arms. Yet, truly, did it to have failed utter? for I had surely saved Mine Own from the terror of the Second Night Land, and she not to have come alone and with madness unto her death; but to have died in mine arms; and she surely to have been comforted within her spirit, because that my love did be so utter about her.

And I to think vaguely and terribly on an hundred sweet love actions that she to have shown unto me; and sudden I did remember with a dreadful pain how that I never to have waked to discover Mine Own Maid kissing me in my sleep, as I to have meant. And a madness of anguish did flash sudden through the numbness upon my brain; so that I did be blinded a little, and surely went crooked in my walk; for I to know, sudden, that the Master Doctor steadied mine elbow for a moment; but afterward did leave me be, as I to have again control of my spirit.

And lo! as I drew nigh unto the Great Gateway, the lights of the Pyramid to begin to glow again more strong, and the machinery of the

Lifts and the Air Pumps to work, because that now the Earth-Current did grow once more to natural strength. And they to have power now to open the Great Gate, which did be done by great machines.

And there to come forth to meet me a number of the Masters of the Mighty Pyramid; and the dear Master Monstruwacan did come before them all, so eager as that he did be mine own Father. And he to have heard somewhat, vaguely, that there to have been a fear for the life of the maid that I did bring.

And surely, he did be told by one near to the Gateway, that the Maid did be dead in mine arms; for he and all the Masters did pause and stand silent for me to go by, and did reverse each his Diskos; and this to have been an Honour shown, than which there did be scarce any greater.

And there went a constant murmuring up in the night, which did be the speech of the Millions, questioning. And the news that the Maid did be dead, went upward through the miles. And my spirit to know, as in a dream, of the spiritual noise which did go outward through all space, and did be the grief of the Multitudes, as they did hear this thing. Yet, truly, there did nothing comfort me anywise; neither I proper yet to know the verity of my loss; for I did go stunned.

And I came in through the Great Gateway, and the Full Watch did stand there silent in their armour; and they made the Salute of Honour. And I went onward with the dead Maid that I did bring out of Eternity.

And presently, they that were around, did guide me, with the Maid in mine arms, unto the Great Lift. And I took Mine Own Maid into the Great Lift; and the Masters came with me, and did be in their armour; and none did speak to me. And the Master Monstruwacan and the Master of the Doctors stood silent to the side of me. And there did be everywhere great Multitudes, that I did see vaguely; but my spirit not to wot of them.

And lo! I stood very quiet and dumb as we did go upward through the miles; and the Millions of the Cities stood about the Great Lift, and there did be a great silence upward and downward through the strange miles; save for the weeping of women in dear sympathy, that did sound far and low and constant.

And presently I to know that the Master Monstruwacan and the Master of the Doctors did look one to the other; and I to be aware sudden that I stood in my blood; for I did be wounded in an hundred parts, and the blood to go alway from me. Yet did the Master Doctor be slow to do aught for me, because that he to perceive that I did be

slain in the heart; and there to be no pain so dreadful as that he should be like to wake me unto, if that he went hastily.

Yet, presently, there did come whirlings into my head; and some-one did surely make to ease Mine Own Maid from mine arms. But I held her, dumbly; and the blood to go the more from me; and they not to know what should be done. And I to look at them. And the dear Master Monstruwacan did be saying somewhat unto me, that I did have no power to hear; but only to know that his face did be very human. And there went a strange noise all about me; and the Master Monstruwacan to seem to hold me up, and to beckon to some that did be to my back. And lo! there came a blackness, and the gentleness of arms about mine armour

* * * *

And I to come presently to quietness and to half-dreams; and did alway to seem that I carried Mine Own Maid in mine arms. But truly there did pass three great days, whilst that I did be thus. And I all that while to be laid quiet, and to be tended by the Master Doctor, and aided by all knowledge that did be known of Humans.

And on the third day, as it might be called, I to come full unto my senses; and the pain to take me in the breast; and the Master of the Doctors did be with me, and they that nurst me; and the Master Doctor watched me very keen and gentle.

And I did be in a bed of the Health Room of mine own city. And I gat from the bed, and the Doctor to say naught; but only to watch me. And I walkt to and fro a little, and he alway to watch me; and presently he gave me somewhat to drink; and I drank. And I was gone soon from all knowledge.

And I to come again unto a knowing that I yet to live; and there went a certain strength in my body. And lo! the first that I did see, was the Master of the Doctors; and I to perceive in a moment that he had wakened me, and had nurst my strength for that moment, that I live through the Burial. For he to be very wise, and to have known from that first seeing of me, that I not to live after that Mine Own did die.

And there was brought to me a loose garment; but I to refuse the garment, dumbly, and did look about me very troubled and forget-ting. And the Master Doctor lookt alway at me; and lo! in a moment he called one, and gave an order. And there was brought in then my broken armour, and a garment to wear below. And I then to know

that I did be content in this matter; and the Doctor alway to watch me. And they drest me in my broken armour.

And surely, as they drest me, my spirit to hear the sorrow and sympathy of the Multitudes, and did know that they went downward by millions, unto the Country of Silence.

And lo! in that moment when I near to be in mine armour, I to mind sudden again that I never to have waked to discover Mine Own Maid kissing me in my sleep. And the Pain gat me in the breast, so that I had surely ended then, but that the Master Doctor set somewhat to my breath, that eased me, and gave something of dullness unto my senses for a while.

And I did be carried then in a sling unto the Great Lift, and there did be a bed in the lift, and the Doctor to have me to lie upon the bed; and I to know that he also to know that I never to need a bed any more; neither should I ever to come upward again in the Lift.

And truly the Mighty Pyramid did be an emptyness; for there did seem to be left only the Stress Masters that did arrange the moving of the Millions. And the Stress Masters did stand about the Lift, as we dropt downward through the great miles unto the Underground Fields. And we came downward in the last unto the Country of Silence, which did lie an hundred miles deep in the world, and did be an hundred miles every way of Silence unto the Dead.

And they that were with me, gat me from the Lift, and did mean to carry me in the sling unto The Last Road. But I stood upon my feet, and made that I should walk, and I held out my hand for the Diskos, which one did carry. And the Master Doctor signed that they should obey me, as my spirit to know. And I walkt very steadfast down the Way that did lead unto The Last Road; and the Master Doctor walkt behind me, a little space off.

And surely, there did be all the Peoples of the World in that great Country; and the Peoples did be spread out forever, so far as my seeing did go; and they to have sight of me; and all the æther did be stirred with the humanness of their sorrow and their kind sympathy. And there grew a murmur, which did be like to a low rolling thunder, and did be the voices of the Peoples. And the rolling of that great husht Sound went to and fro across that mighty Country of Quiet; and there to be afterward an utter silence.

And I saw below me the place of the Last Rest, where did be the beginning of The Last Road; and there did lie there a little figure, covered with a white robe, that did glimmer with the beauteous work of women that had stitcht love and honour into that Last Garment.

And surely, I to rock upon my feet, and to steady myself with the Diskos; and the Master Doctor to be unto my side in a moment, and gave me again something that I breathe-in. But, indeed, I to refuse, after that I had taken one breath of the drug; for I to be able to bear my pain the little time that I now to have to live; and I to mean that I have no dimness of my senses for those short minutes that I should have yet near unto Mine Own. And truly the Master Doctor did not press me anywise, but had a perfect understanding, and went quiet again to the rearward.

And I came soon to that place where Mine Own Dead One did lie; and the Master Monstruwacan stood to her feet, and did be clothed in grey armour, and had the Diskos reversed; and this to be for an Honour unto My Dead Maid.

And there kneeled two maids in white, one to the right and one to the left of Mine Own, and they to be for Faithfulness, and did be maids, because that they watched by a maid; and had likewise been matrons, if that the Dead had been wife unto any.

And the place at the Head of the Last Rest did be empty, and did be for me; and he that stood to the head, did be for Love; for it did be the chief, and did hold dominion over and did make to live both Faithfulness and Honour. And this to be the way of the Burial alway.

And lo! I took my courage into my heart; and I stood to the head of Mine Own Maid; and I lookt down upon the wondrous white glory of the garment, which did be white because that Mine Own did be a Maid; yet did be worked with yellow Flowers of Weeping, as we did call them, because that she had died in love. And I to know that no hand had toucht that wonderful garment, save the hands of maidens.

And behold! as I stood there, from far away over the Land, there did come a far and faint sound; and the sound did come more nigh, so that I knew that afar off, beyond the Hills of the Babes, the Millions did begin to sing the Calling Song, where Million did call husht unto Million, and the sound did come onward toward where we did be, and did go over us, and pass onward in a husht and wondrous breathing of sound, as that all the Love that did be ever in this world, did call in a low anguish unto a lost Beloved. And the sound to pass away and away over that mighty Country in the deep Earth, and did hush and hush unto a great and utter silence, save for a faint murmur of countless women weeping, that did be in the air of that Land of Quiet.

And there to be a space of silence, and again the silence to be broken by a far sound; and there to come again from beyond the far Hills of the Babes a strange and low sound, and did be as of a wind

wandering through damp forests. And the sound grew, and came across the Hills of the Babes, and did be breathed forth by Million after Million, so that in a little I to hear the Song of Weeping sung very low and sorrowful by the multitudes. And the Song came onward over all that great Country, and past over us, and went onward into the far Land beyond the Dome, and did be caught by the voices of Millions that did be hid in great distances, and so to go onward forever, and to die at last unto a mighty silence.

And the Master Monstruwacan lookt at me from the feet of Mine Own Maid, and I to know that the moment did be come when I to part from the Maid Naani forever and forever, even though I to live in some strange future, and to find her soul in some other sweet child. And I stoopt and laid the Diskos beside Mine Own Maid there upon the Last Rest; and the two maids drew back the light wonder of the Garment, and showed me the face of Mine Own, and she to sleep there forever so sweet and husht as a child, and as oft I to have seen her to sleep. And I lookt a little while, and the pain of my heart did be sufficient, so that I knew I died as I lookt. And once more I lookt, and I set my soul about Mine Own. And I fought with myself, and stood upward, and the maids did cover the face of Mine Own Maid.

And the Master Monstruwacan commended Naani unto Eternity. And he raised the Diskos reversed; and lo! the Road did begin to move upward unto the Dome, and Mine Own Maid did be upon the Road; and I to fight that I keep breathing; so that I not to die before she be lost utter to my sight.

And there did rise now a sound from all that Country that had no order in it; and did be like to a low moaning that did fill all the air of the Land; and there to be also a constant sound, as of a little whistling dree wind that did be in all that Country of Quiet; and truly this to be more than any singing; for it to be the true weeping of multitudes, that did sorrow from the heart, with the grief of this thing that did be.

And I stood utter still, and did draw my breath very even, and lookt unto that small form that did be now afar off where it did lie upon the moving Roadway. And I gazed, as that my soul and all my being did have no power else, even as a man that dies, doth set all his strength to a last movement. And I not to wot that the Master Monstruwacan and the two maids did hold me up, because they to perceive that I did be dying; for I only to see Mine Own Little One lying afar off upon the moving of the Last Road.

And the Maid in that moment to come to the place where the Road did pass into the strange and luminous vapour of the Earth-Current,

which did lie all about the base of the Dome; and the vapour to be only as a faint shining smoke, scarce seen, yet to be enough to give something of uncertainty to the Dead, when that they did have past inward of it.

And I stared, with all that did be left of my strength; for Mine Own to be gone utter and forever in but a little minute. And the uncertainty of the luminous vapour did cling about her, and to make her to seem unreal to my gaze; for the vapour did be in constant movement, and to give a seeming of shifting to and fro of all that did be in it.

And behold! as I did stare, with my dreadful pain, there did be sudden a strange hoarse noise from the nearer Millions. And lo! in an instant there came a mighty Shout out of all that Country; and the shout did be made again, and did grow into a mighty hoarse roaring from the Millions, so that all that great Country did be filled with the monstrous sound. And, in verity, I to have seen the thing, likewise; but to have set it to the madness of longing of my heart and to that desperate and dreadful pain which did make me to be crazed and lost from all sane thinking.

And the thing that I did see, had been that the Maid did seem to move, there upon the Last Road, where she did lie; but indeed, this to have appeared only to be the stirring of the luminous vapour of the Earth-Current, which did seem to make things shift, as I have told.

And lo ! I now to see truly that the Maid did move where she was laid afar off upon the Road; and I now to know, and to believe that she did indeed live. And my life came into me with a bounding; yet did my heart seem to be a moment stilled in my breast. And the Master Monstruwacan to have signed already that the Roadway be stopt, and brought backward; but I to be now upon the Last Road, and did run as a madman, shouting vainly upon the name of Mine Own. And I to learn afterward that there to have been a dreadful peril that all the near Millions to rush toward the Last Road, and so, mayhap, to have caused the death of many, and to have been like to have crusht Mine Own. But this danger to have been eased, because that the Watch Master did act very prompt, and set the great regiments of his men to keep back the Millions, and did send a signal abroad over all the Country, that there to be calmness, for that the Maid should be succoured. And alway, whilst this to be, I did run staggering most strangely upward of the Last Road; and surely that great roof did ring and boom with the constant and mighty shoutings of the Millions.

And there did run others also along the Road, to my back; but I to have been the first, and to make a good speed, though I did stagger

and rock so strange upon my feet; and the Road alway to be moving backward under me; and so I to be come wonderful soon unto where the Maid did be. And she to be upon her back, and to have pusht the Garment from her face, and did be lying with her eyes open, and a look of gentle wonderment upon her dear face. And she then to see me, and her eyes did smile at me, very glad and quiet; for there to be yet an utter weakness upon her.

And lo! I came with a falling beside her, and I gat upon my knees and upon my hands, and my heart did shake my lips to dry whisperings. And she to look weak and steadfast unto me, and I to look forever at her; and I did alway try to say things unto her; but my mouth to refuse me.

And understanding did come into her, as a light; and she to know in that instant that she to be truly come into the Mighty Pyramid, and I to have gat her there somewise; and she to wake sudden in her body, and set her hands forth all a-trembling from the Garment, and in dreadful trouble. And I to see then that the blood did go from me, constant; and the Maid to have perceived this thing, so that she was waked the more proper in a moment from her death-swoon.

And surely, I did bleed very dreadful; for all my wounds did be opened with my running. And I to have sudden power with my lips, and did say unto her, very simple, that I loved her. And she to be all in an haze from me; and I to know that she to have come likewise unto her knees, and did have my head upon her breast; and there to be an utter shaking of the air with some great sound, and a mighty spiritual stirring of the æther of the world.

And there to be then the voice of the Master Monstruwacan very dull in mine ears; and the low voice of the Master Doctor; but I never to hear what they did be saying; and did know only that Mine Own Maid did live; and I not to mean to die, but to fight unto living. And even whilst that I made this resolving, I was gone into an utter blackness.

XVII
The Love Days

NOW, WHEN THAT I gat back unto life, I to know that I went upward in the Lift, and did be upon that same bed, where I to think I never to need a bed any more, neither to come upward again from out of the Country of Silence.

And I to know vague and strange, that there rose up from out of the mighty depths of the world, the deep thunder of the Underground Organs, and did sound as that they made a strange and utter distant music beyond death; and there to go alway a rolling chaunting, as that multitudes did sing beyond far mountains, and the sound to be somewhiles as a far-blowing wind, low in the Deep; and again to come clear, and to be that great olden melody of the Song of Honour. And I knew, as in a dream, that the Millions in that deep Country made an Honour and a Rejoicing over this Wonder of Joy which did be come. But yet all to be faint and half hid from me, and mine eyes to be as that they had no power to open, and I to seem to be lifting alway upon strange waters of unrealness. And there to be sweet and lovely odours, and these to be of reality, and to come from the great Fields, where the flowers did alway to grow about the passage ways of the Lifts; for the Lift even then to be going upward through the great miles.

And mayhap I moved a little; for there came the voice of the Master Doctor low and gentle to me; and bid me rest; for that all did be well with the Maid. And surely, afterward, I did be gone into an haze, and there to be then a seeming of days in which I half to live and half to sleep, and to wonder without trouble whether I did be dead.

And then there to come days when I lay very quiet, and had no thought of aught; and the Master Doctor oft to bend over me in this hour and that hour, and to look keen into my face. And in the end, after strange spaces, there bent over me another, and there lookt down upon me the dear and lovely face of Mine Own, and the eyes

did speak love into my soul; yet did she be calm and husht. And I to begin again to live in my body, and I made, mayhap, a little fumbling with my hands; for she to take and to hold them; and life to come from her to me; and she to be ever wordless and gentle; and contentment to grow in me, and presently a natural slumber.

And there came a day when I did be let rise, and they that tended me, carried me to one of the Quiet Gardens of the Pyramid; and they set me there, and did seem to leave me alone. And there came One then around a bush, and lookt at me a moment, as with an half shyness; only that the love that did shine in her eyes, made the shyness to be a little thing. And, truly, I knew that it did be Mine Own Maid; but I never before to have seen Naani drest pretty as a maid. And I lookt to her, and knew that she did be more dainty than even I to have known. And sudden I made that I rise to come unto her; but she to run quick to me, that she stop me of this natural foolishness; and she then to sit beside me, and to take my head against her breast, and she not to deny me her lips; but to be both a maid and a mother to me in the same moment.

And afterward, she had me to be very still; and we to sit there in an utter dumb happiness, until they that did attend me, were come again. And the Master of the Doctors did be with them, and I to see that there went something of satisfaction in his face.

And after that day I saw Mine Own Maid every day; and I gat better unto health with a wondrous quickness; for Love did mend me. And soon I did be let go downward unto the Fields; but yet to go by private ways, because that the Multitudes should be like to follow me alway; and I to need to be quiet.

And the Maid to be with me; for the Master Monstruwacan and the Master of the Doctors did agree upon this matter, and had an Officer of Marriage to wed us; and we to be married very quiet and simple; for I yet to be over-weak for the Public Marriage, which we to have later; when, truly, the Millions made us a Guard of Honour eight miles high, from the top unto the bottom of the Mighty Pyramid. But this to have been later, as I do tell, and did be a Ceremonial of the Peoples, because that they not to be denied that they give me an Honour.

And surely the Maid to be with me alway, and did be now my wife, and my strength to come alway upon me, and Mine Own to grow again unto a perfect health. And, in verity, we did be now in the Love Days which do be the most beauteous, if that the Love to be True.

And we did wander through the mighty Fields at our will, and walkt in the Love Paths of the Fields, which did be alway anear to

those places where did be the villages. And I to hide our name, lest we to be beset by any, out of natural curiousness and kindliness; for we to need to be utter together and quiet.

And we to chose those places for our slumber where beauty of flowers did be most wondrous; and we to carry somewhat of food with us; but also to eat when we came unto the villages which did be here and there in the Fields, which were truly so huge as Countries. And Mine Own did make good her promise an hundred times, as you shall say, and did prepare me a great and hearty meal; and did tease me utter that I did be a glutton, as I did eat, and kist me, lest that I have ever a chance to say aught in mine own defence. And truly, she did be all that my heart and my spirit did desire; and she to have companioned me with Love, and to have entered my spirit into Joy.

And once we to go downward unto the Country of Silence; but not to stay very long at that time; because that my Memory did return upon me. Yet in the after time, we to wander there oft with Memory, and Holiness of great Thinkings, and with Love which doth hold all.

And as we to leave that Country, I to tell Mine Own how that when she had been suspend of her life by the Horrid Force of the House, I to have minded me with a dreadful pain that I never to have waked to discover her kissing me when that I did sleep. And surely Mine Own Dear One did blush most lovely, and had never known that I did be aware of her sweet naughtiness; and she then to have all thought for mine agony, when that she did be dead, ere the Vapour of life of the Earth-Force did set her spirit free of the Silence.

And she to come unto me in dear understanding.

And she then to tell me that the Doctors to say that she had been, as it were, stunned and froze of the Spirit, and all her Being and Life suspend; and the great life-force of the Earth-Current to have waked her spirit, and her body then to live and her blood to flow proper again. And the Doctors had talkt much and searched much of late in the olden Records of their Work; and they to have found somewhat of one such happening in the olden time; but truly, naught such to have been ever through a mighty age of years.

And whilst that we to wander and to rest in the Fields, I oft to tell Mine Own of this matter and that matter; and I to know that she had learned somewhat of odd things, ere I did be come to health; but not overmuch; for she also to have been utter alack, as you shall think; and to have come from her bed, when that I did lie so still; for the Master Doctor to have ordained this, because he to fear that I to be going truly to die, if that he not to do somewhat to awaken my spirit.

And in verity, you shall think upon the deepness of my Love as I to know that she did have held my hands so brave and gentle, whilst that she to have scarce power to her feet. And I to say a little holy praise of Mine Own.

And so do I come to mine ending; and have but one more thing that I tell. And this to happen a while later; after that Mine Own and I had gone through the second marriage which did be the Public Marriage. For it did be, that one day My Wife, that did be Mine Own, did take me with a sweet cunning unto the Hall of Honour. And surely, when I was come there, I to see that many of the Peoples did be in that great Hall, and did stand about in a silence; yet as that they had no meaning to do aught; but yet to be that they did wait upon somewhat.

And My Wife did go forward with me unto the centre place of the Hall; and sudden I saw why that she did bring me so cunning sweet; for there did stand in the midst of the Hall of Honour, in the Place of Honour, a Statue of a man in broken armour, that did carry a maid forever.

And I did be dumb; and how of this Age shall you to know the Honour that this to mean in that; for it did be an Honour that was given only to the Great Dead; and I to be but a young man, and did be so utter far off from greatness; save that I to love with all my heart and with all my spirit, and therefore death to be but a little thing before love. And you to know how Love doth make sweet and brave the heart; and to have understanding with me in my humbleness and my wonder and my natural pride that there did any so think to honour me.

And Mine Own did be weeping with joy and honest pride of her man, beside me. And there to be an utter silence of dear sympathy in all the great Hall of Honour. And they that did be there, to let me go in quietness, with Mine Own, which did be a lovely thing of understanding.

And I to go loving and thoughtful with Mine Own Wife; and she to be very nigh to me.

And I to have gained Honour; yet to have learned that Honour doth be but as the ash of Life, if that you not to have Love. And I to have Love. And to have Love is to have all; for that which doth be truly LOVE doth mother Honour and Faithfulness; and they three to build the House of Joy.

Perilous Romances

The Captain of the Onion Boat

BIG JOHN CARLOS, CAPTAIN of the Santa, stood looking up at the long tapered window in the otherwise great, grey blank of the convent wall, a dozen yards away.

The wall formed the background of the quay, and between it and the side of the vessel was a litter of unloaded gear and cargo. The Captain's face, as he stared upward at that one lonesome window, had an extraordinarily set expression; and his Mate, a little lop-shouldered man, very brown and lean, watched him over the coaming of the main hatchway, with a curious grimace of half-sympathy and half-curiosity.

"Old Man's got it bad as ever," he muttered, in an accent and language that spoke of the larger English. He transferred his gaze from the silent form of the skipper, standing, in the stern, to the long taper of the one window that broke the towering side of the convent.

Presently, the thing for which the two men watched, came into view, as it did twice daily, at morning and evening—a long line of half-veiled nuns, who were obviously ascending some stairway within the convent, on to which this solitary window threw light.

Most of the women went by the window quietly, with faces composed, and looking before them; but here and there a young nun would take this opportunity to glance out into the Carnal World which they had renounced for ever. Young, beautiful faces there were, that looked out momentarily, showing doubly human, because of the cold ascetic garb of renunciation which framed them; then were gone on from sight, in the long, steadily moving procession of silent figures.

It was about the middle of the procession, after a weary line of seeming mutes had gone past, that the Mate saw that for which he waited. For, suddenly, the great body of the Captain stiffened and became rigid, as the head of one of the moving figures turned and stared out on to the quay. The Mate saw her face clearly. It was still

young and lovely, but seemed very white and hopeless. He noted the eager, hungry look in the eyes; and then the wonderful way in which they lit up, as with a strange inward fire, at sight of the big man standing there; and the whole face seemed to quiver into living emotion. Immediately afterwards, she was gone past, and more mutes were making the grey, ascending line.

"Gord! that's 'er!" said the Mate, and glanced towards his master. The face of the big skipper was still upturned and set with a fixed, intense stare, as though even now he saw her face at the long window. His body was yet rigid with intensity, and his great hands gripped tightly the front of his slack jumper, straining it, unconsciously, down upon his hips. For some moments longer, he stood like this, lost to all knowledge except the tellings of his memory, and stunned with his emotions. Then he relaxed abruptly, as if some string within him had been loosed, and turned towards the open hatchway, where the Mate bent once more to his work.

"W'y don't 'e get 'er out," the Mate remarked to himself, "They've bin doin' that years 'n years, from wot I can see an' 'ear, an' breakin' their blessed 'earts. W'y the 'ell don't 'e get 'er out! It's easy ter see she's a woman, a sight more'n a bloomin' nun!" In all of which the little crooked shouldered Mate showed a fund of common sense; but likewise an insufficient ability to realise how thoroughly a religious belief may sometimes prove a stumbling-block in the pathway to mere human happiness.

How a man of the stamp of Big John Carlos came to be running an onion boat, must be conjectured. His name is explained by his father having been a Spaniard and his mother an Englishwoman. Originally, Big John had been a merchant, of a kind, going to sea in his own ship, and trading abroad.

As a youth, he had become engaged to Marvonna Delia, whose father had owned much property, farther up the coast. Her father had died, and she had been an heiress, sought by all the youths about; but he—Big John Carlos—had won her.

They were to have been married on his return from his next trading voyage; but the report went home to his sweetheart that he had been drowned at sea; and indeed he had truly fallen overboard; but had been picked up by a China-bound sailing-ship, and had been a little over a year lost to his friends, before he had managed to reach home, to carry the news that he still lived. For this was before the days of the telegraph, and his one letter had gone astray.

When at last, he reached home, it was to find sad changes. His

sweetheart, broken-hearted, had become a nun at the great convent of St. Sebastian's, and had endowed it with all her wealth and lands. What attempts he made to have speech with her, I do not know; but if his religious scruples had allowed him to beg her to renounce her vows and retirement, and return to the world to be his wife, they had certainly been unsuccessful; though it is quite conceivable that no word had ever passed between them, since she had put the world behind her.

From then onward, through nine long years, Big John Carlos had traded along the coast. His former business, he had dropped, and now he wandered from port to port in his small craft. And twice in every year, he would come alongside of the little wharf opposite to the great, grey wall of the convent, and there lie for a week, watching year by year that long narrow window for the two brief glimpses daily of his lost sweetheart.

After a week, he would go. It was always a week that he stayed there by the old wharf. Then, as if that had exhausted his strength— as if the pain of the thing had grown in that time to be too dreadful to continue, he would haul out, and away, whatever the weather or the state of trade. All of this the little twisted Mate knew, more or less clearly in detail, having learned it in the previous visit, which he had made with Big John Carlos to the insignificant port where the convent stood.

And she—what can the young nun have thought and felt? How she must have fought to endure the grey weary months between the far-apart visits; and day by day glanced out of the tall stair-window, as she passed in the long, mute procession, for a sight of the little onion boat and the big man standing in the stern, watching—tense and silent—for that one brief glimpse of her, as she passed in the remorseless line of figures. And something of this also, the little crooked-shouldered Mate had realised, vaguely, and had achieved an instant though angry sympathy. But his point of view was limited and definite:—"W'y the 'ell don't 'e get 'er out!" was his brief formula. And that marked the limit of his imagination, and therefore of his understanding.

His own religious beliefs were of the kind that are bred in the docks (London docks, in his case), and fostered in dirty fo'cas'les; and now he was "come down to this onion shuntin'," as he would have worded it. Yet, whatever his religious lack, or even his carelessness on a point of ethics, he was thoroughly and masculinely human,

"W'y the 'ell—" he began again, in his continual grumble to him-self; and had no power to conceive that the woman, having taken a certain step, might believe that step to be unretraceable—that usage,

belief, and finally (bred of these two) Conscience might forbid even the thought, stamping it as a crime that would shut her out from the Joy of the Everlasting.

The Joy of the Everlasting! The little twisted man would have grinned at you, had you mentioned it. "W'y the 'ell don't 'e get 'er out!" would have been his reply, accompanied by a profuseness of tobacco-juice.

And yet, it is conceivable that the heart of the woman was, even this long while, grown strong to do battle for dear Happiness—her heart that had known, silently and secretly and dumbly, all along, the unnatural wickedness of her outrage of her Womanhood. Visit by visit, through the long years, her heart must have grown fiercely strong to end this torture which her brain (darkened with the Clouds of Belief) had put upon her, to endure through all her life.

And so, all unknowingly, because of the loyal brain that would not be aware of the growing victory of her heart, she was come to a condition in which her beliefs held her no more than if they had been cords that had rotted upon her, as indeed they might be said to have done. That she was free to come, the little Mate had seen, using his eyes and his heart and his wit. To him, it was merely a matter of ways and means—physical. "W'y the 'ell—!" that was his puzzle.

Why? With an angry impatience, that came near to verging upon the borderland of scorn, the little Mate would question inwardly. Was Big John Carlos bit wiv them religious notions, same as the other dagoes! He did not understand the complaint, or how it was achieved; but he knew, as an outside fact, that there was something of that kind which infected the peoples along the coasts he travelled. If Big John were not troubled in this way, "why the 'ell—" And so he would return to his accustomed formula, working furiously, in sheer irritation of mind:—"If 'e ain't religious, wot is it? Carn't 'e see the way 'er eyes blessed well looks at 'im! Cam't 'e see she's mad an' double mad to be out wiv 'im!"

Why did not John Carlos attempt to win back for himself the one thing that he desired in all the world? Maybe (and I think that it is very possible) in the early years of his return, he had so striven; but the young nun, shaken with the enormousness of the thought, hopelessly weighted with her vows, had not dared to think upon it—had retreated with horror from the suggestion; had turned with an intention of double ardour to seek in her religious duties, the calm and sweetness, the peace and joy, which she felt to be lost to her forever in any more earthly way.

And then had followed the long years, with her heart fighting silently and secretly—secretly almost from herself—unto victory. Arid the man (having lost the force of that first fierce unpenting of his intention to win her—and mayhap having been repulsed, as it would seem to his masculine mind, hopelessly) had fallen back under the sway of the religious beliefs, which ruled him in his more normal hours; and so, year by year, had withheld from any further attempt to win her; striving to content his soul with those two brief visits each year to the old wharf; each time to endure a mad week of those futile watchings for his beloved.

Yet, in him, as in the woman, there had been going forward, without his knowledge, that steady disruption of religious belief—the rotting and decaying of all arbitrary things, before the primal need of the human heart; so that the olden barriers of " Impossibility," were now but as shadows, that would be gone in a moment, when next the Force of his Need should urge him to take his heart's desire.

His first attempt—if there had ever been such—had been the outcome of his natural want—his Love—; but lacking the foundations of Sureness of Himself and of his Power to withstand the Future. Indeed, it is conceivable that had he succeeded at the first, and gained his desire, the two of them would have wilted in the afterblast of thought and fear-of-the-hereafter, and in the Fires of Scruples which would have burned in their path through all the years.

But now, whatever they might do, they would do—if it ever came to pass—with a calm and determined Intention; having done their thinking first, and weighed all known costs, and proved their strength, and learned the utterness of their need to be truly greater than all else that might be set as balance against it. And because of this, they were ripe—wanting only the final stimulus to set into action the ready Force that had concentrated through the years.

Yet, strangely, neither the man nor the woman knew, as I have shown, that they had developed to this. Their brains refused to know; their Consciences looked, each with its blind eye, at their hearts, and saw nothing to give cause of offence to the ethical in them; or, did Conscience catch an odd glimpse, with its seeing eye, of impossible wickedness, there followed hours of imagined repentance, deep and painful, resulting in a double assuredness, within the brain (and "Manufactured" Parts) of a conquered and chastened heart, and of fiercer resolutions for the future Torture of Salvation. But always, deep within, the unconquerable heart fought for the victory that was each year more assured.

And so, as you have already seen, these two, the man and the woman, were but waiting—the man for some outward stimulus, to put into action all the long-pent force in him, revealing to him his actual nature, developed and changed in the course of the long years of pain, until he should be scarcely likely to recognise himself in the first moments of his awakening to this reality. And the woman, waiting, subconsciously, for the action of the man to bring her to a knowledge of the realities—to an awareness of the woman she had become, of the woman into which she had developed, unable any more to endure the bondage of aught save her heart that leaped to the ordering of Mother Nature. Nay, more, fiercely and steadfastly eager to take with both hands the forbidden joy of her Natural Birthright, and calm and resolute and unblinking to face the future, with its unsolvable problem of the Joy of the Everlasting.

And thus were these two standing, as it might be said, on the brink of their destinies; waiting, with blinded eyes, and as that they listened unknowingly for the coming of the unknown one who should give the little push forward, and so cause them to step over the borderland into all natural and long craved for happiness.

Who would be That One?

"W'y the 'ell don't 'e get 'er out?" the Mate had asked the First Hand, who knew all the story, having sailed years with Big John Carlos. But the First Hand had raised his arms in horror, and made plain in broken English his opinion of the sacrilege, though that was not how he had pronounced it.

"Sacrilege be jiggered!" the Mate had replied, humping his twisted shoulders. " I s'pose though there'd be a 'oly rumpus, hey?"

The First Hand had intimated very definitely that there would be a " rumpus," which, the Mate ferreted out, might involve some very unpleasant issues both for the man and the woman guilty of such a thing. The First Hand spoke (in broken English) as if he were the Religious Conscience of his nation. Such things could not be tolerated. His phraseology did not include such words; but he was sufficiently definite.

"Nice 'ealthy lot o' savages, you!' " the Mate had explained, after listening to much intolerant jabbering. "Strike me! If you ain't canniballs!" And straightway saddled on to the unfortunate Catholic Faith the sins peculiar to a hot-blooded and emotional People, whose enthusiasms and prejudices would have been just as apparent, had they been called forth by some other force than their Faith, or by a Faith differently shaped and Denominated.

It was the little crooked Mate who was speaking to Big John Carlos, in the evening of the sixth day of their stay beside the old wharf. And the big man was listening, in a stunned kind of silence. Through those six days the little man had watched the morning and evening tragedy, and the sanity of his free thoughts had been as a yeast in him. Now he was speaking, unlading all the things that he had to say.

"W'y the 'ell don't you take 'er out?" he had asked in so many words. And to him it had seemed, that very evening, that the woman's eyes had been saying the same thing to the Captain, as she looked her brief, dumb agony of longing across the little space that had lain between; yet which, as it were, was in verity the whole width of Eternity. And now the little Mate was putting it all into definite words—standing there, an implement of Fate or Providence or the Devil, according to the way that you may look at it, his twisted shoulder heaving with the vehemence of his speech:—

"You didn't orter do it, Capting," he said. "You're breakin' 'er up, an' you're breakin' you up; an' no good to it. W'y the 'ell don't you do somefink! Rescue 'er, or keep away. If it's 'ell for you, it's just 's much 'ell for 'er! She'll come like a little bloomin' bird. See 'ow she looks at you. She's fair askin' you to come an' take 'er out of it all— an' you just standin' there! My Gord!"

"What can I do," said the Captain, hoarsely; and put his hands suddenly to his head. He did not ask a question, or voice any hopelessness; but just gave out the words, as so many sounds, mechanically; for he was choked, suffocating during those first few moments, with the vast surge of hope that rose and beat upward in him, as the little twisted Mate's words crashed ruthlessly through the shrouding films of Belief.

And suddenly he knew. He knew that he could do this thing; that all scruples, all bonds of belief, of usage, of blind fears for the future, and of the Hereafter, were all fallen from him, as so much futile dust. Until that moment, as I have shown to you before, he had not known that he could do it—had not known of his steady and silent development. But now, suddenly, all his soul and being, lighted with Hope, he looked inward, and saw as the man he was—the man to which grown and come to be. He knew. He knew.

"Would she… would she?" The question came unconsciously from his lips; but the little twisted man took it up.

"Arsk 'er! Arsk 'er!" he said, vehemently. "I knows she'll come. I seen it in 'er eyes to-night w'en she looked out at you. She was sayin' as plain as your 'at, 'W'y the 'ell don't you take me out? W'y the 'ell don't you?' You arsk 'er, an' she'll come like a bird."

The little Mate spoke with the eagerness of conviction, and indulged in no depressing knowledge of incongruities. "Arsk 'er!" was his refrain. "You arsk 'er!"

"How?" said the Captain, coming suddenly to realities.

The little man halted, and stumbled over his unreadiness. He had no plan; nothing but his feelings. He sought around in his mind, and grasped at an idea.

"Write it on an 'atch cover, wiv chalk," he said, triumphant. "Lean the 'atch cover by you. W'en she comes, point to it, 'n she'll read it."

"Ha!" said the Captain, in a strange voice, as if he both approved, and, at the same time, had remembered something.

"Then she'll nod," continued the little man. "No one else ever looks outer that winder, scarcely, not to think to read writin', anyway. An' you can cover it, till she's due to show. Then we'll plan 'ow to get 'er out."

All that night, Big John Carlos paced the deck of his little craft, alone, thinking, and thrilling with great surges of hope and maddened determination.

In the morning, he put the plan to the test; only that he wrote the question on the hatch-cover in peculiar words, that he had not used all those long grey years; for he made use of a quaint but simple transposition of letters, which had been a kind of love-language between them, in the olden days. This was why he had called "Ha!" so strangely, being minded suddenly of it, and to have the sweetness of using it to that one particular purpose.

Slowly, the line of grey moving figures came into view, descending. Big John Carlos kept the hatch-cover turned to him, and counted; for well he knew just when she would appear. The one hundred and ninth mute would pass, and the one hundred and tenth would show the face of his Beloved. The order never changed through the years, in that changeless world within.

As the hundred and seventh figure passed the narrow window, he turned the hatch-cover, so that the writing was exposed, and pointed down to it, so that his whole attitude should direct her glance instantly to his question, that she might have some small chance to read it, in the brief moment that was hers as she went slowly past the narrow panes. The hundred and ninth figure passed down from sight, and then he was looking dumbly into her face, as she moved into view, her eyes already strained to meet his. His heart was beating with a dull, sickening thudding, and there seemed just the faintest of mists before his vision; but he knew that her glance had flown eagerly to the message, and that her white face had flashed suddenly to a greater whiteness,

disturbed by the battle of scores of emotions loosed in one second of time. Then she was gone downward out of his sight, and he let the hatch-cover fall, gripping the shrouds with his hand.

The little twisted man stole up to him.

"She saw, Capting! She 'adn't time to answer. Not to know if she was on 'er 'ead or 'er 'eels. Look out to-night. She'll nod then." He brought it all out in little whispered jerks, and the big man, wiping his forehead, nodded.

Within the convent, a woman (outwardly a nun) was even then descending the stairs, with shaking knees, and a brain that had become in a few brief instants a raging gulf of hope. Before she had descended three steps below the level of the window, even whilst her sight-memory still held the message out for her brain to read and comprehend, she had realised that spiritually she was clothed only with the ashes of Belief and Fear and Faith. The original garment had become charred to nothing in the Fire of Love and Pain, with which the years had enveloped her. No bond held her; no fear held her; nothing in all the world mattered, except to be his for all the rest of her life. She took and realised the change in her character, in a moment of time. Eight long years had the yeast of love been working in her, which had bred the chemistry of pain; but only in that instant did she know and comprehend that she was developed so extensively, as to be changed utterly from the maid of eight years gone. Yet, in the next few steps she took, she had adapted herself to the new standpoint of her fresh knowledge of herself. She had no pause or doubt; but acknowledged with an utter startled joyfulness that she would go—that all was as nothing to her, now, except that she go to him. Willing, beyond all words that might express her willingness, to risk (aye, even to exchange) the unknown Joy of the Everlasting for this certain "mess of pottage" that was so desired of her hungry heart. And having acknowledged to herself that she was utterly willing, she had no thought of anything but to pass on the knowledge of her altered state to the man who would be waiting there in the little onion boat at sunset.

That evening, just before the dusk, Big John Carios saw the hundred and tenth grey figure nod swiftly to him, in passing; and he held tightly to the shroud, until the suffocation of his emotion .passed from him.

After all, the Rescue—if it can be named by a term so heroic—proved a ridiculously easy matter. It was the spiritual prison that had held the woman so long—the Physical expression of the same, was easily made to give up its occupant.

In the morning, expectant, she read in her fleeting glance at the onion boat, a message written on the hatch-cover. She was to be at the window at midnight. That evening, as she ascended in the long grey line of mutes for the last weary time, she nodded her utter agreement and assent.

After night had fallen thickly on the small, deserted wharf, the little twisted Mate and the Captain reared a ladder against the convent side.

By midnight, they had cut out entirely the lead framing of all the lower part of the window.

A few minutes later, the woman came. The Captain held out his big hands, in an absolute silence, and lifted the trembling figure gently down on to the ladder. He steadied her firmly, and they climbed down to the wharf, and were presently aboard the vessel, with no word yet between them to break the ten years of loneliness and silence; for it was ten years, as you will remember, since Big John Carlos had sailed on that voyage of dismay.

And now, full grown man and woman, they stood near to each other, in a dream-quietness, who had lived on the two sides of Eternity so long. And still they had no word. Youth and Maiden they had parted with tears; Man and Woman they met in a great silence—too grown and developed to have words over-easily at such a moment-of-life. Yet their very quiet, held a speech too full and subtle, aye and subtle, for made-words of sound. It came from them, almost as it were a soul-fragrance, diffused around them, and made visible only in the quiet trembling of hands—that reached unknowing unto the hands of the other. For the two were full-grown, as I have said, and had come nigh to the complete awareness of life, and the taste of the brine of sorrow was yet in them. They had been ripened in the strange twin Suns of Love and Pain—that ripen the unseen fruit of the soul. Their hands met, trembling, and gripped a lone, long while, till the little twisted Mate came stumbling aft, uneasy to be gone. Then the big man and the fragile woman stood apart, the woman dreaming, while the big man went to give the little Mate a hand.

Together, the two men worked to get the sail upon the small vessel, and the ropes cast off. They left the First and Second Hands sleeping. Presently, with light airs from the land, they moved outward to the sea.

There was no pursuit. All the remainder of that night, the small onion boat went outward into the mystery of the dark, the big man steering, and the woman close beside him; and for a long while the constant silence of communion.

As I have said, there was no pursuit, and at dawn the little twisted

man wondered. He searched the empty sea, and found only their own shadow upon the almost calm waters. Perhaps the First Hand had held a wrong impression. The Peoples of the Coast may have been shocked, when they learned. Maybe they never learned. Convents, like other institutions, can keep their secrets, odd whiles. Possibly this was one of those times. Perhaps they remembered, with something of worldly wisdom, that they held the Substance; wherefore trouble overmuch concerning the shadow—of a lost nun. Certainly, not to the bringing of an ill-name upon their long holiness. Surely, Satan can be trusted, etc. We can all finish the well-hackneyed thought. Or, maybe, there were natural human hearts in diverse places, that—knowing something of the history of this love-tale—held sympathy in silence, and silence in sympathy. Is this too much to hope?

That evening, the man and the woman stood in the stem, looking into the wake, whilst the Second-Hand steered. Forrard, in the growing dusk, there was a noise of scuffling. The little humped Mate was having a slight difference of opinion with the First Hand, who had incautiously made use of a parallel word for " Sacrilege," for the second time. The scuffling continued; for the little twisted man was emphatic:—

"Sacrilege be jiggered! Wot the 'ell—" The physical sounds of his opinion, drowned the monotonous accompaniment of his speech. The small craft sailed on into the sunset, and the two in the stem stared blindly into distances, holding hands like two little children.

The Smugglers

"I SUPPOSE," HE SAID, looking down on me from his great height, "you think you're going to straighten out all the smugglers in this part of the country!"

The sneer was uncomfortably obvious, and I looked him over carefully, sizing up his weight and possible capabilities. I was the new Preventive Officer, and had only been in the little village of Burget, on the South Devon coast, for a bare week. Yet, already I had heard of this man, who had just stopped me without ceremony to fire this jeer off at me. He was the only son of Squire Rosset of that neighbourhood, and noted as a wrestler, and for his great strength. Also, as I knew perfectly well, he was up to his ears, as the saying goes, in the free-trade traffic.

"Mr. Rosset," I replied, "I dislike the tone of your question." And with that I turned on my heel and left him.

Behind me, as I went, I heard the man's great bellow of rude laughter; but I went on my way, and kept my temper in hand. Yet, in justice to myself, I must tell you that there was honestly no bodily fear at the back of my quietness, for though he was a huge, powerful man, about four or five inches taller than I, and very broad-seeming, I knew that I was probably the stronger man of the two, and possibly quite as heavy; for he lacked both the chest depth that was mine, and the weight of shoulder development. Moreover, if he was famed in those parts as a wrestler, I was by no means without knowledge of the art; and, in addition, I had what I knew he had not, and that was many hard years of ring-training at my back; for there was no fighting man of my time I had not stood up to privately, and I had yet to be beaten. All this in justification, and in no way to be set down to over-conceit. For whilst I would not willingly be drawn into brawling on the question of my duty, I would not have you to think that I was

to be intimidated from carrying out my work to the best of my ability. I had been sent with extra men to Burget to put down the smuggling, which had assumed such prodigious proportions as to have attracted the attention of headquarters; and put down the smuggling I meant to do. Indeed, already I had spoilt two night-runnings; and three men of the neighbourhood were even then waiting their trial as a result. And by this telling you will the better understand the attitude of the Squire's son.

Yet I was sorry for this ill-feeling on his part; for the Squire had six daughters, and one of them—Miss Ruth Rosset, as I had already learned she was named—had taken my eye strangely at church the previous Sunday, so that since then a dozen times I had caught myself thinking upon her.

On this day it seemed that I was to have my full share of the disagreeables; for presently, as I went down the cliff path, there met me full in the way the Squire's six daughters, to whom I had been, formally presented after the service by Parson Wenlock. To these I gave salute, and stood off the path for them to pass. But, indeed, they went by me with their skirts withdrawn and their faces forward, as if I had been but a matter of dirt upon the path-side. And I had thought, foolishly enough, that Hiss Ruth had looked not unfriendly at me on the past Sunday; and now this.

And by such an incident alone you shall see the bitter enmity which I had earned already by the capture of the cargoes and by the arrests. Moreover, it may help you to perceive the curious sympathy which held the peoples of the neighbourhood together, and the inability of any, from the highest to the lowest, to conceive that smuggling was anything but right and desirable. Indeed, it was evident to me that the daughters of Squire Rosset had both knowledge and approval of their brother's secret trading; and no doubt many a dainty foreign gewgaw came their way through their brother, so that they were the more likely to make a personal matter of any attempt to end the free traffic, as you shall think. Apart from this, as I had reason to suspect, smuggling brought a certain ready wealth into the household, which must have been welcome; for though Squire Rosset was plainly well-to-do, he was reported to keep a very close fist on his money-bags.

In the meanwhile, however, I had many things to take my attention from this unneighbourliness of the Rossets (though in this I do not include the Squire, who was always very courteous and friendly); for within the next month I had made seven big hauls; with the result that at the next assizes there were sentenced ten men of Burget; and the

smugglers of that district were beginning to realise that I meant truly to check the free traffic.

There were, of course, several attempts to put me on one side. Twice I was fired at in the dark, and once three men came out of the bushes at me on one of the low cliff-paths. They had heavy sticks, and, I suppose, thought to have done with me in a minute. I broke the jaw of one with my fist, and one of the others I pitched bodily over the cliff, where he was found at daylight with both legs broken. The third man ran; but I meant that the smugglers should learn that this sort of thing was not going to be tried without certain pains attaching. And so I chased that man for three miles. When I caught him I beat him with his own stick until he cried like a child. Then I left him to get well and think. Apart from this little private adjustment of the matter, I did not press the case officially, though I knew the three men who had attacked me. This attitude on my part earned for me, I think, a certain, respect from my neighbours to salt their general hatred of me. Moreover, it went round the district that I had held off the three men alone, and this made me free of such matters for the future.

And now back to my relations with the Rossets, for it will have become plain to you by now that my interests lay much that way. I had several times been invited by the old Squire to come up to dinner, but had always pleaded duty; for it was easy to know that his children would scarce welcome me so freely as I might like. However, one evening, when I was down in the village, the Squire stopped his carriage by me and asked whether I was going to plead duty again as an excuse for unsociability. So that before I well knew what I was doing I was beside him driving up to the manor, with no excuse for dress or dirt allowed. And, indeed, I must say here that old Squire Rosset showed always a curious and strong partiality for my company, which has often pleased and surprised me; for he was a man of considerable character, and, as. I liked to think, discernment, and most certainly not given to over-readiness in the making of friends, as was plain to me.

At dinner the Squire's six daughters were simply brutal, and I was glad the brother was absent. They acted as if I were not at the table, except for a frigid and over-formal attention to my needs. That the Squire was vaguely aware of this at first I am in doubt; but I do know that later their manner attracted both his attention, and his wrath. And here let me say that the Squire at no time showed any sympathy with the free-trade which was rampant all about—and even in his own household, had he but known. Indeed, it is possible that he more than half suspected, and that he was wishful to stand well with the law, in

my person, and to make it plain that he was on the side of order, and nowise concerned with unorthodox doings. This, at least, has been sometimes my thought.

For a long while the Squire tried to hold off the silence from the table by telling anecdotes of the countryside. Finally, as if it had suddenly occurred to him, he said in a jovial way:

"I hear, Mr. Faucett, that you beat three of our local men the other night, single-handed."

I laughed.

"They were not a very dangerous lot," I said.

"If it had been Tom, and just alone," said Miss Ruth suddenly from down the table, "he'd have probably thrown you over the cliff. You mustn't think all the men in this part are babies."

"Silence, child!" said the Squire. He turned to me, as I sat realising how much talk there must have been already about that bit of trouble.

"You see," he said, "they're great partisans for their own country-men. And they think there's no one in the world so fine and strong as my son Tom."

I nodded and turned to the girl.

"Such scoundrels ought to be thankful, Miss Ruth, for such a champion. They certainly need one."

I was aware that the old Squire looked at me with a sudden quick surprise; but I was still looking at the girl. I had intended to be a little brutal, for her cold insolence had angered me, even while her win-some-ness drew me strangely. Yet she made no answer to my remark, but looked down at her plate, as if I did not exist. All the other girls kept the same frozen silence, and I saw their father looking at them with a vague half-anger, and make as if to say something; but instead he took a drink of ale, and joined the general quiet, so that the whole table was uncomfortably silent.

After dinner we moved into the drawing-room, where Miss Ruth played the harp and sang several ballads. It was while she was impro-vising gently to herself on the harp that her brother Tom came quickly into the room. It was evident that he did not know I was present, and, before he had been told, he said in a savage voice:

"That d—d spy has murdered another of our men!"

"What!" said Miss Ruth, very pale in the face; and all the other girls cried out in horror.

"Tom!" called the Squire quickly, before he had time unknowingly to fix the insult on me.

Tom turned and saw me. He made a muttered choking noise in

his throat, and in the same moment the Squire had hastily introduced us. Tom looked at me, and bent his stiff neck to a curt nod, to which I responded with ordinary courtesy; though I had no doubt but that his remark referred to the hanging that day of one Martin Lowther, who had shot Tames Taunton, a man of my patrol, a month previously at a surprise of a cargo-running, and had been condemned on my evidence. Regarding this same Martin Lowther, he was an infernal blackguard; whilst Taunton had been a steady, splendid fellow, and but newly wed to a pretty girl; so that you must understand my heart held little pity, for Lowther, who, it seemed, had been always a low, loafing, tippling, tongue-wagging longshoreman, with a dirty and ugly record to his back. Yet, as you will perceive, I could only ignore Tom Rosset's remark, and pretend, at least whilst under their roof, that I had no understanding of what it was that he had referred to.

For a while young Rosset remained, and the conversation became general in the room; so that presently I felt that the tension had been eased, and that a more sociable spirit was prevailing. It was because of this feeling that, when Tom Rosset left the room a little later, I walked over to where Miss Ruth was sitting idly by the window, and asked her whether she would pleasure me by singing a favourite old love-song. In a moment I saw that I had made a mistake in supposing that there was either grace or courtesy in the girl; for she said no word, but looked silently up at me with a kind of white scorn. Abruptly she got to her feet and went over to her harp. Then, sitting down, she sang the "Hanging of the Spy," with such deliberate and deadly insult, considering my request and the circumstances, that I quietly took my leave without more ado. The old Squire let me go only with reluctance and in bewilderment. I learnt afterwards that when he found out just what had happened beneath his very nose, as we say, there was such a storm in the manor as was not forgotten for a long while. And, indeed, though I did not know at the time, this had something to do with a note of cleverly-worded explanation and apology which was brought next evening to my house by no less a person that Tom Rosset himself. He, to my amazement, made a jovial sort of apology for all, and explained that I must not take them too seriously, but make some allowance for their feelings of partisanship for their own villagers, who had been born and bred on their own land.

All this, as you will understand, quite took the wind out of my sails, so that I could not be stiff with the man, but felt that he must be a decent fellow at bottom. And when he doubly urged me that I simply must come up that night to dinner and a comfortable evening,

to show that I truly bore no ill-will for what he was pleased to term their "local prickles," I agreed in the heartiest fashion, feeling truly that I had, perhaps, been a little foolish to take too much notice of the somewhat undisciplined attitude of a set of young people. And so, with a final word that the carriage would be down for me at seven, he went off.

That night I found that young Rosset had not exaggerated, for I was welcomed courteously by all the girls, though, as might he expected, with a certain reserve which was developed to actual constraint in the case of Miss Ruth. However, during dinner, at which the old Squire paid me the nicest attention, the girl became more natural, and by the end we had arrived almost at a friendly attitude. Yet under her manner there seemed to be always a strange submission, or rather repression, as if she were not being quite truly herself. I know of no other words with which to explain this vague impression I had when speaking to her.

When in the drawing-room after dinner Miss Ruth moved over to her harp, and played the prelude to the very song which I had asked her to sing to me on the preceding evening. Then she began to sing the song itself in a low voice, and the room was utterly quiet, save for the quaint melody of the song, and the deep, mellow notes of the harp. And then, as I sat listening with my feelings a little stirred, my gaze fell on the old Squire, and I knew suddenly a part of the reason for this friendliness on the part of the Rosset family, and the girl's curious seeming of submission and repression of herself; for the old man, not aware that I saw him, was looking at the girl with a fierce, stern look in his eyes that showed me he must have been mightily angered and wakened to mastery by his family's disgracing of all the laws of ordinary courtesy and hospitality. Indeed, it was obvious to me that he was truly master in his own house when he chose; and in this case he had chosen, and his family had been forced to obey. And all this I reasoned out, from a quick flash of intuition, as I sat listening to the song.

At first, as you may think, I had a feeling that I wished for no such forced welcome as this, but after a little thought I saw that it would be foolishness to act upon this feeling and refrain from ever coming near the manor again; for I knew that I was already more than attracted to Miss Ruth; and I made up my mind then that I would make them all to realise that I was worthy of their friendship, and then, perhaps, I might teach the girl to love me. And, indeed, within a week I had reason to feel that I was succeeding; for the friendliness of the family began to have an unstrained note in it, so that I could see that the old

Squire had relaxed his stern attitude to his family, and felt comfort able now to leave me in their hands.

I was now a regular visitor; and, indeed, a place was set always for me at dinner, so that I might truly call myself a friend of the family. Also, perhaps because the others saw my preference, I noticed that presently it seemed to be taken for granted that Miss Ruth and I liked to be together, for often we would find that matters had resolved themselves this way. And truly she seemed not to dislike my company, though always in a quiet, half-shy, half-reserved way that stirred me with more than a vague hope that she had begun to care a little for me.

Sometimes, when the six girls were returning from their daily bathe, I would meet them and walk back to lunch, at such times carrying Miss Ruth's towel, which act of service pleased me in that strange but natural way which is familiar to most who have fallen in love with a maid, for I knew now that I was very much this way, yet quite unsure of the girl.

Then one day Miss Ruth, as I met them, remarked that bathing made her tired, and that she thought it might be as well to drop it for a time and go for some good long walks. This emboldened me to offer myself as an escort; and to my great pleasure she was pleased to accept, so that I felt surely she must care, if but a little.

From thence onward through a short, happy month I took Miss Ruth for a good walk during the time in which her sisters went for their morning bathe; meeting them on the homeward journey, and so with them to the manor, where I had lunch as one of the family. By this time I was thoroughly miserable unless I was with Miss Ruth; yet I could not bring myself to risk the utter misery of a refusal, so that day after day we walked quietly in country lanes, she seemingly shy but content to be with me, and I in a distress of doubt. Yet I felt sure that she must know that I loved her, for I showed it in a thousand ways, possibly clumsily and foolishly, though I felt so dumb.

Then one day I came upon my tragedy. I met the sisters coming down as usual to their bathe, but Miss Ruth was not among them. They told me that she had stopped at the stile on the corner to rest, and that I should probably find her there; whereat I hurried on. As I drew near the bend of the lane which hid the stile from me I heard suddenly .Tom Rosset's voice, raised almost to a shout in anger. He was saying something vehemently, and it sounded as if his sister were trying to reply. They evidently did not hear me as I came along on the soft grass bank bordering the lane; and even as I puzzled a moment how to let them know that I was near, I heard my name, and knew that Tom was

accusing his sister bitterly of being in love with me. I paused eagerly listening to her answer, for it was what my heart had been aching yet dreading to hear for all the past weeks. Then, like a bitter, unbelievable slap in the face, her laughter came hard and scornful, and I heard her tell her brother that she had done no more than she had agreed to do, which was to hold me from the shore whilst the cargoes were run; that she loved me as little as he did, and that if he did not approve of her methods, he had better take me country walks himself, and so combine courtesy to the enemy—thereby obeying their father—and assistance to the smugglers all at the same time; and she hoped he would have as much or as little entertainment out of it as she had gained! And all this with a fresh and bitter accompaniment of scornful laughter, so that my heart was cold and sick and hard within me.

"If I did," said Tom Rosset brutally, "I'd wring his neck for him, and leave him in the wood—the spying, murdering scum that he is!"

I walked round the corner of the lane, and came upon them. The girl cried out something, with a little frightened gasp, and I saw her face whiten.

"So," I said, looking at her with a grim contempt, "you can stoop to break a man's heart for such paltry ends!"

She made no attempt to answer, and indeed I waited for none, but came round swiftly on the brother.

"At last, Mr. Rosset," I said, "you will be able to show off that strength of which you are so proud—you treacherous beast!"

And with that I met his quick rush with a hard body-punch that brought him up gasping. I heard the girl sobbing where, she stood by the hedge near the stile; then the man tried a "hold" on me, which I slipped, and punched him off. A dozen tries he made to grip me, but I hit him cruelly hard, for he was too strong and heavy a man to deal gently with; moreover, I intended to punish, for I was as bitter as gall. And so, in a minute, I had him rocking on his feet, for I had near hit the life out of him. Then I went in quickly and threw him very hard, so that he lay stunned upon the ground. And Miss Ruth just standing near the stile, as pale as death, and bright-eyed, and shaking with strange, dry sobs.

"Oh!" I said, looking at her, and speaking between my gasps, "he's a brute, but he's a man. But what are you?"

Then I turned and went down the lane as quickly as I might.

As soon as I had steadied sufficiently, and fought down the mad, hopeless pain at my heart enough to think, I hurried down to the station, to find out how it could be possible that there had been any

running of smuggled goods in broad daylight, as was obvious must have been done from what I had overheard Miss Ruth say to her brother. Yet no man had the least suspicion that there had been any "running" of late, and unless I supposed that there had been a general slackness among my own men, I could not conceive how the thing could have been worked, whether my attention was withdrawn or not. Yet that goods had come into the district I was soon able to prove by the reports of the inland officers; so that for the next month I was continually round the cliffs, visiting my men both day and night to see that the patrols were not shirked. And glad enough I was for the constant work and watching, for a more sickening month of misery I never passed. I had not merely lost the girl I loved, but all the glamour of love and all my ideals; so that all the world seemed hopelessly grey and sordid.

And yet, so far as the results of my work went, I was failing to stop the smuggling, for the up-country men still reported goods coming in duty-free; but how it was done I could not imagine, and I had almost decided to send for more men, and put out a couple of patrol gigs, when I got a hint that put me on the track.

A note was slipped under my door one night, with this single line printed across it:

Pride, before Fallin', Watch the Squire's Leddies Bathin'.

It was certainly a curious composition, and was obviously written by some woman of the people who had reasons to hate the Miss Rossets. To me it meant one thing— the explanation of the mystery. The secluded little cove where the Squire's daughters went for their daily bathe was quite near, comparatively speaking, to my house, so that it had never appeared necessary to have a patrol over a place that was practically always under my own eye; and, of course, during the time of the girls' bathing, I had been walking with Miss Ruth. Moreover, since I had discovered the heartlessness of the girl, I had taken very good care to avoid that part of the cliff-path during the hours when the girls would be likely to appear, and so, of course, unconsciously doing the particular thing that they desired.

The morning of the following day I kept a watch for the coming of the Miss Rossets, and as soon as I had seen them go down the cliff-path to their bathing cove I took six of my men and placed them on the upper path, with orders not to move unless I whistled twice. Then I took the lower path down into the cove, and went quietly. At

the bend, from which a view could be had downward, I came upon the girls' maid, who ran up to me in a great fluster to tell me that the "leddies" were bathing below, and 'twould not do for me to go down. This, of course, in the ordinary way would have been sufficient to send back any proper-feeling man; but I had come with a set intention, and I meant to go down into that cove though there had been a thousand ladies there disporting themselves. When the maid saw that I took no heed of her warning she made to run before me to warn her mistresses, but I caught her in a moment and set my hand over her mouth to quieten her. Then I went backward up the path with her, and left her in the charge of my coxswain, telling him to plug her mouth if she attempted to shout. A minute later I was back again at the bend of the lower path, and looking below me into the cove. Down there the six maidens were laughing and splashing about in the shallow water in costumes less complete than had before occurred to me, for it was obvious that they had never so much as imagined that they would be intruded upon. And there, as I looked, the whole mystery of the later smuggling was solved; for the six maidens were gleefully rolling and hauling dozens of exceedingly small casks out of the shallows at the foot of the cliff, and dragging them into the mouth of a cave which was evidently only uncovered at low water. The whole method was now clear to me. On suitable nights, Tom Rosset—I presume—and his gang would bring in their stuff quietly and dump it in the water at the foot of the cliff, in the bight of the little cove where his sisters came for their bathe. They, on their part, would make a search each day for any contraband that might have been dumped, and, finding it, they would draw it safely into the low-water cave, from which it could be removed at leisure. And this they had done safely in broad daylight; for who would have suspected them of such a thing? Moreover, all my men were on their patrols, or asleep at the station, and they had accounted for me by the heartless method which Miss Ruth had put into practice.

All the casks, I noticed, appeared to be loosely roped together in the way common to this method of hiding "free goods," but with more line than usual between each cask, evidently done purposely to make them easier handling by the girls, who worked with zest at their unlawful task, their laughter rising up to me clear and shrill through the splashing of the water.

And all the while I was coming clown quickly and silently upon them. I reached the narrow strip of beach that bordered one side of the cove where the cliff-path ended; then I hailed the girls, sternly

bidding them come ashore and submit to the law. On the instant there were loud screams, and immediately all of the maidens had hidden themselves up to their necks in the water, and were looking at me, some very red in the face, and some so scared that they were red one moment and white the next; but when I looked at Miss Ruth, she was white and hopeless-seeming, and looked only at the water.

I bid them come ashore and dress, but they would not until I had threatened to whistle for my men to come and carry them from the water, for I meant to give them the taste of their own mercilessness, that they might learn the meaning of mercy, and know that a man's love is not to be used as merchandise, neither his heart as a toy, for all had been in the plot with Miss Ruth to use my love to their own miserable ends.

Then, when the Squire's daughters saw that I meant truly to use the law upon them and to have no pity, some taunted me bitterly from where they hid in the water, and some broke into weeping; but when I looked at Miss Ruth, she was only white and silent. Then she looked up at me and beckoned to the others to be still, and asked me in a low voice to go out of the cove whilst her sisters and she came ashore and dressed, for she would .give her word that they would not try to escape. But to this I gave only refusal, and told her that I dared not value her word. This set a look of despair into her face, so that I told them of my true intention, which was that they come ashore singly, whilst I would stand behind a rock near by. When each one was dressed, she was to come to me, and I would signal for the next to come ashore. And with this they had to be content, for I was so stern that they felt in their hearts that I would truly call my men if they did not obey.

Presently, as I stood behind the rock, the eldest sister presented herself to me, fully-dressed and defiant, but obviously frightened. I bid her hold out her hands, which at first she refused to do, until I drew my whistle from my pocket to show that my patience was nearly gone; then she held them out with a kind of fierce scorn and fear, and I immediately snapped one of the pairs of handcuffs on her wrists which. I had brought for the purpose. At that her face whitened, and suddenly she broke into crying and turned from me. Then I signalled for the next maid to come from the water; and as each one in turn presented herself to me I put the irons on her wrists, and some, would whiten and some would redden, but all came to tears in the end, for suddenly the realisation was brought home to them that they had truly put themselves within the power of the law, and that they had no reason at all to expect mercy from me.

The last one to come from the water was Miss Ruth, and when presently she came round the rock dressed, and saw how her sisters stood, all ironed, I knew that she gave a little start; then, quietly and without waiting for me to tell her, she held out her hands for the irons, and I snapped them on her little wrists with the strangest feelings stirring at my heart.

Afterwards, I gave the order to march, and took them all up out of the cove by a sheep-track, which they were glad enough to follow, that they might avoid everyone. They went in a sort of quiet despair, save for odd sobbings, for they knew that if they disobeyed I should simply call my men, and this was of all things the thing they dreaded. I brought them up over the cliff, and so into the country-lands beyond, and thence by secluded paths towards the town, where the assizes were held. For three long miles I took them in this direction, and then, suddenly, their despair culminated, for they stopped on the path and gathered round Miss Ruth, and I knew that they were begging her to intercede with me. I stood a little way off from them, and when, presently, the girl came out from among them and walked quietly over to me, I looked at her sternly but silently whilst she made her request, which was that I would let her and her sisters go free, for they had learned such a lesson as should keep, them law-abiding for all their lives to come; but that if any must be punished, let her be punished, and she would come obediently with me, if I would but let her sisters go free. And even as I stood there, looking so grim upon her, I could near have wept to hear her plead so prettily, for I loved her yet so great.

For a moment or two I stood as if pondering, then turning to the maidens where they stood in a miserable group, I told them that I hoped they had learned their lesson, and that in future not only their actions but their influence would be on the side of law and order. Afterwards I took the key of the irons from my pocket and set them free, bidding them go home. But when I came to unlock Miss Ruth, who had remained to the last, she refused me quietly, and, turning to her sisters, asked them to go on, as she wished to speak to me.

For a minute or so she stood before me, until her sisters were a good distance off, then, without a word, she slipped the handcuffs from her little hands, for whilst her sisters were big-made women, she was small and dainty.

I looked at her with a sudden new feeling thrilling in me, for I knew that she had kept them on only for strange reasons. Yet, though I looked always at her, she, on her part, looked only downward, and I saw that her hands were trembling a little.

"Miss Rosset," I said abruptly, "you are free to go. But will you tell me why you kept the irons on?"

"Because I was your prisoner," she said in a low voice, and still looking down.

"Is that all?"

"Yes," she answered.

"Well, you are free now," I replied.

"No," she said, in the quietest voice possible, so that I could hardly hear her, and making no attempt to go from me, "I am still your prisoner."

I came over to her with three quick steps.

"What do you mean?" I asked, almost savagely. "Is this more of your jilt's play?"

"Oh!" she said, breaking into a sudden sobbing, "I shall never be free again. Never, never, never!"

I had her into my arms.

"I loved you without knowing," she said, perhaps half-an-hour later. "I never meant those things I said to Tom; but he made me so angry. Oh, but I've known ever since!"

And I said nothing; for she was still in my arms.

In the Wailing Gully

"DO YOU KNOW," SAID a clear girlish, voice, quite near to me, "I think I should like you if you weren't so conceited." I turned from my painting and stared in among the rocks and great boulders to my right. Then I saw her, a pretty girl of about sixteen, leaning over the top of a large boulder, with her chin resting on her hands. She was regarding me with queer, half-amused mischief.

I stood up gravely and bowed. Then I sat down again on my painting-stool.

"Come and talk to me," I said. "Conceit was always my besetting sin. Help me to fight it."

"You think I'm only a child," she replied quaintly, and came out from among the rocks. "Nobody realises that I'm grown up. I'm seventeen."

I made as if I would rise again to bow; but she checked me with a little gesture.

"Don't be an ass," she said; and I sat down quickly, striving to obey.

"You know," she said, pausing to look at my work, "you knew that I was looking all this time; and you tried to seem unconscious. You thought I was thinking what a nice-looking man you are."

I screwed round on my stool to face her.

"I'm sure I didn't!" I said quite indignantly. "I never dreamt that there was anyone within a mile of me. I understood the natives kept away from the Wailing Gully, as they call it."

"There you go again!" she replied. "Because you're conceited you think all the natives are fools. Why, there's no place all along the shore where people come more. We're always searching round here and in the gully for the treasure, on the sly."

"If you were a boy," I said with decision, "I'd like to shake you. You've no right to say I'm conceited. You don't know!"

"You!" she said, and laughed wickedly. "Why, you're a painter. You couldn't shake anyone. I don't think you even paint very well. Look how you've foreshortened that rock!"

And then, before I could reply, she was off again among the rocks, and gone from my sight.

"Well!" I said to myself, "of all the— Of all the young— Of all the— Who the deuce is she?" I looked suddenly at my painting of the Wailing Gully. "By Jove!" I muttered, "she's right. Who the deuce is she? She's got eyes, and she knows."

After that I sat quiet for a bit. I was only twenty-two, and her suggestion that I was a boneless artist-chap had really annoyed me; for I had been an athlete all my life, and not a toy one either. But after a little while I was not half so much annoyed as curious and stimulated. Who was she, on this lonely piece of Devonshire coast, apparently quite alone and utterly unconventional? She had a sound backing of culture behind all her unusualness; this had been apparent to me. I sat idle for a long time, thinking, Then I climbed on to one of the biggest rocks near by and had a good look lip and down the coast; but only the desolation of the lonely shore met me on every side.

"And the treasure," I said with a sudden memory. "What did she mean? What treasure?" I leaned over the edge of the great gully which goes winding for a mile among the huge rocks and boulders. What treasure? Surely it had been some obscure local jest? The sea went bubbling and making strange cries and eddyings in the deep holes, which one could believe had never been uncovered through a thousand years. Doubtless it was this same curious noise of the tide in the great gut which had given it the local name of the Wailing Gully. I could imagine that it would be a dree place to come near at night.

Why, I asked myself, had the "locals," or natives, given me to understand that it was a place avoided, when, as the girl had told me, everybody came round on the quiet searching for some treasure? Either they or she had been taking a gentle rise out of me, or the "locals" had been genuinely desirous of keeping me from prowling about there. Perhaps they thought I was a treasure prospector in disguise. As a matter of fact, however, I did not really believe either of these things. I thought it far more likely that if any treasure-hunting were being done, it was carried out very slyly, and each man supposed he was the only one on the hunt; with the result that everyone tried to keep up the illusion that the Wailing Gully was avoided, because each believed that this impression was general, and served to keep other people away. In other words, each man was willing to believe that his

neighbours were fools, and he the only wise and unsuperstitious human in that district. Which is a very common form of delusion.

Presently, finding that I could not concentrate again on my work, I went back to my rooms in the "Black Bat Inn" at Dreesthorp, which is the nearest village, about twenty-seven miles from the nearest station. Here, at first, I had intended to make inquiries about the pretty girl who wandered alone among the rocks and spoke her mind so frankly to strangers (or, at least, to this particular one); but somehow, in the end, I could not fancy digging my information about her out of the stolid landlord; so after one or two rather pointless questions on my part, and equally pointless and apparently bewildered replies on his, I desisted, and determined to be back at my painting in good time the next morning, when I hoped that the pretty maid would come again to the attack.

The following day I carried my gear over the intervening desolation of the shore until I came again to my old sketching-place. Here, having set up my easel, I tried hard for a couple of hours to work; but it was impossible, for I could not keep my attention fixed. All the time I was wondering whether the maid would appear; and a hundred times in the hour I would glance round, expecting to see her looking mischievously at me from among the rocks; but never a sign was there.

Abruptly, away down the gully, I saw something flashing in the sunlight. As I stared, I realised that it was the hand and arm of a swimmer. For ten minutes I watched it draw nearer; and suddenly I knew that it was my girl friend of the previous day, coming on up the gully with the easy, strong, swinging stroke of the real swimmer. I stood up in amazement and almost anxiety; for the eddies and swirls of the tide in the great gully made it a dangerous place.

A few minutes later the girl came opposite to where I stood, and, catching at a jutting piece of rock, pulled herself out of the water and sat down some distance below me. She took her hair down and wrung it out, looking upward at me mischievously, but without saying a word.

"Is it safe?" I said at last. "I don't know who you are; but I'm sure your people would be very anxious if they knew. Look at the eddies!"

The girl put her head a little more on one side and looked up at me with a pretty grimace. She began to re-coil her hair upon her head.

"I've come to apologise," she said at last. "Though you really needed it."

Then, with a quick, lithe movement, she slipped into the water, swam a dozen yards below the surface, and came up in the middle of the gully.

"Stop!" I shouted foolishly, but she was swimming steadily with the tide, and so in a few minutes was gone out of my sight around the great rocks and boulders.

I did no real work that day, and the evening found me thoughtful. Later in the day I had followed the course of the Wailing Gully to where it opens out wildly into the sea; but there were nowhere any signs of the girl, nor of any other living creature.

The following morning I was beside the Wailing Gully at an early hour. I had my day's provisions with me, and I resolved to get in a few hours' good solid work before there should be any chance of the maid appearing to disturb my thoughts; for there is no doubt that she was much in my mind, at the expense of my working.

Yet, as it chanced, I could not concentrate; and, finally, I got my bathing suit out of my knapsack and determined to try the eddies of the gully, which was here quite twenty yards across, though in places it narrowed down to about a dozen feet. As soon as I plunged in I found the plucking and pulling of the eddies very upsetting; so that I should have been tempted to climb out at once if I had not seen the girl swim through it all. Later, I found that at certain states of the tide the gully was really dangerous; and, indeed, I felt then that a weak swimmer would have been drawn under and ground against the rocks very quickly. Presently, after I had swum down for about half a mile, I found the plucking of the eddies to ease, and I turned about and came up in the still water; for it was now close upon the "still," between the tides. I climbed out again opposite to my easel, and sat for a minute or two on the rocks in the sun. It was whilst I was sitting here that I noticed suddenly that I could see the bottom of the gully; for the surface of the water had grown temporarily quiet because of the "still" and the utter lack of wind. The bottom, I saw, was formed of masses of round stones as round as big marbles, though some were as big as cricket balls. These seemed to be lying in worn hollows of the rocky bottom. A little upward of the gully I saw a worn, twisted portion of ironwork, and I thought I would go down to examine it. I dived in, and swam under water until I came to the place; but there was nothing peculiar about the ironwork, for it was merely the battered fragment of a ship's iron rail, which had been jammed into a crevice of the rock. Near it I saw that there was a battered and twisted piece of copper-work, which was all verdigris. The design looked old, and I pulled at it, to take it up with me; but it also was jammed tight, evidently by the action of the tide. As I turned to swim back I saw a worn mass of iron, evidently a portion of an old anchor, which had been brought

up by the scour of the tide. Then I was at the surface, panting; for I must have been under water for nearly two minutes. I climbed out and dried and dressed. As I was doing so I noticed suddenly that the eddying movement of the water in the gully had recommenced, so that the bottom was now invisible. I had just finished dressing, and was wringing out my swimming costume, when someone spoke close to me. I jumped and turned quickly. The girl was sitting quietly on a rock, about a dozen feet away, quietly and critically looking at me.

"Do you know," she said, "I believe you could shake me, after all. I had no idea that you were really like that."

I stared at her, utterly wordless. At last I managed to ask:

"How long have you been there?"

"I've just come," she said; "but I saw you swimming when I was on the other side of the gully. If you hadn't been a very strong man you would have been drowned. You should never go in just before the 'still;' you ought to have known that."

"How did you get across?" I asked, still staring at her with a vague uncomfortableness; for I had dried and dressed with no thought of the nearness of any stranger.

"At the Lover's Leap," she said; "about half a mile down. I gave you a quarter of an hour to dress; and then I came along. You must be conceited, or you wouldn't take such an awful time."

"What's your name?" I asked abruptly.

"What's yours?" she replied calmly.

"John Eliot."

"Mine's Betsy Dunton," she said.

"Squire Dunton's daughter?" I asked.

She nodded.

"The madcap!" I said. "Oh, now I understand! You see, Miss Dunton, you've got what the butcher's boy would call a 'repetition' for high spirits. Even the stranger without your gates hears about you."

She made a quaint grimace at me. "What were you diving for?" she asked. "You stayed down a long time. Were you after the treasure?"

"That's a thing I wanted to ask you about," I said. "What is this treasure? Or is it just some local jest?"

"Of course there's a treasure, if we could only find it," she replied. "I thought everybody knew that the Santa Maria was wrecked off this coast in 1757. It's in all the history books, or some of them. She had sixty chests of doubloons aboard. Since that time three of the chests have been found. My grandfather found two of them, but the Government got the third, about a hundred years ago. Since then

people sometimes pick up odd doubloons on the shore, but especially round the mouth of the Wailing Gully. My father has a charter or grant or something to search for treasure; but all the 'natives,' as you call them, also search for it on the sly. Of course they've no right, for if they found anything it would really belong to my father and to the Government. All the same, I know they do find things sometimes, but they keep it all quiet."

"Sounds exciting," I said. "Has your father ever found anything?"

"Yes," said Miss. Dunton. "Or, at least, I have, which is the same thing. Three months ago I found a pocket in the rocks, below the water-line, near the mouth of the gully. It was packed with doubloons and sand. There were sixty in all, and in perfect condition, which, my father said, showed that a chest must but lately have broken up; otherwise, if they had been washing about loose, they would have been all bent and worn. Of course, we said nothing about my 'find' to the people about here; but the news went round, and ever since everybody has been very keen; they're always going lobstering, but they never catch any!"

"And you?" I asked. "Have you found anything since?"

"Yes," she said. "I come down every day, and spend several hours searching. In the last three months I've found twenty single doubloons; and once I found five lying together in the bottom of the gully during the 'still.' I dived in after them with all my clothes on, because, you see, the 'still' only lasts a few minutes and I was going to make sure of them. But I nearly got drowned. My skirts bothered me so."

She stood up suddenly.

"I must be going now," she said, "and you must get on with your work." She walked across and looked at my painting. "It's really very beautiful," she continued, with a quaint knowledgeable air, "and you've truly caught the strange, dree atmosphere of the place. You must forgive me for my rudeness the other day."

She held out her small brown hand abruptly; then, after a firm quick shake, she turned and went off swiftly among the rocks, leaving me looking after her.

During the rest of the day I worked in a desultory fashion, and would often find myself with my elbows on my knees, thinking about Miss Dunton; so that by evening I had done very little steady painting.

As I was going back to the inn I had rather a bad tumble, and caught my watch-chain on a jag of rock, with the result that I jerked off the gold doubloon on the pocket end. The doubloon went tinkling down among the stones, and I very nearly lost it. When I got back to my room I washed, and then rang for dinner. The landlord himself

brought in my wine, as was always his way. He drew the cork and put the bottle gently on the table. In the same moment he gave a muffled exclamation, and half reached out his hand, but remembered himself suddenly, and drew back with a confused apology.

I stared to see what it was that had attracted his attention, and in the same instant I heard the door close as the landlord went out. Then I saw what it was that had drawn him; for the gold doubloon which I had broken from my chain was lying on the white tablecloth, where I had put it on coming in. In a flash I understood the landlord's agitation, for he had seen the doubloon, and evidently believed that I had found it on the shore, and possibly he thought that I had really discovered one of the chests, and that this was but one of a great treasure of coin. The idea tickled me hugely, and I determined to carry it forward a bit, so that when next the landlord came in I tackled him.

"Oh, Mr. Benn," I said, "you look a bit of an old pirate! You should be able to tell me what coin this is which I picked up on the beach" (so I had, after I'd dropped it!).

I said all this in jest, yet with a serious enough face; but the landlord, who was standing a bit to my back, answered never a word; so that I screwed round, wondering, to see why he made no answer. I was amazed to find him looking at me in the strangest fashion, with his big, heavy face almost threatening, and his eyes full of doubt and suspicion.

"What's up, Mr. Benn?" I asked, half getting to my feet, for he looked so strange. Yet, even as I spoke, he pulled himself together and answered stupidly in broadest Devon that he had no knowledge of such outlandish coins. Which was obviously a lie.

However, I let him go; for it was clear that he was no fit subject for a jest. Yet I wondered very much after he had gone whether it was not the word "pirate" which had troubled him quite as much as the belief that I had really come upon some of the treasure. Though I could quite believe it was the latter, and that he had brooded so much upon it, and searched so often, that he had come to look upon it as his own, and to regard all others as being natural enemies.

That night I went out for a long stroll. As I came back I noticed that the lamp in my room was higher than I had left it, and twice I saw figures pass between the lamp and the blind, but I was still too distant to be able to recognise the shadows. When I got back to my room, however, the lamp was low and the place empty. Yet, as you can understand, the landlord's attitude had made me a little suspicious, and I noticed things more keenly than I should have. Of course, someone

might have been in to tidy up; but I did not think so, as I had told the landlord I should want nothing more that night, which was equivalent to telling him that I desired to be left alone.

I had a careful look round, and then an idea came to me, and I went over to my painting satchel. In a minute I saw that my suspicions were correct, for everything was disturbed, as by a hurried search. I took the lamp and went upstairs to my bedroom; here I found that my boxes also had been gone through, but with much more care, so that it was rather difficult to know immediately whether they had been touched. However, I satisfied myself on this point, and also that nothing had been taken; but it was obvious to me that the landlord had a real belief that I had found some of the treasure, and that he was an unscrupulous man. At first I thought of going down and tackling him right away about the matter; but afterwards I determined to say nothing, and to watch his game, which would not be difficult, so long as I was supposed to be ignorant of anything unusual.

Next morning I took rations for the day, and my painting gear, and set off early for the rocks. Through a couple of hours I painted vigorously, for I was in the mood, and the utter silence of a quiet and gloomy day was upon the shore, so that I seemed to catch the spirit of the desolation which held the place. The only sound that across all that stillness was curious, faint noise of the sea ebb in the big gully, which seemed to have truly a low wailing note in it.

"I think you ought to keep ears open more than you do," said a voice suddenly near to me.

I looked up quickly, and there was Mliss Dunton, leaning on an iron lobster-hook and watching me

"How long have you been here?" I asked, rising and offering her my stool.

"Ten minutes, perhaps," she replied, and, refusing the stool, came over and looked at my work. "You've got our Wailing Gully at last," she said. "You've managed to get its loneliness. I believe you're not so conceited as I thought, after all."

She stood silent for a little while before the picture; but presently, with a thoughtful look, she turned to me.

"What I was going to tell you," she said, "before I looked at your painting, was that you are being watched by two strange men, who are hiding among the rocks behind you. No, don't look now; you can't possibly see them."

I laughed, feeling a bit glum, and told her about the doubloon and the searching of my boxes and satchel. She nodded.

"That explains why the men are watching you. They think your painting is merely a 'blind,' and that you are really looking for the treasure. Benn has set them to watch you. I believe that he's really a bad lot. I know that some curious tales are told in the village about him and about a Captain Jutt, who is his friend. They used to be at sea together, and there is a story going about that they were something very like pirates. I expect your saying that rather upset him! Perhaps he believes you are a detective. Anyway, I think you ought to take care and not let people creep in on you quietly, as I have been able to do. You know, Benn and Captain Jutt are always down here on the search, though they have no right at all. I have often watched them without their knowing. I've heard that they have made a chart of all the local tides and eddies to help them in their search. My old nurse, who lives in the village, tells me things when she comes up to the Hall to clean."

Presently, with a final warning to be careful, Miss Dunton left me. As soon as she was gone I climbed up the nearest big rock and had a good look round for the two men who were watching me. I took care to climb up on the side farthest from the men, so that they could not see what I was doing, and in this way, using great care, I managed to discover them. They were both dark men, and looked rather like Spaniards. The bigger of the two was peering out from behind a large boulder about sixty yards away, and the other man was looking through a spy-glass, evidently after Miss Dunton.

Now, all this made me pretty angry, and I thought I would give these two a lesson. I slipped down from the rock, and began to creep in a circle among the boulders until I was at the back of the men. Then I stood up and walked quickly up to the big man.

"Hullo!" I said. "You seem to be rather interested in watching me. Can I do anything for you?"

Both the men jumped and turned like tigers, so that I thought they meant to come for me there and then. I noticed that both of them wore sailors' sheath-knives. However, they just stood and stared at me in a stupid, dangerous fashion.

"Well," I said again, "what can I do for you?"

"For to h-ll you go!" said the big man, and came towards me aggressively,

"Oh, that's it, is it?" I said, and hit him hard in the neck below the ear, so that he went down in a heap, grunting. Then I went for the small man; but he drew his knife and ran like a hunted rat. I chased him for half a mile, and then let him go, for I had evidently given him a good fright. I returned to where I had left the big man, and dragged

him to the nearest pool, where I soused his head in and out of the water until he came round. I don't know whether this was the right thing to do, but it acted all right with him, and he got up and went off, muttering in some foreign language.

That night when I got back to the inn I thought Benn, the landlord, looked at me rather strangely, though this may have been no more than my fancy, for naturally I was wondering what he was thinking. However, after dinner I decided I would test him again, and told him I was going for a mile along the beach to digest my dinner, I took care to wear rubber-soled shoes, and to have my sword-stick with me. Before I had gone far I found (as I had expected) that I was being followed. This gave me a pleasant thrill of excitement, and I set the pace hard for a good mile; then I dodged in among some big boulders to the right of the shore-path, and waited. Presently there came the sound of footsteps, and in a minute two men passed me in the darkness, running cautiously, and panting. I let them go well past, then I got up and ran back to the inn as hard as I could go. As I approached I saw that there were lights in both of my rooms, but they went out suddenly as I came near, which made me think that someone had been watching for me from the inn, and had seen me coming.

When I got inside, of course, my rooms were empty; but a quick examination showed me that a search had been made, which must have been terminated rather abruptly, for some of my gear had been stowed away in rather a hurry. Yet, in spite of this double proof that the landlord was certainly a shady character, and evidently not likely to "stick at anything," I decided to say nothing, but to pretend ignorance and to see whether I could not upset his game.

Next morning Miss Dunton came early to tell me that she had told her father about me, and he wanted to meet me. I asked whether I might come then, to which she nodded, and gave me a hand to get my gear together. She led me along the side of the gully for about half a mile, until we came to a place where it narrowed to about twenty-four feet. Here there protruded upward out of the middle of the gully a spire of rock, which was about nine feet from our shore, and reached to within nearly six of the opposite side. I looked at Miss Dunton, who smiled; then, holding my canvas lightly, which she was carrying, she gave a short run and landed well on to the top of the spire, jumping easily and neatly, I followed, and she nodded approval, looking at me quizzically,

"Not bad for a painter-man," she said, and jumped to the shore on the land side. I came immediately afterwards, and soon we were

going up the cliffs to the Hall, which stood only about a quarter of a mile inland.

When we arrived Miss Dunton took me into the big kitchen garden, where she introduced me to her father, who was working in his shirt-sleeves, as "The Man on the Beach." Then she left me with her father. I saw that Squire Dunton was one or those homely, simple-ideaed men, with plenty of natural shrewdness, but no great ambition. I saw also that he was looking at me keenly, with an almost peculiar interest, and that he seemed satisfied, for he took me all around the garden, lecturing on this and that flower or plant as we went along, so that it was easy to see that gardening was his delight. At the end of an hour he returned for his coat, and as he was putting it on he asked me suddenly whether my father had not been in the army.

"Why," I said, staring, "you're never, surely you're never the Lieutenant Dunton I've so often heard him speak about?"

"I believe I am, or used to be," he said quietly. "I knew your face as soon as I saw you." He paused and seemed to be looking back into his memory. "How the years pass on—how the years pass on!" he muttered presently to himself, and slipped his arm into mine. "Come along in and have a bit of lunch with us," he said. "My daughter, you know, recognised you first from a portrait of your father."

As we went along he told me a hundred little incidents about my father and himself, and you can imagine how happy all this made me; for you must have seen that I had begun to think a great deal about Miss Dunton.

At lunch I found that I was seated right opposite to a portrait of my own father. It was all most astonishing. Miss Dunton showed no surprise. "I've been sure of it ever since I heard your name," she told me. "Before then, the first time I saw you, I recognised the extraordinary likeness. But I don't make that an excuse for speaking to you. I should have spoken to you in any case, you looked so conceited. I watched you three days just to see how long you would remain wrapped up in yourself; but it was easy to see that you thought you were the only person on the earth."

"Betsy's an impudent maid," said her father, smiling; "but from what she tells me you should have discovered that for yourself by this. Now let me know, please, this business about Benn."

I told him, and also gave my experience of the day before. The girl's delight was great when she heard how I had disposed of the two foreigners; but her father was grave, and told me plainly that he thought the sooner I was out of the inn the better, and that the best

thing I could do was to come up and stay with them, and bring my traps. This, of course, I accepted gladly; and so it was arranged.

As we rose from lunch the girl said to me:

"Come and see the old treasure chests." And she led the way out of the dining-room into the lower hall. As we went across it was plain to me that money was not an over-plentiful commodity with them, and for this I rejoiced, for I had a double quantity of worldly goods, and—well, you can see the trend of my thoughts.

On the north side of the hall the girl paused and drew my attention to two small chests, made of some dark-coloured wood that looked as hard as iron. But what was attracting my attention was that they were bound with massive bands of copper wrought in a distinctive pattern. And, you know, I had seen just such a pattern but a couple of days before.

"My goodness!" I said; "I'll bet there's a chest of doubloons in the Wailing Gully. What a fool I am!" And I explained excitedly about the piece of copper which was fast to something in the bottom of the gully, as you will remember.

Miss Dunton called to her father, and as soon as he had heard she went upstairs to get into her bathing costume, whilst I did the same thing in the Squire's bedroom. I borrowed a mackintosh from him; and Miss Dunton came down similarly covered, and so the three of us set off, carrying some rope, a pickaxe, and a couple of iron bars to act as levers.

We were soon at the side of the gully, opposite to the place where I had been painting, and found that we were just a few minutes before the "still." We waited anxiously in the meanwhile, coiling the rope up free of kinks. Then as soon as the eddies and swirls had died away, and the wail of the gully had gone to an absolute silence, I caught up the end of the rope and took a header. I was fortunate in having located the exact spot, for I came down right over the piece of twisted iron rail of which I have told earlier, and the copper-work lay just under my hand. I grabbed excitedly at it, and drew myself down, until my eyes were within a few inches of it. I saw then quite plainly that it was firmly attached to something that looked like the corner of a small chest, from which it had been partly ripped. You can understand how I thrilled.

The next thing I did was to bend the rope securely on to the massive copper-work, and then I was glad to shoot to the surface, where I found Miss Dunton in her bathing-dress, ready to come in to continue the search.

"Found it!" I gasped. "It is a chest. I've made the rope fast to the copper-work; but I don't suppose it's any use pulling yet."

"Hurrah!" shouted the girl, and I climbed out of the water to give a hand on the rope; but though we pulled with all our might we could shift nothing. I took the pick then and went down again; but I soon found that I could do more good with my bare hands by easing the stones and shingle from around the chest. Presently Miss Dunton came down to help me, for she could dive beautifully. In this way we worked for about an hour, coming to the surface every minute to breathe; yet still the chest remained firm, and at last the Squire insisted that we should stop for a rest.

Whilst we were resting he climbed one of the bigger rocks to see whether we were spied upon; and this way he saw the two foreigner upon the opposite side of the gully, watching us from among the rocks. He came down and told us what he had seen; then, as we were rested by now, we began again to dive, and work at the packed shingle about the treasure chest. In the meanwhile the Squire kept a secret watch upon the watchers, and in this way, with rests, another two hours passed; for we were able to work at the chest, despite the eddies and the swirls, by holding on to the rope, which we had hauled taut.

By this time the evening had drawn in, and I refused absolutely to allow Miss Dunton to dive any more, but begged her father to take her home and make her rest and eat something whilst I kept watch. Then he could bring me out something to eat, and I would finish freeing the chest. In an undertone I suggested that he bring down a shot-gun with him, and not allow his daughter to return, as it was quite possible we might have to fight for the treasure.

Whilst they were gone I put on my mackintosh and kept a watch from the top of the rock where the Squire had been spying. This way I saw presently that the smaller of the two men was creeping off among the rocks, evidently taking some message up to the village, which I guessed would bring down Benn and Captain Jutt, and perhaps some more scoundrels. So that you can imagine how impatiently I looked for the return of the Squire with his gun, for I had begun to realise that Benn and his crew would stick at nothing to secure the treasure.

About half an hour later I saw the Squire returning, and with were two men carrying guns. But what troubled me was that Miss Dunton was also with them. When they arrived it was plain to me that there had been some trouble, for the Squire looked stern, and I could see that Miss Dunton had been crying. The Squire told me quite bluntly that he had asked her to remain at home, and she had flatly disobeyed him.

The men he had brought with him were his two outdoor men, who acted also in the capacity of gamekeepers, and could consequently use a gun. These two men the Squire placed to his liking behind rocks, and when I had told him that the smaller of the spies had gone back to the village, probably to bring Benn and Jutt, and perhaps others, he took his post again on the rock to watch whilst Miss Dunton and I began again to dive, after I had drunk some beef-tea and rested a little. You see I did not dare eat anything solid, having to enter the water so soon.

From then onward until dusk we worked at clearing the chest, by which time we were feeling so exhausted that we had to rest for a while, during which the Squire came down to say that a small body of men were coming among the rocks from the direction of the village. He then went back to his post, whilst I begged Miss Dunton to stop diving and get behind one of the rocks, as I could easily finish clearing the chest alone. Yet, at the same time, I told her how greatly I admired her skill in the water and her pluck, and that I could never nave managed without her. But, though I begged her, she still persisted that she would continue to so long as I continued; until at last I turned sharply on her, and told her that I would like to shake her soundly. Then, to my astonishment, she broke abruptly into quiet cryng, Which she did her best to hide. And suddenly I knew that she cared, and that so long as I ran any risk she intended to share it.

"Thank God!" I said aloud. "Oh, my dear, my dear, now will you obey me, and take a great weight off my mind? And I on my part will promise not to be foolhardy."

"Yes," she said, as simply as a child, and went back from the edge of the gully, to show that she obeyed me. Then I dived in again, and ten minutes later, after four short dives and breathing-spaces, I called out softly to the Squire that I believed the chest was free.

At that the Squire came down from his post quickly and signalled to his men to come and give us a pull. He urged haste, for he had discovered that there were nearly a dozen men hidden among the rocks opposite. Then, all together, we pulled, and I felt the chest come away. We gave a smothered cheer, and a minute later, after desperate exertion, we had the chest up safe on the rock at the gully side. In the same instant there came a shout from the opposite bank. It was the landlord's voice:

"Hands up!" he shouted. "Hands up!"

I glanced across the gully and saw that a line of men stood there, and in the half-gloom they seemed to be covering us with guns or rifles. In the same moment I heard the Squire whispering:

"Down! Down on your face and take cover." And in an instant I obeyed, and we got out of sight behind a rock. Yet there came no shots from the enemy; and suddenly I saw the whole scheme, and whispered to the Squire that the demonstration on the opposite side was merely a "blind" to attract our attention, and to hide from us the fact that they had men on our side as well, who were probably even then creeping on to us.

The Squire saw in a moment the probability of this, and faced round to his rear, keeping his gun handy, whilst I looked anxiously for Miss Dunton. Abruptly the Squire shouted to his men: "Look out on our side, lads! Look out!" and, raising his gun, fired at a moving shadow to our right. There came a hoarse shout of pain; and then, from more to the left, but only a few yards away, the voice of Betsy Dunton, calling my name in mad terror. I left my shelter and went over the rocks in my bathing-suit, swift and silent. There was the sound of a struggle among the rocks, and then I was there. It was the big dark foreigner, and he had got his hands on to my maid. I slipped my left hand under his chin, and bent his head back. His grip gave from the girl, and he tried to turn on me; but I caught the back of his head with my right hand, and drew him to his feet. Then I hit him with all my might, and left him among the boulders, whilst I picked up my girl.

All around there was a sound of firing and then of men running. A big man blundered into me, carrying a cutlass, and made a wild swipe. I jumped to the side, with Betsy still in my arms. Then I came in on him, and got him full in the face with my right, so that he went staggering, and staggered right into the hands of the two gamekeepers, who beat him with the butts of their guns and then left him to crawl off.

That was the end of the fight. The Squire told me he shot Benn in the legs, and at least three others of the enemy must have been shot. I had outed the big foreigner, and you know what happened to Jutt. The other men had run, and were anxious, I expect, not to have their names mixed up with a business that had turned out to have all pain and no gain, as you might say.

It took us until midnight to get the chest home to the Hall, and when the value of .the doubloons was "proved," the Squire's banking account was strengthened by over nineteen thousand pounds. For my part, I have the maid, who still insists, in moments of impudence, that I am conceited; and when I would argue the point, stops my speech with kisses. Which, after all, is not an unpleasant way of being silenced.

The Girl with the Grey Eyes

I

"MAN, MAN, BUT YOU ought just to see her!" cried my chum Jack, in a very ecstasy of description. "She's just about five feet two—I hate big girls—and dainty!" He made an expressive gesture with his hands and widened his eyes. "And her hands and feet!" He held out a mighty paw, "Just lost in mine, just lost!" he exclaimed, in an awestruck tone.

"Her feet?" I queried.

"Don't rot!" he exploded. "All the same, I'll bet her two feet'd go on my palm comfortably. Twos, I sh'd think. And her eyes, man; they're—they're—"

But he had to give it up.

"Marvellous?" I suggested.

He shook his head with a sort of hopeless shake.

"No; 'tisn't that," he said, and made a further endeavour to explain. "They're grey—"

"Eat all the world up," I interpolated softly.

But he went on, ignoring my suggestion:

"Grey! I never saw such a grey in all my life! Honest! My God, Harry, the man she takes for her very own 'll have her for his very own, and don't you make any mistake!" He paused and ruminated for a few moments, then abruptly:

"Met her in Bendigo six months back. Shook hands with her right off when we were introduced. No ceremony up there, y'know. Saw her then for the first time, and forgot I had hold of her hand till she pulled it loose from mine. I guess I felt mighty awkward." He was quiet for an instant, then he said: "Never seen her from then until to-day, though I've thought of her heaps of times."

"And now she's here in Melbourne?" I remarked.

"Staying right here with us in this hotel," he amended. "I was as

431

close to her as I am to you; but she didn't notice me any more than if I'd been dirt. I guess she's forgotten me." Again he fell upon quietness, evidently thinking hard.

A few words of explanation here. Jack Venner and I were chums. We had chummed as boys at school, and had since found no reason to be anything else. At the age of eighteen I had gone into my father's office, he being a country solicitor. My chum, who, though of good family, was without better prospects, had declared his intention of trying his luck in the Colonies; and this he had done so soon as his period of schooling had come to an end. In this wise I had seen nothing of him for nigh on six years; then his uncle——whose affairs we managed——died, leaving the whole of his vast estates to him. And we at once advertised for the whereabouts of his nephew, but without success. Because of this it was decided that I should take a trip out to Australia and prosecute inquiries. And this I did, with the result that, after many months of patient inquiring, I found my man away up in the back blocks.

We had come down to Melbourne preparatory to taking the first boat home, and had settled ourselves in a hotel for the few days that remained to us on Australian soil. Then, in the evening, as I was attending to my correspondence, my chum had come bursting into my room to inform me that he had run up against the "grey-eyed girl." That is what he called her; for, as he had explained to me, when he was introduced to her he had failed to catch her name, and had not seen her since. And so here he was, pacing up and down the room, raving about this girl, and preventing me from getting on with my work.

"She'll be at dinner," he said presently. "You'll be able to see her then."

Now, I had intended to have dinner brought up to my room, so that I could continue my work uninterrupted, and I ventured to hint that such had been my intention. But to this he would extend no hearing, with the result that a little later I found myself at table nearly opposite a remarkably pretty girl, very dainty, and full of bright sayings and ways; so that I quite endorsed my chum's good taste. In a little she chanced to glance across the table, and I saw her eyes, grey and clear——amazingly honest and beautiful. I stared, and was suddenly recalled to the rudeness of my stare by her sudden flush and look of cold displeasure. In the same moment my chum kicked me sharply on the ankle, so that I knew he had witnessed my annihilation. Presently he dragged me out into the verandah, and put this question to me:

"What am I to do?"

"What do you mean?" I asked, in turn.

"To get to know her," he explained. "She's forgotten me dead. Never noticed me once, though I sat blank opposite to her through the whole of dinner."

"I'm sure I don't know," I answered. "We won't know a soul who could introduce you. And, besides, I'm not at all sure that she is anxious for any fresh acquaintances."

The latter part of this I added in a meaning, voice, for the girl had seemed very well pleased to leave her entertaining in the hands of a tall, blond, rather fine-looking young man who had been her companion at dinner.

At my suggestion Jack Venner frowned fiercely, and muttered something under his breath that sounded distinctly unamiable towards the person of the young lady's manly friend.

And here for a time the matter dropped, for I had to go back to my work.

II

I was awakened that night from my first-doze by a hand vigorously shaking me, and at that I sat up and demanded whether the place was afire. Jack's voice answered me, assuring me that all was right, but that he had thought of a way in which he might become re-acquainted with the girl with the grey eyes. At that I told him he was a confounded ass to come waking me at midnight to tell me of some fool scheme which, from past experience of John's plans, I knew would be absolutely lacking in reason and the rudiments of common-sense. And all this I told him with some vigour, for I had worked hard all the evening since dinner, and was dog-tired.

Then I turned over on my side, pulled the clothes over my head, and refused to hear another word; so that in a minute he left me, going away in a sort of sullen rage, for which I did not altogether blame him. Yet I knew that if once I allowed him to commence talking he would keep it up through the whole night, so that I was not filled with any very deep feeling of compunction.

In the morning Jack treated me in what is known as a "distant" fashion, for which I thought him rather a fool. During the day he left me pretty much to myself, for which, to be truthful, I was not altogether displeased, although, perhaps, just a trifle annoyed; for I had a mint of work which needed my attention. That night Jack did not come near me; but the next morning I met him at breakfast, and found him in a more reasonable mood, though obviously occupied in his mind with some matter.

"What about Miss Grey Eyes?" I asked, after some preliminary talk. He shook his head.

"She's always with that red-haired fool, confound him!" he burst forth. "I'll show him that——" he began to say further, but pulled himself up.

"What?" I asked, frankly curious. But he shook his head.

"I've an idea," he said, "but you'll only throw cold water on it. All the same, I'll bet that I get to know her within the next twenty-four hours."

"Better tell me your plan," I suggested, half jestingly. "You'll be getting yourself into some scrape. You're not going to run off with her by force?" I asked, for I knew something of the direct character of my chum, and the question held in it a pinch of the salt of seriousness.

"No," he said slowly, and in a voice that suggested that the idea was not displeasing to him, "I'm not going to run away with her."

And that was all I could get out of him.

That evening, as I was hard at work in my room, he burst in upon me in his characteristic, brusque manner.

"Well?" I queried, looking up at him.

"I've introduced myself to her," he said, and waited for me to question him.

"Tell me?" I prompted.

"Paid some larrikins to bail 'em up, so's to give me the chance of playing ' 'Ere the conquering 'ero comes;' but it went a bit flat, I must own," he concluded.

"Yes," I said, and waited.

"You see, my men collared 'em down by the swamp. I'd followed at a reasonable distance, so as to be ready to march on when the band struck up; but the first thing I knew there was a flash, bang, bang, and the crowd of them were running like sheep, with the red-haired chap blazing hot and strong after 'em."

At that I laughed heartily, my chum joining in somewhat disconsolately.

"And so it's the other man who's the hero," I remarked.

Jack nodded, looking rueful.

"I did the best I could under the circs," he explained. "Ran up at a great pelt, and asked what was wrong, and could I be of any assistance, and all that sort of thing; but the red-haired chap said they'd driven 'em off quicker'n they'd want to come back, he guessed. And so there was nothing to do but receive their thanks, which I did gracefully enough, and then walked back here with the two of them. However, I've got

to speech with them, and that's something; though one of the larrys has been sent up by the others to say that they hadn't bargained to be shot at, and the result is I'll have to tip up pretty handsomely."

The next day Jack spent in hunting round after the grey-eyed girl, and in making himself as useful and agreeable as possible. That night he told me he had invited them for a sail in his yacht on the following day.

"But you haven't got a yacht," I protested.

"Haven't I?" he said. "I bought one to-day, after getting her to promise. I paid fifty down, and I'm to pay the other hundred to-morrow."

"But—but—" I said, and halted.

"It's all right, old man," he replied. "I'm making the running, and I'll cut that red-haired chap out, or else drown him. Did you ever know me not get my way when I was set on a thing?"

"This is different," I answered. "If the girl's really fond of the other chap, all the yachts and all the king's horses and all the king's men won't be of any use to help you to get your way."

"Well, my boy," he replied, with an air of tremendous assurance, "you wait and see."

Three days passed, and on each one of them my chum took the grey-eyed girl and "the red-haired chap"—as he would persist in calling her friend—out in his newly acquired yacht. Yet, at the end of the third day, as he informed me in a somewhat disconsolate manner, he was unable to say conscientiously that he had made any visible progress in the lady's affections; whereat I laughed loud and long, and begged him, at least, to try and remember that he couldn't very well expect to cut out "the other man" and win the grey-eyed girl's affections all within a few hours after making her acquaintance. Yet, for all my assurance, I could see that my chum was revolving some matter in his mind, which I doubted not was some plan whereby his end might be the more immediately achieved., That I was right the next day proved, for he came into the hotel all dripping with sea-water, and followed by the grey-eyed girl and her friend, all in equally disconsolate state.

When my chum had changed, I got from him some of the details, and found that he had deliberately capsized the yacht in a squall, intending to take his chance to pose as the lady's rescuer; but, as fate would have it, he got tangled in the wet sail, and would probably have been drowned had it not been for the other man, who, having first assisted the girl to a place of safety astride the keel of the boat, had gone to his assistance and rescued him, practically at the last gasp.

Yet such is human nature in love that my ungrateful chum actually cursed his saviour for a "red-haired devil."

The following day came the climax. My chum, meeting the other man outside, had with intentional brutality offered to pay him for "service rendered" in freeing him from beneath the sail. This the other man haughtily refused to discuss, but my chum pressing it, he grew angry, and soon after that—my chum having chosen to offer his undesired gold at a place where they were quite to themselves— the two of them were plying vigorous fists. Here, as it proved, my chum came out top man, and presently, having come more to possession of his senses, was tending the needs of his less fortunate preserver.

For the next three or four days Jack kept to his room, for he had come off by no means free of damage in the fight, and he had little wish for his desired lady-love to see him all be-battered as he was, his nose puffy and his left eye encircled with blue and purple tints.

At last, however, he was once more presentable, and made his appearance next morning at breakfast. The grey-eyed girl was opposite to him, as usual, and it struck me, by the brightness of those same eyes and the expression of her face, that my chum was in for a bad time when she should have him alone. Nor was I mistaken.

So soon as breakfast was over, she left her man friend, and came right across to us. Me she ignored; but, bowing slightly to my chum, she requested him, speaking in a very quiet voice, to escort her out on to the verandah. The rest I must give as my chum told it me an hour or two later in the privacy of my room.

"Well, she gave me jip," he began, in answer to the question in my eyes. "Just socked it into me for all she was worth, and I'm hanged if I didn't love her better for her temper—she looked like a little angel. And she calmed down after a bit, and gave me a chance to speak, and I told her straight that I was confoundedly sorry and ashamed of myself; and then I said right out that I loved her, and that I would never have been such a cad if it hadn't been that I was so confoundedly jealous of the other chap that I couldn't bear the sight of him. At that I expected her to give me the go-by; but she didn't, only an awfully queer look came into her face, and, somehow, you know, she didn't seem half so angry with me after that, though she was still very much on her high horse. Before she sent me away, I asked her if there was any chance for me, and whether she really loved the other chap; and she said how dare I, and that she loved him very much, and that I wasn't to dare ever to speak to her again in that fashion. And that's all."

From week to week my chum delayed our departure, for he was, as he himself put it, "Dead set on winning." And gradually, it must be said, the little grey-eyed girl ceased to keep him coldly at a distance;

though it was plain to me that my chum had never a chance, for the other man was constantly with her, and seemed to be more in her favour than ever.

Then one day, after we had been in Melbourne something over six weeks, my chum came bursting into my room.

"I've won!" he exclaimed, and thumped the table with one great fist. "Bless her! I'll marry her this week, if she'll only be sensible!"

"But the other man?" I exclaimed, confounded, for I had seen her kiss him but the previous day.

My chum sat down, then he said, speaking with great solemnity:
"He's her brother."

"O-h-h!" I said, and began to see things in their true light.

"And the little beggar kept it back ever since our row, and left me to go on believing that he was her sweetheart. It only came out by chance to-day, and I tackled her right off, and she caved in, and promised never to do it again. Wasn't that like her?"

"You ought to know," I replied.

And directly afterwards that self-willed man went away to arrange the date.

Kind, Kind and Gentle Is She

"Kind, kind and gentle is she,
Kind is my Mary;
The tender blossoms on the tree
Cannot compare wi' Mary."

I

"LOVE!" SAID LITTLE TRIPE Jones gloomily. "Of course I know wot love is. I'm bothered with it. I always 'ave been. It's you great hulkin' brutes as don't know! You ain't got the 'eart, not for all your size! Look at you!"

Jell Murphy, the big man sitting on the next cot, nodded soberly.

"I guess you're right, Tripe," he said slowly. "I never felt it that way, nohow; but I'd like mighty fine to. I used often to say a man hadn't come proper alive until he'd gone and fallen in love, but it's never come my way."

"Garn!" said Tripe jealously. "There's Maggie, the colonel's wife's maid, is proper struck on you. She won't never give me a word, an' me never stoppin' thinkin' about 'er."

Jell Murphy shook his head. "That ain't no use to me," he said. "She don't count with me. I ain't said a word to make her like me, and she ain't my sort. I want someone that'll make me feel I'm going to do some blessed thing. Maggie's a nice woman, but she's not what I got in my thoughts, anyhow."

"A bloomin' princess you wants!" said Tripe Jones, sneering whimsically. "You got some neck on to you, you 'ave! Your idees ain't no sorter use for a bloomin' privit. Maybe you?d like to offer your 'and an' 'eart to the colonel's daughter. Give me Maggie. She's a proper dandy."

An orderly stuck his head in through the farthest doorway of the great, whitewashed barrack-room.

"Jell Murphy 'ere?" he shouted.

"Yes," said the big man, rising, and reaching mechanically for his belt.

"Cap'n 'Arrison wants you up to his quarters immejit!" said the orderly, and departed.

Jell stood a moment, with a slight frown; then began to buckle his belt.

438

"I reck'n the cap'n is goin' to offer you the charnst to be body servant to 'im!" said little Tripe Jones, grinning perversely up at his big comrade; for he knew Jell's fiercely independent spirit. "You'll be a gentleman's gentleman then," he added. "An' the cap'n 'll give you his old clo'es, an' you'll bloomin' well 'ave to see there ain't no creases in 'is best toonic! Ain't you bloomin' grieved we ain't at 'ome, where a white man 'd stand a charnst of a fine job like that? That's the worst of India."

"Hell!" said Murphy; and walked out through the doorway, across the courtyard to where Captain Harrison had his quarters.

He found the captain standing on his balcony, talking to a peculiarly beautiful woman, whom he knew by sight—as did all the station—to be the Lady Mary Worthington, always spoken of as Lady Mary.

"You sent for me, sir," said Jell Murphy, saluting.

"That you, Murphy?" said the captain. Come up on the verandah! I want you to oblige me in something, if you will."

He turned to the lady:

"This is the man I was speaking to you about," he said, as Jell stopped at the top of the steps. "If you can persuade Murphy to sing for you, I can guarantee your concert will be a success. He's got easily the finest voice in the regiment."

Lady Mary Worthington stared at Murphy with undisguised interest. She had only recently come up to the hill station, where she was paying a visit to the colonel and his wife, the latter being her sister. She had never seen the man before, but he was certainly worth the seeing, for a finer specimen of manhood she had never seen. Jell Murphy stood over six feet in height, and weighed nearly sixteen stone of shapely bone, muscle, and sinew, without an ounce of fat to spoil his clean symmetry. Moreover, he had rather a fine head and face; and he was very distinctly young, and in some ways was plainly a little unsophisticated.

Lady Mary, woman of more seasons than she was beginning to want to remember, was impressed, and smiled entrancingly as she spoke.

"Will you?" she asked. And Murphy's big grey eyes grew bewildered as she looked into them. "Captain Harrison assures me that you have the best voice in the station," she continued, still looking at him bewitchingly. "I want you on my programme. Now will you let me put your name down—some good old home-country song? All the songs are to be the old home-country songs. May I put you down, Mr. Murphy?"

Jell Murphy stirred slightly at the title, then nodded his dark head, clearing his throat nervously.

"Yes," he said. "I should be proud to do anything to please you," he ended simply. "When would you want me?" he added.

Lady Mary stuck a provoking forefinger under her lower lip, and pondered.

"I should like to try you over to-day, if possible," she said. "How would half-past five do, if that will suit Captain Harrison?"—turning to the officer.

"Perfectly all right," said the captain enthusiastically. "I'll see that Murphy is free."

"At five-thirty, then, up at the bungalow," said the Lady Mary, bowing slightly to Jell. "I shall expect you, and we can settle your song then. Ask for me when you come Good-bye."

Jell Murphy muttered something confusedly, saluted, and wheeled to the steps, which he stumbled down, though gracefully enough, as the lady noticed; for she was perfectly aware of the kind of impression she had made.

"A fine-looking man," she remarked to Captain Harrison. "Now to get on with my list of names. What a pity you've no voice, Captain Harrison! I should have insisted on having a song from you. My sister will sing, 'When other lips;' and I suppose I must let that old frump, Mrs. Stanmey, put all our nerves on edge with her 'Ben Bowling.' Why can't she sing something feminine? Then there's Miss Tolfrey, and her brother, that young lieutenant. I've put them down," etc., etc.

II

"What are your favourite songs?" asked Lady Mary, as she seated herself at the piano that evening.

"I've lots," he said. "But there's none of them I like as well as 'Kathleen Mavourneen,' and 'Mary, My Mary.' "

"They're both of them love-songs, Mr. Murphy," said Lady Mary, glancing up at him. "Somehow I shouldn't have thought you cared for love-songs."

Yet, really, she had guessed all the time that his taste would run that way. She had seen a good deal of men, and had readily perceived the possibilities that lay but a little way down in this big, rather earnest young man.

"I know plenty of barrack-room songs," hastily said Jell, who had flushed a little at her remark. "Maybe you'd like one of them?"

"No," said the woman, smiling down at the notes, so that he could

not see her expression. "I think one of the two you mentioned will do very well. I like love-songs myself. Shall we try the Mavourneen one?"

She rippled out the prelude, and Murphy broke into the song, a little nervously; but his voice was magnificent, and tears of sheer ecstasy came into Lady Mary's eyes. The song ended, and she let her fingers rest on the notes as she looked up at the man.

"You really have a splendid voice," she said. "Shall we try the second one?"

By this time big Murphy had his voice in full control, and he let himself go; whilst the woman at the piano shivered a little, because of the beauty of the voice and the force of feeling that seemed to be behind the words. Jell was looking down at her head of bronze-gold hair as he sang, and she was perfectly aware of the fact. Probably it was her temperament which made her read more into his accentuation than ever he had any thought of putting there; though, possibly, he was stirred to an expression of vague feelings, that he had no intimate knowledge of at the time.

"Oh!" she said to herself several times, under her breath. "What a voice! What a voice!" But though it was truly a wonderful voice, the man's clean vigour and unspoilt personality had also its effect in helping so to impress her. Somehow, she could not get rid of a feeling that there was something strange, something personal in the accentuation of the words of the song, yet nothing that held the least offence for her. If she felt aright, it was but one more tribute among, oh, so many to her fascination. Quite an absurd number had betrayed "symptoms" at the first meeting!

The song ended; but she did not look up at him. She had been stirred peculiarly; and she turned over the leaves of Murphy's song-book until she had steadied. The beauty that has its primary effect on the emotions reached home to her quickly.

"You have really a splendid voice, Mr. Murphy," she said, for the second time, "It is a real gift. If you were trained, nothing would stop you. I have troubled you enough for to-night, I think. I like the second song best"—she was aware that her choice had pleased the man in some vague way. "We must go through it together a few times before the concert." She rose, and shook hands with him, feeling him quiver, as her firm hand gripped his enormously muscular one. "You must be tremendously strong," she said, without any intention of speaking. Then, hastily: " Good-night; so good of you to agree to sing for me." And ushered him out.

"What on earth did I say that for?" she asked herself, half irritably, half amusedly, as she passed into the next room. "But I'm sure he is."

III

"You're mighty struck on your Lady Mary!" said little Tripe Jones, something like a fortnight later.

Tripe had put one or two details together with his accustomed acuteness. He had dug some unwillingly willing facts out of Jell by the aid of remorseless questions, and, for the rest, he had used his eyes and his ears.

"You're always hummin' an' hummin' that Mary song of yourn!" added Tripe. "You must be struck on the fine lady as is teachin' you singin' better 'n the Almighty knew 'ow!"

The big man, lying on the next cot in his shirt and trousers, stopped his soft humming, and turned his head towards where the little man lay.

"What's that?" he said. "What d'you mean?"

"Well, you ain't never done singin' 'Kind is your Mary,' " replied Tripe, almost pugnaciously. "An' you go about lookin' every blessed moment as if you was kissin' saints in 'eaven—wimmin saints, I mean. I know the signs; and well I should, too. I've 'ad the experience, w'ich you ain't; only I always 'ad the sense to bother with my own sort. An' you can take it from me you has it good an' hard, and the Lord help you, Mister Jell Murphy, privit; for there ain't nothing in it but trouble. You'd 'a better took Maggie, an' got spliced proper an' settled—"

"Shut your mouth!" roared Jell, flinging himself up into a sitting position on his cot, his face alternately white with anger and red with shame that his secret was so thoroughly laid bare. "You're talkin' like a bloomin' mad fool. An', anyway, don't you get using her name so handy, or there'll be ructions between you and me!"

"Sorry, old pal," said the little man, in a voice that was suddenly quiet. "I never meant no 'arm. All the same, if you're feelin' huffy, don't make no mistake, I'm your man, gloves or fisties. Just say so plain out, that's all, old friend."

"That's all right, Tripe," said Murphy. "You got plenty of pluck. Only don't talk like you been doin'. I'm kind of crotchy these last days, with the heat an' not sleepin'."

IV

The singing lessons were continued; for Lady Mary had suggested the possibility of a duet together, which was to be sprung on the audience quite as an extra. She had no definite intention of singing it when

the time came, though, equally, she was quite capable of doing so, if still in the mood. Meanwhile, there was a piquancy about these little informal singing lessons with the great sapper.

"Have you ever been in love, Mr. Murphy?" she asked him at one of their lessons. "You sing like a lover, you know. So many men are hopelessly flat in a love song."

"I'm in love now," said Murphy, surprising himself with the unexpected words. But Lady Mary laughed musically down at the keyboard.

"How nice that sounds," she said. "I like to find a man who's not ashamed of being natural."

She glanced up swiftly, just a flash of her eyes across his, and thrilled with the passion that glowed in him, all pent up, yet seeming on the point of leaping. She had never before fitted herself into quite so interesting a situation. The very restraint of so forceful a masculine as this big fighting man stirred her in a score of vague and hidden ways.

Abruptly, she remembered Captain Harrison. Undoubtedly she loved Tom Harrison; she had gone to the extent of admitting as much frankly to herself. Tom was just a "lovely fine man," and she dwelt a moment on his memory, her fingers picking out odd harmonies. With the thought of Tom, she checked the tendency to lead the sapper any nearer to the snapping point of his restraint; and when next she glanced up at him it was with eyes that were speculative and almost cold.

"My sister tells me that Maggie, her maid, and you are very fond of each other."

Murphy made a gigantic, dumb gesture of denial; but she continued, remorseless.

"I'm very glad," she said quietly. "Maggie seems a thoroughly nice girl." And then, as he would have disclaimed verbally so soon as the right words arranged themselves, she glanced at her watch and stood up. "I'm .afraid I must go now," she said. "Thank you so much for coming!"

She held out her hand. As she did so, unfortunately, she allowed her glance to meet his, and felt herself sway mentally and physically to the dominant force of him. Before she knew what he was doing, he had knelt down on one knee and kissed her hand with all the strange reverence that a good man feels when love comes truly. Then, rising swiftly, he turned and walked out, without a word, leaving her standing, her heart thudding strangely, and the hand that he had kissed still held out loosely in front of her.

"Oh!" she said, almost "with a gasp, after nearly a minute of silence; and went quickly to her own room; for she wanted to analyse her sensations.

V

"Kind, kind and gentle is she—
 Kind is my Mary…"

Tripe was coming up from the canteen that evening, when he caught the words of the song that he was growing to hate. A few moments later he met Murphy himself in a bend of the path, where three lonely sycamores made a kind of natural bower. It was plain to the little man that Jell had been walking up and down there by himself, thinking and singing, and, as Tripe would have put it, "generally carryin' on damn silly!"

"There you are, singin' that bloomin' thing again!" said Tripe irritably.

He had received about his twentieth rebuff from Maggie that same evening, and had tried the canteen to ease his feelings. Thus, maybe, he was a little less careful of his words than he might have been.

"Why the 'ell," he continued, "you make such a blimey fool of yourself, I carn't think!" Then, with a sudden leaping up of all that was biggest in him: "You go along now an' 'ave a sensible talk with Maggie. She's pinin' to see you, as well I know. An' get that silly, high-falutin' rubbige out of your 'ead, 'fore it drives you dotty! You don't suppose she cares a brass tin-tack for you! Not if you went to 'ell this minnit! You take my tip—"

"Drop it, Tripe!" interrupted big Murphy. "You're talkin' out of your neck! I know what I'm doin'; don't get me shirty! I'm like a blessed filed trigger, so leave me alone!"

Tripe looked a moment at his friend; then had the wisdom to go on without another word. Further up the path he met Maggie, looking very bonnie.

"'Ee's down there, Maggie," he said. "Go an' 'ave a talk to 'im."

"I dassent!" said Maggie.

Yet for all that, she went; but when she got near enough to hear him singing, and to hear the steady tramp, tramp of his feet to and fro along the path ahead of her, she truly "dassent." Instead, she cried a bit, and turned back to the station.

VI

Lady Mary told herself that she must put a stop to the practising for

the concert. But when the usual time came, and Jell Murphy presented himself, he found her seated ready at the piano.

Murphy sang his song with a quality of voice and passion that brought strange tears into the woman's eyes. She felt herself to be intensely moved; the man's love was so real, and there was so much force of manhood at the back of all. And, also, he really did look splendid. Perhaps you follow her feelings.

Outside, behind one of the pillars of the verandah, Maggie, the maid, stood and cried as if her heart would break. The love in the man's voice was so plain, and none of it was for her. Presently she could bear it no longer, and went away to the back of the bungalow, to her own quarters.

It was at the end of the practising that big Murphy did suddenly the thing that he had never dared even to think upon. He was singing the last line of the song, and looking down from his great height at the golden bronze of Lady Mary's hair, when suddenly she looked up at him, her eyes wet and full of a thousand vague feelings and temporary abandon. The next moment big Murphy had her crushed in his arms, and was kissing her, at first madly, and then with an infinite tenderness that the woman appreciated with gentle thrills in every fibre.

Abruptly, a memory of Tom Harrison came into her mind, and she pushed Murphy away from her; for he loosed her the moment he saw her wish to be freed. Then, with a curious sound that was half a sob and half a gasp, she ran out of the room.

Big Jell Murphy stood, maybe, a couple of full minutes, with everything grey about him. Once or twice he swayed a little on his feet; then, realising that she was not coming back to him, he made rather blindly for the entrance, and away out on to one of the mountain paths, to be alone.

It was morning when he staggered back into the station, and it would have been the cells and shot-drill for him, only that his night's exposure and the strain of his emotions had brought on a severe attack of his old plain fever, so that, instead of the cells, he was taken at once to hospital.

VII

"The 'Scurries is out on the bloomin' rampage, an' we're a-going to give 'em their medicing!" said Tripe, who had been on guard, swinging his rifle down into the rack. "An' poor old Jell's out of it all in 'ospital!"

"Wotcher mean?" "Who said so?" "Rot!" " 'Urray!" came a storm of cries from men in the barracks, as they rushed round little Tripe Jones.

"'Ands off!" shouted Tripe, at the top of his voice. "Keep yer 'ands off, or I'll not tell yer nothink! I 'eard the colonel read the telegraft himself to the orficers. I stopped near the windy a minute, an' I 'eard it all." (Tripe was shameless!) "The hill devils is playin' blessed murder out beyond the Candy-peel, an' that's twenty miles leggin' for some of you great tallow-fat lads! You'll sweat! I reck'n it'll mean the 'ole bloomin' regiment. There—I told yer so! There goes the alarm"— as the clear, sweet notes of a bugle sounded through the station.

Two hours later the regiment had gone, leaving Captain Harrison with a hundred and twenty men, a sergeant, and two corporals in charge of the station and hospital. The duty to stay had fallen to Tom Harrison, owing to his being on the disabled list with a badly wrenched shoulder. He cursed his luck, but was consoled by the fact of Lady Mary's company.

Possibly Tom Harrison was a little too much taken up with the Lady Mary to attend properly to his duties, and maybe his temporary slackness had its effect upon the discontented sentries who were so hopelessly "out of the fun" there would be presently for the others beyond the "Candy peel," as the regiment called the hump of foothills away to the north-west of the station. Whether Captain Tom Harrison was to blame does not matter now, for he wiped everything clean when the thing occurred. But about two o'clock, six hours after the regiment had marched out, just when everything was at its slackest, there came a harsh ripple of rifle-fire from the edge of the ravine which began about a hundred yards from the front of the station.

Three of the sentries went down, and then, before anyone had any conception of what it all meant, there came swarming up out of the ravine itself hundreds upon hundreds of big hillmen.

The station itself was rushed, and half the company cut to pieces, before Captain Harrison was out of the colonel's bungalow. He jumped the verandah steps, firing his Colt as he jumped; and as he did so, there came the sharp ringing thud of a rifle volley from the windows of the barracks, where the sergeant had already rallied a score of the remaining men.

Six times the sergeant directed his fire into the horde of murdering hillmen, and then came the crack of a single rifle from the hospital. This was followed by the report of three other weapons; for Jell Murphy had got out of bed, in an old, ragged, hospital gown, and was firing from the window of the hospital, with the dispenser and two sick-duty men at his side, each with his rifle. But how they had got the rifles, in the circumstances, is a mystery.

It was this prompt action on the part of the sergeant and Jell that gave Tom Harrison his chance. He looked round quickly, and saw a number of his men, perhaps a round score, penned into the alleyway between the end of the barracks and the cookhouse. They appeared to be fighting with any odd weapon that they had managed to grasp; for one man was certainly swinging a pick, and he saw a heavy iron saucepan being used, evidently in deadly fashion; whilst another man fought with one of the cook's cleavers.

Captain Tom Harrison did a thing then that the regiment never forgot. He charged straight into the thinnest portion of the surge of hillmen, firing as he charged; and they gave way. He came through, fifty seconds later, stabbed in half a dozen places, whirling a native chopping-knife in his usable hand, and the knife running blood to the hilt. His revolver had gone, so had almost every rag of clothing from his body. He dashed in under the rifles of the sergeant's party, and mercifully was not shot to pieces. Then down the whole length of the barracks, to where the heavy end door opened opposite to the cookhouse; for it was through this door that the meals were brought in. As the captain had surmised, the door had been made fast on the inside, and the men outside were just penned up for slaughter in the most hopeless sort of cul-de-sac. As he raced for this door, there was a constant thudding against it with some heavy implement that sounded plain through the hideous native yelling and the shouting of his own men.

Captain Tom Harrison reached the door, gave a quick wrench, and had the great bar back. The door came open with a crash, and his men fell in over each other, dragging the dead and the wounded with them. The last man in was knifed clean through and through from behind by a huge pursuing native; but Captain Tom, naked and murderous, hauled the native in after his victim, and butchered him on the floor of the barracks; whilst the men closed the door, and ran for their rifles.

"The colonel's bungalow!" shouted the captain, staggering up from the dead native. "Lady Mary—the women!" He headed out, naked, through the sergeant's doorway, followed by a dozen of the men, with fixed bayonets. They made one clear charge right up to the bungalow, and found Jell Murphy there, guarding the women with a big sapper's axe, but no rifle. They took up their post on the verandah, where, between the cross-fire from the barracks and their own, they drove every native out of the station front within ten minutes.

"Thank God!" muttered Tom Harrison, a little weakly, for he had bled a lot. A moment later: "Lord! I must get some more clothes on—" He never finished even the thought, for he heard the sergeant shouting:

"There's about a thousand of 'em coming now, sir! Bring the wimmin over, sir. They're almost 'ere, sir! Quick, sir!"

Captain Tom Harrison turned and raced into the bungalow; but the big sapper had been even quicker to grasp the sergeant's warning; for the captain met him coming out, with Lady Mary held like a child in his arms; so that it was her sister, the colonel's wife, that Tom Harrison carried, whilst one of his men would have done likewise with Maggie, the cook, only she told him she wanted no "mauling," and could manage on her "own two legs" as well as he.

They reached the barracks safely, and as they did so there came a tremendous yelling without, and the square in front of the barracks became literally alive with hillmen, charging in huge, unwieldy mobs of them, and every second or third man of them seemed to be carrying a new Service rifle.

"By gad!" gasped the breathless captain, staring down from one of the barred windows of the barracks. "We're done, sure. They've got Service rifles."

"I've got it, sir!" almost shouted the sergeant. "I couldn't make head or tail of what all them bloomin' p'tarns was foolin' round 'ere for. Them's new smuggled-in German or Roosian rifles, same bore as the Service pattern—rotten made they is, too, sir. But the amminition's gone astray somewhere or t'other; an' that bloomin' well explains them monkeyin' in 'ere, like I never 'eard the likes of, not since the bad year. It ain't their way. But they couldn't stand 'aving them rifles and no bloomin' amminition; an' it's all a plant to get the station amminition, so as they can play 'ell with them new playthings they got. I'll bet there's a lot of devilment to the back of this; an' I'll bet there ain't no ructions out beyond the Candy-peel. It was just a trick to leave the station empty; an' someone's going to be hung for this, sir. Look out! Here they come!"

But the soldiers drove the hillmen back time after time during the next ten minutes; for their empty rifles were little better than so many clubs, whilst the remnants of the company shot swiftly and with comparative security from the shelter of the great barracks. At the end of some fifteen or sixteen minutes' lighting, the enemy had ceased to charge up to the windows, and a sudden rush was made to the left.

"They're on to the amminition-house, sir!" shouted the sergeant; and clapped his rifle again to his shoulder. "Clear them from the door, boys!" he sung out. "If they once get in, we're done. Fire low, and keep cool—"

"I'm out of cartridges, sergeant," interrupted a man's voice.

"Get one of the other chaps' belts," snarled the sergeant, without ceasing to cuddle the stock of his rifle to his chin. "There's enough dead men's belts to see us through, Gawd knows!"

"We've been usin' them all along, sergeant," said several voices. "We ain't any of us got more than a few left."

The sergeant ceased to cuddle his rifle, and looked round quickly, a sudden touch of added grimness in his eyes.

"Here," he said, " keep them devils from the ammunition-door while I take a look!"

He glanced at Captain Harrison as he spoke. And the captain, very white, pulled a dead man's coat round his naked, bloodstained shoulders. He had already appropriated a pair of trousers from the same source, and, as his wounds had ceased to bleed, he managed to keep on the go.

"What are we to do, sir?" asked the sergeant, when they had searched the arm-stands afresh.

"We've got to cut through those beggars outside," said Tom Harrison, " and get a box of cartridges out of the ammunition-house."

"It's the only thing, sir," said the sergeant, after thinking a moment. "But we won't never do it. There's a couple of thousand of them p'tarns outside—an' there goes our last cartridge!" For as he was speaking the men had ceased firing.

The sortie was arranged. Captain Harrison picked out a dozen of the biggest and soundest men, and allowed Murphy to join them, though the big sapper's eyes still burned dully with fever. The arrangement was that as soon as the door was opened they should charge through with fixed bayonets, whilst those left at once barred the door and held it for their return

Nothing was said to the three women, who had been put in a sergeant's cubicle away up at the end of the big room. But Lady Mary must have perceived something of their intention, for suddenly she came running out with an inarticulate cry of supreme distress that made the big sapper take a quick step towards her with his arms open; but the next instant he remembered himself. And then the door was open, and they were making the attempt.

Captain Harrison was clubbed insensible on the very threshold, and dragged back by his feet into the barracks just before they got the door closed and fastened. And it was big Murphy who led the charge, swinging the great sapper's axe with its four-foot haft and broad head. The weapon made a circle of steel and blood around him, and a couple of score big natives must have died under its swing before he stood

in the little stone porch of the ammunition-house. But he stood there alone. The dozen men who had been at his back had died in a dozen different ways in that brief, mad charge.

Through all the big, seething square there came a curious silence, and then a kind of ferocious screaming, and a thousand big hill-men rushing on one spot. The big axe swung amid a hail of German rifle-butts, yet the huge sapper was untouched. The porch gave him just room for his weapon, and no more, and not one of the attackers could get in at his side or back. And presently even the hillmen tired of rushing in on that one little spot of certain death, and gave back a while to confer.

Meanwhile, up on the high roof of the barracks, the sergeant was manipulating a piece of broken looking-glass, part of a shaving mirror, and presently, from maybe half a dozen miles away to the north-west, through, the eternal mountain air, there flashed suddenly and burned the blink of an answering helio:

"Coming. Hold on. End."

Twice more during the next half-hour the hillmen rushed Jell Murphy, and each time the big sapper built him a semicircle of dead round about the stone porch, though by the end of the second attack he was bleeding in a dozen places. After the hillmen had backed away for the second time, there fell a most extraordinary silence upon the square, broken only by a curious low rattling of rude castanets from a native "holy man," who had begun to walk round and round the small ammunition-house on the stumps of his knees, rattling the little pieces of slate as he went.

"That shows as they think Jell Murphy's got devils fightin' with 'im," said the sergeant, gravely. "Yon bleedin' fakir is puttin' a spell on to old Jell. He'll go round like that for maybe a hour, an' then them beggars 'll rush 'im, an' nothin' 'll stop 'em then. I guess old Murphy 'll have to go. He's shown hisself a fine lad."

There came a low growl from the half-dozen men who still lived.

"We ain't a-going to let 'im go cut like that, sergeant," said one of them grimly. "We're going out to fetch 'im in, or bloomin' well kick it wiv 'im."

"If you makes a move, boys," said the sergeant, " you'll end 'im and us right off. If only yon chap 'll keep foolin' round long enough we'll be safe, an' Murphy too; the rigment 'll be back then, an' I want to live for that! You can go out then, boys, and kick it as quick as you like, only we has the wimmin now to think of." .

"Sergeant," called one of the younger men eagerly from across

the barrack-room, "I've found some! My God, sergeant, there's fifty bloomin' rounds!"

The sergeant's hands fairly trembled as he took the precious packets from the man.

"Oh, Lord," he said, in tremulous earnestness, " let me kill a man wiv each bloomin' one!"

"Sst!" said one of the men suddenly. "Hark to old Jell. He's singin' summat."

The men craned forward to stare and listen, and so great was the stillness upon the big square that they could clearly catch the words— (blending oddly with the rattling of the fakir's castanets), that the big sapper was singing softly to himself as he stood leaning on the big axe.

"It's yon Mary song of his, I'm think-in'," said a Macdullarg, whose cot lay near Murphy's. "It's the fever in him, I doubt not; an' him been practisin' for the concert that was to be."

Murphy continued to croon and sing to himself. And suddenly the Lady Mary, leaning over the bed, white-faced, where Tom Harrison lay, heard it, and shivered a little.

"Look out, boys!" said the sergeant abruptly. "Yon devil 'as finished, an' now they'm going to rush old Murphy. Shoot slow, an' send as many to hell as you can."

The holy man shuffled away from his persistent rounding of the house, and in the same moment a tremendous yell filled the square as a rush was made. For a moment the men in the barracks saw Murphy clearly, from the waist upwards. Below the waist the semicircle of the dead hid him as a wall. Then the enemy were at the porch in a chaos of intended butchery, through which swung the great axe.

"Now!" said the sergeant; and six rifles were fired methodically.

They fired every cartridge they had, and eased some of the fury and deadliness out of the attack on the big sapper, for still the great axe swung.

"He's done now!" said the sergeant, fingering his useless trigger. "An' we carn't do nothin'. My Gawd, what's 'appening? He's chargin' them!"

It was true. They saw the gigantic form of the big sapper leap up suddenly into sight over the barrier of the dead, and hurl himself into the enormous mass of surging hillmen.

"He'd got to do it," said one of the men, in a husky voice. "Hark to him! He's singing again. Hark to him!"

They saw the gigantic sapper, head and shoulders bigger than any man in the square, driving through the heart of the natives, the big axe swinging and circling and dripping. And as he swung the great axe, in

a voice that could be heard above all the roar of the fight they could
hear him chanting a curious medley of words:

"Ha, ha! Gentle is she,
Mary, my darling!"

And with each chanted word the four-foot axe swung and circled
and struck—a dripping baton beating a melody of death.

"It's the fever," the sergeant kept muttering under his breath, yet with-
out knowing that he said anything, as he stared so tensely with his men.

Still the big sapper went forward, and still across the square there
came the strange "Ha, ha! Gentle is she, Mary, my darling!" and the
eternal swing and circle of the great axe.

But inside the big barrack-room Lady Mary was not even aware
of what was happening. She was holding Captain Harrison's head
against her breast, and crying tearlessly, for the young officer lay so
everlastingly quiet that she began to feel sure he was dead. As for
Maggie, mercifully she had stayed tending her mistress in the cubicle,
and so knew nothing of the immediate happenings.

"They've stopped him!" said a man's voice abruptly, dry and tone-
less. "He's done! My God!"

They saw the great shoulders of big Murphy sink out of sight
under a thousand rifle-butts; then he hove himself upright, and swung
the great axe round once more, striking madly to right and left. There
came just three shouted words:

"Ha, ha! Gentle—"

And he disappeared, finally, and the four-foot axe ceased to strike.

And so, as it seems to me, I see big-hearted, big-bodied Jell Murphy
swinging, his axe of victory, and stepping great and fine and wholesome
and unafraid out of that pasture of death into the Pastures of the
Eternal, still singing in his spirit the words that held for his particular
soul no single trace of irony:

"Ha, ha! Gentle is she,
Mary, my darling!"

* * * *

It was just upon the evening as Jell Murphy died, and, almost as

if it had been the fitting signal of so momentous a dying, there came the crash of a thousand Service rifles. The regiment had returned.

Little Tripe Jones it was who got first to where his big comrade had died. With ferocious energy, and sobbing brutal oaths out of his throat, he attacked the great circle of dead hillmen that lay all around that last stand. Body after body he swung clear by main strength until a score of his comrades were working only a shade less furiously to the same end. And so at last they had him clear. As they lifted him an undersized Cockney voiced his epitaph, standing there in the midst of that quiet but infinitely eloquent circle of the dead: "My word!" said the little man, in an awed voice, "him was sure a bloody man!"

* * * *

Three months later Lady Mary married Captain Harrison.

At breakfast, a few mornings after the wedding, Captain Harrison remarked:

"I see the men still keep Murphy's grave covered with flowers."

"I'm glad of that," replied Lady Mary. "He deserved it. Is your coffee right, dear?"

A Timely Escape

MADGE JACKSON DISLIKED MR. George Vivian, B.Sc., with an intense and thorough dislike. This feeling was conceivably strengthened by the considerations that Mr. Vivian was something of a rival; though, indeed, this sounds a queer thing to say when the saying concerns a man and woman.

But it is correct; for Dicky Temple, her young lover, appeared to consider Mr. Vivian a veritable intellectual god upon earth, upholding his belief with all the generous vigour and blind hero-worship of which a young and boyishly-dispositioned man can be capable.

Against his "guide, philosopher, and friend," Dicky would hear no word—not even from the pretty lips of his pretty Madge. Moreover, he was developing a way of "laying-down-the-law" to his fiancee, which might have been permissable and possibly even pleasant to her, had the said law been "Dicky." But it was not; it was Vivian in structure and utterance. And the woman in the maid rebelled.

This was bad. But worse than this and the curb of silence which Dicky's rather intolerant partisanship put upon the girl's speech, was the actuality that he was passing more and more of his time in George Vivian's luxurious rooms, even to the extent of encroaching very considerably upon certain hours that had been hitherto considered devoted to their daily worship at the altar of love. And this, as all will agree, suggested the base of a proposition, if not in Euclid then in Cupid, which was not likely to end in an exposition of the angles of their natures and tempers, which might conclude at a tangent.

Now, Mr. George Vivian was a writer—to be exact, a novelist and an essayist; and not very wonderful as a literary workman, if we are to believe Miss Jackson. Dicky, on the contrary, would have assured you earnestly of the converse. He would have insisted upon the grace and beauty of his style, and the delicacy and subtle point of his thoughts;

and all the while he would have been totally unconscious of the paucity of ideas, and the general threadbareness and commonplaceness of the material that his older friend was wont to dress up with so much "grace and beauty" of style.

Yet his "style" which so impressed the younger man was considerably less than he imagined it to be. Indeed, when one day Madge epigrammatically described Vivian's work as ancient knuckle-bones dressed in new paper frills, she did that worthy litterateur less injustice than the vehement Dicky could have conceived possible.

The immediate result of this cruel ticketing had been a very decided row between the two young people, which had not yet ended; for the very real reason that Master Dicky Temple was being a thorough young fool, and showing his independence by purposely neglecting his pretty sweetheart, the while that he proved his unwavering loyalty to George Vivian by putting in all his spare time with him.

So far as a labelled worker goes, Dicky was nothing— that is to say he possessed a private income and, incidentally, a vivid and peculiar imagination, seeming to be truly bubbling over with ideas.

He had written some exceedingly good stuff of a somewhat fantastic nature; so that one would be inclined to suppose that the very plenitude of his ideas and natural ability would have enabled him to feel the pretentious glitter of the work that came from Vivian's pen. But, as is so readily the case in the callow years, he mistook the finnicking smartness and re-dressed "mouton" of his friend for something that indicated powers far beyond his own; not realizing that such can be readily attained by some labor, a good memory, and the purposeful cultivation of eccentricity in the telling.

His own abilities he conceived to be of a crude and inferior order— "blood-and-thunder" he was inclined to label them when talking to Vivian; and it is to be noted that Vivian never took earnest means to suggest that they might be otherwise, but would sit in stately content, submitting to the constant adulation of the young man who would be his disciple.

In reality, Dick's gifts were the true gold of imagination, and Vivian was a sufficiently acute man to recognize this fact; though at no time, as I have remarked, did he ever hint that such was or might be the case.

It is a regrettable thing, yet the truth, that Dicky managed to neglect Madge for a full week after their row. What is even more to be regretted is that Dicky achieved this without any personal distress at the separation. It was as if the elder man had really a power to compensate him temporarily for the loss of his sweetheart; and the

thought arises, to what extent might this compensation of attraction have carried the youth? Possibly to a point at which the girl and he would achieve that tangential divergence aforementioned, which might result in their separation through all this life and the eternities to be.

This, to say the least, has a lamentable sound about it, and therefore I join with Madge Jackson in heartily disliking Vivian; for the man knew exactly the condition of affairs between Dicky and his pretty fiancée, and had sufficient experience and general sanity to know that such behavior as Dicky's must lead to a definite and final break way from the girl, unless he altered very speedily. And knowing this, he should, as an older man and one having a wider outlook, have packed Dicky out of his rooms with a little sensible masculine advice.

For her part, Madge had her own ideas. She loved Dicky thoroughly and honestly, and she meant to try to break this friendship; being convinced by intuition rather than by reasoning, that it was undesirable for her love. And this conviction I conceive to have been bred apart from her natural anger and jealousy in connection with Temple's idiotic uplooking to his man friend, and his neglect of her.

Her first step towards achieving her object was a letter sent to Dicky to his rooms, on the eighth day of his absenting himself.

She asked him to call. He replied, with almost childish folly, that he was engaged to spend the next three nights with Vivian; but that he would call on the fourth. She, as of course was most natural, considering the circumstances, allowed him to call; but instructed the servant to tell Master Dicky Temple that she was not at home.

Dicky perceived the rightness of the snub and stood a while upon the step—as it were—fighting a strange, horrid hurt with anger and pride. The latter gained the battle, being aided to victory by his knowledge that he need not endure the evening alone; but might have a good time at George Vivian's rooms.

He turned away from the door and passed on up the street, his head held very high and his heart full of the ready and uncounting foolishness of blind and undeveloped youth. And even as his footsteps sounded under her window, poor little Madge burst into crying, repenting her natural and almost justified pride.

A fortnight passed after this, during which she saw him twice in the street; but he, if he were aware of her, gave no sign to show that he had seen her; but went on his way without so much as a look in her direction.

On each occasion he had been on the opposite pavement; but even at this distance it had seemed to her that he was looking unwell, rather

pallid, and that there was a certain listlessness in his step. At home she had reasoned with herself that she might be mistaken, and that even if he did look unwell, it was because he was fretting to be back with her on the old happy footing. Yet, she did not believe her reasonings. She was convinced in her heart that things were going wrong with Dicky in some way; and no amount of commonsense reasonings would be likely to move her from this state of intuition.

She wrote to him once more at his rooms, asking him to call and explain his continued absence. He replied with a curiously incoherent letter that frightened her, and left her just as lacking in definite knowledge as before; but he made no call.

Ten days later, when she was out with her sister, she saw Dicky again. He was walking slowly down the opposite side of the street; and scarcely knowing what she was doing, she pulled Gertrude to a standstill, while she watched him.

Dicky came on slowly down the street, his step utterly lacking in its old firm briskness, and his face seeming peculiarly white and almost gaunt, so far as she could judge at that distance. He was almost opposite to her, when suddenly she tugged her arm free from her sister's and walked swiftly across the road, so as to meet him diagonally. She reached the opposite pavement and met him face to face.

"Dicky!" she said. "Dicky! What's the matter? What's the matter?" and she stood there breathlessly facing him.

He, for his part, had come to a halt, and stood looking down at her with a peculiar vacant stare, holding out his hand automatically, and smiling almost as though she were some person he could only half recollect.

"Dicky!" she cried again, passionately, staring up into his eyes which were dull and unrecognizing. "Dicky, what is the matter?"

As she spoke, she noticed afresh with shocked feelings how dead white and spiritless was his face, and the utter slackness of his whole attitude.

"Dicky," she said, once more. "What is the matter?"

The young man ceased to hold out his hand in that mechanical fashion and passed it across his forehead hesitatingly, and still looking at her in that blank way that was so dreadful. Then a definite expression took the place of his vacancy. He lifted his chin absurdly, with the queerest little assumption of offended pride, and raising his hat, turned from her murmuring: "Good day, Miss Jackson."

And with that, he went on up the road at a fairly brisk pace.

Madge stood, staring dumbly after him. It was all so strange and

terrible to her. It was as if she had been talking to an automaton that was yet half human, and which had recollected in some queer passionless way, some forgotten anger which it must put on and wear as a garment, rather than that it had exhibited the normal reflex of a natural emotion. She stared after him blindly, because of the unshed tears that made a mist of everything, and all unaware that her white face and intense attitude were attracting attention from passers-by.

Gertrude had followed her slowly across the road, and now she touched Madge on the arm.

"Whatever is wrong with Dicky?" she asked in a puzzled voice, and glancing quickly at Madge's white face. "He looks a perfect wreck. Has—has he been drinking or something?"

Poor Madge answered nothing, but steadied her trembling knees by holding tightly to her sister's arm.

Later that same day, after much sympathy and gentle coaxing, Gertrude persuaded her sister to tell her everything about the separation which appeared to be growing permanent between Dicky and her. This the elder girl forced herself to do, growing easier and happier finally because of the telling; so that she found it possible to go into all the half-thoughts and vague suspicionings and fears which had troubled her so much of late.

"Oh," cried Gertrude when Madge had finished, "I hate that man Vivian. I've always felt there was something bad and dreadful about him. I'm sure of it now."

"Yes," agreed Madge, miserably. "I'm certain too; but we can't be sure." After which contradictory but perfectly intelligible remark she had a good hearty cry.

"We must get him away dear," Gertrude told her later, after she had petted and comforted her sister into quietness once more. "Let's plan. I'll do anything to help you."

For a long while they discussed ways and means, eventually deciding that they would call on Dicky at his rooms in the morning, have a good, serious talk with him, and find out what was wrong and the reason he was looking so ill.

"There must be no tragedies through silly misunderstandings," Gertrude asserted with quaint commonsense. "If we can only be sure whether he is really ill, or not, we shall know what to do. If there's nothing wrong with him, and he's just cutting you and being a brute, you must never speak to him again. If he's ill, we'll take care of him and make him better. Cheer up, dear!"

The following morning they made their call upon Dicky, in force.

"Mr. Temple, mem, is staying at 'is friend's 'ouse in West Street," the landlady told them. " 'E ain't so well as 'e might be, and 'is friend's 'ad 'im over to stay with 'im a bit. Yes, Miss, I sends all his letters over there by my Billy. Yes, Miss, he comes in sometimes in the day. I'll tell 'im you called, Miss. Good-day, mem."

With the closing of the door, the two sisters looked at each other.

"I'm sure there's something wrong," said Madge in a desperate voice.

When they arrived home, Madge wrote a long, straight-forward, loving letter to Dicky, telling him all her doubts and troubles, and asking—even though he wished everything to be ended between them—that he should give her a call and let them talk it over; or at least, that he would write to her some explanation of things. She ended by telling him how worried she was about his looks, begging him to take care of his health. But she made no mention of Vivian, judging it wiser under the circumstances to be silent in that direction.

After the letter was posted, she felt happier. She felt that surely now she would have an opportunity to see him, speak to him, have an explanation, and perhaps win back to the old-time joy of life.

Several days passed, but there was no reply. Twice, she and Gertrude walked past the house where Vivian had his rooms. It was a biggish, old-fashioned house, and the windows, lit up but securely blinded, gave on to a big veranda. Each time that they had passed, Madge had stopped her sister that she might look up at the light blinds behind which was Dicky. Then, after a long, useless, painful gazing, she had dragged her sister forward once more, being now as anxious to hurry away as before she had been hungry to stop.

"Why doesn't he write? Why doesn't he write?" Madge asked her sister, day by day. But Gertrude had no answer; neither did Madge expect one.

At the end of another week Madge declared that she would pay one more visit to Dicky's rooms to see whether he had returned. Gertrude accompanied her. They discovered that Dicky had been there that very day. "Lookin' pretty bad, Miss, I will say," the landlady had assured them. " 'E's still staying with 'is friend."

Madge's next step was to write direct to George Vivian, asking for news of Dicky. She received a reply two days later, in which he assured her suavely that Dicky Temple was in every way well and happy, but a little run down. He hinted with veiled brutality that Dicky disliked letter writing, and that it might be better for him if he were not bothered with unnecessary correspondence.

"Unnecessary correspondence!" cried Gertrude furiously. "I never heard of such a horrid man." Then she broke off to comfort Madge, who was crying. "It's all right, dear," she assured her. "We'll go and see Dicky there. We'll get him away, you'll see." But Madge shook her head, desperate and miserable.

"He's got Dicky, body and soul," she said. "He'll make him do just what he wants. I know it. I just know it. Oh, what shall I do?"

Next day, however, they called to see Dicky at his friend's rooms. But, of course, they never saw Dicky. Mr. George Vivian came down and interviewed them, very politely, very regretfully, exceedingly brutal under a silky manner. Poor Dicky was lying down, and they must forgive him—Vivian—but surely Mr. Temple had made his feelings plain, painful though it had been to him. These things were always painful to both parties. Mr. George Vivian felt sure that the ladies understood. He bowed, coldly apologetic.

Madge turned away with a white face; but Gertrude faced Vivian, furious.

"Do you mean—do you mean that Dicky's there—that Mr. Temple does not wish to see my sister?" she said, panting in her young anger.

Mr. George Vivian, B.Sc., bowed once more and said nothing. Then, as the angry girl stood, searching for words that should sufficiently express all that she felt without unduly uncovering her sister's feelings, Madge caught her arm.

"Come along, dear," she said quietly. "We should never have come. This is a case for Dicky's father. I shall wire for him at once."

As she said this, a strange look came into Vivian's hitherto expressionless eyes, and sent a faint shadow of some unknown emotion across the calmness of his face. But neither of the sisters saw this, for they were walking towards the door, which Vivian silently opened for them.

He bowed to them from the top of the steps; then stood thoughtfully staring after them, his surface-calm lost in an expression of white, intense concentration.

That evening the two girls went for a walk. Neither said anything to the other, but the same thought was in the mind of each; for presently they found themselves walking down the long road where Vivian lived. As they came in sight of the house, Madge drew her sister to a pause, and the two of them looked up the long garden at the lighted windows above the balcony.

It was Madge who presently opened the iron gate and began to walk silently up the grass that bordered the central walk. Gertrude followed

her equally noiselessly. The same feeling was in both of them—that they must come close to the house; yet beyond that, neither of them had any clear idea, plan or intention. It was instinct, longing, possibly something more—psychic-awareness, if I may compound such a term, or a blending of all three. Certainly their minds were empty of any concerted action. They felt vaguely that they might hear something, might do something; nothing definite yet withal sufficient to impel them forward.

The lower windows of the house front were dark and shuttered, being closed up for the winter, so that there was no fear of the girls being seen from the lower story. As they drew nearer, the dark bulk of the big veranda loomed out over them, hiding the row of lighted windows above. Near to them, there went up one of the narrow supporting pillars of the veranda.

"Hush!" said Madge suddenly. Yet there had been no need for the remark as neither of them had spoken. They stood motionless for a while, their faces upturned, listening. Above them there was a faint monotonous sound, continuous.

"Can you hear it?" asked Madge at last in a breathless whisper, and she gripped her sister's arm with a hand that shook. "Can you hear it?"

"Yes," whispered Gertrude, shaking with excitement. "Yes, it's Dicky. It's Dicky! Oh, what is the matter with him?"

"Hush!" said Madge again, and they both listened once more. The night was utterly still, or they had not been able to hear the sound. Even as it was, they heard it only, as it were, in little eddies—a monotonous, dead voice dropping words constantly, so low and toneless and lifeless as scarcely to seem human. Yet it was Dicky's voice, as both the girls knew.

Suddenly they caught each other's hands, shaking and desperate. What devilment was being worked up there in that quiet room over the balcony, behind the lighted blinds? Madge drew in her breath, and her grip on Gertrude's arm was painful in its intensity. Abruptly she said in a fierce tone: "I'm going up," and she began to fumble at the pillar by which they stood.

"I'll come too! I'll come too!" Gertrude whispered, her hands all ashake as she strove now to help Madge to climb. She caught her round the knees, lifting her; then stooped and shouldered her up as any schoolboy might have done. And so in a moment Madge stood gasping on the balcony. Gertrude followed, and Madge reached down to aid her.

The sound of that curious voice came to them plainly now, yet with an even more horrible note of something inhuman and monstrous

about it. It was Dicky's voice, dropping low, toneless words within that light room, and each word came out to them clear yet meaningless as they stood there on the balcony.

The voice reached them here, dead and lifeless, every word spoken without inflexion, with a constant slow drop, drop, as if they fell leaden upon the air from something without life. Madge caught suddenly at her collar and ripped it open so that she might breath; then she put her hand noiselessly to the blind and pushed it back.

"—across the moorlands, pursued by the grey hands—" said the strange voice, as the two girls peered into the long room.

The room was normal enough in its fittings, except for a very low table away to the left, which stood on glass legs. On this table, seated in a black vulcanite chair fitted with switches, sat Dicky. His face was of a dead, pasty whiteness. He was leaning back, his head resting in a cup-shaped vulcanite head rest, and his white face staring up at a dome of bluish metal suspended from the ceiling by thick rods of vulcanite.

From the dome there came down two metal rods with little bright metal balls at the ends, which were pressed lightly upon Dicky's closed eyes. Round his head was an India rubber belt, strapping a peculiar dull-colored ring to the center of his forehead, and within the ring there glimmered and winked a curious green light, flashing and disappearing oddly. His hands gripped tightly two big grey-colored electrodes, which were attached to the arms of the vulcanite chair.

There he sat, with never a movement or sign of life, except for the strange, slow automatic moving of his lips, dropping words like dead things into the room.

By the side of the motionless talking automaton stood Vivian upon a broad stool supported on glass legs, like those of the table. He had a large notebook in his hand, and as the Dead-Alive brought out that constant dropping of uninflexed words, he wrote steadily. From time to time he would lay his fingers gently on the pulse of the man in the chair; but for this, he wrote always, calmly, methodically, evenly.

As Madge looked, trembling with a kind of nerve sickness which had seized her as she grasped all these things, she caught again those words that came dropping so dreadfully from the white, stiff-moving lips.

"—the face rose over the wall—"

Her attention was taken by Gertrude, who was shaking her arm.

"It's Dicky's tale about the Moon-word," she whispered in trembling excitement. "The one he told us he was writing. That man's got him to sleep with electricity or something, and he's making him tell it all, all, all! Oh! I—I—"

She grew incoherent in her excitement. "He'll kill Dicky if we don't stop him!" she got out at last.

"—The three grey figures bowed across the silent breadth of the plain, and there rose something up out of the shadows to the left of the wall—" the voice continued monotonously. And all the time Vivian wrote steadily.

"I'm going in," said Madge in a quiet voice, and she pushed the blind forward.

Vivian turned with the rustle of the blind and now stood looking silently at them with an inscrutable expression.

"What does this mean?" he began at last. But at that moment something in Madge seemed to give way, and she rushed at him with all her might, pushing him with both hands off the low-glass-legged stool on which he stood, so that he fell crashing and rolled bodily on the floor. Then, stretching out her arms she would have touched Dicky, and probably have caused his death, for she was standing on nothing to insulate her, as Vivian had been standing. Moreover, Dicky's death would quite possibly have caused hers; for the current would have "earthed" through her.

It was Vivian who saved her, with most marvellous presence of mind, coupled with characteristic brutality.

"Don't touch him!" he shouted, even as he fell; then, while he still rolled from his fall upon the floor, he kicked her legs violently from under her so that she too came headlong. He was up in a moment and made to raise her; but she refused his hand and staggered giddily to her feet.

"So sorry if I was a little rough," said Vivian with perfect calmness. He stepped to the wall, pulled over a big vulcanite switch, and instantly the glimmering, flickering light died out upon Dicky's forehead; at the same time his hands released their tension upon the big grey electrodes.

Vivian turned to Madge.

"Mr. Temple is safe to touch now," he said quietly. He walked across the table and with the greatest ease lifted the young man down and carried him to a couch. Then he stepped away and left him to Madge.

In turning away he saw his notebook on the floor where he had dropped it when Madge pushed him over. He picked it up, but as he turned round with it, he found Gertrude in front of him. She gripped the book, evidently expecting that she would have to tussle for it, but he gave it up to her without an effort or a sign of emotion. Looking at it, she found it covered with shorthand, which she was able to read.

"Oh, you brute, picking his brains!" she cried vehemently. "You brute! You might have killed him. You wouldn't care a pin if you had."

He looked at her calmly but said nothing; neither did he attempt to take the book from her.

Over by the couch Madge was silently attending to Dicky, who was now feebly conscious. She chafed his hands and kissed him, the tears running quietly down her face all the time. Presently she turned from the couch to Vivian.

"Will you call a cab, please," she said. And he went.

While he was gone, Gertrude had a sudden idea. She stepped across to the writing table where a pile of notebooks similar to the one she held were placed on one side. She picked them up and, glancing through them, she found them all containing parts of the same story set down in shorthand. She picked them up and counted them. There were six in all. Then, as Vivian came into the room to announce that the cab was at the door, she looked her angry defiance at him, but made no pretence to hide the books.

The man said not a word, nor attempted to touch them in any way. He helped Dicky up and aided that still dazed young gentleman down the stairs to the cab. As he shut the door after they were all in, he made one terse remark.

"Of his own free will entirely," he said and turned away into the house, indifferent to their reply, a truly extraordinary man along certain lines.

"Yes," Dicky told them a week later, "that's all right. I was willing to be his 'subject' for that trance mucking about; but I never thought it could harm me. I guess he must be a rotter after all, or he'd never have let me into it. No, I never dreamt he was playing the pirate. He's a queer chap. The funny thing is that I don't even now hate him. But I'll never speak to him again. Too much for me. Why was I like that with you— blest if I know, Madge. I suppose it was with all that trance business. Perhaps there was some 'suggestion' about it. You know what I mean. You see, old Vivian wouldn't want you interfering—eh? Wanted to keep you away and have me to himself till he'd sucked me dry. The old devil!"

"Hush!" said Madge, stopping his mouth with her kisses.

"Anyway," he said, "you'll be able to look after me for always, after next Tuesday, won't you, dear?"

By which remark, I suppose, we are to understand that the inevitable was about to overtake Dicky Temple and his pretty Madge.

A Note On The Texts

WHENEVER POSSIBLE, TEXTS FOR this series have been based on versions that were published in book form, preferably during Hodgson's lifetime. The major exceptions to this rule are the stories that appear in volumes edited by Sam Moskowitz. Moskowitz was known to have access to original manuscripts and other source materials. Some stories were published only in serial form, and have been taken from those primary sources.

Over the years, many of Hodgson's stories have appeared under variant titles, which are noted below. As a rule, the titles used in this series are based on the first book publication of a story, even if the story previously appeared under a different title, in serial form.

Specific textual sources are noted below. The only changes that have been made to the texts have been to correct obvious typographical errors, and to standardize punctuation and capitalization. British and archaic spelling has been retained.

The Night Land is based on the 1912 Eveleigh Nash edition.
"The Captain of the Onion Boat" is based on its publication in *Men Of Deep Waters* (Eveleigh Nash, 1914). It was originally published in *Nash's Magazine No. 21* (Christmas 1910).
"The Smugglers" is based on its publication in *Grand Magazine* (March 1911).
"In the Wailing Gully" is based on its publication in *Grand Magazine No. 79* (September 1911).
"The Girl with the Grey Eyes" is based on its publication in *Red Magazine No. 91* (January 15, 1913)
"Kind, Kind and Gentle Is She" is based on its publication in *Red Magazine No. 96* (April 1, 1913).
"A Timely Escape" is based on its publication in *Blue Magazine* (June 1922).

The Complete Fiction of William Hope Hodgson is published by
Night Shade Books in the following volumes:

The Boats of the "Glen Carrig" and Other Nautical Adventures
The House on the Borderland and Other Mysterious Places
The Ghost Pirates and Other Revenants of the Sea
The Night Land and Other Perilous Romances
The Dream of X and Other Fantastic Visions